THE END OF TRUTH

ALSO BY AVTAR SIMRIT

TRUE TIME TRILOGY:
A Dream of True Time
The End of Truth

TRUE FICTION:
True Fiction (Volume One)

POETRY:
Shackled to Creation
Break Every Chain

THE COMPLETE LYRICS
OF AVTAR SIMRIT:
Nilotic Years
The MC Pan Era

The End of Truth

True Time Trilogy
Volume Two

AVTAR SIMRIT

Apocalyptic Rhymes

For all the ones who ever wondered if they are evil at their core. Your Being is beyond both good and evil. Know within your essence that there is nothing wrong with you.

I Love you.

Word of *Caution* and *Discernment*:
Do not seek to understand this, you may get confused.

CONTENTS

*"This Universe never did make sense;
I suspect that it was built on
government contract."*

- Robert A. Heinlein, *The Number of the Beast*

Convergence of Shadow Forces

*"You wanted connections, and they're there
to be found. But you have to look in the terrible places...
The places where death comes to take love away, where we
lose each other and lose ourselves; that's where the connections
begin. It takes a brave soul to look there and not despair."*

- Clive Barker, *Everville*

PART 12

October Is Gone

*"God is beginning to resemble not a ruler
but the last fading smile of a cosmic Cheshire Cat."*

- Julian Huxley

FOURTEEN

Waking life is a Dream which is experienced as both spacial and temporal. A Dream—waking or sleeping—is an interactive illusion, a hallucination that we string together with our minds one instant to the next. Time is not linear. Past, present, and future are all one moment that eternally exists as an ever-present Now. Every day is the same day. As the Earth rotates and the sun rises and sets, the cycle of life continues as a wheel within a wheel. The Dream is yours; and yours alone. And as you tell your own story, it is yours to create and yours to destroy—then to *rebirth* over and over like the phoenix and the shape-shifting Ouroboros: the dragon eating its own tail infinitely to prove its own perfection.

Out in space, a little ways past Earth's Moon, two spaceships were doing battle. One of these crafts resembled what on Earth was known as a conversion van. To see a red Dodge Ram van zipping through space with thrusters on its back would be a rare sight indeed. The thrusters on its rear wasn't the only obvious modification made to the outside; it was also equipped with long red grappling arms that would fold out from the underside of the van. These grappling arms were used to duel with other ships. This modification had become somewhat of a trend among the beings of the Higher Universe who owned and operated interplanetary spacecrafts. Adding these arms changed the designation of the spaceships into what the inhabitants of the outer galaxies were now calling Grappler Ships.

This Conversion Van zipping throughout space was known as the Quantum Shortbus. And the ship it was currently grappling with was the spaceship Tenchi. The Tenchi was significantly larger than the Quantum Shortbus, which would seem quite obvious. However, the Shortbus seemed to be doing some notable damage to the hull of its target as it came at the Tenchi again and again, using its grappling arms in a way equivalent to a battering ram. The spaceship Tenchi was known to be of the Highest Technology across innumerable galaxies. Its main middle segment resembled a large metal frisbee with several domes of glass around the circumference. Several layers of discs were stacked in the middle of this saucer, and they were capped by a cone that came to a point. Several large windows were wrapped around this upper cone. On top of this cone were several rotating balls as well as what looked like spinning helixes. Directly on the underside of the large saucer, four pillars jutted down and connected to another spinning disc which had a long nipple that jutted out from below. This was the main fusion reactor.

Bracketing the structures in the center of the saucer were two large wing-like protrusions which made it look like the whole ship was collected inside parentheses. They were made of intricately carved wood and metal, and these wing-like protrusions also resembled the wooden part of a bow, pulled back and ready to let an arrow fly.

The Quantum Shortbus had already knocked loose several chunks from these wings. Debris went hurtling into space as flames and smoke shot out from the damaged areas. The Tenchi tried to return fire from a laser gun turret at the edge of the saucer. The Shortbus was too quick—the way it moved in jumpy zig-zags seemed physically impossible, but it was happening.

The Tenchi was retreating, or being pushed further and further toward the Moon and then beyond it toward Earth.

The Tenchi tried to use its thrusters to evade the Shortbus and fly back into deep space, but it was useless. The Shortbus was so small compared to the Tenchi that it could barely get a target on it for more than a second; then it had disappeared to a different part of the gargantuan hull where it proceeded to use its grappling arms to punch holes in it like a UFC fighter. One good ram and the tip of a wing flew off into space, burning as it went.

The Tenchi was done for, and whoever the pilot was knew that it was only a matter of time before they crashed. The Shortbus was determined to push its target closer and closer to the little blue planet until it could throw it into the atmosphere. And they were almost there. The continents slowly became visible beneath the cloud cover. Suddenly, the Shortbus's grappling arm ripped off the nipple of the fusion reactor below the saucer of the Tenchi and hurled it into space with flourish. And after that, it only took one final push to get the Tenchi to be taken by the Earth's magnetic pull.

The Quantum Shortbus hovered just outside of the atmosphere as it watched the Tenchi start to spin out of control as it was taken by Earth's gravity. Down, down, down; hurtling toward the ocean. The pilot had lost control of her spaceship and knew it was just a matter of time before she and her precious Tenchi hit the big blue of the planet below.

The red conversion van, which was now a spaceship, watched for another minute as the Tenchi became a smaller and smaller speck, and then zoomed back off into outer space.

FIFTEEN

Chicago remained in ruins. Buildings crumbled and sank into the earth below. Corpses were strewn around the rubble, mutilated beyond recognition and being hugged by the freezing flood from Lake Michigan. In some areas the water was already beginning to turn a deep crimson. They stood in Daley Plaza, in ankle-deep frigid water. Eden, Darren, Mothman, and Rob; they all stared at Terry as if silently asking him "What next?"

"Circle up and hold hands," Terry said. Without question, they joined hands and expectantly awaited whether there was a way to right all of this destruction. "I was given a spell," Terry continued, "and now is the time to use it."

Everyone closed their eyes intuitively. Their feet were going numb in the freezing water, but none of them seemed to care. This was too important. "Will this reverse all the damage done to this city?" Eden asked.

"I don't know," Terry admitted, "but we have to try." He took a deep breath and squeezed the hand of Eden on his left and Darren on his right. "I will recite this once so you all know the words, then we will repeat it until the damage has been re-paired." Terry took a pause in which all of his friends were in a hushed silence. He took a quick inhale and then recited: "*What's done is done, until it is undone.*"

Then they all chanted:

"*What's done is done, until it is undone.*"

On this first spell cast, wherever there was a specter attached to a human, dead or alive, or even solitary, they got pulled up and thrown into the air. "Again!" Terry commanded.

And they chanted:

"*What's done is done, until it is undone!*"

The specters got sucked up higher into the air and then suddenly disappeared, taken from the Hollow Dimension and put back in their rightful place in the Dark Tethers. In spite of the cold, January morning air, Terry began to sweat from his brow. Steam wafted from the top of his cranium. "Keep going," Terry whispered. "It's working."

"What's done is done, until it is undone... What's done is done, until it is undone... What's done is done, until it is undone..." They all shot the spell out into the Spiralverse in perfect harmony. While they chanted, Terry visualized the buildings being put back together the way they were before Maya ripped the fabric between worlds. He didn't need to tell his friends to keep chanting anymore, they just kept doing it.

Terry opened his eyes while they all continued the recitation. It had become difficult to keep it up, as if the weight of the task was too great for any of them, alone or collectively, to handle. Terry looked over at the building across the street; the one that had been devastated by Darren's Singularity Pulse. The chunks of glass and metal on the street below the building twitched and moved. Sometimes they would start floating up into the air, as if to return themselves to their place before they were rubble, but then they would just fall back into the ruins and water below.

Then he looked farther in the distance, at a skyscraper that was trying to right itself. The top half was trying to levitate and put itself back in place to heal the broken building, but it couldn't muster the strength to get there and fell back to the street below, causing more destruction on impact.

"It's too heavy for us," Darren finally said from beside Terry. "This isn't fucking working." The frustration was evident in his voice. He opened his eyes and they all stopped chanting. They dropped hands in defeat. Darren continued, "At least we could send the specters back to Dark Tethers... But we can't fix a city that is broken... No matter how much we love it." The disappointment was etched on his face. Chicago was his home too. He had made a life here. He had built his club *angelfuck* here and created a safe space for people like him, like Terry, like Eden, and all the other freaks like them. Now Darren was realizing that all of that might be over.

"We had to try," Terry said with a sigh.

"You did your best," Rob said, putting his hand on Terry's shoulder. Tears were threatening to come pouring from Terry's eyes.

"So many people dead," Terry said in a horrified whisper. "And I can't help feeling partly responsible."

Eden leaned in and kissed her lover on his red cheek, burning from the cold. "Come on, love," she said. "Let's get out of this freezing water and go home."

They all started walking back over toward the van that was still angled half-way into the empty fountain. "Can you drop me off back at *angelfuck*?" Darren asked. "It's probably all flooded and I want to get started on cleaning up, and see how much damage there is."

Terry nodded and he looked over at Mothman. "You haven't said much, Mothman. You're never this quiet. You okay?"

"Hmm?" Mothman looked at his friend as if pulled out of a trance. "It's just, I never knew that this could be a possibility of where my life would go. I always thought I would just be chasing pussy and partying for most of my life. Probably die young... I don't know if I should resent you or thank you for activating my Soulmind."

"I didn't do it on purpose, you fuck!" Terry raised his voice, taking out his frustration on Mothman. "Feel free to go back the fuck to sleep at anytime."

"Relax, baby, relax," Eden whispered, rubbing Terry's back as they got into the van. Terry walked around and got into the driver's seat, Darren got in on the passenger's side.

"Yes, it's been fun sometimes," Mothman admitted, scooting in beside Rob. "But it's also stressful. Things that aren't human have tried to kill me. I was stuck in your house with Rob and some bitch-ass cat because we couldn't leave or we'd be possessed by demons from another Dimension. A fat fuck doused me in his semen before I killed him..."

"That sounds like a good day for you," Terry mocked.

"Oh, fuck you, you cocksucker," Mothman shot back.

"Boys!" Eden yelled. "Cut it the fuck out! I don't want to hear your bullshit right now. Yes, we're all stressed out. Yes, Chicago might be Ground Zero now and it was partly our fault. So can we just try to be supportive of each other, not take out our frustration on each other, or be at one another's throats?"

"Fine," Mothman said.

"Good," Eden replied.

It went silent in the van. Terry didn't even bother turning the engine on. He just tuned into the Merkabah field around the vehicle and it began levitating into the air. There was no way they could drive normally on the destroyed downtown streets; they would just fall through the cracks. It looked like a bomb had gone off in the middle of Chicago and it was beyond all hope of repair. The people, or government, would have to build a whole new city and call it *Neo-Chicago*, if they chose to. As they floated through the streets in Terry's van, they sat in hushed silence as the reality of the extent of the destruction really began to set in. There seemed to be no signs of life anywhere.

They made it to *angelfuck* and the flood-water was splashing against the door in little waves. "Thanks," Darren said, and shook Terry's hand. He turned around in his seat to look at Eden as he started to open his door to get out. "It was good to see you, Eden," he said. "I'll call you."

Eden gave a weak smile and nodded. After which Darren got out of the van and opened the door to his club. The water rushed in and poured down the stairs. Before entering, he turned and waved to his friends as they floated away, back towards the suburbs.

In no time they were out of the city, trying to put the remains behind them literally and emotionally. Once the streets were back to normal, Terry brought the tires down onto the asphalt, started the van, and began to drive like a normal person. What had transpired in the city had not touched the suburbs, so Terry didn't want to risk being spotted in a flying car. Most unconscious humans didn't notice things that were out of the ordinary anyway, but he wasn't willing to take that risk.

"You guys tired back there?" Terry asked, glancing into his rearview mirror. Eden looked next to her and Mothman and Rob were leaning on each other with their eyes closed.

She chuckled quietly. "I guess we wore them out," she commented. "Are we almost home?"

Terry smiled. "You're starting to consider my house your home?"

Eden nodded, staring out the window as they got closer to Terry's street. "Yes, my love. Wherever you are feels like home to me... And also I don't know if my apartment in Wicker Park survived after all that. I hope Kat's okay."

"Oh, yeah," Terry responded, "Kat. I'm sure he's fine. I have a feeling we'll see him again one of these days."

Terry pulled up alongside the curb and parked in front of his house. The golden sphere still shone brilliantly around it, and the star tetrahedron spun inside it. However, all of the specters were nowhere to be seen. They had been banished with the first chanting of the spell Jessica had given Terry.

After putting the car into park, Terry sighed loudly and let his muscles relax. It felt like he had been tensed up for a whole year and could now finally let go. "Fuck me, we're here," he said.

Eden nudged Rob with her elbow. "Hey, fudge-packers," she said, "we're back."

The two boys slowly opened their eyes and yawned. Mothman glared at Eden out of the corner of narrowed eyes. "The fuck you call me, bitch?"

Eden laughed. "I was just fucking around," she said as she slid open the van passenger door. "Let's get inside. I think we're all going to sleep for a year."

They were all as slow as geriatric patients, hobbling from the van toward the front door. "God, we look pathetic," Terry chuckled. Rob and Mothman were supporting each other as they shuffled through the snow. When they finally made it into the house and Terry locked the door behind them, they all breathed a sigh of relief. "Sanctuary at last!" Terry said.

"I don't know about you guys," Rob said, "but I'm thirsty as fuck." He rushed into the kitchen to get some water from the tap. "You guys want anything?"

Eden nodded.

Mothman replied, "Some water and some fucking orange juice."

The house was eerily quiet to Terry; in more than an auditory way. He walked up the stairs, presumably going to his bedroom. Eden watched him as he climbed the stairs and then turned the corner out of sight. Rob got glasses out of the cabinet and was filling up water for everyone. A couple minutes later, Terry appeared at the top of the stairs, looking down at them in the kitchen.

"What is it?" Eden asked, looking up at him.

Terry shook his head. "The Octobers are gone..."

SIXTEEN

The soles of Darren's shoes squeaked on the wet stairs as he went down to see what kind of damage had been done to his precious club. He had to hold tightly to the railing as to not slip and fall on his ass. Opening the door at the bottom of the stairs, he walked out onto the dance floor through almost ankle-deep water. The whole place had been flooded and the force of the tremors had thrown the furniture from the balconies literally everywhere. It looked like a monsoon and an earthquake had hit at the same time.

Darren shook his head, grieving. "I'm sorry, my love," he whispered. "You did not deserve what Maya has done to you." Sloshing across the floor, he went through the curtain at the back of the club and into his private office. There was a heavy stone of dread developing in the pit of his stomach, but Darren didn't want to accept the possibility that the golden days of running his club might be over.

There wasn't as much damage in Darren's inner sanctuary. Maybe that was because of the presence of the portal to The Kingdom hiding behind the Little Door. None of the furniture had been thrown around, but the carpet squished underfoot like a wet sponge as Darren made his way over to his desk and plopped his tired ass down in the chair. He closed his eyes and let out a long exhale as he dropped his head back. As he rubbed his eyes, the adrenaline of the fight was finally wearing off and the exhaustion began to grip his fatigued muscles and sink in like strychnine into his bones.

Suddenly the sound of footsteps splashing through the dance floor met Darren's ears and he jerked up in his chair. There was a gun he kept in the top drawer of his desk, and he slowly opened it and put his hand on the pistol. Who could be coming into his club right now? Who was even still alive after all that destruction?

The door to the office opened slowly and four cloaked figures walked in. Two were men and two were women. Their cloaks went all the way down to their feet and they all wore them with the hoods up, obscuring their faces. Their cloaks were also a dark gray color with the letters *LC* embroidered on the right breast in fancy script. When Darren saw them, he relaxed and closed the drawer, hiding his gun once more.

"Comrades," Darren greeted them. Obviously, he knew them. "Come in." They approached his desk silently. Darren continued, "It's pointless to fill you in on the situation, because, obviously, you're all aware."

One of the hooded figures stepped forward—a woman. She spoke, "You've been in contact with the Prophet." It wasn't a question, it was a statement. Seemingly it was apparent that whatever Order this was was keeping tabs on Terry and the goings-on around him. The woman continued, "Our sources tell us that the Shadow Forces are converging on the Prophet and intend to take him."

Darren's brow furrowed in a pensive expression. "Are you sure? Well, that's not good…"

The woman smiled wryly under the shadow of her hood that cast a darkness over her obscured eyes. "No, it is 'not good' as you so aptly stated," the woman said. "Aren't you just the poet? Nevertheless, more is being required of you."

"Yes? I'm listening," Darren replied.

"This is your mission now," the hooded woman stated flatly. "If he is to be captured, you have to be the one to break him free. The Prophet is too vital to our cause to allow him to be locked away. And as the strings we are going to need to pull become clearer, our people on the inside and on the outside will be coming to you with more instructions. Do we have an understanding?"

Darren nodded his head seriously. "I understand my role and I will play it to the best of my ability."

The woman shook her head under her hood. "No," she said with force, "that's not good enough."

Darren was puzzled. "What's not good enough?"

"The best of your ability," the woman answered. "In this case your best is not good enough. You will dig deep into the depths of your Soulmind and pull out more than you ever knew you had. And with the power of the Body, you will be guided. That is all." Without another word, the four cloaked figures turned and left the way they had come.

SEVENTEEN

FROM THE MIND OF TERRY BROSWALD:

The house is silent as I start stirring in my bed. What woke me up? I feel a strange vibration in the air. Then I hear a loud crash and the house shakes as if an earthquake erupted. I jolt upright. "What the fuck was that?" A cool breeze blows through my open door and I shiver, shirtless. Getting out of bed, I pull on a sweatshirt and some black pants. I'm pretty sure I'm dreaming since I went to sleep beside Eden and now she's nowhere in sight. There's an odd absence of noise from Rob and Mothman as well.

How come in my recent dreams I'm always appearing in my own house? Whatever happened to dreaming of fantastic far away places? All I can think is hopefully my dream-parents haven't shown up again. The earthquake that happened in that dream was Sul stomping around outside my house. Maybe he's back.

Rushing down the stairs, I confirm that I am in fact alone in my dream-house. I see a large green shape looming outside my front window. Sul! After flinging the front door open, I bound down the porch stairs. The dragon moves his gigantic head over to look at me. He smiles warmly, as if seeing a long-lost friend. "My boy, you survived," the dragon speaks in his deep bellowing voice.

I laugh. "You had any doubt in your reptilian mind that I would?"

Sul smiles, showing me his impossibly long fangs. "No, I had no doubt in my mind that you would be okay. It is not yet time for the Steward of Time to pass from this life and on to the next."

I ignore the *Steward of Time* thing and say, "There is a next life? You know, after this one?"

Sul nods his giant head. "There have been before-lives. There will be next-lives. And there are next-next-lives." The dragon looks up into the sky thoughtfully. "Or maybe—just maybe—you could become immortal in this lifetime. That doesn't always mean you'll live *forever* in this incarnation, but maybe through millennia."

My mouth hangs open, I'm dumbfounded. My puny brain can't even comprehend such a thought. "I don't know if I would even want to live forever," I say, shaking my head. "And a millennium is such a long fucking time. I can't even comprehend what it would be like to live that long."

Sul changes the subject as he starts to walk down my empty street. I walk next to him, placing my hand on the scaly skin of his leg. "You know," the dragon begins, "dragons used to walk the earth free. Before men in armor started to hunt us down and bring our heads back to impress their girlfriends." Sul presses his lips together in a sorrowful expression. Then he continues, "But... Dragons will walk and fly free on the earth again very soon."

"Why can't you do that now?" I ask.

"Actually," Sul explains, "the Hollow Dimension used to be at a much higher vibration. Dragons are magickal creatures and can only survive on a high vibrational level. When a plane of existence gets to be too dense, we have to go underground and to a different plane of reality. So when the Hollow Dimension became more dense, we had to go into the caves of Meddia and into the Dreamsphere. Back in the times of dragons, there were also other magickal creatures who inhabited the Hollow Dimension: faeries, elves, dwarves, unicorns, to just name a few."

"And they had to go underground too?" I ask, fascinated.

Sul nods. "Yes, they have. And they have migrated to other Dimensional levels like Pangea. And like the dragons, they inhabit the Dreamsphere as well. Those with very sensitive Soulminds, can sometimes be in a forest and penetrate the veil between worlds, especially on times of the full moon when the veil is at its thinnest."

"Wow!" I exclaim. "I want to have adventures with elves and faeries and unicorns!"

The dragon laughs warmly. "Oh, I'm sure you will have your time. Especially since it will be you to open the way for the Hollow Dimension to raise in vibration again. That is when the dragons and the other magickal creatures can emerge again."

"How am I supposed to do that?" I ask. "Raise the vibration of the Hollow Dimension?"

"Timestrus," Sul says matter-of-factly.

"What? That rapist creep?"

The dragon elaborates, "He has a monopoly on the Fourth Dimension, which keeps the human world locked in the Third Dimension. In order for the Hollow Dimension to ascend in vibration past the Fourth, and on to the Fifth, and the Sixth, and Seventh, and so on, Timestrus has to be eliminated."

"And you think that's gonna be me?" I scoff. "I was barely able to wound him last time. And he ripped my arm off and then tried to rape me again. Needless to say, I don't want to go anywhere near that fuck ever again."

"It's okay," Sul says comfortingly. He stops walking as we get to the end of my street. "You don't have to think about that right now."

The dragon looks up toward the sky again. I follow his gaze, and what I see leaves me speechless. High in the sky is some kind of craft. Some fucking alien-looking spaceship. It reminds me of the as-big-as-a-city spaceships from *Independence Day*. The craft is trying to hide behind the cloud cover, but I can see it clearly. "What the fuck is that?" I yell, pointing toward the object in the sky.

Sul doesn't say anything for a moment, then he finally speaks, "There are other Beings in this Spiralverse as well. Not the Magickal creatures of nature and Mother Earth, ones that come from deep out in the Expanse. And as of right now, it is unclear what their intentions are. So be cautious in your dealings with them, Terry. I'd hate to see you played like a puppet by the wrong forces."

"What? Like aliens?" I ask.

"Aliens. Demons from the void..." Sul continues. "Actually, to be honest, we don't know yet whether they are benevolent or malevolent. Their technology is somewhat foreign to creatures like me. We who rely on magick instead of machines. Maybe one day dragons will be able to fly in space as well. That's an ability that we can only dream of evolving into. What that would mean for the Spiralverse, we can only speculate..."

"My head hurts," I say, and rest my forehead against the dragon's bulbous leg. I shut my eyes and listen to his deep, soothing voice.

"That's fine, child, it's time for you to wake up anyway."

Then I'm back in bed, laying next to Eden's warm body. I lay there with my eyes closed, listening to her quiet breathing as she sleeps.

EIGHTEEN

"Hey, Terry, do you see this?" Rob called from near the front door.

"What?" Terry called back. He was in the kitchen making breakfast and had a piece of buttered toast hanging out of his mouth.

"Come here!"

Terry bit a piece off of his toast and took it out of his mouth as he walked over to join Rob at the front window. Rob looked at Terry as he approached, and then pointed out the window. Terry followed with his eyes to where Rob was pointing. Across the street, parked alongside the curb, was a black SUV with the most tinted windows they had ever seen. The vehicle wasn't directly across from Terry's house, that would be too obvious. It was parked a little down the street to the left; but still, the SUV wasn't exactly hiding either.

"Well that is not normal," Terry said, shaking his head. He frowned and looked at Rob. "You've never noticed it there before?"

Rob shook his head. "Uh-uh. You either?"

"No, never," Terry replied. He turned back to look at the ominously black SUV and heard it start its engine. In a moment it was driving away, and it quickly turned the corner at the end of the block and was out of sight.

Terry shrugged and took another bite of his brittle toast. Crumbs rained down from the corners of his mouth and onto the rug under his feet. He squeezed Rob's shoulder and then walked back toward the kitchen. Mothman was sitting on the couch in the living room, and at the sight of him, Terry stopped and stared. Mothman had his pants and boxers down and around his ankles. His erect cock was in his right hand and he was stroking it viciously. In his left hand he held the Hi8 camera and was pointing it at his dick. He watched the monitor on the side of the camera with a wicked grin on his face.

"What the fuck *are* you doing?" Terry asked, raising an eyebrow.

Mothman looked up and registered that Terry was standing there. "I'm filming my magnificent cock for posterity," he answered.

Terry looked baffled. "For *posterity*?"

Mothman continued to stroke his erect member, up and down every inch of the shaft and then rubbing the head like the tip of a mushroom. He licked his lips. "Yeah, Terry," Mothman continued, "why don't you come over and help me? Cum choke on this dick!"

Terry coughed out a laugh, an involuntary reaction, like a spasm. He waved Mothman away and continued to walk back into the kitchen, shoving the last of the toast into his mouth. "Maybe later," Terry answered through a mouthful.

"Awww," Mothman whined. "Don't be such a little bitch, Terry!"

"Who you calling a little bitch, you faggot?" Terry shot back.

Mothman continued, "You know you want some of this dick right now. Come *on*! Let's have some fun and make a video. You know you want to."

Terry rolled his eyes, but smiled in spite of himself. "Fine, you perverted sicko. Let me go see if Eden wants to join in. We could do, like, a group sex video."

"That's the Terry I know!" Mothman said cheerily.

Terry began to walk up the stairs to find Eden. He stopped and looked down at Mothman. "Go see if you can talk Rob into it," Terry told Mothman. "I think he's still at the front window watching out for the *guvment*."

Mothman nodded and Terry went up to his bedroom. When Terry entered his room, Eden was still in bed but she wasn't asleep. She was laying on her back, rubbing her eyes, and yawning with a wide open mouth. "Hey, babe," Terry said.

Eden blinked sleepily. She smiled warmly at seeing him and stretched her arms out in a gesture for him to come to her. "Good morning, baby," she said as Terry crawled onto the bed and hugged her tightly. They kissed, already going at it with tongues and wet lips. "You don't mind my morning breath?" Eden whispered, giggling softly.

Terry shook his head while Eden still had her arms around his neck, face close to hers. "Not really," Terry answered. "You're just too sexy for me to care about that."

"Aww, you're sweet, babe." Eden poked him on the tip of his nose and smiled. "What have you boys been up to?"

Terry was quiet for a moment and then chuckled mischievously.

"What?" Eden said, now really interested.

Terry's grin widened even more. "Do you want to make a porno with us?"

"*Ah-ha!*" Eden half snorted and half laughed. "What? Why?"

"Cause we're fucking bored."

"Oh, that explains it then. And it has nothing to do with Mothman trying to get your hot girlfriend into the sack?"

"Well, yeah," Terry admitted, "that probably has something to do with it."

Eden shrugged. "Yeah, sure, whatever. Let's do it."

"What? Really?"

Eden nodded. "Sure, why not? It's not like it's the first time I'm doing erotic modeling. I've even done a couple solo masturbation videos."

"Really? I didn't know that," Terry responded. "I want to see those!" he said, smiling and bouncing his eyebrows up and down.

Eden rubbed her thumb over Terry's lips and then slipped it into his mouth, rubbing the edge of his bottom teeth. "I'm sure you would... I'll have to show you sometime."

Terry sucked on Eden's thumb as they gazed into each other's eyes. Then Eden pulled her thumb out of Terry's mouth, rubbing it over his tongue as she went. She smacked his cheek playfully and said, "Okay. I'm going to go brush my teeth and I'll meet you downstairs."

Terry kissed his lover one more time and then slipped off the bed and back downstairs. When he got back to the living room, Mothman was completely naked, standing in the middle of the room stroking his huge cock. Rob was in front of him, filming with the Hi8 camera. Terry laughed at the ridiculousness of the scene. "How did you talk Rob into doing this?" he asked.

Rob glanced at Terry without moving the camera away from what he was filming. Rob responded by saying, "I didn't want to be in the video, but I don't mind filming you guys."

"Yeah," Mothman said, bouncing his dick in the air. "Rob likes looking at my cock. Don't you, Rob?"

Rob shook his head, but he was smiling nonetheless. "Eden's gonna come down and join us," Terry said, looking back up the stairs. "I know this is just your elaborate scheme to fuck my girlfriend."

"I would never!" Mothman exclaimed in mock-offense. "Actually, you're totally right. I'm gonna fuck that pussy good. If it's not today, it'll be tomorrow or the next day. But mark my words, Terry, one day I'm going to pound that pussy."

Terry replied, "If I wasn't polyamorous, I'd probably be offended by that. But human beings don't belong to anyone. No one can possess another person. My freedom and her freedom allows for that."

They heard the toilet flush at the top of the stairs and suddenly Eden appeared there, wearing only a t-shirt and panties. She looked gorgeous as she walked down the stairs. Gorgeous in a way where she didn't even have to try. She wasn't wearing any makeup and her long pink hair bounced around her shoulders, still messy from sleep. Her nipples were hard and her small perky breasts bounced under her shirt, braless.

Terry looked over and noticed that Rob had moved the camera away from Mothman and was following Eden as she came down the stairs. Silently, Eden approached Terry, pressed her body against his, and kissed his lips. "Undress me," she whispered.

Eden raised her arms over her head and Terry slowly pulled her shirt up and off. Her tits were perfect and Terry cupped them tenderly in his hands. Eden tugged at Terry's shirt and he allowed her to start undressing him. He unbuckled his belt and then Eden finished unzipping him and pulled his pants down to his ankles. Terry kicked his pants into the corner of the room. Now all he was wearing was a pair of boxers. And Eden was naked except for a pair of black panties.

Terry knelt down in front of his lover, the Perfect Forever, and slid her panties off. The sprouts of a little bush were growing cutely between her legs. When Terry tried to stand up, Eden pushed the top of his head back down and spread her legs. "Lick my cunt, you slut," she commanded. Terry allowed her to press his face into her crotch, and he lapped greedily at her cunt with his wet tongue.

"Oh yeah, this is getting good!" Mothman said lustily. He was staring at the scene from the spot where he had been standing for a while. Drool glistened at the corners of his mouth as he jerked himself off. "God, that's so fucking hot! Yeah, Terry, lick that pussy!"

Rob continued to film Eden and Terry going at it. He once swung the camera back to capture Mothman pleasuring himself, but then he went back quickly to the cunnilingus. Terry's tongue was so deep inside Eden's snatch. He lapped at it and sucked on her clit until she was dripping into his mouth. Eden closed her eyes and moaned as she threw her head back. "Oh, fuck, Terry, just like that," she moaned loudly. "You're so good, you're gonna make me cum!" She clenched Terry's hair in her fists and ground his head harder into her crotch.

Eden started to yip louder, and breathe heavier. Her thighs began to shudder on either side of Terry's head. The nipples at the tip of her tiny breasts were rock-hard, erect and waiting to be sucked.

Rob turned to look at Mothman, without moving the camera. "Fuck, dude, this is really hot," Rob said, his face flushed.

"Oh, I'm gonna cum!" Eden screamed. "Get ready, Terry! Ahhh, aaahhh, AAAAHHHH!" She came violently in that moment; her eyes rolled back up into her skull, showing the whites of her eyeballs, and her whole body trembled with the orgasm. Terry made a muffled moaning sound as he worked his tongue even faster over Eden's clit. Her chest heaved as she breathed, the afterglow of the orgasm sending tingles throughout her whole body. She pulled Terry's head away from her cunt and guided him to his feet. Then they kissed passionately, tongues licking in each other's mouths. Eden could taste the sweetness of her own juices on Terry's lips and tongue.

"Rob got a boner!" Mothman laughed and pointed at Rob's crotch which was tenting out the front of his pants.

"Shut up!" Rob snapped, his face flushing deeply. "That's a natural response, you jerk. Look at your own boner!"

Mothman chuckled again. "I know, Rob. I'm just giving you a hard time. Now I hope I get to join in now."

Eden smiled naughtily and walked slowly, seductively, over to Mothman. She was so close to him that the tip of his erection was almost touching her lower abdomen. Eden bit her bottom lip and looked up at Mothman with pouty puppy-dog eyes. Rob moved in closer with the camera. "Do you want to fuck me with that big cock of yours?" Eden whisper-moaned this, teasing Mothman.

"Oh my God!" Mothman said, an orgasmic chill shooting through his body. His glasses almost fogged up from their collective body heat. Watching from the short distance away, Terry was still hard and stroked between his legs. Mothman continued,

"I want to fuck you in the worst way! Your petite little tits and ass. And that sexy-ass pink hair." He stroked the side of Eden's face and through her hair.

Eden backed up a step. "Too bad, so sad," she said. "If you want to fuck me, you gotta earn it." Mothman frowned and Eden flicked the tip of his dick with her fingernail.

"Ow! You bitch!" Mothman yelled out and grabbed his manhood. "That's dirty."

Eden giggled. "I will suck you off though," she said with a mischievous grin. "Get on your fucking knees!"

"Ooo, she's dominant," Mothman said, looking over Eden's shoulder at Terry. "I like when a woman takes control."

"I bet you do, you little boy. Little brother," Eden said as Mothman knelt down, erection still sticking out straight in front of him. Then Eden got down on her hands and knees. Her ass stuck up into the air, and Terry had a great view of her luscious cunt and asshole.

"What's with that?" Mothman asked. "You have some kind of incest fetish? You want your brother to fuck you?"

Eden nodded and gave the tip of Mothman's cock a little playful lick. "Yeah," she whined sexily. "That's one of my kinks. *You're* definitely not one to judge anyone."

Mothman laughed. "Yeah, you're right about that."

Eden assumed the role of sexy sister again. "Brother, why do you always want to play doctor in the basement? You touch me here and there, and everywhere. If you don't make me cum I'll have to tell Mom and Dad."

"Oh, no! Don't do that," Mothman played along. "I know how to please my big sister."

Eden looked over her shoulder at Terry who was still standing a few feet away with his mouth open and hand on his cock. "Terry, get the fuck over here and fuck me!" she commanded.

Terry snapped out of his trance and went to kneel down behind Eden. "With pleasure," Terry said as he rubbed his lover's pussy which was still dripping from when he was licking her. Eden turned her head back toward Mothman and took his thick cock in her mouth and started sucking it deep.

"Oh, fuck yeah," Mothman moaned. "Me and Terry are gonna treat you like some fucking Chinese finger cuffs!"

"You're seriously making a movie reference right now?" Terry said as he rubbed the tip of his cock over the lips of Eden's wet snatch.

"What?" Mothman said defensively. Then he moaned loudly. "Oh, fuck, yeah that's good, baby. Suck it just like that." He put his hand on Eden's head and guided it down and up on his dick. "That was a fucking good movie," he continued. "That chick should totally have had a threesome with Ben Affleck and what's his fuck—his ugly comic book friend."

"Jason Lee," Terry said as he put his hands around Eden's slim waist and began to thrust deeply into her. "Now shut the fuck up. You're ruining the mood."

Mothman tilted his head back as his eyes rolled into the back of his skull. He started to breathe heavier as Eden sucked and licked Mothman's magnificent member. She was definitely a master. The blowjob was making Mothman feel like he was on the verge of cumming but he wasn't busting a nut, the ecstasy just kept going. She knew how to keep her teeth from scraping his shaft as well. Mothman was no stranger to girls who didn't know what they were doing when it came to sucking dick.

The three of them looked like a wobbly letter *H* as Eden got reamed in one hole on each side of her body. Terry was stroking down the line of Eden's spine with the tip of his index finger as he buried every inch of his manhood into her tight pussy. She moaned through the cock in her mouth. Rob moved to the back and side of Terry so that he could get a good shot of his cock sliding in and out. Eden's round muscular ass slapped against Terry's tight abs right above his pubic hair.

Suddenly Mothman's orange Soulmind erupted from his chest and started illuminating the aura around his body. The bright incandescence of the energy wafted off of him like electric steam. Rainbows of light burst from the top of his scalp and lit up the arcline around his head.

Rob moved the camera up so that all three of them were in the shot now. "Holy shit!" Rob exclaimed, staring into the monitor screen on the side of the camera.

"What? What is it?" Terry asked.

By this point Terry's white Soulmind had revealed itself as well, dancing around his body and stretching into Eden's energy field. Her pink and red Soulmind was also leaking out of her back like her spine was glowing and growing bright tendrils of light.

"I can see your guys's Soulminds on the camera here!" Rob exclaimed, totally in disbelief of what he was witnessing.

"What? Nuh-uh," Terry said incredulously, not slowing the rate of his thrust. "Let me see."

Rob leaned over beside Terry, pointing the camera at Mothman who was deeply enjoying the fellatio. Looking down at the monitor screen on the side of the camera, Terry's mouth dropped open. "Well, fuck me in the asshole," Terry said, stunned. On the little screen he could see Mothman's orange aura growing larger and large, and then tendrils of it reached like fingers to start mingling with Eden's red and pink energy. Terry looked away from the camera and of course could see all three Soulminds with his naked eye as well. But he was flabbergasted that it could be picked up on the camera.

Rob moved again to get a better shot of all three of them as they built up to the Climactic Moment of orgasm. Mothman was breathing shallowly and fast as his cock throbbed all the way to the back of Eden's throat. She choked on it as he felt the cum building in his balls and perineum. Sweat was dripping down Terry's spine and into his ass crack as he felt himself getting close to busting the fattest nut.

"Oh, my god, this is hot!" Rob moaned, and his boner was still bulging through his pants.

"I'm gonna fucking cum!" Mothman screamed. "Get ready for my load, slut!"

Eden moaned hard and didn't take Mothman's cock out of her mouth. Instead she put her hands on his ass cheeks and pulled him deeper into her throat. "I'm gonna fucking cum too!" Terry yelled loudly. Mothman screamed as his hot cum squirted into Eden's throat. She gagged but swallowed every last drop. Simultaneously, Terry pulled out of Eden's cunt suddenly and pumped his cock with his fist tight around his shaft. Five pumps of jiz shot out of his cock and onto Eden's tight little asshole. And as he came, his white Soulmind exploded through Eden's and Mothman's energy, creating a storm of colors: white, orange, red, and pink.

Sliding his already-softening cock out of Eden's mouth, Mothman sunk down to sit on his heels. Eden also collapsed onto her side on the rug in a sweaty heap. She lazily rubbed her clit with her right hand. Terry sat back against the front of the couch. "Holy fuck," Eden said, panting. "I haven't been fucked like that since Kindergarten."

Terry and Mothman exchanged a look and then they burst out laughing. "See! I'm not the only one who quotes from movies during sex," Mothman said, hardly able to catch his breath from the laughing and the heavy sex-breathing.

Rob turned off the camera and closed the screen back into the side. "That was wild," he said. "I'm sure other people with

Soulminds will be able to see your energy on that tape. But non-Soulminds probably won't be able to."

"I think that's a safe assumption," Terry said. Their Soulminds had settled down after the peak of their orgasms and had disappeared back into their warm bodies.

"Did you fucking cum in your pants, Rob?" Mothman joked.

Rob nodded, conceding the issue. "Not gonna lie, I think I actually did."

Mothman and Terry burst out laughing again. "Rob wet his tighty-whities!" Terry laughed, pointing at Rob.

"Shut up, you fucker!" Rob shot back. "I don't wear tighty-whities!"

"Oh, that's right," Terry commented, "you're black, so you wear FUBU boxers."

Rob grinned with his shiny phosphorescent white teeth. "Speaking of BLACK," Rob continued, "I love your new friend Darren, he's so cool.... Cause he's *BLACK*."

Terry rolled his eyes. "I bet he would love to know you think so."

"Oh, no," Rob giggled, "don't tell him I said that, he'd probably kick my ass."

"Yeah, maybe," Eden interjected as she pulled herself up and leaned against the couch next to Terry on the rug.

Terry put his hand on her naked thigh. "You okay, babe?" he asked. "Did you cum?"

"Oh, yeah," she said with her eyes still closed. "I came so hard. A couple times actually." She opened her eyes and looked at Rob. Holding out her hand, she made a grabbing motion. "Gimme the camera."

Rob held the camera to his chest like it was his Precious. "What? Are you going to delete the video?"

"No, idiot," Eden answered. "I'm not going to delete the video. I want to upload it to my Pornhub account."

Terry looked at her, surprised, as Rob handed her the camera. "I didn't know you had a Pornhub account."

Eden smiled and looked at him out of the corner of her eye. "Actually, there's quite a few things you don't know about me," she said, standing up, her legs a little wobbly from the after-effects of sex. She continued, "I think I might change my username on my account though."

"To what?" Terry asked, looking up at her.

Eden looked down at her lover and winked. "*Temple of Cosmic Fuck.*"

FEBRUARY

ONE

The whole Soma trip and ordeal that followed was so traumatic for Jessica that she had to stay in bed and recover for several days afterward. She would sleep for whole days, it seemed, and would only wake up when Magda or Jay brought her some food or healing tea to bring her strength back. Now, she was finally coming out of her transcendent stupor. Jessica yawned and rubbed her eyes, rolling over in the cot. Wrinkling her nose, she realized that she smelled subtly of sweat, even though she had washed off thoroughly before laying down to recover. Laying in bed for almost a whole week could make someone stink.

Throwing her legs over the side of the cot, Jessica laboriously pulled herself to her feet and swiped the curtain aside that separated the little room from the rest of the cottage. She could hear Magda busying herself in the kitchen. Approaching silently, Jessica sat down at the table across from Jay who was quietly reading a book. Upon her joining the table, Jay closed his book and looked her up and down.

"Well, look who's finally joined the world of the living again," Jay said, smiling warmly.

Magda put a mug in front of Jessica and poured her a steaming cup of tea. "Yeah, I'm feeling a lot better," Jessica responded, blowing on the hot liquid in her teacup.

"That's wonderful, dear," Magda said, putting her hand on Jessica's shoulder. "I was just cooking up some eggs. Are you hungry? You must be."

Jessica nodded. "I'm starving."

Magda set a bowl of freshly picked blackberries and raspberries down in the middle of the table. "Here, sweetheart," she said, "you can start on some berries while I finish up the eggs."

Jessica popped a fresh blackberry into her mouth. The steam from the tea was still coming off of it in thick white wisps. "What's the plan?" Jessica asked, eager to get on with her lessons. "What's the next task or thing you're going to teach me?"

Jay smiled at his young student and folded his hands in front of him on the wooden table. He glanced over his shoulder at his companion who was back to cooking the eggs over the fire. "Well," he said, turning back to Jessica, "there comes a time when the Teacher has nothing left to teach you directly, and the student must go off to learn more while questing on their own." Jay's eyes were sad as he smiled.

A raspberry dropped out of Jessica's mouth and she shook her head. "No, I don't want to leave. I like it here with both of you. I feel like we've become family. You've been more family to me than my real parents back in the Hollow Dimension."

"Sweetheart, we understand," Magda said as she set a plate of steaming eggs in front of Jessica. "We've grown very fond of you as well. We ain't sending you away because we want to, but because you're now needed elsewhere."

"Elsewhere *where*?" Jessica asked, anxiety building in the pit of her stomach. "I don't want to go back to the fucking Hollow Dimension!"

Jay reached across the table and touched Jessica's hand. "We know this is difficult," Jay assured her. "And where you're to go is not for us to say."

"*Puh!*" Jessica snorted and jerked her hand away from Jay's touch. "So you're just going to fucking abandon me, is that it? 'Here, Jessica, have fun wandering around the woods.' It's bullshit." Obviously, she was hurt and turned her gaze away from Jay, not wanting him to see the tears in her eyes.

"You will have to travel deeper into the forest," Jay admitted. "But you won't be alone."

Jessica wiped her eyes and looked back at Jay across the table. "What do you mean?" she asked, picking up her wooden fork and shoveling some eggs into her mouth.

Magda stood behind Jay and put her hands on his shoulders. Then she answered the question. "Oh, you'll have lots of guides to show you the way. Enchanted animals, faerie folk, and the like."

Jessica sighed, it was taking too much of her energy to be angry at these two beautiful beings who had taken care of her so selflessly. "I guess I knew that I wasn't going to be able to stay here forever," she acknowledged. "And maybe to go on an adventure with faeries and unicorns maybe doesn't sound so bad. I need something to help me forget what happened to me in that town. Thanatos."

The old witch and wizard smiled and gave each other a knowing look. Jay nodded. "We've put together a little knapsack for you with some food and provisions that you'll need on your journey."

Jessica stared. She chewed slowly and let her fork fall into her eggs. "You're sending me off today?"

"Yes, love," Magda admitted. "That is the way it has been ordained."

"Ordained? Ordained by who?" Jessica wanted to know.

Jay took the reins on this one. "The higher powers of nature and the Spiralverse. You are a key element to the coming spiritual evolution—for all beings of the Spiralverse. Why do you think you survived even after you disappeared yourself from the Hollow?"

Jessica shrugged. "I just figured that I didn't do it right. I was trying to merge back into the nothingness."

Jay nodded reflectively. "The Spiralverse wouldn't let you leave. There was a specific reason for that."

"What reason?" Jessica asked through a mouthful of food. She was finishing up the eggs on her plate.

Jay didn't answer, instead he looked up at Magda and said quietly, "Do you want to finish getting Jessica's pack ready? She's got a long way to go and it's good to get an early start."

"I'm sitting right here, you know," Jessica said, pushing her clean plate a couple inches into the middle of the table, knocking the bowl of berries. Magda kissed Jay and then went to finish putting the last few things into Jessica's knapsack.

"Yes, Jessica," Jay said, looking back at her, "I know you're sitting right there. It wasn't meant to be disrespectful. Now that you have a full belly and some hot tea in you, are you ready to start on your quest?"

"No," Jessica answered flatly.

Jay couldn't help chuckling as he stood up from the table. Walking toward the door, he motioned for her to follow. Quietly Jessica acquiesced, following Jay out into the crisp forest air. As they stood side by side, staring off deep into the forest, Jessica was beginning to look frightened. "Don't be scared, child," Jay reassured her. "The magickal creatures of the forest will protect you and come to your aid whenever you are in peril."

"I sure hope so," Jessica said and shivered even though it wasn't cold.

"Now, that way," Jay pointed in one direction, "is back toward Thanatos. You don't want to go that way. You've already done that quest. But that way," Jay pointed in the opposite direction, "that's the way you want to go. Deeper into the forest."

"I have no idea what I'm supposed to be doing, or if there's something I need to be searching for?" Jessica voiced her questions as Magda emerged from the house with the knapsack full.

"Here you are, dear," Magda said, helping Jessica pull the straps of the knapsack over her shoulders. "There's food in there that won't spoil. And other assorted odds and ends, items, that you may need along the way."

"Where am I going?" Jessica asked, still reluctant to set off on a journey shrouded in so much mystery.

"The way will become clear as you go," Jay said knowingly. "Now, go. You're wasting daylight."

"Uhhh..." Jessica felt frozen, terrified to leave the two people who had always given her answers when she lacked them herself.

Magda smiled warmly and hugged Jessica. They embraced tightly, squeezing each other as if they would never meet again. When they detached, Jay hugged Jessica as well. She felt a little calmer after that. Smiling weakly, Jessica said, "Until we meet again."

Jay and Magda nodded as they smiled and waved her off. Jessica finally turned her back to them and walked deeper into the forest, into the unknown. In a few minutes, Jessica looked back and her two companions and their cottage had disappeared from sight.

The sounds of the forest thrilled her. Birds singing in the trees sounded like beautiful serenades of love. There were also noises that sounded like music from handmade instruments, yet she couldn't see any creatures that could be playing that music. The sunlight shone down in sparkling beams through the tree canopy above. The undergrowth was so green that it almost looked fake to Jessica. She had never seen such a healthy shade of green on any plants in the Hollow Dimension.

Time meant nothing in a magickal forest, and Jessica had no way to discern how long she had been walking. She was sort of taken into a trance from all the beauty and majesty surrounding her. Suddenly there came into view in front of her a clearing with a very still pond shimmering brightly on the forest floor. She approached this clearing with caution. The beams of sunlight shimmered off of the clear water like a sheet of a million diamonds. Jessica abruptly stopped when she saw a large animal drinking from the pond. It was a gorgeous white stallion. Jessica stayed in a hushed silence and watched this magnificent creature as its head bent down to the water and it lapped up the cool liquid with its long pink tongue.

Was it a stallion? Jessica squinted and caught a glint reflected off of something long protruding from his head. The breath caught in her chest as she realized that this wasn't a stallion—in fact it was a unicorn! "Holy fuck," Jessica whispered. "A real live unicorn." She could see its horn more clearly now that she had adjusted to the reality of the magick in front of her. The horn was shiny silver and cast subtle rainbows as it reflected the light. His tail swung side to side, the long white hair blowing through the air. Suddenly the unicorn drew his head up and looked in Jessica's direction. Her eyes went wide and her hands shot over her mouth as she tried not to make a sound.

"Don't be afraid, child," the unicorn spoke in a deep resonating voice that vibrated every cell in Jessica's body. "Come closer so I may look at you."

Jessica inhaled a quick breath and cautiously took a couple steps forward. The unicorn laughed and then whinnied, tossing his head back, mane flying in the wind. "You're so… gorgeous," Jessica said with hushed reverence and took a couple more halting steps toward the creature.

"I knew you were coming, Jessica," the unicorn said. "You got here just in time for when the light through the canopy hits the water just perfectly. Just glorious, isn't it?"

Jessica nodded, struck by the whole scene. Now she was only a few feet away from the unicorn. "You… knew?" she asked slowly. "That I was coming?"

The unicorn nodded. "The trees have ears, you know, and they whisper to me their secrets." He lowered his head as Jessica approached even closer. She reached out slowly and placed her hand on his white fuzzy nose. The unicorn sniffed deeply and then blew air out between his lips. "Artemis is my name," he introduced himself. "I am the guardian of these woods."

"Nice to meet you, Artemis," Jessica replied. "I'm Jessica… But you already knew that."

"I did, yes," Artemis said as Jessica continued to pet his long snout. "Take a drink from the pond of Sacred Knowledge before we go."

Jessica nodded and kneeled down on the bank of the pond. Cupping her hands, she scooped the crystal-clear water into her mouth and drank deeply. After one drink, she was infinitely refreshed and her mind was clear. Artemis knelt down into the soft grass below as Jessica turned back to him. "What are you doing?" she asked.

"Allowing you to get on my back so we may ride," Artemis answered. "We have some traveling to do."

Without further question, Jessica hiked up her skirts to her waist and swung her leg over Artemis's back to straddle him.

Once she was secure and holding onto his mane, the unicorn stood back up to his full height. Then they were off. Artemis walked deeper into the forest. They were in no hurry, so Artemis just strolled along at a leisurely pace.

As they walked, day began to change into afternoon and then the lower light of evening. Jessica had the distinct feeling that they were being watched as they traveled. Sometimes she even thought she caught glimpses of gnome-like creatures peeking out from around the thick trunks of trees. These gnomes couldn't have been more than a foot tall, their heads were stretched out in a kind of football-like shape, and they had large pointed ears. Every time Jessica jerked her head to look, whatever it was disappeared again behind whatever tree it was hiding. She could only see them as flashes out of the corner of her eye.

Night was falling on the rich sounds of the forest and Jessica was starting to nod off atop her steed. Artemis abruptly stopped and Jessica pulled her head up from the sudden movement. "I'm awake. I'm awake." she muttered.

"We should stop and rest for the night," Artemis said. There was a large tree that loomed in front of them. Its huge root system came up out of the ground in waves, forming several spots that could be good for nesting down for the night. The unicorn knelt down onto the grass and moss on the forest floor. Jessica hopped off of his back. Then Artemis walked over to a patch of soft green between two walls of tree roots. He laid down there and leaned against the roots. Jessica swung her pack off of her shoulders and sat down next to her companion. After rummaging through her knapsack, Jessica found some crackers wrapped in a cloth. She couldn't really see what else was in the bag because of the swiftly gathering darkness.

Quietly she munched on the crackers, and her belly was thankful for the food. She offered some to Artemis who ate right out of her hand, grateful for the sustenance as well. The exhaustion was creeping into Jessica's muscles and bones. She curled up against Artemis's soft belly and closed her eyes. Within seconds she was asleep.

TWO

There was still a stinging chill in the February air that was painful when sucking in a harsh lungful of oxygen. A light dusting of snow covered the sidewalk as Terry blew his breath out in puffy white clouds. He had decided to go out for a walk around the block, but not until he had made sure that that black SUV was not lurking around anywhere. Terry had his hands stuffed in the pockets of his parka, trying to keep his fingers from freezing. After getting to the end of his block, he had turned around to circle back to his house.

After getting past a few houses back down the street, Terry heard a vehicle turn onto his street behind him. The breath caught in his chest and the paranoia began to grip his heart, which began to race. Terry dared a glance over his shoulder. What he saw made his stomach sink into his balls. At a quick glance, the vehicle coming toward him looked like the front of the black SUV that had been spying on his house for days now. After quickly pivoting back forward, Terry took off running as fast as he could. The freezing air ripped painfully through his lungs as he huffed and puffed from the exertion.

"Terry! Why are you running?" The voice came from behind him, out of the vehicle. At the sound of his name being yelled, Terry stopped. The voice was familiar. As he turned back around, the black vehicle pulled up to the curb beside Terry. It was apparent now that it was not an SUV, it was a large black pickup truck. Darren poked his head out of the driver's side window. "What are you running from?" he asked again.

Terry sucked in another frigid lungful of air that felt like needles. "There's been this weird black SUV with tinted windows hanging around my house for at least a week," Terry answered.

Darren shook his head and looked forward through his windshield. "That's most likely the fucking CIA."

"How would you know that?" Terry said.

"Nevermind, I just do," Darren responded. "Have you been seeing black helicopters too?"

Terry shook his head. "No. Not since that day Maya destroyed most of Chicago."

Darren nodded thoughtfully, then he leaned out the window and slapped the side of his driver's side door. "Go around and hop in," he said. "There are some things that it's time for you to know."

Terry walked around the front end of the truck and then hopped in the passenger's seat. "How's you club?" Terry asked as they started to drive away.

Darren looked grim. "Not good," he admitted. "It's flooded, the water damage is probably going to be immensely expensive to repair on its own. Not to mention all the furniture was thrown around, a lot of it busted now." He pursed his lips together and watched the road as he talked.

"That's too bad," Terry offered his condolences. "I thought that place looked cool."

"It was, yeah," Darren replied. "But anyway, no one is going to come to a club now that all their apartments have been destroyed by giant black tentacles from another Dimension. That is if they're even still alive. Regular humans without Soulminds probably won't remember exactly what happened in Chicago, but the aftermath is painfully real."

"Did you live there in your club?" Terry asked.

Darren turned to look at Terry, a little smirk pulling at the side of his mouth. He shook his head. "Hell, no. I'll tell you one thing I've learned is that most people with Soulminds can't stand living in the city. And if they can get out, they will. I have a house in Aurora. It's nice, and I like to keep to myself most of the time."

"What about Eden?" Terry said.

"What about her?"

Terry continued, "She still lived in the city. In Wicker Park."

"Yeah, but she's still relatively new to her Soulmind, and the oppressiveness of the city hadn't really sunk into her yet. But now she lives with you, which is more than likely better for her. I'll tell you the thing about cities, Terry. They're too dense, and we're too sensitive. Our energy can't take all the concrete, the big-ass buildings, and the sheer amount of people packed in like sardines. We need open spaces, nature."

"Yeah, that's true," Terry said, trailing off as he stared out the window. "So where are we going?"

Darren took a moment of silence and then answered. "There's a group of people that I get together with now and then. Relatively small, twenty people, sometimes thirty at most. We operate from a nondualistic spiritual plane. And we have our people stationed in all of the major government institutions and agencies. You'd be surprised some of the famous people that we have part of our congregation. They're hiding in plain sight, and that's how we like it."

"So is this like a cult?" Terry asked, raising an eyebrow.

Darren couldn't help but chuckle. "Technically it would be," he admitted. "But that word has a lot of negative stigma around it. So we call ourselves the Body of Lucifer Christ."

"Lucifer... Christ?" Terry said slowly. "Isn't that an oxy-moron?"

"No," Darren answered. "You might think so if you've been conditioned by Christianity. But if you really know about Christ Consciousness, which is complete Oneness, then the ultimate act of Christ is to take Lucifer as itself."

"Interesting..." Terry didn't quite understand.

"Oh, I meant to ask you something," Darren interjected, changing the subject.

"What's that?"

"Jade is gone, isn't she?" Darren asked. Terry nodded. "I should have known I wouldn't get much time with her." He swiveled his head over to look at Terry. "Remius gone, too?"

Terry sighed. "Yeah, they're both gone. I don't know what to do anymore without my October."

"Well, maybe the Body of Lucifer Christ can kind of fill that gap now," Darren said as he turned off the paved street and onto a dirt road surrounded by trees.

Terry didn't respond to that comment. They drove for a couple minutes down this dirt road, and at the end was an old Catholic church in disrepair, surrounded by trees. There were several other cars in the gravel parking lot. Darren parked next to another pickup truck. "This isn't creepy at all," Terry said, staring up at the monstrosity.

"Oh, it's not that bad," Darren assured Terry. He started getting out of the truck. "Come on, I want to introduce you to the others."

Terry reluctantly got out and followed Darren up to the entrance. Quiet voices could be heard coming from the inside of the church. The building looked like it had been abandoned for years, Terry thought to himself. Darren swung the big doors open and they entered the foyer. Then they went on into the sanctuary where the rest of the Body of Lucifer Christ were gathered.

Darren led Terry down the ragged red carpet between the rows of pews. There were about ten people on one side and ten on the other. They all had their heads bowed as if they were praying. Hoods were up over all their heads and their dark gray cloaks hung down their backs all the way to the floor. There was one lone figure up at the pulpit. Terry could see her long hair coming out from either side of her hood, but her face was obscured. This was the same woman who had came to talk to Darren at his club. Behind the pulpit, the whole wall was a stained glass window depicting Jesus kneeling and praying with streams of sunlight illuminating his face. In front of that was a huge cross, but this cross was not like any regular cross Terry had ever seen. Instead of one cross-section, it had three, equally spaced going down the vertical section. It was a *Triple Cross*.

"Welcome!" the woman's voice boomed and echoed in the sanctuary. "Our Prophet has arrived!"

"Prophet? What Prophet?" Terry whispered to Darren. He was trying to hide behind Darren's tall and large frame.

"That's you, Terry," Darren whispered back.

"What?" Terry sputtered, a little too loud in the quiet hall.

"Come, Terry! Approach!" the woman commanded, beckoning Terry to come closer.

There were three small steps to climb to get up onto the raised pulpit. Terry approached the cloaked woman reluctantly. He stood on the floor below the bottom step and looked up at the woman. To Terry, it seemed that she towered above him. Her face was still shrouded in shadow. He swallowed hard.

"I am the Mage of the Meadow," she said, smiling down at Terry and extending her hands toward him. "You may call me Mage, or Meadow. Whichever you prefer." Terry hesitated and then took Mage's hands. She led him up the small steps and onto the pulpit. Mage turned and faced her right side toward the congregation and held Terry out at arms length, her hands on his shoulders. "We have been searching for you a long time," she continued. "When Darren told us about you, we didn't believe him at first. It seemed too good to be true that the Prophet was finally in our midst." Mage looked over at Darren who was still standing in the middle of the aisle. He nodded and went to sit down in one of the pews in the front row.

Terry was nervous and swallowed hard. This whole ordeal was beginning to weird him out. Mage continued, "You, Terry, are the Antichrist Christ Lucifer Christ!"

Terry sputtered and almost choked on his own saliva. "The what?" he finally spoke. "I'm the Antichrist *what*? And the Lucifer *fucking who*?"

Mage laughed, and the congregation laughed with her. "I know this is a lot to take in, but you are *that*."

"No!" Terry said firmly. He pulled away from Mage's hands on his shoulders and looked at Darren. "This shit creeps me out! First I'm the Steward of Time, and now I'm—I'm... the fucking *Antichrist*?"

"You're not the Antichrist," Mage said, trying to reason with Terry. "You're the Antichrist Christ Lucifer—"

"Fuck this!" Terry cut her off and stomped down the pulpit steps and started walking quickly toward the exit.

Mage nodded at Darren and pointed at Terry as he left the sanctuary and entered into the foyer again. "Brother Darren," Mage said quietly. "Keep an eye on him. Make sure he's safe. He'll come around soon enough."

Darren nodded silently, got up from the pew, and quickly followed Terry out of the church. Terry was almost back to the truck when Darren caught up to him. "Wait!" Darren called out.

Terry stopped and turned around, an angry look on his face. He charged toward Darren and pushed him hard in the chest. "Why the fuck would you bring me here?" he yelled, trying to fight back tears.

"Whoa," Darren said, putting up his hands. "I didn't know this was going to make you so upset. If I had know that, I would never have brought you here."

Terry's expression softened and he waved his hand through the air in a dismissive gesture. "Yeah, whatever, it's okay," he replied. "I just don't need a group of people telling me what to do, or who I am. I'm no one's fucking puppet."

"Of course," Darren agreed as they got back in the truck. "I don't want you to be anyone's puppet. Let's just say I might need your help with a few things in the future. I don't know what the missions are yet, but I will soon. What I do for the Body of Lucifer Christ is sort of like a Secret Agent. Doesn't that sound cool?"

Terry shrugged. "I don't know, maybe."

Darren pulled out of the gravel parking lot and started back toward Terry's house. "Well, you don't have to join our cult, but you could always work for me as like an independent contractor —an independent contract agent. How does that sound to you?"

"Yeah, maybe," Terry mumbled. "I'm just not one to join any fucking cult."

"That's fair," Darren agreed.

They sat in silence for a while as they drove on. Terry stared out the window.

"Hey, I got an idea," Darren finally said, breaking the long silence.

"Hmm?" Terry turned to look at Darren.

"Now, more than ever, it is important that humans with Soulminds find each other and work together toward a common goal—a common spiritual evolution."

"And?" Terry asked.

"And now that your October is gone you feel kind of lost, don't you?"

Terry didn't say anything.

Darren continued, "So you could try to find other young Soulminds who have been abandoned by their Octobers. Like, you could put a post up on Craigslist or something, and structure it as a support group for witches who have been abandoned by their familiars."

"Witches?" Terry asked.

"Yeah," Darren responded, "witches, Soulminds, it's the same thing. People with magick who have Dimensional powers."

"That's not a half bad idea," Terry admitted. "I might just do that."

Darren smiled, glad he could at least plant some seeds in the soil of the Spiralverse.

THREE

FROM THE MIND OF JESSICA THORN:

The sounds of the forest at night are even more intense and magickal than they were during the hours of daylight. My eyes are still closed, but I had been stirred from my restless slumber by the sound of rustling in the bushes. Sometimes, if I listen hard enough, the noises sound like Elvish voices whispering to each other from the branches of trees. Artemis is sleeping soundly against me, his warmth is comforting in the cool air of the night.

Then I hear grunting and heavy breathing. My eyes shoot open and I scan the shadows in the moonlight. Finally I spot it. Across the undergrowth, maybe ten yards away, there is a squat figure crouched by the roots of another large tree. At first I think it's a man, but I squint my eyes and notice features that are not human. The creature is as tall as a short man. The moon casts some light and shadow across its face. He has long curls of brown hair that cascade down the sides of his face, a little goatish beard, and protruding from his forehead are little horns!

I try to squish myself into Artemis's furry belly as I continue to watch this creature grunt, and suddenly I notice his hand working furiously between his legs as he stares at me from across the forest. Now I can make out a hairy muscular upper torso, and then lower, instead or regular legs, he has goat legs. It's freaking me out to see a live faun in real life. Even in the moonlight where I could try to convince myself it is a dream. I can't help but think of Mr. Tumnus in Narnia—that faun that gives Lucy tea when she first goes through the wardrobe.

This perverted faun is still staring at me and vigorously jerking himself off as his left hoof beats against the ground. I see his tongue loll out of his mouth and he licks his bottom lip wetly. How I wish he would go away. So I close my eyes tightly and say to myself, *Go away, go away, go away!*

When I open my eyes, the faun has disappeared as if he was never there in the first place. Maybe it was just a trick of the moonlight, or I really am dreaming. Either way, I shiver and snuggle closer into Artemis's warm belly. The unicorn snorts in his sleep. He's obviously not afraid of anything in the night. So I close my eyes again and sink my fingers into his soft fur.

PART 13

No Bounce No Play

*"In a lot of ways, I guess Satan was the first superhero...
In his first adventure, he took the form of a snake to
free two prisoners being held naked in a Third World
jungle prison by an all-powerful megalomaniac.
At the same time, he broadened their diet and
introduced them to their own sexuality.
Sounds kind of like a cross between Animal Man
and Dr. Phil to me."*

- Joe Hill, *Horns*

"Don't say I didn't warn you, if it all goes wobbly."

- Neil Gaiman, *The Ocean at the End of the Lane*

FOUR

"What are you doing, babe?" Eden asked from under the covers on Terry's bed. She yawned and stretched, the sleep from the night before still clinging to her eyelids. Terry was sitting at his desk, typing away on his computer. He swiveled in his chair as Eden scooted her butt back and sat up in bed. The sheet fell lazily to expose her naked breasts. She made no attempt to cover herself.

"Oh, I uh," Terry started, pointing at the computer screen. "Just this thing that Darren suggested I do. I'm putting up this Craigslist post—purposely keeping it vague. I posted it under Community and under groups... I also made a copy under the Pets section." Terry laughed.

Eden shook her head and rubbed her cheeks. "Well, what is it about?"

"Darren suggested that I try to find other young people with Soulminds who have been abandoned by their Octobers. I guess like a support group where we can help each other maybe find a direction... I don't know. The title of the post is: *Magickal Persons Who Have Lost Their Feline Familiars.* Figured that was goodly vague and that ones *on the level* will know what it means. I didn't put my address or phone number, but I put down my email address for people who are interested. That way I can weed out the ones who don't belong. And I capped it at age twenty. It seems like the older a Soulmind gets, their October leaves at a specific time anyway."

Eden laughed humorlessly. "Why?" she asked.

"What?" Terry said. "Why what?"

"You know you don't have to do everything that Darren tells you to do. He doesn't know everything," Eden responded. "Besides, I've gotten along fine for these two years my Soulmind has been active without an October. Why would people need a stupid support group?"

"Forget it," Terry said, turning back to his computer to finish the post. It was obviously no use to try to explain the importance of the group to Eden. She was fiercely independent, and figured that if an October left, then it meant that that Soulmind was meant to be on their own.

"Don't get all butt-hurt and pissy about it," she smirked. "I didn't mean anything by it. If you want to have this *group therapy* for kids who can't survive without their kitty cats, then I'll support you."

Terry finished posting and put his computer to sleep. Glaring at Eden he said, "If you really want to be supportive, then you don't have to be so sarcastic."

"I'm sorry," Eden replied, throwing up her hands. "I just don't think there's a point in turning your house into fucking *Psychology 101* for magicians... *What?*"

Terry snorted and just shook his head, unsure of where all this hostility was really coming from and why she was directing it at him. "You know what," he said finally, "fuck you!" Terry stood up from his chair and started walking toward his bedroom door. "You don't have to be a part of it if you don't want to. I don't give a fuck. Who knows, I might not even get any emails anyway." He turned his back on Eden and walked out the door, mumbling "Fucking bitch" under his breath as he went.

Eden rolled her eyes and groaned. Then she flopped back onto the pillow and covered her eyes with the palms of her hands.

Steaming with irritation, Terry stomped down the stairs to see what Rob and Mothman were up to. Eden could have her period all alone in his room for all he cared. Terry didn't need that energy on him right now. Mothman and Rob were sitting on the couch thumb-wrestling each other. They had two tray-tables set up in front of them with half-eaten slices of pizza on top of grease soaked paper towels.

"No fucking fair!" Rob yelled at Mothman. "You keep slipping your index finger out to cheat with."

"Hey, it's not cheating if I can get away with it," Mothman laughed, then he turned his head when Terry approached. "Yo, bro-ski! There's some fucking pizza over in the kitchen if you're hungry."

"Meat-lovers again?" Terry asked.

"You know it," Mothman answered, shoving a huge bite of greasy pizza into his mouth. "You know how much I like having meat in my mouth," he said and laughed hysterically, spraying chunks of half-chewed crust, cheese, and sausage. Rob punched Mothman in the shoulder as he continued to be a slob. "What was that for, you ass-penis?" Mothman shoved him back.

"That's for being a disgusting pig," Rob answered matter-of-factly.

Terry rolled his eyes and went to go grab a slice of pizza. He came back and sat down on the rug which was beginning to become stained with semen and sexual fluids. "Hey, do you guys think it's a good idea to find other young people with Soulminds so that we can band together and help each other out?"

Rob thought about this as he munched on a bite of crust. Then he said, "That's a great idea, bro. Inspired."

"Thank you!" Terry responded, relieved. "At least someone in this house thinks I'm doing the right thing."

"Yeah," Mothman added wickedly, "maybe there will be some sexy Soulmind girls who are all sad their talking cats have left them, and they'll be hurting for a good fuck! Yeeeah!" He smiled and pounded fists with Rob who chuckled at the idea as well.

"That's not the point of..." Terry started and then trailed off. His two friends stared at him, wondering if he was going to finish his thought. Suddenly, in that moment, Terry got a brilliant idea, but he didn't share it just then. Not yet. He wanted to wait for the idea to mature. To wait for when the idea's time would come. No pun intended.

"What?" Rob asked.

Terry snapped back to the moment. He had almost slipped away and forgot that his friends were sitting in front of him. "Oh, I'm sorry," Terry said, shaking his head as if clearing the fog—the Purple Fog. "I had an idea, and then I just lost it." But he hadn't lost it. It just felt important for him to let it ruminate before he sprouted it. Before its official conception—or *inception*.

"You know what," Mothman started to interject a thought, "after all that excitement with Maya and those three fucking weirdos, this boring-ass day-to-day shit really leaves me wanting more."

"Hah!" Terry couldn't help but laugh. "Dude, you'd rather be fighting demons and entities from other Dimensions every other day? You'd kill yourself, you'd have no time to rest and recover. Trust me, this is just mundane to you because you're used to it. If battling your way through Time and Space became your norm, you'd get bored with that too. Mothman, you're just not satisfied with anything."

"Why do you say that?" Mothman asked, frowning and a little offended.

"I know that," Terry continued, "because you're addicted to the rush. The adrenaline and the high. Once the novelty of that has worn off, you'd try to seek out greater risks and also crazier sexual situations."

Mothman shrugged. "Maybe that's true, but fuck it." He pulled an already rolled up joint out from behind his ear and a lighter from his pocket. "That's why I like to smoke that good weed!"

"Gimme that!" Terry said as he stood up and snatched it out of Mothman's mouth. "Give me the lighter," he commanded as he put the end of the joint in his mouth.

"Yes, ma'am," Mothman joked and threw Terry the lighter. Lighting the end slowly, he took a huge inhale of the sweet cannabis smoke. Leaning his head back, Terry drew the smoke deep into his lungs.

"Pass dat shit, nigga," Mothman whined, stretching his hand out toward Terry.

Terry passed it to him and commented, "You ain't black. Someone might smack you for saying that."

"I might not be black," Mothman responded as he hit the joint, "but Rob here is." He nudged Rob's arm with his elbow. "He likes that Gaping Black." Then Rob took the joint from Mothman and took a hit himself.

"Gaping Black? What the fuck is that?" Terry asked, already too high for this conversation.

"Ha-*ha!*" Mothman laughed, emphasizing the last *ha* like a crazy person. "It's like the gaping anus of a black man," he continued. "Rob just wants to crawl inside and live there. Live in Tupac's butthole. Hee-hee! That's what he misses about not going to school anymore—that he can't see that black guy who works in the copy room anymore. Right, Rob?"

"Shut your gay homo face!" Rob said in a really stoned voice. Poking his fingers into Mothman's face, he smeared greasy fingerprints down the lenses of his glasses.

"You bitch," Mothman yelled as he tried to wipe his glasses on his dirty t-shirt.

Terry had the joint again and was leisurely smoking it, entertained by the spectacle in front of him. "Hey, shut up you guys and watch this," Terry said. Still holding the joint, he leaned back and started to produce a spiral of white light from his solar plexus. "Can you do it? Meet me."

Leaning back into the cushions of the couch, Mothman let out a long breath and slowly a spiral of orange light began to emanate from his solar plexus as well. Terry's Soulmind light darted quickly toward Mothman who jumped a little, startled by the sudden movement. Then he relaxed and began to grow his energy out into a beam to touch Terry's. Their Soulminds collided halfway between both of them.

"Oh my God!" Mothman moaned as if he was having the best sex of his life. "What are you doing?" He closed his eyes and breathed the ecstasy through his veins.

Terry smiled. "Oh, just pleasuring you without touching you," he answered.

"I want to play," Rob whined.

Terry gestured to the point where his and Mothman's energies converged. Rob took that as an invitation and brought his blue Soulmind out to play, too. He speared it into the convergence and almost immediately felt an orgasmic rush take hold of his body. "Holy shit," he moaned. "It's like I'm jizzing without jizzing."

Terry chuckled. "You guys like that?"

"Do we like it?" Mothman blurted out at the ridiculousness of the question. "Does the pope wear pink panties?"

Terry burst out laughing. "Uhhh, I don't think I'd want to know if the pope wears pink panties even if he did... Check this out." Terry pushed his Soulmind energy harder into Mothman and Rob's energy streams, and they began to float up off of the couch.

"Holy fuck!" Mothman said, looking down at his legs dangling in midair. "I'm flying."

"Just relax," Terry cooed. Then his friends closed their eyes again and trusted him as he floated them higher toward the ceiling.

"A weightless orgasm," Rob whispered.

Terry stopped ascending them and pumped more orgasmic electricity into their nervous systems. Both of them started moaning loudly and breathing heavily. "I'm gonna make you cum like you've never cum before," Terry said to his friends—his lovers.

Suddenly the energy of their converged Soulmind energy rushed up Rob's and Mothman's spines, and the orgasm exploded through their brains and out the top of their heads in shimmering fountains of sparkles. The orgasm was so intense that both boys felt like they had melted into puddles of plasma as Terry slowly brought them back down to the couch.

They sat there, totally relaxed as their Soulminds thinned and disappeared back into their bodies.

"Terry, my God," Mothman said, satisfied, without opening his eyes. "You have that magick touch."

"I do, don't I?" Terry admitted, grinning from ear to ear.

"That was just... Wow," Rob was so out of it he was having trouble stringing a sentence together. Then he sighed and said, "Hey, if we have a group of Soulminds here, let's do that with *all* of them."

Terry was already thinking along these lines and he winked at Mothman who looked at him through glazed eyes. "Oh, don't worry," Terry assured them. "It's going to be orgasmically transcendent."

FIVE

In an undisclosed location, underground, the Director of a secret CIA program peered through a large rectangular window into a white room on the other side. The Director was in his early fifties and in pristine shape, he wore a dark blue suit with a black turtleneck, had shortly cropped brown hair, and his square jaw was clean shaven. He held an iPad with some sort of control panel app up on the screen. Standing on the Director's right was a man in a black jumpsuit and a helmet which looked like it would have been worn by a rich Harley rider. The visor on the helmet was completely black. There was a mess of red and blue wires protruding from the side of his helmet, they stretched down and attached to a small monitor that the jumpsuit-man held in his left hand. The screen of this tiny monitor was not a typical LCD, it had to be made of a special kind of plasma—for what they were looking at to show up.

They both stared through the window into the white room beyond. In the center of this room was a metal chair bolted to the floor. A young girl—maybe sixteen or seventeen—was strapped to the chair so she couldn't get up. She was wearing a nightgown, barefoot, and a crown of electrodes and wires had been placed over her greasy, stringy brown hair.

"Fucking let me go!" the girl screamed, sound muffled through the glass. She strained against her bonds. "You can't keep me prisoner here! I'll fucking kill you all!"

The Director smirked, pressed a couple buttons and moved some levers on his iPad. This stimulated the electrodes on the girl's head. No change could be seen with the naked eye. The girl struggled uselessly against her wrist cuffs. "Do you see anything, Lieutenant?" the Director asked.

"Yes, Director," the Lieutenant replied. "There is a yellow glow being produced around the subject's body... See for yourself." He held up the tiny monitor that was wired to his helmet and presented it to the Director.

Leaning his head down, the Director stared into the monitor. "Yes," he agreed. "It looks like the helmets are working better." On the little monitor, the girl could be seen sitting in the chair, and around her body there lapped streams of yellow Soulmind energy like flames from a brush fire.

Suddenly a man wearing a black suit, white shirt, and black tie came into the room and approached the Director. He was also holding an iPad. "Sir, Director, Sir," the new man said, a little nervous. "We've been monitoring the individual that you assigned us to."

The Director looked over at this new man as he handed the little monitor back to the Lieutenant in the jumpsuit. Looking this new man up and down, he gave him a silent appraisal before he spoke. "Ah, yes, the boy—what's his name?—Terry Broswald? What's the status? Have you been able to apprehend him?"

"It's been a little more difficult than we anticipated," the man admitted. "His house is protected by some kind of force field. We aren't able to penetrate it. Look." The man showed the Director energy readings on his iPad.

"My God," the Director whispered, looking at the numbers and graphs on the screen. "I've never seen numbers like this in my entire career. This boy is more powerful than we predicted. Now, more than ever, it is essential that you apprehend him and bring him here for study. Is that understood? Even if you have to put his house under twenty-four-hour surveillance until he slips up and leaves his house. That's when you take him. Have I made myself clear?"

The man nodded, holding his iPad closer to his chest now. "Yes, Sir. Crystal clear, Sir."

"That is all. You may leave now," the Director ordered, waving his hand as if shooing the man out of the room. The man bowed slightly and left. Then the Director turned back to the Lieutenant. "How are the improvements coming on the weapons being developed to affect the energy of these individuals—their Soulminds?"

The jumpsuit-man slid his helmet off his head. He was completely bald and there was a jagged scar that ran down the whole length of the left side of his face. The iris and pupil of his left eye were cloudy grey. He smiled evilly and his teeth were stained from years of drinking black coffee. "Those are coming along swimmingly. We've been making a lot of progress with the technology, Mr. Director. Would you like a demonstration?"

The Director nodded in the affirmative. "Lead the way, Lieutenant."

The jumpsuit-man stuffed the little monitor and wires into the helmet and walked around the Director, exiting through the door and into the hallway. The Director followed close behind, leaving the girl alone in the white room, still restrained to the chair.

"YOU FUCKING ASSHOLES!" the girl screamed at the top of her lungs. "LET ME GO! LET ME THE FUCK GO! WHO THE FUCK ARE YOU PEOPLE?!" Then she let out the loudest, most piercing, blood-curdling scream that shook the entire facility. She fought violently against her bonds and continued screaming with her eyes clenched tightly shut. The crown made of wires and electrodes flew off her head as she flung it back and forth. There was a point when her scream reached an impossibly high octave, and when it did, the window in front of her cracked, and the fractures quickly grew out in a spider-web pattern.

SIX

"Artemis?" Jessica started. It was morning and she was on the unicorn's back; they were traveling deeper into the forest, continuing their mysterious journey. "I had this strange dream last night," she continued. "Or at least I think it was a dream. I saw a faun—a man with goat legs and horns—and he was watching me from the base of a huge tree. It looked like he was jerking himself off."

Artemis snorted and then laughed a horsey kind of laugh. "You saw Pan. Perverted little creature."

"Pan?" Jessica asked, repeating the name as if it sounded familiar. "Like Pangea? The name of this whole landmass?"

"That's right," Artemis replied. "He's the god that rules over this whole Kingdom. Some creatures in this forest have not so benevolent intentions... Pan, I'm not so sure most of the time. He's a trickster god, always playing jokes. And he enjoys playing his little pan flute to seduce the nymphs of the glade. He enjoys sex with all creatures."

"That sounds a little disturbing," Jessica admitted, thinking about Pan fucking a goat in the middle of an open field. She tried to shake the image from her mind. Changing the subject, she tried to take her thoughts away from her imagination going to very perverted places. "Where are we going, Artemis?"

The majestic, divine unicorn was silent for a moment, then finally spoke. "Your mind must be running wild to all different kinds of scenarios, child. I apologize that you are so in the dark about your own initiation. Even I don't know exactly where this all leads, but I have been charged to guide you to your final destination."

"Initiation?" Jessica asked. "What kind of initiation?"

"The initiation to bring your Soulmind into full maturity. It must be at a certain level of operation for when you cross back over into the Hollow Dimension."

"I'm going back?"

"Eventually," Artemis admitted. "When you have completed the initiation."

"What if I don't want to go back there?" Jessica asked, feeling a bit distraught at the idea.

Artemis sighed deeply, as if mourning the hardships Jessica would inevitably have to go through. "Sometimes the quest asks of us things we don't necessarily want to do. That's the nature of the Hero's Journey."

"I'm not a hero," Jessica said without any emotion.

Artemis didn't comment on this. Instead he said, "You have Celtic roots. I can tell they go way back into your bloodline."

"How would you know that?" Jessica wondered.

"Sometimes I can just get a sense of these things."

"Well," she continued, "I do have Irish and Scottish blood."

"And your spirit is still connected to the old country," Artemis said in a way that seemed like he was far away, meditating on days long past.

"So where are we going?" Jessica repeated her question again.

"I didn't want to say anything," Artemis admitted reluctantly, as if the information had to be pulled out of him like rotting teeth from a rancid jaw. "For your first initiation, you must travel into the Underworld."

"What?" Jessica at first didn't know how to respond to this new information. It took her a few moments to even register it, like her mind was trying to protect her from the realization of the realms in which she would have to travel. "The Underworld? I don't want to go there, that sounds scary. Don't you have to die to go into the Underworld?"

"Not necessarily."

Jessica leaned forward and laid her head on Artemis's soft mane. She closed her eyes and hugged his large, strong neck. "Oh, Artemis..." Her voice trailed off as she closed her eyes. "Why is this my life? I didn't ask for any of this. What happened to that good little Christian girl from the suburbs of Chicago?"

"She disappeared when you did," Artemis responded. The truth was undeniable. "Your Soulmind chose you. Being a witch is just in your blood. Sometimes there's no choice involved."

"Maybe you're right," Jessica sighed, trying to calm herself by petting Artemis's luscious mane. "Maybe resisting is causing me more trouble than it's worth. Will I be dragged kicking and screaming toward my destiny, or do I have the strength to surrender and flow with the current easily?"

Artemis stopped abruptly and Jessica opened her eyes. "We're here," he said quietly.

Sitting up, Jessica took in the vision before them. They were standing at the edge of the trees and looking out over a huge lake. The water was crystal-clear and shone with the brilliance of a substance otherworldly. To Jessica's eyes it was almost magickally still. Not even the gentle breeze blowing through the trees could disturb the serenity of the water.

There was an island in the middle of the lake and a massive mountain jutted up out of it toward the sky. Jessica could see a path starting at the edge of the lake that went down into the water and led all the way to the landmass that stretched down into the water from the bottom of the island. "That's the entrance to the Underworld," Artemis said in a reverent voice.

"Not exactly what I imagined," Jessica commented as she dismounted from Artemis's back.

"What? Did you think it would be some gaping pit in the earth with flames shooting out of it?"

Jessica shrugged. "Maybe. Something like that."

Artemis chuckled. "It's not nearly that sinister. The Underworld is not the same as Hell, mind you."

"I guess that's my Christian conditioning coming back to bite me in the ass," Jessica remarked offhand.

"Unfortunately, I can't follow you down," the unicorn admitted regretfully.

"You're going to leave me alone?" The despair was evident in her voice, and she put her hand on Artemis's side, digging her fingers into his warm fur.

"I have no choice," Artemis continued. "But I will be waiting for you on the other side when you emerge."

Jessica didn't want to admit it, but she was afraid. She didn't know what to expect walking down into that water; what creatures she might find there—maybe with ill intent. Maybe Pan would be there, lurking in the shadows, waiting to violate her in indescribable ways. To be honest, she felt a pang of shame that she wasn't more courageous. That she couldn't summon the gall to just give herself over to the quest—this initiation into the God-conscious Soulmind Kingdom of Eternity. Suddenly her thoughts unexpectedly went to Terry. She could see his face in her mind. His handsome features smiled at her in her mind's eye. The awareness that Jessica actually missed him really hit her in that moment, more than in the whole time she had been in Pangea.

Her thoughts wandered back to the memory of when they were all fighting Timestrus in the Dreamsphere. At that time, she had been able to summon the courage to fight—for Terry if not for anything else. Why was it that she could summon the courage when she was fighting *for* someone else, but couldn't when it was only for herself? Maybe that was also dregs leftover from her Christian upbringing. The propaganda that one always had to be selfless, to sacrifice oneself for the good of mankind—like Jesus had supposedly done. It was something Jessica would have to get over one of these days. And today was as good a day as any to start pushing past the last remnants of her religious brainwashing.

"You better get moving," Artemis encouraged. His voice brought Jessica out of her cloud of thoughts and back to the present moment. "That stone path stretching down into the lake is waiting for you."

"I'll drown," Jessica said, the dread felt like a rock in her stomach. "I can't breathe underwater. It's not like I'm going to magickally sprout gills."

Artemis laughed at the image of Jessica spontaneously growing fish gills out of the sides of her neck. "No," the unicorn replied, "but I'm sure there's something in your knapsack that may be of use."

Jessica swung the bag off of her shoulders and flipped open the top flap. Rummaging through the seemingly random assortment of objects and food, she found a curious spherical object resting on top. Pulling it out of the knapsack, she held it in the palm of her hand; it was about the size of a baseball. It was cloudy, milky-white inside and resembled a bubble that wouldn't pop. The skin of the ball was rubbery and somewhat pliable.

"That's looks about right," Artemis smiled as Jessica returned the knapsack to its place on her back. The unicorn continued,

"Hold that in your hand as you walk into the water. Remember, I will be there on the other side when you return to the surface."

Jessica nodded, forcing the courage to go onward. Squeezing the bubble in her hand, she look a couple slow steps into the lake. The water was warm and soon she was up to her waist. Looking back over her shoulder, Jessica made eye contact with Artemis who silently watched her from the shore. Her feet stayed on the underwater stone path as she trekked deeper and deeper, until suddenly her head slipped under the surface. In that moment, in a quick burst, the bubble in her hand expanded and enveloped her whole body. It served as a barrier between her and the water surrounding her. Jessica took a deep breath and found that she could breathe normally inside the bubble.

The water looked green and blue from the algae and weeds growing up from the bottom. Fish of all different colors and sizes darted around her bubble. It was like being at the Aquarium in Chicago, but even more visceral. Some distance in front of her, at the end of the stone path, she could see the mass of rock jutting down into the depths from below the island which floated on the surface of the lake. There was a large entrance in the stone, but nothing could be seen in the darkness beyond.

There was suddenly a feeling which crept over Jessica; the perception of a creature's presence she wasn't familiar with. It made her skin crawl. She looked to her right and saw a woman's upper body attached to the tail of a fish—a mermaid! The creature's long purple hair floated in the water as if she were out in the weightlessness of space. She was slender and her full breasts floated buoyantly in the blue. Jessica admired this creature with stunned silence as it slowly swam past her. Then it suddenly glared at her, its eyes turning completely white and large. The mermaid snarled at Jessica, baring jagged, pointed teeth menacingly. Jessica shuddered, realizing that mermaids might not be the harmless creatures that she had seen in musical cartoons. As quickly as the mermaid snarled at her, it swam away, disappearing into the reeds swaying up from the bottom of the lake.

Jessica picked up her pace and hastened toward the yawning mouth in the rock face in front of her. It was just like the opening of a cave, and once she got there, she stepped through without hesitation. The wall of water stopped at the cave entrance like a membrane stretched over the opening. Once Jessica was sucked into the open air of the cave, the bubble around her shrank and became the small sphere in her hand once again. As she squeezed it, it started to emit a white glow, like a flashlight illuminating the tunnel in front of her.

Stalactites grew from the ceiling. They were damp and water occasionally dripped from the tips at the end. Jessica stared into the darkness of the tunnel in front of her. Then she saw the light from a flame coming toward her. It was close to the ground, and as it got nearer, she could see that the flame was from a torch carried by a three-foot-tall male dwarf. Jessica squinted at the short creature, trying to make out his features in the glow cast by his torch. He was waddling along, slowly toward her. The dwarf's head looked abnormally large on his stubby body with short arms and legs. He had a long pointed nose, long pointed ears, and some sprigs of white hair growing out like grass on his otherwise bald scalp.

Jessica looked down as the dwarf stopped in front of her and craned his neck to look up at her. "My name is Trondlebist," the dwarf spoke. "I shall be your guide through the labyrinth of the Underworld."

Jessica gave a little bow with her head. "Nice to meet you, Trondlebist," she said, greeting him back. "I'm Jessica Thorn."

"Yes, you certainly are," Trondlebist replied. "Well, follow me." He turned and started waddling back through the tunnel the way he had come. Jessica followed him without saying another word. The tunnel seemed to be carved out of the rock. The floor was incredibly smooth, and Jessica admired what was illuminated by the dwarf's torch and her glowing orb. She could see that the walls were engraved with Celtic symbols which felt oddly familiar to her. The energy emitted from these symbols made her feel comfortable, as if she was coming home after a long and difficult journey. The walls also sparkled as they caught the light. Jessica looked closer and realized that the walls of the tunnel were also inset with a myriad assortment of gems. A feeling of awe and reverence for this sacred place took her over.

Even though Jessica occasionally noticed passages leading off from the main path, she stuck close behind Trondlebist for fear of getting lost. As they walked deeper into the labyrinth, she began to hear the soft sounds of harp music. And as Jessica focused on the melody of this music, she began to see images flicker in the shadows cast by the lights they carried. Out of the corner of her eye, she could have sworn she saw Terry smiling and waving at her. But when Jessica turned her head to look, the trick of the light vanished like smoke. However, she unmistakably could feel his presence around her. Whether the sightings of Terry down in that cave were just her imagination—only visions or actually real, Jessica was unable to tell.

The sound of water trickling echoed through the corridor as they came to a wide room in the passage. There was a basin mounted in the far wall and water flowed down to fill it. Trondlebist silently led Jessica over for a drink. "You must be thirsty," the dwarf said. "Drink. You'll be refreshed."

Jessica set her glowing orb down on the stone floor and bent over the basin. The water within shone like silver. She cupped her hands through the cool liquid and brought it to her mouth, drinking gratefully. Then she splashed the water up and over her face.

The dwarf continued speaking, "Have you accepted that you are a Shaman, Jessica Thorn?"

Jessica looked down at the short creature and wiped the water off her lips with the back of her hand. "A Shaman?" she said, trying to wrap her head around what exactly that meant. "A witch, yes," she continued, "I have accepted that. But a Shaman, I'm not quite sure."

Trondlebist nodded with his eyes closed. "Yes, yes, my child," he said softly. "As we go deeper into the labyrinth of the Underworld, it is imperative that you accept your charge as a Shaman. To acknowledge that you have influence in the world of spirits, of gods, which is part of your divination and ability to heal."

"That's a lot to process," Jessica replied honestly.

"That is true, yes," Trondlebist admitted. "However, this is your true nature. Who you really are."

Jessica took another drink of water from the basin, trying to settle herself into the realization of her status as Shaman, and what responsibility that entailed. "Okay," she said finally, courage as well as surrender working together inside her consciousness. "I accept that I am a Shaman, and the responsibility that comes with that power." She said it with confidence and conviction.

Trondlebist smiled. "Excellent," he said. "Now you are ready to meet the Goddess of the Underworld: Cerridwen."

SEVEN

When women get into a moody funk, Terry knew that there was no trying to reason with them. He knew it was just better to keep his distance and let whatever it was work its way out of that woman's system. The vibes in Terry's household had gotten strange ever since he made that post on Craigslist. This was not because of Rob or Mothman—they were still their same silly selves. Terry was also more or less normal, even though he did find himself getting spells of depression every now and then. It was Eden's energy that had changed. She was becoming increasingly pissy and would snap at Terry over any little thing. Then the rest of the time she was in a quiet, sullen state.

It was unclear to Terry what exactly she was sulking about. And after a few attempts of trying to discuss it with her, he gave up. Eden was in the shower now and Terry was relieved to get a few minutes where her dense energy wasn't encroaching on his aura. Sitting in the chair at his desk, he opened up his email to see if there were any new emails about his post. Steadily they had come trickling in, maybe one or two a day for a week since he posted it. Terry was actually surprised at how quickly he was getting responses. Collecting all the responders into an email list, he realized that he almost had twenty people so far.

He composed an email, attaching all the addresses of the people who had responded to his post. The following Wednesday seemed like a good time to have the first meeting. After adding his home address to the email, the date for the following Wednesday, and that they should arrive around noon, he hit send and left it up to the Spiralverse to bring the Soulminds who needed to be there.

As Terry put his computer back to sleep, Eden walked back into the room. She was wearing a t-shirt and jeans, and she was drying off her wet hair with a towel. "Hey, babe," Terry greeted her weakly. "Refreshed from your shower?"

Eden shrugged. "Yeah, I guess," she responded, sitting down on the edge of the bed.

"Hey…" Terry began slowly, "Are we okay?"

Eden stared at him with a blank expression. "Yeah, Terry," she answered finally. "What do you mean? Why wouldn't we be okay?"

Terry shook his head. "I dunno," he admitted. "You've been kinda *different* lately. Just sort of grumpy and quiet a lot of the time. I guess I was just wondering if you're mad at me for something."

Eden laughed bleakly. "Can't a girl be allowed to be fucking moody now and then?" she snapped. "Not everything is fucking about you!"

Terry narrowed his eyes. "You don't have to be so nasty about it," he said, trying to remain calm and not feed into Eden's negativity. "We're in a relationship, aren't we? And relationships are based on clear communication. So, I'm trying to communicate with you—I haven't had much practice with this, so I'm trying to learn. I'm interested to know what's going on with you."

"Oh, please," Eden snorted a short, insulting laugh.

Terry's mouth hung open in disbelief. "What?"

"You're not interested in what's going on with me at all," she said, raising the volume of her voice. Throwing the towel onto the floor, she just let her hair drip onto the bedspread she was sitting on. Eden continued, "You just want to be reassured that it wasn't something *you* did to piss me off."

Terry suddenly felt the heat rise through his chest and into his face. The anger had finally gripped him, even though he had tried to keep it at bay. "Listen, bitch," Terry snapped, pointing a finger in her direction. "Don't you tell me what I want, because you have no clue! If I say that I'm worried about you and that I'm interested in what's going on with you—then that's what I *mean*. I mean what I say and I say what I mean, which is more than I can say for *you*."

Eden stood up abruptly from the edge of the bed. Terry noticed she was barefoot and little damp puddles were spreading out on the hardwood floor around her feet. A frown was etched on her face. "Let's do it!" she yelled. "Let's fight! Come on! You know you've been wanting to!"

Shaking his head, Terry stood up from his chair. "No, I don't," he said, a little calmer. "I don't want to fight. I don't like to fight."

"Why not?" she said, provoking him as she took a couple steps closer to Terry. "Are you a fucking pussy? Too submissive to yell back at me." She glared at him as if willing him to do something.

Terry raised his hands up in surrender. "I'm here for you if something is bothering you. I want to be supportive, whatever it is you're going through. And if it *was* something I did, I want to make it right."

Tears stung Eden's eyes and she shook her head, grinding her teeth together. "Don't be so fucking contrite," she spat at Terry. "Like you're apologizing for something you don't even know you did! It's so pathetic. Fucking—fucking yell at me, you little bitch!" Eden lunged forward and pushed Terry forcefully in the chest. He stumbled back a couple steps, knocking his desk chair into the closet door.

"You crazy cunt!" Terry yelled, finally raising his voice. "What the fuck is wrong with you?"

"There it is," Eden said slowly, a smirk pulling at the corners of her mouth. "Finally I get to see some anger from you! Call me a *slut*, call me a *whore*! I know you fucking want to!"

Lunging forward again, Eden hammered her fists into Terry's chest. He caught her wrists and did his best to restrain her. By this point tears were streaming down her cheeks. "I don't want to fight," Terry said firmly. Eden was trying to squirm away from his grip, but he was too strong. "I want you to chill out and talk to me like a rational human being."

Eden laughed. "Gimme a break! You're saying because I'm a woman that I'm irrational." She kept trying to pull away from Terry, but still couldn't.

"That's not what I said at all!" Terry yelled back.

Eden jerked her right arm hard and finally slipped her wrist out of Terry's grip. Then she slapped him hard across the face. His ears rang and his cheek stung as his vision got blurry from his skull being rattled. Instinctively, he grabbed her wrist before she could hit him again.

Eden spat in Terry's face. "Why don't you hit me, you faggot? I want you to hit me!"

"No," Terry replied softly. He pulled her into him and enveloped her in a tight embrace. "I love you. I don't want to hurt you," he whispered against her damp hair. Eden sobbed harder and her whole body shuddered against him. Terry continued, "Whatever it is you're feeling, whatever it is you're going through, I'm here for you. But only if you want me to be. I don't want to fight you, I don't want to hit you, and I don't want to force you to do anything—even to tell me what's going on with you."

Eden screamed painfully into Terry's chest and gave a couple more choked sobs before she pushed him away. Wiping the snot with the back of her hand, Eden stared at Terry through wet eyes. "I need to get out of here," she said finally. "I'll be back later." After which she stomped out of the room, leaving little wet footprints in her wake.

EIGHT

FROM THE MIND OF EDEN LOCKHART:

What the fuck is wrong with me? There was no reason to pick a fight with Terry. But I feel… I don't know what the fuck I'm feeling right now. I feel like breaking something; like punching someone in the face until they bleed and spit out broken teeth. Where is all this rage coming from?

Stomping back into the bathroom, I pick up the pair of socks I had thrown on the floor before I showered. After pulling them on my still-damp feet, I go downstairs to leave for—I don't know, wherever. The two queers, Rob and Mothman, are rough-housing, wrestling on the rug in front of the couch. I roll my eyes as I walk past them. They stop and watch me as I wander into the kitchen and grab my coat from the back of one of the chairs around the table.

"Hey, sexy, where are you going?" Mothman asks, smiling his idiotic grin at me. He didn't make any move to get up, Rob was still on top of him, poking him in the ribs with a bony finger.

"I'm going out," I reply dryly, pulling my arms through the sleeves of my coat.

"Don't leave our dicks dry, baby," Mothman jokes. "Come over here and we'll have some fun." He starts to dry-hump Rob and moans, too-loud and exaggerated. "*Cum* on, Edie," he continues, calling me by a stupid nickname. "You know you want me deep in your ass!"

I don't respond to any of Mothman's inane comments. After slipping on my shoes that were by the door leading to the garage, I stop and glance up at the landing at the top of the stairs. Terry isn't there, he didn't even come out of his room to try to follow me. Why hasn't he come after me, to ask me to stay? Fuck it then. Fuck him. Fuck all these idiots. Rob and Mothman have already forgotten about me and abruptly go back to dry-humping each other. Shaking my head, I slip out of the door into the mudroom connected to the garage. The garage is empty since the minivan is parked on the street in front of the house. There's a BMX bike leaning up against the far wall. I register it, but I feel like walking today. So I walk out of the door of the mudroom and slam it shut behind me. I hope Terry fucking heard that, his room is directly above.

It's a little chilly so I zip my puffy coat all the way up to the top and stuff my hands in the pockets as I start to walk toward the main street. In one direction it goes all the way to Uptown, and in the other direction it goes to the Blue Line train into the city. I wonder if all the L train tracks were destroyed, or if they were spared in all of the destruction. It doesn't matter, I can use the walk anyway. I get to the end of Terry's block, turn the corner, and start trudging down the sidewalk that goes along the main street.

If the train is still running, I can get off at Damen Avenue and go check to see if my apartment is still standing, I think to myself. As I walk, I sort of space out. The anger and rage I was feeling earlier has dulled out to a low-level numbness. And I just feel kind of zombie-ish, if that makes any sense. Cars zoom past me as I walk, going in both directions to and from wherever, as if Chicago isn't laying in ruins less than twenty miles away. The radioactive rubble of sadness. I don't know if the remains are radioactive, but it seems more dramatic to imagine it that way.

Finally I get to the Blue Line station and there are cars parked in the parking lot, and it looks like the train is still running. How it avoided getting damaged is beyond me. But I consider myself exceedingly lucky that it is. After rushing up the stairs, I slip my CTA card in and go through the turnstile. Then I go to wait on the platform for the train to come.

There aren't *that* many people on the platform waiting. Several look like dirty and drunk homeless bums, and the other ones are silent, their eyes looking like they're in some kind of daze. What the fuck is up with this? The energy of the bums and the dazed people give me a chilling vibe, making my skin crawl. It's creepy.

When the train finally comes, we all pile in. Nobody says a word. The silence is eerie. I take a seat next to a window, and thank God no one sits next to me. Staring out of the window, I sigh as the train starts to roll out of the station. As the fake niceness and nature of the suburbs fades away in the distance, I can feel the coming closer to the city's destruction as weight pressing down on my Soulmind. I feel it heavy on my chest and I struggle to breathe. Squinting painfully, I rub the space on my chest right above my heart. It's beating abnormally fast and I feel like acid reflux is burning the area between my lungs. I cough dryly and try to ignore the pain by watching the landscape zip by outside.

As we come into the city, I look down toward the cracked streets below. There are huge and weird-looking government vehicles all around, trying to repair the roads. I think the buildings might be beyond repair. It's so strange to me that these people aren't talking about what happened. They're all silently walking around like robots. Are they all that traumatized? Or have they been threatened by the government not to talk about what nobody can explain? Maybe they think Chicago was just hit by a huge earthquake and a flood. I don't fucking know. Glancing around, I notice that all the other people sitting in my car are not even looking out of the windows. They stare down at their laps as if they're all clinically depressed.

I don't want to attract attention to myself, so at the Damen stop I blend in with the crowd as we exit the train. Making sure

I don't say a word, I fix a cloudy dazed look on my face as well. Quickly I walk down the stairs from the platform and get to the sidewalk below. My apartment is only a few blocks from here.

When I arrive there, I see that one of the windows on the front of the apartment had been gouged out of the building—maybe by one of those huge black tentacles. The cold February air blows into the living room which is now visible from the street. I walk up the steps and try the door. It's unlocked. The interior of the apartment looks okay, except for the glass and rubble strewn around the living room from the gouged-out window.

"Hey!" I call out into the apartment. "Is anybody here?" I want to be prepared in case there are any squatters waiting in the shadows of my semi-destroyed apartment.

"Eden? Is that you?" A voice calls out. It sounds like it's coming from the bedroom.

In a second I recognize the familiarity of the cadence in the voice. "Kat? Is that you?" I call out in response, slowly walking toward the hallway and the bedroom at the end.

"Yeah, it's me," he answers. "I'm just in the bedroom resting."

I get to the room at the end of the hall and push open the door which was only half closed. My room is pretty bare. I put some stuff in when I first moved here, but I didn't have that much to decorate it with, and to be honest, I was too lazy to care anyway. There is no bed frame, just a mattress pushed into the corner of the room with sheets thrown over it. The floor is hardwood, there is a small closet where I keep my clothes, and a little dresser with figures of faeries on top, which I put there. I don't have any bookshelves, so there are piles of books stacked on the floor against the walls.

Kat is in bed with the sheet over him. He scoots to sit up as I come in the room. The sheet falls to his waist and I see that he is wearing one of my dresses that is pretty much just a long shirt. It's the one with Jim Morrison's face on it. One side of the dress slides down to reveal Kat's smooth white shoulder. He's very thin and his hair falls around his collarbone in a pretty way. There's a silver chain hanging around his neck and what's hanging from it disappears underneath the collar of his dress. But I know what it is. I'm the one who gave it to him. Kat smiles at me, happy to see me as I sit down next to him on the mattress.

"How long have you been here?" I ask, pulling off my shoes and tossing them in the corner. I take off my coat and throw it on the floor as well.

Kat shrugs. "I don't know. A while. All of the days have seemed to blur together." He puts his hand up to his forehead, as if he is trying to remember something that he has inevitably forgotten. Turning to look in my eyes, he asks, "What happened here, Eden? I feel like I just woke up and Chicago was destroyed. Was there an earthquake? A flood?"

"Something like that," I answer. Trying to explain what had actually happened would be useless. Kat wouldn't understand it anyway.

"It's... I don't know," Kat begins. "It's all hazy or something. My apartment—you know where it is—was totally... destroyed." He gives me a miserable little look.

"And you weren't in there when it happened?" I ask. Obviously he wouldn't be here if he had been. He'd be dead.

Kat shakes his head. "No, I guess not. I don't really remember. But... I think I was *here*." He pulls the silver chain out from under the collar of his dress and rubs his fingers along the antique silver skeleton key hanging from the end. Staring off into the distance at nothing in particular, Kat keeps fingering the key as if he's far away in some distant memory—or some vision of the future. It's hard to tell.

"Do you remember when I gave that to you?" I ask, pointing at the key.

That seems to snap him out of his reverie, and he looks at me and smiles warmly. "Yeah, that was when you asked me to be part of your poly-family. You gave them to all your lovers back then..." He trails off and then says, "Did you give one to Terry?"

I shake my head. Kat sighs loudly and flops back onto the pillow, closing his eyes. He stretches his arms up by the sides of his head. I can't help thinking that he looks really cute laying here—vulnerable and girly. Slowly I peel the sheet off of him and toss it at the foot of the mattress. Kat doesn't move as I stroke one of his shaved, muscular legs. The Jim Morrison dress is bunched up a bit and I can see Kat is wearing nothing underneath. I slip my hand between his legs and start to stroke his warm cock. He moans softly as I feel him getting hard in my hand. I push the bottom of his dress up to his belly-button, then I start to use my mouth.

Slipping my wet lips sensually over the tip of Kat's cock, I guide it over my tongue and then down into my throat. Lightly I gag on it, the way guys like, and then I start to suck it. I close my eyes and enjoy the sensation of his thick, warm, pulsing cock on my eager tongue. As I go down on him, I feel Kat place his hands on the top of my head and start to guide the motion of my head bobbing up and down on his erection. Just from how hard he is, I can tell he's enjoying it. Then he gives out another soft, feminine moan. God, those moans really turn me on. I can feel my pussy getting wet in my panties.

After a few more minutes, I slide my mouth off of the long sexy cock and lick the tip as I look up at Kat. He looks down at me and cups my face in his palms. My cheeks are already red from being turned on. "Kat?" I say, quietly in a whisper. He smiles at me, his eyes glazed over in a sexual hypnotic state. "Will you fuck me?"

His smile falters a little. "Uhh..." he hesitates. "I don't usually *do* vagina. Honey, you know that. But your mouth is nice. You can keep doing that, if you want."

My eyes plead with him, like a puppy begging for a treat. I don't know why, but I really want him inside me right now. Maybe a part of me wants to activate his Soulmind. The prospect of that seems dangerous, titillating. I grab Kat's cock and stroke it gently with my hand. "Can I tell you something?" I ask.

"What is it, love?" he says, taking his hands away from my face, but still looking at me.

"I have magick powers."

Kat blinks and stares at me blankly. "Like *you belong at Hogwarts* magick powers?"

I roll my eyes. "It's more like a special energy that allows you to see beyond our normal mundane reality. Into different Dimensions and perceive beings from other realms. And if you have sex with me, your eyes will be opened too."

"Sounds kind of scary," Kat admits.

I shake my head adamantly. "No!" I insist. "It's not. It's fascinating and exciting. What do you say? You want to fuck me and be activated?"

Kat swallows nervously and his dick begins to soften in my hand. That's not a good sign. Whether he believes me or not, I can't really tell. "I just... That sounds crazy," he says. Pulling away from me slowly, he sits back up in the bed and hugs his knees into his chest. "You know, from just waking up to seeing the whole city destroyed—my apartment along with it—I just feel so confused. I don't know what's going on anymore."

"You don't have to feel like that," I insist, touching his leg tenderly, lovingly. "When your Soulmind is connected, you won't be confused about this anymore. You'll understand all that has happened."

Kat shakes his head. "I don't know if I want that. Even if that's true and not just some weird thing you made up to try to get me to fuck you... Muh-m-magick, that's not my world." he stutters this last part. I've never heard Kat stutter before. Maybe he's right. Maybe if I did activate him, that would get him killed. Could I live with that? Could I live with opening someone's eyes and then having them go crazy or being killed by an entity from another Dimension?

"Maybe you're right," I concede. "Maybe I just wanted the comfort of being intimate with you right now."

"I know, love," Kat says as he lowers his knees back down onto the mattress. He opens his arms and I come in for a hug. I feel like sobbing all over again, but I don't. "It's not you," he continues. "I've had sex with a couple women before, but I was never really into it. It's nothing wrong with you, honey."

I lean my head up and kiss him on the lips. We stay there for a few moments, kissing and hugging. Then I pull away and watch as Kat takes the necklace from around his throat. "What are you doing?" I ask.

Kat puts the skeleton key and the chain in the palm of his hand and then hands it to me. "I think you should have this back," he says.

I open my hand and he places it there. "Why?" I ask, looking into his eyes.

"We've been growing apart. Don't act like we haven't," he replies. "It's okay. I don't feel hurt. You've been spending more time with Terry than you have with me. And maybe that's a good thing. I have a feeling that you two need each other more than you realize. Don't let him slip away. Don't push him away." *How is he intuiting this?* Then he continues, "Even though I may not have a Soulmind—or whatever it was you said—I'm not stupid. I could see the connection between the two of you the first day he came here. Maybe you should give that key to him."

I nod my head in agreement and squeeze the skeleton key in my palm before I slip it into the pocket of my jeans. Suddenly I choke on a laugh—it's like a mixture of a sob and a chuckle. "I remember when I first started giving my lovers old skeleton keys. I thought it was a clever joke on my last name... But I guess it's been a while since I've opened any locked hearts."

"What about Terry?"

"Hmm?"

"Haven't you unlocked his heart?" Kat asks. "It seemed like you opened his heart pretty wide."

I shake my head, unsure of whether this was true. "Oh, I don't know. His heart might still be locked. I'm not really sure." I feel myself starting to get sleepy. "I wish I could love him in the way he really needs. I don't know if I can, but I can try." I yawn.

"I think you'll do fine. I can tell you really care about him," Kat observes. "Are you sleepy?"

I nod again. "Suddenly I feel exhausted. I should really be getting back home soon. Told Terry I would be back later tonight."

"I assume *home* means Terry's house," Kat says.

"That's my home now," I whisper as my eyes start to close. "Maybe I could just nap here for a bit and then go catch the Blue Line later..."

Kat falls back onto the pillow and I snuggle up to him, laying my head on his chest. My eyelids feel as heavy as lead, and in moments I'm asleep.

NINE

Jessica was having a difficult time trying to hide her anxiety over the prospect of meeting the *Goddess of the Underworld*. She had never met a goddess before—at least she didn't think that she had. It was taking a while just to process the fact that she was being led through a cave tunnel by a short dwarf named Trondlebist. Traveling for a couple days with a unicorn had been slowly easing her into the reality of living life surrounded by magickal creatures. Her head spun. It seemed like one minute ago she had been a conservative girl sitting in church, wearing a cross around her neck, and the next minute she was an occult Celtic witch who traveled into faerie-land. By now nothing should have surprised her, but it still did.

They had left the chamber with the basin of water in the wall. Now they were walking down a new passage that seemed to be widening as they went deeper. Jessica could feel a strong presence getting closer with each step. The path suddenly started to curve to the right, as if they were going into a spiral. There were still gems inlaid on either side of the path on the smooth floor. They sparkled green as the light from Jessica's orb glinted off of them. *Maybe this is the Emerald Road leading to a Yellow Brick City,* Jessica thought, and smiled to herself. The sound of the harp music was getting distinctly louder as they went deeper into the spiral.

"Are there more dwarves down here?" Jessica asked, breaking the silence. "Or are you the only one, Trondlebist?"

The dwarf glanced briefly over his shoulder and back at Jessica. He shook his head. "No, I'm not the only one," he answered. "We prefer to live underground, and deeper down are miles and miles of mines. We are the ones who dig up all these precious gems that you see imbedded in the floor and the walls. Our kingdom is all under the earth and the God and Goddess of the Underworld take care of us."

They fell into silence again.

As Trondlebist and Jessica went around the next curve, they were met by the light of two torches hanging on the stone wall in front of them. These torches were mounted on either side of a large stone door which was carved with the same Celtic symbols that Jessica had seen on the walls. The orange glow of the torch flames, coupled with the sound of the harp music, was lulling Jessica into a hypnotic trance state. Her anxiety was starting to dissipate and what was left was a feeling of high lightness.

Trondlebist stood in front of the great door with his torch held up to illuminate the Celtic runes. "Trondlebist of the Undercurrent," the dwarf spoke loudly. "We wish an audience with Cerridwen, Goddess of the Underworld!"

The stone door groaned as the Celtic runes lit up with white light which seemed almost like liquid. Then the door slowly swung inward toward the chamber beyond. Jessica followed Trondlebist into the great central cavern. She stood in awe as she took it all in. Stalactites hung down like spears. Their origins in the ceiling high above were cloaked in shadowy darkness. Stalagmites rose up from the floor like ancient stone sculptures. These strange stone columns led to the center of the chamber. Jessica followed these rows of stones with her eyes toward a fire burning on a great flat stone. Beside this was a huge Cauldron with light shining up from the liquid within. As she stared at the Cauldron, the harp music became clearer in her ears. This Cauldron was black with silver beads around the rim. Covering the rounded sides were swirling Celtic designs etched in silver.

There was a throne carved in stone behind the impressive-sized Cauldron. Sitting on this throne was a shadowy figure wearing a hooded robe. Her long dark hair flowed down out of the sides of the hood. The robe was dark green with red around the edges. Jessica could not see this woman's eyes, but the light from the fire cast a glow onto her slim chin and sensual mouth. The hooded woman rested her right elbow on her knee and her hands were covered in bejeweled rings. Next to the throne was a stone bench. On the side of bench closest to the throne were four silver goblets and a beautiful tall silver and glass decanter filled with a mysterious liquid.

Trondlebist led Jessica along the stalagmite-edged path toward the Cauldron. As he did, the robed woman rose from her throne and approached them. "May I present Cerridwen, Goddess of the Underworld. She of many names," the dwarf spoke, his voice echoing in the cavern.

Cerridwen waved her hand and smiled down at the dwarf. "Now, now, Trondlebist. No need to be so formal," the Goddess said. "Jessica is welcome in my Kingdom."

Jessica's head swirled again. Cerridwen's voice was intoxicating; it was so sweet and melodic, like faeries singing while she drank honey wine. Trondlebist bowed low to the Goddess as Jessica just stared in wonder. She felt a sudden punch from a small fist in the side of her leg. "Bow!" Trondlebist whispered harshly.

Jessica came out of her trance and bowed awkwardly. Cerridwen laughed the most pleasant laugh Jessica had ever heard—a laugh worthy of an Elf princess. "Come, come," the Goddess said, beckoning for them to come around the Cauldron and take a seat on the stone bench. They did so as Cerridwen poured the liquid from the decanter into the four silver goblets. She handed one to Jessica and one to Trondlebist.

"I trust your journey wasn't too full of perils, I hope," Cerridwen said, taking a sip from her goblet.

Jessica shook her head as she drank from the goblet, not sure what to expect. The liquid was sweet, a bit citrusy, but also intoxicating. "It was exciting," Jessica answered. "Artemis, the unicorn, was there to accompany me until I descended to here. No one has tried to kill me yet... Well, not since I was in Thanatos." Jessica laughed and then it died quickly.

"Artemis, yes," the Goddess responded. "What a gorgeous creature. He will take marvelous care of you on your journey to the Upperworld and beyond. Why exactly have you come, Jessica? I know but I need to hear you say it."

"I, uh," Jessica began, not quite fully sure herself what this journey was about. However, she was starting to piece it together. "It's the journey of the Shaman... That's what I'm gathering as I go along. To fully own my power and be willing to undergo transformation and rebirth. Is that right?"

Cerridwen smiled, her eyes still in shadow. "I can't tell you what your journey is about, dear," she admitted. "I can only guide you. But you are correct. You know exactly who you are. You do not need to question it. Do not ask me whether that is right. You know in your heart that it is."

Jessica nodded. Trondlebist stared into the fire next to her as he sipped from his goblet. Jessica continued, "When I came through the water that led to the entrance to this cave, I saw what looked like a mermaid, but then it bared these pointed teeth and swam away."

"Were you frightened?" Cerridwen asked.

"Yes, I was. I thought it was going to try to attack me."

"Mermaids here aren't like what you've read about in stories," the Goddess continued. "They are beasts of the Underworld.

Vampires that swim. And they will drain you of your energy and your life if you let them get too close."

Jessica shuddered. "That sounds awful."

"Do you have fear deep within you?" Cerridwen asked with compassion.

"What? What do you mean?" Jessica asked, knowing full well what Cerridwen meant but not wanting to face the fact.

"A deep-seated fear," Cerridwen explained. "A fear of death, maybe. A fear of Hell lingering from your Christian upbringing, perhaps. Maybe you're afraid of what might happen to Terry." She smiled again as the orange light from the fire flickered on her face.

Jessica perked up at that. "What's going to happen to Terry?" she said, feeling anxiety grip her again and her heart pound in her chest.

"I don't know," Cerridwen answered. "But worrying about it doesn't benefit you and that energy doesn't benefit Terry. You will be brought back to him because your work with him is yet to be completed. Tell me, what did you see in the tunnels of this labyrinth as you came closer to me?"

"I saw him," Jessica said slowly. "I saw Terry. Images of him flickering in the shadows and on the walls."

"Tell me what your greatest fear is that is associated with Terry?" Cerridwen asked, slowly and deliberately enunciating each word. "Does it have something to do with why you came to Pangea in the first place?"

Whatever the liquid was in the goblet that Jessica was drinking, was helping to loosen her tongue. Like a truth-serum. It was also helping her realize deep truths that she may have not wanted to face before. "I've been afraid for a while," Jessica admitted, "that if I stayed with Terry, that I might end up causing him to get hurt or even killed. I couldn't live with myself if that happened. That's one of the reasons I erased myself from the Hollow Dimension. So that Terry didn't feel like he had to protect me."

"Are you ready to let that go?" Cerridwen asked. "Are you ready to shed those fears and throw them headlong into the fire?"

"I... I don't know. I'm afraid."

"I know you're afraid. That's what courage is; to push past that fear and move forward in spite of it. That's how true transformation happens."

Jessica swallowed hard. "Yes, I do," she said, very quietly and slowly. "I don't want to have this constant feeling of dread in the pit of my stomach all the time. I don't want to feel like God is going to punish me for *sinning*. I don't want to be tormented by the thought that I'm the problem, that I deserve to be punished. My dad did enough trying to engrain that into me. Now I want to be free of that."

Cerridwen clapped her hands together. "Good. Very good! You are ready for the next phase of your initiation."

The harp music became louder again. Trondlebist and Jessica turned their heads to look down a passage leading off from the central cavern. A Celtic harper came dancing out of the entrance to this passageway followed by an entourage of animals. There were squirrels, and cats, and rabbits, badgers, otters, and foxes, and frogs, there may have been a couple hedgehogs in there, too. The harper wore a brown cap on his head with a striped feather stuck into it. He was dressed like someone who might travel around with Robin Hood. Sitting down next to Trondlebist on the stone bench, he continued playing the beautiful music on his majestic harp. The group of animals mingled and roamed around the cavern.

Following in after the line of animals was another strange creature. The top half of him was a head and muscular torso of a man. He had long hair and a beard like a mountain-man. However, sprouting from the top of his head were a pair of antlers. His legs were the legs of a deer. A hairy animal-like penis swung between his legs.

Cerridwen noticed Jessica staring at him, so she decided to make the introduction. "Meet Cernunnos, Lord of Animals, the Underworld God!"

Cernunnos bowed to Cerridwen then sat cross-legged on the floor. The Goddess walked over to him and presented the fourth silver goblet. He took it gratefully and sipped leisurely. Jessica looked down at him. He met her gaze and spoke, "You're going to be right as Underworld rain, Jessica," Cernunnos said. "You're already beginning to shed that fear and old, stale conditioning from times archaic. And when you see Terry again, you will be a completely different being. An entity unto herself."

"You really think so?" Jessica asked.

"I know so," Cernunnos replied confidently.

"You look familiar," Jessica continued. "Are you also known as *Pan*?"

The Underworld God laughed heartily and shook his head. His voice was deep and bellowed in the cavern. "No, child. Pan is my brother. He is God of Nature, I am God of the Underworld. He is half-goat, where as I am half-stag. Watch out for him, he can get very horny."

Jessica rolled her eyes. "Yeah, I've noticed." She finished drinking the last of the liquid in her goblet and set it down on the stone bench beside her.

"You are stronger than you yourself even realize," Cernunnos continued, moving on to a different thought. "We say that this is a journey of initiation. Know that it is not *we* who initiate you. Really and truly, you will and must initiate *yourself*."

Jessica let this sink in as she stood up from the bench and approached the great Cauldron emitting soft blue light from the liquid within. Cerridwen followed her, and stood by her side. They stared down into the blue liquid which was moving with tiny ripples and waves. "That is your way to rebirth," the Goddess spoke. "Renewal can be difficult, this you need to know. However, it is greatly rewarding. Jessica Thorn, are you willing to be reborn into a new way of life?"

"Yes," Jessica answered without even a moment of hesitation.

She hadn't noticed that Cernunnos had stood up from his seat on the ground and was now right behind her. In the flash of an instant right after Jessica said "Yes," the God of the Under-world grabbed her by her ankles and dumped her headfirst into the Cauldron.

Jessica yelled out with surprise, but she had already been pulled below the surface, into the blue liquid spiral inside the Sacred Cauldron.

* * *

It was dark by the time Eden got back to Terry's house. She let herself back in through the door to the mudroom—it wasn't locked. But she did lock it behind her. It was dark in the kitchen and Eden threw her coat over the back of a chair then slipped her shoes off. The TV was on in the living room, but the volume was really low. Rob and Mothman were snoring as they spooned on the couch. It looked like they fell asleep watching cartoons. Adult Swim was on, it was that time of night.

She tiptoed quietly up the stairs and went into Terry's bedroom. The lights were off and he was in bed, laying on his right side. Eden stripped off her clothes and got under the covers, cuddling her body against Terry's back. She kissed him lightly on the back of the neck. "Are you awake?" she whispered.

"Yeah..." Terry whispered back.

"Baby," Eden continued, "I'm sorry I tried to pick a fight with you today. I love you so much. I don't want to push you away." The skeleton key on the chain was still in the front pocket of her jeans, and she thought about it in that moment. She decided she would give it to Terry in the morning.

Terry sighed. "It's in the past," he replied quietly. "I've been forced to fight recently—you've seen it—even when I don't want to. I don't want to fight with my lovers as well. I care about you. And when I ask what's bothering you, it's not me trying to provoke you. I genuinely care... I don't know."

"I know, baby," Eden replied apologetically. "I've just been stressed... I didn't mean to take it out on you."

"Let's not talk about it anymore," Terry said. "I'm tired." He turned his head around and they kissed. Then he turned back over and settled into the pillow.

"I love you," Eden whispered in his ear.

"I know," Terry said back.

Eden slid her arm over Terry, put her hand on his chest, and hugged his body into hers.

TEN

"Hey, Eden? Did you go into Chicago yesterday?" Terry asked. It was morning, but they were still in bed next to each other.

The sunlight was peeking in through the curtains, waking them from their slumber.

"Yeah...?" Eden replied. Her eyes were still closed and she yawned.

"What was it like?"

Eden opened her eyes and turned over on her side to look at Terry. She looked lovingly into his eyes and smiled. "It was fucking weird," she answered. "I'm so glad to be back here, next to you in bed." Leaning over, she kissed Terry on the lips.

"What was weird about it?" Terry wanted to know. "Was it still totally destroyed and whatever?"

Eden frowned and then nodded, tucking her hands in between her head and the pillow. "Yeah, still completely fucked... There were government trucks that were trying to repair the roads. And then when I was coming home—it was dark already— there were other trucks collecting all the bodies. It was creepy. And the worst part was the people that were alive... They were like zombies in some sort of daze. It was like, you know, in *Men in Black* right after they wipe a person's memory of all the alien shit they saw. It gave me those kind of vibes."

"Bizarre," Terry commented. There was silence for a moment, then Terry continued, "Was your apartment still there? I take it you went to check on it."

"It was mostly intact," Eden laughed dryly. "Except there was like a giant bite out of the front—there was a gaping hole where one of the windows should have been. Kat was there... like, hiding in my room."

"Was he okay?"

Eden snorted again. "Okay is a relative term when you're talking about the aftermath of such a traumatic event. He was unharmed, if that's what you mean. Mentally he was kind of in a daze like the others. He couldn't remember what had happened.

It was like he just woke up to find Chicago totally destroyed. I mean, can you imagine that? If we had no idea what had happened and we only saw the results without any context?"

Terry looked horrified. "That would be awful..." he trailed off and then went quiet.

Eden seemed suddenly anxious to Terry and she took a deep breath and then exhaled loudly. "So..." she began. "Are you gonna ask me if I fucked him?"

"What? You mean Kat?" Terry said, kind of surprised by the thought.

Eden nodded.

Terry shook his head. "No, I wasn't," he admitted. "To be honest, it doesn't matter to me either way."

"Huh," was all Eden said, taking that in. "Well," she said, giving Terry a mischievous smile, "I'm horny now. Are you?"

Terry laughed heartily. "I'm always horny. You should know that by now."

"Mmmm, yeah," Eden moaned and threw the covers off of them, exposing their beautiful naked bodies. "Oh, wait, I just remembered that there's something I have for you."

"Something for me? What is it?"

Eden crawled to the end of the bed to reach down into her jeans bunched up on the floor. Her butt was in the air and Terry had a great view of her round ass and sexy labia squished cutely between her legs. "Are you looking at my ass?" Eden said as she pulled the skeleton key necklace out of the pocket of her jeans.

"You bet I am!" Terry said enthusiastically. Already his flaccid dick was getting hard between his legs.

Eden looked back at him over her shoulder, gave a sultry smile, and wiggled her hips. "You fucking better be!"

Terry laughed as Eden crawled back over and sat next to him. Propping himself up on his elbows, Terry said, "What is it? What do you have for me?"

The light from the sun streaming through the window suddenly glinted off of the silver cross Terry wore around his neck. Eden frowned and touched it. "Have you always been wearing this, Terry?"

He nodded. "Yeah, ever since before we met."

There was a bewildered look on Eden's face as if she had just been forcibly woken from a dream. "That's weird," she said. "I guess I just never really registered it before... Here." She held out her hand and presented the skeleton key on the silver chain.

"What is it?" Terry asked as he picked it up by the key and studied it with fascination. "It's a beautiful key. Where did you get it?"

Eden shrugged. "I dunno, some antique store I think. I used to give all my lovers a necklace with a skeleton key. It's sort of a joke on my last name."

Terry raised an eyebrow. "Your last name? I don't think I know it," he laughed suddenly then continued, "I always just thought of you as Eden, you know, one name like Björk or something."

"What the fuck? Björk? That's who you thought of?" She chuckled at the thought of herself dressed as Björk. "No, baby, I have a last name. It's Lockhart."

"Lockhart..." Terry repeated. "Eden Lockhart, that's a beautiful name. You must have some Irish heritage like me. Now I get the reference of the key. You can unlock my heart any day." Terry smiled warmly at Eden as if to say *Thanks for the gift*. Then he leaned in and they kissed slowly and passionately.

Eden silently took the skeleton key necklace from Terry and clasped it behind his neck. It hung just a little higher than the cross. *Now I have two lovers around my neck*, Terry thought. Eden pulled away from Terry's kiss and laid on her stomach with her ass slightly up in the air. "Fuck me, baby," she said. "I want you inside me from behind so fucking bad!"

Terry got behind her on his knees. He stroked and admired her glorious ass and could already see she was wet and ready for his cock. Slipping his hand over his cock a couple times got him the rest of the way fully hard. Then he leaned in and slid deep inside her.

"Oh, fuck yeah!" Eden moaned as her head went forward toward the pillow. "I want it hard, give it to me hard!"

Terry obliged, thrusting deep and fast into her dripping cunt. Now his hands were gripping her thin hips so he could pull her into him, and his pelvis smacked against her ass with the sound of skin on skin. "Oh my God!" Terry yelled. "That pussy is so fucking perfect!"

"Tell me how much you want that pussy!" she screamed. "Stuff me! Stuff me with that big cock!"

"I want that pussy so bad!" Terry said, moaning every word. His thrust kept getting faster and faster, and he knew that it wasn't going to be long before he busted.

Eden smashed her face against the pillow and crossed her wrists behind her back. "Hold my wrists! Restrain me!" she commanded. Terry held her wrists and pressed them hard against Eden's lower back, enough for it to hurt. She groaned and was enjoying the exquisite pain. It was sending her into a trance-state like she always did for Terry—into Subspace. "Harder, harder!" she screamed in ecstasy. "Fucking stab me with that dick! Call me a *slut*! I order you to call me a *slut*, you submissive puppy!"

Terry didn't mind this, they'd played these games before. "You fucking slut!" Terry yelled at her, not slowing his thrust at all. Grinding his palms harder against her wrists, he could feel the orgasm behind his balls. "Take that fucking cock deep inside you, you dirty whore! You're such a slut for my hot cum! Beg for it!"

"Oh, yeah, Terry! Uh, uh, uh, fuck!" Eden was almost to the point of cumming as well. "Please give me your milky cum! I want it all! I want you to bust your load all over my asshole!" She could feel the orgasm building in her cunt and it was about to explode.

The dirty-talk from Eden was enough to send Terry over the edge. He pulled out suddenly and a long string of semen squirted across Eden's left ass cheek. As he let go of Eden's wrists so he could jerk the last squirts of cum from his cock, she spread her cheeks, exposing her beautiful puckered asshole. Shuddering with ecstatic orgasmic spasms, Terry squirted the last five, or even six, pumps of cum right into that tight little hole.

Eden collapsed on the bed, heaving. "Oh my God," she said between breaths. "When your cum hit my ass, I came so fucking hard! That was just what I needed." Terry sat back on his heels and Eden turned back over onto her back to look at her lover, who was utterly spent, balls drained. Scooting up onto her knees, Eden crawled to Terry and kissed him on the mouth. "I'm gonna go to the bathroom and wash up, love. I'll meet you downstairs." She slid off the bed, winked at Terry, and walked out the door and to the bathroom, still naked.

Rubbing his red face, Terry realized his whole body was still buzzing. That sex was just the medicine he needed as well. He felt like a puddle of primordial ooze and dripped himself off of the bed like slime—the slime created from the Spiralverse's first orgasm. Terry slipped on a pair of jeans without bothering with boxers, and he found a t-shirt from the floor that was relatively clean. After which he went down the stairs to see what his friends were up to.

Mothman and Rob were watching TV, but shut if off when they saw him approach. "What were you guys watching?" Terry asked.

Rob waved his hand dismissively. "Oh, just some news bullshit."

"I didn't know you guys were into politics," Terry replied, raising his eyebrows.

"Pfff," Mothman snorted. "We're fucking not. Politics is dead... Rob was just showing me something that I didn't believe him about."

"Huh?" Terry said. "What's that?"

"You know we were so busy over the past several months dealing with Maya and all that other shit," Rob explained. "Well, there was a whole presidential election that we missed."

Terry shrugged. "So what? Who the fuck cares who the President is?"

Mothman and Rob exchanged a knowing look. "You're gonna want to hear this," Rob insisted.

"What?" Terry asked, playing along. "Who is it then?"

Rob and Mothman spoke at the same time: "Elliot Cage!"

Terry blinked, it took him a second to process that. "Like, *the* Elliot Cage?" he sputtered. "The tranny actor?"

Rob nodded. "First tranny President. Can you believe that crazy shit? Female to male. She got her tits cut off and I wonder what her dick looks like." They laughed.

"Isn't he married, too? He, she, whatever it is. And his wife is the opposite—male to female?" Terry asked.

"Yeah," Mothman answered. "I dunno, I'd probably fuck both of them though. Ha-*ha!*"

Terry rolled his eyes. "You'd fuck anything, Mothman. You said one time that you'd even buy a dog just to fuck it."

"Ewww!" Rob exclaimed and pushed Mothman away from him on the couch.

"You know," Mothman continued, "if they can elect a tranny to be President, might as well elect Sasha Grey's bush to be President!"

There was a beat and then Terry said, "*Impeach my bush,*" and he swung his hips as if he were dancing.

Rob laughed. "Oh, yeah," he said. "That was Peaches, right? We should elect *her* as President! Her campaign slogan would be: *Fuck The Pain Away!*"

They all laughed and started singing in unison: "*Fuck the pain away! Fuck the pain away! Fuck the pain away!*"

While they all were singing in their silly way, Eden came down the stairs to join them. Her hair was still wet from taking a quick shower. Stopping at the bottom of the stairs and staring at the three boys in a bemused way, Eden listened as their song trailed off, "*Fuck the pain away...*"

They went quiet and Eden asked with a smile, "What did I miss?"

Terry smirked and replied, "We have a tranny President!"

ELEVEN

FROM THE MIND OF JESSICA THORN:

The air is a frozen mist. It chills me deep into my bones. It takes me a few seconds to register what had happened; I was dumped headfirst into the Sacred Cauldron. Now I am falling through what seems like dense cloud-cover. All around me is gray and wet. Frigid droplets of water hang all around me in the air, as if suspended in zero-gravity. However, I am falling, slowly. My body feels like it is plunging down through water after jumping from a high cliff. But I am in air—foggy wet air, but air nonetheless.

As I fall in slow-motion, I see shocks of lightning light up parts of the clouds around me. Then images start to appear in the clouds like a projector's image on a cloth screen. They are all the memories I shared with Terry. The first is when we met in Italian Class. Then I see us at Starbucks, talking. The third vision is us sitting in church, listening to Brother Evan's sermon. Another lightning flashes, and I see Maya pursuing us at the school dance, and then me going to get Terry's van and meeting with Remius. In the next burst of lightning I see us all fighting Timestrus in Dreamsphere. Another lightning flash and the loudest crack of thunder, and the image is Terry and I making love in the ice cave. There is one more flash of lightning, almost bright enough to blind me, and a crack of thunder almost deafening; the last image is me and Terry standing on the bridge over the highway. I can feel his pain as he reaches for me, but then in the memory—as it was—I disappear, leaving only the cross necklace.

After this last memory, I break through the bottom of the gray clouds, and find myself in open air. Below me is a huge labyrinth made out of tall hedges. As I fall toward it without control, I start to feel the presence of a pain in my heart—the love and longing that still cries out for Terry in the darkness of the night. He is still a part of me, and that is something I can never erase, no matter how many worlds I eradicate myself from.

My fall slows as I get closer and closer to the labyrinth. It's like once you've reached the bottom of a deep pool after jumping off the high-dive. Slowly I descend between two hedges, stopping briefly in midair, and then I am plopped down on my ass into the grass. "Well, that was fun," I say sarcastically to no one. It seems I am completely alone in the labyrinth—or at least that is my first impression. My stomach sinks at the prospect of there being beasts lurking around each corner. I look up and the immaculately trimmed hedges loom over me, maybe fifteen or twenty feet into the air. The wind is still chilly and wet, the sky is gray and gloomy. I can't help but feel uneasy.

Standing up, I stretch and brush myself off. Not that brushing myself off will do anything, it's just an automatic thing people do. There's a long passage in one direction and a long passage in the other direction. The optical illusion makes it seem like it goes on forever. This makes my head spin, and I feel a slight touch of vertigo. Randomly I pick a direction and just start walking. The hedges are too high to climb over, and they're too dense to try to push through.

As I walk toward what I hope is a turn at the end of the passage, I feel a chill and my skin starts to crawl. My intuition is telling me that I'm not alone in this labyrinth, there is a presence of another creature that sets my spine tingling. I walk a few more steps and then I smell it; the most foul stench that my nose has ever beheld. The odor is like a cow standing in a pile of its own feces mixed with a dead skunk being eaten by a feral dog with mange. Then there is the sound of a low growl. I freeze where I'm standing and I can feel all the blood drain from my face. The piss threatens to exit from my bladder, but I hold it in with all my strength. There is a beast here! I can't see it, but I feel its presence along with that stench and the growl.

Swallowing hard, I turn back toward the way I had come. Presumably the beast—whatever it is—is around the corner toward the way I was walking. Hopefully it hasn't heard me. Oh shit, it can probably smell me though. Terrified, I take off running back the way I came. Through the fear and the adrenaline I feel pumping through my veins, the purple energy of my Soulmind starts to spiral violently out of my solar plexus and illuminates the aura around my body. My Soulmind anticipates the danger and the hilts of the two katanas pop right out of my chest. It's been a while since I've had to use them. Grabbing the hilts, I rip them out of my chest. The purple blades buzz, sizzle, and shine in the low gray light of—wherever I am.

Suddenly I get a brilliant idea. Turning to the hedge-wall to my left, I hack at it with one of my blades. I can't express the extreme disappointment I feel when the Soulmind blade just goes through the thick greenery without doing any damage. It's as if my katana blade is just made of light and no substance. Do they not work anymore? Without dropping the weapon in my left hand, I reach over and touch the other blade with my index finger. I yell and jump at the pain as my finger is burned and left with a small cut. A trickle of blood drips off the tip of my finger. I guess the katanas still work, just not on the hedges.

My stomach jumps up into my throat as I hear another guttural roar, this one louder. The foul stench hits me and I turn toward the direction I had just run from. There in the distance, at the end of the passage, is a Minotaur. *Wait, what?!* A fucking Minotaur! "Oh, fuck..." I say out loud. The creature is huge, probably at least eight feet tall. His upper body is so buff, built like Dwayne Johnson. Veins pulse all down his arms as his muscles ripple and bulge. His head is that of a vicious angry bull—with eyes burning red. The breadth of his horns scares the shit out of me. His tail is long and comes out of the base of his spine like a savage whip. The legs, as you've assuredly already guessed, are that of a bull as well. The Minotaur stomps his right hoof on the ground and I feel the ground shake, a small tremor underneath me. His nails are long and pointed at the tips of his human fingers. I also see a gigantic erection in heat between his legs. It is intimidating and as large as a horse's sex organ.

Fighting against the fear that threatens to root me to the spot, I turn and run away from the great beast. As I sprint, I heave lungfuls of air painfully into my chest. The katanas swing chaotically by my sides and I try not to stab myself. I hear the Minotaur scream in protest and then the ground begins to shake as it runs after me. This fucking thing is about the same size as Timestrus, but now I'm alone. When we fought Timestrus there were three of us! There's no freaking way I want to fight a Minotaur, and I don't want its swinging horse-dick anywhere near me!

I know the beast has to be gaining on me, but I continue to sprint faster than I feel is physically possible, sucking air into my lungs at almost hyperventilation speed. Suddenly I get to the end of this labyrinth passage and it abruptly turns to the left. Not daring to look back and waste even one second, I turn the corner and find myself stumbling into an open area of the labyrinth. It's a large grassy square with several passages leading off of it on all sides. In the middle of the clearing is a large stone fountain. The water shoots up from the top and over an upper basin, then comes down in a thick sheet of water all around the circumference. My legs are burning and I know that I can't keep running. Catching my breath is almost impossible and my lungs scream in my chest. The lactic acid burns like a million tiny blowtorches in my muscles. Quickly I circle around to the other side of the fountain so there is something between me and the Minotaur when it emerges. I grip the hilts of my katanas tighter.

"Jessica!"

I jump and look around for who called my name. The voice is somewhat familiar. I don't see anyone.

"Jessica. Here." the voice says again. Then I look at the water cascading down the fountain in front of me. I mean, what am I expecting to see? But there is a face in the water! It's like a holographic image projected in the waterfall. There's the scraggly shoulder-length black hair, kind and handsome facial features—he's smiling at me. It's Terry's face in the waterfall! Is it just a trick of my mind, brought forth through terror and adrenaline? No time to psychoanalyze it.

"Get ready," the waterfall-Terry says. "It's coming!"

"Terry, help me!" I plead. "I can't fight a giant mythical beast!"

He laughs from the water. "What makes you think that? Remember, you made a guy *explode!*"

"Oh, yeah," I say, remembering that now. "But how do you know about that?"

But there is no time for an answer because the Minotaur stomps into the clearing on the other side of the fountain. I get my katanas ready as it lets out another angry roar. Suddenly it runs at me around one side of the fountain. I run away from it, going around the outside of the fountain, trying to keep distance between me and the huge beast.

"You can't run away from it!" Terry yells.

"Why not?" I yell back, running around and around the fountain, pursued by the Minotaur.

"You're running around in circles!" Terry yells at me. I don't know if he's talking literally or metaphorically—or both. "Just fucking stop and stab him!"

I stop and turn around. The Minotaur closes the distance between us. I'm scared shitless as I face him. Towering above me, the bull's head exhales rancid breath and smoke from his nostrils. Then he takes an open hand and swings it down as if to swat me away. Immediately I slash with one of my katanas and cut a deep gash across the Minotaur's palm. He screams and stumbles back a step or two.

"See," Terry comments from the water of the fountain, "he's not that smart."

I try not to give the beast any time to recover. So I lunge toward him again and attack with both katanas, trying to get the Minotaur on one side and then the other. Unfortunately the giant creature dodges both of my attacks, then rears back and kicks me hard in the chest with one of his hooves. The wind is knocked out of me and I fly back through the air. My flight is suddenly stopped when I hit the side of the hedge-wall behind me. The katana in my left hand slips from my grasp and disappears as its energy goes back into my purple Soulmind which continues to illuminate my aura in flickering violet flames. Luckily I still maintain my grip on the weapon in my right hand. It's extremely difficult to breathe and I fear that at least a few of my ribs are broken.

The Minotaur quickly comes over to where I lay. His eyes burn red as he stares down at me, pure rage. Raising his right hoof into the air, he makes to stomp on my head to finish me. And my head would most likely pop like a grape under his enormous weight.

"Now! Go now!" Terry yells from the fountain.

Without thinking, I know what to do. No time to hesitate, I roll out from under the path of the Minotaur's raised hoof, and in one movement I stab up between his legs. The blade of my katana sinks into his flesh right behind his grotesquely-large set of testicles, in the area of his perineum. The Minotaur screams in pain as I pull the blade out from where I stabbed him. Steaming red blood pours down on me like a waterfall as the beast stumbles forward and falls face-first into the hedge. He tries to recover and blood continues to gush from his perineum. I'm ready this time. The hilt of the other katana suddenly comes out of the purple spiral at my solar plexus and I rip it free, now ready with both.

Moaning in pain, the Minotaur clumsily rolls onto its back to try to get up. But I don't give him that chance. Running up, I jump onto the Minotaur's muscly chest, and in one fell swoop, I hold the katanas with my arms out, as if to embrace the beast, and then I swing the blades together like a pair of scissors. The Soulmind blades slice through his neck as if it's butter, and still roaring in protest, the Minotaur's head is severed completely from his body. Blood gushes like a river breaking through a dam from the stump of neck and the severed head. As I jump off of the creature, his body goes limp, but he still maintains his obscene erection.

Now the pain shoots through my ribcage, I scream, and drop the katanas. They disappear and all the purple energy of my Soulmind is sucked back into my body as I double over in agony.

"You killed that motherfucker!" Terry said, excited, his face looking down at me from the fountain's waterfall. "Are you okay?"

I groan painfully as I curl into a fetal position on the grass. "I think my ribs are broken," I choke out, barely able to talk.

"Drink the water from my fountain. You'll feel better," he says.

It's extremely difficult, but I drag myself over toward the edge of the fountain. Without standing, I reach over the lip and scoop a handful of water into my eager mouth. Instantly I feel the pressure in my chest subside and I can finally take a breath. Gasping, I drink in the glorious oxygen. It is unclear whether my broken ribs fully healed, but at least the water from the fountain seems to take away the pain enough for me to regain my strength. I get to my knees and scoop a couple more handfuls of water gratefully into my mouth. The liquid is cool and refreshing.

"Thank you, Terry," I say, staring at his face in the sheet of water. The image moves as the water moves.

"Why are you thanking *me*?" he asks, smiling cheekily.

"Well," I start, "I don't know if I could have defeated that Minotaur without you being here to encourage me."

"Why do you need someone to encourage you anyway?"

I frown. "Uh... I don't know. I just feel stronger knowing you're with me."

He laughs and smiles lovingly back at me from the screen of water. "That's what's funny," he says. "I'm not really here."

"What do you mean?" I ask.

"You conjured me from your own mind because you felt like you needed me to help you fight," he says, laughing again as if the joke is continuing. "I'm really you. It's really *yourself* encouraging yourself. That strength has been inside you all along. It's okay to feel connected to Terry because that love runs deep. But realize that you don't need to rely on him to use your *own* power."

"So I..." I start and then trail off, looking at the dead Minotaur bleeding on the grass.

"You did that all on your own," he finishes my thought for me. And when I look back at his face in the waterfall, it's already fading. The last thing to disappear is his wide bright smile, like the last fading smirk of a Cheshire Cat.

Suddenly a cold wind swirls around the fountain and blows my hair. I shiver, my skin crawls with a sudden shock of dread as well as temperature. Scanning around at all the paths that lead off from the clearing, I half expect something else to come jumping out, ready to kill me. Then I hear a voice, a whisper, that seems to be coming from nowhere: "Come closer!"

I'm prepared for anything and I assume a defensive stance with my back toward the fountain. "Who's there?" I demand.

The voice is distinctively female and somewhat familiar. Its response is a cackle that echoes around me in the wind. "Jessica," the voice whispers again, "come to me..."

Why does the voice sound so familiar? I shake my head and notice that my Soulmind is becoming agitated again, spiraling out of my chest. A burst of my purple energy shoots out like a spear and illuminates one path that leads off from the clearing. I guess that's where my energy wants to take me. Would my own Soulmind try to lead me to my doom? I hope not.

Reluctantly I take my leave from the clearing and the fountain, and start to walk down the path designated for me. There's a chill in the air and the hedges that loom above me on either side are like ominous giants leering at their captive. The soft green grass underfoot is long and sways in the cold breeze.

"That's it, my pretty," the disembodied woman says, an echo swirling around my skull.

Now I realize what's so familiar about the voice! It sounds like the voice in my head when I talk to myself—my own voice! But how can that be? Who is this other *me* that beckons me on? There is an uneasy sense of malevolence. Actually the vibe is kind of ambiguous.

Courage is acting in spite of fear, not the acting in the absence of it. If there is no fear, then how could it take courage to act? And right now I am pushing through the fear of the unknown—the fear of what might await me at the end of this path. Whoever it is might not have ill intentions, but I can't rule out the possibility. This means I must be prepared to do battle again. My Soulmind senses my restless energy and the hilts of the katanas appear at my solar plexus. I pull them out and hold them by my sides. The purple light of the blades flickers and ripples with power. Part of me hopes that I'm almost at the end of this baroque labyrinth.

Baroque? Is that the right word? I don't know... doesn't matter.

The silence is broken by the cackle again. *My* cackle? Okay, that's too weird to think about. "You are most beautiful," the voice continues. "I wonder how much more beautiful you would be with your red blood flowing into the grass?"

I swallow hard. Now I think it's a safe deduction to think this woman or whatever it is wishes to do me harm. Keeping at my steady pace, I squint into the distance. The light is still gray and hazy from the dense cloud cover, but I think I can make out something in the distance between the hedges. It looks like a huge door, or gate, that stretches up even taller than the hedges on either side of it. As I keep taking cautious steps forward, this giant metal door comes into better view.

Its surface is smooth, impossibly smooth, and silver. It shines even in the dull daylight. The carvings in it are intricate and gold—just as intricate as the ones on the walls of the cave. They appear to be in the same script—some form of Celtic, or possibly Elvish this time. I am several yards away from this barrier when the entity who had been speaking to me materializes. She is intimidating and her energy makes me stop in my tracks. This being looks like me—somewhat. We're the same height and she has my same long black hair. However, she's wearing a skin-tight black leotard like the one I saw Maya wearing. This being stands in a warrior stance with her legs wide and she's holding a set of Soulmind-blade katanas as well. They look as if they are burning with purple flames. Her eyes are nothing but orange flames burning in the sockets, and she wears a necklace of shrunken heads around her neck. The image is terrifying.

"Who are you, entity?" I demand, trying to sound confident.

This other-me sticks her tongue out of her mouth. It's long and pointed, and the gesture seems to be mocking me. "I am…" she hisses, seemingly getting a lot of enjoyment out of my disgust at her appearance, "Kali Ma," she finishes.

"Kali… Ma?" I say back to the Goddess. "Like the Hindu Goddess?"

"The very same," Kali replies, flicking her tongue out and in like a snake. "Do you see yourself in me?" she continues. "Do you see your own terrible beauty?"

I hesitate, not knowing how to respond. "It's sort of disconcerting," I reply finally. "Are you here to kill me?"

Kali laughs as if this is the funniest joke, a jest thrown into the void of eternity. "Kill you? *Yesssssss*," she hisses. "Must one die to be reborn? Must you die to yourself to become a higher form?"

"What?" I say, confused. Her intention of killing me seems ambiguous, so I assume a defensive stance with my katanas out in front to block my body. "Are you being literal, or are you speaking in riddles?"

"What's the difference?" Kali smiles and flames burn ominously from her eye sockets. "Isn't life the greatest conundrum? Isn't life the most divine and terrifying mystery there is?"

"I grow tired of these games," I admit with a sigh. "If you intend to kill me, fucking try it!" Without giving Kali time to attack, I charge her, trying to get the element of surprise. Swinging my katanas toward her midsection, my blades are blocked almost immediately by her own blades. The purple Soulmind energy sizzles as my katanas grind against hers. We are locked together. Kali's smile is like a grotesque clown mocking me with lips that have been sliced off. Then I actually hear laughing, cackling that's so creepy my skin crawls. I look down and the shrunken heads around Kali's neck are in hysterics, convulsing with their laughter.

Pulling away, I retreat a few steps, disengaging our blades. I'm completely repulsed by the cackling of the shrunken heads. My stomach suddenly turns and threatens to come up and out. I almost am too slow to react when Kali makes an attack. She lunges and swings one of her blades at me, and I deflect it with one of my own.

"Why are you fighting me?" Kali asks, grinning as if this is all still one grand practical joke.

I scoff. "Why am *I* fighting *you*?" Grinding my katana against hers, I force her to stumble back a couple steps, putting some distance between us. "Isn't it *you* who is fighting *me*?" I yell. "What exactly is going on here?"

Kali stands to her full height and it seems as if she becomes even more grotesque—even more beautiful. A darkness grows around her and the shadows dance around her like puppets. "I am the Shadow within you, Jessica!" Kali bellows, her voice suddenly taking on an otherworldly quality, as if there are multiple voices overlapping each other. "You fear your own Darkness," the Goddess continues. "You fear your own capacity to be sinister! So you suppress and repress, pushing it down until it must find another way to manifest its destruction. Little do you know that embracing your Shadow is the key to your transformation —your own Rebirth!"

More riddles, goddamnit! "I don't need your fucking psychobabble!" I yell. At this point, I'm so exhausted and ready to be done with this, I lack the capacity to entertain anything that takes any extra brain power. "The Shadow is not a part of me!" I insist. "The Shadow is a demon, an entity, that can be cast out. And I cast it out of me! I cast you out!"

Kali laughs in my face. "Still thinking in Christian terms, are you? You cannot cast me out, because I *am* you. The Shadow is you, and if you treat it with disrespect, it will destroy you. And that time you will not be reborn. I am the Goddess of time, creation, preservation, and destruction! All the power that is yours as well!"

I ignore the monologue and yell, "Stand aside from the door! I want to leave!" Hopefully I sound intimidating enough.

Kali smiles again as if she knows something I don't. "The only way out," she says, "is through me."

"If that's how it's gonna be, I'll gladly oblige," I say and rush her, slashing my katanas in a chaotic way, trying to stab or cut her. Kali dodges all of my attacks and retreats until her back is against the silver door. I try to take the moment to catch my breath.

"Isn't it obvious now that *you* are the one fighting *me*?" Kali says again, as if it's going to mean anything more to me this time. "Just let the Darkness take you and burn you from the inside out."

"Never!" I yell. "I am to be reborn through the Light, not through the Darkness!"

Ah, hell, who am I trying to convince? It seems now that I'm trying to talk *myself* into it. I'm trying to grasp onto the last tendrils of a dying mode of thinking—a dying ideology, gasping its last breaths. There is a darkness in me, and I know it. Why am I uselessly trying to pretend there's not? The fear of it, that's why. The fear that it might consume me. That that Shadowy aspect of my consciousness might be the very thing that could threaten Terry's life. He's too special, he's too much of a key to what is coming—even though I don't know what that future holds. I wouldn't want the damage of my trauma to rear its ugly head and destroy everything.

"Aren't you tired of fighting?" Kali asks. She is holding her blades out in front of her, mirroring my own stance. "Let's just lay down our arms, yes?"

I stare at the Mother Goddess, Kali Ma, as she opens her hands and the Soulmind blades disappear, returning to the purple flames burning in her aura. Then before I even make a conscious decision, my katanas disappear as well, spiraling back into my chest. I nod slowly as I drop my arms to my sides. "Yes," I say finally, "I am tired of fighting. It's so draining and exhausting. I do it when I have to... But combat? Why? It's so tiresome."

"Then *surrender*," Kali says in a booming voice. The flames of her eyes burn into the depths of my Soulmind.

I realize then that I'm done talking; I'm done fighting. It's over. The violence has ceased and I feel a welcome relief wash over me in a cosmic wave. Falling to my knees, I suddenly feel the tears burn my eyes and then flood down my cheeks. I don't know if Free Will really exists; all I know is that this moment feels inevitable, as if it was seeded aeons ago in some distant galaxy, by unfathomably evolved entities. Because I can't speak, I say this to Kali Ma in my mind: *Take me; destroy me if you must.*

In that moment, the violet flames around Kali's body grow to an enormous height, as if it is a mystical bonfire ready to burn the House of the Ego down to the ground. She takes a step toward me and says, "All witches must burn in the Kundalini fire!"

The Goddess jumps into the air and her whole form dissolves into a ball of purple flame, joining the rest of the bonfire. Then this fire takes me, enveloping my whole body. I close my eyes and feel this *Kundalini Fire* burn me down to my very Soulmind. There is no resistance, I *have* surrendered. My flesh melts off layer by layer, taking with it all of the lies I have ever been told; all the false religious conditioning. The trauma inflicted upon me by my father, my mother, comes melting off. It feels like a blowtorch is incinerating me from the inside out. I try to scream but no sound escapes my mouth, there is no throat left to scream with. When I feel the burning reaching down into my core, I know that the Darkness is being released to transform and cleanse my consciousness—my Soulmind. Within that core I realize I am angry, I have all this rage toward my parents that I bottled up to try to spare myself from becoming a monster. I see visions of my father pouring boiling water over my arm; I see him hitting me, and yelling at me. I see a vision of my mother abandoning me and running into the arms of other men.

If this is a surrender, it has to be a *total* surrender. So I allow myself to feel that rage, to watch myself killing my father and my mother over and over again in my mind. Stabbing them to death and then bringing them back to life just to stab them to death all over again. Then I see a vision of myself burning down Brother Evan's church with the whole congregation inside. In the vision people on fire come running out of the church and I spray them with more gasoline. The Kundalini Fire burns and it burns. It continues to burn until I don't even feel the rage anymore. There is no anger, there is no happiness. There is no sadness, but there is no joy. There is no suffering, and there is no Heaven. And that is okay. There is peace in that. I am utterly burnt to ashes and I touch the silence of the void. The blessed emptiness. And it feels like liberation.

The violet flames of Kali Ma and my Soulmind have destroyed me, leaving just a pile of ashes. Maybe not even the ashes. Maybe pure Nothingness. I feel the flames collapse into a dense ball and then implode on itself. Stretching my arm out of the ashes, I claw at the tall grass in front of me. Like a *Living Dead Girl*, I reemerge from the dust. As my head comes through, I spit out a mouthful of ashes, my own cremation. I'm like a witch reincarnating from the urn. Wriggling out of the pile like a worm,

I feel my legs and feet reform. Shakily I get to my knees and then stand up, brushing off the super-dusty remains of whatever I used to be.

Looking up at the immense door, it starts to rumble, then slowly it opens inward. Whatever that task was I just completed, I guess I must have passed. After being burned by Kundalini Fire, I didn't really realize how different I would feel, but I do. Whatever it did to me is unexplainable. What the Soma trip had begun, Kali Ma just completed with her fire of destruction and transformation.

Keeping balance on my new legs, I walk through the open door toward what I hope is the center, or ending, of the labyrinth. As I walk forward, the path starts to widen. Looking up into the sky, I see originating from somewhere in front of me, a white beam of light coming up from the labyrinth and penetrate the gray clouds above. Something tells me that's my portal back through.

After walking the path for a few more minutes, I come to a new clearing a bit larger than the one with the fountain. In the center is what looks like a perfect replica of the Sacred Cauldron through which I got here. The great white beam of light is shining out of this Cauldron into the clouds overhead. Sitting next to the Cauldron, smiling at me, is Cernunnos, Lord of Animals. His deer legs are crossed in a meditative posture. The same group of animals that had followed him through the cavern are playing and grazing on the grass of the clearing.

"Well, well," Cernunnos says cheerily, "you've made it through the labyrinth! Well played, Jessica Thorn! Are you ready to return?"

I nod my head vigorously. "Yes, yes!" I say enthusiastically. "I am more than ready to return!"

Cernunnos laughs. "I can imagine. No one said these tasks would be easy. But you have come through—renewed and reborn! And in this moment you can rest easy in that knowledge."

"Thank you, Cernunnos," I reply, bowing a little to the god. "I cannot begin to explain the significance of what I have experienced here."

Cernunnos puts up a hand. "No need. I already know. Let the mysterious be mysterious. Why try to analyze every little thing, eh? Where's the fun in explaining everything away?"

"Yes," I agree.

"It is time," he says.

I approach the Sacred Cauldron and grasp the rim. All the animals are hushed and they watch me with beady eyes, whiskers and noses twitching. I try to gaze deep into the light coming from the magickal water of the Cauldron, but it is much too bright to see anything within it. Glancing at Cernunnos, he smiles knowing that I don't need his help this time. I swing my leg over the side of the Sacred Cauldron, and then I just let myself fall in.

TWELVE

Wednesday finally rolled around and Terry was going over the list of names he compiled from the emails he had received. He felt like a bouncer going over a guest list, determining who was to be let in and who wasn't. It was about a few shy of twenty people, and to Terry that still seemed like a lot of people to have in his living room. Rob was sitting next to him on the couch and looked over his shoulder to read the names in the notebook. Mothman sat on the other side of Rob and was playing Tetris on his cell phone. Now and then Terry would glance up to the top of the stairs to see if Eden was coming down. She hadn't yet.

"That's a lot of people," Rob commented.

Terry nodded. "Yeah, Rob, and it's going to just keep growing. That's why if anything ever happens to me, I need to be able to rely on you to keep this going."

Rob frowned and looked very serious. "I'll do my best," he said. "What's that?" He pointed up to above the list of names; it said *The Playground.*

"That's what I'm calling our group of Soulminds: *The Playground*," Terry answered.

Mothman glanced over at Rob and Terry and said, "What about me? Don't you need my help too with this if you're not around?"

"Yeah, you'll help as well," Terry responded, "but I trust Rob more to get things done."

"You asshole," Mothman shot back. "I'm just as capable of running shit."

Terry laughed. "Okay, dude, you will be helping Rob keep everything afloat. But we all know how easily you get distracted —especially by the prospect of getting some pussy."

Mothman grinned. "Oh yeah, I bet you there is going to be some hot Soulmind snatch coming here today!"

"Please don't try to fuck everyone in our Playground," Terry pleaded. "We want to keep our fellowship intact, not scare everyone away."

Eden came strolling down the stairs and into the living room. She had slept late into the morning. "What's going on, guys?" she asked.

All three of them looked up at her from the couch. Terry was the one who answered her. "First Playground meeting today."

"Oh yeah," Eden remarked offhand. "I totally forgot about that."

"I've only been talking about it for weeks," Terry shot back with a little edge in his voice.

The only response Eden gave was to shrug her shoulders and then walk into the kitchen to get some juice from the fridge. Terry brought his attention back to Rob and said, "See how I wrote their email address next to each name?"

"Yeah," Rob answered, reading the page.

"I'll make a copy of this for you so you have everyone's information," Terry continued.

The doorbell rang, cutting off their conversation. Terry went to the door and there were a couple guys and a couple girls standing out on the porch. After opening the door, he asked them their names and checked them off of the list. "You guys had no trouble getting through the Merkabah Field?" Terry asked.

A young boy who couldn't have been older than fifteen shook his shaggy dirty-blonde hair. "Nah," he replied. "You gotta teach me how to set one of those up though! I don't know how to do that."

"All in good time," Terry said. "You are..." he looked down his list and got the boy's name again, "Michael, right?"

The boy with the dirty-blonde hair smiled and nodded. Then Terry led them all into the living room. "Hiya," Michael said, waving to Rob and Mothman.

Terry introduced them: "This is Rob and Mothman, and that's Eden in the kitchen." He glanced back toward the door. "You can all get acquainted. I think there are some more people here."

Terry went back to the front door as more members of The Playground came to the door. It looked like some had driven and parked their cars on the curb near the front of the house.

Others had ridden bikes and dropped them on the lawn inside of the Merkabah shield. Terry welcomed everyone and checked off every name as they entered his house. After he checked off the last name on the list, Terry saw one straggler walking toward his house from the end of the block. This boy looked like he was about twenty, and he was wearing plainclothes. There weren't anymore names on the list so Terry was suspicious. He watched from the doorway as this young man approached the edge of the Merkabah Field. The man hesitated when he was about a foot away from it. It didn't seem like the man could see the Field, but he could feel something. When he tried to walk through it toward the house, he was pushed back as if he had been shoved. He tried again, but the Merkabah wouldn't let the man through. Terry looked at the young man and gave him the finger.

"Not supposed to be here, are you?" Terry yelled.

The man stared but didn't say anything. Then after a couple seconds, he turned and walked back the way he had come. After closing the front door and locking it, Terry walked back into the living room where the seventeen new members of his Playground were chattering away like they were in the lunchroom at high school. The boy called Michael was over by the island in the kitchen, talking to Eden.

"Hey, cutie. I'm Michael," he said to Eden, trying to sound suave. "Aren't you, uh," he continued, "*Temple of Cosmic Fuck* on pornhub?"

Eden didn't answer, she just eyed Michael as she took a drink of orange juice. When she didn't say anything, Michael continued, "That video was hot—*you're* hot! And that's the first time I've ever seen Soulmind energy captured on a digital video."

"You could see our Soulminds on the video?" Eden finally asked.

Michael nodded. Then he took a step closer to her and said, "You know... We should do another video, together, we could make it even sexier—way more Soulmind explosions, if you know what I mean." Michael winked.

Eden scoffed and backed away from him. "In your dreams," she said. "Are you even old enough to watch porn? You look like you're twelve."

"Hey!" Michael retorted, looking offended. "I'll have you know I'm fifteen!"

"Yeah..." Eden continued, looking bored by this conversation already. "That would still be statutory rape on my part." She looked over and saw that Terry was watching them. "Hey, Terry," she yelled over to him. "I'm getting the fuck out of here for a bit. Sorry I don't want to stick around for the *circus*, but I'll be back later." And without waiting for a reply, Eden pushed Michael away with the tip of her finger and walked out the door into the mudroom.

Terry stared at Michael and gestured for him to go take a seat with everybody else in the living room. He did. When Terry stood on top of the two steps that led down into the living room, they all stopped their chattering and watched him, eager to know what he had in store for them.

"Welcome, everyone," Terry began. "This is the first meeting of The Playground and I'm very pleased that you all could be here. I've gotten the impression that individuals with Soulminds don't often unite in a big group like this. Sometimes we are unaware where other awakened people are, and without our Octobers to guide us, we can feel lost. Am I right?"

There were nods and murmurs of agreement.

Terry cleared his throat and continued his monologue, "As I stated already, this is The Playground, and the first rule of The Playground is you don't talk about The Playground!"

There were chuckles around the group and others who didn't get the joke. Terry smiled. "Actually, I'm joking," he continued. "We *want* you to talk about The Playground! I—*we*—want this to grow and spread. The plan is to awaken more and more people —as many as we can. But we'll get to that later. I assume you all have lost your Octobers, that's what brought us all together, yes?"

One girl who was sitting next to Rob spoke up. She was totally goth: black hair, black eye makeup, fishnet shirt with a purple spaghetti-strap shirt over it, ripped skinny jeans, lip piercings. "My October, Pearl, left me almost a year ago," she sounded angry and bitter. "What the fuck am I supposed to do? I don't know what to do with this power! The idea of going into other Dimensions all by myself scares the shit out of me. I feel like I still needed Pearl and she just abandoned me!"

"Yeah," Michael chimed in; he was a chatty one. "My Jester disappeared too! I feel like my other Soulmind friends went off on another adventure and just left me behind."

"That doesn't feel good, does it?" Terry asked. There were more murmurs of affirmation. "Well, I say fuck all that! What if in the future, every person you meet has a Soulmind? You would never be alone! You would have companions at every turn, and if the Octobers decide to come back, that would just add to the fun and adventure we're already on! Let's awaken the whole world!" Terry said, getting really excited. "Okay, okay, let's not think about that all at once. We have to start out slow. One step at a time until we can reach critical mass. How many of you here have awakened someone else, you know, sexually?"

The group gave each other nervous glances. Then, reluctantly, a few guys and a few girls raised their hands. "Was it a shock to you?" Terry asked. The ones who raised their hands nodded. "Yeah," he continued. "My October, Remius, didn't fucking tell me that could happen until after I activated *this* guy." Terry pointed at Mothman who blushed and tried to shrink down into the couch. The group laughed and Rob poked Mothman with his elbow. "So, my friends, this is the main tenet of our Playground: *to make love and activate!* This is, and will always be, our mission. To activate at least one other person who's Soulmind isn't awake; and they in turn will go on to activate more people. If we're lucky, this will spread like a blaze and set the world on fire—turning it on in more ways than one! However, mark my words carefully: the sexual activity must *always* be consensual. And it's even better if your sex partner is aware beforehand that having sex with you will awaken special powers within them, but that is not a requirement, just a suggestion. Let me stress this again: all sexual activity *must* be consensual—Mothman!" Terry shot Mothman a burning look.

"What?" Mothman said defensively. "What makes you think *I* would be the one to rape someone?"

Terry rolled his eyes. "Because you can never keep your dick in your pants."

A young man who looked about seventeen or eighteen raised his hand. He wore baggy jeans and a Wu-Tang Clan Christmas sweater. Terry nodded in his direction indicating that he could speak. "So this—*Playground*—is basically like a Soulmind Sex Cult?" Wu-Tang Christmas sweater asked.

Terry blinked, not knowing how to respond at first. Then finally he said, "You don't have to put it that coarsely, but yes, I guess you could call it that. But, no, I don't want to think of our group as a Cult. I'm not the leader, and you don't *have* to do what I say. Is that clear?" Everyone nodded. Terry continued, "And I've come up with a secret password so we know who is friendly and part of our Playground. If you want to test someone, you say: *No Bounce*; and they have to respond: *No Play*. Let's all try that... *No Bounce*..."

The whole Playground replied in unison: "*No Play!*"

THIRTEEN

Slamming the door behind her, Eden let herself out into the mudroom attached to the garage. She hoped that her irritation was apparent in the way she took off so fast, leaving Terry with his new 'friends.' *What the fuck*, she thought, *I liked it when it was just our little family: me, Terry, Rob, and Mothman. Now he's bringing all those* clowns *into our house.*

Eden knew she was being unfair, but she preferred their group to remain intimate. Since she had become aware of her active Soulmind, Eden had never personally activated *anyone*. During that time she had only seemed to have penetrative sex with other people who were already awakened. And the other sexual partners she had did little more than mess around with her; like Kat who never actually stuck his cock inside her. *What was wrong with only having a few companions to travel through Dimensions with?* she thought. *Why does the* whole *world have to be awakened?*

This time she wasn't going to walk to the Blue Line station. Obviously she was pissed off at Terry again; it seemed to be happening more and more lately. So Eden grabbed the BMX bike from the other side of the garage, dragged it through the mudroom, and out the door. Terry had finally given her a key to the house, so she locked up behind her. Before mounting the bike, Eden got out her cell phone and dialed Darren's number.

He answered on the second ring. "Hey, this is Darren."

"Darren, it's Eden," she replied. "Where are you right now?"

"I'm at *angelfuck*, just kicking it in my office. Why?"

"I was hoping you'd be there," she said. "I'm gonna come by."

"Okay," Darren responded. "I'll be here." Then he hung up.

Eden stuffed her phone back into her pocket and hopped on the bike, pedaling hard toward the Blue Line. When she got there, she just dumped the bike in the grass, not giving a fuck whether it got stolen or what. She'd never seen Terry ride it, and really she just wanted to be mean.

The train ride was just as creepy as the last time she went into the city: silent zombie-like people and homeless bums sleeping off their drinking binges. The streets looked like they had been patched up the best they could. Cars were driving through the streets again; not many, but some. The buildings were still utterly destroyed and there was no indication that the city or the government were attempting to rebuild them. The corpses seemed to be all cleaned up though. There were large groups of newly homeless people wandering through the streets, scavenging for whatever they could find.

Eden tried to blend in as best she could: remaining silent and looking as forlorn as she could. The stop closest to *angelfuck* came and she got off. Employing her Soulmind power, Eden did her best to stay somewhat invisible—psychically influencing any people she passed by to *not see her*. In no time she found herself at the entrance to the club. The neon sign above the door no longer lit up and several of the letters had been shattered. Eden pulled on the door but it was locked. Mumbling to herself, she pulled out her phone and dialed Darren again.

When he answered she said, "The fucking door is locked! You knew I was coming, you fuckwad!"

"Take a chill-pill," Darren said with a sigh. "Don't get your panties all in a twist—wait, you don't wear panties!" He laughed at his own joke.

"Hardy-har-har, very funny," Eden snapped. "Now will you come open the door?"

"Jeez, yeah, I'll be right there," Darren responded. "I had to lock the door because of, you know, looters."

"Yeah, I figured. Now just get up here, It's creepy out here." She hung up and pocketed her phone.

Within moments the door swung open and there was Darren, smiling and ushering Eden inside. She walked past him and down the stairs. Darren locked the door behind them and followed her.

"Jesus," she said when they came into the main room. Darren had cleaned up a little bit, but there was still so much water damage. "I guess you won't be reopening for a while." Eden looked at her friend sympathetically.

Darren frowned and sighed in resignation. "I don't know if I'll ever be able to open her again. My little passion project has maybe seen its last days. I hate being out here on the dance floor now, it makes me depressed. Let's go into my inner sanctuary."

Darren swiftly crossed the floor, went through the curtain and back into his office. Eden followed close behind. Flopping down on one of the red couches, Darren didn't mind that it was still a little damp, it was dry for the most part. "So what brings you to my humble abode on this strange day?"

"Oh, I just had to get away from the house for a little bit," Eden said, walking over to the small bookshelf and running her fingers over some of the titles there. "Terry started this Soulmind sex club thing and was having the first meeting today. It was just too much for me, I had to get out of there."

"Soulmind sex club sounds exactly like something that would be up your alley," Darren grinned.

Eden rolled her eyes. "Yeah, you would think so, wouldn't you? I don't know, I haven't been feeling like myself lately. I've been feeling... irritable. Like everything is annoying and I'm, like, above it."

"Huh, interesting," Darren continued. "You know, I knew about Terry's little meeting today."

Eden turned to stare at Darren. "You did?"

He nodded. "Oh, yeah. I saw his post on Craigslist about it and forwarded it to a couple people. Actually, I kind of gave him the idea for it. Some of the members of the Body of Lucifer Christ have teenage children who's Soulminds have just recently come online. I made sure some of them made it to Terry's little *Playground*."

Eden was dumbfounded. She walked over and sat on the couch on the other side of the coffee table, trying to formulate her next question. "How come you never told me about this *Lucifer Christ* cult thing?" she asked.

Shrugging, Darren replied, "You just don't seem like the type for joining cults. I could totally see you pushing your way to become the cult *leader* though." He winked at her like that was the funniest inside joke.

Scoffing at that, Eden responded, "As *if!* I just don't see that ever happening. Where you got that notion is beyond me... So you support Terry in trying to spark some kind of Pycho-Sexual-Spiritual Awakening?"

"Yeah, why not," Darren shrugged. "It's not like anyone else is doing anything really radical. Even the efforts of the Body have been pretty slow. We need something to really shake this baby up."

"Shake this baby up?"

"Yeah, you know what I mean," Darren continued. "I would think you of all people would be for some kind of global Soulmind orgy." He smiled and bounced his eyebrows up and down.

"Okay, fine," Eden smirked. "You got me. That does sound kind of fun. But, no, no, there was this kid there today who had seen this porno I shot with Terry and Mothman. He looked like he couldn't have been older than thirteen or fourteen. How young are kids watching porn these day?"

"Ha! Who the fuck are you to judge? How old were you when you first started watching porn?"

"Touché," Eden conceded.

"And how old were you when you first had sex?" Darren pushed her.

Eden sighed but answered the question. "I was six, with my stepbrother. That doesn't mean I *should* have been having sex."

"I know, I know," Darren said, putting up his hand. "I was just making a point."

Eden shrugged and looked away. "Yeah, I know you were."

"So tell me," Darren continued without a pause, "what's the real reason you come here today."

Suddenly Eden looked at him with lust in her eyes and a mischievous grin. "You know I'm horny and I haven't had you in a while."

"Ah," he said, nodding. "I should have known you needed a fix of that big black cock!" He started to unbutton his pants and then unzipped his fly. Without a moment's hesitation, Eden got up from the couch and pushed the coffee table to the side.

Kneeling between Darren's legs, Eden tugged at the bottoms of his pants until they slid off of his legs. Then the boxers were gone, kicked to the side. Eden stared ravenously at Darren's long, thick cock as it swelled in his hand. "Well, then let's get down to fucking business," he said as Eden took the chocolate-colored cock in her own hand. She stroked it until it was fully hard and then she took it into her mouth. Darren leaned his head back and moaned low and long as Eden continued to deep throat him. Licking the hot shaft swollen with blood, her saliva dripped down onto Darren's balls.

"Yeah, baby, keep sucking that black cock," Darren moaned as he lightly put his hands on top of Eden's pink hair. After a few more strokes, she pulled the cock from her mouth and licked the top as she gave Darren the puppy eyes. "Oh, Eden, I love it when you look at me like that. It makes me so gushy!"

"Can I ride your huge cock, Daddy?" she asked in her whiney little-girl voice. "I need it so bad."

"Beg me for it," Darren said, playing along.

"Please, Daddy?" Eden whined. "I need you inside me. I can't live without your giant black cock destroying my tight little pussy."

"Since you asked so nicely," Darren obliged, "you can have the honor of my cock."

"Thank you, Daddy!" Eden stood up and in less than three seconds she was completely naked. She pretended to act shy and her petite body got Darren so hot. Straddling his lap, Eden guided his massive dick into her dripping and eager cunt. She cried out, taking its entire length into her. As she started to ride it, Eden put her hands on Darren's shoulders. He put his hands on her hips, guiding her bounce up and down on his shaft. His girth was so thick that her pussy was tight around him, as if her cunt could squeeze the cum out of him.

"Oh, Eden," Darren moaned with ecstasy. "It's been so long since I've been inside you. I've missed this..."

Eden leaned in and kissed his wet lips. Their tongues found each other's and they were eager to have their saliva mingle together. Moving her hips like a snake, Eden intensified her thrust and got even wetter at the prospect of making Darren cum. "I love your cock," Eden whispered close to his face. Darren could feel her breath on his cheek.

"And I love your pussy, baby," Darren said, almost unable to get the words out since he was moaning so loudly from the building pleasure.

"I want to make you cum, Darren," Eden gasped. "I want your milky cum all over my tight naked body. All over my abs, all over my tits."

Darren stood up off of the couch. Eden was so small and barely weighed anything, so this was no difficult feat. Wrapping her legs around his hips, she wrapped her arms around his neck, hugging him as she bounced on his cock. Screams escaped Eden's lips as she felt her pussy cumming onto Darren's fat cock. "Oh, fuck, oh god! I'm cumming," she screamed. "I want you to cum too!"

Softly and tenderly, Darren laid Eden down on her back on the coffee table, still thrusting in and out of her tight cunt. She was so wet that her juices were dripping down his shaft and soaking his balls like the flood had done to his precious club. "I'm about to cum!" he yelled all of a sudden.

"Give it to me, baby! Give me your cum!"

Darren pulled out abruptly and grunted as spurts of jiz began to gush from the tip of his cock. The first stream streaked across Eden's tight abs, filling the cup of her belly button. The second pump striped her tiny titties. Then the last squirts got her cheek and into her open, waiting mouth. Eden moaned in delight and swallowed the hot cum that had made it onto her tongue.

Darren collapsed back onto the couch, his dick already softening. "Oh my god, I so needed that," he said, heaving.

"That was so fucking hot," Eden replied wickedly, playing with the ejaculate on her belly. Sitting up on the table, she noticed that Darren was laying out on the couch, tired from their exertion. She joined him, laying with her ass and back against the front of his body.

In minutes she heard him softly snoring. Satisfied that he was asleep, Eden quietly got up and dressed quickly. Glancing again to make sure Darren was really asleep, she was satisfied to see his eyes closed. Then silently she pulled the middle drawer of his desk open and got the extra set of keys to *angelfuck* that he kept there. After pocketing them, she kissed Darren's forehead lovingly and then left as quickly and silently as a looter.

PART 14

Black Helicopters

*"If a government can't keep the roads open,
what good is a government at all?... Wouldn't that be a
sad epitaph for the world? 'Democracy was canceled
on account of rain. The human season will be
suspended until further notice.'"*

\- Joe Hill, *Strange Weather*

*"The city seemed to be inhaling Benzedrine and exhaling light;
a neon-lunged Buddha chanting and vibrating in a temple of filth."*

\- Tom Robbins, *Even Cowgirls Get the Blues*

MARCH & APRIL

ONE

In the captivity of the underground government facility, the girl in the nightgown tossed and turned in her bed. She was locked in her cell. It seemed like she was always locked in her cell—unless they brought her out to preform experiments or medicate her. Body aching from trying to fall asleep yet failing, she felt like she would die of fatigue. Whatever pills they were force-feeding her were making her muscles tremor and sometimes she would break out in cold sweats, semi-delirious not knowing where she was.

Suddenly the door of her cell was unlocked and swung open. A man in a black suit and wearing sunglasses indoors stood there. "Anna?" he said.

Anna sat up in bed quickly and hugged her knees into her chest. She didn't respond.

"It's group time in the activity room," the man in the suit continued.

Sighing, Anna swung her legs out of bed and stood up, barefoot. She followed the man reluctantly out into the hall. The hallways outside the cells were uncomfortably narrow and there were no windows since they were underground. When they got to the activity room, the man shoved Anna inside and locked the door behind her. "Hey! There was no call for that!" she yelled through the door uselessly.

The room was about the size of a living room, carpeted, with a few tables and chairs. There were bookshelves which contained some books (mostly for children) as well as board games. There were boxes of toys on the floor with blocks, dolls, etc. It was set up as if the subjects of the experiments were little children—which they weren't.

There were two other teenagers in the room with Anna. A boy about sixteen-years-old who sat in a chair rocking back and forth, staring into space. He mumbled incoherently to himself, "Tethered Toys... the... the space muffins... Lucifer Christ..."

The other was a girl the same age as Anna. She had long black hair and dark skin, looking Middle Eastern; Indian maybe. This girl was wearing sweatpants and a baggy sweatshirt. Anna turned to her and introduced herself. "I'm Anna. I've never seen you here. You must be new."

The dark haired girl nodded. "I'm Priya. They took me from my home two days ago. I think they may have killed my parents... I don't know." Priya looked like she was still in shock; too shocked to even cry. "How long have you been here?"

Anna snorted. "Fuck me, I think about a year. Who the fuck knows? If you haven't noticed there are no clocks in this place. No calendars. That's part of them trying to break you—take away your sense of time. A week feels like five years. And five years feels like an hour."

Priya cocked her head to the side and raised an eyebrow. She glanced over at the boy in the chair mumbling to himself. "What's up with him?"

"That's Jeremy," Anna replied. "He wasn't always like that. They fucking broke him. Sick bastards."

"What? How?" Priya asked.

For a moment Anna didn't respond, she was silent, looking pensive. Then she finally said, "They raped him. Repeatedly. Trying to get his Soulmind to transfer. Until it fractured his mind."

"They... raped him? Like in the ass?" Priya looked horrified.

Anna nodded. "Like in the ass," she continued. "The fucking people here found out that when someone with a Soulmind has sex with someone who doesn't have one, it activates them. Connects up their Soulmind, awakening their powers. So they figured, fuckin', rape him so they can get the power. However, it didn't work the first time. So then they just did it over and over again to see if they could finally get it to work... I think maybe they were angry it didn't work the first time so they wanted to punish Jeremy in the most torturous way. It's so awful. But now they know—and we know too—that Soulminds cannot be activated through rape. Intimacy with someone with a Soulmind must be consensual for the activation to happen."

"Oh my God..." Priya swallowed hard, feeling sick. It was all she could do to keep her stomach from rebelling and puking all over the floor. "So that's what this place is? The government experimenting on newly awakened Soulminds?"

"That's right," Anna confirmed. "I call it the Facility. Has a sort of ominous tone to it, don't you think? You see those cameras up in the corners of the ceiling?" She pointed to all of them. Priya nodded. "They put us together now and then to see how we interact with other awakened individuals. It's best not to give them anything they can work with. You know, best to not do anything too radical or powerful. Fuckin' eh! They fucking fucked me up!" Anna bent over in pain and her right hand was shaking uncontrollably.

"What's wrong?" Priya asked, concerned. She put her hand on Anna's back. "You're shaking!"

Anna grimaced, and sweat beaded from her brow. "It's just the pills they've been feeding me. I don't exactly know what they do or what they're for, but I fucking for sure know the god-damn *side effects!*" She stood up and forced a smile at Priya as she held her trembling hand against her leg. "They'll be feeding them to you soon enough. I don't say that to be mean, just warning you. And if you refuse to take them, they forcibly inject you. The fuckers! And that's even worse. GOD FUCKING FUCK!" Anna screamed, there was searing pain now shooting from her hand and up through her wrist and forearm.

Priya's eyes were wide, she looked terrified. "What can I do? Oh my God, you look like you're in so much pain!"

"There's nothing you can do," Anna admitted. "I just have to fucking grit my teeth and bare it. Let's talk about something else to try to get my mind off the pain... Did a black cat come and see you before you were taken and brought here?"

"Yeah," Priya answered, surprised someone else knew about her October. "Her name was Jasmine. She was so pretty. And she came to talk to me about my Soulmind only a few times before I was kidnapped."

"Mine was named Enki and he was a boy," Anna continued. "Enki taught me so many things. Fortunately I had quite a lot of time with him before I was captured. These dickheads here fuck with me more because my Soulmind is more developed. They think I could be the key to whatever the fuck it is they're doing. Before Jeremy here turned into a fucking turnip, he had a theory that the government is trying to *weaponize* our Soulminds."

"Weaponize?" Priya said, baffled. "How could they do that?"

Anna shrugged. "We have so much energy compressed into this area between our hearts and our brains that Jeremy thought that they were trying to find a way to detonate one of us, like a bomb."

Priya shivered. "That's creepy. Like a living suicide bomb..."

"Yeah," Anna continued. "We'd be the ultimate weapon of mass destruction. Like globally destructive. And there'd be nothing to hide going through security at an airport since the bomb literally *is* our own body, our own energy. Some World War Three type shit."

"Do you think they really could pull that off?" Priya wondered.

Anna shook her head. "Beats the fuck out of me." Suddenly she shot Priya a mischievous glance. "I've heard rumors in the walls. Rumors of a boy more powerful than all of us combined. The Director faggot is trying to send his lackeys to abduct him I think. This boy..." Anna trailed off, looking thoughtfully over at Jeremy. "This boy, if they pull off bringing him here, might just be our ticket the fuck out of here."

TWO

FROM THE MIND OF TERRY BROSWALD:

Flashes of bluish-white light illuminate the darkness of the night in my bedroom. I can see this intense light through the membrane of my closed eyelids. *Is this a dream? Or is this real?* Slowly I open my eyes and see Eden laying on her side next to me in bed, still fast asleep. The light didn't seem to have woken her. The light is still flickering, bleeding into the room from under the closed door. I hear some kind of shuffling from the other side of the door. Fear grips me like an ice-cold hand reaching up from below a frozen pond.

My body feels heavy and I can barely move. The effect is close to paralysis, but not quite. I stare as the door finally blows open, the light almost blinding as it looks like the reflection of waves off an indoor pool. My body refuses to move as I stare in horror at the four incredibly tall beings that duck in through the doorway. These creatures look to be eight-feet-tall, but seem to be humanoid in appearance. They have insanely long and lanky arms and legs. Their heads are bald, and their eyes large, completely black, and jelly-ish. I try to swallow, but all saliva seems to have fled in fear from my mouth. The skin of these humanoids is grey, yet almost translucent. They wear thin white spacesuits with tubes running off of various places.

I'm shocked that Eden is still asleep and hasn't been woken up by the presence of these alien lifeforms. All four aliens converge on me and pick me up from the bed; I'm naked. *No, no!* Trying to scream, my throat refuses to obey and no sound escapes from my vocal cords. I wish to try to squirm away and escape, but my body is still too heavy to allow me to make any real movements. The aliens carry me out of my bedroom and I can see now where the origin of the light is coming from—it shines through the wall of my house, making an opening made of white and blue energy.

I am carried through this opening of light and out into the cold air of the night. These beings seem to have powers of levitation; maybe they are in possession of the Merkabah technology as well. With me in their arms, we float almost weightlessly down to the ground outside of my garage on the side of the house. Looking up, I see the portal of light shrink and disappear, leaving the house exactly as it was, as if an opening had never been there.

Some sort of small aircraft is hovering about four feet above the dirt road on the side of my house. This craft is white, egg-shaped, and has small wings attached to the sides. There seem to be no openings or windows of any kind. Suddenly the four aliens, and me, dematerialize and then almost instantaneously re-materialize inside the aircraft. The indescribable flash of an instant where I am completely nothing in space is very disconcerting, I must say. Never have I ever traveled through means of Matter-Relocation or teleportation before, and I must say that it instantly gave me a sense of vertigo, even when we reappeared inside the craft.

The aliens let me go and I crouch on my hands and knees on the silver metallic floor. My stomach is on the verge of rupturing and spilling everything I had ever eaten onto the floor. But it doesn't. After a few minutes, the vertigo dissipates, and my body stabilizes. The aircraft seems much larger from the inside. When I saw it from the outside, I didn't even think that eight-foot-tall beings would be able to fit inside it. Maybe that was just an optical illusion, I'm not quite sure. My body is still quite heavy and I can't seem to move much from the spot where they dropped me. So all I can do is sit here and look around.

The room we are in is large and circular, covered by a transparent glass dome that seems to function like the windshield of a car. The floor is shiny and silver. There isn't anything else in this room except for several large quartz crystals which float in the air. I deduce that these crystals have something to do with the navigation system of the ship. Some of the Grey aliens seem to be communicating with the crystals, and others are gazing out through the glass dome.

The craft starts to move, floating higher into the air, and then we start flying forward. I can see through the dome that we are heading toward the high school. The ship seems to be completely silent as it glides through the air. We zip past the front of the school, through the parking lot, and around the side where the pond is. This pond is next to the street that runs parallel to the forest preserve on the other side.

The Grey aliens slow the ship down as we fly over the pond. The water is so still that it looks like an undisturbed pane of glass that might at any moment be shattered, resulting in aeons of bad luck. We hover over the water for a few seconds and then start to descend. The craft breaks the water and then we are submerged like a submarine. As we go deeper and deeper, I expect the craft to quickly crash into the bottom of the pond, but it doesn't. It seems as if there is no bottom of the pond at all. Where the bottom of the pond should have been, we just slip through as if through the side of a bubble. Then we are out of the water and in a pit cave, a vertical shaft that leads farther down into the earth. Looking up through the dome, I see the underside of the pond as if it is just held suspended at the top of the pit cave.

As we descend farther into the earth, one of the Grey aliens turns and walks over to where I am sitting on the floor. The metal is cold against my bare ass. He blinks at me with those black-jelly eyes. Then he squats slightly, offering me his hand. Reluctantly I take it and he helps me to my feet. When I touch his grey translucent skin, it's as if I can feel the aeons and aeons of evolution, of technology, of the crystallization of metamorphosis into a higher form. It feels electric. Still I regard him with suspicion.

"My name is Graeson," the alien speaks, "of the race of the Greys."

"A Grey alien named Graeson," I joke, "that doesn't seem very original. Couldn't come up with anything more interesting than that? Like maybe Jelly-Eyes or something?" The alien looks at me blankly, obviously not comprehending the humor. "Nevermind."

Graeson continues, "We apologize for so rudely taking you from your sleeping quarters. However, this method has been our tradition for many generations."

I smirk. "Abduction? Yeah, I know. I've heard a lot of stories. Never experienced it myself though, until now. Are you going to probe me? You've never had a close encounter with me before so you don't know that I'd probably like it." I wink at Graeson. Surprisingly most, if not all, of the fear I had felt before is now gone.

"No need for a probe test for you, Terry Broswald," Graeson responds. "We have taken you to reveal to you the Hollow Earth, wherein a great many of us reside. Also to show you some parts of our technology, which you have actually been in contact with the Moon Unit but not the Earth Unit as of yet."

"The Moon Unit..." I think about what he could mean by this. The only thing that comes to mind is the Black Pyramid on the Moon which contains that strange sarcophagus. "Why? Are you really supposed to be showing me this?"

Graeson nods. "Your awakening has turned you into a Spiritual Catalyst of sorts. This has put your energy signature on our radar, revealing to us that you have a vital key role in bringing the Earth's frequency up to a point where humanity can join the Galactic Brotherhood."

"We're stubborn and slow, aren't we?" I ask.

"Sometimes your species can be. Way back in Antiquity, the Nefilim genetically engineered Homo-Erectus into the common human you see today. They spliced their genes into the most evolved hominid that was on this planet at the time. They did this, creating you to be slave-animals that would work for them in the mines, bringing them precious metals and gems. The awakening factor—the Soulmind—was a quality imprinted into the DNA as a result of the splice. The lower animal nature reaching for the stars, for the higher nature of racial enlightenment. Homo Erectus-Nefilimus is what you truly are and that created problems for the Nefilim masters. They ultimately allowed you to live since not all of the Nefilim agreed on genociding your race. These Nefilim have all but retreated back to their home planet and disappeared. And the mystery remains."

"How come you can't just help out in human evolution more directly?" I ask, genuinely curious.

Graeson shakes his head. "If you really wish to know, the Greys *are* you in a higher form—a realized or unrealized potentiality. We can make contact with individuals such as yourself, but the fact is that the majority of humans today aren't at a high enough level to even see us, much less *interact* with us. Not to mention that the Galactic Federation of Light has a strict non-interference rule, which we can bend or get around now and then. But they—the GFL—keep a tight monitoring of us."

"The rule of non-interference," I repeat back. "I feel like I've heard about that somewhere before... Hmm, maybe not." I shrug. "It would be awesome if the general population all had Soulminds so they could interact with other beings like you—like the Greys, like the Nefilim, like dragons and faeries."

"This is a very real potential," Graeson admits. "Like I said, *you* are the key. Timestrus still puts a cap on the Dimensional Frequency of the Earth so that the planet is unable to ascend all at one time."

"Wait," I say, "you know about Timestrus?"

Graeson nods. "Timestrus is a Reptilian. A Reptoid-Demoniac being who's origins are unknown to us. The Great Dragon Sul says that you will be the one to destroy him and free the planet so it can ascend beyond the Fourth Dimension."

I laugh. "You talk to Sul too? I'm not surprised he said that," I grumble. "I haven't made any promises to fight that Reptilian bastard again. Once was enough for me. I don't even know how to get to where he is again. I've never been to his fucking Dimension, and to be honest I don't *want* to. Why can't you just blast him with a Death Ray or something?"

Graeson doesn't answer. He looks up through the dome above. The cave formations are getting larger. "We're deep within the Hollow Earth now," the Grey says. "We're almost to the Chamber of Mystical Control."

The ship dips down and we glide out of the pit cave and it opens up into an immense room. It's so huge that I can imagine a small city being able to fit inside it. Many others of the same ship we are in are attached to metal arms that come down from the ceiling. There is a control room built into the far wall. A Grey sits behind the computers within the room and peers out through the windows in front of him. Standing on the floor of this massive chamber looks like *thousands* more Greys. The mass of these beings looks to be in the shape of a circle. The center of the circle of Greys is open, like they are standing in the shape of a living donut around a hollow center. In the middle of the hollow center looks like a perfect replica of the sarcophagus that I laid inside when I was in the Black Pyramid on the Moon.

The three other Greys use the navigation crystals to dock with an empty arm that hangs from the ceiling of the cave. "Now what?" I ask.

Graeson smiles down at me. "Now it is time to take you on a small initiation."

I don't know what he means, but it makes me a little nervous. Without warning a blue portal of energy opens up on the floor between me and Graeson. The blue energy swirls like a radioactive whirlpool. "That's our way down," Graeson comments.

"Is that like a tractor-beam?" I ask.

The tall Grey laughs heartily. "Humans still call them that?"

I don't respond because the comment felt rhetorical. The three other Greys that were manning the controls are now around the portal. Without hesitation, all three jump down into it and disappear. "My turn?" I ask with a deep swallow of the lump in my throat.

Graeson nods. Trying not to think, I just step into the whirling vortex and am taken by the current. I close my eyes, expecting to feel a free-fall, the ground careening toward me at a million miles an hour. But no, it feels like I'm slowly carried down as if on a solid cloud. I open my eyes and look down. Blue light surrounds me and I see that the mass of Greys has cleared the area around where the beam touches down. Looking back up, I see Graeson coming down behind me.

The three Greys who descended before us have already dispersed into the crowd. I touch down, feet on the ground, and then in a moment Graeson is beside me. The beam of blue light retracts back up into the craft above us. "What are we doing?" I whisper to Graeson out of the side of my mouth. "They're all staring at me and I'm naked here with my dick hanging out. Not that I mind that."

"Follow me," Graeson says and starts walking toward the center of the circle. The Greys clear a path as I follow close behind. We come out to the center where the sarcophagus is and the tall Greys fill in the gaps behind us. I peer in over the edge of the sarcophagus and see the same strange black sand that was in the one on the Moon. "Lay down inside," Graeson instructs. "This is your initiation into one of the great Mysteries."

Without question I crawl into the sarcophagus and lay down on my back. Graeson peers down at me through the open top. Laying at the bottom of the sarcophagus, the tall Grey looks like a massive giant looming over me. Suddenly I feel my Astral Body being pulled down out of my physical form. It's only pulled down for a second and then I feel it pulling *up*. A purple spiral of light shoots up toward the ceiling as far as I can see, and my Astral Body is being pulled into it. I don't resist this time, I let the spiral take me.

I let it take me up and through the ceiling of the cave chamber. It feels like it's pulling me at an increasing speed, so I'm shooting through almost too fast to register where I am. It takes me through the hollow chambers of the earth, up through the dirt, toward the sky, through the clouds. For a moment all I can see is dark blue of the night sky and then I'm through the atmosphere, blackness and stars. The moon shines brightly above me and it's coming toward me at speed. Then before I can blink my Astral eyes, I'm laying in the sarcophagus inside the Black Pyramid. That was a wild ride—almost too fast to even realize it happened at all.

"Let there be light!" I command, and the torches on the walls flame to life, casting a warm orange glow inside the pyramid. Crawling my way out of the sarcophagus, I stand up and walk through the wall out onto the surface of the Moon. I'm surprised to see Graeson standing there waiting for me. There is a clear bubble around his head now which attaches to the collar of his white spacesuit. "How the fuck did you get here so fast?"

Graeson smiles and nods. "In the time between when we first built this station here and now, we have developed the technology for self-teleportation. The catch is that we can't just teleport *anywhere*. We have to have been to the location physically at least once, so that map is imprinted into our DNA. We still leave the Spiral Way for certain humans we show and initiatory rituals."

"So what does this all mean?" I ask, staring out and down toward the Earth.

"This, Terry Broswald," Graeson continues, "is one of the secrets to human reincarnation."

"Reincarnation?" I ask. "I don't understand."

"Like your society of humans," Graeson explains, "we Greys have a hierarchy and not all of us agree on the same laws or innovations to be made. The ones in power passed a law that they would not allow human souls to get past the Moon to reincarnate on other planets. Actually, there used to also be a Prison Grid around the Earth, but a very powerful entity destroyed that quite recently. However, our Soul Catcher is still in place here." The Grey turns and gestures toward the Black Pyramid.

I look toward the pyramid as well and ask, "What's a Soul Catcher?"

"Maybe we can have a demonstration," Graeson says. "Perhaps a wandering Soulmind without a body will make its way here—ah, there's one now!"

"What?" I jerk my head over toward the Earth again and see a ball of red light streaming toward the Moon. A tail of red energy swirls from the back of it like the tail of a comet.

"Watch," Graeson says and points toward the Black Pyramid again.

I look and a beam of white light shoots from the apex of the pyramid. Then this beam of light stretches out to form a wide net—a net made of light. Now the red ball of Soulmind energy is approaching quickly. It comes in and is caught directly in the center of the net like a catcher's mitt in baseball. The red energy sticks there in the middle of the net for a moment, seemingly trying to break through, and then it is shot back down toward the Earth.

"Holy shit," I say under my breath. "We can never go to another planetary game except Earth. That's why I feel like I've been here for millions of lifetimes..."

"You have been here for millions of lifetimes," Graeson admits with a sigh. "But all of that is hopefully changing. Through the effort of yourself and the other Soulminds that you've touched, we are on the threshold of a New Age. And it is coming rapidly."

"It is?" I say quietly, still staring down toward the blue planet and where the red Soulmind disappeared. "It doesn't always feel like things are changing."

"It's all coming to a head, to a climax," Graeson continues. "When the Black Mist meets the Purple Fog. Keep trusting yourself and doing what your intuition tells you. Especially what you're doing with this *Playground*, that's key."

I stare at the Grey alien. "You know about that? What the fuck *don't* you know about?"

Smiling warmly at me, Graeson says, "You know, contrary to popular belief, we still have emotion and can feel compassion. We are still human*oid*, don't you know. Just like humans, Greys have the capacity for cruelty as well as love and kindness."

"Who's popular belief? Some think that you're beings of pure logic and no love?"

"That's right," Graeson replies. "Some who have been abducted by us harbor resentments, understandably. Others who are of the more enlightened persuasion, see themselves as participants and not victims."

"That's good to know," I respond. "We hear so many conflicting stories about encounters with alien beings."

The tall body of Graeson approaches me slowly. In a couple strides he's close enough to touch me. "Look down there again," he says.

"What, toward the Earth?" I look down and don't see anything out of the ordinary.

"Do you see them?"

"Hmm, see what?" I ask, then I look again. After a few moments of studying the circumference of the Earth, I blink and my eyes focus. Then I see them! Around the whole Earth, above the atmosphere, hover large spacecrafts. "Holy fucking Godfuckers!" I exclaim. "Are those always there?"

Graeson nods. "We're always watching, always monitoring. Having to obey the law of non-interference, we just bide our time until humanity ascends to the point where we can interact and bring you into a whole new intergalactic world!"

"That's so fucking cool," I say. "I want to travel to other planets and have adventures!"

"And one day you will," Graeson says, as if telling me a secret. "Now you know of our existence and the entrance to our Hollow Earth chambers through the Black Pyramid and vice versa. See you soon, space cadet." Then the Grey alien leans down and touches the center of my forehead with his long finger.

Bright white light erupts from my third eye and I feel myself falling. In an instant I am back in my physical body inside the sarcophagus in the Hollow Earth. I feel the black sand vibrating under my back. Then white light explodes all around me. Temporarily I am blinded. But when the light dissipates, I am back in my own bed, next to Eden who is still sleeping soundly. That was fucking crazy. Was that a dream or did that really happen? The lines between the sleeping Dreamsphere and the waking Hollow Dimension are beginning to blur. Maybe *all* of it is real. Or it is all equally an illusion. Sometimes we just have to let the Mystery be.

THREE

President Elliot Cage enjoyed the power and the forbidden pleasures of being a high-ranking Satanist. He had access to the best and most expensive surgeons who were also high-ranking Satanists. This made it possible to get the best sexual-reassignment surgery available in all of the world. They had chopped his tits off, leaving scars that were almost invisible. Using the inside of her vagina and the clitoris, they constructed a working penis that could get erect and have an orgasm. The technology was so advanced that they were even able to construct testicles and all the organs and glands responsible for ejaculation. Of course, the tranny semen couldn't get anyone pregnant, but the technology was advancing in that direction.

He was laying in bed in The President's Bedroom next to his wife who used to be a man. The First Lady was Imogene Cage. Her surgeons had done superlative work with her. Imogene had the longest and straightest pitch-black hair which had a shimmer that shone even in the dimmest of light. Her face was slender and sensual. The little titties that she was so proud of were all a result of the hormones—no boob-job. Needless to say, they had chopped off and mutilated her penis, reshaping it and warping it in to make the vaginal shaft. The tip of the penis was condensed down to make a clitoris through which she could have convulsive orgasms.

Elliot stroked the inside of his wife's thigh with the tip of her fingers. Imogene was wearing a black silk nightgown. The President pushed the bottom of the nightgown up as he inched closer to between his wife's legs. They kissed as Elliot stroked Imogene's naked crotch.

The only light in the room came from the orange glow of candles and a few salt lamps. The bed was huge and had four posts with a luxurious canopy over the top. It seemed big enough to accommodate an orgy with the whole of the President's Cabinet. The rest of the room was equally palatial. There were a couple antique-looking tables with chairs, a white couch, and a fancy dresser with a mirror against one wall.

As they licked the inside of each other's mouths, they groped at each other's crotches, moaning pleasurably. Elliot suddenly pulled away and smiled mischievously at Imogene. "Are you feeling ravenous?" he asked with a wink. "Should we order a fresh pizza?"

"Uhhh, god yes!" Imogene moaned and tilted her head back. "I'm famished." Her eyes flashed wickedly.

Elliot grabbed a small, strange-looking cell phone from off of the bedside table. He dialed a couple numbers—not enough to be a real phone number—and put it to his ear. After a moment he said into the phone, "Yes... Hold on a second." He pulled the phone away from his ear and put his hand over it. "Should we get a full meal?" Elliot asked Imogene.

"Definitely!" Imogene replied decisively. "Oh, Jesus, I'm cumming just thinking about it!"

The President put the phone back up to his ear. "We'd like the full meal. Fresh pizza and hot dog order too. Send it right up." He hung up and put the phone back on the bedside table.

"Oh, baby," Imogene said, licking the side of Elliot's face. "It's been too long since we had some hard candy."

Suddenly there was a knock on the door of The President's Bedroom. "That was fast," Elliot said, looking at his wife. Then toward the door: "*Cum!*" She said *cum* loud enough for the person on the other side of the door to hear. Both Elliot and Imogene giggled like little schoolgirls.

The door opened, but it wasn't their meal order. It was a short stout woman wearing a hooded black cloak. The inside of the cloak was crimson. Obviously the President and his wife knew who this woman was. She was Harriet Kavanaugh, former First Lady and high-level Satanist. "Mister President," Harriet began. "Sorry to disturb you."

"Yes, Harriet," Elliot replied, playing with his cock through his red silk pajama pants. "You could never disturb us. Do you want to join us for the *feast*? We know how insatiable you are." He smiled with lust and licked his lips.

"However tempting that may be," Harriet continued, "I have other business to attend to. Just wanted to inform you that the boy—the Antichrist—has been found. And his power is even beyond our wildest imaginings! He has enough power to trigger and end World War Three in less than a minute!"

"That *is* very exciting news," the President admitted. "I knew our Brothers and Sisters in the Midwest chapters would not let us down. Have they apprehended him yet?"

"Not yet," Harriet conceded reluctantly. "But they are closing in."

"Good, very good," President Cage said, nodding his head. "This boy is connected to the incident that took place in Chicago, correct?"

"Yes, Sir."

"That was quite obvious," Elliot chuckled. "Well, nice work, Harriet. Have them send more of our helicopters to monitor what's left of Chicago. And to circle this boy's house until the rat comes out of his hole."

"As you wish," Harriet Kavanaugh said, bowing as she retreated through the door. "*Ave Satanas!*"

Elliot and Imogen clasped their hands together, bowed their heads, and said in unison, "*Ave Satanas!*"

Harriet closed the door behind her and was gone. A moment later there was another knock at the door. *"Cum!"* Imogene shouted loudly and then erupted into laughter.

Elliot pinched her inner thigh and teased her by saying, "You're so naughty. What am I gonna do with you, you little pervert?"

"I don't know, daddy," Imogene whined with a look of lust in her eyes. "Maybe you'll have to punish my tight virgin asshole."

They both fell into fits of laughter as the door slowly opened. Two small figures were pushed inside the room and then the door was slammed behind them. Standing there in the orange glow of the candles were two naked children, no older than nine. They were naked except for festive masquerade masks that they wore over their faces. The girl stood on the left with a colorful and sparkly mask that was shaped like a butterfly. The boy stood on the right with a blackish-gray metallic mask that had goat horns sprouting out the top of it. Neither child made a sound and the boy's pre-pubescent penis hung flaccidly between his legs like a dead worm.

Imogene felt her mouth salivate as she appraised the pizza and hot dog they were about to binge on. "Oh, we're gonna have some wicked fun tonight!" she exclaimed, super excited. Pointing at the boy she said, "Before we have our fun with you two, I want to watch you fuck her with that little cock of yours." Imogene pointed to the girl now. The two children exchanged a glance.

"My God, this is so *hot!*" Elliot gushed, barely able to contain himself. "I can feel the epic orgasm already, all the way down in my designer balls."

FOUR

A wave of bright light and energy carried Jessica on its current and shot her back out into the central chamber. She ended up on her butt in front of Cerridwen who was sitting on her stone throne again. Cernunnos was there as well, meditating in a lotus pose on the stone floor. His harem of animals explored the cave. Trondlebist was still there, sitting on the bench sipping from the goblet.

"You have done well, my dear," Cerridwen said, leaning forward toward Jessica. "Although, in matters of inner journeys, there is no such thing as failure. But you, you have exceeded; soared above and beyond expectations. Here, this is for your aid when you need it most." The Goddess produced a small scroll of paper from her hooded robe and handed it to Jessica.

"What is this?" she asked, unrolling the paper. There was written thereon what looked like a mantra in the most beautiful calligraphy Jessica had ever laid eyes on. The mantra was this and she read it silently to herself:

> *Jai Ma, Jai Jai Ma, Jai Jai Ma*
> *Kali Ma, Kali Ma, Jai Jai Ma*

"Use this when you are in dire need, Jessica," Cerridwen continued. "The transformation will be incendiary." The Goddess of the Underworld handed Jessica one of the silver goblets, which she drank from gratefully.

"The transformation... What do you mean?" Jessica asked, not fully understanding the magick the mantra would weave.

Cerridwen shook her head. "That is for you to discover on your own. What form *you* will take is within your own power."

Jessica nodded, still not fully comprehending, but decided not to ask anymore questions. Her knapsack was leaning against the side of the Sacred Caldron and she pulled it to herself. After slipping the parchment with the mantra into her bag, she slung it over her shoulders and stood up. She sensed that it was time to move on.

"Thank you for your presence and all you've shared with me," Jessica said with reverence. She bowed to the Goddess.

"Yes!" the Goddess said loudly with a snap of her fingers. "The hour grows late and Artemis will be arriving at your rendezvous point! That magnificent creature will carry you to your next initiation—your Middleworld Journey. Trondlebist will show you the way out and back up to the water." Now Cerridwen bowed low to Jessica, showing equal respect to an equal Goddess. "And I thank you for gracing us with your presence; the presence of an exquisite Goddess such as yourself." Cerridwen smiled, her eyes still shadowed by the hood over her head.

"I'm no Goddess," Jessica replied quietly, looking down at the floor.

The Goddess of the Underworld laughed loudly. "No?" she said. "Maybe not yet, but you will be. Do not doubt yourself, Jessica Thorn. It's not a very attractive quality."

Trondlebist pulled on Jessica's sleeve and she looked down at the dwarf. "We must go, my lady. Time is thin. Let us away." After saying this, the dwarf turned and waddled toward the passageway where the Celtic harper had emerged from earlier.

Jessica gave one last silent bow to Cerridwen and then followed close behind Trondlebist. Walking past Cernunnos, Lord of Animals, Jessica glanced at him but he didn't stir from his meditation.

"Come, come," Trondlebist beckoned as his torch illuminated the darkness of the tunnel.

Quickly she followed, and soon they were around a corner in the dark passageway, leaving the God and Goddess of the Underworld behind. Jessica took out her orb which illuminated the gems and Celtic runes carved into the walls. It was difficult for her not to get distracted by the shining symbols on the walls. They seemed to be alive, flying off of the walls and swirling around with psychedelic trails of light.

"Trondlebist," Jessica said, "I feel like we're just going further into the passages of the labyrinth, getting us more lost."

"That's just a trick," the dwarf assured her. "Another test for any traveler who has come down to the Underworld uninvited. They will follow where the energy pulls them, to a place where they are faced by their greatest challenge. There they will conquer it or they will perish... Luckily, I know the way out since we dwarves have mined down here for millennia."

The tunnel started to widen before them and Jessica could feel them coming upon something new. "Mines?" she asked. "You mentioned this before, but I haven't seen any mines since we've been down here."

"Truly," Trondlebist continued, "you are about to see them."

Just after the dwarf said this, the cave wall to their right ended abruptly, and the path became a ledge on the side of the cave wall. They were on the side of a huge chasm, an incredibly wide vertical mine shaft. The plunge went down farther than Jessica could see and she felt queasy looking over the edge. "This is where you mine?" she asked, feeling a little woozy so she hugged herself against the cave wall, as far away from the edge as she could.

"This is it," Trondlebist answered, peeking over the edge. "Miles and miles of tunnels, passages, spiraling ledges that go down and down and down."

There were several wooden structures that Jessica could see that had pulleys and ropes, with buckets or large crates to move what was collected. The *chink-chink-chink* sound of hammers on stone reached her ears. And then she saw them—thousands of dwarves working on the ledges below and going in and out of the tunnels that went into the cave wall.

Trondlebist turned and continued walking; Jessica followed. "You all mine for precious stones and metal down here?" Jessica asked.

"Yes," the dwarf answered. "I work down here as well."

"And you don't mind all that hard labor?" she wanted to know.

Trondlebist chuckled. "We're not slaves, if that's what you're thinking. We work these mines by choice. We build up our own kingdom, help out the Goddess of the Underworld, and in turn she takes care of us, protects us."

"Protects you?" Jessica said. "From what?"

"Not all of the creatures in Pangea are friendly," Trondlebist admitted. "Dwarves have enemies, especially from beasts who would want to steal our riches."

They reached the other side of the mine shaft and the tunnel continued. Going into the darkness of the passage again, the sound of the dwarves' hammers against stone faded into the background. Jessica could feel that the ground they were walking on started to have a slight incline, going up, and could feel that they were close to the cave exit.

"We're almost to the water barrier," Trondlebist confirmed. And in a couple minutes, there they were. The blue of the water covered the whole entrance of the cave like the edge of a bubble that wouldn't pop. Jessica marveled at it, placing her hand on the vertical surface.

"This is so magickal," Jessica whispered as she stuck her finger into the water that wouldn't flow into the cave.

"This is where we depart, my lady," Trondlebist said politely. "It has been a pleasure being your guide on this tour of the Underworld." A smirk tugged on the side of his mouth as he held his hand out.

Jessica extended her arm and shook the dwarf's hand. "The pleasure has been all mine, Trondlebist. Maybe we will meet again in one of the infinite streams of Creation."

"Perhaps we shall," the dwarf concurred. He made a slight bow, and without any lingering, turned and set off back toward the mines. Jessica watched him as he went until he disappeared around a corner. He never looked back.

Jessica turned back toward the membrane of the lake. After taking a deep breath, she squeezed the glowing orb in her hand. It expanded into the bubble and enveloped her head like an astronaut's helmet. Then she stepped into the water and onto the path.

Jessica couldn't get over how beautiful it was under the forest lake. So many different kinds of fish swam by, in so many different colors. The plants and the weeds growing from the bottom swayed in the current. She felt so much peace walking along this underwater path back up toward the shore. Surprising even herself, she had expected to feel tired after that whole ordeal in the labyrinth, but she didn't, she felt oddly refreshed. *Renewed* was more the right word. Jessica was renewed and transformed—*reborn*. Through each new experience in her journey, she felt less and less like the old Jessica, and more and more like some new empowered creature that she didn't have a name for yet.

Wrenching her out of her meditation, a large fish dashed past her at an unnerving speed. It hovered in the water and bared its teeth at Jessica, who saw now that it was the mermaid from before. She could feel the dread of the fact that this creature wished to do her harm. Suddenly Jessica's Soulmind became agitated and activated. Purple energy started to spiral out of her chest and illuminate her aura.

The mermaid lunged, striking again. Jessica didn't have time to defend herself before a sharp pain shot through her upper left arm. The mermaid had bitten her, ripping a chunk of flesh out of her arm. The water began to cloud with red blood. At the same time Jessica grabbed her wound, the handles of her katanas popped from her solar plexus. *I don't want to hurt a mermaid,* Jessica thought to herself. *But if it's trying to kill me then I have to defend myself.*

She pulled the katanas from her chest and got ready to attack if need be. The mermaid made a couple more lunges, baring its teeth menacingly, but Jessica swung her Soulmind blades at each attack. The mermaid dodged and retreated from the weapons. Obviously Jessica's movements were significantly slowed down by the density of the water around her. The mermaid took advantage of this. Before Jessica could turn around, the mermaid swam around behind her and flicked its tail, clipping the side of the bubble around Jessica's head.

The bubble slipped off of Jessica's head and shrank back down to the glowing orb. It floated onto the path and began to roll away. Jessica, panicked, had to hold her breath and watch out for where the mermaid was going to attack from next. She tried to swim toward where the orb was rolling away. Maybe she could reach it before running out of breath.

The mermaid snarled and lunged at Jessica again. She stabbed and sliced with her katana, clipping the mermaid's hand, cutting a gash across its palm. Now it was pissed. Blood clouded the water, mixing with Jessica's blood cloud. The water was so red it was getting difficult to see. The lungs in Jessica's chest burned and screamed for oxygen, but she fought it, holding her breath almost violently. The orb was almost within reach.

The mermaid made another attempt, and Jessica thought, *Fuck this.* She pushed off of the path and paddled with her feet toward the creature trying to kill her. It wasn't expecting that, so it was taken off guard for a second. Jessica took advantage of that and stabbed with her left katana, skewering the mermaid through the belly. Then she swung the right katana, cutting the mermaid's head clean from its body.

By now the water was so thick with blood that Jessica could barely see the glow of the orb that had come to a stop on the path. She let go of her Soulmind weapons and they disappeared back into her aura. Swimming with fervor, she propelled herself toward the orb and reached her hand out to grab it just as her lungs felt like they were about to give out. Her fingers were around the orb, she squeezed it, and in a second it was back as a bubble around her head. Gasping for air, she thanked the gods she was alive. She almost was certain she was about to drown or be eaten alive by a bloodthirsty mermaid—or both. Gratefully her lungs sucked in the oxygen, and she held her hand over the bite on her arm, trying to stem the bleeding.

There was no way to be sure that there were no more homicidal mermaids lurking in the weeds, so Jessica picked up her pace as much as the water would allow. Half-walking, half-floating down the rest of the path, she hurried toward the shore. The path curved up into an incline and Jessica started to ascend toward the surface of the lake. By the time she broke the surface of the water and stumbled up onto the shore, she was feeling light-headed from loss of blood. Luckily Artemis was standing there to meet her.

"Artemis..." Jessica mumbled as she stumbled toward the unicorn. "My arm..." Pitching forward, she sunk down to her knees on the pebbles of the shoreline.

"My God, Jessica, you're hurt," Artemis said, showing genuine concern.

Blood gushed from between Jessica's fingers despite trying to cover the wound. "Fucking mermaid tried to murder me," she laughed morbidly. "I always thought they were harmless little Disney princesses. Turns out they're fucking psycho-killers. Ugh!" She winced, trying to fight to stay conscious. "Guess I'll just sit her and bleed to death... Ironic to be killed by a creature little girls are supposed to love."

"Don't be silly," Artemis said firmly. "You're not going to die. I'm sure there's something in your knapsack for healing wounds. Check it."

Jessica took her knapsack from off of her shoulders, gritting her teeth against the sharp pain. Opening the flap, she rummaged around inside through all the seemingly random objects. She stopped when she came across an item she hadn't noticed before. "Wait... What's this? I don't remember this being here before." Pulling it out of the bag, Artemis saw that it was a little glass vial with a clear liquid inside that shone with a silver sheen.

"You have been blessed," Artemis said. "For that is water from the Sacred Caldron. It has healing properties. The Goddess of the Underworld must have slipped it in your bag when you were focused on something else."

Jessica smiled. "Cerridwen comes to the rescue again..." She felt her head spin and she tipped forward, almost dropping the vial onto the stones.

"Whoa," Artemis said, trying to steady Jessica. "Quickly pour some on your wound."

It was a struggle, but Jessica managed to pull the glass stopper from the vial. Then she poured only a few drops over the area of her arm that was still gushing blood. Within seconds she felt her head and vision stabilize to the point she no longer felt like she was going to pass out. Then miraculously before her eyes, the wound began to heal and close up. In less than a minute the whole gouge was gone and there was no trace that she had been maimed at all.

"Thank you, Goddess of the Underworld," Jessica whispered reverently as she returned the vial to her knapsack. Standing up, she swung the pack over her shoulders and stroked Artemis's soft white fur.

"Are you ready to go?" the unicorn asked. "We have a lot of ground to cover. The next initiation isn't going to wait until you're ready. The time is Now."

"What? I don't even get to process my experiences down in the Underworld?" Jessica feigned surprise. "It's just: *done with one battle and right on to the next?*"

Artemis chuckled. "Yes, something like that. We have to catch up to the Timestream."

Jessica rolled her eyes. "Why am I not surprised it's something weird like that? Okay, let's go then."

The unicorn kneeled down and Jessica mounted her steed. He stood up and started trotting off back into the forest. "The Timestream of the Middleworld waits for no one," Artemis continued as he sped up into a gallop. "And we have to catch up with it."

Jessica didn't exactly understand, but she decided that it wasn't beneficial to ask anymore questions. Knowledge would be given soon enough. The trees soon became blurs of brown and green as they continued with speed through the magickal forest. Any sense of time blurred and Jessica felt like they should be intercepting this *Timestream* at any moment.

As the unicorn and his girl got deeper and deeper into the forest, Jessica suddenly felt the presence of a *god*. She couldn't place it at first, but then she remembered waking up in the middle of the night to see that faun—half human and half goat. What was his name? *Pan.* At the same flash of an instant when she thought the god's name, she heard a loud bleat of a goat. Whether this bleat was in protest or in pleasure, Jessica could not tell. Then the overwhelming stench reached her nostrils. She wrinkled her nose in disgust. "What is that?" Jessica asked.

"It's Pan," Artemis answered. "The god is in the vicinity."

She heard the bleat again and her vision seemed to slow down despite the speed they were running. In so doing, Jessica caught a glimpse of the nature god behind a tree in a soft patch of grass. Pan had a goat on its back and he was on top thrusting in and out of the animal's nether regions. Just as quickly as Jessica saw the scene, it was left behind, leaving Pan and his goat concubine to linger in her mind.

"My God," Jessica said, wanting desperately to unsee what she just saw. "He was screwing that goat!"

Artemis laughed. "Yes, Pan is a skanky goat-groper."

"But... but..." Jessica started. "That's bestiality!" She said this with utter disgust in her voice, like she wanted to puke the image from her mind.

"Well, technically Pan is part beast himself—part goat. So him having sex with a goat isn't all that weird," Artemis admitted.

"That's still repulsive, in my opinion." She closed her eyes and shook her head, trying to forget the vision of that molestation that had seared itself in her mind.

"There it is!" Artemis exclaimed. "The Timestream of Middleworld!"

"What?" Jessica opened her eyes, and on her right a stream of shining water had appeared seemingly out of nowhere. The stream went off in front as far as her eyes could see, and also behind them. Bright white light shone off of the surface of the water, making it almost not look like liquid at all. "In which direction is it flowing?" she asked. "I can't tell."

"It flows in both directions," Artemis replied. At this point they were running so fast beside the Timestream that Jessica was having a difficult time hanging on. As she watched the flow of the liquid-light, it started to rise up from the forest floor. Trails of light streamed below it as the stream raised to the height of Jessica's shoulder. She almost felt like she could reach out and touch this stream of light. As Jessica stared into it, she almost thought she saw the shadow and light play of images within the stream. While she was caught within this thought, Artemis suddenly bucked her off and she slipped from the unicorn's back to the right, directly into the Timestream.

"Why do people keep dumping me into the water?!" Jessica yelled right before she disappeared into the Timestream of the Middleworld.

FIVE

"Welcome, welcome! Good to see you again..." Terry was greeting the members of Playground as they entered his house for another meeting. It was Wednesday again. As he checked off the names on the membership list, he noticed a few new faces, which meant that Playground were doing their homework. Terry stopped Michael before letting him in the door. "Michael, my man!" he said enthusiastically. "Gimme some skin!" They high-fived.

Michael was with a new young girl who was very pretty. "It's good to be back around our people," Michael replied.

Terry winked at the girl who smiled back. "Looks like you've been busy, Mike. Who's this gorgeous lady?"

"I'm Emily," she said, and shook Terry's hand.

"We get intimate around here," Terry said and gave her a hug as well. "*No Bounce...*"

Michael and Emily both responded at the same time with: "*No Play!*"

"Good job," Terry said, patting Michael on the shoulder. "Just keeping you on your toes. Go inside, I'll be there in a minute."

Terry finished signing everyone in and then went to join them in the living room. There were an assortment of twenty-two boys and girls crammed onto the couches and on the floor. Mothman and Rob were on the couch squished between the goth-looking chick and a girl with purple hair. Eden was sitting on the landing at the top of the two stairs that led down into the living room. Terry came over and put his hand on her shoulder. "Are you staying for the meeting today, babe?"

Eden looked up at her lover and nodded. "Yeah, I'll stay today."

He sat down next to her and kissed her on the lips. "Okay," Terry began, addressing the group. "I see some new faces today which makes me very happy. That means y'all have been fuckin' and that is how we make this thing of ours grow. The more we awaken people, the more we help the frequency of the planet ascend into a higher vibration. We are doing the Great Work here and we all have an important part to play—in the Playground." He winked at them and smiled. "Our motto is: *Each One Teach One*; and also it's important that we all help each other. We're traveling into an unknown world, building something that hasn't been seen before. Or at least hasn't been seen in a *very* long time. A Great Awakening can be scary, I know. But the more people there are on the same wavelength, the more we can hold each other's hands into the future. It's a lot of responsibility to be one's own authority. No one is higher or lower than anybody else, including me. We all can be each other's companions into the adventures that are to come—the adventures that span Time, Space, and all Dimensions. That can be more preferable for most people than trying to go it alone. Don't you agree, babes?" Terry laced his fingers through Eden's and they held hands tightly.

Eden nodded. "That's so true, love," she said as she turned to look at the group who were eagerly gobbling up every word. "It's important to feel love and have connection. Having a Soulmind can feel isolating at first. But as we grow our community, it's reassuring to know that if we need help, there may be another individual with a Soulmind just down the street or down the block."

"Even though awakening the world is serious business, a lot of things having to be destroyed and rebuilt," Terry continued. "I'm sorry to say there will be a lot of casualties as well; some people just won't be able to make the transition to the New Earth—or they will refuse to, desperately clinging to the old paradigm which will ultimately be ripped from their cold dead hands. This should also be exciting, full of adventure and potential. Full of pleasure and light! Sometimes I just want to turn the whole world on, just for a moment. I want to make the whole Earth cum. In one ecstatic global orgy!"

Eden giggled and squeezed his hand. "You would, babe. And you'd be the one to do it," she said.

"Okay, enough with the seriousness," Terry said. "Who wants to feel good? Who wants to get off?"

A murmur of agreement rippled through the group. Terry clapped his hands together loudly, and at the sound everyone's auras lit up around their bodies. The pleasure of the energy already began to tingle on their skin. Every boy and girl in the room closed their eyes and leaned their heads back, surrendering to the ecstasy of the sexual energy. Terry began building it up again, controlling the sensation they were all feeling with his Soulmind. He looked over at Eden who leaned back and laid down on the floor, breathing deeply. The sex in the air was palpable, a living electricity who's only mission was to make all of existence orgasm. Now he provoked the spirals, pulling the Soulminds out of their chests. Then he connected them. Terry watched, moving his fingers like a conductor, as he psychically braided everyone's energy together, including his own. Terry's aura was playing with Eden's, and their collective merging was stretching toward the center of the group. All of their Soulminds were being connected in arcing waves and then brought into the center where they all converged into a compressed ball of orgasmic bliss.

By this point everyone was moaning and gyrating, feeling the culmination of everyone's pleasure multiplied exponentially. They twitched with breathy sighs, touching themselves, stroking breasts, between their legs, and erections that were fighting against the pants that trapped them. Eden had her hand inside of her pants and was vigorously rubbing her clit. Terry could see drool dribbling from the side of her mouth as she cried out in ecstasy. This was the most beautiful sight he had ever seen— the most exquisite thing he had ever orchestrated. The intensity of each person's pleasure was multiplied by the presence of the others. And Terry was guiding them towards a mutual orgasm. He could feel it also, and could hardly contain himself. The bliss of sexual energy was threatening to send him over the abyss into orgasmic oblivion, but he had to fight to maintain control of the experience. If he let himself go, surrendering into the meditation, the momentum would be lost. Terry was the focal point, the center connecting them all in this orgy of Soulminds.

With his eyes open, to Terry the whole room was like a painting of moving rainbows. The colors of each person's Soulmind danced and mingled with everyone else's. He was reminded of his and Eden's experience in the *Temple of Cosmic Fuck.* It also brought to mind the sounds and mewlings of some deep-space brothel; all whimpering in a melted pool of their own euphoria toward a shared Orgasmic Continuum. *Could you open a portal with an orgasm? I will cum into the cosmos*, Terry thought.

They were all screamers. Terry liked people who were vocal while they were sharing energy. Now they were stroking and caressing each other; tongues and lips on sweating necks. Terry could feel the peak of the climax coming into view. "Yes, yes!" he yelled, feeling it build in his balls as well. It was like his cock was his whole body, his entire Soulmind, and the wisps of all the others' energy was fucking him deep and hard. "I want you all to fucking come for me," he gasped. "Oh my fucking God Fuck! I can't hold this for much longer. I feel you all inside me and it's fucking amazing! Fuck me deeper! Cum with me!"

Instantly the ball of energy in the center where all the Soulminds came together exploded with an interstellar orgasm. Every person in that room screamed with the feeling of transcendent euphoria. The orgasm was indescribable. The colors of all the braided Soulminds exploded out in long tendrils as if reaching to the very edges of the Spiralverse. In that one moment when they all came, their Egos dissolved and they were no longer many individuals, they melted into each other, becoming one entity made of the Void. Beyond Time and Space, they were all One essence of cosmic orgasmic bliss—and that was the Truth of it All. The Truth of the Pan-everything combination. In the Emptiness is bliss.

Clitorises had exploded in the most intense orgasms that these girls had ever felt. Their pussies still buzzed with the afterglow of the energy. The boys had all ejaculated the most semen that had ever come out of their young cocks. After the explosion of the climax, the Soulminds shrank back down and went back into everyone's auras, then disappeared again, leaving only a pleasant tingling.

Terry smiled as he watched his Playground slowly come back to their bodies. They had gone so far in that Tantric Meditation that it took a few moments to connect back to the physical world. "Fuck, Terry," Eden moaned, rolling over and sitting back up. Her face was flushed and her eyes were glazed over. "You just keep getting better and better. Sometimes I just want to stay inside you forever."

"I love you," Terry whispered and kissed her.

"Holy shit," Michael said as he came to, rubbing his eyes. "Best sex I've ever had! Not that I've had that much." He winked at Emily who squeezed his thigh.

"My cock is still hard," Mothman said, stroking his crotch. "Why did it have to end?" he whined.

Terry shook his head. "You can't stay in the orgasmic Void forever," he informed them, "even though you may want to. It's tempting. Just like it may be tempting to become a monk, meditating all day and hiding from the world. But there is still work to be done here."

Rob was frowning, it looked like he was concentrating on something. "Do you hear that?" he said, looking at Terry.

The convergence of everyone's sexual energy created a huge spike on the energy signature associated with Terry's house. This had shown up on the radar of several black helicopters who were monitoring the area. When the intense spike of energy showed up on their instruments, they had all come to hover over the house. Luckily the Merkabah field was still in place to keep them relatively safe. Rob was hearing the propellers of the helicopters chopping through the air.

Terry listened and he heard it as well. The noise of the helicopters was incredibly loud now that they were all coming out of their sexual trance, still with heightened sensitivity. Eden shared a worried glance with her lover. "The government?" Terry asked.

Eden shook her head and shrugged. "Should we go check it out?" she asked.

Terry nodded, suddenly looking serious. "We can't show those fuckers that we're afraid." Holding Eden's hand, he stood up and led her to the stairs. They walked up, heading toward Terry's bedroom. The whole Playground stood up and followed close behind them.

There was a spot on the roof right outside Terry's bedroom window. He used to sit out there at night and gaze at the stars when he was younger. Now he went right over and slid the window open. All the members of the Playground were trying to squeeze into Terry's bedroom. It was like a mosh pit of disheveled people who looked they'd just been having sex for hours. He quickly crawled through the window and stood on the roof. Looking up, he shielded his eyes with his hand as Eden followed him out onto the roof. They stood side by side. Rob, Mothman, and several others came out onto the roof to join them. Not all of them could fit on the roof, so the rest huddled by the open window and tried to crane their necks out to see.

The noise of the propellers was overwhelming now as they stared up into the sky. Hovering at a distance above the house were four black helicopters. They were piloted by ominous-looking men in black suits and dark sunglasses. Terry wanted to make it perfectly clear that they weren't afraid of the government or whoever else came at them. They were rebels, defiant and independent. They didn't take orders from anyone and the Truth was only what they discovered through their own mystical experience.

Slowly Terry raised his fist into the sky toward the helicopters. Then he raised his middle finger in the ultimate act of defiance. *We give the finger to whatsoever powers that be trying to stop us.* In a motion of solidarity, Eden, Rob, Mothman, Michael, Emily, and the few others out on that roof raised their fists into the sky together and flipped off the helicopters—the ultimate *fuck off.*

And Terry whispered under his breath, "*No Bounce, No Play,* Motherfuckers!"

SIX

The night was strange. Darren could have sworn there were voices in the shadows. He was restless. A couple times he even thought he heard the whisper of Jade's voice, but when he went to seek it out, nothing was there. Tossing and turning in his bed at his home in Aurora, Darren was tired but couldn't seem to grasp onto the sweet respite of sleep. Maybe it was his thoughts of Terry making him anxious. Something ominous was approaching; he could feel it in the cold sweat clinging to his clammy skin.

Giving up trying to find the regenerative void of sleep, Darren quickly went to his garage and got into his black pickup truck. What he needed was sanctuary, away from the gossiping walls and the dancing shadows. The abandoned church where the Body of Lucifer Christ had been holding their gatherings; that was the place he needed now.

He drove there, silently with his thoughts, making sure he obeyed all of the traffic laws. The risk of getting pulled over or even arrested, he knew, wasn't worth it. Darren was aware that he needed to be ready at any moment to come to Terry's aid—or the aid of any of the awakened individuals surrounding him. There were a few other cars on the night road, but it was very late indeed. In no time Darren was driving along the little dirt road that led back to the church. There were no other cars parked outside. He wasn't surprised; the thought of any of his cult brothers or sisters being there right then seemed absurd in Darren's mind.

Quietly, he parked the truck and went into the church. It looked kind of spooky in the dark night in the middle of the trees. The door wasn't locked. It was never locked. He went through the foyer and into the sanctuary. It was dark, but the light of the moon streamed in through one of the stained-glass windows. He walked slowly down the aisle toward the pulpit in front of him as he stared up at the Triple Cross that loomed there. When he got to the altar, he fell to his knees.

Now Darren wasn't much for praying, and he didn't believe in God. But he believed in himself; yet he was having trouble seeing what he was supposed to do next within the puzzle of the Great Awakening. So he just meditated there at the foot of the Triple Cross, all thoughts leaving his mind. He had no words to speak, for what use were words when all was just waves of energy?

"I see the Triple Conundrum of this cross has drawn you here as well," said a voice from behind Darren. It was a woman's voice and he hadn't heard her come in. He turned. It was Mage of the Meadow; she stood there in her gray robes with the hood pulled over her head. Darren made to stand up but Meadow put up her hand. "No need to get up. Not yet." She walked up and sat in one of the pews in the front row.

Darren pulled his legs out from under him and sat cross-legged on the floor, turning to face Meadow. "I'm actually relieved that you showed up," he admitted. "For I seek counsel."

"Oh?" Meadow inquired, encouraging Darren to elaborate. "What is it that troubles you, my Brother in Light?"

Darren sighed, putting his hands on his knees. "It's the boy," he continued. "I feel like there's more I could be doing—to protect him, to guide him."

"Yes, I understand," Meadow replied. "However, sometimes we must step back and let whatever will be unfold through the energy of Lucifer Christ Consciousness. The Infinite Collective Intelligence sees more than we can from our limited perspective. You're worried he may be affected or influenced by the Pair of Opposites?"

"The Pair of Opposites?" Darren repeated. "Oh, yes! You mean the other two extreme offshoots of our Cult—the Satanists and the Krystics. Yes, that is a concern of mine that either of those extreme sides of the spectrum could try to use him for their own purposes."

"Luckily we have our spies planted amongst both groups," Meadow commented.

"That's true," Darren responded. "If either group were to try to sink their teeth into Terry, we would be informed right away and could remedy the situation. There are such dangers in extreme thinking—whether it be Satanic or Krystic—that's why we sort of hang in the middle. The embodiment of Christ's love so unconditional that we embrace Lucifer as part of the One Consciousness."

"That's the beauty of our way of life—the Middle Way," Meadow agreed. "And don't get down on yourself that you aren't doing enough. You are a valuable asset to the Body and have done more than most of the rest of us have done concerning the Evolution. When in doubt, the best thing is to do nothing. Clear your mind, and the next move will reveal itself." Darren nodded in agreement, this being sound advice and counsel.

Suddenly Meadow's head shot up straight, stretching her neck as if she had just heard a sound. "What is it?" Darren asked, looking around anxiously.

Meadow spoke slowly, "The Shadow Forces are descending. They will attempt a capture."

"What?" Darren asked, standing up to be ready for anything. "What do you mean? Capture who? Capture Terry?"

"Yes!" Meadow said firmly. "You must go now! No time to waste! To Terry's house now, hurry!"

Darren knew exactly what he needed to do and he didn't wait for anymore words. In a flash he was out the doors of the church and in his truck. Speeding away down the dirt road, the danger of the night drew him to Terry's house again.

Thinking he heard someone calling his name, Terry awoke in the darkness of his bedroom. Eden didn't wake, she continued breathing quietly beside him. He decided to let her sleep as he crept out of bed and slipped on a pair of boxers and a t-shirt that was lying on the floor.

"Terry! Come closer!" There was the whispering voice again. Suddenly Terry recognized the voice as that of Remius.

"Remius?" he whispered into the dark. "Is that you?"

In a semi-trance state, Terry walked out of his room and down the stairs. "Come closer!" the voice repeated. Terry thought it must be coming from outside so he made his way to the front door. Still half-asleep, he stumble-walked out onto the porch, leaving the front door wide open behind him.

"Come closer, Terry! Here!" the voice said again. He continued down to the sidewalk and thought he saw a small furry shape hiding in the shadows at the end of the block. Now he was outside the protective shield of the Merkabah that was around his house.

"Remius?" Terry called out again and walked toward the shape at the end of the sidewalk.

Instantly a black SUV appeared out of nowhere and stopped on the curb right next to where Terry stood. Before Terry had a chance to react, the back passenger door opened and two men in black suits and dark sunglasses jumped out and grabbed him. They zip-tied his hands together behind his back and then one of the men produced a syringe with which they injected him in the shoulder. As the shot began to dull his senses, Terry remembered wondering how these men could see anything wearing sunglasses at night.

At the same moment that the SUV pulled up beside Terry, Darren turned onto Terry's street. He stopped his truck and turned the headlights out when he saw the two men zip-tying Terry's hands and then dragging him into the backseat of the car. "Fuck fuck fuck!" Darren cursed himself for being too late. Terry had been abducted anyway. He desperately wanted to try to get Terry back from these men, but from what he could see there were at least three men—two in the back and one driver. They also had guns. And Darren knew if he tried to fight them, he might end up getting killed; and he knew he was no use to Terry if he was dead. Using the Singularity Pulse had significantly weakened him and he wasn't sure of the extent of his powers, so he wasn't willing to take the risk. Better to follow them so he could know the location of the place they were taking Terry.

The SUV pulled away from the curb and started driving toward the end of Terry's street. Darren followed at a distance with his headlights off. Hopefully they couldn't see his black truck in the darkness.

The injection they had given Terry didn't knock him out right away—he had a very strong will. He was trying to kick at the two men in black suits with his free legs, so they zip-tied his ankles too. Then they put duct tape over his mouth. Terry could feel himself slipping into unconsciousness, but he was fighting it with all he had. Screaming behind the duct tape on his mouth, he wriggled and squirmed as much as he could. The back seats had been taken out of the SUV so Terry was laying on the floor and the two men crouched at either end of him. The man closest to his head reached for some canister of unknown gas that was attached to a tube and a rubber breather-mask.

"If you won't let the shot do its work," the man said menacingly, "then you will huff chem-trails, you little faggot!"

He leaned over Terry and pressed the breather mask against his face. Even though his mouth was covered, he could still breathe through his nose. The gas smelled of exhaust and chemicals. The potency was too strong for Terry to fight this substance. His vision turned blurry and red, it jerked like a bad TV, faded to gray and then the blackness of unconsciousness.

Darren continued to follow at a distance; his focus so intense as not to lose them. It was the Chicago area, so there were cars on the road at all hours of the night. He switched on his headlights again once he felt he was sufficiently camouflaged by other cars, especially when they got onto the highway. So afraid that he might lose the SUV in the flow of traffic, he kept his eyes fixed on the vehicle, without blinking, almost to the point his eyes were in pain and bulging out of his sockets.

The black SUV that had abducted Terry drove all the way into the heart of the Central Manufacturing District of Chicago. This area was mostly deserted, leaving old abandoned warehouses and factories. The streets of the city still looked like the aftermath of the apocalypse, or the rubble of an atomic bomb. A lot of the buildings were destroyed beyond repair and were just left to be looted by the roving bands of the newly homeless.

When there were no other cars around, Darren switched his headlights off again, making sure he was far enough behind not to be seen. The men were probably too distracted by the kidnap of Terry to worry if they were being followed. And besides, their windows were so darkly tinted, how they could even see out of them was beyond Darren's imagination. Finally they came to one large abandoned warehouse, the top of which had been completely torn off by one of the tentacles from Dark Tethers. There was a hole in the brick wall of the building, which the black SUV now drove into, disappearing from Darren's view.

Stopping his pursuit, Darren knew that this was as far as he could go safely. It would be a suicide mission to attempt to break Terry out of there by himself. He needed to get his comrades for help with that task. Getting his GPS out of his glovebox, he punched in the coordinates for the warehouse and saved it so he could find his way back. Then he pulled a u-turn and headed back toward the church where he hoped Meadow still was.

As the black SUV drove through the hole in the wall of the warehouse, a trapdoor raised up from the floor inside. It was large enough for them to drive the car down the ramp that it revealed and down into the depths below. They drove into what looked like a small lower level of a parking garage. There was one thick steel door with a small square window at the top that led into the underground facility which was home to the CIA's *Project S & M.*

The man in the black suit parked the SUV and stepped out. The two men in the back also opened their door and stepped out.

Terry was still unconscious. They stood in front of the steel door which was locked and bolted with a very sophisticated security system. There was a shiny black half-sphere attached to the wall next to the door. This was a security camera. The door buzzed loudly and swung open. Two other men in suits came through the door rolling a gurney between them.

The two men who had put Terry in the car now picked up his unconscious body and dumped it on the gurney. As they pushed him on the gurney into the hall on the other side of the door, Terry began to groan; still unconscious, but he was stirring. There were still zip-ties on his ankles and wrists, so if he woke up he couldn't get very far. The thick steel door swung closed behind them, locking them into the compound. They wheeled the gurney through a maze of thin and incredibly bare hallways. They stopped when they got to a stretch of what looked like cells for the subjects that were imprisoned there. The cell door was also reinforced steel with a tiny square window at the top. There were metal wires cross-hatched through the glass of the window.

The first door beeped loudly and opened. The two men pushed the gurney into the cell which was very small, surrounded by concrete walls, lit by a dim fluorescent strip on the ceiling, and there was a small cot in the corner. One of the men pushing the gurney pulled a knife that was clipped on his belt and cut the zip-ties on Terry's wrists and ankles. Then he peeled the duct tape off of his mouth.

"Don't forget this," the other man said from the head of the gurney. He pulled out a small injector gun from his pocket. It was equipped to punch a tracking device the size of a grain or rice through the skin. He put it against the cartilage at the top of Terry's right ear, directly under where the ear curved. Pulling the trigger, the tiny tracking device lodged itself under the skin of Terry's ear. He groaned and twitched, getting closer to waking up.

Quickly the two men picked Terry up and threw him on the cot. Then they exited the room with the gurney, locking the re-inforced steel door behind them before Terry could fully come to. However, in moments he regained consciousness, taking in his surroundings, and remembering vaguely the kidnapping.

"What the fuck?" he groaned, holding his head which was now developing a migraine from the injection and the gas they made him inhale. The cell was so small that Terry almost felt claustrophobic, especially since there were no windows except the tiny one in the door. Folded at the end of the cot was a pair of gray sweatpants and a gray sweatshirt. He put them on when he realized he was cold in just his boxers and a t-shirt. First he was disoriented, now he was angry.

"Hey, fuckers! Let me out!" he yelled at the top of his lungs, walking over to the door. He pounded his fists against it use-lessly. "Let me the fuck out of here! You can't keep me here, you fucking assholes!"

"It's no use," said a girl's voice from behind Terry. He turned just in time to see the Astral Body of a teenage girl walk through the wall and into his cell. It was Anna. "These fucking fascists aren't known to let their prisoners go until they've thoroughly broken them, rendering them useless to the government any-way."

Terry eyed her suspiciously. He could see the silver cord stretching from her and back through the wall. "Are you a prisoner here too?" he asked.

Anna nodded. "I've been here a fuck long time."

"Here?" Terry repeated back. "Where exactly is here?"

"I call it the Facility," Anna continued. "Actually it's a CIA program, an offshoot of MKULTRA, I'm pretty fucking sure of it. They call it Project S & M."

Terry chuckled in spite of himself. "Project S & M? Like sadism and masochism? BDSM?"

"What? No," Anna answered. "It stands for Soul and Mind."

Terry shook his head in recognition. "Soul and Mind... Soulmind... Of course it does."

"I'm Anna," she said, finally introducing herself.

"Terry," he replied.

"If you're the one that they've been talking about," Anna confided, as if telling a secret, "then they've been seeking you for a fuckin' long-ass time. And they finally got you. But I have a feeling that they can't contain you for long."

"What you mean, they've been looking for me?" Terry wanted to know.

"They're experimenting on us who have Soulminds," Anna explained. "What all it's for is unknown. They don't tell us god-damn shit, fucking bastards. They force-feed me pills that I don't know what in fuck's name they do except give me permanent muscle spasms. I think they like torturing us, sick cocksucking fucks. Anyway, I'm rambling."

"They really fucked you up, didn't they?" Terry said.

"What do you mean?" Anna shot back.

"Nevermind, continue."

"So anyway," Anna continued, "there's talk that what they're trying to do is *weaponize* us. *Weaponize* our Soulminds."

"Can they do that?" Terry asked, raising his eyebrows.

Anna shrugged. "Dunno, but they're sure gonna try. The word is that they want to start World War Three or some such shit. And they want to use you to trigger it."

Terry laughed with no humor in it whatsoever. "Great," he said flatly. "Everyone's trying to use me for something... Say, you are walking through walls and shit, why don't you just escape or go get help or something?"

"This is just my Astral Body," Anna explained.

"Oh, yeah, that's right," Terry concurred.

"So I'd have to leave my physical body for good and I'm not sure I'm ready to do that yet," she admitted. "Besides, I can't get past the walls of the compound. I've explored everywhere *inside* the Facility in my Astral Body, but as soon as I try to leave, I can't get through. They must have some sort of technology that's used to keep our Astral Forms contained. Shit is fucking frustrating."

"If there's a way out of this place, fuck me I'll find it," Terry said confidently.

Anna smiled. "I'm sure you will, and take the others of us with you. Now, I think I'm gonna go back to my room to get some sleep. You should do the same."

"Why?" he asked.

"Because," Anna replied, "tomorrow they're probably gonna fucking ream our assholes harder than they usually do. If you know what I mean."

SEVEN

FROM THE MIND OF JESSICA THORN:

Why do I keep getting thrown into streams of water, energy, and light? It's very unnerving. As I'm feeling right now, tumbling through this Timestream, disoriented enough to not even know what direction I'm being carried. Maybe I'm being carried in every direction at once—to every time period at once. It does kind of feel like I'm being torn apart, yet I remain intact. All I can see is this wash of white; not quite liquid, not quite light.

After riding on this current for an unfathomable amount of time—if time even exists—I find myself stopped, my butt finding solid ground underneath me. This floor, or ground, is pure white. Above me and on every side is stark white as well, with no shadows or grays, like a blank sheet of paper. Standing up, I take a couple steps forward. The sound of my footsteps echoes like if I was in a cave.

I stop because it seems that trying to walk anywhere would be useless in this Oblivion of Whiteness. "Hello?" I say, my voice echoing back to me. Suddenly I feel a Presence. Not a human or creature presence, but a Presence like an Omniscient Intelligence that exists everywhere and nowhere. "What do you wish to show me, Great Spirit?" I ask into the void. The question bounces back to me in echoes, like a record broken and repeating itself to itself.

Colors begin to swirl in the whiteness, like a tornado of running paint. It twirls around me, not yet solidified, colors of a potential image. And this image, my intuition is telling me, is the past; a memory I have almost forgotten, an event I never revisited in my contemplation. Then the environment starts to take shape. The floor beneath me comes into focus to resemble a black and white chess board. I'm in a room with no windows and there is a huge chandelier hanging from the ceiling high above. The next thing to come into view is a round table with eleven women dressed in all white sitting around it. Then I see Terry and myself on our knees on the floor. There are two women standing behind us: one black with long white dreadlocks, the other white with straight black hair that was so long it reached her ankles. I'm starting to remember this now.

This was when we had all broken into the Public Works building, and then found ourselves in a whole other realm, or a fortress for some sort of Order. I don't remember. God, it's been a long time since I even thought about this event. I watch in a sort of detached way as I see the black woman produce a yellow energy rope from her hand and it wraps around my past-self's throat. The woman also puts her foot against my back. The white woman with the black hair wraps a yellow energy rope around Terry's throat as well and proceeds to pull his head back roughly. Even though part of me feels detached from this memory, as if it happened to someone else and not me, another part of me cringes at seeing myself and Terry in so much agony.

Suddenly a woman stands up from the table. She has brilliant blue hair that puffs out around her head like a lion's mane. She walks over to stand in front of Terry and myself. "Your crimes are many, and strictly linear," she says. "You are also denied access to this space, making you in violation of the Ordinance."

Terry doesn't respond to the blue-haired woman. A vague ping of recognition is produced within my memory, and I seem to recall these words, this conversation, as from a deep well of forgetfulness. Then the lion-haired woman continues her monologue by saying, "We have enough of our own problems keeping the balance without you and your little cat friend meddling into the spirals of what you do not understand." The woman kneels down in front of Terry and slides her fingers between his teeth, then pries his jaw open. I flinch a little as I watch this violence unfold. The woman pushes her right hand into Terry's mouth and then extracts it slowly, pulling a piece of his essence along with it. As her fingers come out, a thin stream of white light is pulled from his throat. It is a piece of Terry's Soulmind—dangerous, I feel. She puts the fragment of Soulmind into a small glass cylinder that she pulls from her white robes. Terry gags as the woman seals the cylinder tightly shut.

It's frustrating that this is just a memory, played out like a movie before my eyes. There is no way for me to alter the events that have already taken place—right? Or is there? The thought of that possibility briefly flutters through my consciousness, but I don't act on it. Even if I did wish to try to change past events, I feel glued to the floor, entranced by the scene before me, only able to witness once again.

"Learn your world," the woman says as she stands up. Then she takes my remembered-self's leash out of the black woman's hand. I cringe as I watch her step down on my back. Myself in the memory smashes her face against the floor and blood pours from her nose—or *my* nose, it's gotten confusing. I am the witness, but that's also me in the past. Whatever, I grasp it as much as I can.

"Don't you fucking touch her!" Terry screams, trying to pull against the energy rope around his neck but failing. I smile and tears well up in my eyes as my heart feels the love I still hold for Terry. I can see that my memory-self's aura is blazing purple around me and it's also spiraling out of my chest, even as my face is smashed into the floor. The lion-woman flips me over and rips my shirt open, exposing my breasts. To be honest, I don't remember any of this part at all. Then I watch as the woman waves her hand over the purple Soulmind spiraling out from between my breasts.

Suddenly the energy of my memory-self's Soulmind lunges up and engulfs the woman's face, obviously taking her off guard. Then her hand goes into her white robes again, producing another glass cylinder. My Soulmind energy leaves the woman's face and is sucked into the cylinder. The woman seals it shut with the fragment of my Soulmind inside, then the rest of my aura and spiraling Soulmind disappears back into my body. I can tell that I'm only semi-conscious. That's probably why I don't remember this, after my head had been brutally smashed against the floor.

I look at my body that just lays there, naked breasts exposed. At this point I feel the hot tears running down my face. I wish I could run up and embrace my past self, hug her and tell her everything is going to be okay. But I can't, and I don't know if that would even be the truth. Blood still ran from my memory-self's nose, and my eyes fluttered up and closed, just a reflex. Until now I didn't even know that they had taken a piece of my Soulmind. That must have some sort of significance, why else would I be being shown this right now? My hand goes up to my solar plexus, feeling my energy. I don't feel like I'm missing anything; I feel whole.

But there is no mistaking the memory and the reality of this occurrence. The woman with blue hair stands up, pocketing the two cylinders, one with the piece of Terry's Soulmind, one with the piece of mine.

"He doesn't understand what we are trying to protect him from," the lion woman says to the one with white dreadlocks. "Give him a dose of Dark Tethers so he knows that his world needs us to protect it."

Metal shackles attached to the longest chain I have ever seen descend from the ceiling. They are clamped onto Terry's ankles and they hoist him into the air. As he is pulled up into the infinite ceiling, the whole memory just as quickly washes away into the same tornado of colors that brought me here.

Through the wash of colors another environment solidifies. What builds itself around me are three gray walls and a steel door. I'm in the tiniest cell I've ever seen. Looking down, a cot forms in front of me and there is a figure sleeping there. I hold my breath, almost not believing my eyes. Is this real? Or just another vision? It is Terry sleeping before me, covered by only a thin white sheet. His shaggy black hair falls over his face as he breathes quietly in his slumber. He looks almost peaceful, but not quite. He seems older than he was at the time I disappeared, more world-weary. I shake my head sadly. "Oh, baby, what have they done to you? Locked you in a cell, by whatever forces are working against you? A soul as beautiful and brilliant as yours should never be locked in a cage."

I kneel down next to his cot and brush his hair tenderly away from his eyes. I can touch him! This must be real, not just a memory or a vision. This must be the present. Desperately I want to be able to free him from this prison, but I know deep in my bones that that is an impossibility. Leaning down, I kiss him on the cheek. Terry murmurs in his sleep but doesn't wake. "I love you so much, Terry," I whisper into his ear. "I'm so so sorry that I left you... But I had to. I knew then and I know now that was the only path forward for me, or I would have been faced with a future I didn't want to come to pass. But I promise you, I will find my way back to you, my love." I can feel the conviction of this statement deep within my bones. In this moment, I know it is an infallible truth that I will be with him again soon. I kiss him again, on his cheek, his forehead, his lips.

Terry shudders in his sleep as if he's having a nightmare. I hug him from the side of his cot; it's been so long since I've touched him. It feels like an eternity, and maybe it has been. Then I whisper in his ear, "Find the piece of my Soulmind which is lost. The piece that they stole from me. Wherever it is, I know it is you who can find it. I want you to have it, it is my gift to you. And it will help us find our way back to each other."

In that moment, I know without a doubt this is why I was brought here; to deliver this message. Even in sleep Terry is able to receive it. He will remember this, even if to him it may seem like a dream. Now that this is done, I feel that I must go. But I do not wish to, I want more time with my beloved. The tears continue to stream down my face as I cling to his sleeping form. It pains me to no end to see him locked in a cell like this. A spirit such as him is meant to fly free, forever exploring the limits of time, space, and the imagination—and then perhaps *beyond.*

The walls around me begin to fade into white again; so does Terry under my embrace. "No!" I scream to the void. "Don't take him away! Just give me a little bit longer!" But my screams of anguish go unheeded and I am again swept away into the white of the Timestream.

I am lost for lifetimes again on the Timestream, like a leaf on the stream of creation. Where to next is a mystery. *Where to now, O Great Spirit of the Otherworld? I say to the silence. Or what else do you wish to show me? What secrets will you now reveal?*

Hovering there in the whiteness of whatever ethereal substance this is, a new vision presents itself before me. However, it never quite becomes perfectly clear, like a movie projected into smoke. Is this another memory? Or perhaps a prophecy? Yes, that's it; it must be a vision of a possible future. What I see is three women in a circle around a central figure. I squint and can finally make out—ah, yes!—it's Terry there in the middle. One of the women is me, I can see that now. The next one is very petite and has pink hair. The third is tall—taller than any human I've ever met. It seems strange to see this other woman towering maybe a couple feet above the rest of the figures. But her energy is staggering, even through a vision. She is a pure redhead, with full locks falling down her back like waves of fire. And what is she wearing? I can't quite make it out; it might be a green dress, or something like that. This circle and Terry in the center are at the foot of a beautiful mountain. The energy of this mountain, I can feel, is immensely strong as well. It almost feels like a portal into another world.

After I register all of these separate pieces that make up this one vision, it is swept away just as quickly, like smoke from a campfire. Then I am spinning again. Suddenly I feel the exhaustion in my body and I hope that this journey may quickly come to an end. Yet I feel like it wants to take me to one more place before I am released. In a moment I feel like I'm tumbling head over heels, as if I'm rolling down a steep hill. The momentum increases and I feel dizzy, vertigo gripping my equilibrium. I'm spinning at increasing speed, then quite suddenly I collide with the ground with a *splat!*

"Son of a bitch..." I mumble, trying to drag my body from the ground. There's still white all around me, but it's dissipating fast to reveal a strange landscape. I'm in the middle of a street that looks like it's been heavily patched up. There are buildings looming on either side of me, but they've been devastated, great portions of them have been reduced to rubble, or giant holes have been ripped into the sides of them. It takes me a couple minutes to realize that I'm in Chicago—or what's left of it. Whatever section I'm in seems to be deserted as far as I can tell. There may be droves of homeless people hiding in the remains of the buildings, but I can't see them if there are.

I suddenly hear zooming noises high above me and I cover my head and duck down in fear. Peeking up into the sky, there look to be some sort of flying cars zipping through the sky above me, then they disappear into the distance. "What in the hell?" I say out loud. What kind of place is this? Where have I landed now?

Staring in the direction the flying cars disappeared, I almost don't hear the sound of the engine noise behind me until it's right behind my back. I cringe and turn around slowly, not knowing what to expect in this foreign, maybe unfriendly, environment. To my amazement there is a flying car hovering maybe three or four feet above the street, stopped right behind me. It's body shape is similar to an egg with a flat underside. Two little wings the shape of shark fins protrude from the bottom edge of the vehicle. "That's freaking amazing..." I say when my fear subsides a little. Whoever is piloting that thing hasn't shot me or anything, so that's promising.

The door to the passenger's side opens upwards like the DeLorean in *Back to the Future*. I walk around to look inside, surprised at my own boldness. A friendly-looking man smiles out at me from the driver's seat. He wears spectacles and a snazzy suit with suspenders. I chuckle to myself at the absurdity of this whole scenario. The man pats the seat beside him and says, "Come, get in and ride along."

My intuition tells me that he's friendly enough and I don't get any sinister vibes from him, so I climb up onto the passenger's seat. The door slowly comes down and closes beside me. "I'm Jessica," I say, smiling at the stranger.

"My name is Nikola," he introduces himself in turn. "Welcome to the future!"

EIGHT

The light from the morning sun was peeking over the treetops by the time Darren got back to the church. To his dismay, Meadow had vacated the premises, leaving the sanctuary empty of either Brother or Sister. With no time to lose, he jumped into his pickup truck and drove back over to Terry's house to let Eden and the two boys know what had happened.

When he pulled up and parked at the curb behind the white minivan, Darren could see Rob poking his head out of the front door and looking around. Sliding out of the driver's seat and onto the pavement, he locked his truck behind him as he walked up towards the porch. Rob spotted Darren in a moment and waved in greeting.

"Hey!" Rob called out as Darren got to the stairs that led up to the porch. "This door was wide open when I woke up just a little while ago. I was wondering why it was so fucking cold in the house. And can't find Terry anywhere."

"That's what I came to talk to you about," Darren responded as Rob ushered him inside and closed the door against the chill of the morning. "Terry's been kidnapped."

"Kidnapped?!" Rob said, his eyes wide. "By who? And how do you know?"

"I was there, last night," Darren answered. "Regrettably, I was too late to stop it. Terry wandered out past the safety of the Merkabah Field, and that's when they had a chance to take him. As for *who* took him, as far as I am aware it's some secret program run by the CIA. They experiment on individuals who have Soulminds, and in turn they develop technologies to mimic our powers or suppress them."

"That's fucking insane," Rob said slowly with a shocked expression on his face. "So what are we going to do? How do we get Terry back?"

"You shouldn't worry about that right now," Darren responded with authority. "You, Rob, have some other quite important things to worry about." At that Rob raised his eyebrows. Darren continued, "Let me and my affiliates handle Terry's rescue since it requires a calculated plan and determining what the best time to execute it would be. You can't just break into a underground secret government facility and not expect there to be military personnel trying to stop you."

Rob nodded quietly. Hearing the commotion, Mothman had woken up and was now coming down the stairs to see what was up. Shortly after, Eden came out and down the stairs to join them.

"What's going on?" Mothman wanted to know.

Rob turned and looked at him and then at Eden who had just gotten to the bottom of the stairs where they were congregated. "Terry's been kidnapped," Rob informed them.

"Son of a bitch," Mothman said in response.

Eden crossed her arms and frowned, silent. She looked at Darren, he returned her gaze and they shared a quiet moment. Finally Eden said, "Does this have something to do with those black helicopters?"

Darren's mouth fell open. "You saw black helicopters?" They all nodded. Darren looked down at the floor and said, "That's bad... That's trouble for us... How many were there?"

"There were four," Mothman answered.

"Fuckin'—four?! Right above your house? Lucifer Christ, there's more to deal with than I even realized," Darren said, obviously worried. He put his hand on Rob's shoulder. "Hey, Rob, let me talk to you alone for a second. No offense, you two," —he indicated Mothman and Eden—"but I have a couple things I need to discuss with Rob and it's just easier than having all three of you work on the same thing."

Eden nodded, showing that it was okay and she didn't feel offended. Darren took Rob aside, into the kitchen where they were out of earshot of the others. "What do you want to talk to me about?" Rob asked.

"You know how you've been helping grow this Playground thing?" Darren continued.

Rob nodded and said, "*No Bounce*—"

"*No Play*," Darren finished.

"You know about that?" Rob seemed a little surprised.

"Of course I know about that," Darren replied, but didn't elaborate. "Anyway, with Terry gone and us not being sure how long it will be until we can rescue him, it's up to you if you want to disband your Playground meetings *here*. Appoint at least one person from your group, or more preferably a couple, who can start holding meetings themselves to keep it going. And you, Rob, since I trust you and see potential in you that it quite seems that nobody else does, I charge you with the task of starting up new chapters of Playground around the country and even beyond our shores. I believe in you Rob, and it is more important than ever that we grow our numbers. Make no mistake that we are at war. World War Three is not really between nations, it is between the unconscious and the Awakened. It is the War on Consciousness. And you can always count on the unenlightened to make war on the awakening Soulminds."

Rob stared at Darren for a moment, trying to process what he was being told. Then he said slowly, "So you want me to travel around the country, and then to other countries, setting up new Playgrounds around the globe? Do I have that right?"

"That's the gist of it," Darren confirmed. "Of course, I'm not the boss of you and I would never claim to be or attempt to give you orders. This is completely in the hands of your free will. However, doing this would greatly enhance our cause and make sure we have a foothold to defend ourselves if the Shadow Forces really decide to try to wipe us out to keep their unconscious slave-wage population. There are members of the society that I belong to in virtually every country, and I can set them up as your contact points so you will be taken care of wherever you go. It'll be dangerous, but I believe in you, Rob."

Rob slowly nodded. "I understand what needs to be done."

"Good," Darren said, smiling. He put his hand on Rob's shoulder. "Take some time to think about it and I'll be in touch."

Darren turned and started walking back toward the front door. Rob followed behind him. Stopping briefly where Eden and Mothman still stood at the bottom of the stairs, he said, "I have to be going now, time really is a factor while we're still in this third dimension."

"What's happening, Rob?" Mothman asked, turning to his friend.

Rob waved his hand and said, "I'll fill you in later."

Eden looked at Darren with sorrowful eyes. She felt Terry's absence in her heart more than the rest of them. Wanting desperately to say something to her friend and lover Darren, she opened her mouth but no words were there to speak.

"It was good to see you, love," Darren said, leaning down and kissing Eden on the lips. "Like I said, I'll be in touch." And without another word, he left, making sure to close the front door behind him.

When he was back in his truck, he took out his phone and dialed Meadow's cell. After a few rings, she picked up. "Yes, this is Meadow," her voice spoke from the other end of the line.

"Meadow! It's Darren," he responded back, his voice serious. "The Shadow Forces loom larger than even we anticipated. Terry has been taken. Unfortunately I got there too late to stop them. In light of this, I wish to call an emergency meeting of the Body of Lucifer Christ!"

NINE

The distinct impression of Jessica's presence lingered in Terry's mind as he awoke in his cell. He felt as if she had been right there next to his cot, in flesh and blood. Grasping for her, the last lingering droplets of sleep began to clear from his mind, taking the image of Jessica with it like fading tendrils of a dream. Terry knew that there was something she said to him as he slept, but he couldn't call it to mind.

"Jessica," he mumbled as he sat up and swung his legs over the side of the cot. As he rubbed his eyes, he made note that he felt awake, but his brain was still afflicted by a thick mental fog that he couldn't quite shake.

In another room of the Facility, which had several monitors mounted on the wall, the Director stood next to an older man who had gray hair and circular glasses, he also wore a long white lab coat. They were watching Terry sitting on his cot in his cell on one of the monitors. The Director turned to the man in the lab coat and asked, "He hasn't tried to escape at all? No abnormal spikes of energy from his body?"

"No, Director," the man replied. "That injection he was given on the way here, coupled with the radiation being released into his cell, seem to be suppressing his power quite nicely."

"Yes, Doctor Morkian, it appears to be working quite nicely," the Director continued. "Regulating the pills with the other sub-jects—some to suppress the power and others to enhance it—have been working quite nicely. There's no reason to think that won't work for this subject Terry Broswald, right, Doctor?"

Doctor Morkian nodded. "That's correct, Director. We can fluctuate it as need be for our experiments. And if there's ever an emergency, there are protocols to irradiate the subject. Every room is equipped for that eventuality."

"Perfect," the Director agreed. "Have him prepped and brought into Observation Room 4. The one with the electrode helmet."

"Right away, Director," Doctor Morkian obliged.

The Director nodded and exited the room without another word.

Terry tensed up when he heard the door of his cell unlock. When the door was flung open to reveal three large men in black suits, Terry stood up and backed away, assuming a defensive stance.

"Come on," the man closest to the door said. "Just cooperate and this will go smoothly. We don't want to use force on you, but we will if we have to." This man had a small cup of water in one hand and a small pill capsule in the other which was red and white. Terry eyed the pill warily.

"And if I refuse?" Terry asked.

The man sighed as if dealing with a difficult child. "Just come quietly. If you don't, we'll be forced to hold you down and inject you instead. Do you want that? Because, we can do that too. It's up to you."

Terry took a couple reluctant steps forward. The idea of being forcibly injected again was very much *not* something Terry wanted. He snatched the pill from the man and said, "You're a bunch of pieces of shit, you know that? You're gonna get yours!"

The three men in black suits laughed as Terry snatched the water and swallowed the pill. "Yeah, we've heard that one before."

Terry threw the plastic cup as hard as he could toward the floor to show his dissatisfaction. "You cunts aren't going to get away with kidnapping people against their will! It's fucking illegal!" he shouted.

"Come on, kid," the man said, putting his hand on Terry's shoulder and pushing him out of the cell door. They guided him down the hallway, both men holding Terry's arms in a firm grip. "Don't tell us what's legal and illegal," the man continued. "The one's who make the laws are the very ones who *had* you kidnapped, you dumb little shit!" The three men laughed again as if the whole scenario was the most funny joke.

They roughly dragged and pushed Terry into a plain white room which had a chair in the center that was bolted to the floor. Throwing him down on the seat, they used the cuffs attached to the chair to restrain Terry's wrists and ankles. The electrode helmet that was hanging from the back of the chair was pressed firmly on his head. Terry realized that resistance was useless and any fighting or yelling he could do would just be a waste of energy right then. Once they were done locking Terry in the chair, the three men exited the room, locking the door behind them.

Terry looked up and there was a large rectangular mirror embedded in the wall in front of him. Not being an idiot, Terry knew that it was a two-way mirror and there were undoubtedly people on the other side watching him.

Obviously, he was right about that. The Director stood in the center, staring through the window at the new subject. On his right was the jumpsuit-man with the helmet on and holding the small monitor wired into said helmet. On the Director's left was Doctor Morkian holding an iPad which contained a control panel. He also used the iPad to take copious notes. Terry stared silently on the other side.

"I'll turn on the intercom so you can speak to him," Doctor Morkian informed. He pressed a button on his iPad and nodded to the Director.

"Terry Broswald," the Director began, "we have brought you here because you have the most intriguing energy reading we have ever come across. Cooperate with us and you won't be harmed."

Terry smirked, suspicious of everything this man said, and rightly so.

The Director ignored the smirk and continued, "You are in possession of the Merkabah Technology. Show us how it works."

"I don't know what you're talking about," Terry said, playing dumb. He knew it was a long shot and an unlikely tactic to work.

"Oh, please," the Director responded, "don't be coy! We *know* you are in possession of the Merkabah Technology. That is a reason it was so difficult to collect you. There was one of those fields around your *whole house*, and we *know* you were the one who set it up. Now show us!"

"Go to hell!" Terry yelled.

"Shock him," the Director whispered to Doctor Morkian, who pressed a button on the iPad.

Suddenly bolts of electricity were coursing through Terry's skull and brain. He gritted his teeth and shut his eyes agains the excruciating pain. In seconds it was over, but the pain still lingered through his head. Breathing heavily, Terry hung his head forward and groaned.

"Now will you show us the Merkabah?" the Director said with unwavering authority.

Terry started to laugh, soft at first and then raising in volume to hysterical laughter as he raised his head and stared straight at the mirror. "Like I said—GO TO HELL!"

"Again. Shock him again," the Director whispered to the Doctor.

In seconds the agony of the electric current was flowing into Terry again. It was extended a bit longer than the first time and Terry began to scream in exquisite anguish. Suddenly the golden sphere popped out around his body and the star tetrahedrons began rotating. In conjunction with that, the electricity was cut off by the energy of the field.

"What? What's happening?" the Director asked. The only one who could see any of this was the Lieutenant with the helmet on. He held out the monitor so that the Director and the Doctor could see it. On the screen they could see the golden sphere around Terry as well as the rotating star tetrahedrons—which only appeared as a white shine since they were spinning at almost the speed of light.

"He *is* the one," Doctor Morkian said in awe. "The most fascinating subject I've come across."

"Can we duplicate this technology synthetically, Doctor?" the Director asked.

"Well, yes," the Doctor answered. "I mean, once we've studied it more, gotten the readings of all the wave patterns, then yes, I'm sure our team will be able to create a synthetic Merkabah Technology."

"Good..." the Director said. "Wait... What's happening now?"

Their attention was back on the window and not on the small monitor anymore. Terry was still screaming, his eyes tightly closed as his Merkabah spun around him. His hair blew around as if caught in a whirlwind. As the pitch of his scream increased, the bolts fastening the chair to the floor popped out violently, shooting in all directions. The three men on the other side of the two-way mirror stared in awe as Terry, with the chair he was strapped to, started to levitate into the air.

"He can... fly?" the Lieutenant in the jumpsuit said from behind the helmet.

"Have you ever seen anything like this, Doctor Morkian?" the Director wanted to know.

"Never," the Doctor replied. His mouth hung open as he stared at Terry, who looked, to the non-Soulmind naked eye, to just be hovering in the air as he screamed. They could only see the Merkabah on the monitor.

Suddenly a pulse of energy shot out of Terry's Merkabah and cracked the two-way mirror, but it didn't shatter. The three men cried out, startled, and put their arms up in front of their faces in case the glass exploded.

"Okay, that's enough!" the Director shouted. "Blast him with the radiation! Now! Before it gets out of hand!"

Without hesitation, Doctor Morkian pressed a button on the iPad. They looked at the monitor attached to the helmet as radiation was being pumped into the room adjacent. On the screen they could see the light of the sphere and the star tetrahedrons slowly dim, flicker, and then disappear. Terry fell, still attached to the chair. The back legs hit the floor first and tipped over backwards, knocking the wind out of Terry as his back hit the floor. His scream ceased and he went silent as the electrode helmet slipped off his head.

"That was extraordinary! Quite remarkable!" Doctor Morkian commented.

"Yes... It was, wasn't it?" the Director replied as if deep in thought. What schemes were cooking inside that depraved mind of his? "Maybe," he continued after a long pause, "a little later we'll put him in the playroom with the other subjects and see what they do. Who knows, maybe they'll give us some useful information."

A couple hours later, Terry awoke in his cell again, hearing Anna's voice in his head. "We mustn't let them take everything from us. Resist those fucking cocksucking fucks…" she said, her voice echoing in his mind.

"Anna?" he mumbled, sitting up. A headache pulsed in his brain and Anna's voice didn't speak again. Before Terry even had any time to acclimate himself again—foggily remembering the events in the Observation Room—his cell door opened again. The same three men stood in the doorway. At least Terry figured they were the same men, they all looked the same. He groaned. "What now?"

"The Director wants you to meet the other subjects," one of the suit-men smiled obnoxiously. "All you kiddies can play together. Maybe you can do a little puzzle. Or maybe you can play with some cute stuffed animals." The three men laughed, obviously the bully-types.

Terry shook his head, irritated by their insulting banter. "I'm not a fucking child, you imbeciles. Do I look like I'm four?"

"Oooh," one of the men cooed. "Baby knows a big word. Now come on, you little twit. Don't give us a hard time."

Terry stood up off his cot and glared at them, but he went without fighting them. "You parameciums couldn't even possibly begin to grasp the complexity of the Soulmind," he said under his breath.

"What was that?" one of the men said as he pushed Terry into the hallway.

"Nothing," Terry grumbled.

"That's what I thought," the man shot back as they dragged Terry down the hall.

All the halls looked the same to Terry and he couldn't differentiate between which hall was which and how the layout was set up in this labyrinth of a Facility. They turned down a new hallway and stopped at one of the first doors. It was labeled: Activity Room.

"Behave yourself during group time or they're liable to knock you out again," said the man who was holding Terry's arms.

"Go eat a dick," Terry shot back.

"Oh, aren't you charming," the man said sarcastically as they unlocked the door to the activity room. "Enjoy your time with the others. You don't get it very often," he said as they pushed Terry inside and locked the door behind him.

"You don't have to shove me, you barbarians!" Terry yelled through the door. "I'm not a fucking wheelchair!"

Anna chuckled. "A wheelchair?" she said. Priya was standing next to her and they had been talking quietly before Terry was pushed into the room.

Terry shrugged, eyeing the room incredulously. "That was the first thing I could think of..." He stared at the kiddie toys and games. "What do they think we are," he continued, "little children? What the fuck is with this shit?" Terry surveyed the rest of the room, briefly registering Jeremy rocking in his chair and mumbling to himself.

"Obviously that's what they think," Anna replied. "That should have become pretty goddamn apparent by now."

Terry looked down and noticed that Anna's right arm was tremoring against her leg. "Are you okay?" he asked.

"Yeah, well, these dickheads get off on torturing us," she continued. "And if they can find a way to fucking rape us permanently—with side effects that become the cocksucking gift that keeps on giving—then they sure as my cunting anus will do that." Anna grinned morbidly.

Terry pointed at her, just remembering her visit to him the night before. "You're Anna... right? The girl I met in Astral Form last night?"

"Yep, that's me," she confirmed. "It's nice to meet you *in the flesh*, as they say. Now you can see me in my faggoty, weird, pedophile-ish nightgown that they stuffed me into—since Astral Bodies don't wear clothes, duh. And I kind of suspect that they don't give me shoes or socks because one of these creeps working here has a twisted foot fetish. Hey! Nice to meet you too, Terry Broswald! Welcome to Hell where they're probably going to *fuck* us to death. How are you?" Terry stared at her as if she had two heads. "Oh yeah, and this is Priya." Anna pointed with her thumb at Priya who waved a greeting. "And that turnip over there is Jeremy. *They reamed his asshole to the point his mind split.*" She whispered that last part. Then she raised her arms and put on a fake smile. "Welcome to the candy cane-land where everyone is happy and there's never-ending fucking-fucking-*FUCKING* fun to be had for everyone!"

Priya kind of scooted a couple steps away from Anna at this point. Terry laughed and then coughed. He couldn't help it. This chick was weird, he thought, but he was attracted to her in a strange way that he didn't quite understand. "So wait... What happened to Jeremy over there?" Terry asked.

"I was just telling Priya about that the other day," Anna answered. "They tried to get his Soulmind to transfer sexually—I'm quite sure you're familiar with that, I can tell—but it didn't work. Activation won't work through rape—like, duh! Fucking simple-minded cocksucking fucksticks. Anyway, I'm pretty sure they got mad it didn't work and just kept raping him... over and over, until his mind *exploded.*"

All color drained from Terry's face. "That's"—he swallowed hard—"so fucked... Did they, you know, 'ream your asshole' like you were saying last night?"

"Oh, yeah," Anna confirmed. "They reamed it good like a little whore that wouldn't give her pimp the money she earned. The Director had a hard-on to see my Soulmind weapon today."

"And did you show him?"

"I didn't want to, Terry, I swear I didn't," she continued, "but they have such mouth-watering cock-squirting torture devices here it's almost impossible to resist. You've probably seen that by now. At first I refused—motherfucking motherfuckers!—but they have this thing, this device, that shoots needles into my tits. Oh my Godfucking FUCK, Terry, I hate it so much when they shoot one through my nipple. So I gave in and showed them... My poor little boobies..." Anna massaged her tits through her nightgown.

"And... what is your Soulmind weapon?" Terry wanted to know.

"It's like a battle axe," Anna shrugged. "It's pretty bitchin'."

"That's pretty cool," Terry admitted. "Mine is—"

Anna suddenly rushed over to him and silenced him by putting her finger to his lips. "Shush!" she insisted, looking around at the ceiling. "Don't tell them if they don't know yet. Look, there's cameras up there and microphones. Don't say too much. They like to put us together to see if they can glean any new information they can't ream out of us otherwise."

Terry's face flushed at Anna's touch and a heat shot up his spine from her proximity. Priya sighed and went to sit down at one of the tables. "Oh, okay," Terry said as Anna took her finger away from his lips, but she stayed close to him.

"Did they ream your asshole too, Terry?" she asked, staring into his eyes. Terry squirmed under her gaze. He felt as if she meant to rip his clothes off with her eyes.

"Yeah, they did actually," Terry confessed. "They forced me to show them the Merkabah."

Anna gasped. "You can do the Merkabah?" She was wildly impressed. "You really are the one they were talking about... I've never seen the Merkabah Field produced—I mean, I've never done it either—and I've only heard stories. Some people even whisper that it's a lost technology."

Terry shook his head. "No, my October taught it to me."

"You lucky cocksucker," Anna said smiling. Then she leaned forward and whispered in his ear, "What about the Singularity Pulse?"

Terry leaned against Anna's cheek and whispered back, "I've never done it myself, but I've seen someone perform that, and know one other who has that ability as well."

"I hear whispers in the walls," she replied so quietly that Terry almost couldn't hear her. Then she licked his earlobe and continued, "They think you have that ability as well, so don't tell them that you don't. And they think maybe even something greater... The ability to create worlds... the Spiralverse... it will be was..."

"What?" Terry whispered back, confused. "The way the world was created? Or wait... will be? Which one is it?"

"Don't let them hear..." Anna said slowly into Terry's ear. "It *will be* how the Spiralverse *was* created."

Terry hesitated. If he said that he knew what that meant, he would have been lying. He didn't get what she was trying to tell him, but it seemed to be important—important enough to not let the Director of the project and his associates hear. But she had delivered the message and was already on to another thought. She slid her arms around Terry's neck in an embrace. "Hey," she said seductively, "you know they're already watching us like voyeuristic perverts, why not give them a more spicy show? What do you say, loverboy?" Anna smiled wickedly and stared into Terry's eyes, daring him to be naughty.

He didn't have to think about that for very long. In a second, he leaned in and kissed Anna on the mouth. Their lips parted, and as her eyes closed, her tongue found Terry's. She moaned, her body aching to feel the touch of another body against hers. "I want you, Anna," Terry whispered.

"Oh God, fuck yeah," Anna groaned, practically salivating with anticipation. "It's been so fucking long since I've been fucked. My pussy is screaming for that cock!" She pulled off her nightgown in a flash of an instant and she was completely naked underneath. Terry could see needle marks on her perky breasts from her torture earlier. Her body was slim and pretty, and she had a full bush. Terry's sweatpants and sweatshirt were easy to slip out of also, and in seconds he was naked in front of his new sexual partner.

"What *are* you guys doing?" Priya yelled in protest.

"Shut the fuck up, Priya," Anna shot back, not turning to look at her. "You can watch if you want! God knows Jeremy the turnip doesn't know what the fuck is going on enough for him to enjoy the show."

Terry was already starting to get hard as he admired Anna's hot body. She was taller than any girl he'd had sex with before, at least a couple inches taller than him, and that turned him on incredibly. "You're... so sexy," Terry said.

She smiled and pressed her naked body against his. Stroking his chest, she said, "You like me? I like you, Terry. I'm already getting wet for you. Feel." Anna grabbed his hand and put it between her legs against her pussy. Terry could feel the lubrication wetting her outer labia and then slipped his finger inside almost by accident. "Oh fucking yes!" she moaned, tilting her head back. "I love the way you fucking touch that pussy."

Then she pushed him backwards onto the top of one of the tables—not the one Priya was sitting at. Terry fell onto his back on the table and scooted up onto it. By this time he was fully hard and stroking between his legs. "Yeah, baby," he oozed, "I want to be inside of you so fucking bad!"

Then she pounced on him, straddling his torso, Terry's cock slapping against the outside of her wet cunt. "Let's see how long it takes for them to pull us off each other," Anna cooed. "They probably *want* to see it. They'll fucking save this in their personal porno collection. The Director will take the tape home with him so he can wear women's lingerie while he jerks his cock watching us. What a pervert." She smiled at Terry with lust in her eyes as he smacked his hard cock against her puckered asshole.

"Let's give them a good show then," Terry said enthusiastically. They kissed hard, almost smashing each other's lips between their teeth.

"Do you want to fuck my asshole, you boy-slut? I feel that hot dick against my tight little hole."

Terry shook his head. "I want to feel the juices of your pussy squeeze around me. Your pubic hair is really turning me on, not gonna lie."

Anna reached between her legs and grabbed Terry's cock in her soft hand, rubbed the tip between her wet pussy lips, and then slipped it inside. She gasped as he went deep, all the way in. "Oh God, that's good," she moaned, starting to move her hips. "I love your cock, Terry! Give it all to me! I want to feel your Soulmind!"

Terry could feel the orgasmic energy sparking between them. The yellow energy of Anna's Soulmind started to spiral out of her solar plexus, begging to be joined with Terry's. In response, his white light began to spiral out of his chest. When the energies joined, they both yelled in ecstasy, feeling as if they were melting into one being. At that moment, they were both the one being sought—the one with the highest energy. Both of their auras illuminating, practically filling the entire room. Priya had her hands over her eyes, but was peeking through her fingers. Having a Soulmind herself, she could see their energy as plain as anything solid.

"Anna... Anna..." Terry moaned her name, lost in the euphoria.

As Anna rode his cock, she almost forgot who she was. She had become pure bliss, pure pleasure—the Singularity Pulse ejaculating the Spiralverse into the cosmos. Terry's hands went up to her breasts, squeezing and massaging them. Anna winced slightly as he did. "Oh, I'm sorry," Terry said lovingly. "The needle wounds..." He took his hands from her breasts.

Anna grabbed his wrists and put Terry's hands back on her tits. "It's okay," she whispered. "I want you to touch them. Play with them. Massage my nipples. Love me like you would a life-long lover." She smiled warmly and her eyes shone of compassion. Then the orgasmic ecstasy started to build again and she closed her eyes, grinding her tight pussy against Terry's pelvis. "Oh my God, Terry," she squealed, "what kind of energy are you hiding in this sexy, tight body of yours?"

Terry moaned deeply, his eyes closed and his face flushed. "Uhhh, fuck, Anna! You really knew what I needed."

"Because it was what I needed too..." As she said this, the braid of their intertwined Soulminds impaled both of their bodies, weaving and creating a magnificent tapestry of light. Their auras rippled the air around them and they started to lift up off the table into the air. "Holy shit! Are we floating?" Anna exclaimed as they hung suspended in space by their own energy.

The room became dense with the Kundalini of their Soulminds, and they were floating on that wave. As Anna started to ride Terry again, moving her hips in a way that sent Terry into what felt like a whole other Dimension. Slowly they began to ascend higher into the air.

Suddenly, and without warning, the three men in black suits opened the door and rushed into the activity room. Two of them pulled Anna off of Terry roughly by her arms. She squirmed and kicked, enraged that their lovemaking was so rudely interrupted. "NO! NO!" she screamed. "You fucking faggot cocksuckers let me go! Let me go! FUCKING FUCK YOU ASSHOLES!"

Once Terry was no longer inside Anna, their Soulminds detached quite immediately and Terry fell hard onto the table. "Ow, motherfucker," Terry groaned.

At this point Priya had her hands completely over her face and she was screaming at the top of her lungs. The two men who had pulled Anna off of Terry were now forcing her nightgown back over her head. Once it was on, they dragged her from the room as she kicked, and screamed, and protested.

Before Terry could recover from the fall, the third black suit-man pulled a syringe from his pocket and injected him in the shoulder. "I think that's enough fun for one day," the man said angrily.

"You fucker," Terry groaned in dissent. "Was the shot really necessary? Fuck, I *totally* hate you guys already..."

The man didn't reply, irritated enough as it was to have to deal with the situation. He squeezed Terry's arm hard enough to bruise him. As he dragged Terry toward the door, he scooped up the clothes Terry had disrobed before the coitus. Priya was still screaming as they left the room and the man locked her and Jeremy inside.

"You're just full of surprises, aren't you?" the man grumbled as he dragged Terry back to his cell.

"I don't know," Terry shot back cheekily. "Why don't you take off your clothes and find out?"

The man scoffed. "You're disgusting, despicable human filth. I really hope they dissect you until all that's left are scientific specimens." He shoved Terry in his cell, threw his clothes at him, and slammed the door, making sure it locked completely.

"Yeah, well fuck you too!" Terry yelled at the man through the door, still naked with a hard-on. "At least you could have waited until both of us could cum, you fucking prick! Cutting me off before I can nut is worse torture than anything else you all put me through today!"

… PART 15

Maya Awakens

*"Dreams are gateways to the other worlds... Dreams are the
shadow self let loose... Dreams are where we will meet again.
In love. In yearning. In fear. Dreams, like countries,
are ideas; all reality gestates first inside a dream. Dreams are
information for those who will read their tea leaves come morning.
They are tiny little maps of the soul. Of every secret we push aside
while we are awake... Dreams are miracles. Dreams are portents.
Dreams know you better than you know yourself. They know everything."*
- Libba Bray, *The King of Crows*

*"But here, meaning was dead. Future and past were dead. Love
and life were dead. Even death was dead, because anything that
excited emotion was unwelcome here. Only nothing: once and for all,
nothing."*
- Clive Barker, *The Damnation Game*

*"The darkness is not dark to you; the night is bright as the day, for
darkness is as light."* - Psalm 139:12

TEN

The old city of Chicago had been all but abandoned. This was obvious to Jessica as they flew over the patched-up streets and between the ruins of buildings which had never been rebuilt. Completely stunned into silence, she marveled at the magnificent wreckage. Of course, she had not been in the Hollow Dimension when Maya tore the fabric between Dark Tethers and the human world. This was all new information to Jessica—almost more than she could process.

"Was this done by that lady—Maya?" Jessica asked. "I only saw her once, but I had the creepy feeling that she was planning, or trying, to do something like this."

Nikola nodded grimly. "That is what I've heard. Myself, like you, was not in this Dimension when it happened. I've only heard stories; the spectral entities who were possessing people and making them commit atrocious acts on each other; Maya assimilating a piece of Terry's Soulmind so that she could tear a rift in the fabric between the Hollow Dimension and Dark Tethers, after which she conjured huge black tentacles which tore most of these buildings down. That's the story, however, we can physically see the aftermath." They both looked around at the ghost-city which looked like the remains of a city after war had ravaged it.

"Looks completely deserted," Jessica commented.

"It is for the most part," Nikola continued, "except for the few groups who like to live in the rubble of the abandoned buildings."

"And you're not from the Hollow Dimension?" Jessica asked. "I just picked up that you said that earlier."

"That's right," Nikola answered as they approached the edge of the old city. "I'm originally from the Kingdom of the Stone Queen—er, or it's just The Kingdom now."

"But then," Jessica started, "you must have a Soulmind to travel between Dimensions."

"Yes, you're absolutely correct," he admitted. "However, I didn't always have a Soulmind. To make a long story short, let's just say that I ended up being activated and then I managed to escape my own Dimension, finding myself here."

"That can happen? That's cool!" Jessica commented.

Nikola laughed. "You *have* been away for a while, haven't you? Seems like there is a lot you aren't aware of."

"Then tell me something more about this new future," she said.

"Well, at this point," Nikola began, "most of the population are activated, meaning they have Soulminds. When the Great Shift happened, most—if not all—of the ones who couldn't be activated just died off."

"What? Really?" Jessica was trying to grasp the implication of this. "Like who? Who were incapable of being activated."

"Oh, you know," he answered, "politicians, police, military, corporate overlords, the government—the ones who were more interested in maintaining control of the slaves, meaning the mass population, more than conscious evolution. Those people weren't able to survive in this higher frequency... Oh, look, welcome to Neo-Chicago."

As they flew over the border of the old city and into the new, Jessica stared in awe at how futuristic everything looked. There were buildings that looked like they stretched a mile into the sky. Flying cars zoomed all around them. There was also ground traffic below them and people walking on the bright sidewalks of Neo-Chicago.

"This is amazing," Jessica said in wonderment. "I never imagined to see something like this in my lifetime."

"Your lifetime may be longer than you think," Nikola commented offhand.

Jessica didn't really catch the comment or the implication therein. "How did this come about?" she wanted to know.

"If you must know," he replied, "my personal profession is scientist and inventor—*Technician of High Technology*. I was the architect for some of these buildings you see stretching unfathomably high into the sky. Also, I brought the technology of these flying cars with me from my own Dimension. I perfected it, of course."

"Perfected it? How?" Jessica asked. "How do they not crash into each other all the time?"

"That, my dear, is the very thing I perfected," Nikola expounded. "To be completely honest with you, I borrowed some technology I was shown by the Greys and I mixed it with the technology of the Merkabah field, making it programmable in each of these flying cars. Here." He pointed to a medium-sized touchscreen on the right side of the driver's seat. "The Merkabah is infinitely programmable and you can put in any settings you want into the controller here. The default settings are just to, you know, protect the vehicle as well as adjust course when it gets too close to another vehicle's Merkabah Field."

"Yes," Jessica continued, "I know about the Merkabah Field, but I didn't know that it could be configured around objects and not just living beings. It is the human lightbody after all."

"Very astute observation," Nikola complimented. "That is the very reason that I combined it with technology I got from the Greys. Otherwise every singe Merkabah Field would have to be programmed through a human's field with the meditation. That would be tedious, in my opinion. It's easier to just program the control panel in the factory."

Jessica nodded. Their flying car dipped down and they swooped through an open plaza which looked quite familiar to her. She spotted the Picasso sculpture in front of a new building; it looked exactly like the one that was in Daley Plaza. "Is that the Picasso sculpture?" she asked.

Nikola laughed at this as if it was an inside joke. "No, no," he answered. "This one is a replica. The original one was so defiled and graffitied that there was no way it could be salvaged. So we just made a new one for the people who were nostalgic about the old city."

"That makes sense," she remarked. "So where's Terry? Can we go see him?"

"I really shouldn't tell you were he is," Nikola admitted. "He might even be off-planet right now for all I know."

"Off-planet? What?" Jessica didn't understand. "What do you mean? Why can't you tell me?"

Nikola shook his head and put his finger to his lips. "Shhh," he hushed. "Telling you might compromise the mission. Total discretion is my prerogative. Terry's become quite a legend on Earth, don't you know?"

"He's a legend?" Jessica asked, raising her eyebrows. "I can't say that that totally surprises me."

"If it weren't for him, this future would never have been possible," Nikola said, smiling. Then he turned to look at Jessica. "Now, unfortunately, our tour has come to an end."

"Come to an end?" Jessica exclaimed. "Already? Why do you say that? I want to see more!"

"I know, sweetheart," Nikola said compassionately. "However, you and I know that you're not really here. You're still in the Timestream."

"Huh?—" And before Jessica could utter any more questions, Nikola touched the center of her forehead, producing a circle of white light. In an instant, she was back, caught in the white-light current of the Timestream.

ELEVEN

In the silence between the three, the sound of the front door closing behind Darren's departure seemed just a little too loud. Rob looked at Mothman, gave him a weak smile, and without saying a word turned and walked back through the kitchen. He walked all the way through the house, into the bar area at the far end of the house, and took the back stairs to the top floor. The double doors to Terry's parents' bedroom were closed, as they usually were, since none of them went in that room very often. Even though there were no dead bodies lingering there and rotting, they all agreed that that area was still pretty creepy. An unsettling presence seemed to linger there.

But at that moment, Rob didn't care about that. Without hesitation, he opened the doors and went inside, knowing exactly what he was looking for. There was a fancy wooden chest at the end of the King size bed. Rob knew that there was quite a bit of cash that Terry's parent's had stashed inside. Opening the top of the chest, he looked inside amongst the mementos and souvenirs within. There it was, under a hand-sew quilt, were stacks of hundred-dollar bills. Rob didn't know exactly how much was there, but it was a lot.

"You found the money too?"

Rob looked up, startled, not expecting to see Mothman standing in the doorway. "Yeah," Rob responded. "I guess I did."

Mothman laughed. "You know you're not the only one who's snooped around this house."

"I'm not surprised," Rob admitted. "Knowing you, you probably scoped out the whole damn place the moment you found out Terry's parents were no longer in the picture. I mean, you are known by some people as being a snoop and a thief. Not that I'm judging you. You are my friend, after all."

Mothman took a couple steps closer to Rob and sat down on the carpet. "Yeah, that's fair. I used to do a lot of stupid shit back in the day. But since I've been awakened, I've actually calmed down on a lot of that stuff."

"That's good to hear." Rob took out a couple stacks of hundreds and shoved them in his pocket.

"But I did find some naked pictures of Terry's mom when she was younger in that chest," Mothman said, grinning from ear to ear.

Rob just shook his head. "I bet you did, you pervert. Just don't cum around me when you're stroking off to them."

"So what did he say to you?" Mothman asked, changing the subject. "Darren, I mean."

"Well," Rob sighed, "now that Terry is gone, and we don't know how long until he'll be back, it's my responsibility to take over running the Playground. Terry entrusted me with the list of members, their contact info, and blah blah blah. You know." He stared off into space as if deep in thought. After a while he said, "He wants me to expand. Expand the Playground. Like travel around the country establishing them in specific cities, and also in other countries too. Which reminds me, I'm gonna have to go back to my house to grab my passport..."

"What?" Mothman said, suddenly realizing the implications of what Rob was saying. "You fucker, I want to go travel too! Take me with you!"

Rob shook his head. "It's easier if I just take care of it myself, try to stay under the radar. And besides, I need someone to be my contact here, to protect the house and keep me informed of anything. Especially if Terry comes back."

"You're just gonna leave me here alone, Rob? That's cold..." Mothman said, shaking his head.

"You won't be alone, bro," Rob continued. "At least I don't think you will be. Who knows, you might even be able to get lucky with Eden." He winked at Mothman.

Mothman pushed Rob's arm playfully. "Yeah, I wish. That bitch like wears a chastity belt against me. Bitches usually always spread their legs for me. I don't know what it is with her. She's immune to my charms..." he trailed off.

"She's in love with Terry, that's why," Rob answered. "And maybe you're just not her type. Look at Darren; she definitely likes that big black cock. I know I'm not gay, but I would suck that cock all day just *because* it's BLACK."

Mothman smirked and shook his head. "You and your black fetish, Rob. And you say *I'm* a pervert. I think you might just be the weirdest one out of all of us. You just know how to *act* smart when you need to."

"This is a strangeness contest now?" Rob commented. "And if I know how to act smart, maybe you should take a lesson from me, Mothman."

Bursting out laughing, Mothman shot back, "As if! Take a lesson from a black-obsessed, in-the-closet, trying-not-to-be-queer guy? Rob, you can't fool your best friends. We were all in your basement circle-jerking for years growing up."

"Shut up about that!" Rob said through gritted teeth. "I told you: what happens in the basement *stays* in the basement!"

"What are you two butt-pirates talking about?"

Rob and Mothman both jumped, startled by the surprise of hearing Eden's voice. "Nothing!" they both said at the same time, giggling nervously as they looked at Eden standing in the doorway.

She raised her eyebrows. "Weird to see you guys in Terry's parents' room... Anyway, I wanted to let you queer-baits know that I ordered a pizza. I figured that we all might need some comfort food after the stress of hearing about Terry's kidnapping... I know I do. I miss him already."

"Pizza!?" Mothman exclaimed, almost jizzing in his pants from excitement. "I love yooooou! Did I mention that I love you? You are the *best!*"

"I know I am," Eden quipped. She winked and blew them a kiss as she left the room.

TWELVE

Time was meaningless in the Facility. To Terry, in his cell, it seemed to stretch and then contract in an arbitrary way depending on what his mind was doing. Was this True Time? he wondered to himself. There were no clocks and no windows, so there was no way to gauge what time of day or night it was. Time was, and time was not.

He sat on his cot, in a lotus pose, meditating. Several times he tried to Astral Project, but he couldn't quite get his Astral Form to detach from his body. How could Anna do it? he wondered. As he thought this, Anna's Astral Form walked through the wall and into Terry's cell. "Hey!" he said. "I was just thinking about you."

"I know," she returned. "I picked up on your thoughts." She smiled at him as if they had been lovers for years.

"How is it that you can still Astral Project within these walls?" Terry asked. "Whatever those pills are, or radiation they're pumping in here won't allow me to do it."

Anna shrugged and went over to sit next to Terry on his cot. They turned to face each other like two yogis meditating together. "I haven't the slightest fucking idea," she admitted. "I just can. Despite what those cock-knockers pump into me, I still seem to be able to override it with certain powers."

"Maybe that means you're stronger than me," Terry said, looking down into his lap.

Anna shook her head. "It doesn't mean anything," she insisted. "Just that we have different abilities. One isn't necessarily above or below the other."

"Yeah," Terry nodded. "I can see that. I just wish that I could call forth enough energy to escape. Maybe break through the walls. If we were physically together, our energies combined might generate enough power to blast through this place. Blow it to pieces."

"Maybe," Anna continued. "That would be fucking fantabulous, wouldn't it? Unfortunately I don't think that they're ever gonna let us back in the same room together. After that stunt we pulled."

Terry sighed. "You're probably right... How long have I been in here, Anna? I feel so pilled-out from those capsules they've been feeding us. My head feels like it's swelling and then shrinking at the same time. Sometimes I feel like I've only been in here for hours, other times I feel like it's been weeks."

"Your guess is as good as mine, babes." She smiled warmly, pleased to have the company even if they weren't both in their physical bodies.

Terry rested his hands on his knees with his palms up. Then Anna gently placed her Astral hands on his solid ones. Terry could almost feel it. At least he could feel her presence. "You called me babes," he smiled. "Like we're already lovers."

"We *are* already lovers, aren't we?" Anna said. "You've been inside me in more ways than one." She winked, a mischievous grin pulling at her Astral lips.

Terry blushed. "Stop it," he said, playing with her. "You're so naughty. Don't forget, you penetrated me too."

"Ooh," Anna cooed. "Now who's the naughty one? I wish we had met on the outside, so we wouldn't have these motherfucking cocksucking walls between us."

"You have such a dirty mouth too," Terry laughed.

"I wish I could use this dirty mouth to suck your cock right now," she grinned. "Too bad there's no solidity to me right now." Terry reached out to touch her and his hand went right through her. "See. If I even tried to ride you with my Astral pussy, you wouldn't even feel it. I'd probably just, like, fuckin', sink down and pass right through your body."

"Aww," Terry whined. "And you have such a nice pussy too. My cock is aching to be inside you again."

"I know I have that sweet pussy," she remarked. "She's furry and wants me to sit on your face."

"Oh my God!" Terry moaned. "Don't tease me and get me all horny. Then I'll have to jerk off and get jiz all over my cell." He laughed and then leaned forward to kiss Anna on her Astral lips.

They got the proximity correct, and they stayed still so Anna's head wouldn't just go through Terry's like a ghost. And the memory of what their kiss felt like almost made it real.

The Director stood in a room full of monitors watching the playback of Anna and Terry having sex in the activity room. Momentarily, Doctor Morkian came in to join him carrying the same iPad he had before. The Director stared at the screen, watching Anna ride Terry as he laid on the table. His right hand was stroking his chin thoughtfully, and his left hand was tucked under his right elbow. None of the Soulmind energy showed up on the monitor.

"Doctor, can we put the filter on this so we can see their energy?" the Director asked.

"Certainly, Director," Doctor Morkian answered. "However, this monitor is not equipped to handle that. I'll have to cast it onto this plasma monitor down here." He pointed to a screen in the row below. The Doctor pressed some buttons on the iPad and the image blipped out from the first screen and then showed up on the plasma screen below. Now they could clearly see Anna's yellow aura, Terry's white aura, and their energies braiding together from the solar plexus.

"My God," the Director whispered. "In all my years working in Project S & M, I've never seen *anything* like this. Have you, Doctor?"

Doctor Morkian shook his head. "Never, Director. This is most fascinating. Most remarkable, indeed. I'll have to run some more tests and analyze the wave patterns, but the level of their *combined* Soulmind fields was higher than anything I've ever come across. This bears a lot more study, Director. Before we brought Terry—uh, Subject Four—here, Anna—Subject Two— was our most powerful subject by far. Combining the Soulminds of *both* of them seems to multiply the energy exponentially. Maybe even bringing them up to the level of Super Nova—"

"And that's exactly why we need to keep them separated," the Director interrupted. "We can't risk having another incident like we did before. It's not ideal to have to kill subjects, but we will if we have to."

"Yes, of course, Director," Doctor Morkian said subserviently.

"My God, look..." The Director pointed at the screen. It was the point in the playback where Anna and Terry started to float up off of the table.

"Remarkable. Fascinating. Marvelous..." Doctor Morkian whispered, genuinely in astonishment of what he was witnessing.

"We can take samples from the room readings to study," the Director ordered. "But *this* is dangerous. And we can't allow it to get out of our control."

They sat silently on Terry's cot, trying to hold hands as best they could; one flesh and blood, one ethereal. Anna smiled at Terry, wishing she could physically touch him, and hug him, feeling his heartbeat pound against her chest.

There was a sudden knock at the door of the cell. "Hey! We're coming in! Don't try any funny business!" a voice yelled from the other side.

The abruptness of this interruption shook both of them out of their loving meditation. Anna looked at Terry with a dismayed expression. "You better go," he whispered.

"Why?" she whispered back. "It's not like they'll be able to see me."

"I don't trust them with a ten foot dick," Terry commented.

Anna laughed. "You're beginning to sound like me. Hope to see you soon, my love," she said as she blew Terry an Astral kiss and disappeared into the wall.

The cell door creaked open right after Anna was gone. "Oh, look, it's the triplets again," Terry joked, making fun of the three men in identical black suits.

"Come on, wise ass," the suit-man closest to Terry said. "The Director wants to see you in Observation Room One. Let's go." He grabbed Terry by the bicep and dragged him into the hall.

"So are all you guys clones?" Terry continued the joke. "Or are you all from the same mother? Bastards of course, naturally."

"Ha-ha," suit-man pretended to laugh as he pushed Terry down the hallway. "Shut your faggot-ass mouth or we'll shut it for you permanently."

"Oh, the big meat-head has threats," Terry shot back sarcastically. "I bet you all that aggression is from your latent homosexual tendencies. What? Daddy didn't love you enough? I bet you if all three of you sucked each other off on break, you wouldn't be so uptight." One of the other suit-men smacked Terry on the back of the head. "Ow! So aggressive. So that's your thing? Domination? Gets your dicks hard? I still stand on that offer of you guys coming to my room, take your clothes off, and we'll all have some fun."

They stopped at an open door which was labeled *Observation Room One*. The suit-man squeezing Terry's arm leaned in and whispered into his ear, "You are the most disgusting subject we've ever had the displeasure of working with. You're vile, perverted, and a slut. I really hope they end up murdering you. We would laugh as we watch you bleed out, begging for your life." Then he shoved Terry into the room and locked him in.

"I want my phone call!" Terry yelled, pounding on the door. "Guess they didn't get the joke," he mumbled, turning around to look around the room. It was almost identical to the other observation room except there was no chair in the center, and he noticed some kind of gun mounted on the wall close to the ceiling in the corner. It looked very intimidating. Terry went over to the two-way mirror and cupped his hands around his eyes, trying to peer through it. Frustrated, he realized that he couldn't see the faces of his captors, only the reflection of his own eyes staring back at him. The glass seemed more re-inforced than in the other observation room. Terry guessed that they learned their lesson from his Merkabah almost breaking through. He would bet that Anna was powerful enough to break through the old glass as well.

The intercom buzzed and Terry looked around, waiting for the disembodied voice of the Director. "Welcome back," the voice said through the speaker. "We trust you've been enjoying your stay in the luxurious S & M hotel and spa." The sarcasm was obviously overt, and Terry could hear chuckling from the other side of the intercom.

Terry scoffed. "Oh, yes," he quipped back, "the Metaphysical Massages are just top notch. And the personal escort service—whoowee, I could hardly tell that she was an A.I. robot."

"Okay, enough with the jokes," the Director said, sounding annoyed by the semi-antagonistic banter. "Let's see your Soul-mind weapon."

"What weapon?" Terry played dumb. "I don't know what you're talking about."

The Director sighed. "You're going to try this bullshit again? How well did it work for you last time? Come on, Subject Four, let's see what you got."

Terry laughed morbidly, staring into the mirror. "Subject Four? I have a fucking name you know. It's Terry Motherfucking Broswald! And I won't show you goddamn shit! GO. TO. HELL."

"You're choosing to play it that way?" the Director replied impatiently. "Have it your way."

Suddenly a shot fired from the rifle mounted on the wall. The bullet barely missed Terry and disappeared into the floor about a foot to his right. He flinched from the suddenness and the loudness of the shot. His ears rang.

"That was just a warning shot," the Director continued. "The next one goes through your arm. So I suggest you cooperate."

On the other side of the glass, the Director stood staring at Terry through the thick two-way mirror. The Lieutenant with the jumpsuit and helmet stood on his right. Doctor Morkian wasn't there this time.

Terry stuck his tongue out at the mirror. "What was it you asked to see? My ass?" He turned his back on the glass and pulled his pants down, showing his white ass to the Director and the jumpsuit-man.

"Ugh," the Director grunted, disgusted. "So juvenile. Let's shoot another couple warning shots," he whispered.

In a split second that seemed almost instantaneous, Terry pulled his pants up and flipped around. His aura exploded around him in white light, the handle of his machete popped out of his solar plexus, and he pulled the blade from his chest. When the two shots fired from the rifle, it felt like the machete pulled Terry's arm to the exact spots where the blade could deflect the bullets. *Ping! Ping!*

"Wait! What just happened?" yelled the Director. "That was too fast for me. I wasn't watching the monitor."

To his naked eye, all he could see was the handle of the machete in Terry's hand, and the bullets seemingly being deflected by thin air.

"He's got some sort of light-blade. He deflected the bullets," the Lieutenant replied, holding the small monitor up so that the Director could see.

The Director stared in awe into the monitor. Terry stood in a defensive stance, brandishing his Soulmind weapon, with his aura aflame and spirals of white emanating from his solar plexus.

"We have a girl with a battle axe and a boy with a machete..." the Director said reflectively. "What did Priya—Subject Three—have?"

"She had some kind of, uh, blaster," the Lieutenant answered. "Like a laser gun that shot Soulmind energy. That one was especially strange, I thought."

"Yes, yes..." the Director whispered thoughtfully. "And Jeremy can't do shit anymore... Well, he shits himself but that's about it."

Terry just stood there, ready in case he was shot at again. "Hey, fucker!" he yelled at the glass. "What's your next move?"

"Should we ratchet it up more to see what he does?" the Director asked the Lieutenant.

"Uhhh," the jumpsuit-man hesitated. "Do you really want to push it, sir? You don't want to kill him, do you? He is the one the Agency had been searching for after all."

"I think you underestimate him, Lieutenant," the Director remarked. "Do you have the controls in case I need to shut it down quickly?"

The Lieutenant nodded and handed the Director the iPad with the controls on the screen. Holding up the small monitor again, the jumpsuit-man made sure the Director could see it. "You're sure about this, sir?" he asked one last time.

"You're going to want to watch the show," the Director said, smiling at the Lieutenant. Then he pressed a button.

The rifle mounted on the wall began to shoot bullets in a continuous stream; machine gun fire. It was quick, but Terry was quicker. Instantaneously the golden orb of the Merkabah Field popped out from his heart, surrounding his whole body. The star tetrahedron spun with bright white shimmers. The shield protected him from the gunfire; bullets suspended in midair around the golden sphere like they were caught in a Stasis Field.

The Director watched the monitor in hushed silence with his mouth hanging open. "It's incredible how Subject Four can simply override the effects of the capsules we've given him to suppress his powers in moments of extreme danger and stress. His survival instinct is stronger than anything I've ever seen before. Lieutenant, this subject may just actually be the key to creating the ultimate weapon."

The bullets kept raining down on Terry, getting stuck in his Merkabah Field. He gritted his teeth and squeezed his hands around the handle of his machete. The rage was building and he was beginning to see red. In a minute, the onslaught of the gunfire ceased, and all the bullets clattered to the ground like full-metal rain. The Director continued to stare into the monitor at the image of Terry in all his Pan-Dimensional glory. The sight of him took on an otherworldly atmosphere. The Director couldn't look away; he was mesmerized by this seemingly supernatural being, surrounded by a glowing orb and wielding a blade made of dazzling white light.

The fury swiftly overtook Terry in a brilliant storm of mania and indignation. As if the blade made a decision all on its own, he rushed toward the two-way mirror, pulling the machete back at his shoulder and aiming it at the glass. Without hesitation, he stabbed it straight through with a yell. The Soulmind blade penetrated the two-way mirror, and the Director could see the tip poking through glass on the monitor screen.

"What now, you fascist fuckhead!?" Terry screamed.

At first the Director froze and the Lieutenant yelled, "Director! Shut it down! Blast him now!"

The Director seemed to come out of his trance and pressed a button on the iPad, blasting radiation into the room where Terry was. In seconds all of Terry's Soulmind energy and Merkabah disappeared, and he fell to the floor, unconscious. The handle of his machete clattered to the floor and then disappeared as well.

Breathing heavily, the Director stared at the hole in the glass in front of him. Even the reinforcements couldn't contain Terry's energy. The Lieutenant pulled off his helmet and looked at the Director. They shared a worried look; both of them visibly shaken.

THIRTEEN

It didn't take Rob very long to find the keys to Terry's van. They were sitting on his desk, next to his computer. Terry's bedroom was unoccupied; Eden had apparently vacated the premises. Rob never knew where she went from one day to the next. Mothman was still sleeping in the other room. Without wasting any time, he snatched up the keys and took the van back to his old house to grab a few things he would need for his travels.

The block that Rob's house was on was still in shambles. All of the houses that Trick, Tock, and Tick had destroyed still stood in ruins; their inhabitants long dead. No one had made any effort to rebuild or re-inhabit those homes. He shook his head as he looked at the destruction. Not many people still lived in this neighborhood. It was a strange feeling coming back to his old home. It still stood, and didn't look like it had been vandalized like the other houses. Rob parked in the driveway, wondering whether his parents would be there.

The stench of death still clung to the walls like a cockroach taking a radioactive shit. Rob held his hand over his nose as he entered through the front door. When he made it to the kitchen, he just stared. The air was thick and black with flies. The buzzing was almost defeating. Even though the two dead bodies had almost completely decomposed to skeletons, there was still some black sludge which was being feasted upon by squirming maggots.

"Mom? Dad?" Rob whispered, in shock. Even though it was impossible to recognize these bones without flesh, somehow Rob could sense that these two conglomerations of organic matter used to be his mother and father. Obviously, he didn't want to linger around the death, so he stepped as gingerly as possible to get around the skeletons and the maggots; quickly running up the stairs to get away from the rotting stench.

When Rob went into his bedroom, an eerie feeling fell over him, making his skin crawl. It didn't feel like *his* room anymore. The dominant presence still hanging around was unmistakably Maya. Rob shivered at the thought of her, knowing she was still out there somewhere, even in Dark Tethers, ruminating and biding her time for the next strike. After taking a couple more steps toward his desk, he stopped, feeling the tentacles of another presence. Rob closed his eyes, and the face that came into his mind was Arash. This realization was enough to make his memory jog. It had been quite a while since Arash Khan had entered his thoughts. Where was he anyway? Rob wondered. He never seemed to have come back after their excursion to the Public Works building.

Shrugging off these thoughts, Rob went to find his passport. He rummaged around in a couple top drawers of his desk and found what he needed right away. Strangely enough, Rob didn't open the drawer that contained the little glass cylinder that still held a piece of Jessica's Soulmind.

The house was beginning to give Rob the creeps and he decided he wanted to be out of there as fast as he could. He went to his closet and pulled out a small green duffel bag, and without taking the time to pick and choose, he just threw some clothes in—some t-shirts, jeans, socks, and boxers. Rob figured that was all he would need; he wasn't an extravagant traveler. Without missing a beat, he slung the duffel bag over his shoulder and got the fuck out of there, deciding never again to go back to that house of death.

Rob chewed on his nail distractedly as he drove back to Terry's house. He couldn't seem to get the thoughts of Arash out of his head. "Where the fuck did that guy go?" he mumbled out loud to himself.

When Rob got back, he threw his duffel bag down by the kitchen table. By this time Mothman was up and cooking some sausages on the stove. "Hey, motherfucker," he said, greeting Rob. "I was wondering where your ass went. Stealing the car and everything." He stabbed one of the sausages in the pan with a fork.

"Yeah," Rob said, feeling exhausted already. "I had to run back to my house to find my passport. And throw some clothes in a bag. You'll never guess what I found."

"What's that?" Mothman wanted to know.

"My parents are dead," Rob informed. "Fuckin', almost rotted completely down to skeletons. Probably the work of Trick, Tock, and Tick, I bet."

"Hmm, you don't say," Mothman commented, munching on the end of a sausage. "And how do you feel about this?"

Surprisingly, neither one of them seemed to exhibit any emotion concerning the deaths. Rob shrugged. "I dunno," he admitted. "I don't really feel anything at all. Just kinda neutral."

"Good, that's probably good," Mothman remarked, turning back to the stove and throwing a few more sausages in the pan. "You want some sausages?"

Rob shook his head as he sat down at the kitchen table. "Nah, I'm okay... Hey, you remember that weird Indian kid named Arash? He had us all go on that excursion to the Public Works building—you weren't there, obviously. He thought there was meth in that building. Huh." Rob chuckled, remembering it.

"Oh, yeah!" Mothman replied. "Whatever happened to that fucking guy?"

"That's what I was trying to figure out," Rob admitted. "I haven't seen him at *all* since then."

Mothman shrugged. "Who the fuck knows with Indians? They're always disappearing into their teepees, or their wigwams, or whatever. Maybe he ate some peyote and went on walkabout."

"That's Native Americans, you idiot," Rob said, wanting to smack Mothman over the head. "He's *Indian*. Like from fucking India, moron."

"Hey," Mothman put his hands up, "you don't have to get all aggro on me. Maybe *you* need a little peyote and a walkabout. Just saying..."

Rob tapped the surface of the table with his index finger. "Maybe you're right..." he trailed off for a moment. "Hey, you seen Eden around?"

"Hah!" Mothman laughed. "You kidding? I don't know where that bitch is at half the time. I bet you she's up trickin' in Niles."

"Nah," Rob countered. "She doesn't need to trick. There's enough money in that chest upstairs to support everyone in this household."

FOURTEEN

Dreams are a fickle friend. Dreams can lure you in with promises of pleasure, then deliver your greatest horror. Dreams can be the key to understanding the subconscious. Dreams can be perceived in a multitude of different ways. A nightmare to one person might be an adventure to another. Dreams may contain meaning; messages to be interpreted upon waking. Or dreams may just be a pointless, incoherent jumble of images and symbols. Or they could carry you on the waves of the Taboo Zone, opening you up to your most forbidden desires.

Terry slept fitfully in his cell. His dreams were scattered like the last dregs of butter over a burnt piece of toast. In other words, he felt stretched to the point of almost breaking. Slipping in and out of Dreamsphere, Terry began to unconsciously link a pattern in his dreams: Maya. In this feverish sleep, he kept reliving that moment of falling off the roof of the John Hancock building, finally culminating in the strangest embrace he'd ever experienced. Sweat poured from his brow as he tossed and turned on his cot, unable to awake. One second he was fighting with Maya, both trying for the death of the other, then the next second they were in each other's arms, kissing. Was this a nightmare? Or a sex dream?

Desperately he wished to wake. The thin sheet draped over him was becoming hopelessly twisted and knotted from all of the tossing and turning. Terry started to mumble something in his fitful sleep. It sounded like: "It's inside you... It's inside you..."

It was the storm again: snow and lightning and thunder. On top of the John Hancock they did battle: Terry Broswald of the Hollow Dimension and Maya of the Dark Tethers. However, in the dream Terry just couldn't seem to reclaim the part of his Soulmind that she had stolen. He was blind with rage, wanting to kill the one who had brought so much destruction into the Hollow Dimension—then lighting flashed and the dream immediately changed. Terry was laying on top of Maya and they were making out passionately. Their tongues were all curiosity, like Octobers exploring the caves of Meddia. They rolled around the roof as the snow continued to fall, stroking each other, moaning, licking. Until they just rolled completely off the side of the roof.

Terry gasped and awoke quite suddenly. Bolting upright, he grasped at the air as if reaching for someone who wasn't there. Breathing heavily, he held his fist to his chest as his heart beat into his ribcage like a bully kicking him from the inside. "Maya... Maya..." Terry whimpered, half-delirious, not quite sure if he was awake or still dreaming. "I should have killed you when I had the chance," he grumbled. "Or fucked you... I can't decide which..."

In a sort of trance, he began to untwist his sheet, trying to straighten out the chaos he perceived before him. Then he began to mumble Maya's name again, over and over, almost like a magick spell or mantra. As he repeated the name, Terry was unaware that a black portal was opening up below where he sat on his cot. He said Maya's name a couple more times and then fell through the portal, into the darkness.

"What the fuck!?" he yelled as he fell through what seemed like dark gray clouds. Or maybe it was just thick fog all made up of different shades of fluctuating gray. He couldn't quite be sure, but they almost seemed solid, or at least thick enough to slow his descent. Desperately, Terry tried to tune into his Merkabah and pop out the golden orb so he could fly. It was useless. Wherever he was wouldn't allow him to attach to his lightbody. *Or maybe it's the pills that they've been feeding me*, Terry thought. Either way, his Merkabah wouldn't work for shit.

None of this really mattered since a few moments later, he smacked into the ground. "Uhh, son of a cunt," Terry groaned, not sure if all his bones were shattered. The floor, or ground, was the same gray as the fog all around him. Terry wondered where the hell he was. He didn't recognize it as a Dimension he'd been to before. Slowly, he pulled himself to his feet, a little wobbly. The fog was so dense he couldn't see more than a few inches in front of his face. "Fuckin' fog," Terry complained. "Disperse!" he commanded, swiping his hand through the gray in front of him. Surprisingly, it obeyed.

As the fog cleared, a small hovel-like dwelling made of what looked like clay came into view in front of him. *Okay, that's weird,* he thought. He approached with caution. The door to the hovel was wooden, round, and didn't look like it had a lock. Terry went up to it and knocked twice. The door suddenly swung open inward. An arm shot out from the shadows within and grabbed Terry by the collar of his sweatshirt. All at once he was dragged inside and the door slammed behind him.

"I had a feeling you would come," hummed a familiar voice.

Terry whirled around to stare into that pale face with long black hair cascading down the sides—and those all-black eyes. It was Maya! When Terry felt the anxiety of danger, his Soulmind started to spiral from his solar plexus and the hilt of the machete immediately popped out. He pulled the blade from his body and held it in front of himself in case of attack. "Don't come near me! I'll kill you, I swear I will!"

Maya cackled and waved her hand, dismissing the threat. "Oh, put that thing away. There's no need to try to impress me with how *big* it is. I'm not going to hurt you." She sighed. "That mission was a dismal failure." Maya sat down on the clay floor and crossed her legs. She wasn't wearing that black leotard anymore. Here in her home she was wearing a wispy black dress with bellbottom sleeves.

Terry wasn't sure if he trusted her, but he let go of the machete, and his Soulmind spiraled back into his chest. "Am I dreaming?" he asked, looking around. "This has gotta be a dream, right?" As Terry took in the interior of the hovel, he noted that it was basically bare. They were in a small room that had a small bed in the corner. It sort of surprised Terry, the thought of Maya sleeping. There seemed to be another adjacent room, but its doorway was covered by a long black curtain.

"What is a dream anyway?" Maya said cryptically. "All that we see or seem is but a dream within a dream. Isn't that what they say?"

"That's Edgar Allen Poe," Terry responded, impressed. "How do you know Edgar Allen Poe?"

Maya shrugged. "There is a lot more to me than you would imagine."

"So it would seem," Terry remarked. "And you look... different."

"Oh, yeah? You think so?" Maya continued. "This is my casual outfit. I'm not trying to destroy whole Dimensions right now."

Terry laughed at that. "What's that over there? Past the curtain."

"That's just my temple," she answered. "Where I meditate and do whatever occult things I so choose."

Terry was starting to feel more comfortable, which was somewhat disconcerting. Should he let his guard down? He didn't feel like there was an immediate threat. Feeling a little tired, Terry went over and sat down on the bed.

"Trying to get in my bed already?" Maya joked. "We skipping the foreplay?"

"What?" Terry blushed. "I just ended up here, it's not like I *wanted* to come."

Maya stood up slowly and took a couple steps toward Terry sitting on the bed. "Oh, I think you *want* to *cum*. You showing up here wasn't an accident, and don't play like it was. I can feel you. Remember, there's already been a piece of you inside of me. Now I know you want to put a different part inside." She smiled seductively and closed the gap between them until her crotch was pressing against Terry's knee. His face burned red again, but he made no move to pull away.

"What are you doing?" Terry whispered.

Maya didn't answer, she just slid her fingers through his hair and around to the back of his head. Terry closed his eyes, enjoying the sensation of her touch. Then without warning she clenched a handful of hair and wrenched his head back. Terry flinched, his mouth open in surprise. "Agh," he groaned in protest.

"Are you going to be a good little submissive?" Maya said with authority, her black eyes deep wells of nothingness.

"Yeah..." Terry whimpered.

Maya pulled his neck back more. "What was that? I couldn't quite hear you. Don't make me ask again."

"Yes, mistress!" he said, louder this time.

She smiled wickedly. "Now be a good little boy for me and strip."

"What?" Terry sputtered. He was feeling nervous again, yet completely aroused in a way that felt like he was indulging in a forbidden pleasure.

Maya slapped him across the cheek. "Don't talk back to me, you little pervert! Do as you're told so I can look at you in your nakedness." She licked her lips as if anticipating the most delicious meal.

The buzz from the unexpected blow stung Terry's face, and he touched it with his hand. He looked up at Maya with wet puppy-dog eyes. Then he meekly stripped off all his clothes and tossed them on the floor. Trying to cover his hardening cock with his hands, Terry blushed deeper. Maya swatted at his hands. "Don't cover yourself! Let me get a look at you," she ordered. Reaching down, she ran her fingertips up and down his shaft as it got fully erect. "There's my good little Cosmic Pervert," she whispered.

"A what?" he moaned, the pleasure from her touching his cock shot through his body like electric sparks.

"You're Cosmically Perverted," Maya elaborated. "In every Dimension, in every galaxy, on every planet—beautifully, Cosmically Perverted. But with this air of innocence. And I love it. Lay down, I want to taste you."

Without a sound, Terry obeyed, laying back onto the bed. His legs spread, inviting Maya's mouth to explore his body. She knelt down on the floor so her face was closer to his cock. She licked it, she stroked it, she sucked on the tip. Maya utterly enjoyed it, tasting the sweetness of Terry's rock-hard sex and massaging his balls. "Oh, Maya..." he moaned as she took him all into her mouth, lips circling his thick shaft. Saliva dripped from the seal between her wet lips and Terry's cock. Maya could feel him pulse against her tongue.

She took him out of her mouth and stroked it gently. "I don't know why my mind is telling me that this is wrong, but it feels so natural. How often do enemies become lovers? Maybe more than we would think."

"I wish I didn't *have* enemies," Terry emphasized. "I wish everyone would just be my lovers. That's the Spiralverse I want to live in."

Maya chuckled. "You going to give me the whole 'lover not a fighter' speech? Because you fight pretty formidably."

Terry sat up and forced himself to look into Maya's eyes, which still made him feel a bit unnerved. "Any day, I would rather make love than war. Do you want to make love, babe, or do you want to make war?" He leaned down and kissed her on the forehead.

"Right now," she answered, "I just want to make love with you. Undress me," she commanded as she held her arms up over her head. Terry pulled at the sleeves of her black dress and it easily slipped up and off of her smooth skin. She was beautiful, her skin as pale as a porcelain doll. Maya's breasts were full, not like the teenage girls Terry's age that seemed to be just barely past puberty. Her waist was thin, but she had a set of hips, like a woman ready to bear children.

"You have flawless skin," Terry whispered as he stroked her cheek.

Maya closed her eyes and held his hand against her face. Then she kissed his palm. "That's because I never see the sun, silly," she smiled. "How does it feel to know you're about to share a woman with your friend Rob?" Maya winked.

Terry laughed. "It doesn't bother me. To be honest, I've probably had his cock in my mouth at least a couple times," he admitted. "But let's not talk about that."

"Do you want me?" she whispered.

"Yes," Terry answered without hesitation.

"Say it," she cooed. "I want to hear you say it."

"Maya... I want to be inside you."

That was all she needed to hear to take Terry as her lover. She pushed him back onto the bed. Then she crawled on top, straddling him. Terry realized that Maya was slightly bigger than he was, which was intimidating, but he was the submissive.

Maya laid on top of him as she kissed him and licked his face. His hard-on was aching between her legs, pushing its tip against her pussy lips. Then, before he even knew it, she had guided him inside.

"Oh, your cock is so thick," Maya moaned.

"Mmmm, and your pussy feels so divine as it takes me deep inside," he gasped.

Maya pressed her hands against Terry's chest and began sliding her hips up and down as they merged. He put his hands on her feminine hips, and lightly guided her movements as he slid in and out of her. Picking up on a subtle motherly energy, Terry felt like Maya had the potential within her to give birth to new worlds, hopefully not as destructive as the one she attempted previously.

Maya seemed to have picked up on Terry's thought and said, "Will you call me *Mommy* while I fuck you?"

"What?" Terry gasped. His eyelids fluttered as he felt the orgasm building in his balls. "Do you have some sort of incest kink?"

Maya smashed her hand over his mouth. "Don't you talk back to me! Now be a good little boy for Mommy and make me cum with that hot cock! Are you gonna be a good little boy?" She took her hand away from Terry's mouth.

"Yes, Mommy!" he squeaked.

"That's better," she said as she began to moan louder and ride him harder.

"Slap me," Terry whispered.

"Hmm?" Maya looked down at him, not slowing the movement of her hips on his cock. "Did you say something, son? Mommy is busy pleasuring herself with your perverted little cock."

"Slap me!" Terry said louder.

"I don't take orders from you, you pissant! You are my submissive, don't forget that," she said as she smiled mischievously.

Then Terry felt Maya's pussy twitch just slightly, right before a warm liquid started to flow onto his abs, running down his sides and to his balls. He realized that she was pissing on him, and that really turned him on. "Oh, yes, mistress!" he moaned, feeling the orgasm threatening to explode from his nuts and out the tip of his cock. "That's so fucking hot! Give me all your fluids!"

"Shut your hole!" Maya commanded. "You're not allowed to express gratitude! You serve my clitoris!" Then she smacked him across the face without warning.

Terry's face stung in the most delicious way possible. He wanted more, but this time he begged for it silently. Maya must have picked up on his thought waves because she began to choke him, slipping her fingers around Terry's throat in a sensual way that wasn't violent enough to hurt him. As they both felt their euphoria merging and melting into waves of ecstasy, Terry's Soulmind began to spiral out of his chest. It was reaching for Maya's, even though she didn't have one. His white aura lapped like flames around his naked body. Maya could definitely see this energy, but did not make it apparent whether she felt any way about it.

Squeezing Terry's throat, Maya grinded her pelvis against his, as if trying to swallow all of him into her womb. The braid of white Soulmind energy tentatively grew toward Maya's breasts. This energy was searching for her heart, if she even had one. The sound of their moans and screams filled the inside of the small hovel. Orgasm was imminent. The spiral of white light seemed to gather courage and then pierced the space between Maya's breasts as they bounced with the movement. She gasped and her all-black eyes shot open. In Terry's vision, the whole of their surroundings started to spin as his Soulmind penetrated Maya's body. It filled her up, it traveled her bloodstream, and connected her heart to her brain.

"Are you gonna cum soon?" she whispered.

"Oh my God, yes! Uhh, Maya, fuck me harder!" Terry groaned.

"Come with me baby!" Maya enticed. "Give me all that energy. Melt into me and explode!"

"Oh FUCK!" Terry screamed as he felt the ejaculate explode out of his cock and into Maya's cunt. She moaned so loud as she orgasmed, spasming on top of Terry as the pleasure ripped through her body like a Tantric Tsunami. At the moment they both climaxed, a fan of green energy exploded around Maya's head like a halo. An aura appeared around her body in the same emerald green. A spiral of green grew from her solar plexus to meet Terry's white Soulmind. He was almost frozen with awe, not knowing that he had the ability to activate an entity that wasn't even human. Maya's eyes shot open as she felt this new energy coursing through her body. First her eyes were still all black, then they faded to completely white, then finally a green iris appeared with a black pupil in the center.

Maya sighed. "I grow tired of this dominant/submissive game," she said.

"You're done? Because I could still keep going," Terry admitted, his chest still heaving.

"Hardly," Maya answered. Then she rolled off of Terry, laid on her stomach, and stuck her ass in the air. "I want you from behind. Just slam it into me. Give it to me hard."

Pussy juices and semen mixed together and dripped down Terry's cock as he stroked it a few times before getting on his knees behind Maya. He stared down at her ass and pussy spread open before him. The shape of her was flawless. Each of her ass-cheeks was the size of Terry's hand with fingers spread as wide as they could go. He squeezed and massaged the toned muscle of her glutes as he salivated at the sight of Maya's cunt dripping his and her own juices. Leaning forward, he slipped inside as they both gasped from the sensation.

"You're so beautiful," Terry purred as he stroked his index finger down her spine.

"You have no idea how good it is to hear that," Maya breathed. "I don't hear that very often."

Terry leaned down onto her back, still thrusting in and out of her, and kissed her back lovingly. Then he slipped his hands around her ribcage and cupped her breasts, playing with her sensitive nipples. "Babe," he whispered against her back, breath tickling her shoulder blade, "I don't care what you've done. No being deserves to be condemned. I'm not perfect either. But that's what makes us both perfect."

Going upright again, he grabbed Maya's waist and started thrusting harder, just pounding it in and out. "Oh God..." she groaned. "I love the way you beat that pussy up. I needed you so bad! You fuck like a god, my God!"

Another orgasm began to build between them as their energies continued to dance together. White and green flashed all around them, as if the colors of their Soulminds wished to become one as well. Terry watched in wide-eyed wonderment as his own Soulmind spiral began stretching again from his solar plexus and down toward Maya's back, behind her heart. This white Soulmind braid suddenly pierced her spine between her shoulder blades. Maya arched her back and gasped as she felt the energy connect with her like an electric plug penetrating a wall socket. At the moment of merging, a ring of green light circled the connection point. Then what looked like a DNA strand of that emerald green energy traveled down her spine all the way to the base, then up to the crown of her head. Once the green

Soulmind light traveled up through the center of Maya's brain, it hit her crown chakra, Terry once again saw the glory of the thousand-petaled lotus bloom from the crown of Maya's head. Golden light showered down on both of them like orgasmic leaves falling from the World Tree.

The pleasure threatened to send Terry into the void where he became just a nebulous blob of bliss, merged with the energy of whatever Maya was as well. To bring himself back a little bit, he licked his thumb, getting it wet with saliva. Then he rubbed it around the rim of her anus. Slowly, gently, he slipped it inside. Maya moaned with the new pleasure and sensation. "You like that?" Terry said. "You like it when I finger your tight little asshole?"

"Oh, Terry, fuck!" Her moaning was getting louder. "Uhhh, that feels so fucking good. Don't stop, you're gonna make me cum again!"

"I'm gonna cum too!" Terry yelled as he felt he could no longer contain the torrent of cum ready to explode from his balls. Their screams got lost in each other's as they both orgasmed, the only two beings in all of Dark Tethers enjoying an ecstatic union. As the bliss of the *Little Death* took them to places neither of them had ever been, it seemed to Terry that their bodies lost their solidity. For a moment they were just the energy of their Soulminds, braiding together into an eternally orgasmic Ouroboros, endlessly pleasuring itself in the cosmic oneness of no-time, no-space, and no-mind. Some part of both of them remained in this space of purity forever.

That moment was eternal, and yet in no time at all they were solid again, sweat glistening off of their beautiful skin, shining with the afterglow of lovemaking. Maya collapsed down onto the bed and Terry collapsed on top of her, kissing the sweaty flesh of her back, drinking in her scent and flavor of her essence.

"Oh, Terry," Maya whispered, "thank you for giving me the greatest gift one can give another. And only now do I know it."

Terry rolled off of her and turned his head to look in her now-normal eyes. "What do you mean, sweetheart?" he asked.

"You have made me human, with a Soulmind," she answered. "And only now do I understand what I didn't then. That you must share yourself with one willingly, because of one's own desire and longing to join with that other. That piece of you is a gift, not something to be taken by force. And that piece of me is a gift, and I have given it freely. Now a part of you will always be in me, and a part of me will always be in you. Can you forgive me for my actions before I was awakened?"

Leaning forward, Terry kissed Maya on her forehead. "No need, love," he said tenderly. "Truthfully, I am just as much to blame for creating that situation as you were. Forgiveness is overrated. From a higher perspective, we're all One. There is no need to be forgiven because there is no good and evil. To me, there are no good guys, there are no bad guys, all is part of the Infinite Unconditional Love. And within that, no forgiveness is needed because you are perfect. Do not feel guilt needlessly. I don't."

"Yes, you're right," Maya admitted. "I'm not used to feeling like a human yet—and an awakened human at that. It will take me a while to truly grasp the implications of what I have transformed into. And it will take you a while to harness the gift I have given you."

"Hmm?" Terry murmured, almost falling asleep. His body buzzed from the orgasms. "What gift have you given me?"

"The ability to use Matter-Relocation," she explained. "It is the Dark Tethers form of teleportation. You've seen me do it before. So now you have the connection to here and will be able to call on the black ropes to put you in the pod and transfer you anywhere. However, it might take you a few times before you actually can get the hang of it." Maya sat up on the side of the bed and slipped her black dress back over her head.

"What do you mean?" Terry wanted to know.

"So, maybe the first few times you try to use it," Maya continued, "you might not exactly end up in the place you meant to. That's all I'm saying. But after a while you'll get it."

"That sounds like a cool ability..." Terry trailed off, his eyelids drooping.

"I feel strange, now that I'm a human being," she said, half to herself. "What is my purpose now? I can't stay in Dark Tethers anymore. It's not fit for human inhabitation. I thought I would know my purpose right away after being awakened, activated... but it's just as uncertain as before."

"Welcome to the human condition," Terry mumbled. He stretched his arm out to her and she stroked his palm with her fingertips. "Are you leaving, babe?"

Maya shook her head. "Not yet. I'm going to go into my temple and meditate for a while. Until it becomes clear."

"Don't leave me," he said, almost half-asleep now. "I want to feel your warmth."

"It's okay, sweet babe," Maya purred, leaning down to kiss Terry on the lips. "I'll just be past the curtain, I'm still here. You can rest here. I can tell you need it."

Terry reached for her as she stood up and walked toward the black curtain which separated the bedroom from the temple. Before walking through it, Maya turned and looked at Terry one more time. His arm had fallen back onto the bed, his eyes were closed, and he was breathing quietly.

In a few minutes, Terry awoke a little disoriented. It took him a second to remember where he was and what had transpired between himself and Maya. He was still naked as he swung his legs off the bed and went over to the black curtain. Quietly, he peeked inside. There was Maya, sitting on the floor in lotus pose, meditating with her eyes closed. The floor under her was painted with a large pentagram, and around the circumference of the circle around the pentagram were candles that casted an orange glow on Maya. She looked like the picture of a perfect yogi sinking into Samadhi. Terry didn't want to interrupt her meditation, and he was still a little tired, so he went back to the bed and flopped down onto the pillow, feeling wobbly and boneless like a Stretch Armstrong; stretched to its limit and then left to shrink back to normal.

As Terry sank deeper and deeper into Dreamsphere, he could have sworn that he was in the cave of Meddia, slumbering near the waters of Vivere. The huge shape of Sul was there with Remius by his side. Even in their absence, Terry felt the loving presence of these magickal creatures watching over him; protecting him.

FIFTEEN

Eden was frustrated. As she rode the train into the city, she stared into space and chewed on her thumbnail distractedly. Even though Terry didn't choose to leave, he was kidnapped against his will, Eden still felt abandoned. She also felt abandoned by Darren, who seemingly had taken more of an interest in Terry recently. His attention was elsewhere and Eden wished that maybe he would look after her the way he looked after Terry. *Agh!* Eden screamed to herself. The monkey-mind was going full steam and dragging her along the tracks. Not to mention her rational mind was kicking her in the back of the head and saying, *Hey, bitch, they didn't abandon you, they just have other important things to take care of. Not to mention that Terry is a prisoner in some underground government facility where he's most likely being tortured, and you're thinking this selfish bullshit!* However, her emotions were pulling her in a more irrational direction where she just wanted to blame everyone for making her feel so alone.

As the train neared her stop, Eden abandoned trying to analyze her feelings and actions. All she knew was that she was angry and bitter and the words *Fuck everything and fuck all you people!* screamed inside her head. A break was what she needed; a vacation from the Hollow Dimension. Maybe starting a new adventure would occupy her mind enough to forget about Terry. Who knew if he would ever be back, or if he would even survive? Fuck Rob and Mothman, they didn't need her. They were just interested in getting into her pants, or so she thought at that moment.

Finally Eden's stop came and the train screeched to a halt. After getting off the train in the midst of all the depressed faces and people acting like zombies, she quickly made her way over to *angelfuck. Good thing I swiped that key*, she thought, making sure it was still in her pocket. She had a good suspicion that Darren wouldn't be there since he was occupied with Terry's kidnapping and calling an emergency meeting of the Body of Lucifer Christ. As she got to the black door which was the entrance to the club, she looked around to make sure no one was watching her, and quickly unlocked the door and slipped inside.

Before descending the stairs, Eden locked the main entrance behind her so that Darren wouldn't think anything suspicious whenever he showed back up there. After which she quickly ran down the stairs and through the pink door. Darren hadn't done any repairs or even thought about reopening since the big flood when Maya unleashed the Dark Tethers. Furniture from the upper level was still strewn across the dance floor. Eden didn't pay any attention to the state of the club; she knew what she had come for. In a moment she was across the floor and scooting through the curtain into Darren's office. There was no time to waste and Eden just wanted to be gone as quickly as possible.

With no hesitation or time to rethink her decision, Eden went straight over to the bookshelf and slid it away from in front of the Little Door. After opening it, she admired the spiral of blue energy which was the portal to The Kingdom. "Terry, wherever you are," she said into the spiral, "if you really love me, come find me. I miss you and I can't take it. The separation is killing me, and I've never experienced this before. It's like someone has gouged my heart out with a huge hook. Like Chest Death... I don't even know what that means. Anyway," she sighed and took a breath, "I'm out this bitch! And the Hollow Dimension can *go to hell!*"

Eden's jabbering came to an end, and with no further hesitation, she dove into the spiraling blue portal—and into The Kingdom. After she was gone, the Little Door swung shut and the bookshelf slid itself back into place.

SIXTEEN

One thing that Darren didn't particularly like about the Body of Lucifer Christ was that they all wore the same gray cloaks with the hoods up, hiding their faces. For the most part, he didn't wear them, even during special meetings if he could get away with it. What the gray cloaks represented to Darren was the homogenization of the group—all identifying as one entity, individual identities blending into the collective. This wasn't exactly spelled out in the codes, it was just the way Darren felt about the ritual of wearing the gray cloaks. Freedom and individuality were the most important things which he upheld above all else. Disappearing into identity politics or groupthink destroyed all creativity and expansion of consciousness. Wearing the cloak wasn't a requirement by any means, but most of the members chose to and enjoyed wearing them. The Body of Lucifer Christ *did* encourage freedom, individuality, and nonconformity—just the whole wearing the same outfits thing rubbed Darren the wrong way.

They were finally about to have the emergency meeting concerning Terry's kidnapping. Of course, they met in the abandoned church as they always did. The pews were filled with gray cloaks who whispered to each other from underneath their hoods. Meadow stood at the bottom of the steps that led up to the pulpit so that she wasn't above anyone. Darren sat in the front row nearest to her; he was wearing his cloak, but with the hood down around his shoulders.

"Quiet! Quiet, everyone," Meadow said loudly, raising her hand to silence the chattering crowd. "Now, apparently rumors have been circulating from the sound of your jabbering. Yes, Terry Broswald, the Antichrist Christ Lucifer Christ, has been taken by the Shadow Forces."

There were gasps from the congregation. A man's voice from a couple rows back said, "But he's the Antichrist Christ Lucifer Christ! You told us that he is more powerful than all of us *combined*. How could he have been so easily taken by the retarded powers of government?"

Meadow laughed. "You underestimate the retarded powers of government. They have secret programs that are so sinister that you couldn't even fathom them in your most brutal nightmares. Not to mention they have scientists, engineers, and technology that goes way beyond what most of you here have ever seen—there are a few exceptions, you know who you are. The other thing is that Terry hasn't fully matured into all his powers yet. You forget he's still a young Soulmind, he's still going to be fumbling around a bit while he gets the hang of the extent of his abilities. Anyway, our Brother Darren here saw the kidnapping and followed them to the facility where he's being held. Darren, do you want to tell them?"

He nodded and turned around in the pew, facing the congregation. "I was just seconds too late getting to Terry's house. Witnessing the abduction but unable to do anything about it was so painful for me. I still feel regret. Nevertheless, I followed the black SUV that he had been taken into. Thank Lucifer Christ I wasn't spotted. Anyway, I followed them to an abandoned warehouse in the Central Manufacturing District of Chicago. If anyone is familiar with that area or has affiliation to the CIA in any way that can help with potentially figuring out the layout of the facility, come talk to Meadow and myself after the meeting." Darren couldn't think of anything else to say, so he fell silent and turned back toward Meadow.

"It's okay, Darren," Meadow reassured him. "Don't beat yourself up over getting there too late. It wasn't your fault. The Agency is very crafty... Okay, so, down to business. Of course we must break Terry free. He is pivotal to the evolution of the planet's consciousness, and we can't let him be dissected by a sick and depraved government entity who only care about what technology they can produce based on copying the neural pathways in his brain. It's disgusting. They don't care about human beings, just how far they can take automation, A.I., and whatever synthetics they can use to maintain absolute control of the slave-population who are still unactivated. I'm rambling," Meadow sighed and then continued. "What's important to note is that we cannot strike immediately. This is because Terry is not currently in the Hollow Dimension."

"What?" Darren said, shocked. "Where is he?"

Meadow shook her head. "Unfortunately, he is outside my range of sight. Whichever Dimension he is in now, I know not. However, once his energy signature appears again, I'll be able to detect it. That will be our window of opportunity to free him. We will have to call on all our assets. We'll need vehicles, weapons, maybe some body armor." She smiled at Darren who swallowed hard, sweat glistening on his brow. "Sometimes for the sake of expansion, we must tangle with danger. There is no growth without pain. There is no transformation without purge!"

"Yeah!" the congregation yelled in unison, pumping their fists. "No growth without pain! No transformation without purge! No separation, no duality! We are Lucifer Christ!" they continued to chant all together.

Meadow walked over to Darren and took his hand. "Darren, our beloved Brother," she continued, "you've been such a pillar to this community. And it is commendable that you have taken the task upon yourself to primarily look after Terry's safety. If you are still willing, you will continue to be my point man where this is concerned. Now that it has become painfully clear that many Shadow Forces are working to lay claim to our avatar, we must be doubly on guard. Even within the other branches of the Trinity Cult, I hear rumors that both sides of the pair of opposites wish to trap Terry for their own purposes."

"What are you saying?" Darren asked.

"I'm saying that you must be prepared to *run*," Meadow explained. "To take Terry once we free him, and just go, keeping him safe and keeping him hidden."

SEVENTEEN

"Maya?" Terry yawned and rubbed his eyes. He hadn't meant to fall asleep that deeply, and wasn't quite sure how long he'd been out. At first he thought he had dreamed it all, but once he felt the bed he was sleeping in and saw the clay floor of the hovel, he knew that it was as real as when he had activated Mothman. *Holy shit*, he thought, *Maya is a human now, with a Soulmind... What will she do with her newfound transformation?*

"Maya?" he called out again, toward the black curtain. There was no response. Swinging his legs over the side of the bed, Terry reached down to scoop up his clothes off the floor. After pulling them on, he went over to peek into the temple. He was partially surprised to find the room empty. The candles around the circumference of the pentagram had all but burned down to nothing, and where Maya had been meditating in the center was just an empty space. "She did say that she couldn't stay in Dark Tethers now that she's human," Terry muttered to himself. "But now I have to try to Matter-Relocate myself all on my own. The least she could have done was give me some fucking instructions." Grumbling under his breath, he walked into the temple. Maybe standing in the center of the pentagram would give him a better chance of doing it right.

Terry closed his eyes once he was standing in the center of the sacred symbol. A faint orange glow still illuminated the space from the remains of the candles. He began to think of transporting himself to a different location. Suddenly a black circle opened up beneath him and the tentacles of the Dark Tethers began to grow up out of it. In a few moments the black ropes, or tentacles, created a pod around Terry's body. He was terrified; anything could happen. Anything could go wrong. He could feel his heart pounding in his chest and it was all he could do to keep himself from hyperventilating. As he felt the ropes of the dark constricting him, he tried to visualize his own house, his own bedroom.

"That is where I wish to go!" he commanded, trying to tell the black pod where to take him. "I wish to go home! Now take me there!" The tentacles began to compress him more and more until he felt like all his bones were breaking. Then he disappeared, exploding into a cloud of Black Mist.

In a few moments, Terry felt the pain subside and the tentacles began to unwrap him. Before he knew it, they shrank back into the black circle and were gone. "Am I here? Am I home?" he asked desperately, touching his body to make sure he was all there as the room slowly came into focus. Small room. Three walls and a steel door... A cot. He was back in the Facility, locked in his cell. "SON OF A BITCH!" Terry screamed. Maya had been right, he hadn't done it right on the first try; but couldn't it have taken him somewhere else? he thought.

"You're back!"

"Oh, Jesus!" he squealed, jumping at the sound of a voice he was not expecting.

"Did I startle you?" Anna said, smiling. She was sitting on the cot in her Astral Body.

"Yeah, you did," Terry admitted, sitting down next to her on the cot. "I thought I was alone in here. How long was I gone?"

Anna shrugged. "Fuck me if I know. Like I said before, there are no fucking clocks in this goddamn place. You could have been gone for a couple hours. But then again, you could have been gone for a week. Beats the fuck outta me. Good to see you though."

"You too," he replied.

"Where did you go anyway?" she wanted to know.

"Dark Tethers," Terry answered matter-of-factly.

Anna gasped. "No! You're brave. We stay away from that Dimension. Who would want to go to that hellish place of their own choice?"

"I didn't," he explained. "I was sort of dreaming of this entity that's from there, and I guess a portal opened up and brought me there."

"Gnarly, bro," Anna remarked. "Fuck that noise. Stay away from me with those creepy black tentacles. It's all too fuckin'... weird."

Terry laughed. "Weird is right. I just..." he trailed off, not sure how much he should tell Anna about Maya and the whole activating her thing. "Nevermind. Anyway, what's up with you, babe? It's nice to see you naked in your Astral Body, even though we can't really touch each other, which is a bummer."

She nodded in agreement. "I so wish I could fuck you right now. We never even got to finish—at least I know you didn't get to bust a nut. Fucking bastards had to interrupt us, that's so cruel... Anyway, Terry, what I wanted to ask you about: can you teach me how to activate my Merkabah and use it?"

"Sure, I can teach you the meditation and help you tune into it," he replied. "I'm glad you asked, to be honest."

"Why?" Anna said, curious.

"Because my intuition tells me that you might need that ability sooner than you think."

Inside the room with all the monitors, the Director was intently watching the playback of the feed from Terry's cell. He would play it, then rewind it, then play it again. Doctor Morkian entered the room as the Director stared at the screen as if trying to solve an impossible calculus equation.

"What is it, Director?" the Doctor asked as he entered the room.

"Have you seen this? Look," he said, pointing at the screen and beckoning Doctor Morkian to come closer.

"What are we looking at?"

The Director rewound the playback and hit play. The image was of Terry laying in his cot, presumably sleeping as he tossed and turned. "See?" the Director continued. "He's there in his bed."

"Yes..." Doctor Morkian continued to watch the screen. In a second, the image glitched, showing static and bars of color, then blipped back to the image of Terry's cell; but when the picture stabilized, Terry was no longer there. "He's gone!" the Doctor exclaimed.

"Yes," the Director agreed. "He's just fucking *gone*. Where did he go? Have you ever seen anything like this before, Doctor?"

"No, sir," Morkian admitted. "That is anomalous, indeed."

"I just can't figure it out," the Director said, frustrated. "How can a person just vanish like that? Into thin air."

"Wait..." Doctor Morkian said, looking down at another monitor. "Is this the live feed of Terry's cell?"

"Yeah, why?" the Director responded, still looking at the playback of Terry's empty cell.

"Well, sir, because he's back."

"What?" The Director looked down to where Doctor Morkian was pointing. "When did he get back? What is he doing?"

"I don't know, sir," Morkian continued. "He appears to be talking to himself. Maybe doing a meditation or something. Should we prep him for more tests?"

For several moments, the Director stared at Terry on the monitor. He was sitting on his cot teaching the Merkabah meditation to Anna in her Astral Body, but neither the Director nor

Doctor Morkian could see her. Finally the Director shook his head. "Not yet, Doctor. I haven't quite decided what I want to do with him next."

EIGHTEEN

When a shaman is in the midst of the Timestream, they have the ability to travel back to past periods of history, to the distant future where they can't even recognize what humans have evolved into, or they could just be present, not knowing what the Timestream might show them. Jessica was still tumbling through the white flow of light, not consciously trying to travel to any particular time. For a moment, she thought of Artemis and how she wished to be with her unicorn companion again, taking a rest from all the time traveling and visions. As she thought this, she surrendered to the current, wondering where it would drop her next. Slowly the white light began to fade, and the stream felt like it was slowly bringing her back down to the ground.

Before she was even aware she was back, Jessica came to be sitting on the softest grass under a large, powerful tree. The Timestream disappeared in a shower of crystal pixie dust and floated away on the wind. She looked around to assess where she had ended up. It was the soft glow of twilight and a few feet in front of her was Artemis contentedly munching on the green grass. They were in a large circular clearing with one huge tree in the center. Jessica could see the tree line of the forest ringing the circumference of the clearing. Looking up at the tree, it seemed to tower over her like a giant about to come to life. The leaves were gently rustling in the breeze, and the branches were gnarled like crooked fingers. Also there were what looked to her to be large vines hanging down from the branches which seemed to slither like snakes. The roots in which she sat seemed to make a throne around her.

"You're back!" Artemis said, lifting up his head from his grazing.

"Yes, it would appear so," Jessica replied, making her way to standing.

"How was your trip, my dear?" the unicorn asked, smiling widely.

"Wild," she remarked, brushing herself off and checking that her knapsack was still on her back. "I saw the future." She grinned.

"I bet that was a trip," Artemis returned. "Don't tell me! I want to be surprised when the future comes my way." The unicorn winked at her.

Jessica laughed. "Okay, Artemis. It's good to see you, my friend," she continued as she walked over and began to stroke his soft fur. "Does Pangea ever even become futuristic? I get the feeling it just stays perpetually in like the time of Middle Earth."

"I don't know," the unicorn admitted. "Pangea could possibly develop higher levels of technology and civilization. One day we'll just have to see."

"This has been a wild ride," Jessica commented, "and I have a feeling it's not even close to being over yet. Still more initiations to come, I bet. It's a wild ride, like *Mr. Toad's Wild Ride*."

"Mr. Toad?" Artemis looked at her sideways. "I don't think I know that reference."

"Oh, yeah. Unicorns don't read," she laughed. "It's a book—*The Wind in the Willows*... And speaking of willows, what's up with this tree?"

Artemis whinnied with delight. "This tree?" he said, shaking his mane. "You can't possibly mean this tree," he joked.

"Oh, come on, Artemis," Jessica said, smiling. "Don't joke around. I want to know."

"Well, this tree, my dear Jessica, if you must know," Artemis began dramatically, "is the very most specialest, most stupendous, fabulous, most genius tree there is!" They both looked up into the branches of the tree; the branches seemed to chant mantras in a deep voice, and the vines reminded Jessica of the serpent in the branches of the Tree of Knowledge.

"Don't tease me," she said, scratching behind Artemis's ears. "Just tell me what's so special about it."

"Okay, since you're so curious—how could you not be with the most powerful tree in all of the Spiralverse standing before you," he explained. "This, my dear budding Soulmind, is the World Tree. Also known as Yggdrasil."

"Wow," Jessica whispered in awe of the majestic tree.

"The World Tree is the axis mundi," Artemis continued, "meaning that it is the center or axis of the world. It connects the Upperworld, the Middleworld, and the Underworld. Its energy creates harmony in the cosmos. Yggdrasil connects Heaven and Earth. It is an honor to be so near the Tree's divinity and protection."

"It really is," Jessica commented as she walked closer to the Tree again. "I can feel its energy, as if it has a Soulmind of its own."

Tentatively she touched the bark of the Tree with her right hand. A current of energy like electricity traveled through her arm and illuminated her purple aura and Soulmind. She closed her eyes and felt her whole body tingling. Then she heard a deep voice rumble from the depths, as if the Tree was speaking directly to her consciousness.

"Jessica Thorn," the voice bellowed in her head, "the Shamanic Path has chosen you and you have proven yourself each time with even more poise and power. You have earned a rest in my roots, for tomorrow will begin the third stretch of your journey. It will be perilous, and test you in ways the Middleworld and the Underworld did not. Never forget, you are a shaman and a powerful one. Cease to ever doubt yourself, but I trust that tendency has all but fallen away. Sleep well, child, for the Upperworld awaits you."

The Tree's voice faded inside Jessica's mind and she took her hand away from the trunk. Purple light still glowed around her body as she turned back to Artemis. "I guess we should rest up for our journey tomorrow," she said to the unicorn. "The Tree told me to find shelter amidst its roots and under the shade of its leaves. Sleep sounds nice in the center of the world, between Heaven and Earth. Come curl up with me, my dear Artemis, and we will drift off together, sinking into the center of the Spiral and into Dreamsphere."

BOOK FIVE

To the Inner Limits

"I think you can absolutely have absolute truths, just as I believe you can absolutely never have two people who were there agree on what that absolute truth is. It's the glory and the magic of the way memory works. Memories are being rewritten all the time and the view changes wherever you're standing. So while there probably are absolute truths, I would hesitate to pronounce on what they are. I think that there are definitely no personal absolute truths. Because I think personal absolute truths are coloured by memory and feeling and point of view."
\- Neil Gaiman

PART 16

The Stone Queen's Successor

*"Sweet Jesus, he thought, this was the way the world would end.
A warren of rooms, cars on the freeway winding their last way
home, the dead and almost dead exchanging blows by candlelight.
The Reverend had been wrong. The Deluge wasn't a wave, was it?
It was blind men with axes; it was the great on their knees
begging not to die at the hands of idiots; it was
the itch of the irrational grown to an epidemic."*

- Clive Barker, *The Damnation Game*

*"It was enough to know they had no Devil on their backs. Just old
humanity, cheated of love, and ready to pull down the world on its
head."*

- Clive Barker, *The Damnation Game*

"Motherfucker…" Eden groaned after she smacked down face first into the ground in the middle of Mika'el's field. Muttering more swears, she peeled herself from the dirt and looked around tentatively to see if Mika'el was anywhere to be seen. Preferring not to have an encounter with the old man before she could get back over to the City, Eden darted toward the forest once she determined that Mika'el was nowhere in sight.

The irritation and anger was still festering within her, eating her insides like a cannibal holocaust, and she wished desperately to purge whatever stagnating negative energy had infected her. The love that Eden had felt in her heart now echoed rage like a soulless void. Not knowing if she'd ever feel that warmth again, she was gripped with the overwhelming desire to inflict as much pain and suffering on others as she currently felt herself.

In no time she had reached the trees and now she was far enough into the forest that she had all but forgotten about the Village and Mika'el's farm. The City was her destination, and she walked swiftly toward it; her determination single-pointed, fire blazing in her eyes. When she walked by the entrance of the cave which used to hold the Stone Queen, Eden gritted her teeth and gave it the finger. The cave was now even more overgrown with vines, and though it was empty now, it seemed even creepier than before. A cold wind rustled the leaves and blew Eden's hair into her face. She shivered and began to walk faster the moment she could have sworn that the wind was whispering to her the words: "*Spread... Be its festering wound...*"

A while later, Eden began to grow fatigued and slowed her pace, hoping that the border of the City was near. "Where's a flying car when you need one?" she mumbled to herself. Almost instantaneously after saying this, she heard the sound of whirring traffic. This perked her head up and she got a second rush of energy. The edge of the forest was near.

Seconds later, Eden broke through the last line of trees and stood on the sidewalk staring at the speeding traffic in front and above her. Without a moment to reconsider what she was about to do, she raised her hand toward the cars on the road and threw a flaming ball of red and pink energy at the nearest vehicle. The Soulmind orb incinerated the engine of the car and in seconds it burst into flame, buckling the metal frame as it flipped and started to roll. Eden stared in awe as the other drivers tried to slam on their brakes to avoid a collision, but the pile-up of cars was already beginning. The traffic behind the explosion started to collide, sending other cars spinning and tumbling through the street. The pedestrians on the sidewalk on the other side of the street began to scream, trying to run for cover as vehicles veered off the road into the crowd. Fleeing people were caught under tires and flying shrapnel. Heads exploded in fountains of blood and limbs were ripped off of bodies as they couldn't avoid the hurtling, sometimes flaming, road projectiles.

"Suck a deep dick, you fucking assholes!" Eden screamed over the din of her created mayhem. Cars were still colliding on the street and pedestrians couldn't avoid becoming casualties as they ran for cover. The flying cars above hadn't been affected by the madness yet, but Eden had plans for them as she eyed them zipping above her through the smoke and flames growing higher from the road. Suddenly she ran through the rubble toward the sidewalk on the other side. Standing like a psycho on the remains of a flipped car, Eden began picking off survivors with more Soulmind energy balls which she shot from both hands. She would decapitate bodies, blow holes through stomachs, blast off flailing limbs and send them spinning into flesh orbit. The carnage and gore was staining the City in a matter of minutes.

When Eden was satisfied with that, she turned her attention toward the flying cars. They had begun to thin out, drivers trying to avoid the destruction by flying higher or around through clear parts of the sky. This would not do. She couldn't let them escape unscathed. Calling forth her Soulmind spear, it popped out of her solar plexus. She pulled it out of herself, tip blazing with red and pink light. Aiming true, she threw it into the sky. The huge spear pierced through a flying car that was almost directly above her. The airborne vehicle fell from the sky like a pheasant shot with a hunting rifle. Eden laughed as the car crashed into the rubble below, windows shattering. The madness was intoxicating, and she was becoming drunk with power. Watching with sadistic pleasure, Eden could see the driver of the flying car struggling to pull herself from her seat and through the broken windshield. Blood streamed out from below the driver's hairline and down her face in red rivers; she tried to blink through the red liquid which was flooding her eyes. Eden's spear had disappeared once the car had been felled. Now it was sticking out from her chest again.

Now Eden, blind with power and blood-lust, pulled the spear out of her chest once more and aimed it at the woman who, blinded by her own blood, was desperately trying to pull herself from her totaled vehicle. Without remorse or hesitation, Eden let the spear fly and it impaled the woman through her forehead. The woman fell back dead, her blood-soaked eyes and mouth wide open in astonishment.

"Eden, *stop!*" a man's voice yelled from somewhere nearby.

Who dares to tell me to stop? Eden thought. "You're all fucking weak!" she screamed, whirling around to look for the source of the voice. "Weak people deserve to be killed! If your survival instinct isn't sufficient enough to save you, then fucking suffer!"

"This isn't you!" the man's voice came again. Suddenly a cloud of smoke cleared on the sidewalk and Eden saw who was speaking—it was Nikola. "You defeated the Stone Queen with the Singularity Pulse of your heart, Eden. Do you now wish to exceed her cruelty with your own?"

The expression in Eden's eyes was pure rage and she stared at Nikola as if she wished to kill him. And in that moment, she did. "Fuck the Stone Queen!" she shrieked. "She don't have shit on me! I would rule as the most terrible and beautiful! They're all begging for death, so really I'm doing them a favor. Delivering them to the paradise that they wish to escape to."

Nikola smirked. "You don't really believe that," he continued. "You have a Soulmind. You must know that the majority of these people will just be reincarnated and live the same lives they already have over and over again."

"So fuck it then," Eden spat back. "Then I'm not really killing anyone. They'll just respawn like in a video game. It's all meaningless anyway."

"If that's how you want to look at it," Nikola said with a frown. "But I know there's still compassion in your heart. Stop this madness and come with me. I'll take you back to my apartment, my lab. I can help you. These people didn't do anything to you."

She scoffed. "Nobody is innocent. In my world, there are no good guys. Are you gonna stop me? I could kill you now if I wanted to. What army have you got to bring my reign to an end?" Eden stared as the smoke behind Nikola billowed in the wind. Then it began to blow away, revealing many figures standing behind him. There were at least twenty of them—metal men that looked like the A.I. robot that was in Nikola's lab the first time Terry and Eden came to the City.

"This is my army," Nikola answered. "But I don't use them for aggression or domination or genocide."

"Why the fuck not?" Eden said. "That would be the perfect thing to use them for. What? Is that your new police force? You're gonna arrest me?"

Nikola shrugged. "They could be a police force," he said. "But I'm still tinkering, still perfecting them. The whole system doesn't quite work correctly yet. I'm not fully connected in since we're not at my lab right now. Don't you want to come back there with me? Put all that pent-up energy to productive use? I'm sure you could help with perfecting the technology and coming up with some new creative inventions. You *are* powerful, Eden. No one is questioning that."

Eden sighed and let her arms drop to her sides. Her shoulders slumped and she suddenly felt exhausted. "Fuck it," she conceded. "I grow tired of this game anyway."

"I know you are," Nikola nodded. "I can already feel it ebbing away."

Eden hopped down from the wreck she was still standing on and approached Nikola. Getting very close to him, she stared into his eyes, willing him to judge her malice. He smiled a sad smile and his eyes were all compassion. Embracing her, Nikola held Eden in his arms, trying to take away whatever pain afflicted her. She shuddered, beginning to sob. "Am I evil, Nikola?" she choked out.

"No," he answered lovingly, kissing the top of her head. "Don't ever say that. Don't ever think that. You have a big heart, Eden. You love big, but that's also why your pain is so great."

"Why?" she sobbed. "I don't want to feel like this. It's unbearable and I only want to make others feel what I feel so at least to have that bit of relief."

"Shh," Nikola hushed her. "Let's get you home to rest." He looked around at the mass destruction. "Let's get you out of here quick before someone *else* decides they want to kill you for this."

MAY & JUNE

ONE

FROM THE MIND OF JESSICA THORN:

I wake to find that Yggdrasil, the World Tree, has grown through the sky and into the darkness of the cosmos. Laying on the soft grass, my head against Artemis's belly, I stare up into the branches that look like living vines that stretch to pluck the stars from the sky. It's still night and the steady breath of my unicorn as he sleeps puts me at ease. A full Moon's radiance illuminates the whole area in a silvery luminescence. I've never beheld anything more beautiful.

Without losing sight of Artemis sleeping in the roots of the great Tree, I walk several yards away from the tree so I can just gaze up and admire the night sky. The Spiralverse is so vast— maybe infinitely vast. Suddenly I am overtaken with the desire to explore space, other galaxies, and the limits of the Spiral-verse. That is assuming there *are* any limits. This whole system of Dimensions could be limitless for all I know. Oh, Terry, what planets will we explore next?

"I would build you a galaxy, babe."

I jump, not expecting the voice. Looking down from the stars, I glance around me for the source of the words. And... Oh my God, can this be real? It's Terry, walking out of the trees and across the glade toward me. He's smiling and shining in the moonlight. "How?" I start. "Are you real? How are you here?"

Terry shakes his head as he approaches me. "This is the Pan-Dreamsphere," he explains. "All of Pangea is dreaming. And we are the dream."

"I'm asleep? Dreaming?" I ask as Terry stops right in front of me and touches my cheek.

"But that doesn't mean it's not real," he says.

"I miss you so much..." I whisper, my eyes welling up with tears.

"Hush, my love," Terry says and kisses me lightly on the lips. "Just be the dream with me tonight. Let's enjoy the imagination of the stars, the moon, and this beautiful glade bathed in silver light."

"Yes," I say, smiling, overwhelmed by his presence. My heart feels like it's about to explode and become a galaxy itself.

"Look how it reaches the heavens," he says, pointing back toward Yggdrasil. I turn to look. The wonderment of the vision floors me like a sober hallucination. A dream where you don't know if you're awake or asleep. Or maybe I'm awake within the dream. The branches of the World Tree are moving! They are growing like roots into the sky. Twisting and contorting like a pit of snakes, I see these branches continue to grow past the atmosphere and beyond. I can almost see these branches like arms reaching to touch every other planet, every other star. The green leaves rustle in a subtle breeze that smells of moonbeams. Then all at once the branches expand, filling the entire sky. We are covered by the roof of Yggdrasil, and surrounded by the walls of the circle of forest trees that ring the glade.

I look into Terry's eyes, my own eyes wide in astonishment at the beauty of the spectacle. He smiles back at me with a beam of love. "Have you ever made love under the stars?" he asks.

I shake my head and look up at the branches canopying above, moving like living vines. "I can't see the stars anymore," I reply.

"They'll be out again soon," he assures me as he leans in to kiss me again. Starting to pull off my dress, my body aches to feel him against my skin again. "You are radiant," he says as I discard the last of my clothes and stand naked before him. I feel shy and smile, my hair falling down over one eye. The purple of my aura starts to pulse around my body.

"I will always be yours," I whisper.

Terry shakes his head as he begins to take his clothes off as well. "We share love," he responds, "but you do not belong to anyone. Remember that. Not even me. You are your own sovereign, divine goddess. With powers beyond even your wildest imaginings in the Dreamsphere. The purple of your light intoxicates me." Now his shirt is thrown into the grass and he pulls off his underwear, kicking it aside. His body shines with his white glow. We are two lighthouses calling to each other in a storm. I catch the glint of silver around Terry's neck—it is my old cross, the one that he gave me and I left in the Hollow Dimension the day I disappeared. Approaching my lover slowly, I place a hand on his chest, above his heart. As I feel it beat and the warmth against my hand, I close my eyes.

"We are connected within the light," I say. "I often think of our experience in the ice cave in Dreamsphere. Do you remember?" I open my eyes.

Terry nods and places his hand over mine. "Transcendent. We are," he says, his voice smooth like honey. Pulling me into himself, we embrace. As our bodies touch, our auras merge and our Soulminds begin to grow larger, dancing in the night below the branches of the World Tree. He kisses my neck and I moan softly. I can feel the heat between us and my heart starts to beat faster. His penis presses against my pelvis and I can feel him getting hard. Lovingly and tenderly he lays me down onto the soft grass and begins kissing my whole body; my collar bone, my breasts, my nipples, my tummy, and then before I know it he is between my legs, licking my sex which is already wet and eager to be joined with him.

Moaning, I lean my head back into the soft grass; my mouth hanging open and my eyes closed. As Terry is tasting my clitoris, and my juices, and then lapping deep inside, I stroke my fingers through his soft hair. The movement of his head against my vagina, and the sounds of his soft moans, really gets me going. I feel my cheeks flush and I open my eyes to look up at the writhing branches that have become our ceiling. Watching the purple light of my Soulmind spiraling out of my solar plexus, it braids like a DNA strand and grows up toward the branches above. Terry's white aura has also become vast and a spiral of white light is braiding out of his back as well, right behind his heart. This light twists and turns until it finds my own, fusing in a radiance indescribable on a Third-Dimensional plane. As the two braids of our Soulminds join, a flash of light comes through the branches above us and then small orbs of white luminescence begin to rain down from the branches like a shower of stars. I marvel at the sight.

Terry pulls his head up from between my legs and smiles at me, his chin glistening with saliva and my own lubrication. "I told you the stars would be out again," he says as he crawls on top of me. "To do the dance of love within a shower of stars is cosmic. Wouldn't you agree?" he asks, staring down into my eyes. The silver cross hangs from his neck and brushes my throat between my collar bones.

I nod, still in awe. "It's the most brilliant sight I've ever seen!" I agree as the stars of white light continue to rain down around us. Then he gently pushes inside me. I moan as he begins to thrust slowly in and out, I can feel myself tightly wrapped around his erection. He fills me up and the trails of Soulmind and electricity make their journey up through my veins and nerve-endings. "Oh, Terry..." I wrap my arms around the sides of his ribcage and press my palms against his back as he kisses me passionately and tenderly. He isn't rough with me, and that is how I want him.

Moaning himself, Terry presses his cheek against my own and I can feel his breath against my ear. "I love you," he whispers, and I almost feel like crying from the euphoria I feel. We are together again, merged under the World Tree and bathed in star-shine—even if it is only in Dreamsphere, again.

"I love you, Terry," I whisper into his ear.

As I feel as if our whole beings are melting together into one, he rolls over and pulls me on top of him. I cry out a little in surprise, but then smile as I sit up and begin to ride him. Gazing down at his beautiful face, haloed in white and purple light, I am overjoyed by the ecstasy I see upon it. Feeling the orgasmic bliss building within us, I continue to be amazed by the endless sea of stars raining down around us. I can't help thinking back to the spectacular light show in the ice cave during our first time making love. Each time we've come together this way, there is a fantastic light show, I think, and smile, not slowing the motion of my hips as I take the full length and girth of Terry's cock inside myself.

Then something changes. Everything still feels the same and Terry continues to moan with his eyes closed as I slide him in and out, but suddenly I see two strange dots on his forehead a little above his temples. Then they grow. As I stare, two small goat-like horns grow from Terry's skull. And then I feel the sudden presence of fur on his legs brushing against my own.

Reaching under me, I feel that his legs have changed shape. I cry out in surprise but don't detach from our sexual union.

Terry's eyes open upon hearing my cry. "Something wrong?" he says, still grinding his pelvis against mine, thrusting in and out of my vagina with his goat-dick. His face still looks like Terry; he still wears the cross; and his energy still feels like the one I love.

"Puh-Pan?" I manage to choke out. "Your horns... and... Are you Terry or are you Pan?" Finally I get the question out. If I'm really being fucked by the goat-god, then it kind of disturbs me how much I'm enjoying it.

Pan—or Terry—smiles mischievously. "I am Terry," he answers, "and Terry is I. And you are Kali Ma."

I raise my eyebrows and I feel his penis pulsing inside me—it feels fucking amazing. However, I don't really understand what he meant by the last statement. Is he Terry or is he Pan? Still, I'm confused. And I'm Kali Ma? What does that mean? But fuck it, if this is a dream, does it really matter if I'm fucking the Goat? I can't believe I'm thinking this. What's happening to me? I used to be such a good little Christian girl. Now I'm having sex dreams with a god who is half goat! I sigh and moan as I continue to ride him; the orgasmic ecstasy is just too amazing. "Oh, fuck it..." I mumble.

"I am," Pan-Terry laughs. "Do you trust me?"

I hesitate. "Uhh... I trust Terry," I answer.

"That's good enough for me," he says and points up toward the branches of Yggdrasil. Suddenly the branches above us part, making a circular hole. Shining orbs still fall from the rest of the Tree, but through the hole is the darkness of space and the pinpricks of stars. "Hold onto me as we fuck," Pan-Terry says, and I lean down against him while we're still connected in sexual union. The energy of our Soulminds that has been dancing together produces a sphere of purple and white light completely encapsulating us as we begin to float off of the grass.

"Holy shit," I squeal as I wrap my arms around him.

"Yggdrasil stretches all the way into the heavens," he says as we float up and through the hole in the branches. "And its roots grow all the way through the Underworld."

"This is the most spectacular thing I've ever seen or felt," I say in awe as we continue to float up toward the night sky. The branches of Yggdrasil are all around us, dancing like vines possessed by Dionysus. The silver light of the Moon streams through the cracks in these branches and bathes us in its glory as if she wishes to join us in our lovemaking.

Pan-Terry looks into my eyes and I feel as if he knows the very depths of my Soulmind. "The joining of beings sexually is making love to God—making love to all of existence. It is the deepest meditation and the highest form of prayer. Since we've both come from the same Source, our identical essence is finding itself once again. The beauty and the ecstasy of experiencing yourself over and over again is the wonder of the Spiralverse. The greatest Mystery to be lived forever and into eternity. The cosmic romance played out by yourself wearing different masks."

I have no words to add to what he so eloquently stated. All I can do is look up to the stars as we float past the Moon, the branches of Yggdrasil pushing us up, encouraging us to cum in a gush of stardust. But it feels like we are already having an orgasm—a sustained everlasting orgasm which vibrates in our cells without us even moving. Pan-Terry is still inside me, but we are still now as we float, locked in an embrace, skin burning with the fire of the other's Soulmind.

A star above us in the dark void seems to be shining brighter than the rest and we're floating toward it quickly. The branches of Yggdrasil stretch and dance around this star, as if coaxing us toward it.

"Have you ever cum inside a supernova?" Pan-Terry whispers, looking up at the star in awe.

I look at him questioningly. "What?—" is all I manage to get out before we merge with the light of this star. I feel it swell and then explode out with blinding white light as it pulls us into its center. I cannot see anything other than this light, and it's so intense that I think I'm dying. If it wasn't for the feeling of Pan-Terry's body against mine, I would have sworn my body was being pulled apart. However, as the star explodes with us inside, the most intense orgasm rips through my body and illuminates my Soulmind. Pan-Terry is cumming also, I can feel his cock pulsing inside my vagina, but I can't tell if he's ejaculating or not. All I know is that the euphoric climax of infinite spiritual ecstasy of merger with all of Creation is coursing through our consciousness. And it is heaven.

Then blackness.

The star has died and the afterglow of our orgasm still vibrates within us and without us. It is as if our orgasm is a separate entity living independently of us, but choosing to share itself with us. I see Terry's face as he smiles and kisses me. We float in the black void, our bodies only illuminated by the energy of our purple and white Soulminds braiding together and swirling around us. I never want this to end. I want to stay here forever; one with Terry. But I know it can't be so. Maybe this is what it feels like to die and go back to Source before reincarnating into your next lifetime. But I know I'm not dead and my journey is far from over. Morning will be here soon and eventually I will see Terry in the Hollow Dimension again. And where to after that is still a mystery to me.

"Are we still in space?" I ask. Terry still has the goat horns on his head, but it seems like his legs have become human again; he's still erect inside me and I have my legs wrapped around his waist. He smiles and kisses my face. As if in response, I see a growth of huge roots come into view beside us. They seem to vibrate and hum with the mantra of the Spiralverse. We start floating upwards again.

"As above, so below," Terry says, hugging my body closer to his. "Sometimes in the void it's difficult to know what is up and what is down."

"That's for sure," I agree.

A hole suddenly opens above us and I feel a handful of dirt fall against our skin. Through this hole in the earth, I can see again the orbs of light that continue to rain down from the branches of Yggdrasil. Once we are through and hovering above the green grass, the hole closes beneath us. As we hover in our sphere of purple and white Soulmind light, with stars raining around us, Terry looks into my eyes and says, "A god is one who ascends and descends. We are the connection between heaven and earth. The divine and the terrestrial."

I'm so overwhelmed with bliss in a trance-like ecstasy, I don't have any words to say. The meditation is so profound that I feel that if I talk it might break. Taking my legs from around his waist, I put my feet back on the ground and he does the same. The light of our auras dim to a subtle glow around our bodies. Leaning in, Terry kisses me and I close my eyes, melting into him once more.

Before I can open my eyes again, a bright orange light penetrates my eyelids. It's harsh and cuts through the experience like an intruder. "What is that?" I grumble, squinting my eyes shut harder.

"That is the sun," Terry's voice says and fades away.

I put my hand up to shade my eyes from the light and slowly squint to look. Terry is gone and I'm laying on the grass with my head leaning against the fur of Artemis's white belly. I hear the unicorn snort and feel him start to move his head, waking from the restful sleep. "Morning already?" I mumble. The branches of the World Tree tower over us but they no longer stretch all the way up into space. Smiling, I still feel the afterglow of the orgasm. It's nice that I was able to spend another night with Terry in the Dreamsphere even though I'm not sure he wasn't just Pan in disguise.

"Did sleeping under Yggdrasil renew you, Jessica?" Artemis asks as he begins to stand up.

Sitting upright, I turn to look at my beautiful unicorn in the light of the morning. "Artemis," I say, "you have no idea."

TWO

Rob chewed on the end of a pen as he scanned over the list of the current Playground members. New names had been added at the last meeting and there would probably be even more newbies at today's meeting. Mothman sat beside him on the couch playing a game on his phone.

"Oh! Oh! Oh... Goddamnit, I died!" Mothman squealed as he shook his phone in frustration.

"Can you shut the hell up for two minutes?" Rob said. "I'm trying to think."

Mothman gave him a look. "What crawled up your butt, *Robert*? What do you got to think so hard about? Just, you know, tell everybody when they get here what's going on and then get on that fucking plane and do what you gotta do."

Rob scoffed. "You make it sound so freakin' simple. You're the one who's got the lazy job of sitting on your ass and watching the house. I'm not Terry. I don't know how to be a leader or how to set up groups." He sighed.

Mothman shrugged and went back to playing his game.

Rob sighed loudly and got up from the couch, taking the notebook with him. The Playground members would be showing up any time. A ringing suddenly came from Rob's pocket and he pulled his cell phone out as he walked toward the front door. "What's up?" he said, answering the phone.

"Rob! It's Darren. Are the Playground there yet?"

Rob shook his head and then realized he was on the phone. "No," he answered. "But they should be here really soon. I think I might see some people coming down the block right now."

"Excellent," Darren responded. "It shouldn't be any problem for you to facilitate the creation of an independent sector of Playground run by one of the members there. Anyway, I've booked your first flight for later today. Everything is all set up for you to fly out to Washington, DC. That's your first destination and the most important place to set up a new Playground hub."

"Why?" Rob wanted to know.

"Just trust me," Darren said. "That's like the epicenter for so many pivotal pieces to this whole thing."

"Makes sense," Rob replied. "I gotta go, I think I see some people coming up now. You gonna come pick me up later to take me to the airport? I've got my bag packed and ready to go."

"You bet ya," Darren answered. "See you in a little while. Have a good meeting."

"See ya," Rob said as he hung up the phone and slid it back into his pocket.

The first two people to arrive were Michael and Emily. Rob opened the door and ushered them inside as he checked their names off of the list. "Welcome, welcome," he said. "*No Bounce…*"

"*No Play,*" Emily and Michael responded at the same time.

"Sup, Rob?" Michael said. "Where's Terry?" He looked around, expecting to see Terry who was usually the one to answer the door for everyone.

Rob gave a weak smile but his eyes looked concerned. "That's what I wanted to talk to you about specifically. Terry's been kidnapped."

Michael's mouth hung open. "What?! No way! By the government?"

Rob nodded regretfully. "Mmm-hmm. It's all fucked. Now I'm going to have to go away too in order to set up other Playgrounds around the country and the world."

Emily exchanged a glance with Michael. "That's crazy," Michael continued. "So then who's going to be here to run *this* Playground?"

Rob put his hand on Michael's shoulder. "I was thinking you could—both of you," he said looking at Emily also. "If you choose to accept the responsibility."

Michael was silent for a moment and he looked at Emily, not knowing what to say. She nodded without saying a word. "Yeah… Yeah, okay, sure. We can do that," Michael said finally.

"Good. Great," Rob responded, relieved. "I wanted to run it by you before anyone else came. Anyway, I'll set you up with the list of members and their emails and stuff after the meeting. I'm going to tell everyone else what happened to Terry when they're all here. Then I'll announce that you'll be taking over meetings."

"Okay, Rob, yeah, whatever you want," Michael said. "We fully support you and Terry in whatever you need us to do. We're in this together."

Rob smiled. "Now go take a seat on the couch. Mothman is in there. I think I see more people coming now."

Michael gave Rob an awkward hug and then he and Emily went in toward the living room. Not long after, the rest of Playground showed up. Rob diligently ticked off all their names when they came in. There were a few new faces who had been brought by returning members and Rob added their names and information to his list. When everyone seemed to be accounted for, he locked the front door and went back to the living room to give them the upsetting news about Terry.

Obviously they had all noticed his absence and were chattering among themselves in concerned tones. They all hushed when Rob came in and they looked at him with expectant eyes like a puppy waiting for a treat.

Clearing his throat, Rob laid the notebook down on the floor and took a deep breath to prepare himself for what he had to say. "I regret to have to tell you this," he began, "but Terry has been taken by a government agency and we don't know where he is or when he'll be free. But knowing him, he'll find a way out. I'm sure of it."

There were murmurs of agreement and exclamations of distress from the group. "So what are we supposed to do now? Terry seemed to be the one who knew where all of this was going. Without him do we even have a plan?"

"That's a great question," Rob agreed. "It is important now more than ever to expand our numbers. So we will continue to do what we've been doing. Spreading the word and activating new Soulminds—as per the normal method. You know what I mean." There were a few nervous giggles from the crowd. He opened his hand and gestured toward Michael and Emily on the couch. "Sorry to say I will be gone for a while setting up new Playgrounds, but Michael and Emily here have been kind enough to agree to take over holding meetings every Wednesday. Will they be at your house?"

Michael nodded and gave Emily a glance. "Yeah, that's what I was thinking," he answered. "My mom will be totally cool with it. Luckily our house wasn't affected by the big *event*. We live close to the city, but not *that* close. And, you know," he looked around at the group, "I'll email you all and let you know the address and everything."

"Awesome. Thank you so much," Rob said with genuine appreciation. "Mothman will still be here holding down the fort. Are you willing to keep the lighthouse here and be a safe haven in case anyone is in need?"

Mothman looked up as if he was just now realizing Rob was talking. "Who me?" he asked, looking blindsided.

Rob laughed. "Yes you, you hermaphrodite."

"Hey, don't call me by the pet name you gave your dick," he shot back. Everyone erupted into laughter in spite of the serious vibe developing.

When Rob's laughter subsided he said, "Well, will you? Keep the lighthouse going inside the protection of the Merkabah?"

Mothman shrugged and then nodded. "Yeah, you guys can come by if you need a place or if you wanna hang out. I'll be bored all by myself. Or if any of you chicks are horny, I'm always here." He winked at the hot goth girl and flicked his tongue out like a lizard. She rolled her eyes but was smiling.

"Okay, you horny bastard," Rob said dismissively. "Moving on..." He trailed off and the room went silent for a minute. "Umm..." Rob said, fumbling for words. "I don't really know what else to say. I guess, does anyone have any questions?"

The goth girl raised her hand.

"Allister, you don't have to raise your hand," Rob said. "This isn't middle school."

Allister put her hand down, a little embarrassed. "Yeah, like, where is all this going?" she asked. "Is there like a plan? Why do we even have these powers—these Soulminds? Is there like a point to all this?"

Rob blinked and stared at her blankly. "Well, I don't really know," he admitted. "But I have faith that we're doing the right thing."

Allister scoffed. "Ha! Faith? Are you kidding me, Rob? If someone as advanced as Terry could be taken by the government so easily, what is going to happen to us? Are we all going to die? Will we be killed? If Terry was here he'd know what to do, where all this is going."

The string of questions from Allister started to get the rest of the group agitated to the point they started to talk among themselves, their voices raising to a cacophonous din. Rob couldn't handle it and he put his hands up in surrender. "Okay, this is stressing me out. I don't have all the answers, but I know what I'm supposed to do now and I trust in what I've been told and my own intuition. I have a flight in several hours and I have to finish getting ready. This is getting too much for me to handle right now and Terry usually does this stuff, not me." Without another word, he walked off and disappeared into the rest of the house.

Mothman looked stunned and he just stared after his friend. Allister poked Mothman and he looked over at her on the couch. "Terry had a plan, right?" she asked. "He always seemed like he knew where this all was headed and what we needed to do to get there. I can't be lost again."

"Pffff," Mothman laughed. "I don't fucking know either. Remember, Terry was the one who activated me and not that long ago either. If that fuckstick knows what we're fighting for or what we're trying to accomplish, your guess is as good as mine. And people who don't know him that well don't realize that sometimes he can be just as full of shit as the rest of us. Maybe he doesn't even know any more than we do." He shrugged. "Who the fuck cares anyway? Don't take shit so seriously. I'm just along for the ride, and let's keep this ride fun."

THREE

"Nikola, why didn't you kill me?" Eden asked. She had just woken up on the couch in his apartment. Nikola was in the kitchen making breakfast.

"What?" he said from the other side of the apartment.

"It's just, I was thinking about it," she continued. "And I was having a dream about you murdering me in my sleep. What I was doing was definitely reprehensible. You would have been justified taking me out."

Nikola stopped chopping vegetables and put his hands on the island, leaning forward as he looked toward the back of the couch in the living room. "I couldn't," he admitted. "One reason is that I've never killed anyone in my life and I'm not going to start now. Plus I have a strong sense that you are indispensable to whatever it is Terry is still doing." He took a pause and then sighed heavily. "And if there's one thing I've learned in all my years inventing and living in the City, is that who am I to condemn anyone? Or even condone their actions for that matter. When you condemn someone else, you only condemn yourself... Or at least, that's what I've come to learn."

"Hmm," Eden commented, staring up at the white ceiling. "But you wanted us to get rid of the Queen when we were here last. Wasn't that you condemning *her*?"

Nikola had to think about this. "I don't know," he began. "What I knew for sure was that her existence was causing my people to have difficult and diminished lives, not being able to enjoy all the fruits of their labor because most of their energy went straight to her. So I found it necessary to eliminate her. Do I condemn her actions of enslaving all of us? No, I don't. But does that mean I *condone* her actions? No it doesn't. And besides, I wasn't the one who killed her totally. *You* did. So in my mind I remained neutral."

"Ha," Eden scoffed. "Don't you think that's a little contradictory? Trying to absolve yourself of any responsibility one way or the other?"

Nikola shrugged and threw the chopped up vegetables into a pan on the stove where eggs were bubbling. "So what? Who cares if it is or isn't? That's just the way I see it because I always see points of view that are valid on both sides of any conflict. People are just a mess of contradictions anyway. Don't you agree? Why should I be an exception? You can't get around that fact of the human condition, so why not embrace it instead of pretending that you're internally consistent?"

"You've got a point there," Eden admitted and sat up, looking over the back of the couch toward Nikola. "So you're not going to kill me?"

He laughed. "No, I'm not going to kill you. I thought I made that pretty clear. If I'd wanted to kill you, I would have done it amidst all the chaos you created and then you'd just be one dead body within all the other ones. No, I have other ways you might be able to channel that energy and aggression."

"Like fucking?" she asked, walking over to the kitchen and sitting down at the island.

"What?" he said quickly, blushing subtly, but Eden caught it and thought it was cute. "No, no. That *wasn't* what I was thinking. I figured you could help me with some of my projects. I haven't quite perfected the A.I. of those robots you saw. If you choose to pour yourself into some of this work with me, I'm sure it would help get your mind off of whatever is eating you up inside."

"What's wrong with it?" she wanted to know.

"What're wrong with what?" Nikola responded.

"The A.I. thing. It doesn't work?"

"Oh, it works," he continued. "I can't get them to be self motivated. They seem to need to be connected to a human consciousness in order to have a directive. Otherwise they don't really do anything. You see, I helped create what I call the Brain. It's massive and floats in the sky above the City. Pretty much it's a database of all of our collected knowledge. The robots connect to this Brain wirelessly and they can instantly know how to complete any task or solve any problem. They don't have the ability to give *themselves* an intrinsic purpose. So I had to create a chair in my lab that plugs into the back of my brain stem which gives me full access to the hive-mind. That way I can give them directives to carry out; but it has to come from my consciousness."

"What can I do then?" Eden said. Nikola put a plate of food down in front of her. "What's this?" she said, playing with it with a fork.

"It's an omelet. Just eat it."

"Okay, yeah. I am pretty hungry."

"Anyway," Nikola continued, "I haven't done many trials and I've only plugged into the hive-mind a couple times. Maybe you'd be willing to do some tests with me where you plug into it and control the herd. And through both of our experiences, maybe we can figure out how to make the robots autonomous."

"Maybe," Eden responded noncommittally. "Might be fun and distract me from other shit. Not like I have anything better to do." She shrugged. "You really want these robots to become autonomous?"

"Yeah," he answered, pulling up a chair on the other side of the island after putting his own omelet on a plate. "I think it could be beneficial for society. Especially with the Queen gone, robots could take over the menial tasks and admin positions for factory work. That way more people would have freed up time to pursue what they're really passionate about. I think there would be more scientists that way and our technology could grow beyond anything we could ever imagine." He shoveled a piece of omelet into his mouth and chewed thoughtfully.

"Can we go check out your lab and these robots after breakfast?" Eden asked. "Where do you keep them? Are they all in your lab?"

Nikola shook his head. "No, I keep them in a large garage on the side of the building on the ground floor. I can control the door remotely, so when it goes up the robots can just walk out."

"That's convenient," she commented. "Also, what if I want to go exploring the City? How will I be able to get back into your apartment?"

"I'll get Seyba at the security desk to make you a keycard," he answered. "That'll give you access to my apartment and my lab."

"If I go out do you think that people are going to try to kill me for what I did?" Eden said, obviously worried that was a possibility.

Chewing another bite of omelet, Nikola thought about this for a moment. "No, I don't think so," he replied. "Pretty sure that no one who saw you left there alive—except me of course."

"Okay, good," she said with relief. "Then I don't have to constantly watch my back."

"Besides," Nikola added, "I don't think anyone here in the City is powerful enough to kill you. It was you who took out the Queen after all."

Eden nodded and slowly smiled as this realization sank in. "That's good to know. That's very good to know."

FOUR

O'Hare Airport was packed. It was always packed. Darren had given Rob his boarding pass and was seeing him off before he went to wait in the line to go through security. He was nervous to say the least. Flying by himself to all of these locations he'd never been to, to set up new chapters of the Playground, was a daunting task and it loomed over him like the shadow of *The Thing*. But Terry was imprisoned against his will and Rob knew it was his responsibility to step up and do his part.

"So you've got your boarding pass," Darren said, "and your carry-on bag. There's a couple from the DC chapter of LC who will be there to meet you at the airport. You'll be staying with them for a few days while you set up the Playground there."

Rob swallowed hard. "And tell me again why these contacts of yours can't just set up Playgrounds themselves. Why does it have to be me?"

Darren put his hand on Rob's shoulder to comfort and re-assure him. "Your energy is needed to be the container for each of these new Playgrounds. You are the key that will hold them together once they're established. It is the energy signature of your Soulmind that is the catalyst for this process. You must bring them together and plant the seeds for this new Society to grow. My people from the Body are also too old now to do this work. The LC has other parts to play in this cosmic space opera."

"Yes, I understand," Rob said, nodding in agreement.

"Are you nervous, Rob?"

"Of course," he admitted. "I'm scared shitless."

"Okay, yes," Darren responded, "that's totally understandable. Call me if there is ever a problem. And my people will be there to help every step of the way. Do you trust me?"

"Yes, Darren, I trust you."

"Good, good," Darren said and glanced at the throngs of people swiftly walking past them, anxious to board their flights.

"I trust you especially because you're *black*," Rob whispered while Darren was distracted.

"What was that?" Darren said as he turned back to face Rob.

"Nothing," Rob said quickly. "I didn't say anything."

Darren raised an eyebrow and then said, "You better get going so you don't miss your flight."

"Right," he agreed. "I'm off. *No Bounce—*"

"*No Play*," Darren responded with no hesitation.

They gave each other a hug and Rob patted Darren on the back awkwardly. Then he turned and walked off toward the line to go through security. Darren watched until Rob disappeared into the crowd. He shook his head and walked back toward the exit. "What a weird fucking kid," he said to himself as he left O'Hare Airport.

FIVE

The forest was just as enchanting as always; maybe even more so as Jessica rode on Artemis's back deeper into the trees that seemed to sing the song of magick. Since she had touched the energy of the World Tree, Jessica could see the beautiful creatures of the wood even more clearly. Faeries often flew around them, giggling and trailing pixie dust, then they would fly off into the treetops. Small gnome-like creatures would peek out from behind trees and then disappear again as if back into the imagination. Not to mention that there were a myriad of wild animals that called this enchanted forest home. Does with downy fur munched on the luscious green grass and under-growth. All of these animals and magickal creatures seemed to be comfortable with the presence of Jessica and Artemis, as if they too were part of the mystical landscape, just as much belonging there as any of the others.

Jessica marveled as the trees began to change and grow. The trend toward the way they were traveling seemed to be that the trees kept getting taller, and wider as well. Some trees were even as big around as a house. "Artemis, is it just me or are the trees getting bigger?" she asked.

"That's right," the unicorn answered. "The trees in this part of the forest are giants. Some of them you can't even see the top, they're so tall. We have entered the domain of the Wood-land Elves."

"The Woodland Elves?" Jessica repeated. "Do they make the trees so huge?"

Artemis laughed. "No, they don't *make* the trees big," he explained, "but they do live in them."

"Wow," Jessica whispered in astonishment as she gazed up into the canopy of leaves, imagining Elves to be up there.

"It is pretty spectacular," he continued. "They build beautiful and elaborate villages up near the tops of these trees."

"I'd love to see them!" Jessica squealed. "Do you think we'll see these Woodland Elves?"

"Be careful what you wish for," Artemis warned. "Not all of them are as nice as you would think."

Structures built around the trees and in the branches were now starting to reveal themselves. Jessica could see intricate spiral staircases constructed around the trunks of trees, leading up and up until she couldn't see it anymore. As she stared at the triumph of architecture, suddenly a projectile-net flew through the air out of nowhere, knocked her off of Artemis, and at the same time wrapped her up like a blanket. Jessica cried out as she hit the ground with a thud. Artemis neighed in protest and trotted over to where she was sprawled out, uselessly trying to fight herself free from the net.

"There seems to be some kind of enchantment on this net," Jessica cried out. "I can't conjure my Soulmind enough to help me get free." No sooner had she uttered these words, then both her and Artemis were surrounded by no less than ten Woodland Elves. They had long spears aimed at the unicorn and his human companion.

These Elves were easily the most beautiful humanoid creatures that Jessica had ever laid eyes on. They were all tall and slender; easily over six feet. Their hair was straight and long, either golden or silver, and their pointed ears stuck out from between the cascades of their locks on the sides of their heads. Also they were adorned with jewelry; fine headbands of silver as well as rings with shiny stones on their long fingers. They wore garb that could only be described as regal. Jessica would have admired how gorgeous they were if she wasn't so busy being afraid for her life.

"Should I try something else?" Jessica whispered to Artemis. "Some kind of specific Soulmind attack?"

"I wouldn't," Artemis warned. "They possess magick as well."

"We have been watching you traveling through our forest," the tallest Elf said, looking down at Jessica. His name was Odelliam and his long blonde hair shone in the evening sun. "This is our sacred land. How dare you come to defile it. You are spies of Pan, come to steal from us!"

Jessica exchanged a worried look with Artemis. "We aren't *spies of Pan*, I swear!" she pleaded.

"Then why do you ooze with the stench of Pan?" Odelliam pressed further, moving his spear closer to the net. His blue eyes were suspicious of the two intruders.

Jessica didn't have an answer for that one. Did she really spend the night with Pan, she wondered, or was that a dream? She raised her arm and took a whiff of her armpit. Cringing, she realized that she *did* stink, but wasn't sure if it was *Pan-stink.*

"Raka! Zelda! Take the unicorn to the stables and tie him up," Odelliam ordered.

"Yes, sir!" the two Elves said in unison and then began to lead Artemis away. The unicorn went without protest.

"Now for you," Odelliam said, addressing Jessica again. "We will take you up to The Hole until we decide what to do with you spies of Pan."

It was useless to argue over the fact that they weren't spies of Pan, Jessica knew. Best to just go along and see what mad task was to be set before her this time. "Is this the Upperworld?" she mumbled, looking up into the treetops.

"Yes, we live in the Upperworld," Odelliam answered. "Some cannot survive the higher levels of mysticism required to dwell there. We shall see if you're strong enough to even be among us."

Jessica cocked her head to the side. "So you weren't expecting me, then?" she asked. "This isn't just a test?"

Odelliam laughed loudly. "Expecting you? Foolish girl, we've never seen the likes of you before. If it is a test, it is not one of our design. Nevertheless, we will take you up. Tantel, if you would."

One of the more muscular Elves—Tantel, Jessica presumed—grabbed the net she was trapped inside and heaved it up and slung it over his back. Tantel carried her like a knapsack as Odelliam led them all toward the spiral staircase that climbed the tree into the Upperworld.

SIX

"Can you feel it?" Nikola asked.

"It's weird," Eden replied. She was sitting in a chair that closely resembled one a person would be in for a dentist appointment. A long metal plug was imbedded deep in her brainstem and the thick cord trailed down from the back of her head and snaked along the floor of the lab. "It's like I'm in twenty different people at once."

Nikola chuckled. "Yeah, it takes a little getting used to after connecting into the hive-mind. But you'll get the hang of it. All directives are operated directly from your consciousness. All you have to do is think it."

They were in the middle of his laboratory, surrounded by inventions and electrical odds and ends. Nikola was staring into a large monitor perched on top of a desk. He controlled the monitor-computer with a holographic keyboard. The image on the feed was coming from the camera imbedded in the head of one of the robots in the garage. After pressing a button on the keyboard, the garage door whined and slowly began to open, sunlight flooding in to illuminate the army of robots waiting there.

After a few moments of Eden concentrating, the group of metal-men began to march forward out of the garage door all at once. Every one of them was synchronized in their movements. The garage opened into an alley between Nikola's building and the one next to it. Taking a left down the alley led to the sidewalk and the road where cars zoomed by going wherever it was they went from day to day.

"That's good, that's good," Nikola said, watching the feed.

"I can only move them all together," Eden said with a frown. "Why can't I move the robots individually?"

"That's normal at first," he assured her. "It took me a while to get the hang of it myself. However, the more you're linked into the hive-mind, the more you'll get better with navigating the individual A.I. brains. You can control them synchronized—which is what you're doing now—or you can focus your consciousness into one or more and move them independently of the herd."

"How do I do that?" Eden wanted to know.

Nikola shrugged. "You'd think these things are always scientific, but they're not. When you're dealing with consciousness it's a little more tricky. We don't know what consciousness is, and it doesn't work like a machine. So you'll just have to find your own way to navigate yourself through the synthetic synapses."

"Great, that's very helpful," she groaned. "Luckily my Soul-mind helps me learn things relatively quickly."

"I don't have that advantage," Nikola commented as he pressed a couple keys on his holographic keyboard which illuminated when he touched them.

"Oh, yeah," Eden returned. "I forgot about that. I don't hang around many unactivated people these days."

She used her will to make all the robots turn to the left, facing the sidewalk at the end of the alley. They all turned simultaneously. Through their eyes she could a see a steady stream of people walking in both directions on the sidewalk; and beyond that the cars trying to make their way through the traffic of the day.

"I don't know what their purpose is yet," Nikola continued, "but they can accomplish even complex tasks. I've used them to build structures and machines at a quicker and more efficient rate than even a whole group of construction workers. They can make deliveries. Direct traffic, repair cars. You know, useful things."

"You don't use them as a police force?" she asked.

"There isn't much crime in the City. And the crime that does happen is most likely really covert. I'm not law enforcement, remember, I'm just a simple scientist and inventor. There's so many people in the City—not to mention clones as well. Some buildings are a mile tall. There's so much going on. I can hardly even keep track of what *I'm* working on here."

She thought about this for a while as she explored the herd of robots standing still in the alley. Her Soulmind helped her figure out how to jump from one robot to the next with her consciousness, like a ghost in the machine, possessing them like a conjured entity. But was she a benevolent spirit, or was she a malevolent demon bent on domination?

"I think I'm getting the hang of it," she said as she hopped into one of the robots in the front row of the group. Still she could feel the rest of the horde as thoughts in the back of her mind, but the one she was in was the dominant one. Slowly she began to move this one autonomously from the rest of its metal brothers. Awkwardly it took a couple stumble-steps forward until Eden was able to level it out and get a firm grip on its controls.

Nikola watched the monitor with his mouth open in astonishment. "My God," he said. "I can't believe you got one to move on its own so quickly. It took me two full sessions of jacking-in to do that."

"Well, I'm a quick learner," she replied offhand. "Now what else can these rust-buckets do? Can they fly? Can they shoot guns built into their arms?"

Nikola laughed. "I didn't build weapons into them. They aren't for aggression—what is it with you these days? They're designed to *help* humanity, not destroy them. Anyway, put all that violence out of your head. They *can* fly, to answer your question. I built rocket-powered thrusters into their feet. And vents along their legs so they can control their trajectory through the air."

"So fucking cool," Eden said. "Now I can see how Terry felt when he was flying around."

"Terry can fly?" Nikola asked, raising his eyebrows.

"Yeah," she answered, "he uses this Merkabah Field thing. I don't really understand it and he never taught me how to do it. Shoulda fucking asked him to show me that. Would be the coolest ability ever."

"Merkabah Field?" he shook his head. "I don't know what that is... And I thought I knew about every kind of technology—even Light Technology."

Eden attempted to give the command to *fly* telepathically. She could feel something begin to rumble in the feet of the robot. Blue flames shot from the bottom of the feet and the metal-man began to hover about a foot into the air. Eden was having a difficult time maintaining grip and control on the machine. "You didn't use the same anti-gravity technology in these guys as you did in the flying cars?" she asked.

"Actually, they have both," Nikola answered. "Anti-gravity built in to the whole structure, and the thrusters for more mobility. I'm impressed that you got that function to work so quickly."

"You shouldn't still be impressed at this point," Eden smirked, her eyes still closed as she focused on the machine her consciousness was inside. "You should know by now that I'm a fucking *genius*."

"Ha," he laughed at that. "Oh, I'm not laughing because I don't believe you," he added. "It just sounded funny. You are extremely intelligent, that's why I knew you'd be great to help me with some of my new projects. Not to mention that your Soulmind gives you *innate* intelligence—and astute intuition."

"You're goddamn right, Nikola," she responded. "Now let's get this fucking party started!"

After she said this, she rocketed the robot upwards between the two buildings. These skyscrapers stretched high into the sky; too high for her even to see the tops. She wanted to see how high she could fly this metal-man. Like the *Iron Giant*, she thought. This could be a fun toy; and even things not created to be weapons could easily be used that way or converted into one. The robot kept flying higher and higher like a rocket shot into space. Now the high vantage point gave a great view of the swarms of flying cars zipping through the skies of the City, as well as the sprawl of the districts and buildings of the landscape before her.

"Careful," Nikola warned. "It's more difficult to control the handling of the robot while you're airborne."

Eden smiled to herself wickedly as she stared out through the robot's eyes. It hovered between the buildings facing the flow of traffic that moved like a river through the skies. Suddenly the robot's feet kicked backwards and its metal body was propelled into the midst of the flying cars. "Oh, shit!" Eden exclaimed, feigning that it was an accident. Almost instantaneously, the robot was struck by a car flying at at least sixty miles-per-hour. The explosion was monstrous; and as parts of the robot detached from its body and rained down toward the road below, Eden felt a jerk as her consciousness was ripped from the destroyed robot and deposited back into the robots still standing in the alley.

The flying car that collided with the robot was totaled and it plummeted down through the air like a meteor on fire. Pedestrians ran for cover as the burning wreckage rained down toward them.

"That's okay. That's okay," Nikola said as he watched the destruction on the monitor. "Accidents happen. I've had my fair share trying to get these things to work, to be honest. It'll get cleaned up."

Eden ignored him and took control of the next robot in the front row of the group. She made it run towards the sidewalk at the end of the alley where she could see pedestrians still running to get away from the smoldering wreckage. Reaching out its metal hand, she grabbed a stray woman by the neck and lifted her into the air.

"No, please," the woman begged as she clawed at the metal hand around her throat. Then with one smooth movement, Eden grabbed the woman's arm with the robot's other hand and tore her right arm and head from her squirming body. Blood gushed from the severed neck and shoulder. The headless body twitched on the sidewalk as it bled out, a red pool spreading incredibly fast. The robot chucked the head and arm into the fire smoldering in the middle of the road. All the pedestrians that had been running now were screaming louder in horror at the homicidal robot dripping with human blood. They scattered like roaches trying to get as far from the carnage as possible.

Nikola stared in horror at the monitor. The camera behind the robot's eyes now only picked up images through a haze of red. At first he was frozen in shock, then he regained control of his body and ran over to the control chair Eden was reclining in. Without hesitation, he ripped the long plug out of the back of her neck, instantly severing the connection with the hive-mind. The disconnect from the robots was so sudden that it was jarring. Her head spun and when she opened her eyes, it looked like the room was spinning.

"No!" Nikola said harshly. "No more violence!"

"Ugh," she groaned, putting her palm against her right temple. "The fuck..."

"You can't just go around killing people," he continued, reprimanding her, his face a painting of anger and distress.

Eden narrowed her eyes as the spinning began to abate. She glared at him. "Who says?"

Nikola huffed. "Really?" he responded. "*That's* you're response: *who says?*"

She shrugged. "What authority do you have over me to tell me what I can't do?"

Shaking his head, Nikola went back over to the monitor and pressed a couple buttons on the holographic keyboard. The robots all turned around and marched like wind-up toys back into the garage, after which he closed the door to the unit. "I really don't know what to say," he admitted. "I'm not sure how to feel about this. I'll give you one more chance, but if you're going to be working with me, we need to lay down some ground rules—"

"Fuck your rules!" Eden cut him off.

"Excuse me?" Nikola shot her a look.

She suddenly got a smug smile on her face. "It seems to me that I should really be running this show, and I think you'll come to agree. Maybe you should work for *me*," she continued. "You said it yourself that no one in this world is more powerful than me, so who is there to challenge my authority? *You?*"

The inventor shook his head, mouth hanging slightly open in shock. He couldn't find any words in response.

"Got nothing to say, Nikola?" she prodded. "Cat got your cock? This is how it's going to go, okay. You don't get to lay down any fucking ground rules. *I* make all the rules and there's no way you can stop me. We could make a great team, you and I. If you make the right choice. You could either have a most powerful ally, or you could choose to make me your enemy. But I warn you, if things go that way, it won't end up well for you. And I hate to see a good friend and brilliant scientist end up that way."

Nikola stared at her as if she had just sprouted legs from her forehead. "I don't know what you want me to say," he responded, finally.

"Well, my lovely compatriot," Eden said as she stood up from the control chair and slinked over to Nikola. She placed a soft kiss on his cheek and he recoiled inside. "I'm going to go back up to our apartment to recline and enjoy the luxury. You give this matter some deep thought and I'm confident you will come around to my side."

Nikola stared at her as she walked off toward the door swinging her hips as she went. As she exited the lab, she fingered the keycard in her pocket. Eden smiled, delighted that she could come and go as she pleased; and the realization that no one could stop her brought her even more pleasure than what she felt ripping the head off of that woman and tossing her body parts into the street.

SEVEN

The flying car was parked outside of Mika'el's little farmhouse. It hovered about three feet above the dirt and looked incredibly out of place amidst the fields and animals that grazed there. Nikola had come to see his old friend and get his perspective on the situation with Eden. They were standing in the kitchen; Mika'el was leaning against the counter with his arms crossed and a serious expression on his face. Nikola was standing near him by the table.

"I don't know what to do, Mika'el," Nikola continued apprehensively. "She's out of control. I thought maybe I could reach her emotionally and abate some of her rage by giving her an outlet of helping me with my experiments, but she seems to be hell-bent on creating chaos and killing. Eden seems to be a completely different person without Terry by her side. I don't recognize this person who's sharing my apartment with me. Is she a different entity than the one I met who took out the Stone Queen and freed our people? I can't kill her, my friend. For I know deep in my bones that she's indispensable for Terry's transformation of the Spiralverse. But now, it seems like her intention is to enslave us all again—like the Queen did." He shrugged, exasperated.

"I understand your concerns, Nikola. And I'm hearing all of them," Mika'el said, validating his friend's assessment of the situation. "However, I find it odd that it seems you've spontaneously grown a conscience." Nikola looked at him incredulously. "Not that you have ill will toward your own people," he added. "But it's not like you would sacrifice your own wellbeing for the sake of the masses. Don't you remember how you got that fancy apartment, and all those high-tech toys to play with?"

"What are you implying?" Nikola shot back, narrowing his eyes. "I do not wish to see my countrymen enslaved again by a force asserting its dominance just because it *can*. Eden is not evil, I know that deep in my heart, but her love connection with Terry being severed has turned her into some kind of monster."

"I say we ride it out for now," Mika'el said decisively. "Don't make waves, stay on her good side. Do what she tells you to do, for it is in our best interest to stay close to her. If she kills you that's no good for anyone."

Nikola raised his eyebrows. "You're suggesting I enable her reprehensible behavior? That would be condoning actions I would never do myself."

Mika'el laughed ironically. "Are you serious right now? You don't have a moral leg to stand on. Not that I'm judging you. I'm just as much to blame as you are—of standing around while others suffer."

"What?" Nikola responded, unsure of what his friend was referring to.

"What do you mean *what*?" Mika'el answered the question with a question.

"We're to blame for what?"

"Oh, come on, my brother," Mika'el continued, "don't act like you don't know what I'm talking about. We didn't even try to stop her. Even though *we* were the ones who released her from her prison, letting her have free reign of our Dimension. Yes, neither of us would ever kill people, that's not in our nature, but we remain guilty of letting her free to enslave us all."

"What are you talking about? I don't remember that." Nikola replied honestly. Mika'el searched his face for any dishonesty.

He could find there none. Apparently his friend had no memory of the events that allowed the Queen access to the Kingdom.

"You really don't remember?" Mika'el prodded. Nikola shook his head. "We've kept our secret all of these years. No one except us knows that it was our fault she came. It was when we were experimenting with Alchemy. You really don't remember? The Queen had been sentenced for all eternity in a subspace prison for her intergalactic crimes of destruction of entire worlds. She was completely cut off in solitary confinement in this sub-space, with no hope of escape. However—this is where we made a deadly mistake—one of our Alchemy experiments got out of hand and opened up a Stargate which penetrated into the sub-space coordinates she inhabited. I have no idea what the odds of that are, but it happened. And that Stargate was open just enough for her to come through into our Dimension. We knew she was dangerous the moment she came through, and we did *nothing* to even try to stop her. Admittedly that was mostly out of fear for our own lives, understandably. Our experiments gone awry led to all our people being enslaved for years. That's the guilt we've had to live with all this time. If the people knew, they'd crucify us, my friend."

Nikola shook his head, speechless. "I have no memory of that at all."

"Are you feeling okay?" Mika'el asked, frowning. "Do you have amnesia or something?"

"I don't know," he answered.

Mika'el nodded and gestured for his friend to come closer. "Come here for a moment. Let me have a look at your brain."

Nikola walked over hesitantly and stood in front of his friend. "What are you going to do?" he asked.

"Just a little psychic scan," Mika'el replied. "Close your eyes for me."

Nikola obeyed and Mika'el pressed the pad of his right thumb against Nikola's forehead, between his eyebrows where his third eye was. Mika'el took a deep breath in and let it out with a sigh as he closed his eyes. Projecting his consciousness into his friend's head, Mika'el searched Nikola's brain for signs of damage or memory loss. For a couple minutes, his face was a portrait of pure concentration, determined to understand what was going on with his friend. Suddenly he sighed and took his hand away, opening his eyes as well.

"What? What did you see?" Nikola wanted to know. "Is there something wrong with me?"

"Have you been working on your Artificial Intelligence project?"

"Yeah. Why?" Nikola answered.

"I saw you jacking-in to your hive of robots—the chair and the brain plug," Mika'el continued. "And how that's all connected to the Brain that you set up in the sky above the City."

"And?" Nikola was really interested now.

"And—relax, I'm getting there," Mika'el said, irritated. "Don't be so damn impatient. Each time you jack-in to the robot hive-mind, you lose some of your memories. They get siphoned out and given to the Brain, where they seem to get lost as data."

"What? Are you serious?" Nikola said, disturbed by this new information. "I didn't know that was happening. Maybe I can figure out how to fix that glitch. In the meantime I should warn Eden that she could lose all her memories the more she connects to the hive-mind."

Mika'el shook his head. "No."

"No?" Nikola frowned. "What do you mean *no*?"

"Maybe this could work to our advantage," Mika'el explained, stroking his long white beard thoughtfully. "This is how: I could see the possibility of Eden's rage dissipating along with the loss of memories. In other words, she'll forget why she's so angry, and then she'll forget she's angry altogether. That could possibly allow you to gain some control again. She'll become more docile and open to suggestion."

Nikola furrowed his brow, thinking about this. "Interesting," he said. "You really think that's possible?"

"That seems likely to be the most probable outcome," Mika'el admitted. "So don't rock the boat. Be very agreeable with her, and maybe even encourage her to jack-in more and more. That would speed up the process and hopefully lessen the death and destruction she seems intent on bringing to our Dimension."

"But what if she loses all of her memories and they remain unretrievable in the Brain?" Nikola asked.

"That seems like a small sacrifice to make in the long run, don't you agree?"

Nikola nodded reluctantly.

"That way," Mika'el continued, "we don't even have to entertain the possibility that we'd need to end her life. She'll be alive and there will be minimal casualties along the way. Just make sure *you* don't jack-in anymore. You wouldn't want to lose anymore of your own memories. And who knows, maybe we'll be able to code a program for memory retrieval out of the Brain. Then both of you could get your memories back eventually."

"I'm somewhat relieved," Nikola told his friend. "Your wisdom always comforts me when I feel there's a crisis at hand."

"Come here, my friend," Mika'el said, opening his arms. Nikola came in for a hug. "Trust me, we haven't reached crisis level yet. And if we ever get to that point, I'll know, and mark my words, this time I *will* intervene."

EIGHT

"Where the fuck is it?" Eden mumbled to herself as she snooped through Nikola's lab. After he had driven away in his flying car to see Mika'el, she went down there to look for a device she suspected was real and being hidden from her. She remembered when Nikola showed up amidst the chaos she was creating, he had his hive of robots behind him—but obviously he wasn't connected to the chair set up in his lab to control the hive-mind. So how was he controlling them? Eden wondered. Her deduction was that there most likely had to be a wireless device that attached to the neck, or head, or something which could remote-access the network without having to be stuck in the plug-chair.

Crouching down below the desk that held the large monitor, she rummaged through a couple boxes stored there. These boxes were full of junk: old wires and cords, motherboards and computer chips. Nothing that seemed like what she was looking for. A tingling in her Soulmind suggested that her intuition was sending her a message that she was close though. Out of impulse, Eden turned her head to look up at the underside of the desk—and there it was! It was a small, circular metal saucer-looking device with a round button in the center. A magnet had been rigged to keep it hidden and adhered to the bottom of the desk. Eden smirked and shook her head. "Clever bastard," she commented. "Thought you could hide it from me."

Pulling the device loose from the magnet, she placed it against her neck behind her right ear. When she pressed the button, a thick needle extended from inside the metal and pierced through her neck, deep enough to forge a connection with her brainstem. Eden winced at the pain of being pricked, then she could feel her consciousness connect with the hive-mind once more. As she left the laboratory, she felt high on power and the thought of what she was planning to do.

Seyba looked up from his desk as Eden passed by through the lobby and toward the main entrance. As she walked by, she waved at him and winked. "Good day, Miss," he said in greeting. "How are you this fine morning?"

"I'm flying high, Seyba," Eden responded with a grin. "Everything is falling into place. See you later. Ciao!" As she exited through the front, she fluttered the fingers of her right hand in a playful gesture. Not wasting any time, she walked around the side of the building and then into the alley where the garage was that housed the robots. There was a small gray box on the wall next to the door and Eden swiped her keycard across it. The garage door rumbled and then started to go up, revealing the beauty of her own personal metal army. The robots whirred to life as she gave them the directive to follow her. When they were all out in the alley standing behind her, she swiped her keycard again, closing the garage behind her.

As they walked down the sidewalks of the City, people gave them as wide a berth as possible. The fear on their faces gave Eden such a rush that she vowed never to go anywhere without her entourage in tow. Today she wouldn't tear people apart or blow up cars, she had bigger plans in mind.

Finally they were standing outside Eden's favorite place in all of The Kingdom: The Queen's Wild Orchid Palace—which was just The Wild Orchid Palace now since the Queen was no more, thanks to Eden and Terry. She walked in being trailed by her synthetic army, carrying herself with the most confident authority. Inside, the casino looked pretty much the same as it did the first time she had laid eyes on it. It felt like home, and the only differences she could see were that the waitresses in the transparent bikinis carried cocktails on their platters instead of orchids, and the patrons didn't seem to be in a trance anymore.

"Who the fuck is in charge here?" she demanded of no one in particular. "I want to talk to who runs this place!" Scanning around, she registered all the security cameras and also the patrons who had stopped what they were doing to stare at her. Hopefully her message was getting back to the boss. She didn't like to be kept waiting. Less than a minute later an older man wearing a blue suit with a red tie came walking into the room followed by his security detail, about ten men in black suits wearing sunglasses. They all had guns at their hip.

The older man approached Eden tentatively. "My name is Ross Childe," he said loudly. "I own this place now that the Queen is no more." This man was even uglier up close, and Eden gagged a little inside. He was bald on the top of his head, dark hair around the sides. There were dark spots on his scalp and he had a long hooked nose. He also had a massive overbite, upper teeth protruding from under his top lip like a Satanic rabbit that likes to eat its own babies.

"Ugh, you're one ugly fuck," she said with a grimace.

"Excuse me?" Ross Childe said indignantly, taking offense to the remark. "I'll have you know I'm the richest—"

"I don't give a fuck how rich you are!" Eden spat back, cutting him off. "As of this moment, The Wild Orchid Palace is under new management—me!"

"You little cunt!" he snarled at her, but was eyeing the robots behind her warily. "I'm so powerful I could have you—"

Eden stepped forward and grasped Ross Childe by the throat, wrapping her thin fingers around his old scrawny neck. "You what?" she scoffed. "You couldn't do shit!"

The security detail instantly had their hands at their hips and were unholstering their guns. They pointed their weapons at Eden as her pink and red Soulmind started to spiral out of her solar plexus. The energy wound its way up her arm like a snake and she started to lift Ross Childe off the ground. His feet dangled in the air as he choked and scratched at her hand uselessly.

"I fucking wouldn't, if I were you!" Eden screamed at the men who had their guns trained on her. Obviously they couldn't see her Soulmind, but they could feel how powerful her energy was and they all began to tremble in fear. "I am the one who destroyed the Stone Queen," she continued. "I am a powerful sorceress, not to mention I have an army of robots who will do my every command. In one burst of energy your guts would be dripping from the ceiling. Do you want to keep your jobs and work for me, or do you all want to fucking die?"

She squeezed Ross Childe's throat tighter. He tried to scream but only managed to produce a gurgle and an expression of anguish. The security men hesitated and then began to holster their weapons again, giving each other worried glances. "You're fired, *Ross Childe*," she growled menacingly. "And I'll say it again for the benefit of anyone who didn't *fucking* hear me: the casino is under new management. *Me!*"

In one more squeeze, Eden crushed Ross Childe's windpipe and snapped his neck. The spine severed with a loud *crack*, and then she tossed the body toward the slot machines. A woman screamed and ran for the door. Eden smirked and let her go; let them be scared of her, she hoped the woman would spread the word of the new mistress of The Wild Orchid Palace. "Now," she continued, looking back at the men in black suits standing before her. "You made the right choice. Swear allegiance to me."

All together the men said: *"Yes, ma'am! We swear allegiance to you!"*

Eden waved her hand dismissively. "Yeah, okay, that was good. Just don't call me *ma'am*. Call me *Mistress*."

"*Yes, Mistress!*"

"That's better," she said, cracking her knuckles. "Now if you all would just come with me back to my office, I'm going to need you all to sign your names in blood." She winked at them.

The security glanced at each other again anxiously from behind their sunglasses. "What, Mistress?" one of them squeaked out.

Eden burst out laughing. "I'm *kidding!* I'm just fucking with you," she said, still cracking up. The security guards sighed with relief, visibly releasing the tension. "Jeez, you guys need to relax. And clean this shit up." She pointed with her thumb toward the dead body of Ross Childe. "I could sign your foreheads with my menstrual blood," she continued, still stringing out the blood joke. And as she started walking past the group of security toward the other regions of the casino, she commented: "You don't need to sign contracts in blood for me. That would be unnecessary. Unless you really want to..." Then she disappeared into the rest of The Wild Orchid Palace, followed by her robots, and cackling like a moonstricken lunatic.

It was quick work for Eden to bring the casino under her control. She had the waitresses serve the orchids to patrons once again. Not because she wished to keep everyone trapped in the casino, but just because she liked the high the orchids gave and wished to make it available in case anyone wanted to have a good trip. There was a huge penthouse on the top floor of The Wild Orchid Palace, and she claimed it at once. Eden enjoyed living in the lap of luxury and also having slaves to do her bidding—both living and robotic.

The hive-mind of the robots proved to be very beneficial for doing construction and maintenance tasks. Eden had a special room built in her penthouse which served as her throne room. The throne she had constructed was made using the most expensive wood and stained black. She had the logos of all the most famous corporations from the Hollow Dimension carved into it. It sat in the middle of the floor toward the back of the room. All of the walls were screens and she could monitor any part of the casino where she had cameras set up. The most important place for her to have them was the *Temple of Cosmic Fuck*. Most of the time Eden just had the orgy streaming on the walls of her throne room. The last piece she had constructed was a drain in the middle of the floor for easy clean-up.

Eden never removed the wireless connector from her neck. She was constantly jacked-in to the hive-mind of the robots. They wandered around the casino most of the time, so virtually she had eyes and ears everywhere. However, she was completely unaware that most of her memories were constantly being drained into the Brain hovering above the City.

Sitting on her throne, Eden watched the mass of sexy bodies fucking on all the screens surrounding her. Giving a mental directive to one of her robots, she told it to bring her the man who was head of security. Two minutes later the robot entered her throne room followed by a large man in a black suit. "Ah, yes, my minions," she said as they walked in, "come closer." She gestured a *come here* motion with her finger. The head of security looked around at the explicit sex on the screens and swallowed hard. Then both the flesh-man and metal-man stood in front of Eden's throne, awaiting orders.

"Yes, Mistress?" the man said.

"You," she replied, pointing at him, "bring me a sacrifice. And you," she indicated the robot, "bring me Nikola. I wish to have him."

Both the man and the robot bowed to her, turned, and left the room. As Eden stared at the sex, she got really horny waiting for her human sacrifice. Slowly she stripped off her clothes and sat naked on her throne, rubbing her clit with her legs spread wide. Her juices dripped onto the seat of the throne as she got increasingly wet. Just as she was feeling really hot and bothered, the head of security came back in with a few other security guards dragging a woman by her arms. This woman was protesting and sobbing as they threw her to her knees at Eden's feet. Without a word, the men left the room to let Eden fulfill her forbidden lusts.

"Please, please don't kill me," the woman begged, her hands covered her face as she cried. Eden stood up from her throne and looked down at this pitiful, helpless creature. The woman appeared to be in her mid-thirties. She was thin and wore a pair of jeans and a loose t-shirt. Eden could tell the woman wasn't wearing a bra and had saggy mom-tits. Stepping forward and spreading her legs, she grabbed the woman's brown hair in her fists and smashed her tear-streaked face into her crotch.

"Eat that fucking cunt!" Eden commanded, and she could feel the woman tremble against her naked flesh. That really got her going; it was so hot. Tentatively, the woman began to lap at Eden's wet pussy. "Yeah, just like that," she moaned, tilting her head back as she closed her eyes. "Be my fucking whore, you worthless flea."

The woman sniffled as she switched to flicking the tip of her tongue against Eden's swollen clit. "Please," the woman mumbled through a mouthful of snatch.

"Don't fucking talk," Eden shot back, grinding the woman's head harder onto her pussy lips. "You were doing such a good job that I know you've done this before. You slutty dyke bitch."

The crying woman fell silent again and did what she was told, pleasuring Eden with her wet mouth, tongue, and lips. After several minutes of letting the pleasure build up in her cunt, Eden sighed and kicked the pathetic bag of flesh and bones away from her. The woman sprawled out on her ass on the floor. "I know you like the taste of my cunt in your teeth," Eden continued as she turned back toward the throne. "Strip! I want you naked."

There was a special hidden compartment that Eden had constructed under her throne of logos. She hid a machete in this compartment; she had that specially designed as well. The blade was razor-sharp and also had spikes on the back-edge. The hilt was shaped like an erect cock with two goat horns growing out of it. When Eden turned around again with this weapon in her hand, the woman was sobbing harder, crouched on the floor, and slowly peeling off her clothes. Once she was fully naked, she tried to cover her saggy tits with her arms crossed in front of her chest.

"No covering yourself," Eden snapped, pointing the sharp end of the machete toward the woman's head. Reluctantly she uncovered herself, revealing large nipples that were elongated like the reservoir end of a condom. She also had a hairy bush that Eden found incredibly sexy. "Stand up, you slut!" Eden gave the order and it was obeyed. "Now spread those legs." She used the blade of the machete to push the woman's thighs open wider. "Let me get into that pussy."

Eden flipped the machete over and inserted the penis-handle into the woman's vagina. The woman cried out, sobbing and moaning at the same time. Her eyes were clenched shut as Eden thrusted the dildo-hilt in and out of that cunt. She was getting wet, and in spite of the horrific sexual assault, it felt good. The woman silently cursed her body for getting pleasure from the violation.

While Eden was enjoying the woman's wet pussy, she heard footsteps outside the door of the throne room. As the door swung open, Nikola entered, followed by several of her army of robots. They closed the door behind them and Nikola stared at the scene before him with a pained expression on his face. Eden pulled the machete handle out of the woman and flipped her around, holding her body against hers and the blade to her throat. "You're just in time for the climax," Eden said, smiling. She loved the feeling of her breasts pressed against the woman's back, and the woman's ass pressed against her pelvis.

Nikola didn't say *anything*; he just watched as Eden sliced the blade across the woman's throat. The face of the woman was a silent scream as blood began to gush from the gash. Eden dropped the machete and it clattered to the floor among spatters of blood. She spun the woman around and stood there as the warm blood bathed her naked body. Opening her mouth, Eden could feel the delicious orgasm tear through her body like lightning. She could taste the blood on her tongue and between her teeth. After wiping the blood from her eyes, she watched the woman fall to the floor where the blood pooled and she gave her last few dying twitches before she finally laid still.

Nikola still didn't say anything, he just watched in silence. Eden stared at him with bloodlust and sexual-lust burning in her eyes. Wiping the blood over her tits and down over her snatch, she moaned with forbidden ecstasy. "You know you like it," she said, taunting Nikola. And then something caught her eye near the throne. To the right of the Logo Throne, a small portal was opening up in the air. It was made of Black Mist and couldn't have been more than five inches in diameter. Black tendrils wafted around the edges like dark smoke. "Do you see that?" Eden asked, pointing to the portal.

Nikola looked where she was pointing but saw nothing since he didn't have a Soulmind to grant him Pan-Dimensional sight. He shook his head. "No, I don't see anything. Is there something there?" he asked, pursing his lips.

Eden nodded, approaching the portal slowly. When she was right in front of it, she put out an exploratory finger and touched its black surface. Suddenly another rush of orgasmic ecstasy possessed her body. Instantly she squirted from her cunt, her pussy juice mixing with the blood running down her legs. She knew then what it was. "It's a portal to the Taboo Zone," she whispered in awe.

"The Taboo Zone?" Nikola repeated. "What's that? I still don't see anything."

"Of course you don't see anything," she threw back. "You don't have a Soulmind. You can't see other Dimensions."

"So it's a Dimension?" he pressed, still not sure whether Eden was just hallucinating or not. "Like the Hollow Dimension?"

Eden looked over at Nikola, frowned, and raised her bloody eyebrows. "The Hollow Dimension?" she asked. "What's that?"

Oh no, Nikola thought, swallowing hard. *She must be losing memories faster and at a greater volume than I even realized.* "Oh, I don't know," he answered, trying to shrug it off. "Some other Dimension I just heard of."

Eden was dismissive and turned back to the portal to the Taboo Zone. Slowly she slid her whole hand inside, and then her arm all the way up to mid-bicep. Nikola's jaw dropped open as he saw her arm begin to disappear into thin air. Maybe he couldn't see the portal, but he could sure see that her fucking arm was vanishing into *somewhere. Okay, I guess she isn't hallucinating.*

Eden's legs began to tremble with the growing ecstasy. She moaned in bliss and was almost losing consciousness from the intensity of the euphoria flowing into her body from the portal. The culmination of all of the forbidden pleasures were being condensed into her body as one climactic eruption. Her clit was going crazy—in fact her whole body felt like one *giant* clitoris. "Oh my God! Oh my God! Oh my God!" she screamed and moaned. "God, fuck me hard!" she yelled as she could feel the sweet seduction of the forbidden—every taboo ever indulged in by someone brave enough or insane enough to do so.

Even Nikola could feel the orgasmic runoff of energy; that's how powerful it was. He swallowed hard and could feel activity in his pants. Not sure what to do, he just stood there paralyzed by the strange vision before him. After several minutes of God-fucking the portal, Eden opened her eyes and pulled her arm back out of the dark mists. She stared at her arm which was now stained pitch black all the way up to the mid-bicep point where she had stopped when it was inside. Flexing her black fingers, Eden smiled the smile of power and then made a fist. Her eyes gleamed and she regarded Nikola once more.

In a few quick strides, she was over in front of him, face close to his. Taking her black hand, the right one, she stroked her fingers through Nikola's luscious hair and brought his face down toward her own. Eden kissed him hard, wiggling her tongue into his mouth like a horny teenager. He winced as he tasted the blood in her mouth, but he didn't pull away. Nikola knew that he had to be intelligent about how he handled this whole situation with Eden; she was unpredictable and capable of *anything*, obviously. So he leaned in and kissed her back; plus he couldn't deny to himself that he was attracted to her despite the psychotic behavior.

After the quick make-out, Eden detached her lips and looked Nikola in the eyes intensely. "I can do anything I want," she whispered as Nikola glanced at her black arm, "and so can you."

NINE

The thing about True Time, Terry knew, is that it's *all in your mind.* That means that it doesn't run according to a tick-tock of a clock that didn't exist anyway. An individual's True Time could stretch like taffy, or compress like a skull in a vise. He also knew that one could even find themselves slipping forward into the future (which is just another now point at a different time-space coordinate); or back in 'time' as they're taken by the slipstream. He stared at the blank wall of his cell and imagined the face of an analog clock hanging there. In his mind, Terry could see and hear the tick of the second hand circumnavigating the circumference of the strange imaginary object that didn't measure anything in reality.

Time's a flat circle, he thought, *so I'm always coming back.* That jogged his memory and he thought back to a conversation that he had had with Remius about whether time was linear or circular. The October had told him that time was linear; giving him some crap about timelines and not time-circles. *That was a crock of shit.* Terry now realized that time—whatever that was—wasn't that straight forward. Literally. People's minds have been so conditioned to accept that time is linear so that they can construct some kind of narrative in order to give their lives some semblance of meaning. Yes, happenings in the past affect the future, but also events in the future sometimes can affect the past. How was it that when Terry killed his parents in a dream so much later than when he found them dead did that end up becoming the origin of their demise? He knew he was trying to put pieces of a puzzle together that would never fit. When was the origin point? That dream of murder simultaneously became a point of origin in the past, in fact creating a time loop. A causal loop. When Terry discovered his parents' dead bodies, it planted the seed for the idea that what came after could only happen if they were out of the picture. So when it came time for Terry to recreate the scene in his dream, he knew it must happen, which then became the cause of their deaths in the first place. The Bootstrap Paradox.

Now, Terry wondered, had Remius known about the nature of True Time and deliberately given him false information? Or was the cat really under the false assumption that time was linear? *Knowing that fucking cat, he probably did it on purpose*, Terry thought, shaking his head. There's no way Remius was that stupid to not know about time-loops and paradoxes. Maybe he just needed to come to certain realizations on his own, instead of having Remius spoon-feed him every little bit of knowledge. Terry sighed and let the imaginary clock disappear from the wall. It felt like he had been in that cell for aeons. He was lonely and it seemed like Anna hadn't come to visit him in her Astral Body in a very long time. There it was again: Time. *Fuck you, Timestrus.*

Terry jumped as there was a sudden knock at the door. "It's your lucky day. You get to come out and play," said a familiar voice as the door opened. It was one of the inbred triplets, with the other two standing behind him. "Come on, you disgusting pervert," he continued, gesturing for Terry to get up and follow them. "Don't make us have to drag you there."

Terry narrowed his eyes to slits, glaring at the three men who's black suits always looked like they'd just been picked up from the dry-cleaners. Reluctantly he got off the bed and walked over to them. The suit-man in the front grabbed Terry's arm and dragged him out into the hallway. "That fucking hurts," he yelled. "Do you have to squeeze so *hard*?"

The inbred-clone-man glared at Terry through dark glasses. "Don't be such a pussy," he returned, spraying Terry's face with spittle. "No wonder you take it up the ass, you faggot. Get a move on, let's not keep the Director waiting."

Terry didn't say another word as they dragged him down the hall toward whatever room they were gonna throw him in this time. He was too tired for jokes today, and he'd become weary of the constant captivity with no sunlight or fresh air. They took him down a long hall, around a corner, around another corner, and finally stopped at a door in the middle of that hallway. "How the *fuck* do you guys find your way around this place?" Terry asked. "Do you guys have some sort of invisible leash around the tip of your dicks that the Director just pulls around wherever you need to go?"

By way of response, the suit-man opened the door and kicked Terry inside, slamming the door behind him. "You sadistic fucks just *love* abusing young people, don't you?" he yelled back through the closed door. "Don't you guys ever get tired of violating our goddess-given rights?"

Terry fell silent and turned to see what was so special about *this* room. It was significantly larger than any of the other rooms he'd been it. However, there was no chair in the center, no windows or mirrors as well. The walls were piss-yellow and there were cameras mounted in each corner of the ceiling. There was a larger steel door imbedded in the far wall. *What could come out of that, I wonder?* he thought to himself, getting a sick feeling in his stomach.

As he stood there watching the door, it finally opened and what emerged was more terrifying than he could have imagined.

It was like a whole SWAT team was pouring in to surround him. Each one had on the same gear: a black jumpsuit and a black helmet with a tinted visor that looked like it was made for riding a motorcycle. They were holding strange-looking guns; futuristic rifles with radiation blasters mounted on the top edge. Also a circular metal device was attached to the middle of their armored vests. These discs generated an electromagnetic field synthetically designed to withstand Soulmind energy. Their rifles were trained on Terry as then marched into the room aggressively.

"Fuck this shit," Terry said, and immediately called forth the black circle underneath himself. As quickly as he could, he wrapped himself in the black ropes of the Dark Tethers and tried to direct the pod where to relocate him. He thought of his home, his bedroom, and then Eden's smiling face invaded his thoughts. "Eden," he whispered, and then vanished into thin air before any of the thugs could get a shot off.

For a few moments, he was nowhere within a black void, not exactly sure where he was going to end up this time. Suddenly he felt his body fall into a substance that was cold and wet. The black tentacles disappeared into a wash of Black Mist and then was no more. Terry groaned and sat up. "Where the fuck am I?" he said out loud. His ass was wet and he realized that he was sitting in a couple inches of icy snow. Looking down, he saw that he had appeared on the side of a mountain. From this high vantage point, it was obvious that he had traveled back to The Kingdom. He was on the side of one of the mountains that encircled the entire domain. The closest section to his location was the City. It was strange to see it from an aerial view. The flying cars were tiny specks and looked like a hive of hornets buzzing around the impossibly tall buildings. He could also see the forest that bisected the two sections of The Kingdom, and beyond that, the Village.

As Terry stood up, being careful not to slip on the icy snow, he could unmistakably feel Eden's presence like a huge storm cloud threatening to flood everything below it. At once he was certain she was not far away. Out of curiosity, he turned to face up the slope and took a step. With a shock of surprise, he was pushed back by some invisible field. Stretching out his finger, he touched the barrier and it revealed itself: a neon-green grid of light. Obviously that was the edge of the Dimension, not allowing anything to pass through. The only way to travel in or out was to portal through—and that was only possible for people with Soulminds. After taking an adequate mental note of the grid, he turned back toward the City. Connecting to his Merkabah Field, Terry popped the golden sphere of light out from the anchor in his heart and spun the star tetrahedrons around his body. He floated up into the air, hovered there for a moment, then flew forward and down toward the City below. Eden was there somewhere, and he needed to find her.

TEN

"You want to see something funny?" Eden asked Nikola as she smiled and bounced her eyebrows up and down. Blood was still pooling under the woman's dead body and flowing into the drain in the middle of the floor. Nikola didn't answer, just stared at Eden expectantly. The robots stood close to the wall, motionless and silent.

Without waiting for a response, she walked over to her Logo Throne and pressed a hidden button imbedded in one of the armrests. A small square of the seat slid open to reveal a hollow pocket underneath. In a moment a purple dildo thrusted slowly up out of the hole and then descended back down. It continued this up and down motion as if it was fucking the air. Eden laughed. "My throne doubles as a fucking machine!" She grinned, very pleased with herself. Nikola smiled in spite of himself. "This way," Eden continued, "I can sit up here surrounded by a live-stream of what's going on in the *Temple of Cosmic Fuck* and fuck myself all day if I want to."

Nikola felt a slight twitch in his pants thinking about Eden naked on her throne as the dildo slid into and out of her dripping cunt. He didn't want that to be something that turned him on, but it did nonetheless. "You're the most oversexed person I've ever met," he admitted.

"Ha!" Eden chuckled at this. "You can never be *oversexed*. There can never be *too much* sex. There's never *enough* sex. Sometimes I fantasize about being an immortal sex god. I wouldn't need to eat, or sleep, or drink water. I'd just be in the throws of sex and sexual ecstasy for all eternity—preferably it would be an orgy. A pile of us all gyrating and fucking and licking and sucking forever and ever. A heavenly expression of one euphoric continuous GodFuck."

"Huh," Nikola said, thinking about this. "That's an interesting thought. You don't think you'd get bored only doing that one thing for all of Forever?"

Eden shook her head. "I don't think so. The pleasures of the flesh transcended into the expanse of the Spiralverse. We'd vibrate on every level of existence a consummate orgasm flowing all the way back to Source and then back to us in waves of unending bliss." She walked back over to Nikola, maintaining intense eye contact, and then grabbed his crotch, squeezing his cock and balls through his pants. "You want to put it into practice, you sexy genius?"

Before he could choke out a response, there was a knock at the throne room door, interrupting their erogenous moment. She rolled her eyes and let go of Nikola's dick. "Come-hither!" she yelled, looking at the door. "I hope you brought me something to fuck—or kill. Or both." She laughed and waited as the door swung open. It was Eden's head of security, followed by two more security guards, and Terry between them. Nikola's mouth fell open when he saw him.

"Mistress," began the head of security, "we found this boy wandering around the upper halls of the Palace. He claims he was trying to find *you*."

Eden narrowed her eyes and studied Terry with no recognition on her face. Terry made no attempt to fight the security guards. He exchanged a glance with Nikola and then took in the state of Eden—her nakedness and skin covered in the dead woman's blood. "What the hell *is* this, Eden?"

She raised an eyebrow. "Who are you, traveler?" she asked. "I don't know *you*, but I can feel your Soulmind wanting to fight me."

"What happened to you, babe?" Terry said, sadness and compassion in his eyes. "This Eden I see before me is not the Eden I knew."

"Don't tell me who or what I am!" she scoffed. "You are obviously insane and I have no time for your incoherent ramblings. Judging by your strange gray clothes, all I see is a wayward traveler who has become lost in lands that are not his home." Looking at the head of security and then Nikola, she concluded by saying, "Take him down to the subterranean dungeons. Nikola, go with them so you can set up the Quarantine Seal around his cell. This boy has a Soulmind and we don't want to risk him escaping through use of his Pan-Dimensional powers before I decide what to do with him."

Nikola nodded silently and followed behind as the security guards escorted Terry back out of the room. They took Terry down the back stairs that led directly to the subterranean dungeons. This stairwell, as well as the floors under The Wild Orchid Palace were very barren and industrial compared to the rest of the casino. The stairs reminded him of the ones in a hospital. When they got to the underground level, they were in a dank concrete basement lit harshly by a lone fluorescent tube on the ceiling. There were several cells around the perimeter of the room which were just concrete rooms with a locked door made of bars on the front.

Terry groaned. "I seem to just be going from one cell to the next. Even in other Dimensions," he mumbled to himself.

The security guards ignored his grumbling and opened one of the cell doors. Terry obediently went inside as they locked the bars behind him. The irony was not lost on him that the new cell he was in so closely resembled the one he was in at the Facility. With his face close to the bars, he stared through, intently at Nikola without saying a word.

"Leave us," Nikola said, addressing the security guards without taking his eyes off Terry. "I need a moment to set up the Quarantine Seal and I wish to have a minute alone with the prisoner."

The guards gave a little bow to Nikola and exited the way they had come. Terry sighed and shrugged sheepishly at his old friend. "Well, buddy," he said finally. "It seems like some weird shit is going on here."

"I'm sorry we have to keep you locked up like this," Nikola apologized with genuine remorse. "But when Eden gives the order, we kind of have to obey. Or she's liable to kill us all."

"I was kinda getting that vibe, you know," Terry continued, "especially with all the like blood dripping off her naked tits.

What's up with *that*? She seemed like she didn't even recognize me. Is she possessed?"

"Possessed?" Nikola thought about this for a moment and then shook his head. "No, I don't think she's possessed. Her trauma seems to be rearing its ugly head like a rabid dragon. She mentioned something about being separated from you and it triggered feelings of rage and isolation... Anyway, I'm not going to go into psychoanalytical mode here, but let's just say she was angry when she got here, proceeded to massacre people and just cause unmitigated destruction. I stopped her the first time and tried to encourage her to help me with my experiments to maybe channel that aggression into something less violent. She took over my A.I. robots, meaning she's jacked-in all the time now." He pointed to a spot on his neck behind his ear. "With a little device on her neck right here, she can control the hive-mind of the robots."

"Okay, so she went a little off her nut and now she's power-drunk," Terry commented. "But why can't she remember me?"

"I was getting to that," Nikola returned. "The A.I. of the robots is connected to what I call the Brain which is a database of all our collected knowledge. It hovers in the sky above the City. Unfortunately, the side-effect of controlling the robot hive-mind with your consciousness is that the Brain will siphon off your memories and lose them as data within its internal structure. She's jacked-in all the time, so it's safe to say that she's lost numerous memories. How many exactly, I couldn't say."

"That's totally fucked," Terry remarked. "Couldn't you like get control of the robots back somehow? Don't you have lots of equipment and means to do that sort of thing?"

Nikola shook his head. "There's no way anymore. She sealed up my lab and she makes me live in the casino now so she can use me as an assistant or for whatever other menial tasks she might have. She guards the circular control device on her neck like it's a gem of power, and since she's always surrounded by some of the robots, she's protected on multiple levels of reality."

"That sucks... And I take it you haven't figured out a way to recover memories from the Brain." Nikola shook his head. "Fuck me, I should have just stayed in the Facility and let all those jumpsuit guys shoot me."

"The who in the what?" Nikola asked.

Terry slouched and hung his arms out through the bars of his cell. "Fuckin', where I teleported here from. I was being held prisoner in some underground government Facility where they were doing experiments on me and other young people who have newly awakened Soulminds. I try to escape and I end up just going from one cage to another." He knocked his forehead against the bars a few times in frustration.

"Wait..." Nikola started. "So you didn't portal through near Mika'el's farm?"

"Nah," Terry answered. "I used Matter-Relocation with this black pod thing from the Dark Tethers that I apparently have access to the energy now. But I keep fucking it up, can't get the hang of it, and it sends me to places I don't intend to go. I ended up on the mountain looking down over the City. There's a barrier up there, like an energetic force field which is the border of your Dimension... Anyway, might as well stay in this cell for a while instead of risking another teleportation trip. For all I fucking know I could end up in Canada."

"Canada? What is this Canada?" Nikola inquired, raising his eyebrows. "Is that like hell?"

Terry laughed. "I dunno. It very likely could be. I've never actually been there. Anyway, I'm going off on tangents. The memories. How could we help restore Eden's memories and bring her back to herself? Maybe if I kiss her. That always works in Disney movies and shit."

Nikola looked at Terry as if he was going a little nutty himself. "I think that only works in Fairy Tales. Not so much in real life."

Terry hung his head again. "Well, then I'm fucking out of ideas, bro." He looked back up at Nikola. "Are you really gonna leave me in here? What if I psychically acquire the ability to walk through these bars and escape?"

"I'm sorry, my friend," Nikola replied remorsefully. "You won't be able to once I activate the Quarantine Seal." He walked to the middle of the floor between all the cells. Now Terry noticed a saucer-shaped silver control panel built into the floor. Nikola leaned down and punched in the number of the cell Terry was in on the keypad. Then he pressed the spherical button in the center of the saucer. Immediately a holographic grid of red plasmik light superimposed itself over the bars of Terry's cell like a glowing chess board.

Terry shook his head and laughed morbidly. "How the fuck did you develop that one, Nikola? I smell foul play afoot."

The inventor wore an expression like he had been caught with his pants down. "Can you ever forgive me? The first time you and Eden were at my lab, I secretly took readings of your energy signatures and invisible Soulmind consciousness waves. Those readings were what I used to create the Quarantine Seal which suppresses the powers of your Soulmind. I can't—I..." he stammered. "It's not my fault that my inventions keep being stolen and appropriated for negative purposes. Don't hold me accountable, please. I never wanted any of this to happen." Nikola looked up at the ceiling and closed his eyes. "Maybe this *is* my Karma and I don't even know it... Oh, Great Source of All Creation, please forgive me."

"Spare me," Terry said with a smirk. "It's time you take responsibility for your part in the unfolding of the Current... Wait, the Current?" Terry questioned what he just said. "Whatever, you know what I mean. Fucking own your shit and don't blame other people for what you create in this Dimension."

"You're right. You're absolutely right," Nikola conceded. "I have to acknowledge my part in these events and strive to make it right. Not sure how I'm going to do that exactly, yet. But I promise you, Terry, that I won't let Eden hurt you. I give you my word. And I'll see what I can do to facilitate you getting out of here."

"Great, I have a lot of confidence in you," Terry replied sarcastically. "I can see how well you've maintained control of the situation. Speaking of the crazy bitch that I love, what's up with the black arm? I noticed her right arm is like stained black."

"Apparently she put her arm into a portal that opened up in her throne room. I couldn't see this portal, obviously, but I did see her arm disappear into thin air, and when it came out it was stained black."

"The Taboo Zone," Terry mumbled almost to himself.

"Yeah," Nikola said lighting up. "That's exactly what she called it. How did you know that?"

Terry shrugged. "I dunno. Sometimes my Soulmind just tells me these things."

"Right, right," Nikola said nodding as he contemplated this. "Sometimes I wish I had that energy activated within me."

Terry didn't comment on this. Instead he just said, "Now leave me to marinate behind these bars until you have some beneficial ideas about how to help Eden. Otherwise I'm going to have to do everything myself, as usual." He went over to the cot in the back corner of the cell and flopped down on it. "You know, I should be getting used to being locked up by now, but

I still fucking hate it." He closed his eyes. "I want to explore nature again, see the sun instead of concrete walls, and maybe even travel into space one day."

"I'm so sorry," Nikola apologized again. "I swear I'll figure something out to remedy this situation, to help you and Eden. I care about you both, I really do. I'll come again soon. Be safe."

Terry snorted at that without opening his eyes. "I guess I'm the safest I can be considering the circumstances. But what is safety and security anyway? It's just an illusion to maintain the facade of stability..." Terry trailed off as Nikola took his leave. He quickly walked back toward the stairwell and then ascended to the upper levels of the casino with the seed of a specific purpose planted deep in his mind.

Eden paced around her throne room, still covered in blood, debating to herself whether she should go take a shower or just let the blood seep into her skin a little longer. Several of her robots still stood frozen at attention in a group by the door to the room. Absentmindedly, still pondering over the strange traveler who seemed to know her but whom she herself did not know, she stared at the images of the orgy taking place in the *Temple of Cosmic Fuck* as it was streaming on the walls surrounding her. Suddenly there was a knock at the chamber door. "Cum!" Eden commanded, smiling to herself.

The door opened and in walked another one of her robots, and it was carrying a pillow on its palms like a waiter might carry a tray of food. Sitting on the pillow very regally was a crown-shaped electronic device. Eden had ordered this crown to be made by the robots themselves, and her eyes lit up when she saw it. The crown was made of what looked like computer chips and when she wore it on her head, she could control the hive-mind with it, replacing the device that stuck into the side of her neck. "Oh my God! It looks so amazing," she cooed as she approached the robot to take her new crown. Picking it up reverently, she held it above her head and said, "I now crown myself Queen! The Queen of Cyber-Fuck! I control the hive-mind of my metal minions and I control multi-Dimensional coitus of the world! Let us fuck and be inside each other for Eternity!" She laughed confidently as she slowly placed the crown on her head. When the device encircled the crown of her head, she felt a rush of energy and electricity shoot through her skull and down her spinal cord with an orgasmic chill. "Yes," she whispered, looking at the robot in front of her. "I can feel the power surging through my spine and my Soulmind."

Even though she had the crown now that would control the robot hive-mind in a more comprehensive way, she didn't take off the device from her neck, not yet. Eden's head jerked toward the door as she heard it creak open. Nikola poked his head into the throne room. "Sorry to disturb you, Mistress," he began and then stopped talking as he registered the computer-chip crown resting on top of her head. Making a mental note of it, but not commenting on its existence, Nikola continued, "The prisoner is locked in his cell with the Quarantine Seal activated to keep his Soulmind suppressed. Do you wish me to do anything else, Mistress?" he asked subserviently.

Eden shook her head and made a dismissive gesture with her hand. "No, Nikola, thank you for all your help today. You are dismissed to do as you wish or go back to your chambers for the night. I know how to find you if you're needed."

"Good night, Mistress," Nikola replied, bowing and closing the door as he left to go back to his own quarters in the casino.

Grabbing the pillow from the robot's still outstretched hands, Eden tossed it into the corner of the room. It bounced off the bottom edge of one of the screen-walls that showed a slender older woman with long white hair having an orgasm as she rode a very fit man's cock as he laid on the floor below her, his chest heaving with the existential pleasure. Sweat glistened off of their beautiful bodies.

Eden sighed and stroked the cheek and chin of the robot who had brought her the crown. "Oh, what to do when you have absolute power? What do you think, my metal friend?" She looked into the eyes of the synthetic A.I. being, and they studied her back; but it was only her own consciousness looking back at her from within. "I suddenly feel weary," she said, her eyes falling to the floor for a moment and then she glanced back up at the robot in front of her and the others standing by the door. "Maybe I'm getting tired of killing and destruction." She shrugged her shoulders discontentedly. Then she started walking toward the door. "Come, my friends of me. Just a couple of you, too. The rest of you stay and clean up this bloody mess." She pointed to a couple of the robots standing by the door. Those two, and the one who brought her the crown, followed her out of the room with the Logo Throne. Closing the door behind them, leaving the screens to broadcast the orgy continuously into the night, all four of them retired to Eden's bedchamber.

The three robots kept guard inside her bedchamber and in front of the door in case anyone tried to break in. She placed her newly-crafted crown on the sink in her bathroom so she could take a shower and scrub all the gore from her body. However, the circular device remained lodged in her neck; she wasn't quite comfortable enough yet to take it out since she had grown accustomed to being *always* jacked-in.

With her eyes closed, she let the water rain luxuriously over her face and drip down her naked skin. The dead woman's blood flowed down like red rivers amid the cascades of warm water. Eden caressed her breasts as she moaned softly, massaging her body and slipping her fingers between her legs. The feeling of the water and blood turned her on, exciting her nipples and her clitoris. Crying out with pleasure, she rubbed one out while the flows of water carried all the blood down her legs and into the drain below. To Eden's surprise, she found herself thinking about the traveler she had thrown in the subterranean dungeon. *Had he given his name?* She couldn't remember. *Who is this sexy mysterious stranger?* she wondered to herself as her fingers sped up rubbing her clit and then sliding two fingers deep inside her wet pussy. Face turning red, she got so hot as she saw his smiling face in her mind's eye; then she imagined what his body might look like naked. That really got her going. This fantasy was getting her so hot and bothered that she had to put her left arm out to brace herself against the wall of the shower. Her body trembled as she moaned loudly, getting close to orgasm.

"Uh God..." she moaned with her eyes still closed. Her face was tilted down as she leaned her weight against the hand she had on the wall. Water dripped from her nose and open mouth. Imagining herself touching the traveler, and then laying him down as she got on top of him and put him inside her, she screamed as the orgasm tore through her body. Her legs went all wobbly and her eyes rolled up in her head as she lost herself into the orgasmic bliss of Eternity.

As Eden caught her breath and came back to her body from the euphoric orgasmic outskirts of the Spiralverse, she turned the water off and felt the cleanse deep in her cells. Maybe even on an atomic level. Flicking water off of her hands, she stepped out of the shower and toweled off. She liked being naked so she just left the towel in a heap on the tiled floor of the bathroom, picked up the new crown from the sink, and went back into her bedroom.

Lovingly, she placed the crown down on the small table next to her enormous bed. Still she did not detach the device from her neck. The room was huge just like the bed which was fit for a Queen—or even a Goddess for that matter. This bed was shrouded by a canopy of semi-translucent white curtains. Eden crawled through the curtains and onto the soft bed, her clit still buzzing from the intense orgasm.

"Who is this strange traveler?" she said to herself, still thinking of the boy she sent to be locked away. "Did he say his name?" She pondered this, thinking as hard as she could. Undeniably there was something vaguely familiar about him, as if they had been lovers in a past life. From somewhere deep within her, she remembered. "Terry? Was that it? Did he say that when the security brought him in? He must have, because I don't know that boy." She seemed pretty certain of this, and other than his name and an obscure sense of familiarity, there was no recollection in her mind of Terry whatsoever.

She shrugged and laid her head down on the soft pillows. Carrying her own Soulmind off into Dreamsphere from the exhaustion she felt, Eden fell asleep with Terry's loving face still lingering in her consciousness.

PART 17

Neither Condemn nor Condone

"Put on the whole armour of God, that ye may be able to stand against the wiles of the devil. For we wrestle not against flesh and blood, but against principalities, against powers, against the rulers of the darkness of this world, against spiritual wickedness in high places."

- Ephesians 6:11-12

*"Continuing to breathe the breath of God,
I slip into Eden alone."*

- L.F. Falconer, *Beyond the Veil*

ELEVEN

"So you're the goat-fucker, huh?"

The bars of Jessica's cell were made of ornately carved ivory and were enchanted with the same spell used on the net that the Elves had captured her in. She had been dozing off slightly and it took her a few moments to realize that someone was addressing her from outside her cage.

"Hmm?" she groaned as she yawned and rubbed her eyes. Still sitting on the stone floor, she scooted closer to the bars to see who was talking. "What did you say?" Gripping one of the ivory bars, she peeked out between them to see who it was.

There were stone steps outside of Jessica's cell that led down farther into the Tree Village, and it also ascended up more toward the higher levels. There was a youngish male Elf, maybe about eighteen-years-old, sitting on a step with his legs dangling over the side. He had long dirty-blonde hair and was whittling a stick with a small dagger. "You're the goat-fucker," the Elf said again, briefly glancing up at Jessica and then back down at the stick he was carving.

Jessica steamed. Her face suddenly flushed red and burned hot with fury. If she could have produced smoke from her ears, she would have been billowing like a chimney. "What!? I don't—I didn't—" she said haltingly, stammering for lack of a comeback.

The young Elf laughed at Jessica's sputtering protests. "I think the lady doth protest too much," he commented. "It's true.

I can smell the odor of Pan clinging to your skin—in your flesh and in your sweat." He wrinkled up his nose in disgust.

"I would never!" she whispered harshly, pressing her face between the bars. "I would never ever f—*have sex* with a goat!"

The Elf shrugged and chuckled again. "Whatever. That's not what Odelliam says. And he knows all that goes on in this forest."

Jessica glared furiously at the Elf once more. "Screw what Odelliam says! He can't possibly know *everything* that goes on in the forest. He doesn't know *me*."

"You are Jessica Thorn," the Elf said matter-of-factly and stopped his whittling to look at Jessica through the bars of her cage. "My name is Josh-oo'el." He gave a little nod of his head as he introduced himself.

"I don't give a shit who you are or what your name is," Jessica hissed back, still pissed about the goat-fucker comment. "Just let me out of here!" She shook the ivory bars of her cell with frustration. "I'm not a freaking spy of Pan, or whatever it was he said. Whatever all you Elves think I am is wrong!"

Josh-oo'el raised an eyebrow and smirked. "But you *are* one of those witch types. Odelliam said—"

"Forget what that guy said!" Jessica shot back, cutting him off. "What, is Odelliam like your god or something? Omniscient, omnipresent?"

Josh-oo'el didn't answer, he just shook his head and said, "No matter, apparently there is a task for you yet."

"A task? What task?" Jessica wanted to know what this vague statement meant in regards to a decision made without her awareness about something she was obligated to do. That didn't sit well with her. "I'm not doing jack!" she snapped, folding her arms over her chest. "Especially since you have me imprisoned against my will."

"We'll just have to see once you've met with Odelliam," Josh-oo'el remarked authoritatively. Jessica rolled her eyes. "Fine, don't take me seriously. That's no nevermind to me." He let his gaze fall again to the stick in his hand and began chipping away at it with his blade once more. "And I wouldn't try any witch stuff to try to escape. We have magick too. It would just be a waste of energy on your part... Say, you're not a Maleficer, are you?"

"A who?" Jessica asked, not quite fully paying attention to the Elf anymore, she was thinking of scenarios that might help her escape, despite Josh-oo'el's suggestion not to even try it. "Maleficent? Like in *Sleeping Beauty*?"

The Elf cocked his head and looked at Jessica as if she was speaking some kind of unintelligible looney language. "I don't know what this *Sleeping Beauty* is, but a Maleficer is one who spins and weaves evil tapestries. One who is a worker of wickedness, their magickal working is to harm, maim, and to curse."

Jessica snorted as if this was the most ridiculous thing she'd ever heard. "No, I'm not a Maleficer," she said after a moment. Then she sighed and leaned back against the side wall of her cell, still feeling exhausted, physically and spiritually. "I wasn't even a witch until recently." She closed her eyes and leaned her head back to rest against the wall. Speaking not necessarily to Josh-oo'el, but maybe just to speak in general, she continued, "I used to be a Christian." Jessica laughed dryly. "I'm not anymore... Or, I don't know, maybe I still am and have just added a new dimension to my spirituality. It's not so easy to define something like that, I guess, is what I'm learning."

"You use strange words that I know not their meaning..." Josh-oo'el began and then trailed off as he looked up to see two tall male Elves walking down from the stairs above. It was Zelda and Raka, looking very militant with their hands on the hilts of their swords that hung at their hips. Josh-oo'el stood up quickly and looked nervous like he wasn't supposed to be there. He bowed to the two senior Elves as they stopped on the landing in front of Jessica's cell.

"Josh-oo'el!" Raka said firmly. "You know you are not to be hanging around the prisoner. Run along back to your mama."

Josh-oo'el glared at Raka and said, "I'm not eight-years-old anymore, Raka! You can't boss me around!"

"Yes, I can," Raka replied with a smirk. As a response to this Josh-oo'el just huffed and started to descend the stone steps until he was out of sight.

Zelda started to unlock Jessica's cell. She stood up in anticipation of being let out. "Odelliam wishes to see you, Miss Thorn. We've come to escort you to the Upper Room," he said, and his green eyes flashed with a grace almost feline.

Jessica stepped hesitantly out of her cell. "Now it's Miss Thorn?" she remarked. "So you found a little bit of decency and respect down in there somewhere, did you? I don't appreciate being kept in a cage. I was in one before, and trust me, it doesn't bring back the fondest of memories, if you know what I mean."

Raka and Zelda positioned themselves behind Jessica and pointed toward the stairs leading up. They still had their hands at the ready on their weapons; they didn't need to acknowledge that they would use them, but Jessica knew that if she tried to make a run for it that it wouldn't turn out very pleasant for her. So shrugging in surrender, she turned and started climbing the stairs that continued to go up and wrap higher around the top part of the tree. It was getting to be dusk and beautifully carved lamps and torches lined the edge of the steps as they spiraled around the trunk of the great giant. The whole architecture of the Elven villages in the trees were on a whole higher level than merely stunning. To Jessica the whole experience was breathtaking. If she hadn't been in the unfortunate position of playing the prisoner, she probably would have been able to enjoy it more if she hadn't been locked in a cell or escorted everywhere by militant looking Elves who were intimidating already even before taking into account that most of them were about a foot taller than her.

Soon they got all the way to the top and entered the Upper Room, which was really a large observation deck where Odelliam stood alone, staring out into the forest as he contemplated the challenges faced by his fellow Elves and the tree villages at large. This Upper Room was enormous and circular with the trunk of the tree running through the center. The inner portion of the tree had been hollowed out to create a meeting room with several gorgeously carved chairs which had been cut right from the tree itself. The floor was made of black marble and there was a whitish ceiling about twenty feet above Jessica's head which seemed to undulate with energy waves of all different colors. Around the edge of the deck were arches made of the same ivory as the bars of Jessica's cell. They stretched from the marble floor all the way to the shimmering ceiling. And stretched across the space inside the arches was not glass, but a transparent, biological, membrane-like substance. Lanterns and torches lit the interior of this space as well.

Odelliam was standing on the far side of the room, his back facing Raka, Zelda, and Jessica. She could see him through the space hollowed out of the tree. The Elder Elf raised his right hand without turning around. "Thank you, Zelda and Raka. You may leave us. I wish to speak to the traveler alone."

"Yes, my lord," the two Elves said in unison, bowed, and then turned and departed the way they had come.

Jessica hesitated, studying the back of Odelliam's tall figure. His blonde hair was immaculate, straight down his back and majestic like an angel's. He was wearing a long black cloak. There were dark purple patterns on the surface of the cloak, but since they were both such dark colors, it was almost indistinguishable. "Why did you come to our part of the forest?" the Elf asked, still staring out at the forest and the villages in the other trees.

For a second Jessica was taken aback. She didn't know what sort of question she was expecting, but it wasn't that. "W-what?" she stammered.

"Why…" Odelliam repeated patiently, "did you come to our part of the forest? It's a simple question."

"Well I—I don't know," she replied honestly. "I mean, it's the journey, the initiation, right? Artemis was taking me where I needed to go."

"Do you always go where other people take you?" the Elf asked without missing a beat.

Jessica felt a little offended by that insinuation. "No!" she snapped back. "I don't always go where people tell me to go." This last part she grumbled almost inaudibly.

"You seem to be uncertain about quite many things, Jessica Thorn," Odelliam astutely observed. "You should really work on that. For a being as powerful as yourself, you don't want to be used or taken advantage of if you can discern when people or entities are trying to do that to you."

"I *don't* let people take advantage of me," she said resolutely.

"Good, that's good. At least you make that your intention. That's a good start," he responded, turning his head just slightly to look at Jessica over his shoulder. "But it seems you still don't know who you are, or what you are. Are you a Christian? Are you a witch? Are you a god? Are you a human? These are the questions you need to start answering for yourself. And answer them decisively, not in an ambivalent wishy-washy way."

"What do you know about me? You don't know me," Jessica said, but it was weak. Odelliam's words were hitting home and she didn't have the strength to try to fight the truth.

"I know a little more than you think," Odelliam smiled and made a come-here motion with his finger. "Come closer, child. I'm not going to hurt you."

For a moment Jessica stood frozen, feeling comfortable at the distance she was away from this powerful Elven Lord. Then she took a couple reluctant steps through the hollowed-out tree and toward where Odelliam stood staring into the forest outside. He turned around to fully face her as she approached him. "Do you wish to return to the Hollow Dimension to be reunited with the young man named Terry Broswald?"

Jessica stopped when she was a few feet away from Odelliam. He looked down at her with a soft expression on his face. She fumbled for words again, having not expected that question either. "Huh?" was all she managed to squeak out.

"I don't like having to repeat myself," Odelliam spoke without any emotional indication in his voice. "You need to do some more thinking about what it is *you* really want. Are you just going along? Letting the journey jerk you around; or are you going to make the choices of where this journey is going to go?"

"I don't...think I know how to do that," she said slowly, finally realizing that she had the choice to exert more of her will if she so wished.

"Now let me ask you again," Odelliam continued with deep patience. "Do you wish to return to the Hollow Dimension to be reunited with Terry Broswald? If so, we can help you. If that is not your desire, we can let you go free with your unicorn and you can continue wandering around the forest to blindly search for something you yourself doesn't even know what it is or even if it actually exists."

Jessica didn't understand everything that Odelliam was saying, but she thought she was finally getting the gist of it. And to her surprise, she wasn't feeling angry, she was feeling empowered. "So you don't think I'm a spy of Pan?"

Odelliam smiled subtly at the corners of his mouth and shook his head. "No, I know now you are not spies of Pan. You do seem to have a strange relationship with the Goat, though, which I do not understand, and frankly, I don't think I want to know. But you are not spies."

Against the urge to argue about not having a relationship with Pan, she kept her mouth shut. At least he didn't call her a goat-fucker, she thought. Finally she said, "Yes, I really do," and she could feel the conviction as a reality within her Soulmind.

"*Yes you do* what?" Odelliam asked, pushing her to articulate her true desires.

"Yes, I want to go back to the Hollow Dimension and find Terry for the next stage of this strange inter-Dimensional, inter-planetary mission that we seem to find ourselves on."

Odelliam smiled and laughed, turning back to look out of the membrane around the observation deck. "Inter-planetary, huh? Now that will be something to see. Okay, now that we've established that common ground through you articulating your true desires, we can start working together." He pointed out of the window, down, and to the left a bit. "Do you see that tree over there?"

Jessica fell in next to Odelliam on his right side, slowly feeling more comfortable being close to him. Following his finger toward where he was pointing, she tried to see what he was indicating. A couple trees away there was a village that seemed to be in ruins. The spiral staircase around this other tree as well as the dwelling places attached to the upper portion of the trunk looked like a chunk had been ripped out by a giant hand. Wood, ivory, and stone were splintered and hanging off the tree in ruin. "What happened?" Jessica asked, eyes wide. "It looks like that other village there got bombed or something large crashed into it. Holy shiitake mushrooms..."

"There is a creature that continuously threatens our fellowship of Elven tree-dwellers and what we've built here," Odelliam explained. "It only comes in certain seasons, but we still haven't figured out a way to rid ourselves of this pestilence—or even appease it if that's possible."

"What is it that's doing this?" Jessica asked, looking up at Odelliam's concerned expression.

"A giant of immense grotesquerie," the Elf continued. "We still don't know what he wants or for what reason he has targeted our community as an outlet for his destruction."

Jessica swallowed hard, anticipating what was coming next. "So..." she started slowly. "Why do I get the feeling that I'm going to get roped into this somehow?"

Odelliam smiled warmly as he weighed his next words. "This giant," he continued, "lives on the Great Plains far to the West of here. At certain times of the year he comes into our forest and destroys one or two tree villages, and then he goes back to his land on the Great Plains. Why he only destroys one or two at a time and not our entire structure is uncertain."

"So what can I do about this?" Jessica suddenly felt the pit of her stomach sink and her legs went all noodly. She dreaded the truth of what was now dawning on her. "No way. Uh-uh. Nah effing way. I can't kill a fucking giant!"

The tall Elf looked down at Jessica with compassion, as if he knew something that she herself did not. "After all you've been through and experienced," he said, "you still underestimate your own power? I find that to be an intriguing mystery. It's like you embrace some of your abilities, and yet push others away like you don't want them. You don't trust yourself enough to wield that amount of energy so you in turn deny its existence."

"Maybe you're right," she admitted. "I don't know how far my power can go. I guess I'm a bit scared of it really. What if I inadvertently unleash something—a force—that I can't control. And then it takes ahold of me instead of my will having hold of it. I don't know. I'm afraid of losing myself."

"You can never lose yourself, my child," Odelliam said in the voice of confidence and deep knowing. "You just come to know and accept *more* of yourself, empowered."

"Empowered..." she repeated back, contemplating this. "Why would I want power? I don't want power. I just want love. I guess, yeah, that's what really matters."

"That power *is* love," he continued. "The power *of* love. It is the most powerful force in existence."

"So I'm just going to love this giant to death?"

Odelliam laughed. "That's funny. It'll take you a while to get my meaning, but you'll understand what I'm talking about sooner than you think."

"But really though," Jessica said seriously, "I can't kill a giant. That's just—I'm—I'm just a little girl. I know it doesn't seem like it, but I'm nearly pissing myself right now just thinking about standing in a field looking up into the drooling face of a man the size of a mountain."

"You are *not* just a little girl," he emphasized. "You are becoming a wise woman, a Shaman in your own right. However, you also have the ability to connect to and run the god-body of Kali Ma."

"The who what now?" she asked, almost losing this train of thinking now.

"I hope you'll forgive me for invading your privacy, Jessica," the Elf continued with a small nod of his head. "But I went through your bag after we confiscated it. The Goddess of the Underworld gave you a great gift. The mantra—"

"The mantra?" Jessica said, cutting him off mid-sentence. "That one on the little scroll that goes like 'Jai Ma, Jai Jai Ma' something something something? What? It's like a spell or what?"

"It—" he started. "It runs the god-body. We call it *running the god-body*. It's your higher consciousness god-form. And Kali is yours."

"Wait... So I *am* Kali Ma?"

"Something like that, yes," Odelliam answered. "It's a way to bring *yourself* as a higher-dimensional frequency temporarily down to a denser plane in order to utilize its powers. You can't keep it here though, can't just exist in your god-body down here in the physical."

"Okay, this is wild," Jessica commented. "My brain is trying to shut down because its having difficulty processing all this craziness."

"The experience will anchor in your DNA once you've fully connected with your god-body. Then you won't have to think about it, you'll just know on the deepest level, beyond thought." He turned fully toward Jessica now and was very serious. "This is the pact. You destroy this giant, ridding us of a pest that threatens our way of life, and we will bring you to where you can travel back through to your own Dimension. Do we have an understanding?"

She nodded in acknowledgement. "Yes, Odelliam, I will at least try to carry this out for you. Whether I am Kali or I'm not, I guess we will find out. And if I don't come back, just know I was a snack for a giant." She laughed and shook her head. "I'll tell ya," she continued, looking out the window at the destroyed village again, "if I had been sitting in church before any of this happened, and my older self came to me—sitting right next to me on the pew—and told me that I could connect to the god-body of a Hindu deity and that I was going to have to slay a giant like David in the Bible, I definitely would have punched myself in the face."

TWELVE

The Facility had been on high alert and complete lockdown since Terry disappeared the second time. In the room with all the monitors, the Director stood watching the video of Terry vanishing over and over again to try to decipher whatever he could from what he was witnessing. The video was filtered through the plasma that could visually show multi-dimensional energy. On the screen he could see the black circle opening up under Terry's feet, the black tentacles that wrapped him up in a pod, and then his complete disappearance in a cloud of Black Mist which soon dissipated into nothing. The Director watched this repeatedly, trying to solve the mystery that it presented, but it only served to confound him more.

Standing next to the Director in silence was Doctor Morkian. He himself didn't understand much more than the Director did, which was frustrating to both men. "What is this energy?" the Director asked. "How can it just envelope him and carry him somewhere else? You've never seen this before, Doctor?"

"No, sir," Morkian replied. "I've never come across this in any other subjects or in any of my work during my entire life. This is just as baffling to me as it is for you. Even the energy readings are inconclusive."

"Explain," the Director demanded.

"Well, sir," the Doctor continued, "I can't seem to figure out the type of particles that these black tentacle things are composed of. The machines just can't compute it. It's as if the matter is so dense that it overloads the sensors picking up the waves. But at the same time the matter is so ethereal that it's as if it doesn't exist at all. In effect the particles are confusing the machine, making it unable to determine whether this *black-matter*—let's call it—is so compact that it belongs on a higher density of reality, or conversely it's so delicate and light that it belongs in a more 'heavenly' realm, let's say. Basically, it exists in both states simultaneously, making whatever these particles are to be present on all levels of cosmology—but all in one, not different forms on different planes. This is paradoxical, so this material cannot in actuality exist anywhere. However, we see it here on the screen plain as day. To put it more simply, this black-matter exists everywhere and nowhere, that's why my machines can't get a reading on it. It gets no reading—and *every* reading." Doctor Morkian frowned, trying to piece the theory together more in his mind.

The Director shook his head. "I don't understand a word of what you just said, Doctor. Try speaking English more often, I find it's more effective. How can something not exist if we're seeing it on the screen right here? It's right goddamn there!" He pointed to the screen where he was rewinding the video feed, so they could see it in reverse: the pod of black tentacles appearing again out of the Black Mist. "If something exists, then it exists! If something doesn't exist, then it doesn't fucking exist! You *cannot* have both at the same time."

"Well, sir," Morkian continued, "that's not exactly true. From the time you've spent working with this Project, I would think you'd know that by now—"

"Do I hear disrespect in your tone?" the Director snapped, cutting the Doctor off.

"No—no, sir," he stammered. "I didn't mean anything by it. Just wanted to air the fact that it is possible for something to theoretically exist and not at the same time. You know Schrödinger's paradox with the cat..."

"Right, right," the Director acknowledged with a wave of his hand. "I admit it's *possible* for something to simultaneous exist and not exist. Now let's move on. The tracking device in the Subject's ear—have you located him? I know we weren't able to track him the first time he disappeared from his cell, but maybe this time we'll pick up a signal."

Doctor Morkian nodded, acknowledging the possibility. "Yes, sir," he continued, "we're getting closer this time, trying to triangulate the signal. The Lieutenant is out in the field doing some reconnaissance to see if we can pinpoint where the Subject might be. Unless he's slipped into some other Dimension." The Doctor stroked his chin. "But even then, we might be able to still get a reading."

"What?" the Director asked. He was still having some difficulty keeping up with this stream of thinking. "I can understand maybe teleporting from here and then re-materializing in some other location in the city—or even the world maybe. But to not be in existence in the same plane of reality as the rest of us, how is that even possible? I've never seen any of our other subjects spontaneously blip out of here and re-emerge into some 'spirit world,' of whatever this other Dimension that you refer to would be called."

"Sir, there are multiple layers to our quantum reality," the Doctor tried to explain. "This was all in the report I wrote up for you several months ago."

"Yeah, yeah, yeah, reports," the Director remarked with a wave of his hand. "Just explain it to me."

"Theoretically," the Doctor continued, "having a Soulmind gives the individual access to these other Dimensions that normal people don't have the capabilities to interact with. This has just been my own theory up until now since we hadn't seen any definitive proof. But now with this Subject—Terry Broswald—we are that much closer to having that solid proof of the existence of other layers of reality."

"But what good does that do if we can't apprehend him and bring him back here?" the Director replied, exasperated. "The evidence has escaped and all we're left with is video footage and some energy readings. We can't use him to work for us if he's hiding in limbo-land."

Suddenly they were interrupted by the Lieutenant walking into the room. He was wearing his normal black jumpsuit and still had the helmet on his head. "Director, I have some information," he said, his voice muffled through the black helmet.

The Director looked over at him like he was an imbecile. "Take off the helmet if you want to talk to me, you look like a lunatic."

"Sorry, sir," the Lieutenant said as he took of his helmet and cradled it under his arm. "We've detected a faint signal from the Subject's tracking device. We picked it up when we were out in the field."

"Yes, and where is it?" the Director asked.

"Somewhere in the vicinity of Boy's Town in Chicago, sir," the Lieutenant returned. "We have a specific location with the coordinates, but we didn't want to move on it without your approval."

"You did the right thing, Lieutenant," the Director said. "Get the arsenal together and we'll move out. This is a highly sensitive situation."

"I could come too, Director," Doctor Morkian said softly. "This is a monumental day for science and I'll love to see this in action and take some readings. Especially if the Subject is in a trans-planal state."

"Sorry, Doctor. You'll have to stay here," the Director ruled. "This is now a military operation, not a scientific one."

"But, Director—"

"This is not a discussion," the Director cut him off. "You will stay and we will retrieve the subject. That's final. Let's go, Lieutenant."

Without so much as a final parting word, the Director and the Lieutenant left the room with all of the monitors, leaving Doctor Morkian to sink into disappointment. His excitement had all at once been deflated, but he still held out hope that one day he would be able to bring his work out into the field.

The Director was in the passenger's seat of one of their black SUVs. One of his thugs in the all-black suit and sunglasses was driving and the Lieutenant was in the backseat on a thick laptop trying to pinpoint the signal from Terry's tracking device. He had a bluetooth device in his ear and he was talking to Doctor Morkian back at the Facility to get more information about the location they were tracing. Driving close behind them was a black Humvee wherein was their 'arsenal' with the weapons technology that they had developed based on all their research of the Soulmind subjects.

"Lieutenant, do we know what the location is that we are going to?" the Director asked.

The Lieutenant punched a couple buttons on the laptop and replied, "Sir, it seems to be the location of a nightclub by the name of *angelfuck.*"

"Angel—what?" the Director sputtered, seemingly shocked by the name of the club. "Nevermind... Why would the Subject be at a nightclub?"

"Beats me..." the Lieutenant trailed off. "It's what?" he said suddenly.

"What?" the Director asked, turning around in his seat to look at the man in the backseat. "What is it?"

The Lieutenant held up his hand and then pointed to the bluetooth device in his ear, indicating he was talking to the Doctor back at the Facility. "Inside the nightclub? Are you sure, Doctor?"

"What is it? Talk to me, Lieutenant," the Director demanded.

"Okay, hold on a second," he said and then looked up from the laptop screen and back at the Director. "I sent the location back to Doctor Morkian in the lab so that he could maybe connect to the satellite to get some reading of the space at those coordinates."

"And what did he find?" the Director wanted to know.

"So apparently, sir," the Lieutenant continued, "there is a pocket-dimension built into the nightclub."

"In English," the Director snapped.

"A pocket-dimension means that the building of the nightclub itself shares space with a connected, yet separate, reality. They share the same space but not the same time or level of frequency. These two planes of reality seem to be accessible back and forth through a portal of some kind."

"And Terry somehow traveled from our underground government Facility into this pocket-dimension that's part of this obscene nightclub?"

"That's the working theory, sir," the Lieutenant answered. "It's the most likely explanation. Since the signal from his tracker is so weak, we are speculating that it's being picked up *through* the portal somehow. The Subject could also be hiding out in this nightclub in physical reality, meaning he'll be there in the flesh, but we think this is a less likely scenario."

"We'll find out soon enough," the Director remarked as he turned to face out the front windshield again. They were turning the corner onto the street where *angelfuck* was located. The street was mostly deserted except for a couple homeless looters at the end of the street who quickly ran for cover when the SUVs started rolling down the block. Most of the buildings had been abandoned or were in ruins. Garbage and discarded food wrappers blew across the road on the stench of the city breeze.

The Director's driver parked their vehicle right in front of the entrance to the club and the Humvee stopped close behind them. Glancing out the side window, the Director caught a glimpse of the neon sign above the door which bore the name of the club, but didn't light up anymore. The *g* and *e* in the word *angel* had been smashed and someone had used pink spray-paint to draw a letter *a* on the wall behind the busted letters. Now it read *analfuck* above the door. The Director grimaced when he saw the profanity. "Ughh," he said in disgust. "There are only animals living in this city now. Humans not much higher than apes flinging their feces at one another."

"Sir?" the driver said, turning to look at the Director, anxious for further instructions.

"Nothing," the Director replied, brushing off his previous comment. "Let's move out, men. You come with us," he indicated the driver, "and, Lieutenant, go get the enforcer from the Humvee so we can break this door down."

"Sir, yes, sir!" the Lieutenant said excitedly as he flipped the laptop closed and placed it on the seat next to him.

"Oh, and one more thing," the Director said to the Lieutenant, "tell the arsenal to stay put and await my orders in case we need them to storm the castle."

The Lieutenant nodded and exited the car, holding his helmet under his arm. When he came back to the door with the enforcer—a handheld battering ram—he was wearing his helmet again and the Director and driver were standing there waiting for him. They backed away and let the Lieutenant do his work. He swung the enforcer back and then into the door with all its weight, busting the lock from the door jamb. It swung open violently and hit the wall inside. The jumpsuit-man took a little bow as the other two men entered through the broken door and began to descend the stairs. The entrance at the bottom of the stairs was unlocked and they unhesitatingly let themselves in.

They stopped on the dance floor, looking around at the empty room, almost expecting to see Terry and an army of Soulmind kids jump out of the shadows. "So, is he here? Where is he? I'm beginning to get impatient," the Director warned.

"Uhh, let me see," the Lieutenant started, observing something in his helmet that the other two couldn't see. "The reading seems to be coming from over there," he mumbled, his voice muffled through the helmet. Then he pointed toward the direction of Darren's office where the portal to The Kingdom was hidden.

"I can barely understand what you're saying with that thing on sometimes," the Director added. "We need to get those helmets equipped with a com and a speaker on the outside..." he trailed off as they walked the length of the floor and to the black curtain. The Lieutenant brushed it aside, leading the way. Then he opened the door to Darren's office, not sure exactly what to expect. But the room was quiet and empty—Darren wasn't there and neither was Terry, which was a disappointment to the Director.

"He's not here!" the Director yelled. "What is this shit? We came all the way out here to this shithole for nothing?" He was obviously angry and stormed around the room looking for any clues that could help them. "I'm sick of having to hunt this kid down—especially *after* we had him in custody! We can't even keep him in a secure Facility!" Walking over to the small bookshelf, he swatted a stack of a few books that were on top of it, sending them scattering and bouncing to the carpeted floor.

"Just stop for a second! That's it!" the Lieutenant said with anticipation. "That's it! There's something weird about this bookshelf here. Wait, look..." He pulled the small monitor from the pocket of his jumpsuit, trailing wires behind it, and plugged it into the back of his helmet. Then he went over to the bookshelf, the Director backed up a few steps, giving him some room. Sliding the bookshelf along the wall to the right, the Little Door behind was revealed.

"What in God's name is that?" the Director asked rhetorically. "A secret passage? He's hiding in the walls?"

The Lieutenant shook his helmeted head. "I don't think so, sir. This is otherworldly."

The driver stood back silently, just watching the surreal scene unfold before him. Slowly, the jumpsuit-man opened the Little Door, trying his best to be on alert if anything came jumping out at him. "Wow! That's...amazing," the jumpsuit-man said in awe.

The Director snorted. "It's fake!" he exclaimed. "There's nothing but drywall behind that tiny-ass door. Unless... What are you seeing, Lieutenant?"

As a way of response, the jumpsuit-man Lieutenant held up the small monitor attached to his helmet. The Director stepped closer to see what was on the screen. There, plain as day, in the image on the plasma monitor, was the blue vortex of energy spinning and spiraling inside the Little Door. "My God..." the Director uttered in a hushed whisper. "What in the name of Science is that?"

"Remember how I mentioned that there was a pocket-dimension built into this nightclub?" the Lieutenant asked. The Director nodded. "This must be the portal that leads through to a different plane of reality. The Subject must be on the other side of this." For a moment he stared at the blue energy within the frame of the Little Door. The Director had fallen silent as well; and the driver was too in shock to do much of anything.

The jumpsuit-man was wearing protective gloves and now tentatively stretched his hand out toward the portal. "What are you doing, Lieutenant?" the Director demanded, a warning in his voice. "You don't know how dangerous that energy is or if it's emitting toxic radiation!"

"I just want to see," the Lieutenant whispered as if he was in a trance. He was still holding the monitor in his left hand so the Director could see it, and his right hand was slowly getting closer to the portal. When his fingers touched the blue energy, he cried out and pulled his hand back as if he'd been bitten by a wild animal.

"What's wrong? What happened?" the Director demanded.

The Lieutenant shook his hand out and blew on his fingers. The fingertips of his glove had been singed and burned, and the jumpsuit-man could feel it like a chemical burn on his skin. "It burned the fuck outta me!" he said, wincing in pain. "What did you see, sir?"

"All I saw with my naked eye was your hand hitting the dry-wall behind that tiny doorframe," the Director explained.

"And yet it burned me," jumpsuit-man replied, holding up his burned glove and twiddling his singed fingers in the air.

"Well," the Director continued thoughtfully, "if the Subject is on the other side of this portal, he won't come out, and there's no way for us to get to him, there's only one thing to do." He turned to look at the driver who had been frozen where he stood in stunned silence. Pointing at the man, the Director said, "You, go up to the Humvee and have them bring the Reversal-of-the-Spiral Annihilator."

The driver nodded and started to walk back toward the door of Darren's office. The Lieutenant looked dumbfounded behind the tinted visor of his helmet. He held up his hand to the driver and said, "Wait a minute!" The driver stopped and looked at the jumpsuit-man and back at the Director for instructions. "Let's *not* do that," the Lieutenant continued and then looked at the Director. "Sir, what are you thinking? That's a very powerful weapon and this is special," he indicated the portal. "You really want to destroy it like that? Sealing off the pocket-dimension? We don't know what kind of repercussions that might trigger."

The Director glared at the Lieutenant, angered by his insubordination. Then he turned back to the driver and said, "Do as I say. I have the highest authority here, not the Lieutenant. Go!" He shooed the driver out of the room, and the driver left a little bewildered to go get the arsenal and the weapon. Once the driver was out of the room, the Director turned back to the Lieutenant who was now regretting having questioned his superior's authority. "Take off your helmet," the Director demanded in an even voice, but the anger seething beneath his calm demeanor was palpable. The Lieutenant swallowed hard and slid the helmet off of his head; his knees suddenly felt all rubbery and the anxiety was more than apparent on his face. The Director cleared his throat and continued with the calm only rage can produce, "Never ever *ever* question my authority again—especially in front of another employee. And if it ever happens again, I can assure you that you'll be facing more than a firing. Maybe even a firing *squad*. Do you get my drift? Are we understood?" The Director gave the death-stare that would have made any man crumble and send piss running down his leg out of pure fright.

"Y-yes—yes, sir," the jumpsuit-man managed to sputter out. "It won't happen again, sir. Please accept my apologies. I forgot my place for a moment there, but I've come to my senses again."

"Good," the Director returned. "That's how it should be."

"But why destroy the portal?" the Lieutenant still wanted to know.

"What I have deducted—this is my theory," the Director continued. "The Subject disappeared directly from our Facility, correct? He teleported, for lack of a better word, into this so-called pocket-dimension on the other side of this portal. This is just my own feeling, mind you. If my deduction is correct, however, the Subject would be able to leave that Dimension via this portal in front of us. If we destroy this portal, then that in fact eliminates one alternative means of escape for him. If he portaled out *here*, and we weren't here to apprehend him, he's likely to escape our nets and maybe get out of our reach for good. So—again, this is in theory—if we seal off this exit, there's a possibility that the Subject would have to travel *back* along the *same* route that he came into that Dimension through. Do you see what I'm getting at? If he can't get out of this pocket-dimension through *this* portal, then there's a possibility that when he tries to teleport out of that plane of reality, he'll end up back at the Facility. Is that a sufficient explanation for your pea-sized brain?"

The Lieutenant nodded, "Yes, sir," he confirmed, "that is more than sufficient explanation." Even though the Lieutenant could follow that string of logic, and it did make sense as a possibility on some level, he still didn't buy it as the absolute of what was going to happen when the Subject decided he wanted to leave the pocket-dimension.

In a moment the driver was walking back through the office door followed by a man in full SWAT riot gear and carrying a strange weapon that closely resembled a rocket launcher. The Lieutenant put his helmet back on and got out of the way of the Little Door. He held the small plasma monitor up so that the Director could get a view. "You're going to want to witness this, sir," the jumpsuit man said.

The man in all the riot gear was also wearing a helmet like the Lieutenant, so he was able to see the energy of the portal himself. "Destroy it. Seal it up," the Director said, giving the order to destroy the spinning blue vortex of energy. The Reversal-of-the-Spiral Annihilator looked like a strange cannon, yet the soldier held it from the underside like a rifle. He approached the Little Door and the portal with his weapon raised. Swiveling his helmeted head, the soldier looked at the Director, awaiting orders. "I thought I already gave the order!" the Director snapped. "Do it already!"

The soldier nodded and turned back to face the portal. The Director watched the plasma screen as the man pulled the trigger of the cannon. When the weapon went off, it emitted a strange audible tone that was high-pitched and almost unbearable to the human ear. The Director put his hands over his ears but still kept his eyes glued to the screen. Then, only visible on the monitor, a burst of subtle radiation and artificial frequency light shot from the weapon directly into the center of the spinning vortex. The portal ruptured, shaking the whole room as it absorbed the negative radiation and light waves. First it started to ripple and boil like the surface of water, bubbling violently. As the surface of the vortex bubbled, it turned black like it had become diseased. Finally, after the boiling bubbles became so rapid that it was hard to discern what was happening, there was a loud popping sound and the now-black energy began to evaporate into a Black Mist and disappear into the air.

All four men stood in silence for a moment, trying to process what they had just witnessed. The only thing that could be seen now on the plasma monitor was a small ordinary door with drywall behind the frame. The soldier lowered the weapon and all three men looked at the Director as if to say "What now?"

"Now it's just a waiting game," the Director answered their unspoken question.

"But, sir," the Lieutenant started. The Director gave him an annoyed look but he continued speaking anyway. "What if the Subject never comes back? What if he stays in this whatever Dimension forever?"

"Ha!" the Director laughed. "Who would possibly want to stay in another Dimension forever? They always come back to reality sooner or later."

THIRTEEN

The next morning, Terry was slowly pulling his consciousness back from Dreamsphere as he awoke. While he was still half in the dream, he suddenly found himself in Eden's bedchamber. He'd never been in there before, and like in a dream, the location was a little blurry, but he knew right away intuitively where he was. In the dream, or projection—Terry wasn't quite sure which it was—he couldn't see his body; he was more like a floating field of awareness.

Hovering in the air at the foot of Eden's bed, Terry saw her emerge from the bathroom brushing her hair. All she was wearing was a tight purple turtleneck and a pair of white panties. It looked like her pants were a pair of baggy jeans that were bunched up on the floor. When Eden came out of the bathroom, she stopped abruptly near the night-table by her bed and looked around as if expecting to see someone there other than her few robots stationed by the door. After she looked around enough to satisfy herself that she couldn't see any physical form attached to the distinct feeling of a presence she was subtly picking up on, she put her brush down on the night-table and bent down to slide her jeans up over her legs.

Terry stared, in his non-corporeal blob of conscious awareness, at the inherent beauty that was in Eden. Even when no one was watching her and she thought she was alone, she still possessed this charming sort of sloppy grace which Terry found endearing. As Eden tucked in her turtleneck and buttoned her jeans so they would stay up over her hips, Terry had a sudden thought of that beautiful amethyst crystal that he had bought for her the day that they had went out to explore the Village, the first time they came to The Kingdom. He visualized it in his mind's eye as if he was really looking at it, really rolling it around in the palm of his hand. He could see the innumerable facets of deep purple, shining and sparkling its beauty like a talisman imbued with energy from Source itself.

If Terry had a face within his field of pure consciousness, it would have registered shock as he watched Eden while simultaneously picturing the amethyst crystal in his mind. The right side of her jeans were slowly starting to slip down off of her hip as if there was something abnormally heavy being carried in her pocket. Eden registered surprise as she tried to pull her pants up and at the same time her and Terry both became aware of a bulge in her jeans made from an object in her pocket the size of a baseball. *Was that crystal the size of a baseball?* Terry asked himself, trying to think back to the day he had bought it in the marketplace. After slipping her hand in the pocket for the object that clearly was trying to get her naked again, she pulled out the baseball-sized amethyst crystal and admired it like it was an alien artifact.

"Now how did you get there?" she cooed at the rock. "Wow, so pretty..." Staring into the purple crystal, the individual shimmers from each facet reflected themselves like sparklies in Eden's wide eyes. After admiring the stone for an appropriate amount of time, she slid open the drawer of her night-table and put the crystal gently inside. Then she pulled off the metal circular device from her neck and placed it in the drawer beside the crystal. As she closed these objects in the drawer, Terry finally noticed the strange crown sitting on top of the night-table. Now Eden picked this up and placed it dramatically on her head, knowing with every fiber of her being that she was a queen.

With her regal-ness intact, she walked—almost gliding—over to the three robots standing in front of her bedchamber door. She indicated for one of them to accompany her, and the other two to stay and guard the bedchamber just in case anyone tried to get their slimy hands on something they shouldn't—especially the neck-device which was the only other accessible way to get control of the robot hive-mind.

After Eden had exited the room with her robotic escort, Terry felt his consciousness being pulled back into his physical body. In no time at all, he wasn't seeing the reality of Eden's royal bedchamber anymore, he was experiencing the uncomfortableness and hardness of the cot he was sleeping on. And the bars locking him in was a good wake-up call in the morning as well. As he yawned and stretched, Terry wished for once that the prison cells would turn out to be the dream and not the reality he continued to wake up to. Terry could feel the depression trying to take hold of him. A lot of things seemed to be going wrong. He knew he was building something special with the Playgrounds, but letting himself get captured threw a wrench into the whole thing. *Is my building crumbling now?* he wondered. *Like the sky-scrapers of Chicago...* Each new layer laid on a little bit more bewilderment. He never in a million years would have predicted that Eden would go on a massacring rampage like this—or he didn't want to accept the fact that inside she was capable of such atrocities and cruelty.

"Am I fated to be roped into all this destruction?" Terry mused out loud. "I'm not about killing and annihilation. I like love. I like change and making the world a more fun place to live in. Oh, Eden, I love you no matter what you've done... I just wish you'd come back to me. Remember me..." He trailed off thinking of all the times that he and Eden held each other in each other's arms—endless compassion and warmth. That Eden was still buried deep within the guise of a deranged fascist dictator. He had to believe that. Sighing, he mumbled, "I wish Nikola would come back to see me. He'd know how to put some of this into more perspective."

Eden did not feel the need to hide the black stain on her arm. Sitting on her Logo Throne, she stared at her pitch-black right hand that sprouted from the sleeve of her purple turtleneck like a burnt aloe plant. She could feel the Taboo Zone's mark sinking deeper, below her skin and into her meat like an injection—like a tattoo that saturated the body all the way down to the bone.

In a way, she was proud of it, like a badge of honor. It was like literally wearing the blackness of the soul on your sleeve. Now and again Eden would also see the portal to the Taboo Zone pop back into existence, hovering in the air next to her throne. It would pop into the air like Black Mist, expand and contract for several minutes, and then blip back out of existence. But Eden could still feel the pull—could still feel the connection that she had made with all forbidden pleasures. She was wearing it on her skin, after all.

However, even surprisingly to her, she seemed to be growing bored with the daily dosages of debauchery. There must be something more risky, more rare, more dangerous, more... forbidden. More *Taboo*. *To indulge or not to indulge?* that was the question. *How far down the Taboo Hole do you want to go?* she asked herself. *Could you go so deep that you wouldn't be able to pull yourself out again?*

She sighed and slouched down in her throne, leaning her cheek against her black fist as if absolute power had become a hassle—thinking up new and interesting ways to be hedonistic had almost become like work. The novelty and charm of being the villain was beginning to wear off, and the spiritual hangover was threatening to overtake her. Because of this creeping reality threatening to burst her bubble of barbarity, she knew that she had to find a way to be even *more* extreme, or she'd have to come to terms with her lack of creativity and start backing off on her *reign of terror*. Even some of the things she loved were beginning to make her feel sick. Staring at the screens that completely encircled her, she wondered how much more fucking she could watch before all enjoyment was drained out of it. She didn't even feel like having fun with the fucking-machine dildo she had built into the throne. How many orgasms could she have in a day before she got tired of cumming?

Should I just destroy this entire Dimension along with myself? Eden asked herself. After thinking about that for a moment, she mumbled, "That's so fucking depressing. I don't want to kill myself. I know I can have more fun with these useless people." After she came back to the present moment after really zoning out into her thoughts, Eden glanced up at the small group of robots that stood by her throne room door. They were silent and obedient, only existing to await orders. Using the computer chip crown on her head, she sent a directive to one of the robots in the casino to notify the head of security that his presence was required in the throne room.

It took the head of security only three minutes to get the message and come through the door into Eden's throne room. He knew what would happen if he kept the Mistress waiting—and he knew there would be pain involved if he was slow following orders.

"Yes, Mistress," the head of security bowed to his new Queen as he came into the room. "You wished to see me?"

"I did, yes," she began, staring into the blackness of her right hand as if it was an abyss that had adhered to her skin. "I want you to bring me a child," she said slowly and deliberately.

The head of security swallowed hard. "A child, Mistress?" he said shakily.

"Did I stutter?" Eden snapped. "Yes, I said a child. Bring me a girl. Not too young, maybe ten or eleven. Do you understand?"

The head of security hesitated, as if this might be the one order he was unwilling to follow. "Are you sure, Mistress? A child is an innocent. I don't know much, but doing something like that may stain your soul forever. Yes, granted, when I was working under Ross Childe, I was aware of some of his more licentious activities, but I didn't support some of the evil things that man participated in." He was shocked to hear these words coming out of his own mouth, and he knew that questioning his Mistress was enough to get him put to death. With knees knocking, he almost pissed himself from fear.

Eden glared at him. It was a look intense enough to make him lose control of his bowels, but he did his best to maintain his composure. "Don't forget your place, slave! Your job is not to ask fucking questions—especially not to question *me*, your Mistress. Now go find me a child or I will have my robots tear you limb from limb. Is that understood?"

The head of security's face went white and he bowed nervously as he began backing up toward the door again. "I-I'm sorry, Mistress," he stuttered. "My-my apologies. Right away, I will bring you what you request." Without another word, he left to go kidnap a child for his Mistress. The door slammed shut and Eden was alone again with her robots and orgy livestream. There was a faint pop and she looked up in the air to the left side of her throne. There was a small black dot that began to grow to the size of a baseball and then a grapefruit. Tendrils of Black Mist wafted out of the portal to the Taboo Zone like living smoke. Eden could feel that the energy from the Taboo Zone was communicating with the black skin on her arm. The skin prickled and rippled like goose-flesh. Rolling up her sleeve all the way to her shoulder, she stared at her arm as it began to bubble, then the black of her skin began to have little points that stretched into the air like little plasma spikes.

The sensation she was feeling through this energy activity was not painful or uncomfortable, just strange, and she watched with fascination. As if in one moment the whole blackened part of her skin seemed to become a living liquid. This living black plasmik liquid began to drip off of the muscles in her arm like water in zero-gravity. When this black liquid floated in the air above her arm, it had liquified her skin with it, leaving bare tendons and muscle. Eden stared at her skinless arm in wonderment. Still, there was no pain and she was fascinated by being able to see her own veins and the blood pumping through them. Also, there was a presence of another substance that didn't seem natural inside a human body—some kind of black sludge.

As she watched this black sludge trace its way between her tendons, there was a swift knock at the door and the head of security let himself in. Eden's attention on the material from the Taboo Zone was broken and it assembled itself back on her arm as her blackened skin. The head of security came into the room dragging a young girl by her arm. The girl sobbed as he pushed her into the center of the room and toward Eden sitting on her throne. She surveyed the prize. The child must not have been more than ten; she wore a yellow dress and pressed her palms against her face as she wept pitifully.

Eden stood up from her throne dramatically and gave a dismissive gesture to the head of security who bowed and exited the room. Sniffing the air, she almost believed that she could smell the little girl's tears in the air. Such delicious agony. Sliding the drawer out on the bottom of her throne, Eden retrieved her cock-machete from inside. She aimed the point of the blade at the girl and said, "Take your hands down from your face or I'll gut you like a pig!"

Shaking like a frightened dog, the girl slowly took her hands down from in front of her face. She blinked a couple times to get the tears out of her eyes and then she looked at Eden as if begging for her life, her face soaked and red from crying. "Please don't hurt me," the girl squeaked.

"What was that?" Eden said, putting her hand up behind her ear. Then she pressed the tip of the machete into the flesh of the girl's neck. "I like that. Beg me more."

"Please, Miss!" the girl pleaded, water starting to fall from her eyes again. "I beg you not to hurt me! Please don't kill me!"

Eden could feel the girl's fear like it was electrical; energy that she could feed off of. It tingled the skin of her black arm. As she pressed a little harder, one small drop of blood rolled down her neck from where the point was piercing her. "Are you afraid, little girl?" Eden hissed, her voice full of gushing malevolence. "Because I want you afraid. I want you to imagine that I'm your worst nightmare come to life. Imagine all of the scariest torture you can think of and see me doing it to you. *Feel* me doing it to you."

The little girl's eyes got really wide and then she screamed at the top of her lungs while a waterfall of pee dribbled down her leg and began to pool on the floor next to her foot. "No! No! No!" the girl yelled as she clenched her eyes tightly shut.

Eden chuckled as she watched the puddle of piss grow between the girl's legs, and she felt a little turned on by the sight of the bodily fluid. As the new Queen was about to put her hand between her legs, the door to her throne room flew open and in ran Nikola. When he saw that Eden had her machete to the girl's throat, he froze in his tracks. "What's the meaning of this, Nikola?" she demanded. "How dare you interrupt me during my rituals!"

Nikola laughed grimly. "Your rituals? This is some sick shit, Eden. There are some roads that when you decide to walk down them, you can't decide not to have walked down them later."

"What the fuck are you babbling about? I almost didn't remember who you were at first when you came barging in here. You're liable to get killed," she warned, pointing the blade at Nikola now.

"I'm just saying you don't want to hurt a kid, Eden, come on," Nikola replied, he was begging now.

"You will address me as Mistress!" Eden barked.

"I'm sorry. Forgive me, Mistress," he blubbered. "Please let me say, some actions will mark you forever. Like that black on your arm—permanently staining you. One day you might look back on this and wish you chose something different. You're really close to the edge here."

"Ha!" she laughed in his face. "I've gone over the edge long ago! I massacred a whole street. I blew up cars. I had blood sacrifices and rapes played out right here where we're standing. All the mess immaculately cleaned up by your lovely robots—*my* lovely robots. What's one measly little girl in the midst of all the rest of my deeds?"

"Trust me, it's different," Nikola implored her. All he needed to do was stall her a bit until Mika'el showed up. Well, he hoped that he would show up; he sure was praying to whatever God there might be to bring him to help intervene. "A child is an innocent," Nikola continued. "It's different than killing an adult."

"That makes their energy all that much more potent and delicious," she returned with a lick of her lips.

"They're uncorrupted, a ball of pure potential," he kept talking, grasping for words. "Are you willing to deny her the experience of living her life and discovering the joys of learning?"

"That's why it's such a rush to corrupt them," Eden replied, her eyes wild and ravenous. "To enjoy them in a way that we know will leave an indelible mark on their soul is tantalizing, a temptation that beckons like a dangerous lover. An itch like blackened skin that will never peel. A child is an unparalleled forbidden indulgence. No others come close. Something we know we should *never* do, but we do it anyway. What sort of permanent mark would that make on me as well?" She raised up her black arm. "Something like this?"

Nikola was out of material and couldn't think of anything else to say to convince Eden to not do what she was thinking of doing. The portal to the Taboo Zone still puckered and pulsed in the air by her throne, as if daring her to take the plunge of killing or molesting an innocent. "Don't kill her..." Nikola whispered, it was the only thing he could think to say.

Eden pointed the cock-machete at the girl again and ordered, "Take off the dress!" Body still shaking from the tears of terror, the girl slowly pulled her dress up and over her head. When it was off, she dropped it onto the floor next to her. Standing there naked except for a pair of white panties, the girl shivered and continued crying. Eden grabbed the girl's shoulders and turned her to face the door where Nikola was standing. "Don't move," she snapped at the girl who was too terrified to move even if she wanted to. Stepping behind the girl, Eden faced her bare back, the girl's skin all goosebumps.

Stretching out her arms, Eden could feel the portal pulsing behind her, as if it was about to cum and spew a fountain of semen to soak her like an inter-Dimensional bukkake party. There was a popping in the grapefruit-sized portal and a thin tentacle-like band of energy shot out and attached itself to Eden's skull at the base of her neck. Nikola couldn't see any of this. Several other black ropes whipped out of the portal and attached to the same spot on her skull. She started to moan as dark energy started to flow into her skull from the portal and down her spinal cord. Her aura illuminated around her in red and pink flames. Wafts of Black Mist were seeping from several points down Eden's spine and the blackness danced into her aura to play with the pink and red energy as well.

Suddenly Eden's eyes were fierce and she stared deep into Nikola's soul. As she maintained eye contact she recited this spell: "Light is blinding, light is bright. I give the gift of

Soulmind Sight!" And as she said *Soulmind Sight*, she pointed her machete directly at Nikola. A shot of red and pink energy went down Eden's arm, through the machete, out of the tip, and into Nikola's eyes. He stumbled back a couple steps as if he'd been punched in the face. After rubbing his eyes, his jaw dropped open from what he was now witnessing. He could see the portal, the black ropes attaching to Eden's skull, her aura, and the Black Mist. Then he saw the little girl's aura pop out as white light around her body. She didn't have a Soulmind, but everyone has an aura even without a Soulmind. The white light within the girl's aura was chaotic and now Black Mist was oozing off of her skin to invade her aura. Nikola knew intuitively that this black energy was a manifestation of her fear.

Eden looked at Nikola again and gave a toothy grin like a seasoned psychopath. As she blinked, her pupils grew to overtake her entire iris, and then the black expanded to cover her whole eye. Nikola grimaced and jumped back as Eden began to speak with her voice taking on a slightly electronic cadence. "Children produce the most delicious agony, don't you think?" She opened her mouth wide as if she was going to take the biggest lungful of air, but then a vortex of the Black Mist started to grow its way out of her throat chakra and stretch out toward the girl's aura. "Her fear is food for the black hole," she said as the vortex from her throat chakra plugged into the backside of the girl's aura and began to siphon the Black Mist from her energy field like a vacuum cleaner.

The child's fear was like black sludge being slurped up through the vortex tube and into Eden's throat chakra. As all of that black-energy coursed through her, she began to feel the orgasmic euphoria of the forbidden building inside her again. The black-energy of the girl's fear trailed through Eden's throat-tube, through her Soulmind and body, then up her spine and out the black ropes at the back of her skull; all this energy going back to feed the black hole inside the Taboo Zone.

As Eden was feeding like a psychic-energy vampire, the door to the throne room suddenly flew open again. Her eyes—still all-black—shot open to see who the new intruder was. Mika'el stood in the doorway and he looked like he meant business. He took a couple steps forward and looked at Nikola. "Step back, my friend. Sometimes we gotta intervene when shit gets too hairy." He winked at his friend.

"I knew you'd come, Mika'el! I just had a feeling and a futile prayer," Nikola said with a smile.

"Who the fuck is this old-ass guy?" Eden asked, pointing her machete at Mika'el. "You look like you belong in Merlin's lair milking a toad." She laughed at her own strange joke.

"I'm not surprised that you don't remember me," Mika'el remarked but didn't elaborate. "And *this* has got to stop. Right now." He glared at Eden with intense eyes.

"Oh yeah," Eden snapped back, narrowing her eyes. "What are you going to do about it, old fuck?"

Without hesitation, Mika'el lunged forward, picked up the girl's dress and then took firm hold of her arm. She was still crying violently and paralyzed with fear. "Let's go now!" he said firmly as he pulled the girl toward the door, severing the connection between the throat chakra tube and the girl's aura. Eden felt the disconnect as if she had been unplugged from a power source. As her eyes went back to normal, she growled at Mika'el but made no attempt to stop him as he ran toward the door with the girl. As quickly as he could, he put the dress in her arms, pushed her out of the door, said "Run!" and closed the door as the child ran off down the hall, still crying as she went.

The ropes attaching Eden's skull to the Taboo Zone portal suddenly began to rip out of her painfully and retract into the hole of Black Mist. "Son of a bitch," she mumbled as she rubbed the back of her head.

"I can't allow you to bring harm to anyone else!" Mika'el said, puffing himself up as if to get ready for an attack.

Eden laughed at him. "And what are you going to do about it, *old man*?"

Mika'el suddenly ran towards Eden with the index finger of his right hand outstretched. Poking Eden's breast bone where her heart chakra was three times, he said, "I bind you! I bind you! I bind you! I bind you now so that you may not bring harm to yourself or to others around you! I bind you!"

After working the spell, Mika'el retreated from Eden back next to Nikola. At first she feigned like she was frightened, like the spell had injured her. Then she stood up tall, laughing like a fairy tale villain. Suddenly the lights in the room dimmed and in the low light it seemed like Eden herself became a shadow and grew to an enormous height. "You stupid, stupid fool!" she bellowed. "Don't you know that you can't bind God?"

Mika'el never even saw Eden cover the distance between herself and him. The next thing he knew was a sharp pain in his gut and the illusion that Eden just appeared out of thin air in front of him. She had skewered him through the stomach with her cock-machete. In disbelief he sputtered as blood dripped from his lips and he looked down at his own gored abdomen. After Eden slipped the blade out of his guts, Mika'el held his hands over the wound as if to keep his intestines from spilling out. Nikola was in shock and his old friend turned his head to look into his eyes and smiled. "It's okay, my friend. I tried my best to bind her, but maybe there's more to the mystery of the Spiralverse that even I don't know." He coughed and blood spattered out of his mouth in drips and mist. "I've finally paid my karmic debt for releasing the Queen the first time. I'm okay with it. Now I'll finally get to see the other Dimensions that we always talked about." He grimaced as blood seeped from the wound in his belly.

Mika'el sank to his knees as he continued to choke up gobs of blood. Nikola wasn't paying attention to Eden anymore, his whole attention was focused on his dying friend. Eden stepped back and watched with amused detachment. Thick crimson liquid dripped off her blade and splashed onto the floor. In a second, Nikola was on his knees next to his best friend, wishing to comfort him in his final moments. Instinctively, he put is arms out and caught Mika'el as he started to fall backwards, losing strength to keep himself upright. "I'm so sorry, Mika'el," Nikola whispered, unable to keep the tears at bay any longer. "I should have done more. This never would have happened."

Mika'el smiled and then winced from the pain. He reached up and stroked Nikola's cheek with an affectionate touch. His hand smeared blood over his friend's face. "Never hold the burden of guilt, Nikola," he said through the blood still soaking his tongue and teeth. After coughing, he continued, "It's poison—that guilt. It'll eat away at you like termites eating the trunk of a tree, until there's nothing left for you to stand on. It'll have gnawed at you so much that there's nothing left for you to do but fall. Nikola," Mika'el said, staring up into his friend's wet eyes, "we were like two peas in a pod, weren't we, in the best days of our lives? We were discovering the mysteries of the Spiralverse. We were learning the secrets of transformation within the consciousness and the world around us. I was ancient wisdom, and you were the progress and march of the future." He cut himself off with another coughing fit, then he gritted his teeth together against the pain.

"Shh, don't talk," Nikola said, trying to soothe Mika'el as he pressed his hand against the freely flowing wound, trying to stem the bleeding, but it was useless. "Maybe we can get you to medical and they can fix you up. Maybe even transfer your consciousness into a clone if your body can't be repaired. You don't have to die. There's technology—"

"No!" Mika'el said forcefully, cutting Nikola off in mid-sentence. "I'm okay with death. Somehow I've grown old and tired. Now I'm ready for the next adventure." He smiled bloodstained teeth and picked his next words carefully because he knew death was creeping over him quickly. "I know I never said this enough, and maybe I should have said it more," he continued, "but I love you. I love you, my friend, truly."

"And I love you," Nikola whispered in turn.

"I'll see you on the other side," Mika'el replied, not afraid to travel ever on into the unknown.

"*The untold want by life and land ne'er granted,*" Nikola quoted from one of their favorite books, a poetry collection by Walt Whitman that Darren had given them as a gift one time he came to visit. "*Now, voyager, sail thou forth to seek and find.*" As Nikola finished reciting the quote, Mika'el exhaled in a long wheeze. There was no inhale breath to follow. Mika'el's eyes stared ahead into space, unseeing. Nikola wept as he closed his friend's eyelids and quietly mourned the loss.

Eden cackled and then began to clap, mocking the two men's display of affection. "Wow, that was some of the funniest shit I've seen in a long time," she said, still chuckling. "Great performance, you should win some award for that or some shit."

Nikola glared at Eden, still kneeling on the floor covered in his friend's blood. His face was also bloody and tear-stained. *He looks kind of cute and pathetic sitting there*, Eden thought to herself. "You killed him," Nikola said in a strained whisper.

She shrugged, spinning her machete around through the air. "I've killed a bunch of other people too. Are you really that surprised?"

Nikola huffed as a way of reply. In an attempt to wipe the snot dripping from his nose, he just smeared more blood across his face. He'd seen more killing and torture recently than he had in his entire life, and he was getting tired of it. His mind reeled with thoughts of escape.

"You know why you could never stand up to me?" Eden continued. Nikola didn't reply but his eyes studied her like she was a foreign life-form from a distant planet that might be dangerous. "Why you could never stand up to me, and why your friend is dead now, is because you're a coward. You're a little bitch, Nikola."

He could feel his face get hot and he gritted his teeth. "I—" he attempted to start but was cut off by Eden.

"Oh, are you mad I called you a little bitch?" she teased. "You know how much of a loser you look like kneeling there covered in blood and blubbering like the little girl I didn't even get to kill? You are such a little sissy faggot," she continued relentlessly; she wasn't going to let up. "I thought you two were gonna start making out like the little queer-boys you are. I can just see it now: you two doing alchemical experiments and you two get horny, you bend this old-ass guy over your lab table and fuck him hard in the ass. That actually sounds kind of hot," she admitted, taking a couple steps closer to the dead man and Nikola. "You know, there's an experiment that I always wanted to do. I always wanted to know if a man can get hard after he's dead."

As Eden kneeled down next to Mika'el's dead body, Nikola stood up with a start and backed away from her a couple steps. He knew she was liable to try to kill him next. Staring in disgust, he watched as Eden laid her machete down next to her and began to unbutton Mika'el's trousers. Roughly pulling his trousers and underwear down, she exposed his flaccid penis to the air. Mika'el's soft cock was longer than Eden had expected, and his pubic hair was sprigs of white like his beard. She cupped his balls in her hand and then squeezed the shaft of his cock. It was still warm; it took a little while for a dead body to go cold. While jerking the dead man's dick, she could feel the blood starting to flow into his sex organ. Nikola watched with an expression of repulsion on his face, but he couldn't seem to look away. Eden smiled with delight as the penis in her hand began to become erect. Once it was fully hard, she began to jerk it harder and faster, looking into Nikola's eyes as she did it. He was disgusted by the fact that he could feel himself getting aroused. There was a feeling of being dirty accompanied with these necrophiliac activities.

"Won't you stop?" Nikola finally spoke up. "You're defiling his body! You've already killed him, do you need to bring dishonor to his memory as well?"

Eden scoffed. "You're so full of shit, Nikola. I've seen it in this time that you've been close to me here in my palace. I see that you hold lots of secrets—including secrets you are most ashamed of. You carry a hidden guilt that you try not to let anyone see. But I see right through you. You won't try to stop me from molesting your butt-buddy's body, and you know why? Because you're a fucking *coward*, that's why. I've seen the way you look at me. You don't think I know that you want to fuck me? That you're attracted to me? But you're too much of a pussy to make a move. You want to know what it feels like to be inside me. And you're intrigued to know what it's like to have a Soulmind. It's okay, you don't have to lie to me. You put up a good act that you're mortified by the things I've done, however, revulsion often covers up an extreme attraction."

Nikola swallowed the lump in his throat, but he couldn't argue against what she was saying. Apparently he was more transparent to her than he had realized. "I-I-I—" he stammered.

"Oh, come off it," Eden said with a laugh. "Don't even try to deny it... Speaking of cum..." She looked down at the dead hand-job she was giving and could feel the dead man's balls twitch against his taint. The eruption was about to gush. In a second she felt the cock twitch in her hand and three long strings of semen squirted from his urethra, white milky liquid that tried to fly up into the air but then fell back down onto Eden's hand. After finishing the last stroke, she brought her hand up to her lips and licked the semen off of her knuckles. In that moment, Nikola didn't know how to feel; it was all a mixture of aversion and desire. Eden stood up and walked over to Nikola. This time he didn't make an attempt to evade her. Grabbing the front of his shirt, she pulled him close to her. With a mischievous smile, she looked into his eyes. "Do you want to taste your friend on my tongue?" she asked seductively. And before he could answer either in the affirmative or the negative, Eden pulled him down to her face and kissed his lips sensually, parting them and then slipping her tongue into his mouth. There was a glob of semen on her tongue which she now transferred to Nikola. For a moment he tasted his friend's spunk on his tongue, trying to will it not to bring back memories, and then he swallowed.

"I don't know who I am anymore," Nikola whispered as Eden brushed her fingers through his soft hair. He didn't fully know what he meant by that statement, but it felt like an authentic statement that came from the depths of his soul. He had always been so scientifically-minded; if there was something to be figured out or solved, logic was always there to reason it out through hypothesis and experiments. The inner life—the stuff of the heart and emotions—were not as cut and dry as his left-brain wished them to be.

"Does anybody really know who they are?" Eden replied. "Who is this Eden, anyway? Am I a wicked Queen, my destiny to bring suffering to people and to fulfill my every desire regardless of the harm it causes? Or am I a lover? Someone who wishes for connection, who is strong yet wants to be held, comforted, and told everything will be all right? Or am a Goddess? One who's strong beyond all measure, one who can help the Spiralverse to expand its awareness and to move up levels of empowerment?"

"You are what you are," Nikola responded, even though her question was rhetorical. "And I am what I am. Whatever that may be. We can always change and grow. I can strive to be less of a coward in the future. To stand up for myself and what I believe in. And you can strive to heal that pain that's inside you, eating away like a cancer. You can strive to be whole again to the point you don't want to cause suffering anymore. When you have no pain, so you don't wish to inflict it upon others... But only if you wish, Eden. You have the freedom to choose. No one is beyond redemption. Not even the Devil himself."

"Stop talking now," Eden whispered and kissed him again. "Do you want to fuck me, Nikola?" He nodded nervously. "I need to hear you say it out loud. It has to know you've consented."

Nikola didn't know what she meant by that—by what *it* was that needed to know. "Yes—yes, Eden," he spoke now with re-solve, "I want to f—to have sex with you. To lay with you like a lover." This was all Eden needed to hear in order to ravish him. She fell to kissing his neck, nipping his skin and licking it as she stroked down his blood-stained shirt and into the waist of his pants. He gasped as she took ahold of his cock beneath his underwear. Closing his eyes, he moaned as she stroked him. Nikola's member swelled with blood and strained against the front of his pants, almost bursting to be let loose. Moaning loudly, he surrendered to enjoying the sensation of Eden's warm hand wrapped around his sex organ.

Slowly slipping her hand out of his pants again, Nikola looked at her like *Why are you stopping?* "Take 'em off," she demanded. "I want to see your nakedness."

Without saying a word, Nikola slipped his suspenders off of his shoulders, unbuttoned his pants, and slid them off. Eden watched as the man before her took off every piece of clothing except for his glasses. He made sure to put his clothes over by the door so they wouldn't get wet with the puddle of blood that was slowly getting bigger and beginning to run down the drain in the middle of the floor. Underneath the square science teacher-type clothes, Nikola was surprisingly fit. Eden felt an attraction, a twitch in her clitoris, as she surveyed his muscles. He wasn't super-ripped, but he was lean and had nice muscle tone. His pecs were taut, like a tight drum, its skin tanned to perfection. Moving her eyes down his body, Eden admired his abs which were flat against his torso and she could see the muscles rippling beneath his smooth skin. Just the subtlest layer of sweat glistened on his flesh. The contrast of him standing naked in front of the sex taking place on the screen behind him turned her on. His cock stood out straight in front of his body, aching to be inside of her as he took some slow, deep breaths.

Now it was Nikola's turn to watch Eden get naked. Only for a second, she removed her crown so she could peel off her purple turtleneck up over her head. She placed the crown back on her head as she tossed her shirt carelessly on the floor. Then her jeans and panties were off and kicked aside as well. Nikola liked Eden's sexy, athletic body. Her small, perky tits were so hot, and her hard nipples pricked outwards into the cool air. There was a stubble of pubic hair around her pussy since she hadn't bothered to shave it in a while. Nikola was still under the effects of the Soulmind Sight spell Eden had casted on him, and he could feel a change in the energy in the room.

"Watch this," she said, putting her arms down by her sides with her palms facing out. Suddenly a layer of subtle energy rippled over her skin and then her aura of pink and red burst out around her body like spiritual flames. Nikola stared in awe as he witnessed her aura expand even wider, the pink and red tendrils dancing inside her light field. Then the spiral of her Soulmind light began to slowly spiral from her chest—tantalizing, as if calling him to come closer. "You see this now because I temporarily bestowed on you the gift of Sight. But after we do this, you will have it forever. Lay down on the floor," she demanded.

Without a word, he laid down on the floor on his back. The surface felt cool against his warm skin. His cock was rock-hard and aching for a release. Tentatively he began to stroke himself as he looked at Eden's gorgeous body standing over him looking like a human torch. "*Don't* touch yourself," she ordered, putting one finger up in the air. Nikola stopped, fearing that he might incur her wrath. As he laid there in painful anticipation, Eden stepped over him and straddled his pelvis with her legs. He stared up at her tits, her tight abs, and then lower, admiring the pretty slit between her legs. Her clitoris was large, Nikola noted. He could see it quivering out from between her lips, the pink skin glistening with her own lubricant. As she squatted down slowly toward his cock, he almost couldn't contain himself; he felt like he was already on the verge of gushing. Before he was even aware of it, she had guided herself down to him and slipped his cock inside.

"Oh my God," Nikola moaned, closing his eyes and tilting his head back from the potent ecstasy he was feeling from their merger. Touching his chest softly with her hands, she began to ride him, slowly at first. Eden looked into her new lover's face as she took all of his swollen member inside of her. His pupils were dramatically dilated and there was a cute hue of crimson burning on his skin over his cheekbones. "Oh, Eden," he whispered as his hands found their way up to her breasts. She let him touch her and caress her nipples as he stared at the Soulmind energy still rippling and spiraling between her tits. The reality of his fantasy coming true almost made him forget about the presence of his best friend's dead body just a few feet away. He told himself that he must not get distracted from his true purpose. There was even an inkling of a possibility that Eden was aware of his purpose behind wanting to have a Soulmind of his own.

"Do you like that? Is this what you needed?" she whispered seductively.

"Yes, Mistress," he panted, sweat beading more along his six-pack abs. "I needed to be inside you. Needed to be your lover."

"So then," she continued, not slowing her motion of sliding up and down on his thick cock. He felt nice inside of her. She had to admit that he was beautiful to look at, and his mind was at a level of genius worthy of being envied. *Maybe as I transfer energy to him, some of his intelligence will transfer to me*, she thought to herself. "Do you love me?" she finished her question. "*Could* you love me after all I've done? After murdering your friend?"

As Nikola contemplated this question, Eden's aura expanded to encapsulate both of them. He felt this as a warm tingling along the entire surface of his skin. "I don't condemn you," Nikola finally replied. "How can I condemn anyone without condemning myself first?" he continued between panting sex-breaths. "I'm not blameless, I'm not perfect. Even though I don't support some of your actions, I'm just as guilty of standing around and doing nothing to stop harm from being done. But no matter what anyone has done, they are still worthy of love. I have love *for* you, Eden. Even though I might not always do the right thing, or the noble thing, I still have compassion in my heart. Those times that I may have enabled someone to do evil, or harm to others, it was because of that compassion in my heart—oh, Jesus, that's good!" The sheer amount of pleasure he felt building within his body and energy cut off what he was saying and gripped him with another bout of moaning and getting lost in the bliss of Eden's divine cunt. "So, yes," he said, finally opening his eyes again and looking up at her. *Were those tears in her eyes?* "I do love you," was his definitive statement, no hesitation in his voice.

"Uhhhh! Ahhhh!" Eden screamed with pleasure. Declarations of love always got her even more excited. The spiral of Soulmind energy popped at her solar plexus and began to stretch farther toward Nikola's heart chakra. Smiling mischievously, she looked into his dilated pupils and said, "Are you ready, my love? After this you will never be the same."

"I'm ready," he whispered, not really sure what to expect. Suddenly all the chakras of spiraling vortex energy became visible on the front of Nikola's body, along his central vertical column. These centers of energy mirrored on Eden's body also, glowing with light. The spiral of red and pink energy was still dominantly coming out of her third chakra. Nikola leaned back and surrendered. At the moment of his utter surrender, spears of light shot out of all seven of Eden's chakras. These beams of energy traveled toward Nikola's body and at once plugged into all seven of Nikola's chakras. Once the contact was made, he gasped from the sudden rush of sensation up his spine. It was orgasmic, yet he didn't feel like he was about to ejaculate. The energy of Eden's Soulmind was being fed through the energy currents and into Nikola's body and into his auric field. There was a definite sensation of energy being pulled up toward his brain from the base of his spine. As if with inner vision, he could see this burning coil of energy travel up his spine, illuminating each chakra more as it traveled. When it reached his crown chakra, Eden gave a deep energetic push with a groan. As she did, there was a pop at Nikola's seventh chakra and a white thousand-petaled lotus exploded out the top of his head. Eden marveled at its beauty as a point of green energy hovered above the lotus, raining down showers of sparking light into the petals and down into Nikola's brain. He never felt more connected to the Spiralverse in his whole life as an explorer and a scientist than he did in that moment.

After a few minutes of just existing in the pure bliss of their connection, the perception of themselves as just pure Soul-minds joined into one field raged strong and made them almost forget their finite identities for that long—they were one with the infinite intelligence field of the Spiralverse. Sometimes Eden wished to remain in that connection for all of Eternity, and each time she entered into that feeling, she tried to stretch it out for longer and longer. Now she watched as the small ball of green energy went into the center of the lotus as it folded up and pulled itself back into Nikola's skull. This green energy was his Soulmind activated, and he could feel its spark traveling back down his central vertical column to come to rest at his heart chakra. Their seven centers of energy still remained plugged together, their energy circuit running liberally back and forth between them.

Eden began to ride Nikola's cock with a faster motion. Her mouth hung open and she began to moan and breathe harder. "Are you gonna cum, baby?" she asked, eyes half-closed and glazed with the high of their fucking.

"Yes, Eden," he moaned, feeling the orgasm building in his perineum right behind his balls.

"You're not ready for this," Eden giggled, grinding her clit against Nikola's pelvis. "Your brain is going to melt... Uhhh, fuck... Oh my God, yes... Fucking fuck me just like that!" Her eyes rolled up into her skull as she faded in and out—connecting with her physical body, then her Astral Body, and then merging her consciousness with purely her Soulmind as if she existed as just that energy. "Ready? Ready?" she panted. Nikola nodded, mouth hanging open in a moan. "*UHH FUCK JESUS!*" she shrieked with pleasure. "I'm gonna cum! Cum with me, babe!"

Nikola could feel the energy coming to a peak, and they both screamed as their orgasms were in perfect unison. It wasn't two separate orgasms, it was one orgasm stretched between two beings connected on every level of existence. When they both came with an explosion, Eden leaned back a bit, feeling a mini-orgasm in each of her chakras. As the climax flooded into each other through their central vertical columns, the energy feed-lines connecting their chakras together ruptured, exploding with sprays of energetic colored sparks. These spiraling energy lines pulled free from Nikola and retracted into Eden's body. And as that light went back into her, another energy erupted from Nikola—his newly activated Soulmind. This green spiral of energy now began emanating from his chest, stretching toward Eden as her aura shrank back to only contain her body; Nikola's aura began to illuminate green around him now.

As they both slowly came back to their bodies from having their consciousnesses projected out into the orgasmic bands of energy that are shared by all Creation, both of their Soulminds started to stretch toward each other's again. Nikola's spiral of green Soulmind light reached out to touch Eden's red and pink one. They braided themselves together, not ready to detach from each other quite yet. As Eden sat on top of Nikola, his hard cock still inside her, she could feel the love pulsing through his Soulmind and into her. Suddenly that sensation of love made her feel uncomfortable as she stole a glance over at Mika'el's dead body which was still bleeding on the floor. The tears were threatening to come upon her again—this time not from joy or love, but from a feeling that she should mourn for herself; mourn her loss of innocence. For her soul was stained black, and she had it plain as day on her right arm to prove it.

Unable to stand Nikola's love any longer, since she felt totally undeserving of it, she stood up, sliding his prick out of her still dripping cunt. Taking a couple steps back, she forcibly tore the Soulmind braid apart, breaking the energetic connection between them. Her Soulmind retracted and disappeared into her solar plexus again. Nikola's did the same. He felt permanently changed, his awareness expanded and his power greatly increased. Eden didn't want Nikola to watch her cry from the sorrow and emptiness that she felt, so she turned her back to him as they began to stream down her cheeks. "Leave me alone now, Nikola," she sobbed. "I gave you what you wanted, now get the fuck out of my sight."

Nikola knew that there was nothing else to say. She was right, of course, he had gotten what he wanted which was an activated Soulmind. That was the beginning of his real plan, which was to escape The Kingdom altogether. He did love her, that was not a lie, but he wasn't *in* love with Eden—at least not the way Terry was. If anyone was going to bring her back from the abyss, it was all on him now. Maybe it was his cowardice that made him want to run away; he felt helpless that he couldn't do more for her. He had done all he could, he knew that, and tried not to beat himself up over his shortcomings, but his journey now called him ever ever on. That he knew for certain: that *the road goes ever ever on.*

Eden hugged her arms around herself tightly and Nikola watched her black fingers curl around her left bicep. The nails on her fingers were blackened as well. As she sobbed, her shoulders shuddered, but she tried to be as quiet as she could until she was alone with her haunted thoughts. As quickly as he could, Nikola got dressed and without hesitation exited the throne room. After he had closed the door behind him, he whispered, "I'm sorry," very quietly and then rushed off to the subterranean dungeons.

Inside the throne room, Eden stood naked and alone with just robots and a dead body to keep her company. Her weeping grew louder; she screamed and wailed in frustration. After such a deep sense of connection, the vicious feeling of separation afterward was getting more and more excruciating, like a cross that you're cursed to drag over your own grave for all time. Looking at Mika'el's body through a mist of tears, suddenly something hit her like the undeniable sense of déjà vu, almost like she had known this old man. At that moment she knew definitively that she had interacted with this man in some capacity beyond what she could recall. In her mind's eye she got the flash of an image of herself in Mika'el's kitchen, him serving her food. And there was a boy sitting next to her at the table—she couldn't make out his face but he had shaggy black hair. She knew then that this man had been her friend at one point. And she had killed him without hesitation. Gutted him right through the stomach with no remorse.

Now, surprisingly, she *was* feeling remorse. Her wails and sobs became louder, high pitched from a deep pit of torment. Slowly she knelt down next to Mika'el's dead body, making sure her crown didn't fall off of her head. Then she laid down next to him, her naked skin now wet in the still-growing puddle of blood. As she embraced the dead man, her weeping and lamentations of grief continued unabated. Her unbearable inner turmoil was finally bubbling to the surface.

Terry was meditating in his cell when Nikola rushed in to see him. Sitting on the floor lotus-style, he opened his eyes as his friend approached. "Nikola," Terry said, staring through the bars. "What hap—You're glowing! There's a green light ar—No, you didn't!" he said, the reality slowly dawning on him. Nikola looked sheepish. "You fucked her! You did, didn't you?"

Nikola nodded, a little ashamed of himself. "That's why I've come to say goodbye," he started, getting closer to the bars of Terry's cell. "You've been a great friend and both of you have opened my eyes to realities I could only have dreamed about before."

"Goodbye?" Terry repeated back. "Where are you going? Don't go," he continued, standing up and approaching the bars.

"I have to," Nikola admitted. "My journey here is at its end. Now that Eden has activated my Soulmind, I can do what I have always been meant to do—explore other Dimensions and planes of reality. The outer reaches of the Spiralverse."

"You'll come to find that you have to explore the inner limits as well," Terry informed him.

Nikola nodded. "Yes, I know. It's been my duty as a scientist to explore space—both inner and outer."

"How are you going to leave?" Terry wanted to know. "Are you going to portal out at Mika'el's farm?"

Nikola shook his head. "No, I think I know another way. What you said about where you appeared on the mountain at the edge of our domain gave me the idea. Hopefully it works, but I have a feeling it will work. No doubt we will meet again, my friend. I'm sorry I couldn't do more for Eden. It's up to you now."

"What? No! No!" Terry yelled, stretching his arm out of the bars and toward Nikola as he started to back away. "You gotta let me out of here! Nikola, please!"

The scientist gave Terry another sheepish look and grabbed his hand that was reaching for him through the bars. Nikola squeezed Terry's hand affectionately and smiled at his friend who had surprisingly taught him so much, even things about himself he didn't know. "I'm not supposed to set you free right now," Nikola continued, and Terry didn't understand what he meant by that. "I love you both truly. Pull Eden from the edge of the abyss, please, or she'll plummet forever... But now I must go." He winked at Terry and his final words were, "I'll see you on the other side."

He gave Terry's hand one more squeeze and then he slipped his fingers away from his friend's grip. Turning away, he ran out of the room and back up the stairs. "*NO! NIKOLA!*" Terry screamed after him. "*YOU GOTTA LET ME OUT! NIKOLA! NIKOLA!*" He continued yelling his friend's name, pleading for him to come back and release him, but it was useless since Nikola was already out of earshot—his escape the only thing on his mind.

In the parking lot of The Wild Orchid Palace, Nikola had one of his flying cars. He felt time pressing in on him so he didn't even bother to run back to his apartment to put some supplies together. With the realization of an activated Soulmind, Nikola knew he was a traveler now, like Eden and Terry, and he would have to rely on the Spiralverse to provide for him as he found himself going through different worlds. Jumping into the driver's seat of his flying car, he fired it up and took a deep breath. If his plan didn't work, he'd probably explode in his vehicle and be dead anyway. *For science it was worth it.*

Exiting the parking lot of the casino, Nikola zipped in amid the air traffic. When he was close to the edge of the City, he veered off of the normal flow of City traffic and headed toward the mountains. No other cars were in his airspace now and he pulled up, trying to get as much altitude as possible. These flying cars weren't really meant to go that high, but Nikola was going to test it to its limits. It seemed like it took no time at all to cover the distance to the mountains. The car was still climbing and he was approaching the peak of the mountain range. Suddenly Nikola started to perceive a neon-green grid of light connecting to the topmost part of the mountains, and stretched up into the sky as far as he could see. *This is it*, Nikola thought, *I only get one try at this.*

His aura lit up green around his body and a wisp of a spiral of light started to emerge from his heart-space. Condensing the Soulmind light coming out of his chest down into an orb of energy, he exhaled forcefully and expanded the green orb to encapsulate himself and the entire flying car. This was just in time because when the orb reached its full size, the car flew directly into the grid of light. The whole car was carried through the grid inside the safety of the Soulmind sphere, disappearing into another world as it slipped through, leaving only a wave of green like ripples on a pond.

FOURTEEN

There was a chilling mist hanging in the air the day that Maya came through into the Hollow Dimension, leaving Dark Tethers behind for good. Stumbling slightly in the low visibility, she was disoriented, confused, and unsure of what to do next. The Hollow Dimension was a mystery to her, especially when she wasn't here on a mission to destroy it. Maya stood still, trying to get her bearings. She was surrounded by trees and the whiteness of the chilly fog. *Which way to go?* she thought. *What am I doing?*

As she walked deeper into the woods, she started noticing things hidden in the mist between the trees—tents, blankets, remains of a fire, cooking pots and utensils. This was evidence of people living in these woods, or camping, but she didn't see anyone up and about yet. Suddenly a fatigue gripped her; a weariness like she'd never felt in her life. *Is this what being a human feels like?* she wondered. *Weak and in need of replenishing?*

Walking farther away from the area where the tents were set up, she thought it may be wise to stay within the shelter of the trees for now until she regained her strength and figured out what her next move would be. She took a deep breath, breathing in the cold mist. It chilled her lungs and gave her a rush of energy running up her spine. Her pace slowed and she dragged her feet as she approached a large tree in front of her. This magnificent giant called to her as if its energy was vibrating to the point it magnetized her. Stepping toward this tree, she slowly placed her hand on its trunk, feeling the bark with a soft touch. She could feel it singing, and she closed her eyes. This was something she'd never experienced before. There were no plants in the Dark Tethers and she'd never imagined that something that grew in the ground could have such a rich consciousness and inner life—maybe this majestic tree even had a soul. She wasn't quite sure.

As Maya let this wondrous entity sing its song to her, she saw with her new Inner Vision strange lights, patterns, and geometries that she didn't have any words for. This was definitely not the geometry that Dark Tethers was built on. These patterns she was now witnessing felt a lot less dense and more *sacred*. Like she should be in awe and reverence to the blueprints that the *Infinite Intelligent Source of All Life* used to create the Spiralverse. Maya knew then that she possessed quite a bit of knowledge, but little wisdom to put that knowledge to much use, especially in the Human World. Maybe this wisdom would come to her within deep meditation. So she took her hand from the tree's bark, still hearing the hum of its song, and sat down in front of it with her back against the sturdy trunk. The strength of the tree was comforting to her, and its aura encircled her in a protective embrace. In lotus pose at the base of this powerful being, Maya closed her eyes and could feel the newly activated green energy of her Soulmind stirring as she sank deep into her meditation.

FIFTEEN

Laying naked on the couch, Mothman was enjoying his time alone in Terry's house—with company. Allister was laying beside him, naked also, with her head on his thigh. Her head was right next to his flaccid penis and she played with the rubbery thing absentmindedly. "Hey, Mothman?" she said, flipping his dick between her fingers.

"Hmm?" he said by way of reply.

"Do you think Terry's okay?" Allister asked, concern in her voice. "What if he's already dead and all our efforts are for nothing?"

Mothman snorted. "Terry dead?" he laughed. "If anyone can survive a government abduction it would be that fucking guy. He'll emerge victorious bathing in the blood of his enemies like the valiant knight that he his!" Mothman concluded dramatically.

Allister smirked. "You watch too much *Game of Thrones*," she joked.

"The ring of power, my precious," Mothman continued in a bad impression of Gollum's voice. "I put the ring around my cock and I fuck you like Lord Sauron!"

"You're so weird," Allister laughed. "I say *Game of Thrones* and you think *Lord of the Rings*? You're more like Samwise and Terry is Frodo and you're on Mount Doom having a bromance with him. *Brokeback Mount Doom*." She laughed heartily at her own joke.

"Fuck you," Mothman returned. "Why does Terry get to be Frodo? And I'm the fat Hobbit trying to fuck him? Fuck you twice!"

"You already did," she said, smiling up at him as she cupped his balls in her warm palm.

"Yeah, yeah," he continued, "but you were probably thinking about Terry the whole time." Allister didn't respond, she just kept smiling up at him with his cock in her hand. "You were, weren't you!"

Before Allister could answer, Mothman's cell phone rang from the pocket of his jeans that were laying in a heap next to the couch. After digging the phone out, he answered it saying, "Who the fuck dares do disturb my royal coitus? I shall have your head on a pike for this! You will never bear children again!"

"That sounds like the Mothman I know and love," came the voice at the other end of the call.

"Rob?" Mothman asked.

"Yeah, it's me," Rob answered. "Been sucking any penis lately?"

"Ha ha," he laughed sarcastically. "Only your mom's."

Rob laughed. "That's a good one. Anyway, how are things there? Darren said they haven't tried to rescue Terry yet, but they are prepping for the strike. You're keeping the safe-house ship-shape?"

"Oh, yeah," Mothman replied. "Everything's good here. I've been leaving little loads of my cum all around the house. And I just got laid." He winked at Allister who was looking up at him as he conversed with Rob.

"Oh yeah?" Rob scoffed. "Who is he? Was it Michael? I knew you liked his tight little ass."

Mothman rolled his eyes. "*He*? Suck my asshole, Rob. I'll have you know I just made sweet cosmic love with the beautiful and sexy Allister."

"That Goth girl?" Rob said, surprised. "Nuh-uh. You lie. The only thing you're fucking is your own hand."

Mothman took the phone away from his ear and put it up next to Allister's ear. "Rob?" she said.

"Holy shit, you really are there," Rob replied. "Mothman's always so full of shit."

"I'm keenly aware," Allister smiled. "There was just something I couldn't resist. Maybe it is his big dick." She stroked down Mothman's shaft and he was starting to get hard again. "You've had him in your ass, haven't you, Rob?"

"That's funny," Rob said dryly as Mothman took the phone back from Allister.

"So, where are you now, Robert?" Mothman asked, changing the subject.

"I'm in New York," he continued. "Met up with this other Lucifer Christ couple here and the Playground meeting is scheduled for tomorrow. I don't know how they're coordinating this so well, but they are. There are young Soulminds everywhere thirsty for companionship and a purpose. That's what we're giving them. The Lucifer Christ people are kinda weird though."

"What do you mean?"

"I don't really know. I guess they're okay," Rob admitted. "They're nice and all, but I just get weird vibes from them sometimes. I dunno, maybe it's just me."

"It's just you, Rob, you're the weird one," Mothman laughed. "I know you want to get in bed with all these older couples, but they'd be horrified to see that crooked dick of yours."

"It's not crooked!" Rob huffed. "I'll have you know my dick is perfectly flawless, smooth and circumcised."

Mothman burst out laughing. "Yeah, your brain is circumcised."

Rob waited silently as Mothman fell into a fit of laughter. When he finally quieted down, Rob said, "Are you finished?"

"I don't know," he responded, wiping tears from his eyes. "I quite thoroughly enjoy making fun of you. You get so pissed off it's hilarious."

"I'm glad you enjoy it," Rob mumbled.

"So did you get to see the Twin Towers?" Mothman asked.

There was a silence on the other end of the phone. "Are you fucking for real right now?" Rob replied. "Where have you been since 2001? Has your head been so far up your own ass that all you can see now is your own colon?"

"I was just joking," he said quickly, trying to recover.

"Yeah, sure you were," Rob chuckled. "Just like you know that those Twin Towers were destroyed by alien spaceships."

"They were?" Mothman's eyes widened.

"Yeah, flew right into 'em," Rob continued. "Then they self-destructed with plasma bursts, triggering a controlled demolition of both buildings. And number seven which didn't get hit at all but somehow fell as well."

"What? No way," Mothman said, riveted by Rob's story of 9/11.

"Are you a fucking retard?" Rob said.

"No!" Mothman snapped back.

"The question was rhetorical, you moron."

"I knew that," Mothman said quickly, not wanting to sound like an idiot but suspecting that he still did. "How was DC?"

"The District of Corruption?" Rob said. "That place is fucking weird. There were quite a few Soulminds there aching to unite with each other though. They were so grateful to be brought together. It was beautiful to see."

"That's awesome," Mothman commented. "What was weird about it though?"

"I feel like it's definitely a location of a vortex of power," Rob explained, "but there is also a very dense energy hanging around, created by the misdeeds of the government. A spiritual wickedness—it felt very *Satanic*."

"That sounds creepy."

"Yes, it definitely is," Rob confirmed.

"So where are you off to next?" Mothman wanted to know. He looked down and realized he was completely hard again. Allister had taken him into her mouth and was gently sucking on him, caressing his cock with her tongue.

"I'm a little nervous about traveling overseas," Rob admitted. "My next destination is London. Then Darren wants me to go to Florence in Italy."

"I'm totally envious, Rob," Mothman replied, trying not to moan from the pleasure building as Allister continued to go down on him. "You get to be on vacation and visit all these amazing places."

"Trust me, it's not all fun and games," Rob confessed. "It's stressful and I'm not really able to enjoy these places since I'm off to the next one so quickly."

"Oh my God, babe," Mothman said, starting to moan from the pleasure. "Cute little Robert, I have to go. The slut calls me hither and I have to heed the pussy's purr." And before Rob could say goodbye, Mothman hung up and tossed the phone back into the pile of his discarded clothes. Allister smiled and stared up at him with wide, seductive eyes as she stroked his shaft, lubricated by her own saliva. "Oh, yes, baby," he said, knowing what was about to come next. "I am going to fill you like a Thanksgiving turkey on Christmas!"

SIXTEEN

It was going to be a couple days journey through the forest and onto the Great Plains where the giant lived. The Elves decided to keep Artemis locked in their stables until Jessica returned with her mission complete in case she was tempted to run away without keeping her end of the bargain. Jessica would never abandon her unicorn companion to be prisoner of the Elves forever, and Odelliam was keenly aware of that fact. He had allowed her to take her knapsack with her on the journey, but also charged the young Josh-oo'el to be her traveling companion. This Elf knew the way to where the giant slept and could also vouch for its death to Odelliam once they returned to the trees. Jessica was trying to tolerate Josh-oo'el despite her growing annoyance.

"So what's it like to fuck a goat?" he asked, grinning cheekily.

"Shut your mouth!" Jessica snapped as they traipsed through the wood side by side. "I have *never* done anything like that *ever!*"

Josh-oo'el shrugged his shoulders. "Well, that's not what I heard." He adjusted the large pack he was carrying to be more comfortable on his back. "You are the Goat-Fucker," he stated matter-of-factly.

Jessica gritted her teeth, "Shut up," she growled.

"Goat-Fucker," Josh-oo'el repeated with a smirk.

"Shut up, you impudent little shit!" she shot back, her voice raising in volume.

The Elf cleared his throat loudly and then said, "Goat-Fucker! Goat-Fucker! Goat-Fucker!"

"Ugh!" Jessica screamed in frustration. "*SHUT UP! STOP SAYING THAT!* I swear to God, Odelliam made you come along just to torment me."

Josh-oo'el laughed at her perturbation. "You should have been at least allowed to take a shower," he continued. "You still reek of goat nuts."

Jessica stopped walking and glared at her companion as if she wished to burn holes in his skull with her eyes. "I swear, if you make one more comment about this I will slug you!" she threatened.

The young impudent Elf stared at Jessica in silence for a moment. Her face was red and she looked like steam was about to start shooting from her ears. Suddenly, after the moment of silence, a smile slowly crept over his face and he said, "Goat-Fucker..."

"Agh!" Jessica yelled in exasperation, then she punched Josh-oo'el in the arm to show that her threat was not empty. After hitting him, she turned and started stomping off in the direction they had been walking.

"Ow, that hurt," he mumbled, rubbing his arm tenderly, and then rushed to catch up with her.

"I hope you have stuff for two tents in that pack of yours," Jessica commented as Josh-oo'el caught up to her again, "because I'm *not* sharing a tent with you."

"No tents, my lady," he replied. "I have enough for us to make a little bed for ourselves to sleep side by side under the stars. It'll be so romantic."

Jessica was not amused. "You're not funny, you know," she said, deadpan.

The Elf shrugged. "*I thought it was funny...*"

"Anyway, tell me more about this giant, Josh-oo'el," she said, trying to change the subject to something less irritating.

The young Elf was silent for a moment as they continued walking West through the forest. Jessica glanced over at her companion who looked like he was deep in thought. "Well," he started finally, "the giant is not really a giant. Well, I mean, he is—but he's not, too."

Jessica was confused. "What are you babbling about?"

Josh-oo'el shook his head. "You see, it's, uh, a Troll—a giant Troll."

"Huh?" Jessica said, raising an eyebrow. "I thought Trolls were small—smaller than humans even."

"Some of them are," he continued explaining. "But there are many different races of Trolls. And one certain race of Trolls are giants. They aren't very smart and they can't speak—they more just growl, roar, or make grunting noises. You said you were a Christian?"

Jessica mouth hung open a bit, not really sure anymore about how to answer that question. "No, I—" she started haltingly. "I'm a witch—a Christian witch? Er, I don't know, it's all become sort of muddled up. Not sure what I am anymore, but I'm figuring it out."

"Hmm," Josh-oo'el was thoughtful, rubbing his beardless chin. "Well, regardless," he continued, "I'm not very familiar with this concept of *Christian*, but what I understand is that it is some kind of faith or belief system."

Jessica nodded slowly. "That's right. Christians believe that Jesus is the Son of God and *is* God."

"Huh," Josh-oo'el responded. "I'm not familiar with this Jesus person, but there is a legend of a traveler who came through these parts long ago... His name was Jeshua. I wonder if there is any connection between the two figures..." He glanced over at Jessica briefly and continued. "Do you believe in God?" The Elf was quite enjoying this discussion because it was rare that he was able to wax philosophical since he was young and most of the older male Elves that he looked up to laughed at him and didn't take him seriously.

Jessica shrugged at the question. Earlier in her life it would have been so easy for her to answer that question. "It would be nice," she answered honestly. "But I'm not sure anymore. I'd like to think that God exists. However, I've been forced to question that as of recently. Do you believe in God, Josh-oo'el? Do Elves even have concepts like that?"

Josh-oo'el nodded. "Some Elves believe in God and others do not. Which I assume is the same among the humans. We don't have *religions*—which is what I've learned exists in the Human World—but we do have spirituality and different systems of Magick. As for me, I don't know if I believe in a God. Like you, I think it would be a nice thought that some being is watching over and taking care of you."

"Yes, it can be comforting at times," Jessica admitted. "Hey, what does this have to do with the giant Troll?"

"Oh, yeah, that's what we were talking about," he continued, coming back to his original thought. "The legends about the Troll giants say that they have the ability to sniff out the scent of any creature that believes in God, and it is their instinct to kill that creature, or person."

Jessica swallowed hard. If she still believed in God deep down, they were in trouble because it would rouse the giant's attention. "Is that true?" Jessica squeaked.

"I don't know," Josh-oo'el replied honestly. "I've never had the opportunity to test that out. But I guess we'll find out, won't we?" He smiled and winked at her. She wasn't amused.

The sun was beginning to set on their first day of hiking and Jessica could feel the fatigue creeping into her muscles. "Night is coming fast," she commented.

The Elf nodded in agreement and stopped his stroll abruptly, looking around at the trees and the soft greenery on the forest floor. He took the pack from his back and set it down on the ground. "This seems as good a place as any to set up camp," he said.

"Oh, yeah?" Jessica asked, stopping as well. "I am feeling a little tired."

"We're not that far from the edge of the forest," Josh-oo'el informed her. "By midday tomorrow we should make it to the end of the forest and the beginning of the Great Plains."

"So, you're not afraid at the prospect that you might be killed by this giant Troll?" she wondered, for the fear in her was starting to creep back into her belly like a sinking nausea.

"Oh, rest assured, Jessica, that I probably should be quaking in my boots right now, were it not for the fact that I'm willfully trying to push that thought from my mind," the young Elf admitted reluctantly.

Jessica concurred. "Yeah," she said, "me too..."

PART 18

Lucifer Christ

*"Why should their bodies start to shine in this way?
If these people were really no different from
the stones on the riverbank, then they would not shine
no matter how hard they were polished. However, the fact that
they do shine shows that even malicious spirits,
even Satan himself, are diamonds at heart."*

- Ryuho Okawa, *The Laws of Eternity*

SEVENTEEN

Even the sights and sounds of a palace, which were once so wondrous and novel, could fade to the dullness of day-to-day monotony. Arash Khan knew that he was the guest of honor—the next Mahan Tantric—but he was beginning to feel more like a glorified prisoner. Not that the Order of the Transcendent told him explicitly that he was forbade from leaving the Palace Temple or its grounds, but he was young and still had the drive to run around, be silly, and play with his friends from school. Life had suddenly become more serious after agreeing to be Leeah's successor. Along with that, sometimes he felt strange being the only male in a spiritual body consisting of all women. In a way, he felt like somehow he had cheated his way to become the Supreme of an all-female witch coven. Even though the Mahan Tantric wasn't a ruler in a traditional sense, it would be a strange phenomenon—in the Hollow Dimension—for a women-only organization to elect a man to be their leader.

Sitting on the edge of his bed, Arash felt restless and wiped his clammy hands on his pants as he felt like the walls were closing in on him. Closing his eyes, he took a deep meditative breath as he tried to ground himself into the moment and not let his thoughts take him to places where he would feel discontent. There was a sharp knock on his chamber door and opening his eyes again he said, "Who is it?"

"It's Rahjiah," came the voice from behind the door as it was tentatively cracked open.

Arash shook his head. "Come in," he responded with an edge of irritation in his voice.

Rahjiah let herself in and as if floating in her white clothes, she swooped over and sat down next to Arash on the bed. "Are you okay, Lord Khan?" she asked with concern in her voice. "You've been spending a lot more time in your quarters."

Arash nodded slowly. "Are there other options I'm not aware of?" he snapped and then softened his tone. "I mean, yeah, I have been going out and meditating in the garden. I practice my yoga and the techniques you all have taught me to work with my Soulmind. But..." he trailed off for a moment. Rahjiah listened in respectful silence. "There hasn't been that many more activations recently. Have you all sort of left me on my own? I feel like you don't know what to do with me anymore. I don't know who I *am* anymore," he continued, his voice getting more frustrated. "Out there I knew who I was. I was Arash fucking Khan! I was the fun kid who would come up with mischief to get into and the one who would always make everybody laugh. But, who am I *here*? You call me *Lord Khan*, but I don't feel it. Am I supposed to *feel* like the Mahan Tantric? Because I don't know what that's supposed to be like."

"We haven't forgotten you," Rahjiah replied softly, placing her hand comfortingly on Arash's leg. "The activations have slowed down because you're almost to the end of your training. Hence, we've been giving you more time to work with your Soulmind and new Magick on your own without our guidance. You'll be the leader of all this one day."

Arash swallowed hard. "That's kinda what I'm afraid of. I don't know what that person is going to be like. Will I still be me?"

Rahjiah nodded in acknowledgment. "It's natural to feel uncertain. Don't feel ashamed of yourself if you feel frightened or think that you should have it all figured out by now. It's okay that you don't know exactly what you'll become. But have faith in yourself that you will handle any situation to the best of your own ability, and that's all you can strive for. The transfer of power between you and Leeah is approaching very soon. And you are most likely picking up on that psychically, which understandably would cause some anxiety. After the Transference, she will be gone and it will be only you. You will then officially be Mahan Tantric."

"Speaking of Leeah," Arash continued, "I don't feel like I've seen her in a while. Like a week or something."

"Leeah is off-world right now," Rahjiah answered. "But she's due to return in the next week or so."

Arash's eyes widened. "*Off-world*? Like off-*planet*?"

Rahjiah nodded. "There are many other sentient beings in the Spiralverse other than humans, animals, and plants."

"Plants are sentient?" Arash asked, eyebrows raised. Rahjiah nodded in answer. "And we go to other planets to take care of business and interact with aliens?"

"Yes, that's right," she returned. "Sometimes there is politics, and business, and all that boring stuff we have to tend to with other races and civilizations on other worlds. This is all in maintaining the order of the Spiralverse. We can't have things spiraling into chaos, now can we?"

Arash shook his head. "I guess not, no. Maybe someday I'll be able to go into space and be a diplomat to aliens." He smiled.

"Someday you will," she said, smiling back. "Anyway, I'm sorry that it may have seemed that we were not spending as much time with you and on your training these last few weeks. As you know, there has been much unrest within the Order of the Transcendent. This has been taking up a great amount of my energy and time as of late. There is quite a lot of disagreement and internal politics that I've had to deal with. Leeah being off-world, it is just on me to at least make an attempt to keep some sort of semblance of peace. Goddess Sophia knows how difficult that is for me, and it is only through Her strength that I can maintain as much as I do."

Arash sighed. "And I'm going to be inheriting that disfunction. Sounds like I'm getting the butt end of the deal. Maybe I don't want the job. Maybe I just want to go back to school and make my friends laugh by doing my impression of a Chinese flight attendant..."

"I know it may seem like you're inheriting the leadership of a broken organization," Rahjiah admitted, "but maybe you'll do better than Leeah did. Maybe you're the catalyst which will unite us again. Some of the other women and I have been saying that. You are the difference that we need. We have faith in you. Are you really considering going back to your old life? If you want out now, no one would blame you. But once the Transference is complete, you are the Mahan Tantric for life."

Shrugging, Arash said, "No, I'm not seriously considering going back to my old life. I was just saying..." he trailed off, hoping that Rahjiah understood what he meant. Arash looked up and met her gaze. "So what, did you want to talk to me about something specific? Or you just came to check on me? Cause I'm good—I'm okay, just maybe a bit anxious. But I'm processing. Getting through..."

"Yes, there is something specific I want to ask of you," Rahjiah admitted, getting to the point. "What I'm going to ask of you will be very difficult, and I know you are going to be resistant to it at first, but hopefully you will see the necessity in it in order to keep the balance of the Spiralverse."

"What is it?" Arash asked, his stomach sinking deep into his guts. "I'm scared to even ask."

"You know your friend Robert Blackguard from the Hollow Dimension?"

"Yeah, what about him?" Arash asked, curious now.

"Well," Rahjiah continued slowly. "He's been going outside the parameters of his current incarnation. Meaning that his power and influence is expanding beyond where it should be. He's creating ripples way beyond his limits."

"Ripples beyond his limits?" he repeated, furrowing his brow. "What does that mean?"

"To maintain order in the Spiralverse, events need to follow a certain plan, you see," she explained. "As the Order of the Transcendent, when an individual begins to overstep their limits, it is our job to rein them in. If you know what I mean."

Arash rubbed his chin and frowned, trying to understand the implications of what Rahjiah was describing. "So if someone is going 'off plan' and creating these 'ripples' that are over their limit, then we have to intervene to get the trajectory of the Spiralverse back on plan."

"Right, right, I know that much," Arash replied. "However, I know that the Order have guidelines and rules that you have to follow. So legally—in terms of Cosmic Law—you can only interfere up to a certain degree, then you hit *your* limit." Rahjiah nodded. "So..." Arash continued, "You need me to do something that you aren't allowed to do."

"That's right," Rahjiah smiled. "You're very smart. Have I told you how smart you are?"

He waved his hand dismissively. "Just tell me what it is you want me to do, don't butter me up first."

"We need you to kill Robert Blackguard," she said flatly.

"What?!" Arash's jaw fell open. He didn't know what he was expecting to be asked, but it wasn't that. "I don't want to kill Rob! Are you nuts? Why can't you do it?"

"I just explained that to—"

"Right, right," he said, cutting her off. "You have to get me to do your dirty work since I'm not under the Laws of your Order yet. Isn't there a way we can just get Rob to stop what he's doing? What is he doing anyway? I mean, I can't imagine Rob is out there murdering people or creating mass chaos. What has he done to warrant a death sentence?"

"Trust me, if there was any other way, we would have found it," Rahjiah said with a sigh. "We don't like having to kill people or physically stop them from taking actions that they want to in their lives. It can be a curse to be able to see the full picture—the entire Plan. Sometimes a few deaths are necessary for the greater Plan. We have seen the future where Robert does not stop—he's been putting Soulmind groups together all over the world which is accelerating the trajectory of Earth toward a timeline that we don't want it to be on. If things go that way, even *more* people will die. But he thinks he's doing a good thing. They usually do."

"I wish Leeah was here," Arash whispered, looking over at the burning incense on his altar. The smoke wisped and wafted toward the ceiling in a fragrant leisurely way, and Arash wished life could be as simple as lighting a stick of incense.

"Well, Leeah's not here," Rahjiah remarked. "And we don't force you to do anything. You have free will to refuse, I simply ask as a request."

Arash thought for a long while. He didn't want to kill his friend Rob, but he was also committed to becoming the next Mahan Tantric. Whatever he had to do to transform into that roll, he wanted to do it. And if killing Rob would accelerate him into becoming who and what he was to become, then why not do it? He shrugged. "Fuck it," he said finally. "If I want to be in, then I have to be in all the way—not just half-assed. And if what you say is true and I'm to undergo Transference and become the next Mahan Tantric very soon, then I have to commit to being whatever that role needs me to be."

Rahjiah smiled. "There's the Arash Khan confidence that I'm used to. I understand that it's natural to get down sometimes, to want to see more progress than you do. Have faith, my lord. You are and will be all that you can be. I see the seeds beginning to sprout. But you can't grow an oak tree overnight."

"I don't *want* to kill Rob," Arash admitted. "And I know I haven't made an official oath, but I am committed to the mission of the Order of the Transcendent. I do what needs to be done, not what I *want* to do."

"That's called discernment," Rahjiah commented. "Do not judge what you must do as either right or wrong when there is a higher order at play."

"I don't want to dwell on it," Arash said. "I want to do it, then it's done, and feel detached from the act, knowing that it must be carried out. How will I do this anyway?"

"Robert will be in Italy in a few days," she explained. "We will show you how to portal where he will be in Florence. That's where you will intercept him and take care of it."

"Okay," Arash answered somberly. "At least I'll be somewhere nice when I murder him." He laughed dryly.

"Speaking of not having many activations this week," Rahjiah said, changing the subject. "We actually have a Crown Chakra activation to do with you today." She stood up and gave a little bow to Lord Khan. "Get yourself ready and please grace us with your presence in the Grand Hall, my lord." With that, she turned and floated out of the room, the waves of her flowing white clothes reminding Arash of a magic carpet flying through the air to explore the Cave of Wonders.

JULY & AUGUST

ONE

FROM THE MIND OF TERRY BROSWALD:

This isn't the cell that Eden threw me into. As I blink my eyes and my surroundings come into focus, I flex the fingers of my right hand to make sure I am in my body and in control of it. Sometimes it is difficult to grasp a dream at first—to take control of it. The whole flexing your fingers technique is a helpful one to start the process of lucid dreaming. That way you can maintain conscious control of your dream-self while in the Dreamsphere. It is similar to controlling an avatar in a video game.

Taking a couple wobbly steps forward, the ground is hard and cold beneath my bare feet. The substance is gray concrete, with dark stains and differently shaded patches. As I take steps, tiny cracks spider along the concrete underneath where the pads of my feet touch down. As my vision goes in an out of focus like a camera trying to capture an image in low light, my head feels wonky like it's pulsing with a high-pressure heartbeat. In this dream I am still wearing the gray sweatsuit which has been my only clothes since being taken to the Facility.

Fighting the pulsing in my head, I raise my face up to stare into the distance. As I squint my eyes through the hazy smog, I see the ruins of Chicago buildings in the far distance. The buildings look like they are almost toppling over onto each other, crumbling and tipping over like the leaning tower of Pisa, yet stuck in a forever freeze-frame. As I continue to walk toward the ruins of my city, I begin to hear a loud chopping noise, a *whoop-whoop* sound like the rotor blades of the black helicopter that hovered above my house while we held our Playground meeting.

Before I even have a chance to react, three black helicopters come flying toward me from within the desolated buildings. A couple of them definitely look military, and one may be a police helicopter. Within seconds they are upon me. I hold my arm up to shade my eyes as I gaze up at them through squinted eyes. The wind from the rotor blades blows my hair like the threat of a hurricane. Dust and pebbles from the debris swirl around me and I choke as the grit finds its way between my teeth. The police-looking chopper suddenly blinds me with a huge spot-light. My vision explodes in bursts of stars and the pulse from my heartbeat still pounds in my temples.

Even though this is a dream, I can feel very real terror that now I'm going to be ripped apart by a rain of bullets from three war machines hovering in the sky. Letting a scream loose from my throat, I struggle to maintain focus on the helicopters through the blinding light. "NO BOUNCE, NO PLAY, FUCKERS!" I yell as the white of my Soulmind becomes agitated. It explodes into my aura like a supernova and the spiral coming from my solar plexus is ready for combat. In a flash of an instant, I aim my palms down toward the ground and create an energetic electric-blue Star of David beneath my feet. In the same instant, the golden sphere of light pops from my heart space and encapsulates my whole body.

Now I can open my eyes a bit more. The glare from the spotlight has suddenly diminished and I notice that the light from the helicopter cannot penetrate the golden bubble—it just bounces off like light reflected into a mirror. The helicopters descend lower to the ground as if closing in on me. I feel as though at any moment one of them could fly through me and rip my body to shreds.

As a voice starts to boom through a speaker attached to the outside of the helicopter with the beam of light, I jump at the enormously loud electronic-sounding voice that starts to yell at me. "Terry Broswald!" the voice bellows. "You are under arrest for crimes of cosmic proportions!"

"What the fuck?" I mumble. "Crimes of cosmic proportions? I didn't do shit!"

"Because of this you are hereby held prisoner of the Astral Plane!" the voice continues.

"Prisoner of the…" I start to say back. "Yo, fuck this shit!" I yell louder. "This dream sucks! Where's tech support when you need 'em?"

"If you do not comply, we will be forced to use deadly force!" the voice yells that last part like he definitely means business.

"No power in the Spiralverse can stop me, you fucking cock-suckers!" I scream, the golden sphere around me pulses and starts to grow larger. Holding my arms up and palms toward the helicopters, I will my Soulmind energy to help the sphere of protection grow. The white light dances around me inside the sphere like pixies in a ballroom. Almost imperceptibly, I watch as one of the helicopters—it reminds me of the Black Hawk helicopter from that movie *Black Hawk Down*—descends slowly closer to my sphere of energy. Now it is low enough for me to make out a figure leaning out of the door on the side of the helicopter. This man is wearing a black jumpsuit and what looks like a motorcycle helmet on his head. The weapon he holds in his hands looks strange, like nothing I've ever seen before, yet it does resemble the look of a flamethrower.

Suddenly a feeling of terror grips me all the way down in my saggy ballsack. Why is it saggy? Because despite the fact this is a dream, it terrifies the shit out of me. Is that the warmth of piss running down my leg? My knees start to knock together and my body begins to shake. The spiral of white Soulmind light stretches out of me like a Slinky and lashes around like an octopus's tentacle that has been cut off. My energy has never acted this erratic before. Is it frightened? Is it trying to save me? Is it waiting for permission to break through the golden force field and tear the helicopters and their crew to shreds?

I can feel the air and the energy on the outside of the sphere like it is part of my own body. Like my aura is extending distances to the sides of me and high into the sky. So as the rotor blades of the helicopters *whoop-whoop* through the air, the sensation is that the blades are slicing through my own body. I guess my light body extending way past my skin can feel pain as if it is my flesh as well—invisible flesh. The pain becomes too unbearable as I start to scream. Clutching my temples, I fall to my knees, trying to hold the pulsing of my brain inside my skull so my head won't explode. My vision bursts like a blood vessel and what I can see becomes obscured by red and spiderwebbing veins. This is worse than any hangover I've ever felt. I almost can't think to keep the golden orb stable, and it begins to ripple and shake as if it's struggling to maintain its structure. And all the while the blades—*chop chop chop*—of the helicopters are butchering me like a meat cleaver taken to a slab of beef.

Trying desperately to gain some semblance of control, my hands fall to the ground and I'm on all fours struggling to pull myself back to my feet. The concrete begins to fracture more below me, sinking down into a small crater as the cracks split around me in circles and fault lines. Gritting my teeth, I force myself to my feet again. The feeling of warm liquid dripping down my cheek compels me to wipe it instinctively. My fingers come back smeared with red. I'm bleeding from my fucking eyeballs! There is a sharp pain in my brain and extreme pressure building up on the inside of my skull. Then the blood starts to gush from my ears and all I can hear is a deafening ringing that echoes forever.

"*No Bounce, No Play,*" I say to myself through gritted teeth. Tilting my head up, I see the jumpsuit-man readying his weapon to fire toward me and my protective shield. At the exact moment he pulls the trigger, I stretch my arms up again and push all my Soulmind energy out through my palms to try to stabilize the sphere against the attack. What comes out of the weapon is a long beam of blue-black light. My Soulmind can read the frequency vibration of the light and it feels like it has been manipulated. It is no more natural light, it is *artificial* light. This artificial light collides with the outside of the sphere and sparks in a burst of refracted energy. I can feel it pushing in, trying to penetrate my shield. So I push back with all my strength, letting a scream cut through the noise of the helicopters and the ringing in my ears. "Help me, Remius, please..." I whisper, begging quietly to the nothingness as I feel my hold on keeping the sphere stable begin to weaken. Of course, Remius doesn't answer me. He's not here. Even in Dreamsphere he has abandoned me. Maybe it is just as well. My shoulders are beginning to crumble from trying to hold up all this weight—hold at bay what is trying to crush me. It feels like the weight of the entire government is sitting on my back and crushing my skull, and it is only a matter of time before my body ruptures under the pressure.

The golden orb shakes and tremors as the blue-black beam of light continues to barrage it. My arms begin to quiver as well and I know that it's only a matter of time before I collapse and can't hold the shield anymore. "Fucking government assholes invading my dreams," I grumble as my arms begin to seize up and cramp. "You may have gotten me in my nightmare, but in the Hollow Dimension you won't be so lucky."

Suddenly there is a pop and the whole top of my skull explodes like a pimple. Blood and bits of brain shower me like a rainbow of carnage. The ringing in my ears stops and all I can see are drips of viscous red liquid. Then my arms fail me, completely useless. As my arms fall to my sides like dead weight, the golden sphere gives one final shudder and collapses into a mist of golden dust, leaving me vulnerable.

Without even a second of hesitation, all three helicopters fire upon me with machine guns. It is the strangest sensation as my body is reduced to tatters, like my whole being is being fed through a paper shredder. Even in a dream, pain can be felt by the brain. The imagination making the fantasy into a tangible, visceral experience.

"Holy shit! Am I dead?" I wake with a start, in a cold sweat, with my heart racing. Clutching my chest and heaving to catch my breath, I check to see if my body is still intact. It is. I still have all my limbs, thank Goddess. And my skull is back in its place, no bits of brain leaking out. "Fuckin' eh, that really sucked." Blinking my eyes, I rub the crust of sleep out of them and register the familiar surroundings of my cell and remember where I am—and what Eden has been up to. Even though I fucking hate being locked up, this is probably at least preferable to how I was treated at the Facility.

I don't have to worry about the government torturing me and experimenting on me here, but I still may have to be worried about the possibility that Eden might kill me if she can't remember who I am. And Nikola is gone who the fuck knows where and can't help me anymore. As I bring an image of Eden's smiling face into my mind, I feel my consciousness being pulled elsewhere again—not back into a dream, but to somewhere else in the casino.

With a gasp, my awareness diverges from my body and I am again without form, hovering in space. Where am I now? I wonder as I perceive my surroundings. Oh, I'm back in Eden's bedchamber, like the other time this happened. Eden lays on her side on the huge bed. My awareness is hovering near her bedside table and I see the smooth pale skin of her back as she breathes quietly in sleep, her ribcage expanding and contracting as her lungs fill and then deflate. The bedsheet is only lightly draped over her up to her waist, and the beautiful curve of her naked shoulder reminds me of the wonderful times where I caressed her skin.

It is a strange feeling to float through space as pure aware-ness—with no form whatsoever. Different altogether from Astral Projecting since in that case I still have an Astral Form. This is more like... What do they call it? *Remote viewing.* That's what it is. Remote viewing, since mostly what I can do is be a witness, an incorporeal fly on the wall. I'm sure there are still ways to affect reality with pure will, but that may be slightly above my skill level at the moment.

Using intuition to guide me, I float down and then into the drawer of the bedside table. Inside, I can see the baseball-sized amethyst and sitting beside it a small metal disc-like device. Was that the device Eden put on her neck to control the robots? Nikola told me about that, right? I can't remember. If I had shoulders, I would be shrugging them right now.

But the amethyst is gorgeous! Even within the darkness of the drawer, the gem still seems to shine and sparkle with an ethereal aura. It draws me in. In an instant my consciousness is swirling within the facets of the crystal—each one a unique universe. The deep purple of the stone, and the vibration of the particles, reminds me of Jessica's Soulmind. Jessica... She still owns a piece of my heart. Wherever she might be, she is loved. Maybe we'll retrace each other's path and meet again in outer space.

I stare through from the center of the amethyst, and through the distortion of the purple, I can still make out the shape of the robot control device. Suddenly a small bubble forms and pops up from the center of the device like soap spheres forming above the water of a bubble bath. With my awareness, I try to call this bubble into the amethyst where my presence resides. The bubble floats tentatively, as if unsure whether it wants to enter or not. Then with a *bloop*, this bubble travels through the surface of the crystal and hovers within my field of awareness. As I stare, contemplating this bubble, an image appears within the transparent sphere, like a movie clip on a tiny circular screen.

The image slowly becomes clearer like watching another person's dream. I see Eden's room in her old apartment. Kat is sitting on the mattress wearing a cute dress which has been pushed up to his waist to reveal his beautiful penis. Eden is playing with it, stroking it in her hand. They are talking, I can see their mouths moving, but I can't hear what they're saying. Only the visual comes through. Continuing to stare deeply into the bubble, I see Kat suddenly pull away from Eden and hug his knees to his chest. After that, the image fades out and the bubble disappears. Before I even have a chance to register that the bubble has gone, another one floats from the device and into the crystal.

This one shows me an instance I am familiar with. The scene I see now is of me strapped to the table in Eden's basement. I am being flogged by her. Her mouth is moving and I see her speaking emotionally—I remember all the things she said to me that day. Tears are streaming down her face and her body shudders as she deals each blow to my naked back. After a few moments of watching this snapshot of time, this bubble disappears as well. Another bubble bloops from the center of the circular device and comes toward me, next in line.

This one is from way farther back. As the sphere comes into my space within the crystal, I see the image of a young girl take shape; she couldn't be more than six or seven. It takes me a second to realize that she is Eden as a little girl! She is naked and in a dank, dark basement. A dirty and tattered blanket has been thrown down on the stone floor. Little Eden lays on her back on this blanket with a pained expression on her face, her eyes clenched tightly shut. There is a larger figure on top of her—a boy looking maybe to be thirteen or fourteen. He is fucking her. I feel sick even though I lack a body or digestive system at the moment. And in my pure awareness I lack eyes so I am unable to shut the image from my consciousness. It triggers me and reminds me of the time Timestrus violated me against my will. How it felt having his long cock inside me, like thick tentacles of an alien rapist. It was as if his monster dick was so expansive, so all-encompassing, that it could pulverize my entire insides. Traumatizing yes, but luckily the experience didn't leave me as a hollow husk. For some people who have been so hurt like that, they never recover. I hope that Eden isn't so deeply wounded that she is beyond my love.

I don't want to watch anymore. As I think this, the memory of Eden's rape disappears along with the bubble it was floating in. Obviously that is what those bubbles are—*memories.* They are coming through the device and collecting in the amethyst. Maybe this is how Eden can get her memory restored! I could feel the suffering in that last memory since I have been through similar abuse. Oh, how it would be so amazing if there was a way to filter out the bad memories and just give Eden back the pleasant ones. Unfortunately, I don't think it works that way.

Floating in my field of presence, I exit the crystal and hover over the disc-shaped metal device. Then I pull myself into the center of the disc. Instantaneously, I find myself in a new location. Looking down, I realize that I am hovering high in the sky above the City. Cars zip through the air way below, and the ones on the street even lower than that. Next to my field of awareness is a huge machine suspended in the air. This must be the Brain that Nikola had mentioned—the database that controls the hive-mind of the robots as well as siphons all Eden's memories away. The amethyst crystal must be powerful enough to re-extract all of her lost memories. This metal Brain really does sort of resemble a real brain. Even though the outside shell is made up of different types of metal welded together, it does seem to have what could be called a left hemisphere and a right hemisphere. And a strange-looking brain stem type of thing trails down and out the back of it, blowing slightly in the wind.

As I watch, the bubbles that I had seen come out of the device in the drawer are being produced from the underside of the Brain. These bubbles then travel down the 'brain stem' and assumedly through the ethers and out out the control device before collecting in the crystal. I wonder what is *inside* of the Brain? I feel my curiosity increasing as my awareness floats closer to the shell of the Brain. When I try to fly through into the inside, I feel a force pushing me back as if something denies me access to that space. Trying to push harder, to force my way into the interior, I force my will to let me in. Suddenly I feel a release and I think that the repulsive power has succumbed to my efforts. But instead of the momentum pushing me into the interior of the Brain, I feel this electromagnetic force pull my consciousness through, but then shove me—and when it shoves me, it feels like an giant invisible hand is pushing me back into my body through the top of my head, the crown chakra.

Gasping, I open my eyes to witness the surroundings of my prison cell again. "What the fuck was that?" I say, catching my breath. The feeling of having my consciousness pushed, pulled around, and manhandled is not something I'm used to and is *not* pleasant. I wanted to see the inside of the Brain, I pout. But I guess something doesn't want me to. My stomach gurgles and I realize, now that I'm in my body again, how hungry I am. I haven't had any water either, so my mouth is incredibly dry—almost so bad that I'm willing to drink my own piss. "Does anybody even fucking remember I'm down here?"

TWO

"So who is this Terry person? Is he some boy you like?" Josh-oo'el looked over at Jessica walking beside him. He was curious about what his hold over her could be that it was so strong that it made her quest all over Pangea just to find a way back to the Hollow Dimension. Their trek through the forest had been quieter today and the young Elf felt like breaking the silence.

Jessica looked down at her feet as she stepped cautiously through the thick undergrowth. "Terry..." she said out loud in a dreamy far-off sort of way. "Like isn't strong enough of a word," Jessica continued. "I think he may be the love of my life. My *true* love. You know, the kind that most people think only exists in fairy stories."

"If he's so special to you, then why did you leave the Hollow Dimension in the first place?" Josh-oo'el wanted to know.

Jessica shook her head. "I thought I could detach from him. I thought my leaving was best for everyone. I was afraid. Afraid that if I stayed near him, it would only cause more pain to him and myself. There was a vision of a possible future that I was shown—a horrible, horrific future in which I die a brutal death. And Terry possibly would have met a similar fate. Through erasing myself completely from the Hollow Dimension, I thought maybe I could save us both from that torturous end."

"But now you've changed your mind?" the Elf inquired, glancing over at his traveling companion with his eyebrow raised.

"I—" she started and then stopped to gather her thoughts. "Trying to detach from my feelings for him didn't work. I was unable to forget the connection and let it go. We are psychically linked somehow and have contacted each other inter-Dimensionally somehow a couple times."

"Mm-hmm," the Elf nodded in recognition. "But how do you know that if you go back to the Hollow Dimension that it won't trigger that same horrible future to be created again?"

Jessica frowned and a darkness fell over her eyes. "I don't know for certain," she admitted, "but all I can say is that the pull to be with him is stronger than the fear of death."

"Have you ever heard of a Twin Soul?" Josh-oo'el asked.

"A who?"

"A Twin Soul," he repeated. "It is when the incarnation of a soul gets split and put into two separate bodies, but your souls are basically identical. That could be a reason why you are psychically linked to each other. It's sort of a paradoxical concept—and you can take it or leave it, it's just something to think about. It's paradoxical in a way that it implies you are un-whole; that you are only half of a soul and he holds the other half. But this is a fallacy, since you can't be anything other than whole. A soul always remains intact throughout Eternity."

"But Terry's Soulmind is white and mine is purple," Jessica continued. "If we were Twin Souls, wouldn't our Soulmind's be identical?"

Josh-oo'el shook his head. "Not necessarily. I don't think."

"It doesn't seem like you know all that much about what a Twin Soul is at all," she remarked.

The Elf shrugged. "Eh, It's just something that I've heard the High Elf Mystics talk about sometimes."

I wonder how much longer until we get to the edge of the forest and the beginning of the Great Plains? Jessica asked herself.

Josh-oo'el took a deep breath and then said, "Shouldn't be too long now until we reach the edge of the forest and the beginning of the Great Plains."

Jessica snapped her head over to look at the young Elf walking beside her, her mouth slightly hanging open. "How did you?—" she started. "I swear to God I was just thinking that! Did you read my mind? Stay out of there."

Josh-oo'el laughed as he adjusted the straps of the heavy pack on his shoulders. "I'm not psychic," he assured her. "I can't read your mind. That was probably just a likely thing you'd be thinking about."

"Well... Okay..." she eyed him suspiciously, not quite sure she trusted that he *wasn't* psychic. Suddenly she shivered, feeling a chilling wind blow toward them from the direction they were walking. "Is it just me or did it get cold all of a sudden?"

"Yes," Josh-oo'el answered. "There is still probably some snow on the Great Plains."

"It's wintertime?" Jessica asked, her eyebrows raising. "Seasons must work differently here in Pangea. I could have sworn that it was Spring or Summer. I don't know."

The Elf snorted. "There is snow on the Great Plains most of the year. It only gets warm and truly green for only a short stretch of time per cycle. Ah, we've made it."

In a couple more strides, they were clear of the tree line of the forest. They stopped when the sky opened up above them, no trees to canopy overtop now. Jessica stared in silent wonderment at the landscape stretched out before her. It was a vast expanse of rolling hills, meadows, and valleys. Most of the ground was blanketed in white with only a few patches of green peeking through where spots of snow had melted. The frigid chill of the air made her shiver, but it definitely wasn't cold enough that they needed to be concerned about dying of exposure. The sky was overcast with gray clouds, giving the whole day a gloomy feeling.

"It's amazing," she said, her breath puffing out of her mouth in white clouds. "Too bad we can't enjoy it. I'm already on the verge of pissing in my skirts thinking about what we have to do. Speaking of which, how are we going to find this this Troll—this giant—this giant Troll?"

"Well, I suspect," Josh-oo'el replied, "that it shouldn't take us very long to find it. There is nowhere to hide on the Great Plains. However, that may not be the only possible way that we come in contact with it."

"Meaning?" Jessica said, looking sidelong at her companion.

"Well," he continued with a nervous smile, "that is unless it finds us first. Then we would lose the element of surprise, which would slightly give us an advantage."

"And if it turns out that we don't have the element of surprise?"

"Then you better start praying to whatever god it is you believe in," he said grimly.

After a moment where neither of them spoke, Josh-oo'el again set his sight forward and began walking again. Jessica quickly scrambled to keep up. The young Elf seemed to be speed-walking for some reason and she was having a little difficulty keeping up with his pace. Was he nervous? Was that why he was basically running? Jessica wondered. She didn't have a chance to get a word in since she was breathing heavily from the attempt to keep abreast with him. The ground began to slope up to the crest of a hill and it became increasingly challenging to climb without slipping on the melting snow.

"Slow down," Jessica finally panted. "Why are you in such a hurry? What's the rush?"

Before Josh-oo'el had a chance to respond, there was a sudden rumbling and the ground shook like an earthquake. The Elf swayed with the tremor, almost falling over. Jessica wasn't able to keep her balance so well. Toppling over forward, her knees hit the cold, wet snow and she threw her arms out in front of herself to break her fall. "What in Heaven was that?" she shrieked.

Josh-oo'el held up his hand for silence. "That's gotta be the Troll."

"It can cause the ground to shake so violently like that?" Jessica asked, her eyes wide in terror.

There was no time for an answer since a deafening, high-pitched roar ripped through the wintry air. Josh-oo'el swallowed hard. "Quick, we must get to the top of this hill. We're almost there. Come on!" He scrambled up, going the last few paces to the top of the ridge. Jessica crawled on all fours the rest of the way until she stood up next to her Elven companion. He was staring, frozen in terror, looking down into the valley below.

"What? What is—" But she couldn't finish her question since her gaze strayed from Josh-oo'el's panic-stricken face and down toward the valley in front of them. Standing in the snow a long distance down and ahead of Jessica and Josh-oo'el stood the monstrosity. The hideous creature towered easily two hundred feet high—almost as tall as the giant trees that the Elves made their homes in. The sight of the thing made Jessica think of the Titans in the Greek myths she had read at school. However, this giant Troll resembled a hairy, ugly man. Its body was covered in shaggy gray fur somewhat like an ape, with a long tail trailing down behind it from the point at the base of its spine. A huge, grotesque dick hung flaccidly between his legs. His nose was bulbous, like the snout of an elephant seal, and he had so many wrinkles on the skin of his face like an old man that the monster's eyes could barely even be seen. Suddenly the Troll looked directly in their direction and opened its mouth to let out another high-pitched roar. Hot spittle spraying out of his mouth as he bellowed.

"I guess now we know that you still believe in God," Josh-oo'el commented without taking his eyes off the Troll in the valley below. "And it is safe to say that he has picked up that scent. How he can smell anything over his *own* stench is beyond me." The Elf wrinkled up his nose at the foul odor and risked a glance over at his companion. She was holding her hand over her nose to try to ward off the stench of Troll since she felt her stomach threatening to expel its contents.

After the Troll's roar ceased its deafening din, it was on the move, running in great strides toward the hill the companions stood upon. As the earth began to quake again from the giant's footfalls, Jessica and Josh-oo'el were knocked off balance and fell to their hands and knees so they wouldn't be pitched forward down the hill from the violent tremors of the ground.

"Oh my God!" Jessica screamed, wishing beyond wishing that this was all a horrible nightmare and that she would wake up before her bones were crushed between a giant's jaws. "And if there really is a God," she continued to yell over the loud rumbling of the ground shaking, "we could really use He-She-Its help right about now! If not, we're definitely gonna die here!"

THREE

FROM THE MIND OF EDEN LOCKHART:

Another day, another opportunity to terrorize the citizens of The Kingdom. I groan as I awake in my luxurious bedchamber that is swanky enough to befit a Goddess of Fuck. As I sit up in bed, naked with only the thin sheet covering my legs, I reach up to my head to make sure my crown of robot power stayed on all night like a sleeping cap. Pleasantly, the device's snugness around the crown of my skull is still making contact. Could it even be possible to control the robots while in a dream? That would be so freakin' crazy.

I look around my bedchamber, blinking the sleep out of my eyes as I yawn and stretch, not jumping to get out of bed and start the day. What is there to do anyway? The two robot guards by my door stare at me blankly through the part in the curtains that sweep down from the canopy above the bed. I don't think the metal men are leering at my naked tits since they don't have little robot penises between their legs with coded mechanisms to make them get hard. Looking down toward my own chest, I enjoy the small size and perkiness of my tits. Squeezing them, I take my erect nipples between my fingers and play with them a bit as I slowly stave off the tiredness enough to get up.

After a few minutes of caressing myself, I toss the sheet off of myself and swing my legs out over the side of the bed next to the night table. I stare at the drawer as if it is calling to me to open it up—like there is an audible whisper pleading with me to release it. Suddenly my head gets dizzy and my vision becomes slightly blurred. Why can't I remember what I did yesterday? Or the day before that? What was it? Clenching my eyes tightly shut, I press my fingers up to my temples as if the very act could bring back what I had forgotten. But my head just keeps spinning, in turn making the room spin, like I'm really drunk and my stomach lurches and I am afraid I might vomit onto the floor.

Panic sets in as I grasp for even my own name; it seems to be slipping out of my mental warehouse of information and knowledge. Who am I? Who the *fuck* am I? In my imagination, it's like my hands are grasping for the word—trying to take hold of it before it drains like water through a sieve. Then I grab it and pull it back before it escapes. *Eden.* That's my name. *Eden Lockhart.* What is this? Why does it seem that my memories have been leaking out like brains oozing out of an ear hole?

Holding tightly to my own name so it doesn't escape me again, I try to recall the events of the previous day. A blurry picture begins to take shape in my memory—it is my throne room. I can't see what's going on in the scene, but I can make out the red of blood and I can feel the atmosphere of what took place— deep pain. Frustrated, I open my eyes and kick the bedside table. It totters back and forth, the drawer rolling open and shaking up its contents, before becoming still once again. The items in the drawer peek out at me as if they have beady, curious eyes, and their whispers began to chatter again. Reaching in, I push the neck device to the side and pick up the large amethyst. The whispering gets louder and more intense as I bring the crystal closer to my face.

"Are you speaking to me?" I ask the stone.

The reply is not physically audible words, but I can feel its answer directly in the clairaudience of my Soulmind: *Yes.* I get goosebumps and chills run up my arms and then down my spine like a million tiny spiders. Bringing the amethyst closer, I gaze deeply into it like a crystal ball, daring it to show me its secrets.

"Can you show me what took place yesterday? Show me what I've forgotten," I implore it. I feel some energy release within the crystal and I know that whatever consciousness is within it is acquiescing to my request. Slowly the image of the throne room solidifies within the center of the amethyst. As the memory emerges within the purple of the stone, it also duplicates in my own mind, re-instilling it in my memory.

I watch in horror as the scene plays out. There is a sickening feeling in my stomach as I watch myself commit acts that I have lost the memory of. A strange feeling overtakes me—a feeling like I'm watching a stranger who wears my skin. Like I was possessed by some other entity who is *not* me. Unfortunately, I have to come to terms with the fact that this person is me and I willingly committed atrocities with a shit-eating grin.

A piece of my history is returned to me. The reality that I almost murdered a child, then *actually* murdered Mika'el when he tried to stop me. On top of all this, I stood there taunting Nikola as his best friend bled to death in his arms. I'm disgusted with myself. How could I do these awful things? Perhaps my propensity for evil is far greater than I had thought...

The last part of the memory was me fucking Nikola—activating within him the power of his new, green Soulmind. *Hmm*, I think to myself, *clever of Nikola to have me activate him.* I think it's safe to say that Nikola is no longer in The Kingdom. Why else would he want that Pan-Dimensional power, other than to escape this pocket of a Dimension?

Still staring intently into the crystal, the image of the memory fades from inside the purple. Before I have a chance to grasp ahold of the memory and keep it within my own consciousness, it is whisked away like dust through a fan. "What the fuck?" I yell in frustration. "Ugh! I know I just held the memory of what happened yesterday. Now it's gone!" Squeezing the amethyst hard and then shaking it as if I can get the crystal to dump the memories out of its shining facets, I kick the bedside table as my mind begins to go hazy again.

There is a strange *bloop* sound and I look down at the open drawer. The neck device is still in there shoved to the side. At the *bloop* noise, a bubble is produced from the center of the metal disc and floats in my direction. *What the fuck is this now?* As the bubble hovers in the air in front of my eyes, an image forms inside it. *No way!* I know at once that this is the same memory that I watched inside the amethyst and then lost again, having it slip out of my own mind like sand spilling through the cracks.

"How could..." I wonder, baffled, looking down at the hive-mind neck device that the bubble popped out of. "No..." I say, the realization finally dawning on me. The connection between the hive-mind, the Brain, and the loss of memory becomes painfully obvious in light of this *looping of data*. Tentatively touching the crown still atop my head, I finally know the culprit and why I have been losing myself more and more.

With a flourish of my hand, I sweep the memory bubble down and crush it into the amethyst, returning the memory into the crystal. After placing the stone gently down on the bed, I take the computer-chip crown off of my head and hurl it toward the floor. The crown cracks and splits into two pieces. I stand up, rage burning red at the tips of my ears, and stomp on the two pieces of the crown, shattering it into even more tiny fragments. The metal computer chips splinter and cut into my bare feet like shards of glass. Small spatters of blood stain the floor.

No more hesitation. No more bullshit. Let's be done with this. I scramble to the bathroom, leaving bloody footprints as I go, and scoop up a t-shirt and jeans that I had tossed in the corner.

Dressed, I return to the bed and slip on a pair of shoes. I scoop up the neck device from the drawer, drop it to the floor, and stomp on it until it is in a million irreconcilable pieces. *I will never lose myself like that again*, I vow to myself. Now it is time to become whole once more.

Sitting back down on the edge of the bed, I clutch the amethyst between my hands, holding it like it is the most precious gift. As soon as I close my eyes, all the memories come rushing back like the torrential winds and rain of a monsoon. Within mere minutes, my mind becomes clear once again. I am Eden Lockhart, from the Hollow Dimension. My Soulmind has taken me on a long and labyrinthine journey, and now I remember it all. With my eyes still closed, feeling the wholeness of my being return to me, tears threaten to leak from my eyes like a broken dam. God, I've hurt so many people—the atrocities I've committed. Nikola would have been justified in taking my life. Maybe I *am* evil. *Could I ever be forgiven for these crimes?* With all my memories restored, so is the deep existential pain. The hurt that the rage manifests from has been a driving force in my life. Is there a way to not let it drive anymore? There is pain within the well of sadness, but there is also love—*love!*

Oh my God! *Terry!* My love, my light, my strength... And I just threw him in the subterranean dungeons like a common deranged vagabond thief. What have I done? Let's get out of here! Not letting the amethyst out of my grip—which is now shining with its own purple light—I jump up with resolve. Terry and I rid The Kingdom of its thorn once, and I'll be damned if I'm going to replace The Queen as The Kingdom's bane.

Rushing over to the door of my chambers, I look at the two robot guards—frozen and lifeless without a controller. "Fuck you, metal dicks!" I growl as I push one over. It topples like a domino and clangs to the floor. I do the same to the other one.

The robots look stupid sprawled out on the floor like this. I smirk and fling the door open. After taking a couple steps out into the hallway, something pulls me back. Curiosity makes me poke my head back through the door of the bedchamber for a quick peek since I could have sworn I heard some rustling just now. "What in the fuck?" I say as I look back into the room.

The robots are moving! Slowly, but there is no mistaking that both metal men are now squirming like turtles on their backs trying to get on their feet again. *I didn't think they could move on their own!* Well, fuck this, it's not my problem anymore. After slamming the door on the two robots that are obviously struggling to evolve in a way in which they could achieve autonomy, I waste no time rushing down to free my lover from the dungeon.

As I rush into the subterranean dungeon, I am unable to hold back my sobs once I see Terry locked in a cage. "Oh, Terry, my love," I choke out through the flow of tears. "What have I done to you?" He gets up slowly from the cot and approaches the bars as I kneel down to the circular device on the floor in order to deactivate the Quarantine Seal. After punching in the numbers, the plasmik grid disappears from overtop of the bars. Then I put in the code to open the cell. There is a loud buzzing as the door is unlocked. Terry begins to push it open and I run to him, throwing my arms around him, full of remorse and pain in my heart.

"You remembered," Terry whispers as he squeezes me tightly.

I pull away from his embrace and wipe my wet eyes with my left hand, holding out the amethyst with my right. "I don't know how, but this crystal..." I start, trailing off as I stare at the shiny purple of the stones facets. "You bought this for me that time we went to the Village during our first visit to this realm." He smiles and nods knowingly. "And somehow this stone, connected to your love, has brought me back to myself... Oh, Terry,

I feel like I lost myself there and committed so many horrible, awful things out of a deep well of pain within me. I have to think that I lost myself, because if that turns out to be the real me, I don't think I could live with myself. Maybe I don't deserve to be forgiven. But you... Can you *ever* forgive me?"

As Terry takes my left hand in his right, squeezing it affectionately, he kisses me lovingly on the forehead. Tears continue to glisten as a mist obscuring my vision. "You don't *need* to be forgiven," he says slowly. "And one day you'll understand what I mean. All that matters now is that you know I love you. I love you unconditionally—no matter *who* or *what* you are. All beings have the proclivity for doing evil, but also the ability to act out of the greatest love. Every time you find yourself in the present moment is another opportunity to make a different choice, a more conscious choice, an enlightened choice. Your soul is always worthy of love, no matter what you've done. The past is past, now let us move forward."

I smile in spite of the tears. Terry's kind words sink into my heart, warming it with the love stretching between us. "You're right, Terry," I respond. "Now is a new moment and I wish to return to the Hollow before I have the chance to become the monster that wants to burst out of me."

Before anymore precious seconds can slip away, I pull on Terry's hand and, without another word, we run up the stairs, out of the dungeons, and straight to the car park outside, trying to avoid running into anyone if I can help it. The lot is deserted of people, thankfully, and still leading Terry, we run up to one of the flying cars that is property of the casino.

"What are we doing?" Terry asks as the red and pink of my Soulmind spirals out of my chest toward the lock on the car door.

"We're getting out of here. What does it look like?" After a few seconds of my Soulmind penetrating the lock, it pops and the door swings open. I push Terry toward the open door, and without question, he crawls in over the driver's seat to get to the passenger's side. Before he can put his seatbelt on, I'm already in and slam the door shut. I hesitate as I study the foreign-looking nobs on the dashboard. The steering wheel is like a normal car and so are the pedals for gas and brake.

"Do you know how to drive one of these things?" Terry asks.

"Shut up!" I snap. "I'm trying to concentrate. How hard could this be to drive?" When he doesn't say anything, I look over with a softened expression. "I'm sorry, love. I didn't mean to snap at you. There's just a lot of stress right now."

"I wonder if this will work," he mumbles, and I can see the white of his Soulmind coming forth from his heart, not his solar plexus this time. "*On!*" he yells and there is a flash of Soulmind energy as the flying car revs to life.

"Ha ha! I can't believe that worked," I say, very pleased. The vehicle starts to hover and float a few feet higher than it had been. Putting it in gear, I rely on my intuition to guide me as I pull out of the car park to join the flow of traffic in the sky.

"Where are we going?" Terry asks again.

"We're going to portal out of here, and I didn't feel like trekking through the whole woods again to get there," I answer as I swerve between two flying cars which start beeping their horns at me. Narrowly avoiding a collision, I yell toward the other drivers, "Get out of the fucking sky road if you can't fucking drive!"

"Jesus," Terry comments, "you got sky rage. Stay in your freakin' lane or we're liable to be killed before we even get to the farm."

"Lane?" I repeat back to him, risking a quick glance in his direction. "What fucking lane? There is no fucking lane! We're in the sky, are you on crack?"

He didn't reply to that, and once we take the next left at the 'sky intersection,' we are parallel with the forest that divides The Kingdom in half. Breaking off from the flow of traffic, I increase our speed and zip easily over the treetops. In no time we make it to the other side of the forest, the farm and the house coming into view. That was *a lot* faster than having to hike the forest on foot.

"That was quick," Terry remarks.

"That's just what I was thinking!" I return. "Don't you be reading my mind now! You may not like what you find in there." I chuckle and look down at the amethyst wedged safely between my legs. My black-stained hand grips the wheel and that too reminds me of the darkness within.

"I love all that's inside you," he responds with sincerity. "Because what is inside you is inside me as well. Know thyself, and if you know yourself, then you know me well." As he says these loving words, the tears threaten to begin the waterworks again. I try to fight them back as I park the flying car hovering three feet above the dirt road next to the field of wheat.

"Ready to blow this popsicle stand?" I say, smiling over at Terry.

He laughs. "Who says that anymore?"

I point to myself triumphantly. "Me, that's who," I say. "I'm bringing it back. It's gonna be the new trend."

After grabbing the stone from between my legs, I throw the door open and hop out. I circle around the vehicle as Terry jumps out of the passenger's side. It is with despair and wretchedness that I glance over at Mika'el's old farmhouse, knowing that he will never again enjoy his quiet life. And there will be no one to tend to the farm and the animals. Terry must have seen it in my face because he gives me a knowing glance. I hold up a finger, indicating silence. "I don't want to talk about it," I say. Terry nods, respecting my wishes. "I don't want to talk about it *ever*."

We turn and walk side by side into the middle of the wheat field. Stopping, I hold up my hand into the air and command, "Rope!" When nothing happens—no silver rope falling from the sky—I give Terry a nervous look. I snap my fingers and yell "Rope!" again. Still nothing. "This is how we portaled out before, right? It's gotta work. I could have sworn that's what Darren did —called down a rope that pulled us back up through the portal and the Little Door."

"Yeah, that is how we did it last time..." he replies warily.

"Then how come the fuck it's not working? Goddamnit!" I yell in frustration. "I want to get the hell out of here!" Feels like I'm on the verge of breaking down again.

"I think I might have another way to get out of here," Terry says slowly.

"Oh yeah?" I perk up at this.

"Do you remember how Maya could like teleport? Matter-Relocation in that black pod and she could travel wherever?"

I shrug. "Maybe, I don't know. Why? You know how to do that?"

He nods. "It's how I got here this time. I didn't come through the portal."

"How did you learn how to do that?" I want to know.

"It's a long story," is his response. "But I don't really see any other options."

"And you can do this on *me*? Send me first and then come yourself?" I ask.

"Yeah," he affirms. "I've never done it before, so you're gonna have to trust me. Do you trust me?"

"Yes, I trust you, my love," I respond without hesitation. "Can you send me through and make me materialize anywhere? If so, let's end up back at your house within the safety of the Merkabah."

"I can try," he says. His aura begins to glow with the most brilliant white light and he holds up his arms, palms toward me. As he closes his eyes, a black circle appears under my feet and I jump with surprise. Then these long, black tentacles start to emerge from the circle, wrapping me up like a cocoon. "This may hurt a bit. Possibly. Just be prepared," he warns me.

In seconds, the tentacle ropes completely obscure my vision, leaving me in a black void. Then comes the pain. At first it is like a crushing pressure that threatens to rupture my entire organism. I start to scream but no sound escapes to find its way to my ear. Then I swear my bones are snapping. The excruciating pain as if my body is being pulverized and ripped apart at the same time is, in reality, no less than I probably deserve. And just when I think I'm surely going to die, I gasp one last time, surrendering to my death.

Then it's over. The pain is gone and I open my eyes to see the Black Mist dissipating into the hot, humid air. I'm on my back, staring up at a hazy sky. The dry ground is hard against my aching bones. Rolling over onto my right side, I see that I am high atop a hill looking down onto a smoggy, ugly city. *No way*, I say to myself, recognizing the city. Just to be sure, I roll over onto my left side, finding myself staring up at a tall manmade structure that is a white letter *O*. Sure enough, it's the Hollywood sign and the city below is Los Angeles—the gates of Hell itself.

Making sure I still have grip on the amethyst in my hand, I groaningly make my way to standing and brush the dust off of my clothes, turning to stare out in disbelief over the city. From the top of the Hollywood hill, it looks like space. And then I yell out loud into the smoggy, muggy air, "You've got to be fucking kidding me!"

FOUR

"There's no place like home," Terry whispered to himself, hoping he could control the Matter-Relocation this time. Closing his eyes, he tried to will himself back to his own house, inside the protective shield of the Merkabah. With this thought in his mind, the rope tentacles grew out of the black circle and enveloped him in its pod. In a flash of an instant, Terry was gone from The Kingdom once more, dematerialized, only leaving behind a cloud of Black Mist which quickly dissipated, leaving no trace that Eden and Terry had been there other than the flying car hover-parked on the dirt road.

"I'm becoming increasingly irritated with this situation, Doctor," the Director of the secret CIA S & M Project said to Doctor Morkian who sat across the table from him. They were in the break room at the Facility; Morkian was eating his lunch—a sloppy BLT sandwich—and the Director sat there with no food, his arms crossed over his chest.

Doctor Morkian wiped his mouth of the tomato juice trying to dribble down his chin. "I apologize, Director," he responded, contrite. "I know we've been making slow progress. However, the absence of our main Subject makes it difficult to implement changes in the Project. Without new data, there isn't much more we can do at the moment. I am pleased to say though that the technology that we have helped create based on our findings is still well underway. The manufacture of these weapons and devices are being implemented for government use and will soon be introduced to the military as well as police force."

"Well, that's at least something," the Director grumbled, staring at the white wall behind the Doctor.

Morkian dropped the sandwich slovenly to his plate and wiped his fingers on an already stained napkin. "Have you considered switching your focus to our other Subject, Anna? She is very powerful as well. If Subject Terry Broswald is never re-apprehended, we need to explore other options. I feel Anna has the same potential to be weaponized—if that is indeed what you are trying to accomplish here."

"Hmm," the Director grunted, staring off into space. "Well, I'm tired of sitting on our hands," he continued. As if to illustrate the point, he stood up from his chair. "Have that Subject—Anna—prepped and brought to Observation Room 8. We're going to get our weapon, even if it kills her in the process."

Doctor Morkian stared with a blank expression as the Director exited the break room. "But," the Doctor began, "how will we get our weapon if she's dead?"

There was no response, the Director was already gone and out of earshot.

Several minutes later, three suit-men were opening the door to Anna's cell. She was laying on her cot, staring at the ceiling. The bottoms of her bare feet were stained black with dirt, and she still wore the same greasy nightgown that hadn't been washed since they forced her to wear it. As the three men in black suits and sunglasses entered her room, Anna's eyes moved to look at them.

"Time to go, slut," one of the suit-men said with a snarl. "You're wanted in Observation Room 8. Maybe this time you'll really die." The man laughed as he walked over to Anna's cot and grabbed her bicep in a painfully strong grip. He pulled her to get off of the bed and come with them. She glared at him but didn't say a word as she was dragged to her feet and toward the door. Another suit-man waiting at the door held out a black pill as Anna was brought to him.

"Take the pill," the suit-man ordered. Anna stuck out her tongue in defiance. The suit-man scowled and forced the pill over her tongue and into her mouth. Forcibly, he held her jaw shut and pinched her nose closed until she reluctantly swallowed the pill as she tried to wriggle out of his grip. When the suit-man let her face go, she gave him the death-stare and spat directly into his face. He slowly wiped the spittle from his eyes and then punched Anna as hard as he could in her gut. She doubled over, the wind knocked out of her, and a spatter of blood was projected from her mouth.

In her weakened state, the three suit-men half dragged, half carried Anna to Observation Room 8. They unlocked the door and brought her inside. From the trauma of the punch in the stomach, coupled with the pill that they had force-fed her, Anna could feel herself slipping in and out of consciousness. She felt extremely weak and was unsure whether she had the strength to fight back against this experiment. Maybe that was their intention, she didn't know. The room was large and white, with cream colored linoleum flooring. Anna wondered if that was for easy blood cleanup. At the far end of the room was an empty black chair. All standing on the other side of the room, facing the chair, were about ten men wearing riot gear, the motorcycle-looking helmets, and held an assortment of strange weapons— new ones that Anna didn't recognize.

As the three suit-men dragged Anna over and threw her into the chair, she noticed that there was no two-way mirror in this particular room, only cameras and obviously a live feed going to another room where the Director and Doctor Morkian were watching. The three suit-men left the room once Anna was securely in the chair. Before they closed and locked the room behind them, the suit-man that Anna had spat on gave her the finger, silently cursing her to suffer extreme torture.

As Anna sat staring at the intimidating men with weapons pointed at her, she was half-paralyzed and could feel the warmth of urine draining from her bladder. Tears began to silently fall as her eyes peeked out through her greasy hair. Suddenly the intercom crackled and the Director's voice boomed with a old radio quality. "Don't hold back this time, men," he gave the order. "Give her everything you've got. With the upgraded weapons, let's see if her shields and Soulmind weapon can hold against it. We may have our suicide bomb yet, fellas." The intercom clicked off and the men in riot gear readied their weapons, aiming them directly at Anna who looked so weak and helpless that even Doctor Morkian, who was watching on a monitor next to the Director, doubted that she would be able to survive.

As Anna sat there in silence, staring out at her own personal firing squad, she made a final decision. She was exhausted, she was spent, she was done—ready to be rid of the Director and this whole godforsaken hellhole of a place. Embracing the idea of death, an escape from this torment, something released inside her and her whole body relaxed. As she closed her eyes, she brought to mind what Terry had taught her about connecting to her Merkabah field. Enacting the meditation, she activated it, first popping the golden sphere of light out from her heart to encompass her whole body. After that she began spinning the star tetrahedrons. Soon they were going so fast that they only appeared to be a shining white light. The yellow energy of Anna's Soulmind was also illuminating, spiraling at her solar plexus.

The men standing in front of her could see all of this energy activity in their helmets. They raised their weapons and trained them on Anna. The intercom crackled again and one word was spoken: "Fire!"

In the split second before the men pulled the triggers on their weapons, Anna locked her Soulmind in place inside her Merkabah vehicle. Then, using the force of the spinning star tetrahedrons, she took her Soulmind and exited through her crown chakra. Now she was pure Soulmind hovered above her body inside the Merkabah lightbody. This all happened too fast for the men to realize before they blasted her body with radiation cannons. After the one second of radiation blast, the others unloaded round after round from their automatic rifles, ripping her body to tatters. Still fully conscious as her yellow Soulmind inside her Merkabah, she watched her own body be reduced to bloody ribbons and bone fragments.

Anna knew she was dead—*what a relief!* And in that moment, she loosed an electromagnetic pulse from deep within her Merkabah. This energy pulse ripped through the crowd of men in riot gear, their bodies rupturing like water balloons. An impossible amount of blood painted the white walls completely red, congealed organs and bone splinters dripping from the ceiling and walls. After ripping through the men, the electromagnetic pulse continued its journey through the Facility. Anna then took her leave, flying in her Merkabah vehicle up through the ceiling and out into the sky.

The Director was completely pale, staring at the monitor where he just witnessed all ten of his men ripped to shreds after Anna being killed. He swallowed hard and looked over at Doctor Morkian who was looking down and tapping frantically on an iPad. "This is unprecedented... Unprecedented," the Doctor mumbled to himself. There was a loud buzzing and then a click.

"What was that?" the Director said, looking around frantically, panic beginning to kick in.

"Uhh," Morkian started as he swiped his finger across the iPad screen. "It appears that the electromagnetic pulse has disabled our security system and unlocked every door in the Facility."

"What?!" the Director yelled—now the panic was a visceral reality pumping through his veins. Without giving the Doctor a chance to reply, the Director turned tail and ran, fleeing the Facility.

"Wait! Wait!" Doctor Morkian called after him. "Where are you going?" He gave one last glance at the carnage on the screen and then fled as well.

Moments before Anna released the pulse, Terry reappeared in the middle of his cell, Black Mist dissipating as he figured out where he ended up. "Fuck! Again?" he yelled. "Why can't I Matter-Relocate to where I fucking want to go? I'm out this bitch if it's the last thing I do!" With his aura raging white all around him, Terry approached the door of his cell and threw up his hand. "Open sesame!" he screamed, trying to will the door to open. In that exact moment was when Anna's pulse ripped through the men and then the rest of the Facility.

Terry was shocked when he heard a buzz, a click, and the door swung open. He could have sworn that he felt a strong energy flow through his body as the lock released. It had the feeling of Anna and Terry remembered the feeling of how nice it was to be with her intimately. Without a moment's hesitation, he ran out into the hallway before the door had a chance to lock him in again.

The pulse that Anna released also affected the two other Subjects in the Facility in a profound way. When the energy passed through Jeremy's body, connecting back together fractured pieces of his Soulmind, he was instantly restored to full mental, physical, and spiritual health. The light came back into his eyes and he looked around his cell as if awakening from a very long dream. He stared at the open door of this cell and knew liberation was upon them.

Priya wasted no time running out of her cell once her door unlocked. There was a strong pull from her Soulmind to find Jeremy so that they could escape together. Without question, she ran down the hallway, using her intuition to guide her to Jeremy.

The black pickup truck flew down the highway toward the Manufacturing District. Darren had felt the pull today and his Soulmind was telling him that today was the day to help Terry escape the Facility. The last time he had gone to *angelfuck*, he saw the destruction to the portal—that it was sealed up for good. The Agency was doing more crazy and shady shit, Darren knew, and that made it even more imperative that they break Terry from their clutches.

The cellphone in Darren's cupholder rang and he picked it up after the first ring. It was Mage of the Meadow. "Darren?" she said after he picked up.

"Yeah, I'm here," he replied.

"Terry is back in the Hollow Dimension and now is time for a jailbreak!" she responded with urgency in her voice.

"I know," Darren agreed. "I'm on my way to the Manufacturing District as we speak. I'll drop you a pin of the location."

"Great," Meadow said quickly. "I'll meet you there with a few other members of our Body in case we need backup. Don't do anything until we get there!" She hung up.

Darren sent her the location without missing a beat and then dropped his phone back in the cupholder.

As Terry made his way toward the exit—the entrance where he had been wheeled in on a gurney—he prayed that he would not encounter any interference. Suddenly an extreme pressure began to build in his head, like his Soulmind was feeding too much energy into his third eye. Turning the corner with his fingers to his temple, feeling like his head was about to explode, he ran smack dab into a small group of personnel wearing riot gear and holding weapons. They looked just as confused as Terry felt. They weren't wearing those helmets, so Terry knew they wouldn't be able to see his Soulmind energy.

As the men froze and readied their weapons with terrified expressions on their faces, Terry noticed a man in a black jumpsuit wearing a helmet come into view behind the group of men, walking down the hallway that was perpendicular. The jumpsuit-man glanced briefly at the ensuing scene and then disappeared again, quickly running away to save himself from the inevitable violence about to commence.

Terry didn't even give any of the men a chance to put their finger on the trigger. "Out of my way!" he screamed through the pounding in his head, sweeping his hand through the air in front of him. In the same way Anna's pulse did, Terry's projected energy ripped through the men, their bodies exploding in a steaming bloodbath. His gray sweatsuit was now turning red from the spray of blood and entrails. Being careful not to slip on soggy intestines, Terry wiped the blood from his eyes and continued along his escape route, more than ready to be free of this madness.

As Darren drove up onto the dirt patch next to the abandoned warehouse that the Facility was under, he saw a black SUV speed toward him, emerging from the huge hole in the brick wall of the building. The vehicle didn't pay him any mind, it just sped around him and disappeared in an instant. "That was weird," Darren commented. A minute later, a small silver car came speeding out as well, following the same route as the black SUV.

After turning off the truck's engine, he hopped out of the driver's seat, the dust clouds kicked up from the cars were still settling. In another moment, fresh dust was kicked up into the air as a brown minivan appeared almost out of nowhere and parked behind Darren's truck. Meadow appeared out of the driver's seat and then two women and two men emerged from the back. All five of them wore the customary gray cloak of their cult.

"That was fast," Darren said, walking up to Meadow and the others. "I haven't been here but a minute."

"Given the precariousness of the situation, it was necessary to get here with speed," she responded concisely. "You haven't seen anyone come out yet, have you?"

Darren shook his head. "Well, not on foot," he admitted. "There was a black SUV that came out and sped away, as well as a small silver car that followed right after."

"Mm-hmm, mm-hmm," Meadow nodded. "Well, let's not waste anymore time." With that statement, she began to walk quickly toward the hole in the brick wall.

Terry was just walking out of the open entrance to the underground Facility when Darren and his companions reached the top of the ramp that went down to the underground parking lot outside the entrance. They stared at him as he began walking up the ramp toward them, leaving bloody footprints in his wake. He definitely looked like he had been caught in a massacre.

"Terry! Thank God!" Darren exclaimed. "Are you okay?"

Terry waved a bloody hand. "Yah, it's okay," he said. "Don't worry. It's not my blood. Let's get the fuck out of here."

Darren reached out and took Terry's hand, helping him out. He could feel with his own Soulmind that Terry was in a weakened state from expending energy to escape and defend himself. "I got you," Darren assured him, leading him slowly toward the outside. Meadow and the other four members of Lucifer Christ followed in silence in case their help was needed.

"Ugh, my fucking head," Terry groaned.

"Your head?" Darren asked, concerned. "It could be your Soulmind trying to detox your brain and withdrawals from the pills they were giving you."

"You know about that?" Terry mumbled in response. Darren nodded and then Terry suddenly stopped walking, pricking up his ears. "Do you hear that?"

"What? What? What is it?" Darren sputtered, adrenaline starting to surge in his veins. Then the *it* was unmistakeable—the noise of cars converging on them outside.

"Fuck! Not now," Meadow cursed. Darren shot her a questioning look. "It's *them*," she answered.

Darren knew exactly who Meadow meant. And as they brought Terry out into the hot air of summer, four new vehicles surrounded them, led by a white SUV with a decal of the letters KRST on the back windshield. In no time they were surrounded by strange people wearing all-white clothes.

"Who the fuck are these clowns?" Terry asked, looking up into Darren's face.

"They are the Krystics," he answered without any more exposition.

Terry looked back toward the people dressed in white. One woman with short, spiky gray hair approached Meadow. This woman was obviously their leader. The group of at least twenty of their members stood around like thugs behind her.

"Mage of the Meadow," the woman with gray hair greeted the head of the Body of Lucifer Christ. "Hand over the Antichrist!"

"Fuck me! You guys too?" Terry groaned.

"Lucia," Meadow replied, greeting the woman back. "How kind of you to pay us a visit," she said flatly. "However, we cannot honor your request. The boy is not yours to do with as you please."

"He is not yours to do with either," Lucia shot back. "And that is a shame you won't hand him over quietly. Trust me, you don't want to risk a conflict here. You are hopelessly outnumbered. And I think it is safe to assume you would like to suffer no casualties to your Body, just as *we* do not wish to suffer casualties."

Darren shot a worried glance over to Meadow, but she didn't take her eyes off of Lucia. "What a shame," Meadow said slowly. "It would appear that we are at an impasse then."

Lucia shook her head. "You don't want to force our hand, but we will if we have to. You are not an idiot, Mage, so don't act like one."

Meadow's eyes fell and then she looked over at Darren, her face wearing a pained expression. Terry began to shake his head. "No! NO! *NO!*" he yelled. "You can't let them take me! Please don't let them!" He screamed again in frustration, his stomach sinking from the thought of what they might do to him—this cult that thought he was the Antichrist.

"I'm sorry, Terry. I really am," Darren whispered. "But I'll come for you, I promise."

Terry tried desperately to connect to his Merkabah, or even bring his weapon forth from his Soulmind, but in his weakened state and pressure pounding in his head, his energy and power just wouldn't do what he wanted it to do. Darren let go of Terry's hand, and with regret he took a couple steps away from him. In an instant five of the white-clad people surrounded him, grabbing him and pulling him toward their vehicles.

"NO! NO! NO!" he continued to scream helplessly. Darren began to cry and he had to look away.

After they subdued Terry and got him into the back of the white SUV with the letters KRST on the back, Lucia gave Meadow a wry smile and returned to her vehicle. After revving up the SUV, Lucia rolled down her window and yelled, "You better not try to follow us! Don't even get back into your vehicles for at least ten minutes!" Rolling up the window, she sped away in a cloud of dust, followed by the cars of the other Krystics.

"Fuck! Fuck! Fuck!" Darren yelled, squeezing his fists tightly. "Goddamn Krystics! You had no idea that they were planning this?" He looked over suspiciously at Meadow. She shook her head.

"No, I didn't. Otherwise we would have conducted this differently," she admitted. "I didn't even think that the Krystics knew about Terry."

Darren scoffed. "Well, obviously they do. Now all our rescue efforts were in vain. We might have gotten him killed!"

"It's not your fault, dear. It was just an unknown. Sometimes that happens," Meadow responded with a sigh.

"I'm gonna fucking save him," Darren said resolutely. "But I don't want to put any of you in anymore danger. I do this alone."

"Are you sure?" Meadow asked with concern. "You know what you're doing? And you know how vital he is."

He nodded gravely. "Do you trust me?" he asked slowly.

Meadow studied her brother in Lucifer Christ in silence for a moment and then finally said, "Yes, I trust you."

That was all Darren needed to hear. Wasting no more time, he got back into his truck and sped away after the Krystics.

Then Meadow turned to her four companions, their eyes peeking at her from under their gray hoods. "Do you think he'll be able to save Terry?" one of the two women asked.

"Yes, I do," Meadow answered with unshakable resolve. "I have faith in Darren, and also faith in Terry." Without another word, they got back into the brown minivan and sped away through the cloud of dust.

A few minutes later, Priya and Jeremy emerged into the sunlight of the day. They were holding hands to comfort each other. Jeremy squinted against the light, holding his hand up to shield his eyes. "My God," he said. "I can't remember the last time I saw the sun."

"We're free now," Priya said, smiling at her new friend. "Let's go home."

Jeremy looked at her, cocking his eyebrows, and said, "Unless the place that we're from doesn't exist anymore..."

FIVE

The skies above Chicago were gray and overcast when Nikola came through into the Hollow Dimension. For a moment he was in a tunnel of swirling black and gray, but then a green neon light grid showed up in front of him. There was a slight popping sound as he went through and found that all he could see out of the windshield was white. Nikola yelled out in surprise, disoriented, and tried to steady the flight of his flying car. As he pulled up, he realized that he had only been inside of a cloud. Exiting the top of the cloud, the sky became clear and blue; the orange sun shining brightly down on the almost unbroken blanket of white clouds.

Nikola had no idea where he was, or even what time period he might be in. Suddenly he started to hear a deep rumbling, a roaring of some mythic mechanical beast. In a flash of an instant, an enormous airplane came careening through the air, barely missing Nikola's flying vehicle. "What the hell was that?" he yelled as his flying car was hit by the slipstream, sending him spinning out and down through the clouds.

The nausea started to kick in and he had difficulty seeing since everything in his vision was spinning like a possessed dreidel. As he wrestled to get the steering back under control, Nikola could see the Chicago skyline now that he was below the clouds. He chuckled to himself since the buildings seemed so short compared to the ones in the City which were a mile high. Finally he got the flying car righted and flying straight as he kept descending. On closer inspection, he could see that quite many of the buildings in the city below were in ruins; and the streets had recently been patched up.

There was suddenly a loud dinging noise and Nikola glanced down at the dashboard. The battery light had lit up and was now flashing red. *Shit*, he swore to himself. This warning light meant that the battery was almost completely drained and would need to be recharged. He needed to find a landing spot quick, or he would fall like a rock out of the sky. Circling around as fast as he could, he brought the flying car down in a rapid descent, weaving between the destroyed buildings. Spotting a large flat area near the center of the city, Nikola brought the flying car down and parked next to a strange looking sculpture covered in fresh graffiti. He had found Daley Plaza and eyed the Picasso sculpture with curiosity as he hopped out of his vehicle. As he stared into the ape-looking face of the sculpture, he could hear the sound of a couple helicopters coming closer.

Before Nikola was even prepared, two black helicopters were hovering above Daley Plaza, the wind kicked up from their rotors was blowing his hair and clothes violently. Without even a moment to wonder what type of flying machines these were, four police cars with their lights flashing and sirens blaring sped over the patched-up street and stopped in a semi-circle around Nikola and his parked flying car.

The doors of the police cars flew open and cops stepped out, taking cover behind their doors as they raised their guns. Nikola began to walk slowly toward the police cars. "STOP!" a voice yelled through a megaphone. "FREEZE!" the voice yelled again. "GET YOUR HANDS UP! AND DON'T RESIST ARREST!"

"Arrest?" Nikola mumbled to himself as he opened his hands and raised them above his head. Without missing a beat, he was surrounded by cops who were roughly restraining him as they wrenched his arms around his back and cuffed him like a common criminal.

SIX

The meditation had become so deep that it took Maya a few attempts before she could pull herself back from that place so far within her own consciousness. As she stirred, the hard texture of the tree bark dug into her back. The air had become hot and humid; beads of sweat were collecting on the skin of her neck and around her hairline. What brought her back was the soft sound of movement and the crunching of dead sticks and leaves on the forest floor. Maya peeked her left eye open and caught a glimpse of a figure in front of her. The person kneeling down in front of her was a teenager who looked very hippie-ish. Her long brown hair was greasy and tucked behind her ears.

She was wearing cut-off jean shorts, and her no-sleeve t-shirt definitely used to have sleeves. This girl was quietly placing a bowl of food down on the ground in front of Maya.

Now, as she opened both eyes and glanced around, there was a small group gathered around her, sitting cross-legged on the forest floor. They all looked like hippie teenagers—clothes in tatters and skin dirty from camping in the woods for who knows how long. The whole group had their eyes closed as in meditation, and looked like they were patiently waiting for Maya to start teaching a yoga class.

"What is this?" Maya whispered, looking down at the bowl of food.

The girl with the greasy brown hair looked up and smiled warmly at Maya. "She said that you would come," she whispered back.

"Who? Who said I would come?" Maya asked, curious about this group of kids who had gathered around her.

The greasy-haired girl shook her head. "In time we will all speak," she responded. "My name is Kendra. Eat, you need your strength." Kendra pushed the bowl closer to Maya.

"What is it?"

"It's just some rice and beans with a little salsa on top. It's good," Kendra encouraged.

Maya picked up the bowl hesitantly. After spooning a bit of the food into her mouth, she smiled, finding the food to be very delicious. "Thank you for the food," she said. "I didn't realize how hungry I was. Why—uh, what are you all doing here? It can't be because of me."

Kendra smiled and replied, "Eat up and gain your strength back. We will finish our meditations and then we will talk. It seems there is much to discuss. It's not everyday that a bunch of our parents would die in a freak cataclysm in downtown

Chicago. Then we start living like the lost boys out in the forest preserve next to our high school." Kendra shrugged and went back to sit with the others meditating.

Maya swallowed the bite of food she had in her mouth and wondered if these kids knew that she was responsible for the 'cataclysm' that Kendra was referring to, and subsequently the deaths of their parents. *If they don't know, maybe it's best not to tell them*, Maya said to herself as she finished up the camp food that had been served to her.

SEVEN

"Y'all look like fuckin' morons wearing all white like that," Terry grumbled from the backseat of the white SUV he was being kidnapped in. There was a woman on his left and a man on his right, both looked like they were in their thirties. His hands were restrained with zip-ties so as to deter him from trying anything violent. "And these zip-ties," he continued, raising his hands, "what's with people liking to use this shit now?"

The woman on Terry's left glared at him and snapped, "Well, don't you look like a moron covered in blood and wearing a gray track suit?"

"Hey! We'll have none of that petty squabbling," Lucia said sternly from the front seat, glancing a couple times in her rear-view mirror. "Terry, if you must know, what we do is a very precise technology. Wearing all white expands your aura by nine feet."

"You don't say?" Terry mumbled, looking out the window and not really paying attention. He turned back forward and looked toward Lucia in the driver's seat. "So you're these Krystic sons of bitches, huh?"

Lucia nodded. "That's right. We are Krystic—or *Christed*—beings. We connect with the higher Kryst extraterrestrial races and align with their agenda. There's been quite a lot of anti-Krystic shit going on, especially since the Atlantean period. The Lucifer Christ," she snorted, "they think that they're part of Christ Consciousness, but they don't realize that they are still Satanists with just a bit of glitz and glamor."

"So there are Satanists, Lucifer Christ people, and Krystics," Terry remarked. "How is anyone supposed to keep all that crap straight? What? You're all part of the same cult? The Trinity Cult or some shit?"

Lucia snorted again. "The Body of Lucifer Christ *thinks* that we're all part of the same cult. But they're sadly mistaken. We're the only ones who align with the Kryst, all the others are working an anti-Krystic agenda, just cogs in the BeaST machine. Unfortunately, you have fallen prey to being their puppet."

Terry shook his head and rolled his eyes. Sometimes the things these cult people said just sounded like a jumble of crazy-talk. "Yeah, they're so evil and you're all so perfect," he said sarcastically.

"It's not that simple," Lucia replied with a sigh. "It's not that necessarily what they're *doing* is evil. They choose to use technology and a system of geometry that is anti-Krystic. They all connect as different control mechanisms of the BeaST machine which is vampiric—it's a reversal of the natural flows of energy, creating a finite system where death is the inevitable result. The Fallen Angelic races, spearheaded by the lies of Metatron, use the Fibonacci—the death spiral. The Krystic spiral is natural and creates a natural back-and-forth flow of energy to and from Source. Not to mention they've duped everyone to think the Daisy of Death is the Flower of Life."

"I don't know what you're babbling about," Terry said with an irritated sigh. "I was told that the Spiralverse was based on the Fibonacci—we live in the Fibonacci Spiralverse."

"We do now," Lucia admitted. "But it wasn't originally meant to be that. The natural Krystic Spiralverse got perverted and distorted, reversing the natural pattern into one based on the 'Golden Meanie' spiral."

Terry laughed. "Golden Meanie," he repeated, shaking his head. "You got quips for everything."

"I'm sorry you've been deceived and used," Lucia said sadly. "But the Metatronic technology is deep within you, it's hard-wired into your electromagnetic field now. I can feel that your Merkabah is spinning fifty-five."

"It's doing what now?" Terry asked, leaning his face closer toward the front seat.

"You're using the Metatronic blueprint to work your energy. To run your Soulmind—your Magick. It's stuck in the ratio of fifty-five which connects to the Deathstar Technology."

Terry snorted, he couldn't help himself. "Deathstar Technology? Are we in fucking *Star Wars* now? This is just stupid! Just because of the way my Merkabah is spinning, it makes me the Antichrist?"

"Well, you are running technology that works in reversal of the natural eternal life of the Krystic blueprint," Lucia explained. "Basically, your operating system is anti-Krystic."

Terry burst out laughing. "My *operating system*? So I'm not just the Antichrist, but I'm an Antichrist *computer*." Terry shook his head. "Unbelievable..." he muttered.

The car fell silent and Terry stared out the window at the passing scenery. They had long since driven past what remained of Chicago. They were now in a suburb. It could have been Wheaton or Aurora, Terry couldn't tell for sure. Lucia started to reduce her speed, like they were getting close to their destination. The entourage following them slowed as well. "Sometimes we must do unpleasant things in order to keep the anti-Krystic from making the planet Fall anymore than it already has," Lucia said softly as she turned down a back road.

"So you're just gonna kill me then?" Terry said, staring out of the window in a spaced-out manner. His question was met with no response.

They pulled into the parking lot of a small church. There were no other cars or signs of people when they arrived. The white SUV and its entourage parked close to the entrance to the church. It was a plain-looking building, not extravagant or adorned with stained-glass windows. There was a small sign near the entrance of the parking lot which simply read: *Church of KRST.*

Lucia turned around in her seat to face Terry and the man and woman on either side of him. "This will go easier if you don't resist," she warned. Terry felt so exhausted in his bones, in his muscles, in his Soulmind that he wasn't one hundred percent sure he could resist even if he wanted to. They got out of the car and the man and woman continued to stand on either side of Terry, holding his arms in case he tried to run. As the rest of the entourage approached from out of their cars, several others from the congregation—wearing all white as well—came out of the entrance rolling a stretcher.

Terry groaned. "God, I have to be put on one of these fucking things *again*? What did I do to deserve all this torture? First it's being dragged from one cell to another—cuffed and zip-tied, drugged up and injected."

Lucia didn't say anything, she just gave Terry a look. He had no choice but to surrender to the moment as they cut the zip-ties from his wrists. Then they laid him on the stretcher, restraining his wrists and ankles with the cuffs that were attached. The woman who had been by Terry in the car leaned over to Lucia and whispered, "What are we going to do with him? We never really made a concrete decision. We're not going to kill him, are we? That's not our way."

Lucia gave the woman a pensive glance but didn't respond as they began wheeling Terry into the church. There were much more in this congregation than there had been at the abandoned church with the Body of Lucifer Christ. The pews were probably about half full. All the congregation wore white and they stood as the 'Antichrist' was brought in. There were hushed whispers and gasps. Terry heard one person say, "But he's just a boy!"

There was a ramp going up to the pulpit and Terry was rolled up this and brought to a stop in the middle of the stage. Terry looked around, surprised that there wasn't more fear present within him. Maybe he was too exhausted to feel afraid. Maybe death would be a relief. Behind the pulpit, instead of a huge cross like a normal Christian church, there was a banner hanging from the ceiling. On this banner was depicted a Kathara Grid. Terry wasn't exactly sure what this figure was, he just knew it resembled pictures of the Tree of Life which he'd seen from the Kabbalah.

Bending down to whisper in Terry's ear, Lucia said, "For the good of all beings everywhere, you must die. I'm sorry."

The whole congregation was now sitting back down in the pews. The only ones left on stage with Terry were Lucia and the man and woman who had been in the SUV with him. "Behold! The Antichrist!" Lucia bellowed, her voice reverberating off the acoustics of the old church. There were cheers from the crowd.

"You are *all* fucking crazy," Terry protested, his voice cracking and his throat felt incredibly dry. "I'm *not* the Antichrist! How many times do I have to say that?"

"I can see the connections and the energy in your auric field," Lucia said to him. "You are running anti-Krystic energy and you are the main key to activating the BeaST machine for the Earth's galactic system."

Terry groaned. "I don't know anything about this BeaST machine that you're babbling about, but if you can see my aura, then you must have a Soulmind." Lucia smiled. "But how someone with a Soulmind could be so stupid is beyond me. I guess having a Soulmind isn't a prerequisite for being smart."

Before the leader of the Krystics could respond, Darren burst through the door into the sanctuary brandishing his Soulmind weapon. The majority of the congregation of the Kryst had Soulminds, only a few of them didn't. So as the congregation turned to look at the intruder, most of them could see the shining yellow light-sword that Darren was pointing toward the pulpit.

"Darren, come to save your little puppet?" Lucia chuckled. "I should have known you would try to interfere." She lunged over to the lectern that was on the stage and pulled out a long, ornately carved dagger from one of the shelves inside it. Running back over to Terry, she raised it above his heart. "He will die! The Antichrist will die!"

The other woman up on the pulpit tried to nudge Lucia with her elbow. "We don't have to kill him," she whispered through gritted teeth. "I thought we talked about this."

"I swear to Lucifer Christ, if you move that dagger one millimeter, I will blow us all to Hell with a Singularity Pulse," Darren threatened. "And you know I'll do it, too! Terry isn't the Antichrist you're talking about. He's the Antichrist *Christ* Lucifer Christ."

Lucia spat a laugh at that. "Lucifer Christ mumbo-jumbo," she shot back. "You can't be so unaware that you don't know that he's preparing to bring the BeaST machine online through a Magickal Working connection with the Whore of Babylon."

"Are you smoking crack?" Terry scoffed. "The Whore of Babylon? That's not a real thing. You nutcases just sound like Bible Thumpers repackaged with New Age bullshit. Maybe I should just let Darren blast you all to pieces." As he was talking, Darren started to slowly approach the pulpit, not lowering his sword one bit. The yellow blazing energy of his aura burned around him like the hottest flames, and the spiral coming out of his solar plexus was itching for some action. Lucia opened her mouth and her bottom jaw quivered as the knife became not so steady in her hand.

"It's true. Murder is not the Krystic way," Darren said slowly. "Trust me, you don't want to have blood on your hands. Especially if the Satanists are looking for Terry as well."

Lucia hesitated, looking nervous. The young woman standing next to her implored her by saying, "Yes, there must be another way. I don't feel right contributing to violence like this. Free Will never goes away. As long as he is alive, he has the choice to realign with the Kryst."

"Let him go," Darren ordered. Lucia slowly lowered the dagger in defeat. She didn't say anything, she didn't protest as the man and woman standing next to her on the pulpit began to unfasten the cuffs restraining him. They helped Terry off the stretcher and then let him free to go to Darren.

"You'll regret this when the BeaST machine is siphoning your Soulmind in the most painful way imaginable," Lucia warned. "Don't let him join energy with the Whore of Babylon: she who comes riding on the back of a dragon."

"I think it's a little late for that," Darren shot back and then grabbed Terry's hand. "Come on, Terry, we're going." They turned and Darren hustled Terry out of the church as fast as he could. It was twilight when they emerged into the parking lot again.

"Just get me out of here, Darren," Terry said wearily. "I'm so sick of all this shit—people trying to kill me, me being locked in jail cells, people saying I'm the Antichrist. I'm fucking done!"

Once they were by Darren's truck, he finally relaxed and let his Soulmind weapon disappear back into his aura. "I'm sorry you have to go through all this, Terry," he said as they climbed into the truck. "And I'm afraid we're gonna have to go on the run. I don't think we should go back to your house, too conspicuous and Mothman will start asking questions. Better that nobody knows where you are or where you're going. Since there are quite a few groups after you—the Krystics now, the government who will want you back for their experiments, and the Satanists who want to use you too."

Terry groaned as Darren pulled out and started driving. "Great... I can never get a break to just breathe and relax anymore. I'm a most wanted man, and not in a sexy way."

"We gotta get you cleaned up," Darren remarked, looking at Terry's bloody clothes and the blood caked in his hair and on his skin.

Terry thought hard, squinting his eyes. Then two things happened—first he saw Jessica's face in his mind, and as he looked at her smile, it was as if her energy was telling him to go to Rob's house. "Oh, yeah!" he said, eyes widening. "Can't go to my house. Stop by Rob's old house so I can take a quick shower and grab some shit to take."

After Terry was the human GPS, they pulled up outside of Rob's old house. Night had fallen completely by that point. "I'm just going to run in and grab a few things after showering off. Stay in the car, I shouldn't be long," Terry said as he hopped out and ran to the door of Rob's house. It was unlocked and he let himself in. The bodies of Rob's parents were nothing but skeletons now, but the stench of death still clung to the walls. Holding his nose, he ran through the kitchen and up the stairs to the bathroom. After tossing off his bloody sweatsuit and discarding it in a corner, he jumped in the shower, so grateful to scrub the gore from his body.

Once clean and toweled off, Terry walked naked into Rob's bedroom. There he hurriedly threw on some clothes—zip-off cargo pants and a t-shirt. He spotted an empty backpack thrown in the bottom of Rob's closet. Taking it, he stuffed in enough clothes to last about a week. Zipping it up, he threw it over one shoulder. And just when he was about to leave—

"Terry!"

It was definitely a voice. He froze and looked around for the source. It sounded like a woman's voice. When he looked over toward Rob's desk, it spoke again, *"Terry!"* That time it was unmistakably Jessica's voice.

"Jessica?" Terry said hopefully as he approached the desk. A magnetic pull was drawing him closer to a specific drawer and Terry didn't know why. But when he threw it open, he marveled at the purple light that illuminated his face. Picking up the glass cylinder with the dancing purple energy, he remembered at once what it was. "This is a piece of Jessica's Soulmind," he whispered in awe. "She meant for me to find this."

As he smiled and felt affection for his absent lover, he crushed the glass cylinder in his fist. Before letting the Soulmind piece get away, Terry shoved his face into the purple luminescence and inhaled deeply. This dancing shard of Jessica's energy was sucked in through his tear ducts, nose, and mouth. Once it was assimilated to his own Soulmind, he could feel Jessica as a tangible presence, as if she was actually there in the room with him.

"Thank you, Jessica," he whispered, "for giving me that piece of yourself—and your heart."

Confident that he had gotten what he had come for—Jessica's Soulmind was what really had called for him—he ran back toward the stairs. To his surprise, Darren was standing there at the bottom looking up at him. "We have to go now!" he said with urgency.

"What? What's up?" Terry asked as he descended the stairs, adjusting the backpack on his shoulder.

"A black SUV parked up a block behind where I'm parked," Darren answered nervously. "I'm pretty sure it's the CIA wanting to re-capture their asset."

"A black SUV? Like the one that was used to kidnap me," Terry returned. "Let's get the fuck out of here." When they came back through the front door, Terry glanced down the block for the black SUV, but it was no longer there. "Where is it? It's gone."

Darren shook his head. "It was here a second ago. What they're up to, I don't know. But I don't trust them one iota. Come on, let's boogie."

They hopped back into the truck and Terry put the backpack down on the floor between his legs. As Darren began to drive away, Terry asked, "You weren't gonna ask about those skeletons?"

Darren gave Terry a sideways glance. "I don't know. Didn't really seem important. What, do you even know who they were?"

Terry shrugged and stared out the window as the houses of his suburb flew by outside. "One more stop before we blow town," he added. "To my house. I gotta get something out of my van. It's late and Mothman probably won't even notice we've been by."

Nodding in recognition, Darren whisked them away to Terry's house under cover of darkness. Pulling up along Terry's van which was parked on the curb in front of his house, he hopped out with his backpack and went over to the other side of the van. He slid the door open, it was unlocked. The Merkabah around the house was still stable and Terry made a note that it was rotating properly and the shield still held in place. After a few moments of rummaging under the seats of the van, he came back and got into Darren's truck.

"Find what you were looking for?" he wondered.

Terry shook his head. "Nah," he said and pointed straight ahead. "Now let's get the fuck out of Dodge before the black helicopters come back to rape me. *No Bounce, No Play*, right?" Terry winked at his friend and then they were off, planning to leave Illinois as far in the dust as possible.

EIGHT

A heavy darkness, greasy with smog, had descended upon the City of Angels. Eden sat there still, on the hill in front of the Hollywood sign. Gazing down at the sparkling lights below, she sat with her knees up and arms hugged around them. From the top of Hollywood, it looked like space. The buildings shimmered with an ethereal presence that to Eden brought to mind forbidden cities on distant planets. A civilization and people that were utterly foreign would make *her* the alien.

"The City of Lost Angels," she whispered to herself. "Where extraterrestrials fall and become gods of the silver screen. Stars that fell from Heaven to then ascend to become a star once more..." Trailing off, she rested her cheek on her arm and listened to the steady drone of traffic. Eden had been sitting here since she came through from the Kingdom, which was only a few hours earlier, just to meditate and contemplate the heaviness of the chaotic energy that surrounded her.

Then, as if waking her from a dream, she heard familiar noises close up the hill behind her. The sounds were unmistakably the sweet din of two lovers in the throes of passion; the giggling of a female, the deep, heavy breathing of a male. Making sure she still held her amethyst firmly in her right hand, she scrabbled to her feet, brushing off the desert dust. The call of sex was always upon her and she went to seek it out.

When Eden reached the top, flat part of the hill behind the Hollywood sign, she saw a couple, under the cover of night, making love on a large fuzzy blanket. The young woman was thin and had brown hair so long that it went all the way down to her butt. She moved her body in the most sensuous way as she straddled her lover, on top of him with him deep inside her. Moaning, the young woman tilted her head back toward the sky as she closed her eyes in euphoria. Her lover was fit as well, sweat glistening off of his taut muscles. His mouth hung open as he breathed and watched her on top of him, his hands caressing up her body.

Eden tried to stay in the shadows, so she could be a voyeur without being spotted. They must have heard her rustling up the hill or sensed her presence, because the woman said softly, "I hear you back there." She titled her head and looked over toward Eden with a smile. "Join in if you want." Turning her head back to look down at her lover, she began to ride him faster, moans increasing in volume. Eden hesitantly took a few steps toward them, not sure whether or not she *wanted* to join in. The woman turned her head again to get a better look at Eden. "You're hot," she remarked. "I'm sure the three of us could make some sparks fly." She winked.

"Maybe," Eden replied slowly, not sure if the sparks comment was a secret reference to the Soulmind. "You both are incredibly sexy, too. Maybe I'll just watch for a minute or two to get in the mood."

"Suit yourself," the woman said. "The show is always very juicy. Sometimes watching can be just as titillating." Suddenly she stopped the movement of her hips and looked at Eden with wide eyes.

"What is it babe?" the young man asked. "It's okay if she joins in. I'm game. Just don't stop." He chuckled and then started to moan again as his lover resumed the movement of her hips. But the woman didn't take her eyes off of Eden.

"Are you," the woman started, "*Temple of Cosmic Fuck?*"

Eden laughed. "What? You saw my video on Pornhub?"

The woman nodded and glanced down at her lover. "God, that video was hot!" she said. "Damian here and I got off so hard watching that video with you and your friends. Didn't we, hun?"

"Oh, we totally did," Damian agreed. "Not gonna lie, I came so fucking hard watching your tight little body. My lover here—Lana—is a connoisseur of that type of erotica. Well, any type of erotica to be specific."

"I'm just insatiable, aren't I?" Lana giggled as she played with Damian's nipples. "Come, *Temple of Cosmic Fuck*, there is more than enough room on our blanket."

"My name is Eden. Nice to meet you two," she said as she sat down next to them on the blanket. Placing the amethyst down gently in the fuzzy blanket, there was a deep purple glow originating from the center of the crystal, almost detectable by the naked eye.

"That's a beautiful stone," Lana noted.

"Yes," Eden said, gazing softly at the stone and thinking of Terry. "It helped me regain my memories when they were stolen from me."

"That sounds like some occult shit there," Lana returned.

"Yeah, maybe it is," Eden said, looking down at the blanket. Then, when she looked back up at Lana she asked, "Did you see any strange lights and colors in that video of mine on Pornhub?"

"Light and colors?" Damian muttered back, and Lana shook her head.

"No light and colors," Lana answered, "but you are a strange one. Very powerful, I feel. Then it's settled!" she said resolutely, her head thrown back toward the sky as if communing with a higher consciousness. Then slowly she brought her gaze back down to look at Eden with a blazing blue flame behind her eyes. "Eden? No," she said with authority. "You shall now be known as Mystery, Babalon the Great!"

Eden furrowed her eyebrows and gave a puzzled look. "Babylon?" she said.

"No," Lana shook her head. "That's not 'Babylon' with a *y*, but *'Babalon'* with an *a*. The Great Mother! The Goddess!"

"Okay," Eden replied, as if what Lana said was suddenly supposed to explain everything.

Lana laughed long and lightly. "Now let's cum deep into the cosmos!" she said, whipping her incredibly long hair back and forth seductively.

Eden slipped her pants and panties off. Spreading her legs, she exposed her pink pussy to her new friends, but she didn't take off her shirt. As she began to rub her clitoris vigorously, her Soulmind began to light up her aura in the most brilliant display of red and pink. And as they all moaned with ecstasy, Eden came with bursts of pink and red luminescence shooting into the night sky of Hollywood like orgasmic fireworks.

NINE

Yelling out as if in pain, Terry awoke with a start. He was slightly disoriented as he came back to consciousness in the passenger seat of Darren's truck. The pain again shot through the tip of Terry's right ear like shocks of electricity. His hand shot up and he rubbed the area that was in pain. The tip of the ear was red, hot, and inflamed. "Fuck," Terry muttered.

"What is it? What's wrong?" Darren asked, turning his head to glance at Terry a couple times and then back to the road. It was light out and there were a good number of other cars on the highway.

"My ear," Terry groaned in pain. "It fucking hurts like shit in the tip here. How long was I out?"

Darren shrugged. "I dunno," he admitted. "Maybe five hours or so. I was able to stop at a rest area that had gas and took a fifteen or twenty minute nap myself, just to recharge."

"That's good," Terry replied, still rubbing the tip of his ear. "Where are we going?"

"East," was all Darren said for an answer.

"And where are we now?" Terry wanted to know.

"We're near Stony Stream in Ohio. Right outside of Cleveland."

Terry nodded and looked out the front windshield very intently, still rubbing his ear, making it more inflamed. "Ow... Motherfucker," he grumbled.

Darren glanced over at Terry, concerned. "I don't want to alarm you," he said, "but can you feel like a bump where your ear is hurting? Like a small sort of hard thing the size of a grain of rice?"

"Uh-huh, yeah. Why?" Terry answered slowly.

Scowling, Darren said, "I don't want to freak you out, but they may have equipped you with a tracking device. They're very small and could easily be punched through the skin at the tip of your ear like that."

"What? Are you serious?" Terry yelled. "Then no matter where we run it doesn't matter! They'll fucking find us anyway! Here, gimme a knife and I'll cut it out!"

"No!" Darren snapped back. "At least not right now. Neither of us know medical procedures, so you'd bleed a lot and I don't have the supplies to bandage it up in my fucking truck."

"Agh!" he screamed in frustration. "They could be onto us right now! Have you noticed any suspicious vehicles following us?"

"No," Darren shook his head and glanced in the rearview mirror. "Not since that black SUV outside Rob's house... Wait..." he said, trailing off and looking intensely in the rearview again.

"What? What is it, for fuck's sake?" Terry said, agitated.

"There's a police car coming up behind us," he answered, worry was audible in his voice.

"Are you speeding? We don't want to get pulled over for some stupid shit like that," Terry warned, turning around in his seat to look out of the back window.

Darren jumped in surprise when the blare of the police car's siren was turned on. "Fuck," he muttered to himself.

"Shit, he's pulling us over!" Terry yelled. "What do we do?"

"Shut up!" Darren shot back. "I can see he's pulling us over. Be quiet and let me think how we're gonna get out of this."

In silence, they pulled over to the dirt on the side of the highway and stopped the truck. The police car parked behind them, turned the siren off but left the red and blue lights on. Terry was panicking now. "Should I hide? Should we make a run for it?"

"Shhh," Darren hushed him. "If they're tracking you, they already know you're right here. Hiding would do no good. Just be quiet and let me handle it."

He rolled down his window as the police officer approached their vehicle. The cop was wearing sunglasses and Darren couldn't see his eyes, which made him feel disconcerted. As he approached the truck, he had his hand on his gun. This was an indication that he felt there was the possibility of an altercation.

"Good day, Officer," Darren said politely as the cop came up to his window. "What seems to be the problem?"

"Well," the Officer replied as he looked the truck up and down. "There is an AMBER alert out on a vehicle matching this description. A young male with long black hair has been kidnapped." That's when the cop spotted Terry sitting in the passenger seat. Suddenly he backed up a few feet from the truck and drew his weapon. "Exit the vehicle now with your hands up! Both of you!" he said, barking the order.

Darren swallowed hard, not knowing what to do next. In a split second, as if miraculously, Terry noticed that stretching about one hundred feet in each direction were no cars at that exact moment. "Timestrus be damned!" Terry muttered.

"What?" Darren said, but before he could even get the whole word out of his mouth, Terry threw his arms up, facing East and West down the highway. This created a time-bubble about one hundred feet in each direction from the center point which was Terry. The outer film of this bubble was neon pink and wobbled like a spectral entity. This bubble created a Stasis Field right outside of the area contained within the bubble. So as cars would approach from behind, they would freeze in time within the Stasis Field.

As if in one flawless movement, Terry set up the Stasis Field and reached into his backpack. Even though all of this was happening within the span of a couple seconds, Darren saw it as if it was in slow motion. Turning his head, Darren saw the gun come up and he flattened himself against his seat. When the driver's window wasn't obstructed with Darren's body, Terry squeezed the trigger of the Beretta. The cop didn't even have time to get a shot off before the bullet from Terry's gun went right through the center of his forehead.

Darren was in shock as he watched the police officer's body fall to the ground and blood fanned out from the exit wound in the back of his head. "Let's get the fuck out of here!" Terry yelled. "I don't know how long the Stasis Field will hold!"

Without missing a beat, Darren put his truck back in drive and sped off toward the pink film of the Stasis Field in front of them. When they crossed through the spectral light, the Stasis Field instantly collapsed, and the cars in front of them and two hundred feet behind them returned to their normal motion. Terry was breathing heavily, obviously adrenaline was pumping through his veins as sweat beaded on his forehead.

"What the fuck, Terry? Are you fucking serious right now?" Darren snapped, holding out his hand toward Terry. "Give me that." Terry reluctantly handed over the gun and Darren securely slid it under his own seat. "That's what you were getting out of your van, wasn't it?"

Terry nodded sheepishly, like a child who'd been caught stealing. "Yeah..." he said really softly.

"And you lied to me," Darren continued. "That's not cool, Terry. We have to be able to trust each other. You could have told me you had a gun. We can have it as a weapon and use it in a safe way."

Terry snorted. "There's a safe way to use a weapon?"

"You know what I mean," Darren replied, still a bit irritated. "*I* try not to kill people if I don't have to."

"Was there another way out of that situation?" Terry said, with a little more edge in his voice now. "I'm sorry, I thought that I was the one who just saved our asses back there from being arrested! Do you want to go to jail? Obviously you're wanted as a kidnapper now. And the CIA wants to lock *me* up again. As far as I can see I got rid of the problem. And my Stasis Field made it so that there were no witnesses. You're welcome."

Darren laughed. "Yeah, that was a nifty little trick," he jabbed. "But police officers have body cameras and cameras in their vehicles. That's all recorded. Yeah, there were no physical witnesses, but we're on video now. And you're on video shooting an officer of the law."

"Oh," was all Terry could manage to say.

"Okay," Darren said, softening a bit. "Yes, you forgot about all their cameras and shit, but I guess the important thing is we got away. So thank you for that."

There seemed to be nothing more to say as the adrenaline started to wear off. Terry's legs felt weak and his hands began to shake. Reaching forward, he opened up the glove compartment and started to dig around inside.

"What—What are you doing, Terry?" Darren asked, shooting him a glance that looked like a warning. Terry didn't answer, he found what he was looking for. It was a folding knife and he pulled it out, opening it quickly. "No. No." Darren said, trying to grab the knife away from Terry's grasp. The truck swerved on the road and he quickly put his hands back on the wheel to straighten out and not hit a car in another lane.

Before Darren could try to stop him again, Terry sliced off the top of his right ear with a shriek. Blood started to pour from his mutilated ear as he chucked the cut off piece out of the window. Grabbing a t-shirt out of his backpack, Terry squeezed it around the wound, trying to slow down the bleeding.

Darren shook his head in disgust. "I *told* you not to *do* that! Now I'm gonna have to get bandages at the next stop and get you cleaned up again..." he trailed off, ranting.

Suddenly Darren's cell phone rang. Terry was glad of the interruption and squeezed the t-shirt around his throbbing ear as he stared out the window. The phone rang again and he looked down at the number. "California?" Darren mumbled. "Who could be calling me from California?" Terry looked over at him with his eyebrows raised.

Darren opened the cell phone and put it to his ear. "Hello?" There was silence for a second, then he said, "Eden? Where are you?"

"Eden?" Terry said, eager to know where she ended up.

"She's in Hollywood. Yeah, that's crazy," Darren said then paused, looking over at Terry. "Yeah, Eden, hang on. I'll put you on speaker-phone." He clicked a button and Terry could hear some white noise coming through the cell phone speaker.

"Terry?" It was Eden's voice as if from the other end of a walkie-talkie.

"Oh my God, Eden! It's so good to hear your voice and know that you're alive," Terry said, relief in his voice. "When we teleported I didn't know where the hell you could have ended up."

"Yeah, I got spit out on the hill in front of the Hollywood sign," she said through the speaker-phone. "Crazy, right?"

"Yeah," Terry said.

"At first I was like 'are you fucking kidding me?'" she continued. "Like, I'm so far away from everything. Then I met these two cool people, Damian and Lana. I'm crashing at their place and they have connections in the porn business. They saw our video, Terry! They recognized me! Isn't that wild?"

Terry nodded and then remembered that Eden couldn't see his face through the phone. "Yeah, that's crazy," he responded. "Could they see our Soulminds on the video?"

"No," she answered. "Neither of them seem to be activated. They are into the occult and Magick though."

"Be careful around there—Hollywood, I mean," Darren warned. "There are a lot of Satanists working in different facets of the entertainment industry."

"Yes, I'm aware of that, thank you," Eden snipped sarcastically. "You know I'm not one for joining cults."

"Yeah," Darren continued, "but that doesn't mean that you won't fuck around with them."

"What I choose to do is none of your business!" she snapped at him, the annoyance audible in her voice.

"Okay, okay, I'm sorry," Darren conceded. "You're an adult and can do what you want. Just remember that you are responsible for your own actions. No one can force you to do anything you don't want to do."

"Thanks, *Dad*. Are you done with the lecture?" Eden shot back.

Terry was rendered almost speechless by the back and forth between the two of them. "Can you two just chill the fuck out?"

Darren shot him a look. "Sorry, I'm just a little on edge," he offered as an explanation. "Tensions are still high especially since you just—" But he cut himself off and didn't finish the sentence.

"What? Terry just what?" Eden wanted to know.

"Nevermind," Darren returned quickly. "We shouldn't say anything over the phone."

"Well, anyway," she continued, "I know this is a crazy ask, but there's no chance the journey might bring you two over to this side of the country?"

"We're actually heading East," Terry said. "Opposite direction from where you are."

"I know which direction is East, babe," she said with a laugh. "Where the fuck are you two going?"

"Our destination is Providence," Darren said, this being the first time he voiced where exactly they were headed.

"Providence? Where the fuck is that?" Terry asked.

"You know, Providence," Darren continued explaining. "Rhode Island."

"Is that even a real state?" Terry said, wrinkling up his nose. "Is it an island?"

Darren shook his head and laughed. "You must be terrible at geography."

"Providence?" Eden said, injecting in a word between Terry and Darren's back and forth. "Why the fuck are you guys going there?"

"At this point, that's unknown to me," Darren admitted. "But the information came from higher ups in my Society."

"Oh, I see. So you're just following orders like a good little cult member," Eden quipped, not losing an opportunity to send a jab at Darren. He grumbled inarticulately. "And you warn *me* about joining the Satanists. You don't have to do everything those Lucifer Christ people say either."

"Touché," Darren replied. "I should learn to take my own advice more often. However, even when I'm advised by another member of my Body, like by Meadow, I always run it by my own intuition before acting on it. And I know from the information biofeedback that I'm getting from my own Soulmind that there is an energy in Rhode Island and especially around Providence that is magnetizing Terry's Soulmind to it."

"Wait, really?" Terry asked.

Darren looked at him and then back at the road. "Yes. This is the next location the Spiralverse means for you to be. I'm just helping you be where you need to be. That is how the next phase will be catalyzed."

"I don't really understand all that," Terry admitted, "but, okay. I'll have to trust you."

"This is all very fascinating," Eden interrupted, "but I have to go. I'll call you again soon to check in." There was a click and the line went dead.

Darren closed the cell phone and tossed it in the cupholder. "At least we know that's she's okay and where she is," he commented.

"Yeah, I was worried since I haven't got the hang of using Matter-Relocation yet," Terry mused, looking out the window again as he squeezed the t-shirt around his bloody ear.

"I was wondering how you acquired that skill," Darren said, fishing for information.

"It's a long story," Terry responded with a sigh. He didn't want to get into explaining his whole encounter with Maya and how that transpired.

"Okay, that's okay," Darren assured him that he wasn't going to pry for information. "You'll get the hang of it soon and be able to travel to the destinations you wish by pure will."

"That could be a handy skill..." Terry trailed off for a moment and then said, "Darren, do you feel like time is speeding up? Like, I feel like time is flying by. The year is flying by. It's almost August. Where the fuck did July go?"

Darren laughed. "You're right. Time is accelerating. And that's partly because of you."

TEN

The prospect of making all this progress on the journey of initiation just to end up being killed by a giant Troll was now smacking Jessica in the face like a bag of severed dicks. The huge monster was charging them on their spot on top of the ridge, but it was still a little ways away in the valley below. Josh-oo'el and Jessica had fallen to their hands and knees because of the tremor of the earth with each one of the giant's footfalls.

"Do you have a plan?" Jessica yelled over to her companion over the din of Troll shrieks and the pounding of his feet.

"Truth be Trolled, I have a couple spells up my sleeve," Josh-oo'el said quickly.

Jessica laughed in spite of their impending deaths. "You said *Truth be Trolled*. That's funny… Oh shit, we're gonna die!"

The young Elf took off his pack and tossed it out of the way. "That Troll will be up to the top of this hill in like three strides," he informed. "You better start praying. Or chanting that mantra. Or whatever method you use to cast your Magick spells." Before Jessica could respond, Josh-oo'el ran across the top of the hill away from Jessica, trying to draw the Troll's attention away from her. "Hey, you ugly oaf! Over here!" he yelled, getting the attention of the giant. It roared and turned in the Elf's direction as it reached the bottom of the hill.

"Oh, Jesus, please come to us in our time of need," Jessica started to mumble in a totally manic fashion, speaking so quickly it would have been unintelligible to anyone listening. "Deliver us from our enemies," she continued rambling. "Oh God, I don't know what to do. Grant me the full armor of whatever…" she trailed off. In her panic, she had completely forgotten about the mantra that the Goddess of the Underworld had given her as a divine gift.

"This is for my people, you overgrown bully!" Josh-oo'el screamed at the Troll's hideous face as it climbed the hill toward where he was waiting. As the Troll's head came up into view, the Elf jutted his hands out in the direction of the Troll's eyes and yelled, "*Mistafah!*" Jessica knew at once this was a spell and could see a sort of mist of bubbles fly from Josh-oo'el's fingers and into the giant's eyes.

The Troll was temporarily blinded, roaring in protest as he was thrown off balance. For a second, the giant beast collapsed on the side of the hill. He wouldn't be down for long. "Way to go, Josh-oo'el!" Jessica yelled in encouragement, some of her panic giving way to a rush of adrenaline. The Elf jerked his head and looked in her direction as she called out to him. The distraction was just enough time for the Troll to shake some of the Magickal mist from his vision. Jessica watched in horror as the Troll swung his arm down from the side. Unfortunately, Josh-oo'el didn't have enough of a chance to get out of the way. Screaming in terror, the Elf's whole body was scooped up in the palm of the giant's hand, and he proceeded to just swat him off of the top of the hill. Josh-oo'el went flying through the air, over the valley below, like a shrieking projectile. When his forward momentum ended, he fell like a stone to the hard ground below.

"No!" Jessica screamed. That definitely drew the giant's attention, and he readied to rush her as he cleared the last of the blindness spell from around his eyes. "What was that mantra? What was that mantra?" she mumbled to herself as she backed away. There wasn't enough time to take off her knapsack and rummage around inside for the paper. She would have to pull it out of her memory. The Troll was closing in on her, so her remembering mechanism would have to work fast or she was going to be a bug on the bottom of a Troll toe. "Shit, shit, shit," she cursed. Then a lightbulb suddenly illuminated her Soulmind, igniting her purple aura and spiral from her solar plexus in the same moment she remembered the words of the mantra. "*Jai Ma, Jai Jai Ma, Jai Jai Ma. Kali Ma, Kali Ma, Jai Jai Ma!*" she blurted out. Nothing happened and the Troll had already halved the distance between them. Desperately, she repeated the mantra. Then she said it once more as the Troll was almost upon her. The third recitation was the charm.

Now Jessica could suddenly feel the words of the spell working their Magick on her, transforming her, body and Soulmind. She felt less dense, like there wasn't as much gravity pulling her down to the Earth. This feeling in turn gave way to a feeling of expansion, like there was a great force of energy pushing her skin from the inside. With the strangest sensation she'd ever felt in her life, Jessica's body physically stretched and expanded like she was made of clay, malleable. With a cry, she grew to about nine feet tall, her black hair blowing out behind her like a sovereign mane, her radiant body. With a whoosh, her purple aura spiraled around her like a violet tornado. When it came back to just flickering around the edge of her skin, she was now wearing a skin-tight black leotard with a necklace of shrunken heads hanging around her neck. Jessica's bare feet connected with the grass and the Earth below her.

Just as the Troll got to her, it became a little disoriented by her transformation and slowed its pace. Taking advantage of this hesitation, Jessica wasted no time pulling her katanas from the spiral emanating from her chest. As she brandished her Soulmind weapons in front of her, she noticed that the blades of the katanas were twice as long as they normally were, almost feeling like long spears in her hands. She felt strange, like she was a completely different person but the same all at once. There was no mistaking the incredible power that now ran through her like the combined potential of lightning *and* water.

Even after growing to nine feet tall, the Troll's two hundred feet still towered over her intimidatingly. Lunging forward, she scooted quickly between the giant's legs to stand behind him as he dipped down to try and swat her with his enormous hand. He missed and Jessica wasted no time making her attack. Slicing with both of her katanas which burned with violet flames, she severed the area right on the back of the Troll's left ankle. He shrieked out loudly, almost deafening Jessica as he began to wobble off balance. The ankle that she cut was closest to the incline of the hill that led down into the valley below. The Troll's foot slipped and his immeasurable weight began to pull him back down the hill. Flailing as he tried to regain his balance, the giant's fingertips clipped Jessica and she was easily sent flying off of the hill in the same manner Josh-oo'el had been.

As Jessica, in the form of Kali, sailed through the air like a paper plane, she watched the Troll finally topple all the way over onto his back, sliding down the hill as he was dragged by his own momentum. Finding that she could slow her own descent with pure will, Jessica guided herself carefully and gracefully down to the grassy valley almost as if she was flying or gliding. *I wonder if in the form of Kali I can fly?* she thought to herself. Even though Jay and Magda had taught her the Merkabah technology and how to use it as the personal lightbody vehicle, she hadn't ever really gotten the hang of it.

The Troll had slid down all the way to the bottom of the hill and was now struggling to get back to standing. This was Jessica's opportunity to finish him and she didn't know if there would come a better opportunity again. Without further ado, Jessica began to sprint dramatically toward where the giant was wriggling like a turtle on its back. She looked like she was gliding on rocket-propelled ice skates, with trails of purple light dripping off behind her as she ran. When close enough to the giant, she leapt an impossible distance into the air, the flickering energy of her Soulmind carrying her like Magickal wings. She squeezed the handles of her katanas together in her hands, pointing the blades downwards. Guiding herself flawlessly, she came down onto the Troll's forehead, her bare feet feeling the clamminess of his skin. Then in one movement, she stabbed her Soulmind blades down into the Troll's skull, right between his eyebrows. The giant shrieked out in pain, grasping uselessly with his hands as he flailed them through the air. Pushing the light-blades deeper into the giant's skull, she penetrated it, going all the way through into his brain where the third eye would have been. Jessica didn't know if giant Trolls had third eyes or not.

Once the katanas were fully impaling the Troll's head, its arms fell lifelessly to the ground and he gave one final exhale, expelling the last of his putrid breath. As Jessica let go of the handles of her katanas, she slipped off the giant's forehead and fell to the grass below, shrinking back to her original size as the god-body of Kali dissolved back into the ethers. For a few moments, Jessica just laid there on her back, next to the giant's big-ass head, too stunned and exhausted to move. She had connected to and transformed into the body of a Hindu deity. It was so unfathomably impossible that Jessica could hardly even believe it herself even though she experienced it.

As some of her strength returned, she thought about Joshoo'el and how he'd given his life to help her and to help his own people. Assuredly he had not survived the fall into the valley. Pulling herself to her feet, she went over to where his body laid motionless in the grass. Blood ran from the corners of his open eyes and mouth. Jessica thought about bringing back a piece of the giant's body to prove he had been killed, but carrying any piece of the giant back with her seemed to be size and weight prohibitive. Besides, she was going to have to carry the dead body of this young Elf back with her, of course.

"I'm so sorry," she whispered as she closed her fallen companion's eyes. Even though Josh-oo'el had been young and annoying at times, Jessica couldn't help but recognize a certain fondness that she had developed for him, whatever that meant.

ELEVEN

FROM THE MIND OF EDEN LOCKHART:

I've done pornos before, but this is definitely the strangest one that I've ever been a part of. Standing here in the soundstage, I wait with bare feet and wearing nothing but a short, pink, silk robe. The set is built to look like the inside of an alien spaceship. There is a very large control console underneath a window that is draped with a blue screen. I assume this will show the exterior of space, to be edited in during post-production. There is also what looks like an operating table—or 'probing' table. There are several monitors next to this, what is going to be the sex table. These monitors have lots of wires trailing off of them. These wires don't seem to go anywhere, but they look good for props.

Damian is behind the camera ready to shoot the scene. He's the one who hooked me up with this gig actually. I've never acted out a Martian scenario, so this may be kinda fun. There is a director here too, and he stands next to Damian as they discuss how to set up the shots. The director's name is David. Most of the time he's very quiet—like spookily quiet. He doesn't even seem to like to give many directions when he's directing. We did a read-through of the lines with my co-star and David didn't say much more than that we did a good job. I guess he just likes to give the actors freedom to bring their own creativity to the table.

My co-star walks onto the set. He's young, around my age, but still a hunk of a man. Wearing a tight one-piece outfit that has different sections of puffy material that are different shades of purple and black. They put blue makeup on his face—mostly streaks, dots, and patterns—to make him look more alien; as well as making the tips of his ears pointy and blue.

"Take your places. We're about to start shooting," David says in a quiet voice.

I walk over and lay down on the alien operating table. This is my starting point, where I'm supposed to be waking up after abduction. My co-star Marcus is off camera; he is supposed to enter when I wake up.

"Camera rolling..." David looks at Damian to make sure he's rolling digital. "And action!"

After laying still with my eyes closed for several moments, I start to blink my eyes open as if coming out of a deep trance. I look around me at the alien environment and start to panic. As I sit upright on the table, one side of my silk robe falls open, revealing my left tit. Making a show of false modesty, I pull my robe closed to hide my nakedness as I say, "Where the hell am I? I don't think I'm on Earth anymore. How will I get home?"

As I stand up off of the table, Marcus enters the scene, looking very alien and stoic. Wary of this creature, I scoot back as he approaches. "Do not be alarmed, Jezebel of Earth," the alien speaks in an even tone. "If I was going to harm you, I would already have done so. Your abduction was carefully planned. And I would never probe you unless you were fully conscious, as you are now."

I'm still skeptical that this creature doesn't want to rape and murder me—not necessarily in that order. Holding my robe tighter around my body, I say, "Don't hurt me, alien!" I say, trying to keep the quiver out of my voice. "I'm a very important person on Earth," I continue. "Don't think I can't have you killed by a satellite within five minutes! I have those kind of connections, you know." I wag a finger at the alien, hoping it looks threatening. He approaches closer to me without any expression on his blank face.

"I am King of planet Tartarus!" he says with authority, his voice raising in volume. "And I would take you as my Queen. To be my mate and rule by my side."

My eyes are wide as he takes my hands in his. "But I'm a virgin!" I say in protest. As if! I laugh to myself and then throw in an ad lib by saying, "Well, an interstellar virgin at least." He comes in for a kiss and I make myself blush. Marcus presses his lips against mine. His hands are still gripping my own, pressing them against my breasts as we make out. I part his lips with mine and start to taste his tongue.

After a moment, he pulls away and says, "We will mate physically and inter-dimensionally."

"Oh, my!" I squeal as he picks me up and sits me down on the side of the probe-table. My robe starts to come open again and this time I let it fall off my shoulders, revealing the smoothness of the flesh over my collarbone and then the perkiness of my breasts, nipples are already sticking out like plugs trying to find an outlet. I moan as he fondles my tits in a way that denotes an alien without much experience with Earth women. Then he quickly unties my sash and opens my robe to reveal me in all my naked splendor. I am really fucking hot, I gotta say.

Marcus turns around to face his back toward me. "Unzip my Transmigration Suit," he says. Scooting to the edge of the table, I pull the velcro apart to open the collar part of his alien costume. Then I unzip the back that goes all the way down to his buttcrack. He peels the one-piece outfit off and discards it like rubbish on the floor.

"Will I be able to rule over people as your Queen?" I ask as he turns to face me with his alien cock. After wrapping my legs around his waist, I pull his whole body toward me. "Because having subordinates really turns me on," I moan, pressing my forehead against his before we start passionately making out again. Of course, my pink and red Soulmind is dancing in ecstasy around the surface of my skin. The spiral of color is coming out of my solar plexus and I can feel it itching to penetrate Marcus. Not one of the three men in the room can see my Soulmind energy since not even one of them is activated—but one *will* be very soon. I start to stroke Marcus's dick which is starting to get hard and even bigger than it already was flaccid. His tight muscles ripple and it looks like he might have just recently gotten a tan. The dark richness of his skin tone is a good contrast with my milky-pale flesh. Damian walks around us to get a better shot of the action.

As I continue to stroke Marcus into a full erection, I press my cheek against his on the side the camera can't see and I whisper, "Do you consent to having sex with me?"

"What?" he whispers back through the moans he's eliciting.

"I have to hear you say it," I coo seductively.

"Yes," he says, not having any idea what's about to hit him. "I consent to having sex with you."

"Now probe me, you alien stud!" As I say this, I grab the sides of his waist and pull him into me. "Oh my God," I gasp out as I feel his whole length and girth penetrate my eager pussy. Marcus, as the alien, begins to thrust slowly in and out of me as he leans in to kiss my moist lips once again. The pink and red spiral of Soulmind light coming out of my solar plexus is now dancing with ecstatic elation in anticipation of transferring into Marcus to activate his Soulmind.

"My favorite pussy in the galaxy is Earth pussy," he says as he pulls my ass more toward the edge of the table so he can get a better thrust.

"I may be from Earth," I reply breathily, "but when we fuck, I can take you to the Moon." I smile and stare into Marcus's dilated eyes. "We will dance among the stars to reach an orgasmic place where there is no good and evil, where we are one."

As I say these words, I swear tears glisten around Marcus's eyes. "This is why you were always destined to be my Queen. I am King of the galaxy, from my planet Tartarus, and you will be my Queen. This will ensure good relations and love making between our planets."

"Yes!" I gasp, pulling at his waist to make him fuck me harder. "Let me feel the weight and spirit of your entire planet inside me!"

Marcus then looks down at my cute little tits as he makes love to my hungry cunt. His eyes go wide and I know that he is seeing the pink and red spiral spinning toward him out of my solar plexus. Slowly he starts to open his mouth and I put my finger up to my lips—the Sign of Silence. Closing his mouth, he moves his gaze around in wonder, taking in the brilliance of my aura. Then suddenly the spiral of my Soulmind pierces his chest and through his heart like my spear would have if I were here to bring him his death. Tilting his face up toward the ceiling, Marcus moans in exquisite ecstasy as the spiral of my energy laces through his heart chakra and out the point on his back between his shoulder blades. As I watch, the red and pink light that exited through his back is now twisting up and around. A beautiful red lotus made of light blossoms on the top of his head and the spiral of my Soulmind suddenly comes down, slipping through the center of the lotus and into Marcus's crown chakra. Again he gasps and a burst of light shoots out from his third eye—this light is pure crimson. I know that this is the color of his new Soulmind.

I can tell that Marcus is disoriented and doesn't know how to process the subtle energy that he now finds himself seeing. Slipping my hand around the back of his strong neck, I pull his face down closer to my own. *"No Bounce, No Play,"* I whisper into his ear. "Don't forget that."

He gives me the slightest, almost imperceptible nod. Without warning, Marcus pulls out and then flips me over onto my stomach so he has a good view of my ass. Spanking my right asscheek, he says, "You've got that sexy little Earthling ass."

"Uh!" I squeal out as he spanks me again. Looking over my shoulder with lust to see him fuck me from behind, I am struck by the beauty of our light display. Since my Soulmind is pink and red, and his is now crimson, the mixing of our auras almost looks like it's only *my* aura. I am the one encapsulating our passion. I am the one who has sucked him into myself, my pussy like an energy transferring nebula of power.

His hands feel so good squeezing my ass right now as he positions himself to enter me again from behind. I feel the tip of his dick teasing at the edges of my lips and it's an ache for him to be inside me again. When he finally slides himself in, stretching out my tight hole, I see the bright pink and red of my own Soulmind explode around and in front of me. Time for an interstellar orgasm.

"Do you want to feel my alien seed on the sweet meat of your Earthling ass?" he asks as he thrusts into me. The pleasure is almost putting me into a psychosexual trance, threatening to shoot me out into the Astral Plane with the force of an orgasm.

"Oh, fuck... Yes, please! I beg for your seed!" I can barely get the words out because he's literally fucking my brains out. "Oh God, I'm really gonna cum soon! Cum with me, my King!"

"Yes, my Queen!" Marcus agrees. Suddenly with a cry, he pulls out. In the exact moment I feel the wetness of his semen squirt against the soft skin of my ass, I cum too with the most violent tremor. My legs lose control and they start to shake with the immense pleasure. "Ahh ahh ahh!" I squeal so loud and the bright illumination of our Soulminds explodes in a wash of colors, bathing the room in our sexual radiance.

The orgasm swirls quickly through the room and through our bodies and then comes down as both of our Soulminds come back to us, disappearing into the point at the third chakra. I roll over and slide off of the table, pressing my naked, sweaty body against Marcus. "Our sex was your initiation, my Queen," he says, bending down to kiss me. "Welcome to a life of royalty."

"Cut!" David yells and Damian turns off the camera. "That was great, you two. Perfect," he says as he looks at me, winking and giving the okay hand sign.

"That was good?" I ask, still not quite back from that out of body orgasm. "You don't need to get anymore coverage? Different angles?"

David shakes his head as he goes over to the table on the side of room and picks up a towel. "With Damian's handheld shot and the other stationary cameras we have set up here," he points to the cameras on tripods, "I think we're good to go," he continues as he walks back over to me. Damian is breaking down the cameras and Marcus is already changing back into his street clothes. There's no need for changing rooms when you like having sex while other people watch. "Turn around," David says to me.

I turn around and let the director gently wipe the semen off of my ass and back. It feels nice as he does it. When he is done, he tosses the towel toward the table that it came from and then helps me slip back into the silk robe. "Thanks," I say, turning around to look at David. "That was really fun. Maybe next time we can do another installment of the alien thing and do it in zero gravity."

David laughs. "I would love to do that if I had the budget for it." With supreme confidence, he leans into me and kisses me on the lips. "You are pure perfection, Eden. I definitely want to work with you more," he says after the kiss. "Now I have to get this footage down to the editing suite. You and Damian can lock up, yeah?"

"Sure thing," Damian responds as he hands David a duffel bag with all the camera stuff neatly inside. The director throws the bag over his shoulder and heads for the door.

"Till next time," David says, blowing me a kiss as he closes the door behind him.

Damian is still collapsing tripods and breaking down equipment, so I go over to where I laid down my own shoulder bag that I brought a change of clothes in. As I'm changing into my jeans and t-shirt, Marcus comes over to me. He's wearing his normal clothes now, with his backpack slung over his shoulders, but still wearing the blue makeup on his face. "What did you do to me?" he whispers. "Did you slip me something before we started filming?"

"Slip you something? Like what?" I say as I zip up my pants.

"Like acid or something?" he says, straining like he is nervous.

I shake my head. "Welcome to a life of Magick."

"Magick? This is crazy. I didn't ask for this," he says, obviously having a difficult time processing that he is now irrevocably transformed.

I smile and chuckle as I slip my shirt down over my head. "Just remember that if you want to find other people like us, the pass-phrase is *No Bounce, No Play*. That's how you'll find the rest of us out there on the Playground. And you did consent to it, remember?"

"Yeah, but—" he starts, and then all color drains from his face. "I gotta go," he says nervously as he glances over at Damian. Quickly high-tailing it out of there, Damian waves as Marcus all but runs away.

Having finished changing, I put my bag over my shoulder and look expectantly at Damian. "I'm pretty much done," he says. "That was a great shoot, by the way. You are excellent. Acting skills aren't bad either."

"Well, thanks," I say, smiling.

"Hey, I want you to meet our editor before we head out of here," Damian says as we get ready to leave. "The editing suite is just down the hall. That's where David went to drop off the footage. He's probably gone already though, dropped off the cameras to Emmanuel there and then he had some other stuff he had to take care of today."

"Okay, sounds cool," I say as I follow Damian out of the door. He locks it up and I walk close behind him as he leads to the editing suite. When we get there, the door is open and Damian knocks.

"Come in," Emmanuel says. He's sitting there at his editing bay, in front of lots of monitors and control panels that all looked pretty foreign to me. He turns his chair to greet us as we come it. "Oh hey, Damian," he says.

"Hey, bro," Damian replies. "This is Eden who I wanted you to meet," he indicates me and I shake Emmanuel's hand.

"It's nice to meet you, Eden," Emmanuel says politely, "but nobody calls me Emmanuel—except for this guy." He points his thumb at Damian and rolls his eyes. "But that's because we've known each other since Middle School. Everyone else calls me Darkstar."

"Okay, Darkstar," I say. This young man appears to be in his late twenties. And I would definitely describe his facial features as *fierce*. He has platinum blonde hair which he has slicked back with some sort of gel. His face is thin with a very pointy nose. He seems to be about average weight; not particularly thin or heavy. His pants are black cargos and his t-shirt is for some band I've never heard of.

Damian puts his hand on my shoulder and says, "Lana and I also have a studio space in this building. I'm going to pop over there and see how she's doing. You two can get acquainted and I'll be right back."

"Okay," I say as he ducks out of the room and down the hall.

Darkstar rolls up another chair. "Sit down, *Temple of Cosmic Fuck*. I was just editing up another porno, but I have time for a little break."

I laugh as I sit down because obviously he knows who I am too. How many fucking views is my video on Pornhub getting? I haven't even looked at it since I originally uploaded it. "Obviously you've seen the video," I remark.

"Oh, yes," he continues. "It was quite fascinating, I must say. There were quite a few—how should I say?—light anomalies involved. Something involving soul and mind." Darkstar grins at me knowingly.

My eyes go wide. "That must mean—" He nods. "And you must have a—" He nods again and puts his finger up to his lips to indicate silence. "But Lana and Damian, they don't have them," I continue.

"Yes," he agrees. "I try to keep mine somewhat under lock and key. Even to others who may have online Soulminds as well... Nice tattoo," he says after trailing off for a second.

"Huh? What?" I say and then look down at my right arm that's stained black. "Oh, right, my tattoo." Looking back up at Darkstar, I say, "*No Bounce...*"

He gives me a questioningly look and then says, "No *what*?"

Obviously he isn't part of a Playground, or the Playgrounds haven't spread to this area yet. I shake my head. "Nevermind."

"Anyway," he says, changing the subject. "I have something that I think might interest you." He clicks his mouse and a couple keys on a keyboard. "You see, I'm also an animator," Darkstar continues. "I've always been interested in making what I call *spiritual pornography*," he explains. "See, what I can do is animate over the subtle energy that you and I can see on the video, but the unactivated cannot."

"That's brilliant," I comment.

"I know," he returns with a smile. "So I have been using your video as a model. I downloaded it and put it into my animation program where I basically can paint the digital image frame by frame. Normies can then enjoy watching the energy play even if they don't know it's real. Or I can animate it into videos where it wasn't even there in the first place. Here, check out this clip. These two don't have Soulminds."

Darkstar hits the space bar and a video starts playing on his middle monitor. There are a young man and woman naked on a set that's meant to look like a throne room. *If Darkstar only knew the things that went on in my throne room.* When the two start to have sex, the man lights up with a blue aura and the woman lights up with a white aura. Before long, there are the bright lights of the energy swirling around them as they make love. Darkstar even animated the spirals coming out of their chest and the braiding together of it.

"That's so fucking wild!" I say, genuinely impressed with his work. "I think this is genius! And it looks so real! Like those two really have Soulminds!"

"Thank you," Darkstar says modestly. "That appreciation means a lot to me. Especially since your video was in part the inspiration for me to actually start doing this animation. I really like the word genius. Can you say it again?"

"You're a genius," I say, amused by how much he likes it. His eyes close and an orgasmic tingle runs through his body when I call him a genius.

"Oh, that's delicious," he says. "Eden. You're a wild card."

Before I can ask him to clarify what he means, Damian pokes his head back into the editing suite. "Hey, Eden, do you have that beautiful amethyst with you?"

I nod. "Yeah, it's in my bag here." I pat the bag that I have slung over my shoulder.

"You know, Lana likes making custom clothing and costumes," Damian explains. "She wants to make you a special cloak for this party we're going to take you to this weekend."

"Okay," I say, taking the amethyst out of my bag.

"Wow, that is one serious rock," Darkstar comments. "Be careful with that thing. Could be dangerous." He turns back to his monitor and minimizes the video we had been watching.

"Lana wants to make a Celtic brooch for your cloak using the amethyst," Damian continues. "You wanna come? We can hang out in our studio space for a while. Let Emmanuel get back to editing porno."

Darkstar rolls his eyes. "I tell you not to call me that anymore, you nematode," he snaps, trying to sound like he's joking. "But do you listen? No, you have to keep calling me the name of that boy who used to give you charley horses in the schoolyard."

I stand up from the chair and go to start following Damian off to where his and Lana's studio is in the building. Before exiting the editing suite, I turn to Darkstar and say, "It was nice to meet you. Are you going to be at this party too?"

He folds his arms across his chest and leans back in his chair smiling pompously. "Oh yeah, I'll be there," he says as if it was a stupid question to ask, like of course he's gonna be there. "I'm always there. Because I'm the motherfucking Darkstar."

TWELVE

Your gender isn't beauty or ugliness. I mean—that's all your ideas. Gender isn't something you can encapsulate in concrete terms. If you find yourself to be a penis-person, that doesn't make you a man. If you find yourself to be a vagina-person, that doesn't make you a woman. In the days of the new True Time, there are boy-pussies and girl-cocks. This is the most beautiful thing in Creation. However, despite what they may say, the way a person gender-identifies has a lot to do with what they're horny for. And if you want to fuck everything—or *get fucked* by everything—then it may be fun and sexy to see yourself *as everything*. The embodiment of this wisdom is the creation of the Pan within.

The President's Bedroom was full of girlish giggling and laughter. President Elliot Cage was playing dress-up with his wife Imogene, and they seemed to be having a blast doing it. The irony, to be sure, was not lost on them. The President was wearing tan-colored pajamas that were made of silk. The texture of the fabric felt nice against his constructed penis.

"Would I look pretty in this?" President Cage said playfully as he pulled a dress out of the enormous closet. The dress looked like something a First Lady would wear to a ball. The skirt of the dress was long and puffed out at the bottom. The color was dark green and the neckline was low. The President pressed the dress against his body and frilled around the room.

"You look so sexy with that dress," Imogene agreed. She was wearing nothing but black lingerie. The First Lady's abs were tight like a drum and her hips were thin, something that the President found incredibly erotic.

Elliot laid the dress down on the Presidential bed and began stripping off his pajamas. Imogene came closer as her husband slipped his pants down and kicked them off from around his ankles. The President had a cute girly butt that Imogene just found completely adorable and irresistible. Pressing her body against her husband's naked back, Imogene began kissing his shoulders and neck sensually.

"We are Unity," President Cage said poetically. "Whether I am inside you or you are inside of me, we are one collective entity. A powerful force, great enough to be feared, greater than the sum of our parts." As he was waxing philosophical, Imogene had slid her hand down her husband's thin back and between his sexy asscheeks. Now her finger was gently slipping into the orifice located there. The President started to moan as he relaxed his sphincter muscles around his wife's finger.

"I should bend you over and fuck you with a strap-on like the hot slut you are," Imogene said with a smile of lust on her face.

"God, you are so turning me on," the President gasped. His Frankenstein penis was beginning to get hard between his legs as his wife continued to finger his tight asshole. Suddenly he pulled away and turned his body around to face Imogene. He kissed her hard on the lips, sliding his tongue almost far enough into her mouth to taste her tonsils. "Go dress," he said simply.

As the First Lady went over to the closet to put on an outfit, Elliot pulled the green dress over his head. He looked sexy as a pretty woman. With a smile, he watched his wife put on a nice gray suit over her black lingerie. The bagginess of the fit on her small frame was incredibly titillating to the President. Imogene found a costume mustache in the closet as well and stuck it to her face above her upper lip. Keeping the pants of the suit unzipped and open, she found a lovely pink strap-on and harnessed it to her pelvis. Then she buttoned up her pants so that the rubber penis was sticking out of the unzipped fly.

"You know, I like this being President thing," President Cage mused as his lovely cross-dressing wife walked seductively back over to him where he was standing near the bed. "I get to fuck anytime and anything I want," he continued. "I get to drink blood and adrenochrome to boost my youthfulness and occult powers. And we can torture or kill people if we feel so inclined. It's good to be a Satanist."

Imogene smiled. "Yes it is, my love," she said as she grabbed her husband by the bare shoulders and spun him around to face the bed. Then she shoved him down onto it, his face smashing into the soft sheets. Without wasting any time, Imogene pulled up Elliot's dress to expose his cute ass again. "You're gonna take this dick like the whore you are," she said, spitting into her hand and rubbing it along the length of the strap-on. Spreading the President's cheeks to expose the tight puckered hole between, she leaned forward and rammed the dildo into his ass.

The President cried out with both pain and pleasure. "Yes, Daddy," he moaned as the pink rubber penis filled his rectum. "I've been a bad girl, Daddy," the President continued to whimper. "Punish me with that huge cock of yours."

"You like that, little girl?" Imogene said with sadistic lust. "You like taking Daddy's dick in your tight virgin asshole?" She picked up the pace of her thrusting, slamming the strap-on deep into the depths of the President's ass. He continued to moan loudly as he took that thick cock. Squealing and squirming with pleasure, he could feel his little prick getting erect again, dribbles of semen dripping out of the tip.

Suddenly there was a knocking at the door of the Presidential Bedroom. "Cum!" President Cage yelled, smiling to himself. Imogene began to slow down. "Why are you fucking stopping?" he said, looking over his shoulder at the one filling him sexually. "Don't stop! Keep punishing that asshole!" The President ordered.

Imogene was breathing heavily and continued to pound away once her husband ordered her not to stop. The door opened and in walked Harriet Kavanaugh wearing her usual black cloak with the hood up, obscuring her face. "Mister President," Harriet began. The President tilted his head over to look at her and she watched as he literally got the shit fucked out of him. "The boy is here—right outside of Washington, DC. My informants were able to relay his whereabouts to me since somehow he discovered the tracking device that was planted in him and got rid of it."

"Excellent," the President replied. "Uh, uh, uh, oh God, that's good. Fuck that ass just like that..." he trailed off, eyes rolling up in his sockets from the anal ecstasy. "Go get the boy," Elliot continued without opening his eyes. "Get him. And Turn him."

Harriet Kavanaugh bowed low and said, "Yes, Mister President. It is done." With those last words, she left the Presidential Bedroom, closing the door behind her to let the President get fucked deep into the night.

It was already night when Darren and Terry were driving through Washington, DC. Terry was nodding off in the passenger's seat, barely able to hold the blood-soaked shirt up to his ear. The bleeding had almost completely stopped. Darren had picked up a first-aid kit from a Walgreens pharmacy and was now looking for a hotel to crash for the night.

They ended up stopping at Ivy City Hotel, not very far from the border of Maryland. Tomorrow they would start driving north toward Rhode Island. But for tonight, it was important to get rest and bandage up Terry's wound. Darren parked near the office of the hotel and left Terry to snooze in the truck as he went in to get a room. The young woman at the front desk was black and very pretty. She had really long braids that swung when she moved her head. Darren found her really attractive, especially with her thin waist and thick ass.

"Hey, good evening," he said as he approached the desk.

"What can I help you with?" the woman asked. Her name tag specified that her name was Naomi.

"I'd like a room with two twin beds," Darren answered. "Thanks, Naomi."

"No problem," she replied. As she typed in information on her computer, Darren noticed that she had Tarot cards spread out on her desk next to her computer keyboard. It looked like she had been doing a late-night reading for herself. Naomi noticed him studying the cards. "It's the Thoth deck," she informed Darren and then she stared intently at him, studying the space just around his body. "You have a very powerful aura," she commented. "Stronger than anyone I've ever come across. Tell me, what do you know about Aleister Crowley? You do kinda have that look."

Darren leaned in, his elbows on the top of the counter. "Nigga, I'm black," he whispered. "Do you think I care about some old white guy who liked to jerk off in black robes?"

At first Naomi stared at him with a blank look, not knowing if what he said was a joke or not. Then she smiled and laughed. "Right, of course," she chuckled. "But you do obviously know who he is." She winked at him and then clicked a couple times on the computer. "You have a room on the second floor. Two twin beds. How many keys would you like?"

"Let me have two," he said.

"Cool. Two keys... Okay, here you go..." she trailed off, putting more stuff in on the computer and then looked back at Darren. "Cash or card?"

Darren pulled out a wad of cash from his pocket.

When Darren got back to the truck, Terry was waking up. "What's up, bro?" he said sleepily. "We staying at this hotel tonight?"

"Yeah, buddy," Darren answered as they drove to the other side of the parking lot so he could park closer to the room. Yawning as he went, Terry threw his backpack over one shoulder and followed Darren as he led them to their room. After climbing the stairs on the outside of the two-story hotel, they went down the walkway a little ways and Darren used his keycard to let them into the room.

"Well, this is a trip," Terry remarked as he walked into the room and threw his backpack down on one of the beds. One wall of the room was entirely a picture of the head of the Lincoln Memorial statue, and he was wearing a red, white, and blue bowtie. "That's creepy," Terry said, pointing at the picture.

"Yep, that it is," Darren agreed as he put his stuff down on the other bed.

A little while later, Terry emerged from the bathroom after taking a shower. His black hair was still damp and slicked back. He was wearing a fresh t-shirt that didn't have any blood spatter on it. "My ear started bleeding a little again while I was taking a shower," he told Darren. "But I think it's pretty much stopped again."

"Come sit on the bed here and I'll bandage it up," Darren replied as he pulled out the first-aid kit. "Now, I've never really bandaged up an ear before so I don't know exactly what I'm doing, but I'm sure it will be fine," he continued as he took some butterfly bandages out of the kit. After putting some Neosporin on the cut, he used three of the butterfly bandages to wrap around the tip of his ear. After having used those to close the wound, he put a piece of gauze over it, just enough to cover the wound. Then he used medical tape to secure the whole thing to his ear. "That should do it. We'll probably need to change it in a day or so."

"Thanks, Darren," Terry said. He looked exhausted. "I know my behavior can be erratic sometimes and I'm impulsive, and I'm sorry that can sometimes make things more difficult for you. Just, I want you to know I appreciate you—everything you do for me."

"Ah, don't mention it, my man," Darren said, brushing it off like it was no big deal. "You'd do the same for me if the roles were reversed." He patted Terry on the shoulder. "Now get some rest. We have a long drive to Providence tomorrow."

Some time later during the night, Terry awoke feeling paralysis like he had the night the Greys abducted him. As his eyes came open, he could see blue-white light all around his body, but he couldn't move his limbs at all. Darren was breathing softly in his sleep on the other bed. Terry tried to cry out but no sound came from his silenced throat. Suddenly his body began to levitate off of the bed and float toward the window. As he got closer, the same blue-white light was a dot in the center of the window, and then it expanded, making an energetic opening in the wall of the hotel room. Floating through this opening, Terry was taken up and over the railing and then glided down toward the parking lot.

The blue-white energy that had paralyzed him and levitated him was being produced by a massive machine that had been backed into the parking lot on the back of a flatbed truck. This machine was constructed to be the shape of a black cube. A slit on one face had opened and the blue-white light was being produced from this slit in the machine. Standing next to the black cube was Harriet Kavanaugh, obscured by her black cloak. Behind her stood about six or seven other Satanists wearing black robes.

The beam of artificial blue-white light pulled Terry in through the slit on the side of the cube. Once inside, the slit closed up and he was in complete darkness, still fully conscious but paralyzed. Terry could hear commotion from the group of cloaked abductors. It sounded like they were getting into another vehicle—or multiple vehicles. The flatbed truck was then fired up and began pulling away from the parking lot of the Ivy City Hotel.

There was no way for Terry to judge how much time had passed since he'd been imprisoned in the cube. *Would the kidnappings ever end?* he wondered, because he was starting to get tired of it. Suddenly the truck halted and Terry could hear voices again. The slit on the side of the cube opened, the blue-white light illuminated, and he was levitated out into the muggy summer night air. He was in the backyard of a large mansion. The backyard was surrounded by tall fences and the truck and car had come in through a large gate. Harriet Kavanaugh whispered in a huddle to her little band of Satanists. They surrounded Terry in a circle as the blue-white artificial light slowly brought him back down to standing on the ground.

"What the fuck do *you* clowns want?" Terry snapped as they restrained his arms at his sides. "I was already molested a couple days ago by some people who think they're crystals. I bet you guys think that you're living demonic rainbows or something." Without responding to his comments, the Satanists began pulling him toward the mansion. There were some stone steps that led down to an underground section of the house. This was where they took him.

There was a heavy iron door, and Harriet escorted Terry inside as the others stayed out. A tall man in a long black cloak walked over to Harriet and said, "Everything is prepared for you, Mrs. Kavanaugh—I mean, White Serpent. If you need anything, I'll be outside with the others." He gave a little bow and dismissed himself from the room, closing the rusty door behind him. Now it was only Terry and Harriet alone in the room with a third—a little girl no older than nine shackled to a Saint Andrew's cross. She was completely naked, blindfolded, with a ball-gag in her mouth. Terry could see her visibly trembling, sobbing, as tears rolled down her cheeks from under the blindfold. The light in the room was low and creepy. The rest of the room was bare with a concrete floor, and there was a steel table in the corner with an assortment of knives and torture instruments.

"What is this sick shit?" Terry said, disgusted by what he was seeing.

"This is your initiation as the Antichrist," Harriet hissed.

"Why the fuck does everybody keep saying that?" he grumbled in frustration. "Listen, lady, I'm *not* the Antichrist. Like I keep telling everyone, sorry, but you've got the wrong guy. Now that we know this is just a misunderstanding, you can just let me go. Right?" Terry laughed nervously as he felt a bead of sweat roll off his brow.

Harriet ignored his comments and continued by saying, "We are going to use your Soulmind to open a portal to a New World. It will be glorious." As she opened up her arms, her cloak opened as well, revealing that she was naked beneath. Terry swallowed hard as he witnessed Harriet's flabby body; her belly almost sagging so low as to obscure her hairy gray twat.

"I'm going to have to stop you there," he said, putting up a finger. "If you're going to use my Soulmind to open a portal, have you ever thought about what might come through and bite you in the ass?"

"You ever thought about biting into the innocence of an apple?" Harriet asked as she walked over to the table with the knives.

"I'm not quite sure I know exactly what you're referring to," Terry said, feeling anxiety.

"To drink the blood of the innocent—it changes you," she said, as if recalling her best sexual experience. Looking over the knives, she finally picked a dagger that looked almost Arabian. "Tonight is when you drink the blood."

"Uh... I don't think you quite understand," Terry started babbling. "I'm vegan—well, vegetarian—well, I'm moving in that direction. Anyway, what I mean is that I don't really think the idea of drinking the blood—especially the blood of a human— really seems that appetizing." He laughed with nervous energy again.

Harriet walked over to the naked girl, shackled and terrified on the Saint Andrew's cross. Teasing the blade along the inside of the girl's thigh, he said, "The trick is getting the blood when they're at the peak of terror. When they're so consumed with fear that their veins are flooded with delicious adrenaline."

"You know, I don't really *like* killing people," Terry responded in a neutral voice. "I'm really, really trying not to do it anymore especially since I've killed *a lot* of people recently," he continued rambling. "There was that cop, and that group of military guys..."

"I'm not the one who's going to die tonight," Harriet said, supremely confident that she was right. "This little girl is going to die tonight. You're going to fuck her, drink her blood, and then sacrifice her to complete your transformation into the embodied Antichrist!"

"God, lady, you got me so wrong," Terry said, shaking his head. "You really don't know who you're dealing with."

The little girl sobbed behind her blindfold and ball-gag. Then she started to piss, the warm liquid dripping like a stream down her trembling leg. "Ah, look, now you've gone and made her pee herself. That's just mean," Terry commented.

"And now she's going to bleed!" Harriet yelled and cut a gash along the bottom of the girl's left bicep, right above her armpit. As the blood began to gush out, the girl screamed and Harriet put her lips to the wound, drinking deeply.

"Oh look," Terry started. "Now... Now I can't... let you live." He started pacing anxiously, knowing the inevitability of what he needed to do.

"Take your cock out and fuck her little pussy!" Harriet hissed like a reptile, her wicked grin dripping with the girl's blood like juice from a watermelon. "You know you want to," she added.

"I don't think what I want has anything to do with this situation right now," Terry said, his anger rising along with his aura. Suddenly the white flames of light burst around his body, igniting the Soulmind within.

Harriet Kavanaugh's eyes widened. "That's the power I've been waiting for," she cackled. "Get angry! Show that rage, boy!

Even though I don't possess a Soulmind myself, I can see the fire raging around you and within you! The rising of the great beast inside you, the 666, the Antichrist breaking free!"

"Shut your mouth, you sick twisted fuck!" Terry screamed as he threw his arms out in front of him. A burst of electromagnetic force shot from his hands and hit Harriet, carrying her up in the air. She continued to cackle as Terry's Soulmind energy held her suspended in the air, her arms and legs splayed out in an X shape. He squeezed her hand with his energy, causing her to drop the knife. It clattered loudly to the concrete floor.

Harriet tilted her head down to look at Terry, her eyes were wild, her grin crimson, and her laugh maniacal. "It is an honor to be killed by the Antichrist," she whispered. "I exist to serve your vision. *Ave Satanas!*" Flinging his hands up toward Harriet, Terry brought his hands together and then apart like he was miming ripping a piece of paper in half. As he did this, the energetic force holding Harriet in the air tore her limb from limb. Her legs and arms flew off, ripping from their sockets, and smacked wetly against the walls then hit the floor with fans of blood pouring out.

Letting go of the energy that was holding her up, Terry let Harriet's truncated torso fall to the floor. She sputtered through her dying breaths and said, "The dragons... They're coming..." Terry had had enough of her voice, so he squeezed his fist closed in the air. At the same time, Harriet's skull exploded like a crushed grape.

Terry sighed, and as the blood continued to pool and flood the floor, he unshackled the girl from the Saint Andrew's cross. She had fainted and was now unconscious. After taking out the ball gag, and the blindfold off, Terry took her in his arms and carried her to the door. The group of Satanists stared at him as he opened the door and stood there with the bleeding girl cradled in his arms. They looked over his shoulder and saw the dead and mutilated body of their fellow cult member. "Run!" Terry said ominously. They all screamed like little girls and turned to run. With their cloaks flapping, they all sprinted out of the gate that they had driven in through and disappeared into the night.

After finding his way to the street, Terry connected to his Merkabah, began to spin it, and popped the golden sphere out around himself and the girl in his arms. He used his Merkabah like a GPS and let it lead him to the nearest hospital. As he approached the entrance of the Emergency Room, he attempted to with his will call someone out to take the girl from him. A moment later a man wearing scrubs rushed out of the entrance, and without question, took the girl from Terry's arms and rushed her back into the Emergency Room to be taken care of.

In the same moment that Terry turned back toward the hospital parking lot, Darren drove up in his truck, screeching his brakes to a stop. "Terry, thank God I found you," he said as Terry opened the passenger door and hopped in. "I grabbed all our stuff and checked out of the hotel. Let's get the fuck out of here."

"I couldn't agree more," Terry said with a weary smile as they sped off back toward the highway to continue their journey north.

THIRTEEN

Time had been rendered meaningless as Maya sat in meditative trance. She was beginning to slip into what Terry had come to know as the True Time State—the eternal nowness of the present moment. Kendra still sat in front of her in rock pose with her hands folded in her lap, patiently meditating and waiting for Maya to come forth from her own meditation and speak. Letting her eyes flutter open, Kendra noticed that Maya was glancing around at the rest of the group of teenagers sitting silently with their eyes shut.

"Great Mother," Kendra began. "She said you would come."

Maya raised her eyebrows. "Who said I would come, child?"

"Allister," Kendra answered.

"Who is this Allister? A powerful witch?" she glanced around the group of meditators. "Is she here?"

Kendra shook her head. "She isn't here, Great Mother. She is already *Become*. She says that you have the power to enlighten us all."

Maya laughed. "I don't know about that. How do you all know that I even know who *I am* within myself? Maybe I'm not even human."

"That does not matter, Great Mother," Kendra continued. "You don't need to be human in order to help heal this planet. At least, that's what Allister says."

"I don't even know fully what this power is," Maya admitted. "I thought I did before, but now... I'm not so sure."

"You are *immensely* powerful, Great Mother," Kendra replied. "Allister has the ability to see it *all*. I can only see a small part currently, since my Soulmind hasn't been activated. Allister— she is fully realized. But I do have eyes enough to see the great majesty of your aura. It is a brilliant green and stretches as high as these trees." She looked up high into the treetops.

"You can see that?" Maya asked. Kendra nodded, her pupils so dilated that barely any iris could be seen ringing the black. Maya looked up and indeed saw her own green aura stretching all the way to the tops of the trees, undulating. When she brought her face back down to look at Kendra and the group meditating, she also noticed that this green Soulmind energy of hers had also expanded out horizontally, encapsulating the whole group within its embrace.

"Can you not see our potential for awakening?" Kendra asked, craving deeply a lifting of the veil from her eyes.

With deep compassion the likes of which she'd never known in her whole life, Maya gazed out over the congregation of young people looking so desperately for something to believe in—something to give their lives purpose, especially finding themselves newly orphaned, the closest city in ruins, and unexplained and strange events taking place at an accelerated pace. And then Maya saw it—as flickering flames burning about an inch above each of their heads were every color of the rainbow. She knew at once that these flames represented the potential for an awakened Soulmind.

Without knowing really what she was doing, Maya, through an act of pure will, energetically grasped ahold of the coiled Kundalini energy at the base of all of their spines. Forcing this energy up their spines, she traced it directly from the root chakra contacting every other chakra, through the crown, and connected with the flames of potential burning above their heads. In the moment when their Kundalini merged with the flickering flames above their heads, they all sighed with a release of orgasmic energy—activating through a burst of cosmic cum. Their newly awakened Soulminds bursted forth from their slumber and illuminated the newly expanded consciousness of every individual present.

Kendra looked hopefully, with huge pupil puppy-dog eyes, expecting the same. Maya could see a white flame flickering above her head, her potential Soulmind color. Grasping Kendra's Kundalini energetically through her own Soulmind power, Maya pulled the energy up, instantly activating her. With a huge grin on her face and the look in her eyes of euphoric trance, Kendra beheld Maya for the first time how she really was now, basking in the splendor of her fully transformed body and Soulmind.

FOURTEEN

The cloak that Lana made for Eden was gorgeous. It was long with a deep hood, but it was short enough in length that it wouldn't drag on the ground when Eden wore it. The back of the cloak was embroidered with the image of a glorious red dragon, flying out of the earth, mouth in a snarl, ready to release its fire. The brooch holding the cloak together was bronze and very large. The amethyst was housed in the deep well of the brooch, firmly held in place. The bronze of the brooch was also carved intricately with Celtic symbols and runes.

"Holy shit, Lana," Eden exclaimed at seeing her new cloak. "That is so beautiful! I have no words. And the way you incorporated the amethyst is so genius. Thank you!" She hugged her friend and gave her a little kiss on the lips.

Lana already had on her black cloak, but kept her hood down until they made an appearance at the party. "Now you really are Mystery," she said as she helped Eden slip into her new cloak. "The transformation is complete." She smiled, smoothing down the fabric of the cloak and brushing off any dust or stray strings that might be clinging to it. "I think you're really going to be in your element tonight," Lana commented as she squeezed Eden's shoulder.

Damian emerged from the room in the house that he and Lana shared. Although he was wearing his cloak with the hood down too, he already was wearing his mask. This mask only covered the top half of his face and was carved to look like a monkey. Oddly enough, it brought to Eden's mind the image of Hanuman from Hindu mythology. Lana's mask was laying on the coffee table in the living room where they were standing as they finished getting dressed for the party. Her mask covered the whole face and resembled a cat. However, this mask was customized to have two looks—one in light and one in darkness. In the light it looked like a white cat with big black alien-looking eyes, pink inside the ears, and a lightning bolt on the left side of its face. In the dark, the outline of the mask and the ears was a neon pink strip of light; the ears, nose, and mouth were outlined with blue neon strips of light.

Not surprisingly, Eden's mask, which Lana had picked out for her, was a beautiful but fierce pink and red dragon. This mask wasn't exactly a realistic representation, it took some artistic liberties and was a bit abstract, even with feathers to make it more graceful and stunning. "Don't we all look the regal bunch of Satanists?" Damian said as he came to join them.

"Yes, dear," Lana agreed. "We are the most fabulous. How do you like Mystery's look?"

Damian stood there admiring Eden in all her dark glory as she picked up the mask and put it over her face.

"I must be reptilian," Eden said, referring to the mask, "but am I enigmatic enough to be a Mystery?"

"You are more than enigmatic, babe," Lana assured her. "Beyond enigmatic. You are like the Mystery of the Spiralverse as it embraces Her children with love and then spanks us, beating us with the rod to teach us the difficult lessons—as any good Saturn Teacher would."

Eden smiled under her mask, feeling more and more that the name Mystery really did suit her well. "It wasn't an accident that we met, was it?" she asked.

"It's only an accident if you believe it was an accident," Lana replied cryptically. She winked at Eden and then slipped her own mask over her face. Now they were three beasts: the monkey, the cat, and the dragon. "You both ready?" she asked. "I'm pretty sure our ride is out front waiting for us."

Damian and Eden followed Lana as she walked out of the house to meet with the transport to the party. There, waiting at the curb, was a long, black stretch limo. "We're going to the party in a limo?" Eden squealed, almost too excited to contain herself. "Who *are* you guys?"

Lana chuckled as they piled into the back of the limo. "We're just like you, love," she answered. "And we accept you. That's all that really matters."

"Where is this party? The Playboy Mansion?" Eden said, laughing. They were getting closer to their destination and the houses they were driving past just seemed to be getting bigger and bigger.

Lana chuckled at the comment. "It might as well be," she admitted. "We are in the heart of Beverly Hills."

"That totally makes sense now," Eden said, staring out the window as she marveled at the fancy architecture of homes that she would never be able to afford. The only throne she ever occupied was one she stole by force.

"You've never been to Beverly Hills, Mystery?" Damian asked.

Eden shook her head. "Nah, I've only seen it on TV. It's way more impressive in person though."

The limo turned down a more secluded dirt road and they quickly arrived at a high gate which was the entrance to the mansion in which the party was being held. All three quietly got out of the limo and approached the gate. There were two men as gatekeepers. They wore the traditional long black cloak with the hoods up and their faces were covered by plain white theater masks.

"The password if you would, please," one of the men spoke, muffled a little by the mask.

As the limo drove out the way they had come in, Lana spoke up saying, "*Mother was a Lovely Beast.*"

"Very good," the other gatekeeper said. "Now give us the *house password.*" His eyes looked expectantly out through the holes in his mask.

Damian stepped forward and spoke this phrase just then, "*The Khabs is in the Khu, not the Khu in the Khabs.*"

"Excellent, my friends," said the first gatekeeper.

"You have spoken, and now you may enter," said the second gatekeeper.

The great metal gate creaked as it swung open. Eden, Lana, and Damian gave a small bow to the gatekeepers and then proceeded to enter the grounds of the mansion. Walking around the fountain at the front, they made their way to the massive front doors. They were double doors, deep cherry wood, with a carving of a lion head on both. Lana pushed them open and led the other two inside. Everyone was wearing a black cloak, there wasn't one exception. And everyone's face was covered with a mask. Eden felt a certain comfort in hiding her identity—becoming the Mystery. No one knew who she was, no one would judge her, and no one knew of her deeds in The Kingdom. All of this brought a certain level of ease, as if she already belonged to this group.

A shining chandelier hung from the ceiling in the foyer, and Lana led Eden underneath it and down the main hall toward the rest of the house. A large room opened off to the left and Damian disappeared into the crowd there. A group of hooded figures were standing in a circle around the center of the room. In this center was drawn a pentagram in deep crimson. A magician was standing in the center of the pentagram wearing a blue cloak with moons embroidered on its surface. He was surrounded on all sides by naked women wearing different masks.

"What are they doing in there?" Eden whispered to Lana.

"That's one of the Sex Magick rituals we do here. Damian always likes to participate," she added. Grabbing Eden's right hand and led her on. The blackness of her right arm was covered tonight by a long white glove, and underneath the black cloak, she was wearing a white dress. "We can always do Ceremony some other time," Lana continued. "But tonight I have a present for you."

Eden didn't know what the surprise could be, but she could feel the excitement building in her cunt like a typhoon of potential sexual contact. One of the rooms they walked through was a large library with a wooden table in the middle of the room. An orgy was taking place on this table while a group of hooded figures stood around enjoying the show. Eden was starting to feel more and more at home. Almost without realizing it, she found herself stopping to look at the scene. Her eyes fell on quite a beast of a manly specimen—tall with bodybuilder muscles—fucking a petite blonde from behind. She moaned behind her mask of ostrich feathers as he pounded her wet pussy. Eden could feel the arousal and the wetness already starting between her own legs.

"Come on, babe," Lana said, pulling Eden on. "We can be voyeurs later. Right now I'd much rather participate, wouldn't you?"

"Well, since I'm so turned on now, yeah," Eden replied.

Down a small hallway, they found a staircase with red carpeting that led upstairs. Lana took Eden upstairs and to a special discreet room near the end of the hall on the upper floor. After letting them in quietly with a special key, Lana locked the door again once they were inside. It was definitely a sex room. The carpets were red shag and there were mirrors on the ceiling. The bed was the biggest that Eden had ever seen—even bigger than the one she had at The Wild Orchid Palace. This bed was also the shape of a heart, with red sheets. Laying on top of the sheets, against the assortment of fluffy pillows, was a girl no older than thirteen. She wore a half-face mask that looked like a Monarch Butterfly. This girl was thin, blonde, with the budding of small breasts as well as sprigs of pubic hair around her petite vulva. She smiled, her mouth visible under her butterfly mask; she didn't seem to be in any physical or emotional pain.

Eden looked over at Lana questioningly. "This is Kara," she said, answering Eden's unspoken question. The girl caressed her hand down her own body and then between her legs. "Damian and I like to play with her," Lana continued. "She plays with us. We're *regulars*."

"I know how to make you feel really good," Kara said. "Don't worry, I like to play." The girl moaned softly and squeezed her right nipple between her fingers.

"Well, Mystery?" Lana said, peering out at Eden from behind the black eyes of her cat mask.

Eden, with the face of a dragon, took a long deep breath, and then she had sex with her.

PART 19

The Perfect Spirit

*"Magic is the ability to affect change
in conformity to the will."*
- Aleister Crowley

*"Now he has departed this strange world a little ahead of me.
That means nothing. People like us, who believe in physics,
know that the distinction between past, present,
and future is only a stubbornly persistent illusion."*
- Albert Einstein

*"It felt more like magic than magic. As though it could
make everything all right. As if the whole world
had become a different place. But it hadn't...
and all the miracles in here come with a price tag."*
- Naomi Novik, *The Last Graduate*

FIFTEEN

"I'm sure this was already apparent to you, but we are in the midst of a spiritual war that is very real—very real indeed," Darren commented after Terry had filled him in on what had happened after he was kidnapped from their hotel room by Harriet Kavanaugh's group of Satanists.

Terry sighed and stared out the window. The sun was peeking over the horizon as they drove, and there was still a slight chill in the morning air. "Yeah, but it's just magicians fighting other magicians," he said finally, "because they can't fucking agree on how the world should be. That doesn't seem like a good enough reason to be killing each other. What are we fighting for, Darren?"

Darren didn't hesitate in his answer. "*Literally* World War Three," he answered with conviction. "World War Three *is* the War on Consciousness. We're fighting for an awakened humanity. I think that's the highest reason to fight these spiritual battles."

Terry shrugged and fingered the two necklaces around his neck—the cross and the key. "Idealism at its finest," Terry mumbled.

"What?" Darren said, shooting him a glance.

"Oh, nothing," Terry responded, adjusting the backpack between his legs. He felt burned out over the whole ordeal and couldn't see anymore where they were going or their reason for going on and fighting senselessly.

They were on the highway heading northeast toward Providence, Rhode Island. It was still early enough in the morning for there not to be too many cars on the road. Darren kept glancing in his rearview mirror nervously. "I don't want to alarm you," he started.

"What? What is it?" Terry asked, the nervous tension ratcheting up as he craned his neck around to look through the back window.

"There may be someone following us," Darren answered, glancing again in his mirror. "It's a black SUV just like the one I saw when we were by Rob's house."

"Fuck, what should we do?" Terry said, a slight hint of panic in his voice. "I don't want to go back there! I don't want to go back to being locked up and tortured because of my powers. Darren, don't let them take me!"

"I'll do everything I can to not let that happen," Darren assured him. Pressing on the gas pedal a little deeper, he sped up, trying maybe to get some distance between his truck and the black SUV.

Terry had his eyes closed and hands together at his chest like he was praying when Darren glanced over at him. Suddenly Terry popped the golden sphere of light out from his heart to envelop the entire truck. Connecting to the star tetrahedrons of the Merkabah, he began to spin them so fast that they only appeared as a shimmering white light.

"What are you doing, Terry?" Darren snapped, a warning in his voice. Terry didn't reply, he just began to levitate the truck up into the air. "Don't fucking do that! Somebody might see!"

Opening his eyes, Terry softly put the truck back down on the road and Darren continued driving normally, but Terry still maintained the Merkabah Field around the vehicle. "Sorry," he said to Darren. "I figured flying away would be the quickest way to get away from them."

"Yeah, and all the people seeing a car flying through the air probably wouldn't be able to handle that type of truth all at once," Darren remarked. "Okay, that's weird," he said after a pause.

"What?" Terry said, looking out the back window again.

"There was a man leaning out of the passenger window of the SUV back there," Darren continued. "He was wearing like a motorcycle helmet with a completely tinted visor."

"Oh, no," Terry said, his stomach sinking with dread.

"Hmm, you know that guy?" Darren asked, shooting Terry a questioning glance.

"I think I might," Terry answered, still trying to spot the black SUV out the back window and only catching glimpses as the traffic weaved in and out.

The jumpsuit-man then again leaned out of the passenger window of the SUV, this time he was holding a pistol aimed at the back of Darren's truck. As he began to fire, the bullets ricocheted off of the spinning Merkabah like it was a hard surface.

"Fuck me! They're shooting at us!" Darren yelled. Other cars in the flow of traffic began to swerve out of the way of the SUV with the gunman hanging out of the window. This began the beginning of the crashes. One car trying to get out of the line of fire sideswiped the car in the left lane, causing him to spin out and crash hard against the concrete barrier on the side of the highway.

The SUV was gaining on them. "Give me the gun," Terry ordered.

"What?" Darren yelled back, trying to pay attention to the road as he increased his speed to way over the limit.

"Give me the fucking gun!" Terry yelled firmly.

Reluctantly, Darren reached under his seat and produced the Beretta that Terry had recovered from his own van. Without much practice shooting a gun, Terry just leaned out of the window and shot in the general direction of the black SUV in pursuit of them.

"Do you even know how to use that thing?" Darren asked, shooting Terry a glance as he hung his top half out the window.

Without having time to pull his head back in the truck and glare at Darren, Terry opted to yell, "How hard could it be? Just aim and pull the little trigger..." He continued firing wildly. Darren rolled his eyes and kept focus as best he could to drive fast without getting into an accident. After squeezing off another round, the bullet from Terry's Beretta somehow missed the SUV and lodged itself in the front tire of the car following behind. This caused the driver to start swerving erratically on the flat. The wheels cut to the left and then the car flipped, rolling violently toward the side of the highway. There was a great cacophony of honking and squealing of tires as other drivers tried to avoid the chaos and debris building up on the road.

"Shit!" Terry cursed, pulling his body back into the truck. "I wanted to avoid a million-car pile-up," he commented as he popped the empty clip out of the gun.

Darren glanced in his rearview mirror and saw the ensuing mayhem. "This is totally insane," he said. "So much for an inconspicuous getaway and roadtrip..." He grimaced.

"I'm out of bullets," Terry said, sliding the empty magazine back into the grip.

"Did you check your backpack?" Darren asked.

Terry raised his eyebrows but unzipped the backpack at his feet in spite of his skepticism. Sure enough, there were two full magazines sitting on top of the clothes in his backpack. "How did you—?" he started and looked over at Darren.

Darren smiled. "I didn't do anything. Just had a feeling they might have a tendency to materialize there."

Terry didn't have time to question it. After reloading, he angled himself out of the window again. Because of the chain reaction of car crashes and road carnage, the traffic behind Darren's truck was thinning out, their progress permanently slowed or stopped because of the pile-up building. It took all of Darren's flooring the gas pedal to gain on the traffic ahead and try to weave in to lose their pursuer.

The black SUV was gaining on them since there were barely any cars between their two vehicles. They were so close that Terry could see the details of the jumpsuit-man's helmet and the deep inky abyss of its tint. Busting off a couple more shots from his Beretta, Terry aimed as best he cold for the Lieutenant hanging out of the SUV window. He wasn't a very big target, and the Lieutenant dodged the shots all too easily.

As Terry was trying to think of a different strategy, the jump-suit-man returned fire, missing Terry twice and then clipping him in the arm. Red blood started to ooze from the wound. "Ow! Motherfucker!" Terry screamed.

"What? Are you okay?" Darren yelled over the din of the traffic and gunshots.

"Yeah, just grazed," Terry replied, pulling his head back inside the window. "But it hurts like fuck. I don't know how his bullets got through my Merkabah Shield. It must be a frequency technology built into the bullet itself..." he mumbled to himself.

"This is fascinating, Terry," Darren snapped, "but we need to take care of the problem at hand."

"Oh, yeah," Terry said as if awakening from a trance. Suddenly there was a loud *boom* and then a *shatter* as the back windshield exploded after being hit with a bullet from the Lieutenant's special gun. "Fuck this!" he yelled as they both ducked down trying to avoid the shower of glass. Closing his eyes, Terry focused on his Soulmind as his aura illuminated in a warm white glow. The spiral began to emanate from his solar plexus and with pure Magickal will, he popped a sphere of white light out of the spiral and it wrapped itself around the bullet that was in the chamber. In one fluid movement, Terry ducked up and out of the window and aimed the gun at the black SUV that was almost on their bumper now. Squeezing the trigger hard, with more force than natural, the bullet infused with Soulmind exploded from the barrel with a deafening crack, causing Terry's ears to ring like meditation bells. The kickback was enormous and Terry's arm shot up and back as the Magick bullet found its true mark in the engine of the black SUV.

When the bullet pierced the engine of the vehicle, the Soulmind energy detonated with a violent electromagnetic pulse. This caused the engine to explode and then the back end of the vehicle flew up, carrying the car into the air as flames lapped around the front. With a nasty crunch, the top of the SUV collided with the pavement and slid forward as it became more enveloped in flames.

The Lieutenant was still hanging half out of the passenger-side window and his helmet scraped along the highway as he was dragged with the burning car. The side top portion of his skull could be seen through the helmet once the SUV came to a stop. Quickly he pulled the helmet that had saved his life off of his head and chucked it into the street. Blood trickled down the side of his face from the abrasion that had come from his head scraping the asphalt. The Director had been driving the vehicle and he now hung unconscious from seatbelt. The Lieutenant was quickly able to unbuckle him. As the Director's unconscious body fell onto the roof of the upside-down SUV, the Lieutenant pulled him toward the open window.

The jumpsuit-man pulled the Director free of the vehicle just as the flames began to consume the front seat. Frantically trying to get as much distance between them and the burning vehicle, he dragged the Director to a safe spot on the empty highway and shielded his body as the black SUV exploded, shooting geysers of flame high into the sky.

After a few minutes, Darren and Terry blended into the flow of traffic continuing north. Terry decided to leave the Merkabah permanently around the truck even though it was vulnerable to whatever weapons technology that jumpsuit-man had. Sighing heavily as he zipped the gun back inside his backpack, Terry still felt jittery from the chase. Shards of glass crunched under the soles of his shoes. "I'm so tired of having to fight to stay alive and outside of a fucking cell," Terry groused. "I don't know what it is we're doing anymore," he continued mumbling, right leg bouncing up and down hyperactively. "*No Bounce, No Play,* fuckin'—"

"Hey," Darren cut him off and put his hand on Terry's knee. "Calm down. We're alive. I'm gonna get off and pull into a gas station because we need to chill out for a second. At least I know I do."

Terry nodded silently. One imperceptible tear rolled down his cheek as he stared out of the window. "I hope the Playground will be okay without me," he said quietly, almost to himself.

After getting off the highway, Darren pulled the truck up to the pump of the nearest gas station. "I'm going to get some tea or something to drink to calm my nerves," he said to Terry after shutting off the engine. "Do you want anything?"

Terry nodded. "Yeah, get me the same thing. Like a tea." He closed his eyes and leaned his head back against the headrest.

"Cool," Darren said, slamming the door shut and locking it.

When he came back out of the store with the drinks and gas paid for, Darren's phone rang in his pocket. Stopping outside to the right of the entrance, he answered his cell. "Hello?"

"Darren?" the voice at the other end of the phone said. "It's Rob."

"Oh, hey, Rob, how are you doing?" Darren responded. "You should have gotten to Florence by now. Everything's been going well?"

There was a slight pause and then Rob spoke up again. "Yeah, uh, Italy is beautiful. I'm loving it here and the food is amazing. But, uh..."

"Yeah, what is it?" Darren asked, urgency in his voice.

"Well," Rob continued, "I've met up with Paolo and his girl-friend Gabriella and have been staying with them at their flat. Had the first Playground meeting today and there are several Soulmind kids here eager to help and grow."

"So what's the problem?" Darren wanted to know. He eyed Terry as he rested with his eyes closed in the passenger seat of the truck. "Sounds like everything's going well."

"Mostly... yeah," Rob admitted. "But I've been having this dream again—I had this dream a couple times about a year ago, now it's starting up again. And I'm scared, Darren. In this dream I'm being chased by someone with a chainsaw trying to kill me. I'm running across rooftops to try to lose him and he's following me close over these rooftops. What scares me is that the city rooftops I'm running over in this dream look exactly like the roofs of these houses here."

Darren was quiet for a moment, trying to weigh whether this dream was indeed an ill omen or just the product of a teenager's anxious mind. "I'm sure you'll be all right," he comforted Rob. "It's just a nightmare. And besides, Paolo and Gabriella have you protected along with other brothers and sisters of the Body. It's understandable that you're frightened, in a new country and meeting new people, some of whom you're not sure if you should trust. But, Rob, believe me, you're doing important work, and I'm proud of you."

"Thanks, Darren," Rob said weakly. "*No Bounce, No Play*, right?"

"*No Bounce, No Play*," Darren responded with enthusiasm. "Listen, I have to go. I have Terry with me and we're sort of in a time-sensitive situation."

"You have Terry!" Rob said excitedly. "That's great news! The others will be glad to hear that too."

"Talk to you soon, Rob," Darren said, trying to end the conversation.

"Yeah, see ya," Rob replied. Then there was a click and the phone went silent. Darren slid the phone back into his pocket as he went to fill up his gas tank.

"Who was on the phone?" Terry asked when Darren got back in the truck. "Was it Eden?"

Darren shook his head. "Nah, it was Rob."

"Rob?" Terry said, sitting up in his seat. "How is he?"

"He's okay," Darren replied, starting the engine before pulling away from the pump. "He's in Italy right now. When you got kidnapped the first time by the CIA guys in the black SUV, I sent Rob out to different destinations to set up new Playgrounds here in the U.S. and overseas."

"That's crazy," Terry commented, eyes widening. "Rob has some balls to do that traveling by himself. Wait—this was your plan all along, wasn't it? To increase our numbers."

Darren nodded. "Yep. So we have a foothold—representation and Soulmind power everywhere around the globe."

"Smart," Terry remarked, a smile at the corner of his mouth.

SIXTEEN

FROM THE MIND OF JESSICA THORN:

What have I done? This is exactly what I was afraid of—putting someone I care about in danger to the point they lose their life. Huh, I guess I really did care about the somewhat annoying young Elf. I'm kneeling down over Josh-oo'el's body in the grass that is frosted with a thin layer of snow. White puffs of breath come out of my mouth as tears stream down my face and I sniffle as snot starts to drip from my nose. I had retrieved the pack that the Elf had been carrying as well as my own knapsack. They lay in the snow next to me. The Troll's giant body also lays still some distance away.

"Wake up... Wake up, Josh-oo'el," I sob, lowering my forehead down on his chest which had ceased to move up and down with breath. "I'm so sorry..."

"Do not weep, Jessica Thorn," a high sort of chipmunk-like voice breaks through the mists of my sorrow.

Pulling my head up from Josh-oo'el's lifeless chest, I see a group of four little faeries hovering in front of me like a flock of hummingbirds. I don't think hummingbirds travel in flocks, but whatever. These creatures can't be more than four inches tall. I wipe the snot from my face and look at these lovely faeries with a sad smile, wishing I could enjoy their presence and existence in spite of the death in the air. But I can't.

"This is not your fault, Jessica Thorn," another faerie chortles and flies closer to my face. This one appears to be male wearing a little blue tunic and green tights. His wings are a blur at his back. "You must not put this on yourself," he continues in his high voice. "He had the choice to say no to the journey, but he honored Odelliam by agreeing to be your companion. Little Josh-oo'el knew the risks involved with wrangling with the Troll."

"Thanks," I reply, wiping my wet eyes now too. "But I still feel regret," I admit, feeling the pit deep in my stomach.

"You must not question yourself," the faerie with the blue tunic continues. How does he know that I am feeling the doubt creep in again? That I'm questioning whether or not it really is a good idea to travel back to Hollow Dimension to align with Terry again. I would hate to jeopardize whatever it is he is trying to accomplish in this dream of existence. "You must stand firm in your convictions. Stand firm in your power. Do not waver for your strength will be utterly tested once you leave this realm."

"And what? My strength hasn't been being tested already?" I say, wondering how much worse it could possibly get.

"The ordeals are many and not yet known for their are many possible futures," the faerie says cryptically.

"I guess I must surrender to the fact that this is how it's going to be from now on," I concede. "To be honest," I continue, looking down into Josh-oo'el's lifeless face with nothing but compassion now, "I can't always see. I don't have the sight to see so far into the future of where this is going, but the one thing I do know for sure is that my vision is always toward Terry. Always toward Terry..."

"That is your path. Keep going towards him," the blue tunic-ed faerie counsels me. "Deal with your internal resistance before continuing."

"Like, right now?" I ask. The faerie nods in confirmation. Closing my eyes, I take a deep inhale and long exhale, gaining a more meditative mind-state. I can feel the resistance and I can visualize it as a knotted rope constricting my Soulmind. There is the vivid image solidifying to me in my third eye. Trying to will the purple energy of my Soulmind to break the ropes, I only feel like I'm in resistance to the resistance.

"You're resisting the resistance," the faerie says. *How does he do that?*

I huff, not opening my eyes. "Then how am I supposed to defeat the resistance without resisting it or fighting it? Seems paradoxical."

"You can't resist resistance," he answers. "Just relax, don't fight it. Let the ropes fall, don't try to untie them."

Without fully comprehending the faerie's words, I try as best I can to let my intuition guide my internal working. I take another long deep breath, trying to relax even more. Now I'm just observing the resistance, symbolized by the rope, as bright flashes of purple energy shines through the cracks in the knots. *It's okay to feel resistance*, I say silently to myself. *I love you, rope, for trying to protect me from possibilities that might not be so desirable. I surrender to whatever it is that is.*

In that moment, it is okay that the ropes of resistance are constricting my Soulmind. It's a mechanism of myself and is just as valid as anything else. With this thought, I see the ropes loosening around the purple luminescence of my Soulmind. Without fight or force, the ropes drop away and disappear back into the void. Suddenly I feel lighter, as if I had been being squeezed by a Boa Constrictor that just decided to leave me in peace right before strangling me to death. A weight feels like it has been lifted from me too, leaving me with more expansive awareness and the possibility for *more* growth and expansion.

With a contented sigh, I open my eyes and see the tiny smiling faces of the faeries. "Now tell me, Jessica Thorn," blue-tunic faerie says, "what is it you *really* want?"

"I want to see Terry again," I say with confidence, standing up tall resolutely with a renewed sense of certainty as to where I'm headed on this adventure of consciousness.

The four faeries smile, seemingly pleased by my progress. They fly down around Josh-oo'el's body and lift him into the air. "We will help you, Jessica Thorn," the first girl-faerie speaks again. "We will fly Josh-oo'el's body back with you to Odelliam and also relay that we witnessed you defeating the mammoth Troll."

After shoving my knapsack into the top of the larger pack, I throw it over my shoulders and we begin to trek back toward the hill from which the young Elf had been knocked to his death. The faeries fly with the Elf's body close by my side as we go. There is a somber silence that surrounds us like a dark cloud. Shouldn't this feel like a victory? I did kill the giant after all, and now I am going back to the Hollow to find Terry, but the death weighs heavy on my mind. Even though I hadn't known Josh-oo'el for more than a few days, I still feel it is appropriate to grieve.

By nightfall, we've made it about halfway through the journey. I don't bother setting up the tent from in the pack. I choose to sleep open under the trees while the faeries protect us with their charms.

At the fall of evening the next day, we arrive back at the tree villages of the Elves. Odelliam is waiting stoically for us at the bottom of the spiral staircase that leads up the main tree that has the Upper Room at the top. Standing next to the tall Elf is Artemis, smiling as I approach. It is as if a shadow falls over Odelliam's face when he sees Josh-oo'el's body.

"I couldn't save him. I tried," I say, starting to weep. Rushing over to Artemis, I embrace his long furry neck and cry into his mane. "I'm so sorry... So sorry..." Now it really hits me and the sobs come harder, wracking my body, gasps, wailing, and snot running down my face.

"Oh, Jessica, my darling," Artemis says soothingly. "It's okay. You did all that was in your power to do. Just rest in the fact that you aren't able to save everyone."

Unexpectedly the sadness turns to anger momentarily. "Why can't I save everyone, Artemis? I'm supposed to be the Imitation of Christ... I'm the Imitation of..." I can't finish the sentence before I trail off into sobs again, soaking the unicorn's mane in my mucus and tears.

Artemis is silent, letting me release all that I need to. Allowing myself to really feel the grief, it tears through me like a hurricane, leaving me drained but lighter. "Jessica Thorn killed the giant Troll," I hear one of the girl-faeries say to Odelliam.

"Yes, very good," Odelliam responds. "We owe you a great debt, Miss Thorn. And we will make good on our agreement. But first we will have rites for the dead, to put Josh-oo'el to rest, back into the embrace of the forest from which we all come. Then we go north to the coast and set sail, bringing you to where you can travel back through into the Hollow Dimension."

Slowly I pull my sticky face away from Artemis's mane and sniff loudly. "It's in the ocean?" I ask.

"It is indeed in the ocean. And you will have to find great courage within yourself to trust that this ocean vortex will bring you to your destination," Odelliam explains.

"Okay," I say, wiping the last of the tears from my eyes. "I think I'm ready to go home."

"And this is where we must part ways, Jessica," Artemis informs me. I'll miss him dearly.

"You've been a great companion to me, Artemis," I say, planting a kiss on the end of his snout. "I love you." When I hug him on his side and nuzzle into his fur, I can feel his massive heartbeat drumming out a comforting rhythm within the heft of his Magickal form.

"I love you as well, Jessica," he replies, a single equine tear runs down his cheek. "And I will always cherish the time we spent together."

I give him one final squeeze before I let him go. The great unicorn smiles at me, as if silently saying that I've done well. Without another word, he turns and trots off, disappearing once again into the Magick of the forest.

SEVENTEEN

The beauty of New England is spectacular any time of the year, but this is especially true in the Fall. It is so ancient, full of Magick. The trees in their splendor of red and yellow. The deep green of the grass which is ecstatic to feel between bare toes. And don't forget the majesty of older architecture—especially the baroque style of churches and certain houses. On the coast of Rhode Island, the imminent approach of Fall could be felt crisply in the air and from the breeze that came lazily off of the steady waves of the ocean.

The spaceship Tenchi, who's operating systems had been so damaged by the assault from the other ship, the Quantum Shortbus, had inevitably fallen to the Earth on the coast of

New England. Specifically, it ended up sinking into the Atlantic Ocean right next to Colt State Park in Bristol, Rhode Island. The Tenchi's owner and operator, Vespyr, sat on the rocks of the shore with her knees up, arms hugged around them, and her head laying on the fabric of her dress which stretched up and over her legs. She had the most gorgeous curly red hair, so long that it touched the ground while she sat. Her physique was lean and muscular, and when standing, she was actually between seven and eight feet tall. The dark green dress which she wore came down to her ankles, had long sleeves which belled slightly at the end, and sported a patch of a lighter green over her chest in the form of a clover which seemed to shift between having three leaves and having four.

Originally she had been traveling to Venus from her home planet known as Tar when she had been intercepted by the Quantum Shortbus which for some reason felt it necessary to force her to be stranded on Earth instead. What was she to do? Her ship was inoperable and sunk to the bottom of the ocean. She had no way of communicating—except psychically— for some type of rescue from her own planet. However, part of her was too ashamed that she had been defeated by a pint-sized spaceship to even attempt to contact her people for assistance— especially her mother. Oh, her mother. The society on Tar was matriarchal and her mother, Maeve, was the current ruler. This made Vespyr in direct succession to the throne of Tar, which she wasn't really sure she wanted. Yes, there was the masculine by the side of any matriarch for the best use of the feminine and masculine principles, as well as for reproduction, obviously. However, since the beings of Tar were virtually immortal, living for thousands and thousands of years, they reproduced selec- tively and infrequently. This is not to say that they did not enjoy sex as an ecstatic experience of gnosis independent of the reproductive component.

Vespyr, in her despondency, was unaware of how long she had been there stranded on the shore of the Atlantic. And as for the humans who drove through Colt State Park or took walks there, they either didn't notice her at all or they registered her presence for a moment but then never gave her a second thought. Vespyr had a Soulmind which was green like her dress. All Tarans possessed Soulminds, but didn't use that term for it since the phenomenon was ubiquitous between all members of their race.

Releasing a deep sigh, she let her knees drop to a cross-legged position, stretching the fabric of her dress. Closing her eyes, she assumed a meditative posture. The Moon overhead could be seen getting brighter and brighter as day became night. As Vespyr felt the radiance of her own aura and green flickering Soulmind, all thought dissolved away as she attempted to divine what her next move should be.

Feeling as if a presence was approaching her, she opened her eyes slightly into the inky gathering darkness. Through the glaze of meditation, eyes dilated, she saw a movement in the air in front of her like the mirage of water flickering in the heat off of a desert highway. As she stared, not thinking at all, an image of two figures appeared in this flickering hallucinatory vision. One figure was herself, and she was standing next to a young man with shaggy black hair and piercing eyes. The two were holding hands.

"Vespyr," the vision of herself spoke. "I am you in a future to come and am here to communicate with myself."

The meditating Vespyr nodded her head in a self-hypnotic way. "Yes," she said. "I am open to your message." This was very important for Vespyr to solidify the Magickal link between her present self and her potential future self.

"This young man will become of great import to you," the image of Vespyr standing next to Terry continued speaking. "Hark! In two days time, just after sun-fall and the beginning of moon-rise, you will see him"—she indicated Terry—"run past you on the rocks and dive like a dolphin into the sea here."

The meditating Vespyr nodded to show she understood. "Yes, and what is the missive you would then give to me now?"

"You are to wait a few moments—but only a few, no more—then you are to leap yourself into the blue abyss. While submerged, you will retrieve him, bringing him back to shore and reviving his breath. However—and this is the most important part for which the why will be revealed later in turn—you are not to linger by his side at that juncture. You are to flee so that he may then regain consciousness *alone*. Do you discern the import of this task?"

"I do," Vespyr replied from her seat on the rocks, gazing at the vision as if seeing it flicker only on the periphery. "Rest assured, I will complete the task as you have asked with no deviation."

"Brilliant," the vision of her responded back to herself. "Now our missive is complete and our communication is at an end. Farewell!"

Vespyr sat there and watched the vision fade back into the darkness of the night. At the conclusion of this divination, she burst into hysterical laughter which echoed into the New England night and could be heard far away on the Moon.

EIGHTEEN

A gentle breeze coming into the room stirred Rob from his slumber. Slowly opening his eyes, he was a bit disoriented at first, not remembering where he was since the environment he found himself in was so new and unfamiliar. He sat up in the soft bed of the Italian guest room in which the Lucifer Christ couple had been so hospitable with letting him stay. Yawning, he looked over to see where the source of the breeze was coming from. The doors to the balcony up on this second floor were wide open and the curtains were dancing like slow-motion whirling dervishes. Rob couldn't remember whether or not he had left those doors open when he went to sleep, which gave him momentary pause.

The sunlight streamed in, illuminating his face with golden radiance. However, this feeling was fleeting and was soon re-placed by a chill of foreboding in his blue Soulmind. The balcony was open on his right, but suddenly his head jerked to the left and he spotted a small point of yellow energy flickering in the air like a wickless flame. All his muscles tightened as he watched this energy grow until it stretched to about six feet up from the floor. Then it expanded to get wider. Now the yellow flickered only on the edges and it was like looking through a window into another world. Who he saw staring back at him was Arash.

"Arash?" Rob said with a shock. "Where the fuck have you been, bro? Haven't seen you in like—" He shut his mouth, cutting of his stream of dialogue once he saw Arash's yellow Soulmind growing around him violently, and Rob knew that his friend's intentions were not benign.

In a moment of spontaneous instinct, Rob bolted out of bed and straight for the balcony. His blue Soulmind immediately illuminated his aura, assisting him with a burst of strength to jump up onto the railing and then off of it toward the roof of the next house. Behind him, Arash let out a yell and the handle of his chainsaw popped out of the spiral at his solar plexus. Pulling it out, he flourished the weapon through the air and ran in pursuit of his target.

Rob was scared shitless of death. He could feel its pursuit with a cold sweat and wished to his activated Soulmind to save him from Arash's clutches. Would he be sent back into the Gaping Black? That was unknowable, which terrified Rob in a very real existential sense, even though he could not fully comprehend that at the time.

The roofs of the Italian village were slanted and tiled, the color of burnt orange. It was challenging, but with a bit of instinct and luck, Rob ran across them, leaping from one roof to the next hoping to lose his pursuer. A few times his foot slipped, but he was able to quickly pull it back to himself avoiding a slide down and off the roof to inevitably be a pile of shattered bones once on the ground. Rob dared a look back over his shoulder. Goddamn why? Rob groaned to himself, seeing that Arash was not that far behind him and Rob was feeling his strength beginning to wane.

The fight or flight response sometimes seemed to work in inexplicable ways for Rob, making him uncertain whether he should do both—or neither for that matter. Stopping abruptly, he wobbled with his arms out in a cross-shape trying to regain his balance on the inclined surface. A tile slipped out from under his foot and slid down all the way until it shattered on the concrete below. Rob's Soulmind was blazing and ready to assist in anyway that he so willed it. So he pulled his longbow out of his chest and strung a blazing blue arrow, leveling it at Arash who stopped to face him.

"I don't want to hurt you, Arash," Rob said, "but I have a feeling that you've come here to kill me. I don't want to die. And I don't want to kill you either. Wha—"

Before Rob could finish his question, Arash lunged forward and pierced the spinning yellow chainsaw blade through his third chakra and into his physical body. Arash's lips were pressed together tightly and he stared into Rob's wide, unbelieving eyes. His bow dropped from his hand and disappeared back into his Soulmind. Even though Arash didn't say anything, Rob recognized something growing within him—doubt. This Rob could see in his eyes.

"Why, Arash? Why?" Rob whispered as a few tears found there way to flow down his face. Arash's face changed in that second, his jaw relaxing from its clench. There was an almost imperceptible shrug of Arash's shoulders and then he pulled the chainsaw from the wound it had made in Rob's flesh.

Suddenly there was a feeling of release, Rob exhaled, and his blue Soulmind exited his body through the top of his head. Arash looked up and watched it soar and disappear into the sky.

From the surface of the Moon, Anna, as pure Soulmind within her Merkabah, watched the Earth. She had assumed the rough shape of a human being with her yellow Soulmind energy just for the sake of familiarity and walking around in that weird state. When she had chosen to take herself out of her body before being killed, she had floated in her vehicle all the way through the atmosphere, out, and then finally toward the Moon. When she got there, she had recognized that the Black Pyramid's net was a Soul Catcher and thus avoided it.

As Anna walked away from the Pyramid, she felt a presence approaching. Soon, the blazing brilliance of Rob's blue Soulmind came streaming toward the Moon like a projectile. Turning to look back at the Pyramid, Anna saw the beam of white light shoot out of the apex and then stretch out into the energetic net. "Oh, no," she said to herself, knowing that this Soulmind would be caught by the Soul Catcher and forced back to Earth. With a burst of pure inspiration, she extended the golden orb and spinning tetrahedrons of her Merkabah and flew up into space to intercept it.

Catching Rob within her own Merkabah, Anna brought him down safely to the surface of the Moon. Once there, she released him to his own individuality, taking her Merkabah away from him. He wasn't yet aware of what was happening, and Anna could see he would need a little nudge. The blue of Rob's Soulmind hovered there in the air, flickering like a fireplace. Anna didn't possess physical components for human speech in this state, so she would have to improvise. *Assume your form,* she project to it. Rob's Soulmind then assumed a human shape, mirroring her own. *Hey, what's your name?* she asked.

At first this blue light in the shape of a man-beast made no response, for it knew not how. Then there was spontaneous stirring, as if by Magick, of something deep inside being recognized. *My name,* it said. *Well, I... I don't know.* It seemed to be bumbling, for the shock of changing dramatically from one state to another had shook him. *Rob? I think, yeah.*

Anna smiled, for she too had to learn this new thing as well. Although, the assistance of having learned about the Merkabah beforehand helped immensely. Rob didn't seem to have this luxury, which made Anna sympathetic. *Good,* she responded. *You can call me Anna.*

Anna, ha, I love you, Rob said strangely.

As I love you, Rob, Anna returned in kind. *Your uniqueness was in jeopardy of being obliterated. I couldn't let that happen.*

Thank you, I think, Rob said. He didn't know for sure, but it seemed like the right thing to say.

Anna started walking a bit farther from the Pyramid and Rob followed her and where she was looking toward the Earth. *Look closely around the Earth, here, down there or up there,* she said. *Do you see them?*

At first Rob didn't see anything except for the blue planet. *See what?* he asked. Anna didn't answer, so he looked again, trying to discern with different, more mysterious faculties. Then they just sort of popped out—the spaceships of the Greys that were surrounding the Earth. *Holy shit,* Rob exclaimed, *have those always been there?*

I don't know, but they're there now, Anna answered.

Why are they just, you know, waiting there? Rob wanted to know.

It's my guess, Anna replied, *that there is some kind of energetic Seal preventing them from making direct contact on Earth.*

Well, that's good, right? Rob said, expecting an agreement.

Eh, was Anna's comment. *This Seal might be breaking sooner than we think.*

SEPTEMBER & OCTOBER

ONE

Biting her fingernails and staring off into space, Eden sat on the couch at Damian and Lana's place. Every subtle noise or movement of shadow made her dart her eyes and culminated with a feeling of dread seeping through her pours, creating a strange odor of orgasmic terror. In her paranoia, she couldn't contain herself and stood up abruptly, going to the closed door of the couple's bedroom. She knocked timidly.

"Yeah, come in," Damian said from within the room.

Eden slowly opened the door and entered like a meek mouse. She looked at them with her chin slightly tilted down, eyes up toward them. Lana and Damian were sitting next to each other on the bed, naked, reading their respective books. "Hey, can I borrow your cell phone? I need to call a friend."

Lana nodded. "Yeah, sure, dear." She grabbed her cell from the bedside table and tossed it to Eden. "Just put it on the table in the kitchen when you're done."

"Thanks," Eden replied, closing the door quietly as she took the phone with her. Rushing into the bathroom, she locked the door and frantically dialed Darren's number. It rang a few times and then Darren's voice answered.

"Yeah?" he said.

"Darren?" Eden said, unsure she had the right person at first, but then she recognized his calming voice. "It's me."

"Uh-huh, yeah," he replied distractedly. "I'm kind of busy at the moment. Is this really important?"

"Terry's not around you right now is he?" Eden asked, still feeling the terror making her heart pound.

"No, not at the moment. He had to go to the bathroom or something," he answered. "What's wrong? You sound agitated."

"I think I'm gonna go to prison," Eden said in a strained whisper.

"What? That's ridiculous," Darren said in a slow, even tone. "Don't worry so much. You'll be all right."

"No, no, Darren, you don't understand—"

"Let me just interrupt you right there," he said, cutting her off with authority. "Have you been hanging out with any Satanists?" Eden nodded and Darren picked it up psychically. "Okay," he continued. "Don't tell me. Don't tell me *ever*. And I advise you to run. Get the fuck out of there as soon as possible." There was a click and the line went silent.

Eden's eyes widened and she left the bathroom as quickly as she had come in. Throwing the phone down on the kitchen table, she grabbed a new backpack that she had bought. She unzipped it and stuffed her black cloak that Lana had made her inside. No reason throwing away a nice piece of clothing that was gifted to her just because she was frightened. Besides, the amethyst was attached to it and that was a gift from Terry, her beloved. That she never wanted to part with. Zipping up the bag, she threw it over her shoulders and left the apartment like a ghost in the night.

It was close to eleven o'clock and it was super dark outside. Well, super dark for a city, which was kind of a strange mix of light and shadow. Eden walked down the sidewalk toward the end of the block, very uncertain of where she was going. This uncertainty created what she perceived as an existential terror which was currently making her body perspire profusely. Her own stench wafted into her nose, making her high in a way. Periodically, she would forget that she was in possession of a Soulmind, therefore she didn't realize she was using it. Nevertheless, it protected her and guided her intuitively. Even through the sometimes enormous overwhelm of uncertainty, her faith that she was being sort of shown where she needed to go was unshakeable.

Something weird began to come into view for her at the end of the block, illuminated by a street lamp. It was an old-timey VW bus. The side doors were open and there was a couple sitting on the edge. One was a young blonde woman who was thin and very fit. Her hair came down roughly to her shoulders; the roots dark and the ends blonde. Her partner sat next to her smoking a cigarette. This woman was a bit older, Eden's guess at how much was arbitrary. The two lovers sat next to each other in silence and turned to look as Eden approached.

"Ahoy there, matey!" said the older lady as a greeting.

Eden stopped and smiled, this unexpected greeting momentarily knocked her feeling of terror away. "Huh-hey," she stammered. "You two aren't headed out, by chance, are you? I need to get out of here. There's some toxicity I need to distance myself from. If you know what I mean."

The older woman smiled and took an inhale off of her cigarette and looked at her partner knowingly. "As happenstance would have it, we are. I'm Celeste," she said and then pointed to her younger counterpart. "This is Bethany."

"I'm Mystery," Eden responded.

A spontaneous burst of laughter erupted from Bethany and she looked at Eden, extending a fist. "Nice to meet you,

Mystery," Bethany said as Eden bumped her fist against hers. "Ready to Rock?"

"Yes," Eden answered, glad to be leaving Hollywood behind for now.

Celeste stubbed out her cigarette on the sidewalk and then deposited it in a small trash bin behind the passenger seat. "We're headed to Mount Shasta," Celeste informed Eden. "You ever been there?"

Eden shook her head.

"Oh, you're gonna love it," Bethany said confidently. "Let's get on the road. I'm not really that tired. I could drive, honey. Yeah?" She looked over at Celeste.

Celeste shrugged. "Yeah, sure." They leaned in and kissed each other, then Bethany climbed into the driver's seat, ready to rumble.

"Load up," Bethany said to Eden. And Eden obeyed. Hopping into the VW bus, she slid the door closed behind her.

TWO

New England was indeed beautiful, Terry marveled as Darren drove them into the city of Providence. An amazing park with a statue of some dude on a horse was in the middle of the city. Terry gazed out of the window as they drove past. There were many people enjoying walks in the park, nice sits on the benches to talk with friends, and other families having fun during their leisure time in the park.

"Oh, that looks so amazing," Terry said, smiling at the in-between of summer heat and fall chill. The sun was shining and it was the perfect temperature for a walk. "Oh, Darren, can we stop, please?" He folded his hands in front of his mouth and gave his friend the puppy-eyes.

Darren smiled and laughed. "Yeah, sure, why not."

They parked on the curb by a meter and hopped out of the truck. Darren popped a couple quarters into the meter and locked up his vehicle before they embarked on their walk in the park. "It's such a nice day," Terry said, taking a deep inhale of the good-ass prana.

Darren chuckled and playfully nudged Terry on the arm. "Stating the obvious, don't you think?"

"Yeah, I guess," Terry agreed as they strolled past the fence into the park where everyone else were enjoying the day. "But sometimes I like to say that, you know. I don't know. I just think sometimes it can be useful to be reminded to notice the beautiful and pleasant aspects of things."

"Very wise observation," Darren commented.

Terry sort of skipped merrily up to the statue of the guy on the horse raised on the pedestal to read the plaque thereupon. Darren watched over him from a distance as he felt his cell vibrating in his pocket. Pulling it out, he saw that it was Meadow ringing him. "Yeah? Uh-huh?" he said as he answered.

"Darren, I'm sorry," she started, "but I'm afraid I have some distressing news. So do you want the bad news or the bad news first?"

"Pfff," he made a noise blowing air through his teeth and lips. "What, there's no good news?"

"Well, there's always good news," Meadow said. "Yeah, but um..."

"Just tell me," Darren replied, his feeling of momentary bliss from the walk in the park was quickly shattering.

"You're gonna have to let Terry go," she said in a serious tone.

"What? But you sent me on this trip to protect him!"

"I know, I know," Meadow returned. "I'm asking you to please trust me. I know that may be difficult. And I understand that."

"Fine," Darren intoned. "What's the other bad news?"

"Rob is dead."

Darren didn't say anything for a long while. "Are you sure?" he asked finally.

"Yes, I received a call from Paolo and Gabrielle saying that they had recovered his body."

"Well, that's *not* so great," Darren responded, his confidence beginning to waver.

"Shine on, my dear," Meadow said, trying to help him see the silver kind of thread thing around all of this. "I know I don't need to say this but, be careful."

"I will," he confirmed. "Keep me in your prayers, yeah?"

"We always do." Then the line went silent.

Darren felt the heavy weight of this knowledge as he walked back toward the horse statue. He didn't see Terry. Then suddenly, he reappeared from behind it, walking back toward Darren with a smile. Darren smiled back in spite of the doubt he felt. Terry held up the peace-sign and Darren asked, "Hey, what were you doing back there?"

"Oh, just some strange dude wanted to talk to me. I listened respectfully, of course. But I didn't understand any of it. He was like babbling about money, and the one percent, financial backers—whatever *that* is—and I don't even *know* what else!" Terry sounded stimulated by the whole experience. "It was very entertaining."

"Yeah, I'm sure it was."

THREE

In the caverns of Meddia deep below the surface of the Earth, the great dragon Sul gathered his brothers and sisters within a great crystal room where the stalactites shone down from the ceiling and the stalagmites might one day become stalactites. He had gathered them there to make an announcement. The enormous green beast was just one of many magnificent creatures that rimmed the circle of their group. He stared around at the expectant eyes of his peers, and within their ring, all of the Octobers played and purred.

"My fellows," Sul bellowed. "The time is nigh when we will once again fly high. To what heights we can go, I do not know. Since they have descended we have been forced below. But now know what we do not know. Which is this—thus! For what is to come is at last at once! Allamalagula!!"

They all laughed uproariously as the Octobers purred and mewed in their ecstasy.

FOUR

To say that Arash felt torn from the act of destroying Rob was an understatement. In his chambers again, he sat in meditation on his sheepskin rug before his little altar trying to clear his mind of the clutter. Taking a deep inhale, he sighed out of his mouth. As he did so, Leeah entered his room unbidden. Startled, Arash was stirred from his contemplation and turned to see the huge mane of blue hair wasping in through his door. Seeing the fierceness on her face, his eyes widened and he shrunk back in terror.

"W-what is it?" he stammered.

"Stand up," she commanded. Arash stood as she pointed a finger at him. "What did you do, Arash? While I was away. You could have at least contacted me and asked for my advice."

"C-contacted you—how?" he stammered, backing away as she towered over him intimidatingly.

Suddenly her features softened and she relaxed, and it was as if her whole white dress relaxed with her. "Perhaps it was inevitable that this could happen. However, Rob is not to be hurt. Do you understand?" Arash did not understand. So she repeated: "Rob is not to be hurt, is that understood?"

Arash slowly nodded and relaxed his defensive posture as well. "Yes. He is not to be hurt."

"Good, now let's get the fuck on with it," she said as she put her hands on his shoulders and drew him into her breast. Her arms were tight around him, holding him in the most loving embrace he'd ever experienced. He had no word for it. So he began to weep uncontrollably. It was almost as if his sobs were to the point of convulsive. "Yes, get it all out. Shh. Shh." She soothed him by stroking his hair and holding him within the strength of her embrace.

Arash wasn't aware of how long he cried in her arms, but it felt like he was lifting the weight of the world off of his own shoulders and tossing it into the ocean. When the cry was finally culminating, Arash tilted his face up and looked into Leeah's eyes. She smiled and then kissed him softly on the lips. Leading him over to the bed silently, he stood before her and she pulled his white kurti up and off of him gently. Standing before her, his thin figure shivered and his tan skin prickled with gooseflesh. Pulling down the top of her dress, she exposed her breasts. Arash marveled, taking them in his hands. Then, leaning down, he kissed them tenderly, with the most affection he'd ever felt for a counterpart.

Bending down, Arash slid off his white yoga pants, exposing his flaccid penis between his legs. He could feel his body hair standing on end. In turn, Leeah removed the rest of her dress by sliding it down her legs. She had been naked under the dress. Arash was uncertain about the process by which he would transform, but he felt within her, towards him, what he felt for her. And this gave him a sense of protection. So he let go.

Laying down on the bed, Arash allowed Leeah to work her Magick on him. As she sat between his legs, she grasped his penis that was not much more than a stick of chewing gum. He closed his eyes as she touched him. Stroking up and down with care as he became erect. She continued as he became more aroused. She was building him up to it. He bit his lip and furrowed his eyebrows as he tried to force the energy to come under his will.

"Don't do that," she said. "Just relax, breathe."

He relaxed. He breathed. Inhale. Exhale. And slow. Breathing slowly in and out down into his belly or heart, he found that that worked better. She smiled even though his eyes were closed. He began to make sounds, deep from inside, finding he wasn't afraid to just release. She straddled him, guiding him into her. She let out a yell as he entered. He opened his eyes, pupils dilated. She was the same. She *is* the same. And so in kind, he brought his hands up to her breasts, caressing them then sweeping them down her body. She swiveled her hips back and forth gracefully.

He could feel it about to happen. She could feel it about to happen. Then—she evaporated—shining stardust.

Arash opened his eyes, perplexed. "Hmm."

FIVE

Night was gathering in time and space between as Darren drove in silence. His window was rolled all the way down and the cool breeze of the darkness blew his dreadlocks like self-animating tentacles. He couldn't help feeling somewhat heart-broken that Terry would have to momentarily be separated from him. But he had faith that Terry would be all right. Looking over at his companion, he smiled without his eyes. However, Terry was blissfully letting the wind coming through the window blow his hair as well. He was grinning in ignorance and his eyes were closed as he felt the air wash over his face like cooling waters.

"Where are we going, Darren?" Terry asked, turning his head to look across the truck at his friend.

"Oh, just this cute little park I know of," he replied.

"Nice," Terry said.

When they arrived, Darren exited the vehicle. He was very silent. Terry walked around the front of the truck to join him. The night was young, but deeply dark like the ink of an octo-pus. There was silver light of the bright Moon illuminating the choppy waves of the Atlantic below the celestial body. Darren looked out somberly toward the ocean and slipped his hands into his pockets. Terry could tell from his friend's face that he was feeling blue.

"What's wrong?" Terry asked, wondering what had suddenly changed Darren's mood.

Darren shook his head. "Oh, it's nothing. I'm just a little tired, that's all."

Terry didn't buy that and turned to follow his friend's gaze out toward the waves at the edge of the rocky shoreline. They had parked in the small parking lot off of the road that ran parallel to the water. When Terry looked back at Darren's dark eyes, his expression suddenly changed as well to one of frustration and anger. "I know why you're upset," Terry snapped.

"What?" Darren said, shocked by this sudden outburst. Backing up a step, he was uncertain whether Terry might unexpectedly get violent. "I'm not upset with you, man. Chill."

Terry gritted his teeth and glared. "You're just upset I won't fuck you!"

Darren wrinkled up his nose. "Dude, what? I'm not trying to fuck you—you're my friend."

"Everyone wants to fuck me," Terry bit back. "You're just butt-hurt that you're not my type. I'm sure you want to whip it out right here to make me suck it. Perfect time—night, with no one around. Pervert."

"Terry, calm down. You're talking nonsense," Darren said, putting his hands up in a kind of surrendering gesture. "Why I'm sad has nothing to do with sex. And I care about you. I'd never want to do anything to hurt you. I know that you've suffered abuse and manipulation. That's not a trauma I'd want to repeat giving to you. Please believe me."

Shaking his head and ticking his finger, Terry clicked his tongue through his scowl. "You can't pretend you don't want me," he said in a low demonic voice. "What?" he said suddenly and looked up into the sky. "No, you can't control me!" Then Terry leveled his gaze back to Darren. Without even a warning, Terry began to strip off his clothes.

"What are you doing?" Darren asked, raising his voice. "Don't *do* that!"

"*Don't tell me what to do!*" Terry screamed and he pulled his pants off and kicked them aside. Shoes off and every other article of clothing, he stood there naked and shivering. Goosebumps prickled his chilled skin and his penis tried to shrink up for warmth.

Darren shrugged in resignation. He *had* to let Terry do what he was going to do even though it was painful to witness. "Okay," he responded, opening his hand as if releasing Terry into the wild.

Feeling the cold air like needles on his flesh, Terry's eyes opened wide in an expression of horror. "They're trying to terminate my contract," he blabbered.

"Who did what?" Darren asked.

"The Greys," Terry returned. "They're upset that they're implant programming is losing its control over me. Fuck your contracts! You don't control me!" he screamed to the sky, spinning on his bare feet toward the Moon.

A puff of white condensation materialized a few feet from Terry, and Graeson, the Grey alien, appeared from within. Darren's jaw went slack and he all but jumped backwards at seeing the extraterrestrial. This being was taller than both of them, and Darren could feel the fear grip his stomach. "Holy shit! An alien!" Darren squeaked.

"You've become a threat to our agenda, an unpredictability!" Graeson bellowed, pointing down at Terry. "So you will die! Kill yourself!" he commanded and then disappeared again in a puff of white.

"No! No!" Terry whispered in terror, backing away with his hands in front of him.

Darren's mouth hung open in the shape of an *o* and suddenly he had the impulse to try to change the course of events. "Terry, wait!" he yelled, lunging toward his naked friend to try to stop him, but it was too late. Turning back toward the ocean and its waves, Terry bolted, sprinting toward the water.

Sighing, Darren let his hand drop and knew what was to happen was bound to happen. He *had* to have faith, otherwise he would be lost. The vulnerable soles of Terry's feet cut on the rocks as he ran, leaving bloody footprints in his wake. He ran across the street, down onto the rocks of the shore, and then dove head-first into the frigid water of the Atlantic.

Vespyr turned her head at the sound. She was sitting in the same spot on the rocks, almost invisible within a shadow, and saw Terry run past her as he ran and plunged himself into the baptismal waters of the ocean.

SIX

On the deck of the Elven mast ship, Jessica rode on fearlessly with Odelliam by her side. She looked up at his mystic countenance as the sails billowed in the sea wind. She wasn't sure exactly how far they had sailed out since they left the shores of the North. Harkening back to the rites of putting Josh-oo'el to rest in the beauty of the Magick of Mother Nature, she marveled over the simplicity of the ceremony—just giving back to the forest in return for how much it gave them. They had wrapped Josh-oo'el's body in a simple shroud, dug a small grave in a faerie circle within a ring of royal trees, and lowered the body in, covering it with loose dirt. The Elves chanted eulogies and celebrated the young Elf's short life. Nourishing the leaves of the trees that gave them shelter and life was paramount to maintain a balanced flow between Elves and the natural world.

The ocean was precarious at times to navigate—choppy in places and calm in others. Jessica was unsure whether a sudden storm would violently come upon them. As they approached the thinning between worlds where she could portal back to the Hollow Dimension, Jessica prepared herself. What Artemis had mentioned to her about not being able to save everyone had created within her a disconcerted feeling, but in a way the comment was comforting. The unicorn's horn had shimmered with silvery light like the scales of a dragon of wisdom—with eyes opening on every shining scale. As Jessica stood on the deck of the ship, gazing out at the blue, she attempted to focus her meditation on the principle of being unshakeable. Whatever that meant. She wasn't quite sure. But it reminded her of a verse from the Bible about building a house upon the rock and not the crumbling sands.

Suddenly she was pulled from her reverie and saw a towering pillar of light—as if spontaneously appearing from nowhere and from no-thing. This pillar of light stretched up into the clouds from the center of a spiraling vortex of ocean current. It reminded Jessica of one of those tornados she had made in school out of two plastic bottles and water inside them. Afraid that if she dove in that she might be sucked to her death, she looked up at Odelliam who was still by her side. Several other Elves stood on the main deck and one of course was manning the helm.

"Fear not, Jessica Thorn," Odelliam said in a comforting voice, smiling down at Jessica.

"But I *am* afraid," she admitted, feeling her ankles shaking in her boots.

The Elf steering the ship had to maintain a small distance from the edge of the watery spiral vortex as to not have the whole ship be pulled in. Odelliam put his hand on Jessica's shoulder and asked, "Do you love Terry Broswald?"

"Yes, without a doubt in my mind or my heart," Jessica answered without hesitation.

Odelliam smiled again. "Then focus on that love instead of your fear when you travel through the vortex back to your home world."

Swallowing the lump in her throat, Jessica looked out over the seemingly gigantic whirlpool spinning around the white pillar of light. In her mind's eye, projected into the pillar of light, she imagined Terry's smiling face and she thought of how much she wanted to kiss him again—to wrap him in her arms again—to make love to him again.

When Odelliam took his hand from her shoulder and nodded silently, she knew it was time. Awkwardly, she climbed up onto the parapet that came up around the deck of the ship. Turning one last time to look at the High Elf, she mouthed the words "Thank you" and then pitched herself overboard into the water.

Instantly the current took her, spinning her in a circle around the circumference of the vortex and then down and in toward the center where the white light emanated. Jessica could feel herself getting dizzy as she splashed around in the cold water. Sputtering, she felt herself being taken by what she thought was an undertow, which pulled her in the opposite spin from the surface spiral. Then she was almost to the center. The light was so bright it was blinding.

Then, as she held onto the warm feeling of love overwhelming her, she merged at once with the pillar of light.

Sputtering, she found herself in a freezing pool of water that was off of a remote hiking trail on the side of a mountain. "Greetings, friend!" came a voice from in front of her. It was definitely a forest on a mountain, she thought as she took in her new surroundings. There were a smiling couple looking down at her from atop a rock that was a bit above the small lake. "How are you?" the man asked Jessica. "The water is so cold this time of year," he laughed as Jessica shivered and swam toward the edge of the lake below the boulder the couple sat upon. She climbed up over the rocks to join them.

The young woman sitting next to the man extended her hand to Jessica to help her out of the freezing water. "Come here, dear, you're shivering. This lake is from the snowpack runoff up there on Mount Shasta. So cold. Good for hydrotherapy," the woman said, wrapping a blanket around Jessica's shoulders to warm her.

"Thank you," Jessica replied through chattering teeth.

The man and woman hugged her from both sides, helping to warm her up through their shared body heat. "This mountain is so beautiful, isn't it?" the woman said.

"It really is," said Jessica, admiring the elegance of Mother Gaia's wonders.

SEVEN

After seeing the splash which was Terry's naked body plunging into the ocean, Vespyr waited a few moments before going in to save him. Not wanting to get her clothes wet and freezing from the frigid water, she stripped off her dress and laid it down next to where she had been sitting on the rocks. Her gorgeous pale skin shined in the moonlight; her full breasts and slender body looked so perfect she could have easily walked out of a painting of an angelic being. Gracefully she ran to the edge and dove in.

Terry had inhaled the water and was now sinking like a stone toward the bottom of the Atlantic. Kicking her feet in a graceful stroke, Vespyr propelled herself quickly next to Terry and looped her arms around his chest, under his armpits, her breasts pressing against his back. Her red hair was weightless in the water and looked like the red locks of a mermaid. Pulling him with her, Vespyr Tar got Terry back to shore and pulled his body easily from the water.

After laying him down on his back, she kneeled next to him to help expel the water from his lungs. All she had to do was place her hand over his heart, glowing the green of her Soulmind in the palm of her hand, and Terry began to sputter and puke the water out of his mouth like a survivor of a snorkeling accident.

Once she was sure that he was breathing, Vespyr stood up and walked away while Terry's eyes were still closed. Her future self had told her that she must not let the boy see her when he regained consciousness. After pulling her dress back down over her head, hair still dripping her curls to be straight, she walked in long strides up the rocky shore and across the road toward the parking lot.

The shock on Darren's face was priceless as he saw the eight-foot-tall woman with long red hair approaching him. His eyes widened and he stepped back jerkily, not sure whether this being was friendly or malicious. Even though Darren was a tall man, he still felt intimidated as this woman's stature towered over him. However, there was a soft side to her that he noticed at once, so he relaxed.

"Hey," Darren spoke, holding up his hand in greeting as Vespyr stopped in front of him. "Do you speak English?" he wasn't so sure if she did.

"Yes," Vespyr answered. "I speak the language of men."

"Whoa," Darren responded. "Your English is very eloquent. Are you royalty?"

Vespyr nodded. "I am heir to the throne of Tar, my home planet. My name is Vespyr Tar. What be thou moniker?"

"My name? Yeah," he continued. "My name is Darren. Nice to meet you, Vespyr Tar." He raised his arm to shake her hand, but she did not return the gesture.

"Your custom of hand shaking is peculiar," she commented, bowing instead. Darren dropped his hand and returned the bow. "I just saved a boy from drowning," Vespyr continued. "Are you acquainted with this young man?"

Darren nodded. "Yes, he is a friend and a very powerful being."

"I felt his energy," she acknowledged. "In a divined vision I spoke to myself from the future. I saw myself with this boy, we were holding hands. I bid myself to save him and then leave him. Strange, no?"

"Maybe not so strange," Darren answered. "I wasn't sure how he was going to survive. You were meant to be here. But he probably needs medical attention. However, we aren't supposed to interfere directly right now. I should call for an ambulance." He pulled his cell phone out of his pocket and called for an ambulance, giving the location and description of Terry.

"My Tenchi is downed in the bottom of this body of water," Vespyr added once Darren hung up the phone.

"Your Tenchi?" Darren said, raising an eyebrow. "I don't know what that is."

"My starship. My spaceship. My transport; you know what an enormous vehicle for traveling through galaxies is, I presume," she explained.

"Oh, right, your spaceship," Darren said, realizing she was saying her ship was out of commission and sunk off this shore. "Weird that I'd see two aliens in one night," he added.

"You have seen another extraterrestrial non-Earthling to-night?" Vespyr asked.

Nodding, Darren explained by saying, "Yeah, he was tall as well—not as tall as you. His skin was like translucent gray and he had big black eyes."

"That is not benign," she said, looking worried. "That is a Grey. If they are already trying to make contact, then it is only a matter of time..." She trailed off. "Do not trust them, they are full of deceit."

"Good to know," Darren said, making a mental note not to trust the Greys.

"I know you are only a human with limited technology," Vespyr said, coming back to the subject of her ship. "Would there possibly be a galactic outpost on this planet where I could gain equipment to repair my Tenchi?"

Darren thought about this. "North," he said finally. "If you go north up into New York state. There is a place called Montauk Point. Find it and you will have what you are looking for." In the silence that followed, they could hear the siren of the approaching ambulance.

Vespyr looked over her shoulder and because of her tall stature could see Terry laying on the rocks. He had begun to murmur and stir, rocking his body against the ground. The heir to the throne of Tar looked back at Darren and said, "This is when we must part separate ways into the world. It was lovely to meet a being such as yourself. Our paths will again cross."

"And it was an honor to meet such a royal and divine being such as yourself, Vespyr Tar," he returned. They bowed to each other and Vespyr began to levitate into the air, then she was gone, flying off in a northerly direction.

Without hesitation, Darren got back into his truck and pulled out of the parking lot. Speeding down the deserted street and out of Colt State Park, he made sure he wasn't anywhere near when the ambulance arrived to pick up Terry who was now semi-delirious and hypothermic.

BOOK SIX

The Climactic Moment

"But then nights and skies are meaningless/to their unearthly eyes./They are our children:/playing chess on the sunburnt backs/of one-eyed turtles/checkmating a lifetimes/slow crawl to enlighten-ment/cashing in their crown/and glory for magic/and contradiction/the children of fiction/born of semen-filled crosses/thrust in calvary's mound/with memories of mañanas millennium:/the gravity of the pendulum/the inscription of the grail/the rumors of war and famine/diseases and storms of hail./All hail the new beginning!/Behold the winter's end!/Bring on the puppets and dragons!/Let the ceremonies begin!/For they have come to shatter time and bring back the dead newborn,/an army of me./Bearing change in the frontlines and shadows in the field mines,/the wilderness and the lights in the city./I have seen them./A tumultuous army of bastards and beggars, mad-men and idiots,/witches and harlots, dancers and lunatics, sinners and

singers,/losers and lovers, students and teachers, poets and priests./Orbiting the realms of the ordinary through the ordinances of those ordained by the beast."

\- Saul Williams, *Children of the Night*

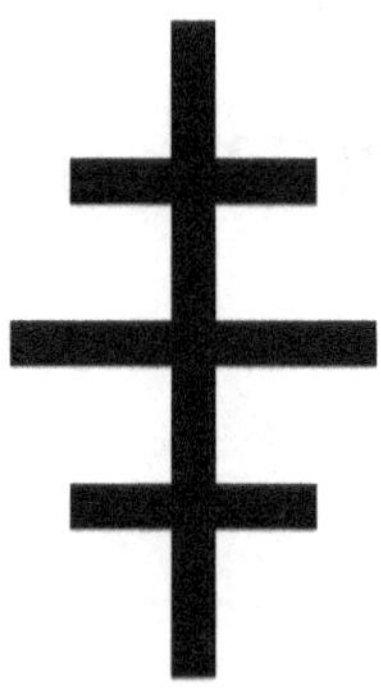

PART 20

Resurgence of Dragons

"A conscious soul in the Inconscient's world,
Hidden behind our thoughts and hopes and dreams,
An indifferent Master signing Nature's acts
Leaves the vicegerent mind a seeming king.
In his floating house upon the sea of Time
The regent sits at work and never rests:
He is a puppet of the dance of Time;
He is driven by the hours, the moment's call
Compels him with the thronging of life's need
And the babel of the voices of the world."

- Sri Aurobindo, *Savitri*, Book VII, Canto II

EIGHT

Moaning in pain with his eyes still shut to the darkness of the night and the Moon shining overhead, Terry squirmed in his nakedness; his skin lacerated upon the rocks. He was struggling to regain consciousness, but he definitely was not all there quite yet. Darren and Vespyr had vacated Colt State Park and now Terry was alone as the ambulance approached blaring its siren.

Suddenly Terry's eyes opened, but his vision was a blur—a wash of grays and blacks. Stumbling to his feet and dripping blood from several cuts and scrapes, he staggered toward the road between the shore and the parking lot. As he neared the paved road, he saw headlights approaching—it was *not* the ambulance. Walking into the street, he stretched his arms out as if begging to be rescued. "Help... Help me..." he mumbled as best he could.

The car approaching slammed on its brakes and honked the horn violently. The passenger door opened with a loud sound, frightening Terry with a chill that shocked his system. A large man got out of the car and approached Terry menacingly, his face in complete shadow. Without any time for Terry to retreat, this man punched him in the jaw and then kicked him in the chest, causing Terry to stumble backwards, trip, and fall sprawled out on the rocks again. He cried out in pain as the man got back in the car and it sped away.

Within moments of the brutal attack, the ambulance arrived. The paramedics wasted no time picking Terry up and getting him on the gurney. They were gentle as they wrapped him in blankets to warm him from the freezing water in which he had been submerged. The paramedics could see the mark from the punch on Terry's chin as well as a boot-print on his chest.

"Poor kid," said one of the male paramedics. "He looks like he's been mugged, beaten, and maybe someone attempted to drown him. Turn the heat up on that blanket," he said to his colleague. "He might have hypothermia."

As they attached monitors and an IV to Terry's arms, the ambulance doors slammed shut and they began rushing him to the hospital. As if in the vision of a foggy dream, Terry saw the face of a beautiful woman with long red hair flowing all around her face like the mane of an Irish lion. She smiled at him from above. He knew that he did not know her, but she felt familiar somehow. Then she spoke saying, "Do not trust those who are Grey." She smiled and then the image of her vanished from his mind. For a moment before falling into dreamless unconsciousness, Terry thought he saw Darren's face as well, smiling in his friendly way.

"He's been through a lot," the male paramedic continued to say. Terry could hear their voices still softly, but all he could see was darkness. "He's still alive, which is what matters. And we can give him the care he needs to come back to his full power. This one is very special..."

Waking up in a hospital bed, Terry rubbed his eyes and then his head. His feet felt like ice cubes, hollow and heavy. Blinking a few times, he breathed deeply then stood up from the bed. Wearing a hospital gown and attached to IVs and monitors, he felt similar to when he woke up in the hospital after his bike accident. Holding his aching head, he ripped the IVs out and pulled off the oxygen reader from his finger. There was the sound of soft breathing from the other side of the curtain which separated him from his roommate. Sweeping the curtain aside which separated the two sides of the hospital room, Terry saw an elderly man laying there as if sleeping. He seemed peaceful enough, though Terry wasn't quite sure.

He approached timidly, not wanting to wake the man if he was in a deep sleep. Touching the man's arm, he suddenly saw a vision of the old man in a desert, barren and windswept. The old man was sitting in the sand, staring in the distance, mostly catatonic. In the close distance was a huge stone ziggurat. Its long stone steps led up to a doorway covered by a purple curtain that flapped in the breeze.

When Terry took his hand away from the man's arm, he was back in the hospital room, the vision gone. Intuitively he knew that this man was suffering from Dementia, and Remius had told Terry that this was one of the Dimensions of the Spiralverse—which meant he could potentially travel there. He didn't know where he was or what hospital he was at in Rhode Island, but something told him that *the way out is through.*

Closing his eyes, Terry touched the old man's forehead lightly between the eyebrows. With his True Will, he summoned the black circle below him and the tentacles came up, wrapping him in the matter relocation pod. It collapsed him, shrinking him down to a speck of black light, and in this vehicle, he zipped through the old man's third eye and into the deserts of his Dementia.

Once Terry's feet touched down onto the sands of Dementia, the Matter-Relocation pod dissolved in a puff of Black Mist. He was standing next to where the old man sat in silence, staring into the distance, mumbling incoherent words. "I do not envy you the Desert of your Madness," Terry remarked as he noticed he was still wearing the hospital gown with his bare ass hanging out. Snapping his fingers once, the hospital gown spun around his body in a blur of blue and white light, transforming into a more appropriate jeans and long-sleeve shirt. "That's better," he said and looked up toward the ziggurat.

He wished that he could help the man, to alleviate the pain of his demented brain, but he knew that wasn't his mission now. So he turned, leaving the man behind as he walked toward the ziggurat's stairs. Terry climbed them all the way to the purple curtain which seemed to be silently inviting him in. If he was to walk through, he knew he would no longer be in the Dimension of Dementia. *I have been avoiding this confrontation all year*, he thought. *But now, as Sul said, I must face my demon once again.* Then he went through the curtain into the interior of the stone structure.

Once inside, he found himself in a strange array of green numbers. This wasn't so odd since Remius had mentioned this. Terry was now in the Fourth Dimension: the so-called Dimension of Reason. It was disorienting being inside the dense green mist of numbers and Japanese characters trailing down and across his vision. Hearing a low growl, he knew Timestrus was here, ready to kill him for taking his most precious parts.

As if parting like a fiberoptic curtain, the green array opened to reveal Timestrus in all his sinister glory. Even though he seemed more haggard and scarred, he was more fully rage. He was pure *reptilian* rage. Terry had made the giant demon into a eunuch and now he wanted revenge for his severed cock and balls. Shrieking, he stretched his wings out to their full span and lunged toward Terry.

As he dodged the attack, Terry's white Soulmind instantly illuminated like a pilot light around his body. The hilt of his machete popped from the spiral at his solar plexus and he pulled it out with flourish and a war-cry. "You can't kill *me*, motherfucker!" he screamed as he lunged for an attack on Timestrus. The demon was in disheveled shape—no eyes and no cock and balls—which gave Terry an advantage, but Timestrus was still formidable even with these limitations. Terry stabbed his machete up toward Timestrus's chest, but the demon flew up into the air, flapping his wings until he was out of range of Terry's weapon.

When the curtains of green numbers and characters had parted to reveal the demon, it cleared a circular space on the stone floor of the ziggurat. The wall of green circled the circumference, but Terry could see clearly within that cleared space within it. As Timestrus descended back down to the ground, Terry could feel the Matter-Relocation Magick click into his Soulmind, giving him mastery over the ability. When Timestrus lunged an attack at him again, Terry instantly summoned the black-tentacle-pod and disappeared himself in a puff of Black Mist and he puffed back in at a different location in the circle where they battled. Timestrus stumbled around, baffled, trying to pinpoint Terry's location.

At this point, Terry was just taunting the black reptilian demon as he popped in and out through the Black Mist in circles around his enemy. Spontaneously, Terry began to cackle with uncontrollable laughter. *What had I been so afraid of?* he thought. *This dickless fuck stands no chance against an advanced magician such as myself... Wait, don't get cocky.*

Terry realized what he was doing was just like a cat playing with its food before killing it. So he decided to be done with it. Appearing through the Black Mist right in front of the bewildered Timestrus, Terry thrust his machete of light up and through the bottom of the demon's chin, piercing all the way through his brain and out the center of the top of his skull. Timestrus shrieked in pain and shock that he had just been killed. Pulling the light-blade from his enemy's skull, green ooze and bile gushed from the enter wound and the exit wound. Terry was splashed in the face with this green blood as he jumped back, away from the reeling Timestrus.

As blood squirted like a geyser from the reptilian's chin and crown chakra, his hands shot up to his jaw to try to stopper the bleeding. It was useless, Timestrus knew his time was up. With one final shriek, the blind and castrated demon fell to the stone floor, his skull smacking with a wet and hollow sound. After a few moments of the green ooze pooling around his head, the whole form of Timestrus began to become transparent and then disappeared completely.

The seal on the Fourth Dimension had been broken, thanks to Terry. As he heaved lungfuls of breath, he let his white aura shrink back to close to his skin and dropped his weapon; it dropped toward the floor and then vanished into his solar plexus spiral with a flourish of white light particles. Simultaneously the whole consciousness of Earth ascended into the Fourth Dimension and then past it into the Fifth Dimension, which was known as the IM. This Terry could feel as a subtle change in pressure. As they all went from the Third, to the Fourth, to the Fifth, he felt the density becoming less and his body becoming lighter.

As all of this shift was happening, the curtains of green numbers and characters fell like discarded Scrabble tiles. What was revealed in the transformation of the location out of the circle of battle in the ziggurat was now a ruined city. Terry stood in the center of this rubble. Several yards in front of him was a sculpture of a golden horse on a pedestal rearing up on its hind legs. On the belly of this golden horse was a circular analog clock. After walking over to this peculiar statue, he studied the clock and saw that it contained no hour hand, minute hand, or even a second hand.

"That's fucking weird," Terry said out loud. "Where in the glorious fuck am I *now*?"

As he looked around at the destroyed buildings encircling the central plaza with the horse, he wondered where to go now. As if as an answer to his question, a carving suddenly appeared in the stone of the horse sculpture's pedestal—an eight-rayed star. Terry raised an eyebrow and there was a rumbling of the stone. A section the size of a door, with the eight-rayed star in the center, slid back into the pedestal and then down into a slot in the ground, revealing a stairway leading down into semi-darkness.

"I'm supposed to go in *there*?" Terry said with a deep swallow. One last time he looked around at the ruined city and didn't see any other viable option for getting out of this realm. So he shrugged. "Guess the only way out is through," he mumbled and then began to descend the stairs into the Underground.

NINE

The caves of Meddia rumbled with excitement and activity. The one that Terry and his friends had entered in Arkansas was only one of several Meddia caves around the globe; each one containing their unique Octobers and dragons, but inextricably linked through the Dreamsphere. But now, since Earth had suddenly been released from Timestrus's seal on the Fourth Dimension and thrust kicking and screaming into the IM, the Fifth Dimension, the dragons and Octobers were again able to survive on the surface of the planet.

In the forest of Arkansas, the opening of that cave of Meddia let out a dragon's roar, and suddenly a swarm of Octobers were released from its depths. Hundreds upon hundreds of Magickal talking cats ran into the forest and out into the world to roam free. Then after them came Sul, bursting with a roar from the mouth of the cave. He ran along the fallen leaves upon the ground; his great green body looked massive between the trees. As he began to flap his wings, he gained lift, bringing his whole heft into the air. In seconds he was overtop of the trees, soaring into the sky as he released a stream of fire from between his fangs.

Then came his fellows, following in suit. One after another, every color and every beautiful shape of dragon-beast came pouring from the open womb of Meddia into the Hollow Dimension once again as they had in the ancient days long past. The resurgence of dragons was a glorious sight to behold as they all took to the sky, finally, after centuries of being confined to the Inner Earth.

Far below the flight of dragons, Remius smiled as he looked up to the heavens in wonder. His comrades swarmed around him, a blur of black fur as they ran. *He did it*, Remius thought with love. *Terry really did it!*

TEN

Meanwhile, in Providence, Rhode Island, at RISD, Rhode Island School of Design, a strange young man sat three rows back in a class who's subject was *Modern Poetry*. The room was small and there weren't may students attending this particular class. The said young man was Benjamin Sanderson; more commonly referred to as Benny. In the desk behind him sat an antagonistic young woman named Kelly Moriarty. Benny was paying close attention to the lesson at hand and taking copious notes.

The teacher was Mr. Malign, a tall black man who wore slacks and a white dress shirt with a tie shaped like Africa. He stood at the whiteboard upon which was written 'Children of the Night.' In his hand was the book in which this poem was written: *The Seventh Octave* by Saul Williams.

Kelly looked down at her notebook paper which was still glaringly blank and white. She began to slowly tear little pieces off of it, crumpled them up, and nonchalantly started throwing them at the back of Benny's head. He flinched each time he felt a little ball of paper hit him, but he didn't turn around. Leaning forward to whisper in his ear, Kelly said, "You're such a faggot. Such a stupid man. I hate men; they should all die."

Mr. Malign was facing the whiteboard, writing a quote from the Saul Williams poem. He spoke without bothering to turn around. "Miss Moriarty," he began scoldingly, "this isn't high school. We don't throw things in my class. Furthermore, I *will not* tolerate any misandry whatsoever. Do I make myself clear?" he asked, turning around to face the class once again.

Kelly pouted her lips and slumped back in her chair with her arms crossed. "Yes, sir..." she grumbled. She was a thin woman with long, straight blonde hair; her features were pretty—almost too pretty—allowing her to somewhat slide through life without much hardship. Benny, on the other hand, didn't bother to keep up with his appearance very much; he hadn't gotten a haircut in a while, and his brown locks were uncombed and greasy. Being nearsighted, he wore black plastic-rimmed glasses with thick lenses.

Satisfied that Kelly had ended her childish game, Mr. Malign smiled as he opened *The Seventh Octave* and began reading out loud 'The Children of the Night.'

Later, Benny was back in his dorm room working on his experiments. The dorm was like a two-bedroom apartment. The common area had a kitchen and a living room with a TV. His roommate Jason had the room on the right and Benny occupied the bedroom on the left. Jason was laying on his bed resting with the door open. Benny's room was simple, with a desk and a twin bed. He was hunched over this desk where he had what appeared to be a chemistry lab setup. There were test tubes, and beakers, and tubes that went through an apparatus which finally came out to an opening where a purple liquid dripped into a beaker.

Benny wore rubber safety goggles over his glasses. As he worked his alchemical concoctions, the poem they had gone over in class recited in his mind. Imagining Mr. Malign's voice, he watched the purple liquid drain into the beaker up to the halfway mark. There was a sudden knock at his open door and he looked up to see Jason standing there. Irritated that he was being interrupted from his Work, Benny said, "Yes?" in an annoyed tone.

"What the *fuck* are you doing in here?" Jason said, wrinkling his nose as he folded his arms and leaned against the door with his shoulder. "It smells like pure Gonzo in here," he continued griping. "No, wait. Maybe if Gonzo had a case of syphilis, that's what it smells like."

Benny just looked at him, trying to telepathically tell Jason that he was an idiot. "I wouldn't expect you to understand what I'm doing," he said dismissively.

Jason scoffed. "I understand that no girl wants to come in here and *fuck me* because of your smelly skanky experiments, Benny. Fucking shit. God."

"Then go to the girls' dorm and play with your vagina," Benny bit back, trying to wave Jason away. But then he just got up and began closing the door on his roommate. "Buh-bye," he said, closing the door in his face.

Jason screamed one last thing before he went back to his room: "I'll report your science-fair-project-magical-voodoo-experimentin' ass, Benny! I will!"

Benny laughed. "Yeah?" he said indignantly. "With all the coke you got up in here? I don't think so! Shove it up your ass!" His voice trailed off and he went to sit back down at his chemistry setup. "Prick..." he mumbled. Picking up the beaker, he sniffed it; his reaction being on par with getting sprayed by a skunk. Then he held the beaker in both hands. Closing his eyes, he uttered these words: "*You are my muse, my spirit. And you've made me rich beyond reason. Because you've spit these colors into my eyes; making my retinas shatter and my pupils dilate; in order to make a larger whole for your soul. My muse. My spirit. My guide. My myself. Because you are me and I am you. And that is a picture of me. Even though it was developed as you, it bears my face. My muse. My spirit. You've made me rich beyond reason; because even though I can't have children, you aid me in giving birth. And for this I thank you.*"

After he recited this spell, Benny swigged the liquid in the beaker like it was a shot of vodka. Coughing violently, he dropped the beaker, causing it to shatter as it hit the floor. Then he fell backwards, his head clipping the corner of his bed, rendering him unconscious.

Benny was now floating in a dark space. Purple and black colors spiraled around him like a sea of paint. His face was tranquil—eyes closed and mouth slightly slack. Slowly, he opened his eyes. Before him was Luce the Goddess of Light. She was age-less yet beautiful; pale of skin and pale of hair. Her long locks blew around her face as if there was a strong wind. The dress she wore was long, flowing, and white which sparkled with blue stones. Stretching her right index finger out, she touched Benny's forehead. "You are here," she said.

Luce spiraled her finger as she pulled it away from Benny's forehead. Violet threads of light leaked from his third eye and connected to the tip of Luce's finger. Momentarily the light transformed into a long purple cylinder about seven inches in height. She grabbed it and held it to the side for the flash of an instant. Then she opened her hand and let the violet light cylinder dissipate into nothingness.

Benny just stared, speechless, in awe of the glory of this Goddess of Light. Luce pointed her right index finger at Benny's chest and said, "Open like a lotus to the sky." This time she spiraled her finger out from his heart, pulling green light. This green light came to hover in a vertical line between them. Luce then touched the center of the line of light and it began to open and become a circle. Benny looked at the Goddess through this circle of green light. "Don't ignore the feminine side," she said simply. Then she reached through the circle and tapped Benny's forehead lightly.

He fell back through space.

ELEVEN

Shivering against her two new friends, Jessica could feel the chill leaving her bones and the warmth returning. They had introduced themselves as Jared and Kara. They both had long, gorgeous dirty blonde hair; Jared's was curly and his partner's was straight all the way down her back. They continued to hug Jessica as her teeth chattered comically. Subtly, her purple aura was pulsing around her. Both Kara and Jared had Soulminds as well and all three instantly recognized this fact.

Kara looked at Jessica with a smile and Jessica returned her gaze, smiling with chattery teeth. "*No Bounce...*" Kara began expectantly.

Jessica frowned. "The what?" she asked.

"I don't think she knows about the Playground," Jared commented.

"What's the Playground?" Jessica asked, curious.

"They're spreading all over the world," Kara continued in awe. "Alliances of young people with newly awakened Soulminds. It fosters solidarity and also facilitates the activation of new Soulminds."

"Whoa, that's radical," Jessica remarked.

"It's been spreading like wildfire," Jared said. "Just recently found its way here to the West Coast. The founder of Playground is a legend. I don't know who's actually met him."

"Some say his dick is thirteen-inches and that he can fly around in his Merkabah all the way to the Moon," Kara continued, wonder in her voice. "His name is Terry Broswald."

Jessica snorted and could not contain her laughter. "Pfff! His di—*penis*—is not thirteen-inches long," she said.

Jared and Kara exchanged a glance. "Wait... You *know* Terry Broswald?" Kara asked, a bit of envy in her voice.

"Oh yeah," Jessica replied nonchalantly, as if knowing him was no big deal. "We are lovers."

"Holy shit!" Jared exclaimed. "Did he activate you?"

"No," Jessica shook her head. "My Soulmind was already online, I just wasn't aware of it at the time we met."

"But you *don't* know about the Playgrounds he set up?" Kara asked. "Where have you been?"

"I've just come through from being in Pangea for a time. A strange Dimension I found myself in after erasing myself from the Hollow Dimension," Jessica answered. "Which is weird now because technically I don't exist in this Dimension anymore. My parents are still here, I assume, but would have no memory of me."

Jared and Kara did not understand that. "Well, now you're part of our Playground. We'll be your new family," Kara said with a big smile as she squeezed Jessica's shoulders in a hug. "The Playground here in Mount Shasta is small, but we're very close and supportive of each other. Before discovering the Playground, we became part of the Sophia Dragon Tribe."

"Sophia Dragon Tribe?" Jessica said. "What's that?"

"We are mentored by the Ascended Masters," Jared answered. "And we commune with these great, beautiful dragons of wisdom. The keycodes were channeled by Kaia Ra in The Sophia Code; this activates your divine genome and Feminine Christ Consciousness."

Jessica's eyes widened. "That's amazing. Sounds like very powerful spiritual technology."

"It is," Kara responded. "I've seen some of these Sophia dragons in the Dreamsphere. There's this one gorgeous one that comes to me—she's silver and every scale contains an eye that watches all around."

Suddenly Jessica turned her face to look up toward the sky. In that moment, she saw a great silver dragon fly above them quickly and then disappear again over the treetops. Each scale sparkled with an open eye. "Did you guys see that?" Jessica said, pointing up.

"Huh? See what?" Jared asked as he and his lover looked to the sky. They had missed its presence. Only Jessica had witnessed the magnificence of the creature.

"Oh, I don't know," Jessica responded with a shrug. "Thought I saw something."

"Hey, you can stay with us for a while if you want," Kara offered. "What is your plan, your mission?"

"I came back to be with Terry," Jessica admitted. "But I don't know where he could be. Have you two heard anything concerning his whereabouts?"

Jared shook his head. "Last rumor we heard was that he had been taken by the government—the CIA!" he said ominously.

Jessica's stomach sank. "Oh, Terry... Oh, my love..." she whispered despondently. "Please be all right, my darling." She threw her hand up suddenly into the air. "I cast a spell of attraction!" she cried out. "To use my Soulmind to call him hither! So mote it be!" She let her hand drop and brought it back into the blanket after casting the enchantment.

"Whoa, that was some improvised Magick," Jared said in awe. "You must be at a high level. We haven't yet gotten to the point where our Magick can manifest spontaneously. Currently we're still working with already-made rituals and spells. But that—that was impressive."

Jessica was silent.

"Come," Kara said after a moment of silence. Standing up, Jared and Jessica followed suit. "Let's get you out of the cold, Jessica, and back to our house."

TWELVE

Back at RISD, two young women were in the embrace of sexual passion. These two women were Kelly and her lover Alice. They were in Kelly's bed in her dorm room with the door closed so they would not be disturbed. Both were fully nude, skin on skin, moaning in their erogenous ecstasy. Alice was a petite young woman of twenty-two. She had short blonde hair and her breasts were tiny, almost flush with her ribcage. Kelly was straddled on top of Alice, fingering her gently as they kissed passionately.

Leaning down to her lover, Kelly bit Alice's bottom lip. Alice moaned and tilted her head back, her eyes rolling up as she lost herself in the psycho-sexual trance. "Suck on my titties," she moaned breathily. Kelly obliged, moving her head down to suck on Alice's erect nipples. She started on one then moved to the other, tracing her warm saliva between the areolae. This drove Alice wild. Licking her tongue down the slim torso, Kelly traced down all the way until she tasted between her lover's legs. Spreading her legs more, Kelly's tongue went to work on Alice's clitoris and then deep inside.

After Kelly worked it for a while, Alice's moans started to increase in volume. They increased in crescendo until she was almost an orgasmic screamer. "Oh my fucking god, Kelly... Uhhh," she moaned. "I'm gonna fucking cum! AHHHHHH!" Alice came violently into Kelly's mouth, squirting her sweet lubricant onto her eager tongue. After the climax, Alice sighed and sunk back into the bed; her sweat outlining her body like a wet aura. Kelly pulled her head up from her girlfriend's crotch, smiled, and wiped her glistening mouth. "Cuddle me, Kelly," Alice said cutely.

As Alice held her arms out for a hug, her face was flushed from their lovemaking. Kelly crawled up her body and kissed her on the lips. After Alice turned over onto her side, she pressed her back against Kelly's body, feeling her breasts against her sweaty skin. Kelly put her arms around her lover and pulled her close. They both closed their eyes in contentment and Kelly kissed Alice's shoulder with infinite tenderness.

Benny laid where he had fallen beside his bed. A little blood dribbled down his scalp and vomit dribbled from his mouth. His roommate Jason was standing over him, frowning. Leaning down, he slapped Benny right in the face. "Wake up, you raving idiot," he said.

Benny slowly opened his eyes. "Muffins... Muffins..." he muttered.

"Dude, you're keeping me awake jabbering about phalluses and vaginas," Jason continued, annoyed by his weird roommate. "Fucking gross, man. Go wipe the cum off your face." Without another word, Jason turned and walked out of Benny's bedroom.

Benny wiped his mouth with the back of his hand and yawned. His eyes blinked wide, not really taking in his surroundings yet like coming out of a deep sleep suddenly. After shaking his head vigorously, he put his hand up to the wound on his skull and his hand came away wet with blood.

Later that school day, Benny was sitting in the college therapist's office. Her name was Dr. Thurman and Benny sat across from her bouncing his leg nervously. It was a small office; with a little desk, a couch, and a leather chair. Benny was sitting on the couch, Dr. Thurman on the leather chair. The therapist was wearing a white dress shirt and a long black skirt. She studied Benny intently. "Why are you here?" she asked.

Benny huffed and looked away. "I think you know why I'm here," he snapped.

"I want you to say it," Dr. Thurman replied.

"Fucking Jason gave you my name," he said, turning back to face the therapist.

"And you came when I called for you."

"Yeah, well, I don't think I need a therapist," was Benny's reply.

"You could have refused to come," Dr. Thurman continued. "No one is forced to see me."

Benjamin Sanderson was silent for a while. Then he slowly leaned forward closer to the Doctor. "Have you ever heard of Magic Muffins?" he asked in all seriousness.

Dr. Thurman just looked at Benny. After he leaned back onto the couch again, Dr. Thurman spoke saying, "And by Magic Muffins I assume you are referring to the female genitalia."

Benny looked puzzled. "Huh?" he said. "No. Hell no. I think I might have discovered the recipe for Magic Muffins."

"And what exactly do these Magic Muffins do?" Dr. Thurman asked.

Slowly, Benny answered. "Once ingested, they speak. Sharing with the chef, or the eater, the meaning of life."

THIRTEEN

The Underground creeped Terry out to say the least. He felt the stone walls as if they were closing in around him like he was trapped in the trash compactor in that one *Star Wars* movie. Chills ran up and down his spine and prickled his skin with goose-flesh as he walked deeper into the tunnel. Since it was fully dark in this Underground, Terry had to use the white light of his aura to illuminate his way through the passages. Walking past several metal cages that seemed to scream of past atrocities, he hugged himself to feel the warmth of his Love against what felt like the yuckiness of the dark and sinister deeds carried out here. A cacophony of noises from the past flooded his ears with the screams of young boys being tortured, brain-wiped, and reprogrammed. Terry began to cry as he felt the pain of the horrific deeds that took place in these tunnels. Pressing his hands up to his ears, he quickened his pace to escape and leave this terrible past behind him.

Passing through another room that contained metal tables and old electrical equipment, he could hear the clanging of things banged on the metal to terrorize the boys into a state of shock—and the screams, the screams were unbearable. Terry continued to weep as he pushed on, praying that he would find the way to the surface soon, or the madness threatened to soon overtake him.

Hoping that something of the natural world would show him the way through this cold, heartless, and malfeasant Underground, he spotted a drawing of an animal on the wall ahead of him. Relief washed over him. The drawing was of a beautiful turtle, and underneath were the words *Turtle Cove* with an arrow pointing the way. "Thank Christ," Terry breathed, the terrifying grip on his heart loosening as he felt himself gettin closer to the surface of the Earth.

Following the way the arrow pointed, he found himself in a huge room filled with abandoned electrical equipment and machines with lots of coils. Some of these contraptions were quite large, about the size of a cottage that someone could live in. Coming down to the floor in the center of the room was a ladder that touched the ground and went up into the room above. Grasping a rung of the ladder, Terry looked up and climbed into what seemed to be a small storage closet or something of the like. The door to the outside was locked and there was no handle on the inside to open it. He kicked this door once but it wouldn't budge.

Suddenly he was determined to break free from this hellish underground, back into the glory of the Moonlight. Cupping his hands around his heart chakra, he produced a shining orb of white light, and with each word he threw out in front of him, he brought his hands out, out, out and then threw his arms out in the shape of a cross saying: "I am the Anti*Christ Christ* Lucifer *Christ!*" At this point the shining white ball of light was as big as his whole torso. He grabbed it and threw it at the door screaming: "By the Spirit of the Risen Christ, I say: *Let Me Go!*" The orb of light struck the door with the backing of Terry's True Will and Love, causing it to rupture and explode off of its hinges, freeing him back to the soft green grass and the light of the Moon that shone over Turtle Cove.

Letting out a sigh of relief, he dropped his hands back down at his sides and stepped out of the storage closet, basking in the silver light of the Moon. The grass he was walking on quickly gave way to a sandy beach where the waves splashed lazily against the shore. As he looked out over the water with a soft gaze, a portal began to open, hovering above the ripples. The edges of this portal was white-blue flickering flames of energy. It grew from a small circle to the size of a doorway. Taking a step forward, Terry put his foot down on the water and found that he didn't sink through it. Placing his other foot next to it, he stood there on the surface of the water, gawking. He had no words for how it felt to walk on water, so in silence he continued toward the portal.

Stepping through this doorway of energy, he found himself on the other side, which seemed to have just turned him back toward the shore he had come from. Shaking his head, he looked up at the Moon for guidance and took a couple more steps on the water toward the shore of Turtle Cove. When Terry looked back down from the Moon, there was a tall figure standing on the shoreline watching him. The figure illuminated and Terry cried out in surprise to see this seemingly giant woman with long red hair. She was gorgeous, yet somehow terrifying.

"We meet at once, again," Vespyr said with a smile as Terry reached the shore. Her expression was warm as she looked down at him, yet Terry just gaped in awe, unable to find words. Vespyr laughed. "Do not be afraid. I have saved your life once over. If I was meant to do you harm, I would have let you drown."

"Y-y-you saved me?" Terry stammered.

"Yes," Vespyr answered. "Which reminds me of what I must do." Grabbing Terry's hand, she levitated them both into the air and floated over to the portal still open above the water. They hovered, hand in hand, and stared through the portal. The image of Vespyr meditating on the shore of Colt State Park appeared on the other side of this portal now. Terry was in shock and could do nothing but watch and listen as Vespyr relayed her message to her past self.

Once the task was done and the portal closed, they flew back through the air to the shore of Turtle Cove. "Holy shit! Holy shit!" Terry sputtered, letting go of Vespyr's hand and dropping to his knees in the sand. "That was you! You saved me! If it wasn't for you, I'd be dead. Thank you... Uh, what's your name?"

"I am Vespyr Tar," she said, smiling with Love beaming from her heart and green Soulmind. "Heir to the throne of Tar," she continued, "and you, my friend, have immense power that you've only begun to grasp. Terry Broswald, you were not meant to perish, for your next journey has hardly begun!"

Terry swallowed as he came back up to standing, staring up into the beautiful face of this eight-foot-tall alien Goddess. "Why do I have a feeling this is going to get even crazier? Vespyr, who am I?"

Vespyr shook her head. "I cannot tell you that. *No one* can tell you that. Only you can know who you truly are, whatever or whomever that may be. However, whereupon you do tread, you spread your Love; and that is your Light which shines like the brightest Star!"

Terry looked up at the Moon again and raised his hand into the silver luminescence. "My Goddess," he spoke, "the One whom fills me with Love to the point of overflowing my Cup; I Love Thee unconditionally!" The tears ran down his face as he closed his eyes, feeling the rapture of this Love radiate from his heart and into his entire aura.

Vespyr gave Terry a moment of silence to integrate the intense power of *Agape* into his Soulmind. When he opened his eyes, he wiped the snot from his nose and laughed. "Now, to further business," Vespyr continued. "My Tenchi—my spaceship —has been plummeted below the ocean and will not fly. Your friend Darren told me I might commandeer the parts to repair my spaceship at a locale named Montauk. Is that this time-space coordinates?"

Terry shrugged. "I have no idea. I've never been here before. There was a sign that implies that this beach is called Turtle Cove, but beyond that—Montauk? I don't know what that is. But!" he said suddenly and enthusiastically. "I came up through this storage closet over there and the room right below contains huge pieces of electrical equipment. Maybe what you're looking for is there. Worth a try, right?"

"What are we waiting for, then?" Vespyr replied, looking in the direction Terry was pointing. "Show me the way. Time may not be of the essence anymore, but that does not give us the excuse to procrastinate." She winked at Terry who gave her a strange look.

"I don't know what to make of you," Terry said as he led the way back toward the entrance to the Underground. "You're a giant woman. Part of me is scared of you and part of me wants to hug you and kiss you."

Vespyr laughed. "I am not giant," she responded. "You are just a short human. On my planet, I am average height."

Terry snorted. "Oh yeah, that makes me feel *a lot* better."

FOURTEEN

The breeze of the Providence morning contained a biting chill. Darren was sitting on the bench in the park watching the early walkers go by with puffs of white breath exhaled from their lungs and then the cold air going back in for another inhale as they exercised. He sighed, keeping Terry in his prayers, but knowing that he would be good and protected. Vespyr, this new unexpected player, he knew, was also full of Love and would help Terry in her own way. What that may entail, he was unsure, but he could feel that she played a vital role in events to come.

Darren was shaken out of his prayer and meditation by his cell phone ringing. It was most likely Meadow; she was his friend who contacted him the most. Picking it up, he said, "Yeah, Meadow?"

"Darren, are you all right?" Meadow asked, compassion in her voice. "You sound... I don't know..."

"It's just heavy on my heart, Meadow," Darren replied. "I have faith and trust, for we are in Christ, but I still feel pain when Terry—or anyone—must face challenging ordeals. You know what I'm saying, Meadow."

"I do," she returned. "Which is why it is difficult for me to ask what I am going to ask of you."

"Here it comes," he said with a sigh.

"Don't do that, Darren," Meadow said. "You know I don't ask you to do these things to hurt you."

"Yes, I know, love," Darren assured her. "What is it?"

"You're still in Providence, right?"

"I haven't gone anywhere in case Terry is still here and needs my assistance."

"Good," Meadow replied. "We need you to stay there a little while longer. And there is one task for you. You know our brother and sister that go by Sunshine and Moonbeam? They live in Pawtucket; the couple."

"Uh-huh."

"Go stay with them while you're there," she continued. "They have a temple space you can use for the Working you will be doing. There are two individuals who have come onto our radar—Benjamin Sanderson and Kelly Moriarty. They are students at RISD."

"Okay, do they have Soulminds?" Darren asked.

"No, they don't," Meadow answered. "However, they are on the edge of Magick and Benjamin has been experimenting with Alchemy—some chemistry and spells. He is communing with Luce the Goddess of Light and has tapped into a method to travel into a realm called MERARI."

"I thought only individuals with Soulminds could travel to other Dimensions," he commented.

"That is what we thought too," she agreed. "However, I feel that since he is evoking the power of Luce, he is using her archetypal force to travel."

"Whoa, okay," Darren said, blinking his eyes wide. "And so..."

"And so," Meadow continued with a sigh. "The Working we need you to do is to awaken *temporarily* their Soulminds so that you can connect them energetically."

"Shit, Meadow," he said, rubbing his forehead. "Is that even possible? Isn't that kind of unethical? I just...ah...I don't know about this one."

"Do you trust me?" Meadow asked.

"Oh, Meadow, you know I trust you and Love you," he answered without hesitation.

"Don't think of it as manipulating their Free Will," she explained. "They have already chosen to take this journey that they've started to its end point—which is part of the larger picture—we are just *assisting*."

"But from the shadows?" Darren said, he was still conflicted. "That doesn't seem right."

"I know this is difficult and I know your compassion is strong," Meadow continued, with understanding and love in her voice. "The Body of Lucifer Christ never forces you to do anything. If you choose to not participate in this Working, we will respect you. If you choose to carry this task out, there will be more information and details for how this can be accomplished once you're with Sunshine and Moonbeam. I Love you, Darren."

"I Love you, Meadow," he said and hung up the phone. Then under his breath he mumbled, "Son of a bitch..."

FIFTEEN

"Benny, did you see this crazy shit?" Jason said from the kitchen of the dorm room.

"Hmm?" Benny grunted from his bedroom. He was sitting in front of his chemistry setup writing down strange formulas on a sheet of notebook paper. The door to his room was open and he glanced out toward Jason who was sitting at the island in the middle of the kitchen looking at his phone.

"Dude," Jason continued, not looking away from his phone screen. "Some *dragon* just crashed into the World Trade Center —you know that weird fucking building that looks like a giant syringe."

Benny's head jerked up away from the mathematics he was deciphering. "What in the illustrious Kraken did you say, Jason? A fucking *dragon*? There aren't any real dragons. What, are we in fucking Middle Earth?"

Jason gestured for Benny to get up and come see the video clip. Benny stood up with a groan and went to look over his roommate's shoulder. Looking down at the clip Jason was playing, Benny could tell that it was a handheld cell phone video, but it was high definition and very good quality. The video seemed to have been filmed from an upper floor of another building in New York. This enormous red dragon could be seen flying erratically toward the World Trade Center, possibly wounded. Suddenly it expelled a burst of fire which consumed the upper half of the building and then the dragon smashed headfirst into the structure, causing the top half of the building to rupture and then fall; debris and rubble raining down toward the street below. The red dragon went all the way through the building, then crashed down into the city on the other side, causing insurmountable devastation. Then the video cut off abruptly.

"Dude, isn't that fucking insane?" Jason said, eyes wide and looking at Benny.

Benny laughed and shook his head. "Fake news is getting *crazy*," he replied. "Obviously that's fake." The confidence in his voice was tinged by just a hint of doubt, but imperceptible to Jason.

Shrugging, Jason went back to swiping through videos on the phone. "I don't know, man. It would be cool if dragons were suddenly real, don't you think?" Benny shrugged and then Jason continued by saying, "I've been watching some news clips and shit on Instagram. Apparently there's a group of protestors gathering outside the Whitehouse too. Like teenagers and young adults."

"That could be fake news also," Benny responded, shrugging it off. "Don't believe everything you see on the internet. You know what, I'm really not interested in all that fake news anyway. I'm working on something that really demands my full attention." He glanced out the window; it was fully dark outside. "What time is it anyway?"

"Mmm-mm," Jason mumbled, eyes glued to the phone. "Like three in the morning."

"Shit, really? I lost track of time," Benny said, looking around and then grabbing his coat from the back of one of the island chairs. "I'm gonna go take a walk."

"Suit yourself, bro," Jason said dismissively. "Go be weird somewhere else..."

Without wanting to dignify that comment with a response, Benny left the dorm room to take a walk around campus in the cool morning air. After walking halfway down a sidewalk in the middle of two grassy fields on the campus, he stopped and sat down on the bench that was there. The sounds of the night filled his senses with delight, and thereupon he pulled a small notebook from his pocket and began to scribe within.

Out of nowhere, Kelly appeared and swooped around Benny like a bird of prey. Her eyes were vicious as she sat down beside him. "Hey, fag," she said with a sneer.

Benny pulled his head up slowly to look at her. Staring with a neutral expression, he didn't give a response to her nasty greeting. Then he dropped his head back down to his notebook and continued to write. Kelly continued to taunt him by saying, "What are you writing? Getting all of your teenage angst out on paper? How precious." She stuck her tongue out at him.

Looking up irritated, Benny said, "What do you want? We're not friends."

"Oh, so harsh. You're such a little boy," Kelly spat back. She began to pet his hair like he was a dog or a small child. "What are you writing?" she asked again.

"A poem," Benny answered without looking up. "It's called *My Mother*."

Kelly contemplated this, pretending to be pensive by putting a finger up to her chin. "Do you have a good relationship with your mother?" she asked.

"She's dead," he answered, deadpan.

"Metaphorically or literally?"

Benny looked at Kelly like she was stupid. "Metaphorically is literally..." he said sarcastically. "Of course fucking literally!"

"Okay, jeez, I'm sorry," she said, not really sorry.

"She died when I was three..." he whispered softly.

Kelly suddenly put her hand on Benny's thigh and slowly began to caress it. "I just got laid," she said with a wicked smile, taunting him again.

Benny, dumbfounded, responded by saying, "What? Wow! We're fuckin' talking about my mother and you—Nevermind, fuckin' forget it." At that he stood up and turned to face Kelly. "Why are you even talking to me? I thought I was a fag to you."

"So am I..." Kelly replied; the only truthsome statement she had made all night. Benny shook his head and turned to walk away. She yelled to stop him: "Benny!" He stopped but didn't look back. After which she quoted from *Children of the Night* by Saul Williams: *"What will become of me? Children of the night. Only some will star the sky."*

Benny walked away.

Benny barged back into his room, visibly agitated. Throwing his notebook on his bed, he whirled around to face his chemistry set. His eyes got big and he breathed very deeply, pressing both hands against his forehead, covering his eyes. Then suddenly he yelled out and swept his hand through his chemistry setup, shattering and scattering glass throughout the room. As the glass shards hit the floor, the floor started to crack and cave in. Pieces of the floor began to fall into the black abyss below. Benny plummeted as the cavernous floor swallowed the room.

He found himself then in completely black space, but still aware of himself. A voice came to him from the divine darkness —it was Luce the Goddess of Light. "Do you honestly think you have nothing to give?" she said.

"It just seems to melt away and I transform into a tongue-tied poet with nothing to say," he replied and then took a breath. "I add nothing to the world."

"You add yourself," Luce pronounced with authority. In that flash of an instant, blinding white light illuminated Benny. His arm covered his face to shield himself from the light. The Goddess continued speaking. "I know you are not afraid of the darkness. But you must also not be afraid of the light!"

Benny slowly pulled his arm down from in front of his face. He was still blasted with light, but he faced it. Suddenly what became revealed were two figures standing on a black lake: Benny and Kelly, facing each other. The white light was coming from her body; all else was blackness. The vast water below them looked black as pitch except for small ripples around their feet. Kelly then approached Benny, presenting her hands to him palms up.

Benny raised his right index finger which was glowing orange like a fire poker. Then he pressed the finger into Kelly's palm, slowly burning a spiral into her hand as if he was branding her with his mark. After he was done, a giant white sheet swooped around Kelly, pulling her away as the light created a channel—a current—between them. As the white light shot out of the sheet, it speared itself through Benny's chest and into his heart. Now *he* was the source of the light.

Kelly was gone now and Benny fell back into the water. He was pulled down through the surface and found himself swimming in the Expanse. Too quickly he was running out of air, so he decided to go back up to the surface for a breath. But as he was trying to break through, he found that there was a wall above him, trapping him beneath the liquid. He couldn't escape the water. Trying to break the barrier with his fist, he struck it repeatedly. On the eighth hit, the barrier shattered and he shot up out of the water.

Benny's hand poked out of the middle of his bed as if it was a small pool and he was breaking the surface. Water swirled around over his white covers. His head popped out of the water and he pulled himself to the wooden bar on the side of his bed. Coughing and sputtering, he puked water onto the floor. Finally he pulled himself completely free of the water-bed and laid on top of the covers, soaking wet. Panting heavily, Benny turned over onto his side and faced the wall.

In the morning, Benny was awakened by a pounding on his bedroom door. He snorted and was jerked out of his slumber. "Benny, wake the fuck up!" Kelly screamed from the other side of the door. Benny's eyes opened and he rolled over. Staring at his desk, he blinked the sleep out of his eyes, not believing at first what he was seeing. His chemistry set was not broken, it was still intact and on his desk. He and his bed were dry.

As Kelly continued to pound on the door, Benny got up to unlock it with a groan. As soon as he did, she barged into the room like she owned the place. The anger on her face made her whole countenance a wash of redness. She held her hands out to Benny. "What the fuck is this?" she shrieked.

He looked down at her palms. There appeared to be brands on both her left and her right. On the right palm was a spiral. On the left palm was what looked like the outline of a muffin. Benny put his hand over his mouth to stifle a laugh, but it came out anyway.

"You think this is funny, asshole?" she screamed like a possessed demon, getting all up in his face. "What the fuck did you do?" she demanded.

Benny shook his head slowly and shrugged. "Shiiiiiiit..." he intoned.

Then Kelly slapped him in the face.

SIXTEEN

The VW bus ride to Mount Shasta was quiet for the most part. Eden stared out of the window feeling melancholy as Celeste snoozed and Bethany drove listening to some Hip Hop music playing on a low volume. Eden sighed heavily and rested her chin on her hand.

"You seem to have something heavy weighing on your Soul there, Mystery," Bethany commented, glancing in the rearview mirror to catch a glimpse of Eden.

"Mmm," Eden grunted. "I'm okay—I'll be okay," she said quickly. "You know how sometimes you just need to get away from certain energies for fear that they might consume or subsume you?"

Bethany nodded knowingly. "Yes, I know that feeling very well," she answered truthfully. "I almost became absorbed in the agenda of the Greys—also known as Zetas; alien beings who sometimes appear benign, but have a sinister agenda lurking below the surface. Fortunately, the Guardian Alliance had my protection in mind and I learned how to activate my Maharic Seal. Zetas can't harm or use anyone who is protected by their Maharic Seal and the Guardian Alliance."

Eden didn't really understand what Bethany was talking about. She had never encountered the world of aliens and UFOs as such, or deeply like that. Eden shrugged. "Protection is always important," she said softly, staring out the window again with sad eyes. "I haven't always been the best at protecting myself. I've allowed a lot of things to be done to me that I shouldn't have—should've been stronger. And at the back of it, sometimes I was even unable to protect myself from myself..." Eden trailed off. "Maybe I should learn this Maharic Seal ability."

"It most likely would be very beneficial for your journeys to come," Bethany replied.

It was still night and darkness sprawled out along their route with only splashes of light from street lamps to light their way. They were almost to downtown Mount Shasta, but Eden didn't know since she'd never been there before. Celeste began to wake up from her nap as Bethany pulled into the middle of town. The sidewalks were deserted and the shops were dark and empty.

"Well, this is where we part ways, Mystery," Bethany said as she parked along the edge of the sidewalk.

"You're just going to leave me here alone?" Eden croaked, swallowing hard.

"You'll be okay," Bethany responded, twisting around in her seat to look at Eden. "Besides, we have other business to attend to that doesn't involve you—no offense. Don't worry, Mystery, there are quite a few from our tribe here. If you're ever lost, just find the Playground." She smiled with a twinkle in her eye. "*No Bounce, No Play*, right?"

Eden coughed a laugh. "Yeah, hah, *No Bounce, No Play*," she replied in kind.

Celeste slid the side door open and invited Eden to exit the vehicle. Eden did, stepping onto the sidewalk on the side of the VW bus after grabbing her bag. She turned and looked back at her two companions who had been gracious enough to give her a ride. "We Love you, Mystery," Bethany said. "Farewell and Godspeed."

"Yes, we Love you," Celeste reiterated. "But mark my words, you will be reckoned with."

Eden's stomach dropped like a stone, she felt all warmth drain from her body, and the dread invaded her every muscle. Her mouth hung agape but she couldn't find the words. Before Celeste slid the door closed, Eden thought she spotted a black cat sitting next to Celeste, smiling. She pointed at the feline, but the door was already closed and they had already begun to drive away.

Eden shivered, hugging her arms around herself and looking around in the darkness and dead of the night. Then she glanced up at the sign above the establishment she found herself in front of. Above the entrance were the words: *Chai Shop*.

SEVENTEEN

"Answers, damnit!" Kelly Moriarty demanded of Benny, still holding out her palms which were branded with a spiral and a muffin.

"Who let you in?" Benny asked, scowling.

"Jason," Kelly replied flatly.

Without responding, Benny sat down on his bed heavily. Kelly closed the bedroom door gently and went to sit down next to him. She sighed loudly to get the message across to Benny and then she looked over at his chemistry setup. "What the hell is that?" she said, studying it like it was some alien apparatus.

"All right... You want to know what's going on?" Benny asked, resigning himself to the fact that Kelly was involved whether he liked it or not.

"That's why I'm here," she said, nudging him with her shoulder.

"I'm trying to mix science and magic," he explained. "But, obviously, I'm not very good at it yet. I don't really know how it works." Kelly looked at him like he was speaking a foreign language. He grabbed her right hand and traced the spiral with his finger. "The spiral is my tag," he continued. "My symbol. Last night I burned it on your hand in a vision I had."

Kelly held up her other hand and said, "What about this FUCKING muffin?"

Benny burst out laughing, holding his hands up in bewilderment. "I truly have no clue. I really don't know. I didn't put it there."

"You're seriously fucked up," Kelly said, glaring at Benny with her eyelids halfway down her eyeballs. She got up suddenly and went to open the door to leave.

"We're connected now whether we like it or not," he said with truth laced in his teeth.

Kelly turned back to him slightly and said, "No, we're not." Then she left.

Kelly's lover Alice was in her dorm room working on homework at her desk. She was scribbling some smath into a notebook when Kelly barged into the room. "What's up?" Alice said, not looking up from her work.

Kelly flopped down onto the bed and covered her face with her hands. "Fuck..." she breathed out in a puff of frustration.

Alice swiveled around in her chair to look at her lover. "What is with you?" she asked, not really appreciative of being interrupted while she was working.

"I think I'm losing my mind," Kelly admitted.

"What's that supposed to mean?" Alice shot back, folding her arms over her chest.

"Crazy. Loco. Bonkers," Kelly replied.

"Explain," Alice demanded and then looked down at Kelly's hands. "Oh my god, what did you do to your hands?"

Alice tried to take her lover's hands in her own, but Kelly snatched them away and hid them behind her back. "Oh... That's... Just some guy..." she trailed off, looking away from her girlfriend's eyes.

Alice gave her a look. "Some *guy?*"

"Yeah, just some guy," Kelly said quickly, trying to brush it off like it was nothing.

"Well, *Kelly*," Alice continued slowly and firmly, "I think I should know if you're messing around with some guy."

"Jesus, Alice! I'm not fucking him!" Kelly snapped. "I hate men, they're retarded!"

Alice gave her partner another look of judgment and disgust. Then she started packing up, putting her notebooks into her backpack. "I have to go to class," she said dryly. Standing up, she started walking toward the door then stopped. "I knew you liked cock," she spat venomously.

"Wha—!"

Alice looked back over her shoulder and at Kelly now. "And to think I was considering baking you muffins," she said with no emotional intonation. Without another word, she turned and left the room.

Kelly flopped back down on the bed releasing a shriek of exasperation. "Ugh! *FUCKING MEN!*"

Back in Benny's dorm room, he was in the kitchen heating himself up some Spaghettios in the microwave. Jason walked in out of his own bedroom and sat down at the island. "Sup, cuz?" Jason said.

"Uh, hey," Benny replied awkwardly.

"I was wondering," he started. "When are you going to get a girlfriend so you're not always here and in my hair?"

"Yeah, I don't think that's gonna happen."

"You're gay, aren't you?" Jason asked, assuming he already knew the answer.

"What? I'm not gay," Benny returned.

"Admit it. You're a fucking queer. You're a fudgepacker," he continued with the insults. "You're a rectal flamer."

"A rectal what?!" Benny responded, raising his voice as he took the Spaghettios out of the microwave. "Forget it."

"C'mon, man," Jason said, continuing the onslaught. "What the fuck are you doing in there all day when you're not in class?" He pointed to Benny's bedroom. "When do you even have time to do your photography? That is your major, isn't it?"

"Yeah, it is," Benny answered.

"Alls I'm saying, man, is that maybe you should get a girl to open you up a bit," Jason said, giving Benny a wink that was uninterpretable.

"I don't need anymore girls to hurt me..." Benny said under his breath.

"Oh, I see."

Benny grabbed his Spaghettios off of the counter with a jerk and started back toward his bedroom. "And you're not in a place to lecture me, you degenerate!" he snapped. "I think I see some coke boogers you missed!" He ran to his room and slammed the door.

"Fine. Do what you want!" Jason yelled after him. Noticing a stray Spaghettio on the counter, he picked it up and ate it.

Later that day, Benny was sitting in Dr. Thurman's office again, on her couch, looking at her and sitting in silence. They stared at each other, almost in a battle of wills to see who would speak first.

"You're back," Dr. Thurman stated.

"That's how it appears," Benny retorted.

"Why is it appearing that way?"

"Because I decided to grace you with my presence."

"I'm so honored," Dr. Thurman said, the sarcasm palpable in her voice.

"You should be," he replied, not joking.

"Any luck with your magic muffins?" Dr. Thurman asked. She was radiating the impression that she just wanted Benny to leave her alone.

"Uh, yeah," Benny said, his eyes flashing away from the counselor's face. "Forget about that. I'm trying to cross over."

"Cross over?" she asked, but she really was not interested.

"To the realm of the feminine," he explained. "But it seems to be eluding me."

"Ohhhhhh..." Dr. Thurman replied, thinking that she had it all figured out even though she didn't. "Crossing over? As in cross-dressing?"

Benny looked at her and blinked to indicate she was not getting it. "What? No," he said, wrinkling his nose. "Just learning how to play the game. But it seems as if I don't know the rules yet."

EIGHTEEN

The Temple room which Sunshine and Moonbeam had been so kind to let Darren use was dark except for a few candles and a Himalayan salt lamp which cast a warm orange light over the marble floor. This Temple was not in the basement, as one might think, but on the upper floor of the house. The white curtains were drawn over the windows for the purpose of Darren's Working, however, the windows were great for bathing the whole room in the warm shining light of the Sun.

Darren had donned his gray cloak of the Body even though he really didn't like wearing it very much. One of the glories of being self-realized was the process and journey of individuation, not the mindless absorption into the herd. However, he refused to hide his face with the hood, and always kept it down even during ceremonies or rituals. Shaking his head at the prospect of what he was about to do, he whispered, "Please forgive me," then he shot his hands up, cupping them around his solar plexus. A spiral of his yellow Soulmind light began to whirl, expanding out from his third chakra. Then, pulsing his hands, he shot out countless spheres of yellow light into the room. They hovered and surrounded him, casting more of a yellow luminescence which mingled with the orange glow of the candles. Throwing his hands out to his sides in the shape of a cross, he held the Soulmind spheres suspended in space as the enchantment conjured a holographic image of a sidewalk that went through the RISD campus.

As the image solidified in the field of spheres, Darren could see that the campus was bustling with people. On either side of the sidewalk were grassy fields which looked like parks. Benny was walking through the campus and stopped at the beginning of this long stretch of sidewalk. Kelly was walking from the opposite side and stopped at that end of the sidewalk.

Darren stretched his arms out toward the holographic images of the other students walking through campus and yelled, "Cease temporarily in your stasis!" The image trembled as it was held within the yellow orbs and all the other students except for Kelly and Benny stopped in mid-walk as if someone had pressed pause.

Kelly pointed an accusatory finger at Benny, the hatred and rage evident on her face. "You! Motherfucker!" she shrieked like a banshee. "You desecrator of everything feminine, maternal, matriarchal, truthful!"

Suddenly every student in stasis dissolved into the air, leaving only Benny and Kelly at a standoff on the sidewalk. Darren raised his arm dramatically with a flourish and then pulled it back down through the air, bringing the darkness of night with it. Now as Kelly and Benny stood face to face, the stars twinkled in the dark void above them.

"Go fuck yourself!" Kelly spat maliciously at Benny.

"What the fuck is this?!" Benny said, looking around bewildered. "Are we having a standoff?"

Suddenly Darren jutted his finger at the image of Kelly and mouthed the words that then came out of her mouth: "Yeah, nigga! Prepare yo-self!"

Kelly assumed a martial arts stance. Benny did the same. Darren extended his arms; right arm toward Benny, and left arm toward Kelly. His palms were open toward them and it was as if he was feeding energy into them, and yet holding them stable at the same time. The energy currents of yellow Soulmind light spiraled their way into the solar plexus of both individuals, in effect simulating temporarily a Soulmind within themselves. Darren then squeezed his right hand into a fist and an explosion of white light burst from Benny's chest in a beam emanating from the center of his ribcage. He lowered his hands to his sides, dropping his martial arts stance, and looked up toward the starry sky.

Kelly at once began to scream after Darren squeezed his left hand into a fist. Holding her arms up in an X across her chest, Kelly looked as if she was trying to keep a demon inside of herself. But it was no use. The same white light exploded out of her chest as well. She lowered her arms and looked up into the night sky as the white light speared out of both of their chests, headed for an inevitable collide with each other.

In the flash of an instant, the spears of white light collided with two claps of Darren's hands. Each beam of light pushed its counterpart with equal force as if in a battle of luminescence. Darren swept his hands down in another flourish and then up and up. Benny and Kelly's feet lifted up off the ground, floating them suspended by the tether of their shared light. They continued to float up toward the stars of the night and the few wispy clouds that flew across the sky.

They were floating high above the campus now. The holographic image casted within the yellow Soulmind spheres had followed their path so that Darren still could see them as if he was floating there too; the point to the triangle trinity of their three. As Darren witnessed, the light stretching between Kelly and Benny began to braid through itself, overlapping, and tracing back to the opposite person as if they were connected as one soul. They were at once Connected Within the Light.

Benny's hands shot up to the sides of his head and he started to shriek a blood-curdling scream. Blue lightning bolts shot from his top jaw to his bottom jaw, lacing between his teeth like electrical dental floss. Kelly's hands shot up to her temples as well and she started screaming with the same blue electricity tracing between her teeth. As the pitch of the screams assim-ilated, the noise took on a quality that almost didn't sound human anymore; it became electronic. As the sound hit the area where it sounded like the ringing a person got in their ears, the sky ruptured and became purple—as if at once alight with a violet flame.

Right at the moment the sky turned to violet, the ropes of light snapped inward—Darren using his hands to pull the two towards one another—and pulled Kelly and Benny into a col-lision. As their bodies became one Within the Light, there was a colossal explosion of pure white light that tore through their bodies and the entire sky. The sky was still violet beneath, and as the white brightness dissolved, it became the shining stars that speckled that purple expanse.

Darren was utterly spent; exhausted. He fell to his knees, unable to control the sobs now ratcheting through his body, causing the tears to flow freely. "I don't want them to die... I don't want them to die..." he whispered as the yellow orbs of Soulmind light dissolved and went back into the bright yellow light of his aura.

NINETEEN

The Moon was bright over Camp Hero as Terry took Vespyr back toward the storage closet he had emerged from to find Turtle Cove. Vespyr hovered in the air, flying next to him slowly as they got closer to where parts for her spaceship were. "I can do that too," Terry said, smiling at the giant princess of Tar.

She looked down at him and replied, "You can?"

Instead of answering, Terry popped the golden sphere of light out from his heart to encompass his body. The star tetrahedrons were already spinning so fast they were a blur of white light as he lifted up off the ground to float beside Vespyr.

"Your Spirit possesses immense strength," she responded as they neared the storage closet. The door that Terry had blown off was mangled, charred, and laying in the grass some distance away. He adeptly floated into the small room and then down the ladder into the underground room full of electronic parts. Vespyr flew in after him and they both touched down in the middle of the room. The ceiling was high enough for the alien to stand to her full height. They illuminated the room with white and green light.

Terry cocked his head and looked up at Vespyr with her long red hair and flowing green dress. "How old are you?" he asked. "Because I get the feeling that you are ancient, yet you have the beauty of a young woman."

Vespyr chuckled. "I ceased to keep count of birthdays after the first couple millennia," she answered. "I see the parts I need," she continued, studying the huge pieces of equipment in the room. "However, I am hesitant to think I have the power to levitate all of these back to my Tenchi while we fly with them."

"You can't teleport objects?" Terry asked.

Vespyr shook her head. "Do you have that skill, Terry Broswald?"

"Yes," he answered with confidence. "It took me a while to sort of get the hang of it. But I'm pretty sure I can teleport them back to Colt State Park where your spaceship is sunk."

"And then we fly back?" Vespyr continued. "I am only able to teleport short distances; not the entire way from Camp Hero, here, and Bristol, Rhode Island."

Terry grinned. "I can," he said. "I can teleport us both back along with the equipment."

Vespyr's eyes widened. "A human who contains more advanced skills than a Taran princess? Goddess, who is this being which I see before me?"

"Are you ready?" Terry asked.

Vespyr nodded and pointed to the pieces of equipment which she wished to take with them. Terry closed his eyes and clapped his hands together twice in front of his heart. Then he folded his fingers together, leaving the index fingers pointing up. The black circles instantly appeared below the pieces of equipment which Vespyr specified, as well as under both her and him. The black tentacles shot up quickly, enveloping them and the equipment in the flash of an instant. Vespyr cried out as she was encapsulated in the black Matter-Relocation pod.

The Taran princess had never teleported in this manner and it frightened her. She could feel the tentacles crushing her, as if compacting her bones; splintering them into fragments of creation. And just when she thought she was about to die, it was over. The black pod dissipated around her in a puff of Black Mist.

Vespyr looked down and there was Terry smiling up at her, the Black Mist disappearing from around him as well. They were again on the rocky beach of Colt State Park where Vespyr had saved his life; which seemed like only mere moments ago to her. There also was the equipment, giant contraptions of machinery, on the rocks next to them.

"Ah my Goddess!" Vespyr exclaimed, touching herself to make sure she was all there. Her heart was racing. "That was wild! Terry, you are something inexplicable."

"Well, it worked," he said. "And that's all that matters, right?"

Vespyr suddenly lunged down at him. Terry thought she was about to strike him, but instead she wrapped him up in a big hug, lifting him up off the ground, squishing him into her bosom. "Okay, okay, Vespyr," he croaked. "You're squeezing me pretty hard."

She laughed and set him back down on the ground with a kiss to the top of his head. "Forgive me, I did not mean to squeeze you that hard. I was merely overcome with joy and excitement."

"Yes," Terry replied, catching his breath. "It's okay. I like you too and your spaceship is about to be functional again. Are you ready to fix it?"

TWENTY

After Darren was done sobbing on the floor of the temple, he stood up, wiped his eyes, and went downstairs to talk to his friends Sunshine and Moonbeam. They were sitting at the kitchen table, next to one another, sipping green tea. They were a couple who had been together for a long while and their relationship was strong. Sunshine was the name of the woman, and Moonbeam was the name of the man. Darren pulled his gray cloak off and hung it over the back of the chair as he sat down across from the couple. They were not wearing their cloaks, they were in plain clothes yet wore white turbans on their heads.

As Darren sat down, his silver kara slid down his right wrist. "Would you like some tea?" Moonbeam asked, looking at Darren, noticing the redness of his eyes and knew he had been crying.

"Yes, thank you," Darren replied. There was an extra mug next to the teapot in the middle of the table. Moonbeam poured Darren some green tea and slid the mug closer to him. The man with the long black dreadlocks picked up the mug in both hands and sipped graciously. When he put the mug back down on the table he said, "I don't know if I can do it anymore." His tone was weary. "This task is demanding too much of me. All I wanted was to help Terry, but I'm not sure if what I'm doing really is anymore."

Sunshine smiled warmly. "We are helping Terry," she said.

"We really are?" Darren responded, relief washing over him. "Because I was maybe beginning to doubt the faith there for a moment."

"It's okay. You're okay," Moonbeam assured him.

"But some of these things I have to do, I question the ethics of," Darren continued.

"Well," Sunshine started, "you don't *have* to do anything."

"But aren't we supposed to be the second coming of Christ?" Darren asked, opening up the true nature of what it meant to be part of the Body of Lucifer Christ.

Moonbeam shrugged and sipped his tea. "We're not *supposed* to be anything."

Darren was silent for a long while, focusing on his long, slow, deep breathing and sipped his tea. "Lucifer Christ," he said in a whisper.

"Have faith that the Spiralverse will always provide the synchronicity necessary for expansion, growth, and evolution of consciousness—whether you participate or not," Sunshine stated slowly.

"Then what's the point in doing anything?" Darren asked.

Moonbeam smiled and laughed. "Following the Tao is not an excuse to do nothing. We take things as they come. That's all we can do for now."

Darren let out a puff of air through pursed lips. He felt the energy settle back into his heart chakra. "This is—Wow." He shook his head. "So is Terry going to be aright?"

Both Sunshine and Moonbeam nodded. This was music to Darren's ears. "He is with the Perfect Spirit, who will bring him back in harmony with the Violet Light which is already inside him, guiding him."

"So is our Work done?" Darren wanted to know.

"I don't know," Moonbeam replied.

Then Sunshine spoke saying, "We'll just have to see."

TWENTY-ONE

FROM THE MIND OF JESSICA THORN:

Kara and Jared have been more than hospitable. Their guest room is warm and comfy; I'm very blessed to have met them upon my return to the Hollow Dimension. *Oh, Terry, my Love, let my Violet light guide you back to me.*

The couple has a little yoga room which is their living room set up with enough open space to accommodate a small group of yogis. However, it is just us three meditating in a circle facing each other at the moment. We open our eyes at the same time and smile warmly as friends do. "Have you ever gone on an Astral Projection journey?" Kara asks me.

I move my head from side to side. "I've learned the ability," I answer. "However, I don't really use it that often."

"Would you be open to going on a journey with us?" Jared asks. I hesitate, unsure. "Don't be afraid, Jessica. You are among friends, you will be safe and protected. That is what the Sophia Dragons are here for." He smiles at me, but doesn't seem attached to whether I answer in the affirmative or not.

Feeling the warmth radiating from my heart, the spiral of my violet Soulmind light begins to move, radiating a pleasant sensation through my body. I nod my approval. "Yes. I feel Sul's presence—the great Dragon whom used to rule over the

Octobers when they were in Meddia. Now, I'm not quite sure whether he rules them or just plays with them."

"Let us fly," Kara says, and instantaneously our Astral Bodies become visualized, superimposed over our physical forms. Our Astral hands reach toward the center of our circle and we hold onto each other as we start to float up toward the ceiling of the room. Then we're through, outside and above the house, looking down on Kara and Jared's beautiful home with its luscious and green backyard.

Where are we going? I ask wordlessly.

To the height of Mount Shasta, Kara responds.

We fly over the landscapes of California; it is even more beautiful from the air. And before I can even take in all of the stunning landscapes, Mount Shasta appears before us like a smiling giant, waiting with loving arms. Continuing to float up and up, we make it to the apex where there is already a group of other Astral Forms gathering. They are all awakened Soulminds—of all different colors and individualities. We float down gracefully and join the circle of friends.

The three of us sit next to each other, cross-legged in our Astral Bodies, as we smile through our Soulmind energies. *Look, there's Kaia Ra,* Kara says to me, indicating a luminescent figure across the circle.

How do you know? I ask.

We just know, Jared and Kara answer back simultaneously, as if they are one Soulmind.

What are we supposed to do now? I wonder.

Just enjoy it, Kara responds, placing her Astral hand on my shoulder. *You're among Loving friends.*

My heart is so full I almost burst into Astral tears—and then I do; weeping for pure joy. Suddenly there are the flapping of wings and a great wind swirls around us. I look up, and before we know it, there is a circle of Dragons flying overhead—us in our Astral Bodies, the Dragons in physical form. There are Dragons of all shapes, colors, and sizes—all stunning, beautiful, and radiant with the light of wisdom. These are the Sophia Dragons. And the greatest one of all is Sul, smiling and green. I had thought previously that Sul was just a regular dragon, *Under Whom the Octobers Run Wild.* But now, as Sul opens the shining eyes of his scales, he reveals that he is, in fact, a Sophia Dragon.

Terry! I transmit psychically. *You are protected forever and always by my Love!* Then I shoot a beam of Violet light from my third eye out into the sky; sending it to wherever Terry might be, since he too has a piece of my Soulmind—and my heart—within him.

This beam of Violet light rockets into the blue sky above us, through the flight of Dragons, guided by the infinite wisdom of Sul. There is a flash and the sky becomes the color of wine. I smile with my heart, knowing that Terry and I—our Love—is united.

TWENTY-TWO

"Now that we have the parts and equipment at our disposal," Vespyr continued, "how are we going to raise my Tenchi out of the ocean to assimilate the changes?"

Terry looked up at the Taran princess and extended his right hand. "Will you take my hand, princess?" he asked with a smile.

She blushed and then extended her left hand down towards Terry. "Yes."

They held hands, Terry's right in her left, and faced the ocean where her spaceship had sunk. They both closed their eyes. The spirals of their Soulminds began to emanate from their hearts, his White and Violet, hers Green. Then the energy traveled up to their third eyes, the pineal gland, and they projected a beam of light that contained White, Violet, and Green. This beam expanded to create a field that swam with those colors. This field of vivid, beautiful colors extended deep down into the ocean and encapsulated her spaceship, the Tenchi, and started to lift it up towards the surface.

At the moment that they both opened their eyes, Vespyr's magnificent spaceship of Tar was breaking the surface of the water. They watched—Terry in awe and Vespyr in joy—as the huge ship began to float in the sky above them. Without letting go of Terry's hand, Vespyr extended her right hand toward the equipment that she would use to repair her ship. A green circle of light appeared in her right palm and she shot an orb of green light out at each of the gigantic pieces of equipment.

"What are you doing?" Terry asked.

"I'm repairing my ship, Terry-sama," she answered.

"What did you call me?" he responded, eyes wide.

Vespyr grinned at him, her teeth sparkling in the moonlight. "Don't worry about it, Love. Now, can you help me assimilate these parts into my ship?"

Terry nodded with a serious expression on his face. Closing his eyes, he visualized the pieces of equipment going to where they needed to be on the ship's exterior and interior. The green orbs around the pieces of equipment vanished as he visualized the repair. "Is it working?" he asked, eyes still closed.

"Incredible!" Vespyr exclaimed.

"Is that good?" Terry wanted to know.

"Yes," she answered. "The parts are materializing into the areas of the hull and interiors which were wounded in the battle with the grappler ship."

Terry opened his eyes and looked up at Vespyr. She smiled at him again; her red hair looking especially radiant in the blue-white glow of the Moon. "Did it fix your ship?" Terry asked, hoping that what he had initiated with his Soulmind had helped heal the Tenchi.

Vespyr laughed. "Hahahahaha! Thank you, Terry-sama! Now we can reach the stars!"

TWENTY-THREE

Kelly Moriarty's moans of pleasure could be heard loudly as she merged with Benjamin Sanderson. Benny was laying on the bed, naked, with Kelly on top of him, riding his cock. Kelly bobbed up and down on it, feeling indescribable ecstasy as their temporarily awakened Soulminds began to braid together.

Slowly the spirals that were emanating from their hearts began to unbraid from each other; but they stayed wafting out of their fourth chakra, reaching for each other. Their white auras illuminated around them as well. Kelly leaned backwards and pulled Benny up with her; finally pulling him on top of her. As Benny continued to thrust in and out of his new lover, he slipped his right hand into the ball of white light at her chest. He slid his whole hand into the light and grasped her heart. She gasped, her eyes shooting open, but she didn't look Benny in the eyes. As Benny held Kelly's heart in his hand, he forced it to stop beating. Kelly went limp, but Benny continued to thrust into her. After a couple seconds, Benny let go of her heart. The second it started beating again, Kelly shrieked as a violent orgasm tore through her body.

Benny pulled his hand out of the ball of white light at Kelly's chest and kissed her on the lips. "I want you to cum," she said.

Benny continued to thrust. The light coming from his chest stretched out toward Kelly's neck. The end of the light split off into three prongs and wrapped around her neck. She closed her eyes and tilted her head back, moaning as the light strangled her. "Oh god! Oh god! Oh god! Oh god! Oh god! Oh god! Oh gaaaaaaaaahhhhhhd!" Benny moaned as he ejaculated inside of her and collapsed on top of his girlfriend. As their physical bodies came together, the light that had been emanating from their hearts was now extinguished; leaving them in darkness.

Later that night, Benny was sitting on the edge of his bed. He was still naked. He had a piece of an old blanket in his hand and he was absentmindedly playing with it. He was off wandering somewhere else in his head.

Kelly was asleep, her back facing Benny. She rolled over and opened her eyes sleepily. "What's that?" she asked.

Benny was pulled out of his daze and looked down at Kelly; then at the blanket. "Hmm? Oh, this? It's just part of an old blanket... A blanket that my mom gave me when I was a baby... I hold it sometimes when I can't remember her." he answered.

"Oh, you," Kelly said.

"Hmm?"

"How come?"

"How come what?" Benny asked back.

"You," was Kelly's reply.

Benny turned and closed his eyes. In his mind he imagined a dark, empty stage. The curtains were closed and there was a microphone on a stand in the middle of the stage. A spotlight suddenly illuminated the microphone and its stand. Still in his mind, Benny emerged from behind the curtains and approached the microphone. He tapped it twice and feedback could be heard.

Benny looked into the distance as if looking for the audience. He got his composure and spoke.

Kelly was laying on the bed now, on her stomach with her chin resting in her palms. She listened intently and Benny recited a poem he had written, still with his eyes closed. He recited:

"I can't be your mother," she said.
"Emotionally you're dead, and in bed you have issues."
"Save your 'I miss yous' and let your tears find their way into
Some other girl's tissues."

Your name is my name
And even though I don't blame
You for how I am, it's still a shame
That I can't break away from this game
Of broken intimacy

But I'm complaining again
Whining to the ones who don't really
Want to hear about it
But then again, I'll fucking shout it out
I might just sit on this stage and pout

The first said she wasn't going to baby me anymore
The second said she couldn't be my mother
But I still clung to her breast
And couldn't bring myself to leave the nest
Or put to rest my best effort
To force you to cradle my head
With thumb in mouth and puppy eyes
I don't know why you call my lies

When I was on top of you, you said,
"Yes, Daddy. I need it."
Then I cut open my hands, and tried to stitch your scars as I bleed it
My intimacy distress, I confess, runs deeper than where they get
Fiji water
And I know that cutting your belly is not Forever or the way that I
taught her
To love me, I guess I am that baby crying for milk
But your tit is sour and I scream for soft silk
And receiving nothing but delayed abortions
Kill me 20 years later because you don't like my alterations
That I've made to myself
Because I guess that untidy shelf
Holds the books of my selfish ways

And I bring it back to the fetus
Tearing it out in order to feed us
I've blocked the sun with the dead babies piled
High to the sky, you killed your own child
But it feels like it was my dick that you cut out of yourself
But I, I know what I am
And I know what you are not
I'm still four years behind
With an undeveloped mind

The Eden, the Forever, the rape victim
The one who said she loved me after we fucked
Is no longer near me but with luck
She won't forget me the way I'm forgetting her
In every way except how she fucked like a hooker
And squeezed my arms as she came
I remember how she loved brother-sister incest play

And I still think of her name every fucking day

I thought that cross dressing would make me feel closer to females
But I guess it makes it seem like I'm just on sale to old males
And they think that I can be their new mother fucking toy
I'm not something you can crush under your belly, I'm still a boy
A little boy just searching for his mother

I know now I can't get what I need from a man
And in this dimension I will forever stand
The realization happened in that moment when I had my hand on
your penis,
You turned to me and said, "You ever heard of the second coming?"
I sink and continuously feel like a gooey piece of afterbirth running
Down my leg to come to rest on the brink of enlightenment
However, that will not come through orgasm or excitement
Astral Penis Projection into the universe's uterus
I can feel myself dying, how come god won't remember us

God is my mother
God is my mother
We are God's failed experiment
I've been going down
Spiraling down
You let the girls pound me into the ground
And the answers for me still remain unfound

Bam I hit the ground!
Making craters and cavities riddling through expanses
Of polluted air, making me impotent and sequentially pensive
And I live, still live, even if you won't help me open the seventh
chakra

I'm still searching for that explorer who will aid me on the road to tantra

To help me dig deeper into the earth in order to hold my hand as we shoot

Into the celestial universe together, but she's gone and in my hand is a boot

A boot that falls into ashes and leaves my dreams for love-making dry

And my mother lands next to me, but I don't want her to touch me even if she tried to love me,

I reject but suspect her of something deeper

Some spirituality I don't wish to be a keeper

Of, I'm a sleeper, a dreamer, a philosopher

Of sexual fluidity, but I remain alone

With no one to become one with, I'm still as a stone

What will happen to our sexual identity when we are blind in the mixture of purple and black?

Fallen trap, I'll drink the sun sap, till I know how the weather speaks, then I fly and fall back

Into nothingness and I become sexless, unsex me here, and fill me from the crown

To the toe topful of direst understanding, because I am that slave bound

But with roots of energy striping and penetrating the ground

I have found what it really means to be inside of the spirit

Soul love, soul sex, souls weaving together, and I don't wish to tear it

Apart and tear the heart, the chakra that eludes my touch the most

But I guess, I'm still that failure, and can't seem to become more than a parasitic host

I am the only one who put these motherfucking scars on my mother-fucking chest

*Please tell me why I still can't figure out how to put these thoughts
to rest
My sex is just a mess, and again I confess, about my intimacy distress
And why I cum less that you wish for me to
But this is nothing new and I always knew
That blue was the color of death
I feel lost when I can't hear your breath
Or watch you as you sleep, thoughts intermingling
Time universe, still searching for the sublime unwinding
And the unbinding from all the ropes that tie me to my mother*

*I don't want to fuck my mother
I don't want to fuck my mother
I don't want to fuck my mother*

*But I guess, when I'm fucking you,
I'm really just fucking my mother*

PART 21

Parliament of Power

*"Don't seek masters.
You are the ultimate master magician in your own life."*

- The Book of Magic

The bottom line is that his magick has reverberated and created effects beyond his own ordinary mortal means. Both men encountered dark forces in their work and neither were afraid to deal with them. They have also chosen dark vehicles by which to communicate. But, ultimately, what did they communicate? That all creation manifests from the light, also defined as the electromagnetic spectrum which is just another word for Mother Nature.

Crowley offered us a clue when he announced he wouldn't officially assume the name "Phoenix" until the work was completed. In this regard, the true Phoenix Project would be to redeem mankind by purging the forces of ignorance and oppression that have ruled during the last 13,000 years.

Armageddon awaits us all, but not in the sense it has been perpetrated on us by the merchants of fear and those with ulterior motives. For each of us, it will be a personal encounter, if it hasn't been encountered already. In one corner will be the Christ with all the angelic forces he can muster. In the other, will be the Antichrist with his demons. Those of us who invoke the wisdom of Babalon will not be rooting in the corner of either side. We'll be functioning as the referee and ensuring that each side fights fair with no bribes being offered to the World Boxing Council by some of those notorious mystery school people who sit in the expensive front row seats. If we can accomplish that, the fight should go the distance and be declared a draw. Ascension will occur.

On the Day of Judgment, there shall be no judgment. At least, if there is, those who are doing the judging won't be following Christ's words: "Judge not, lest ye be judged".

So, as they say at Caesar's Palace: "Let's get ready to rumble!"

- Peter Moon & Preston Nichols, *Pyramids of Montauk*

TWENTY-FOUR

Kelly had woken up in Benny's bed. She was now listening intently to him recite his poem. She was laying on her stomach on the bed, with her head propped up on her hands. She was looking at Benny.

"Wow. Shit... I dunno if I can help you," she said.

"Yeah? Why is that?" Benny asked.

"Because you hate women too much." She rolled over onto her side, turning her back to him.

"What's your story then?" Benny asked.

Kelly sighed long and loud. "There's really nothing interesting to tell," she continued. "Some dude knocked me up when I was fifteen. I didn't really have enough money for an abortion and I didn't want to tell anyone... So I drew a hot bath for myself, and dug the fucker out with a coat hanger. End of fucking story."

Benny looked over Kelly's beautiful slim body as she smiled up at him.

The next morning, Benny was taking a shower. He looked happy. After drying off his hair, he walked out of the shower room wearing a robe and went into the kitchen area where Jason was making himself cereal. They didn't say anything to each other, but they shared a glance which signified mutual knowing.

Benny walked back into his room and Kelly was sitting at his desk studying his chemistry setup. "Will you take me next time?" she asked.

"Where?" he asked.

"Wherever it is that you go," Kelly continued.

"I'm still in the experimental stages," Benny continued. "I'm not sure if that would be safe."

"Pfff. Not that it's safe for you anyway," Kelly said, trying to provoke Benny so he'd take her with him on his journey to wherever.

"Good point," Benny replied, scratching his chin. "I'll think about it. We should probably head to class soon though."

They walked to their poetry class together. The other students pushed past them in the hallway. Benny felt someone brush past his hand and he turned to see who it was. It was Jenny who had brushed his hand. She was a blonde overweight young woman. She looked back at Benny as well. Their eyes met for a second, wordlessly. Then they turn back in opposite directions and continued walking.

When Benny and Kelly got to class, the other students were all already there and Benny sat down in his normal seat with Kelly sitting behind him. Mr. Malign stood at the front of the class. "Today we are going to be talking about Hip Hop," he said. He turned to the chalkboard and wrote the words *Hip Hop* in giant letters."Hip Hop. Hip Hop," he continued. "Benny! What do you know about Hip Hop?"

"Well, shit. I know that hip-hop got me back into writing poetry," Benny responded.

"How so?" the teacher asked.

"When I listen to hip-hop," Benny continued, "I focus more on what is said than how 'phat' the beat is."

"True. True," he responded. "Who are some Hip Hop artists you admire?" he asked.

"To name a few," Benny answered, "I'd have to say Saul Williams, who we've been studying, and KRS-ONE."

"Very good, very good. They are negro. Yes negro. Negro from necro. He overcame it so they named him after it. Any others want to speak about their experience with hip-hop?"

A young man in the back row raised his hand.

"Yes, Timmy," Mr. Malign said.

"I find it really ironic that blacks used to get whipped and chained for free, now they're rapping about getting whips and chains. And probably paying for it," Timmy said. Everyone stared at Timmy in silence. "What?" he said.

Mr. Malign turned back to the white board and spoke saying, "Today specifically I want to talk about a hiphoppa named Sebastian Archaic." He wrote the name on the white board. "Sebastian was around during the 1800s. And I know what you're thinking. You don't believe me that there were hiphoppas back in the 1800s. He was one of the ones who paved the way for us today. He was not a slave. Everyone thought he was a white man, because he had something similar to what Michael Jackson had." Kelly raised her hand. "Yes, Miss Moriarty?"

"And no one questioned his rapping? Suspected him? Seems kinda odd to me," she said.

"Haven't any of your previous teachers taught you about suspending disbelief?" he asked.

"But isn't this a true story?" Kelly asked.

"Even in reality we must sometimes suspend disbelief," he stated. "And I must share the story of the white nigga."

"Michael Jackson?" Timmy said.

"Sebastian Archaic," the teacher responded. "Who wrote what he saw. He truly could travel into other worlds, other planes, other realities. And he wrote about what he saw. There was one specific place he would always talk about." He turned to the white board and wrote the word: MERARI. "Merari," he continued. "He would speak of traveling there through time space to trek down the rainbow of reflection. That's what he called the road that leads through the worlds. You see, the way that he saw the world was as one giant glass walkway in space, stretching off into the distance and riddled with obstacles and enemies."

"Sounds like rainbow road in mario cart," Timmy commented.

Everyone stared at Timmy. "Must you interrupt the story, young man?" the teacher responded. Timmy sat there and didn't react. "So this, this *merari*, was where Sebastian would find Solstice Will I Am. And they would speak together as one."

At the end of class, as the students were walking to their next class, Benny turned to Kelly and said, "Hey, Kelly, I'm going to talk to our teacher for a moment. Let's meet up later, yeah?"

Kelly nodded and went on to her next class. When all the other students had gone on to their next class, Benny approached the teacher. "What can I do for you, son?" the teacher asked.

"What do you know about this *merari*?" Benny asked.

"Pretty much what you heard me say in class," he said, shrugging. "What do you really want to know?"

"How would one go about crossing over?" he wondered.

"Sebastian never specifically detailed his methods of travel," the teacher said. "I don't really know."

Benny looked thoughtful. "So he believed in the spirit and supernatural realms? By meditation he would commune and be transported?"

"I don't know if I'm sure of what you're asking," the teacher said.

"If we discover a substance, and have it blessed by G-d," Benny continued, looking up and then back at the teacher, "and then commune with god, that may open a portal to this *merari*?"

The teacher looked down, unsure. Then he looked back up at Benjamin Sanderson. "I'm not sure I can continue this conversation," he said.

"Why not?" Benny asked.

"I could possibly lose my job," the teacher said.

Benny looked kind of bewildered for a moment, then reacted as if something struck him as ironic. "WaheGuru! I just had darko deja-vu," he exclaimed.

"You what?"

Benny shrugged and smiled. "I'll see you later," Benjamin said and walked out of the classroom.

TWENTY-FIVE

Kelly was sitting at the island in the kitchen of Benny's dorm room eating a salad. Benny's room door was closed. As Kelly turned, she saw Benny emerge from his bedroom. He was decked out in full cross-dress. He had on a red plaid skirt and red checkered knee-high socks. He also had on a tight black shirt which underneath he was wearing a brazier. He held three roses in his right hand.

Wordlessly, Kelly Moriarty stood up and approached Benny who looked a bit shy. As she approached him, she held his hands, squeezing them around the stems of the flowers, then she leaned in and kissed him.

TWENTY-SIX

Mrs. Thurman and Benny were in their usual places in the office.

"I presented my feminine side with flowers," Benny said.

"So you cross-dressed for Kelly?" she asked.

"Yeah," Benny replied.

"You know what?" Mrs. Thurman said.

"Hmm?"

"I think you should bring her somewhere special to you," she continued. "Some place you've never shared with anyone before."

Kelly was laying on Benny's bed. She was naked except for a pair of shorts. Benny was sitting on the edge of his bed next to her. He looked down at her. "Close your eyes," he said. Kelly closed her eyes. "Do you trust me?" he continued.

"No," Kelly said, "but I will for right now."

"Can you promise me something?" Benny asked.

"What?" she said.

"Try not to move at all," he continued.

Kelly shrugged. Benny reached under his bed and pulled out a long bowie knife. He began to rub the blade down her skin, playing with her sensations. Kelly shivered and moaned with ecstasy. She smiled. Benny continued with the knife play down her arms and across her breasts. She moaned. This went for a little bit, but Kelly grabbed Benny's hand and stopped the knife. She opened her eyes.

"That's a little intense," she said.

Benny smiled and pulled the knife away. They kissed. "I want to see what you've seen," she continued. Benny was hesitant.

Kelly squeezed Benny's hand. "Share your world with me?" she asked.

"Are you sure you want to become part of this?" he asked.

"I think I'm already part of it," she said, "but I don't know."

Benny got up and went over to his chemistry set. There was already a full beaker of the purple liquid sitting on the side. He picked it up and brought it over to Kelly. "Sit up," he said. Kelly sat up. "Repeat after me. Rage war in heaven. Rage war on earth."

"Rage war in heaven. Rage war on earth."

"Show me the stars, galaxies, violent explosions of Spirit."

"Show me the stars, galaxies, violent explosions of Spirit."

"And if I don't return, I have committed my soul as a warrior and succumb to eternity."

"And if I don't return, I have committed my soul as a warrior and succumb to eternity."

Benny held the beaker out to Kelly and she took it. She drank it down and gagged, holding back her vomit. "Ugghhh! What's in—" she started but couldn't finish her sentence because the room dripped away like paint. She was swimming in the giant black lake. The only light was coming off of her. She was treading water. She looked around and saw little shapes bobbing in the water all around her. They were muffins. Kelly felt a hand wrap around her ankle and she was pulled down under the water.

As she was dragged continuously down, her belly swelled to the point of being five months pregnant. She was pulled down through the water and down through the ceiling of an old warehouse. She was pulled through a suspension rig where she now hung from her wrists. She was nude, her legs spread open and her ankles were tied by a length of rope. Benny approached Kelly. He decked her in the face. Her head snapped back and blood poured from her nose. Benny stroked the side of her face lovingly. Then he trailed his fingers down her pregnant belly. Benny started to rub between her legs. He shoved his whole hand into Kelly's vagina and began to dig around inside. Kelly began to scream out of fear and pain. Blood and afterbirth poured onto the floor as she gave birth.

Benny held the baby in his arms lovingly. Kelly was on the verge of losing consciousness. Slowly he unzipped his fly and began to make love to her again. This time for another child. Suddenly he cut the ropes that bound Kelly and she fell free, panting to the floor. Then he kissed the top of her head.

Kelly was laying on Benny's bed as she slept soundly. Then he woke her up and gave her a big hug and a kiss.

TWENTY-SEVEN

As Terry watched the Tenchi raise up out of the Atlantic Ocean, he stared in suspense as he held Vespyr's hand tightly. Vespyr's green Soulmind enveloped the both of them, Terry's white and violet Soulmind as well, and they were instantly beamed up into the spaceship. Jessica, Terry's Twin Soul, was calling him back to her in safety and peace, knowing in her heart that he was back with her, connected soul to soul and heart to heart.

When Terry found himself on the Tenchi next to Vespyr, he Loved her even more! "Jessica is back here with us in the Hollow Dimension, which is now the IM," Terry said to Vespyr.

"Yes, I know, My Love," she continued. "Let us go to her."

TWENTY-EIGHT

"You ever heard of the Babalon Working?" Allister asked Mothman as they sat nude together on the couch at Terry's house, still protected by the Merkabah Field.

Mothman shrugged and shook his head. "Did you mention that to me before?" he asked.

Allister said, "Perhaps, but this is how." She pushed Mothman back on the couch gently so that she could mount him once she had gotten his cock erect. He leaned back, placing his head on the pillow, and closed his eyes as Allister began to massage his penis. She slid her hand up and down his shaft until he was erect. As he began to moan, his orange Soulmind began to emanate from his heart in pulses and spirals. "That's good, that's good," she said as her green Soulmind began to spiral out of her heart as well.

She mounted Mothman slowly, easing his erect penis into her vagina. She moaned as her head tilted back and up toward the ceiling. As they both began to moan in unison, their Soulminds began connecting, braiding together into a beautiful tapestry of colors; green and orange.

As their mutual orgasm began to build; in Mothman's penis and Allister's cunt, she visualized the Moon. When she did, she instantly saw Anna's and Rob's Astral Forms there, looking down at the spaceships surrounding the Earth. Instantly they both orgasmed; Mothman ejaculating into Allister's vagina. As they shared the mutual orgasm, a beam of light which was a mixture of orange and green shot out of the braid of light connecting their hearts. This light shot toward the Moon.

On the Moon, Anna, in her Astral Form, looked down and saw it rocketing in her direction. She turned to look at Rob's Astral Form, and before she could say any psychic words to him, the Soulmind light of orange and green enveloped her, pulling her back down toward the Earth. Rob watched as Anna's Astral Form was pulled back to Earth by the energy of the Soulmind orgasm of Allister and Mothman.

Anna didn't really know what was happening. She was still safe within her Merkabah Field and her yellow Soulmind energy was pulled by the green and orange Soulmind energy toward Vespyr's ship which had just risen out of the Atlantic ocean. Anna's yellow Soulmind light went straight through the outer hull of the Tenchi and into Vespyr's body. She gasped and went down on her knees on the floor of the spaceship.

"What, what happened?" Terry asked, startled by her sudden movement.

Vespyr gasped a deep breath and then stood back up to her full height, a couple feet taller than Terry. Her long red hair swooped back and forth with her head movement. "I don't really know," she said as yellow and green Soulmind light spiraled from her heart chakra.

Terry looked down at the energy emanating from Vespyr's chest. He saw that it now contained the yellow along with the green. "Whoa, that's Anna," Terry said.

"Who's Anna?" Vespyr asked.

"She is that yellow Soulmind energy that's mixed with your green Soulmind energy," Terry responded.

"So she's with us in her Soulmind form?" Vespyr asked.

"Yeah," Terry continued, "and Jessica is with me in Soulmind form. Soon I'll be reunited with her physically."

"How do you know that?" Vespyr asked. "Where is she? Shall we fly the Tenchi to where she is waiting for you?"

"Yes," Terry said decisively. "She is near Mount Shasta."

"Do you know how to navigate there from here?" Vespyr asked.

"We are connected at the heart and connected at the Soul-mind," Terry continued. "So trust me, and I'll take us there."

"Yes, My Love," Vespyr said. "You all are Connected within the Light. You to her and also you and I, at once, now."

"To Mount Shasta!" Terry exclaimed.

TWENTY-NINE

The Whitehouse fence was surrounded by newly awakened Soulminds. They were all very angry and pushed up against the fence like a huge mosh pit. The SWAT team had just arrived and were pouring out of their black trucks. They all wore black jumpsuits and those black motorcycle helmets which allowed them to see the Playground's Soulmind energies. They all stared through their helmets and were terrified of how large and pow-erful the Playground's collective Soulmind energies had gotten. They trembled in their black boots as they raised their artificial light weapons to aim them at the mob of Playground Soulminds.

Each of the SWAT guys had a small disc attached to their vests which would put an artificial plasma field up the front of them like a shield, but they knew that the real Soulmind energy was even more powerful than their artificial plasma energy.

The Playground still kept their attention on the Whitehouse, pushing against the fence like a mob of hungry cattle. They all yelled, raising their fists into the air. They had combined all of the colors of their Soulminds into a giant field of rainbow color which became a golden sphere, a Merkabah spinning around the whole mob in a bright white light at almost the speed of light.

The SWAT team were too afraid to attack because they knew that they would be overpowered and destroyed. Suddenly they looked up into the sky and saw a huge flying saucer with lights beaming down from it. When it was hovering just above the Playground and the SWAT team, a staircase opened up from the bottom of the flying saucer and Graeson started to walk down the stairs. The bottom of the staircase touched the ground in the middle of the group of SWAT guys. They parted the way because they had never seen a flying saucer before and didn't know what to make of it.

The Playground didn't really pay any mind, they kept yelling and rushing against the fence of the Whitehouse, trying to break it down. When Graeson stepped down into the middle of the group of SWAT guys, who all had their weapons aimed at him now, he said, "Take me to your tranny!"

Graeson was seven-feet-tall and taller than any of the men in SWAT uniforms. When he said those words, they all dropped their weapons and fell to their knees, trembling. Graeson laughed and then disappeared with a puff of wind.

In the exact moment when Graeson disappeared, the yelling of the Playground increased in volume so loud that their collective Soulmind energies extended to envelope the SWAT guys and the flying saucer that the Grey had just descended from. The SWAT guys screamed as they were instantly vaporized. The flying saucer was vaporized in that moment as well. Then the energy of their collective Soulminds became so strong that the fence of the Whitehouse fell and the whole Playground rushed toward the Whitehouse.

Elliot Cage knew that the Playground was outside the Whitehouse and charging for it, so she had gone into the tunnels underneath to try to escape. Suddenly Graeson materialized before her. She trembled in his presence. Graeson smiled, looking down at the pathetic creature he saw before him and reached down to touch the top of her head. Then he squeezed her head until it was crushed in his giant Grey hand.

The Playground was still running toward the Whitehouse. Their tribe was so massive that the amount of Soulminds involved were almost uncountable. Their collective Soulmind Merkabah was one giant ball of white and golden light. Once they reached the Whitehouse, their collective Soulminds were so powerful that they instantly were able to decimate the Whitehouse; reducing it and everyone inside to tatters.

The Playground stood, on the rubble of the Whitehouse and cheered. Every color of their Soulminds flickered and spiraled and braided together in a beautiful tapestry of light that reached high into the heavens.

THIRTY

Dr. Thurman and Benny were sitting in their usual spots in her office. He looked nervous and was biting his fingernails. "I think I may have hurt her. Kelly, I mean," Benny said.

"How do you suppose?" Dr. Thurman asked.

"Psychologically. Unintentionally. Subconsciously," Benny replied, not really fully comprehending the definitions of those words, but he liked the sound of them.

"Why do you think that is?" Dr. Thurman wondered.

"Uhhh, I dunno..." Benny continued, trailing off. "Maybe she was right, you know. Maybe I do hate women. She said she hated men. But to tell you the truth, I don't hate women."

Benny looked up at Dr. Thurman for answers. She didn't have any and she didn't say anything. "What do you think?" he asked.

Dr. Thurman held out her hands with her palms up. They were empty. "I have no answers for you, young man," Dr. Thurman answered. "You can go back to your dorm room if you wish. I don't think you need to come see me anymore. Okay?"

Benny stood up to leave the room. "Yeah, well, I didn't really want to come talk to you either. I don't need therapy."

"I agree," Dr. Thurman agreed.

Benny walked back into the hallway to return to his dorm room. Many other students—young men and women—trailed past him as they made their way to class. Benny reached the end of the hall as the crowd of students was thinning out. There he was confronted by Jenny, the overweight young woman who had brushed past him earlier. Benny stopped and they looked at each other. "Hold out your hand," Jenny said. Benny held out his right hand, palm up. Jenny placed a folded piece of paper in his palm. "Come find me when you're ready," she said.

As she walked away, Benny unfolded the paper. On the front, the note read: *I am waiting for the Climactic Moment when the Black Mist meets the Purple Fog.* Benny flipped over the note and on the back it read: *Lot seven, Purple Convertible.*

THIRTY-ONE

Arash, the new Mahan Tantric, had just pulled his Kurti and white pants on when Rahjiah rushed into his little yogi room. "Lord Khan," she said breathlessly, looking frantic.

"What is it, Rahjiah?" he replied, with the authority now that Leeah once had.

"The Greys are invading!" Rahjiah exclaimed.

"The who?" Arash said, not knowing what kind of being the Greys were.

"They're extraterrestrials who have genocided whole planets in the past," she continued.

"What? That's awful," Arash said.

"I know, Lord Khan," Rahjiah continued, briefly looking toward the open door of Arash's little yogi room. "It is *imperative* that we get you to safety *now!*"

Arash nodded. "Where?" he asked.

"There is a portal that leads to our spaceship," Rahjiah answered. "I will stay with some of the others of the Order of the Transcendent to protect you." She grabbed Arash's hand and led him out of his little yogi room and toward the Grand Hall. Once they were there, there were the rest of the goddesses of the Order gathered there. "You," Rahjiah said, sweeping her finger in a circle around six of the goddesses of the Order, "go take Arash to safety. I will stay with the others to hold off the Greys so that you can get Lord Khan to safety. Go now!"

The six goddesses that Rahjiah indicated nodded and surrounded Arash. He was a little bewildered, but allowed them to escort him toward the portal which was hidden on the other side of the Grand Hall. They took him around a hidden corner. Arash looked up at the giant chandelier that was hanging over the Grand Hall just before he pulled his face back down to see a huge portal with spinning purple energy before him. The six goddesses were behind him, pushing him toward it. Then they shoved him into it. He was sucked through and then all six of them followed.

Rahjiah stood in front of the remaining goddesses of the Order of the Transcendent. She had her arms out in the shape of a cross as the hoard of Greys poured into the Grand Hall in front of them. The Greys were taller than all of the goddesses of the

Order and they were intimidating with their weapons trained on them. Their gray, juicy, translucent skin and large black gooey eyes watched the beautiful goddesses as they put up a white force shield around themselves.

The Greys opened fire upon them, shooting their high-powered plasma weapons at the goddesses. There were too many of the Greys and they were overpowering Rahjiah and the remaining goddesses of the Order. Rahjiah looked back at her comrades, a tear trailing down her cheek. Her white dreadlocks glistened in the light of their force shield. "I'm sorry," Rahjiah said to her comrades, "but Leeah told me that it has to be this way to protect Lord Khan." She turned back to the huge hoard of Greys that were still opening fire. Rahjiah screamed and released the greatest blast of energy from her heart that she could produce. The white light instantly vaporized the hoard of Greys, but vaporized Rahjiah and the remaining goddesses of her Order in order to save Lord Khan's life.

THIRTY-TWO

Benny was standing over his chemistry set, studying it. He pulled his cell phone from his pocket and dialed a number. Benny heard Kelly's voicemail message which said: "Hey, it's Kelly. I'm so glad you called. Leave me a message."

"Hey, uh, Kelly," Benny said, "I miss you. Hope we get to talk sometime soon. Call me back if you wish. Or stop by. I'm in my dorm room if I'm not in class. See you later." Benny hung up the phone and looked at the beaker that was full of purple liquid. "It's missing something," he said to himself.

One syringe was laying next to the beaker. Benny started to slowly unbutton his pants and unzipped his fly. He pulled his boxers down and his penis hung flaccidly between his legs. Benny picked up the beaker with the liquid in it and put it under his penis. He began to urinate, adding about a centimeter or two of his urine to the purple liquid. Holding the beaker in front of his face, he sloshed it a bit, mixing the contents.

He put the beaker down on his desk and opened one of his drawers. He pulled the bowie knife out of the drawer. Cutting the tip of his index finger just slightly, a drop of blood started to form and he squeezed it into the beaker. After which Benny put the knife back into his drawer. "Perfect," he said.

Picking up the syringe, he stuck it into the beaker and filled it with the liquid. He put the syringe back down on the table next to his chemistry setup and held the beaker in both of his hands tightly. Then he recited:

"I call upon the spirit of Sebastian Archaic. Speak with me this hour." Wind started to blow from nowhere and tousled Benny's hair about his face. "Allow me entrance to the domain in which you communed with Solstice Will I Am. And I shall be the passage from then to now! And speak always with my own authority; sharing that land with this land!"

Benny placed the beaker back down on the table and picked up the syringe and kissed it just as Kelly threw his door open. "Take me there with you!" she yelled, rushing into the room.

He was startled and looked over at Kelly, surprised to see her. She was breathing heavily and soaked in sweat. "What the eff happened to you?" Benny asked.

"Don't worry about it," Kelly said dismissively. She stepped closer to him. "I know you know how to get to MERARI, Benny. Take me with you!"

Benny glanced around the room and then out toward the kitchen to see if Jason was there listening to their conversation. "Not here," he said. "We'll travel through in the car park. Go take a quick shower to wash that sweat off and then I'll take you there along with me."

Kelly nodded and went to Benny's shower. Not bothering to close the door, she took off her clothes and got under the water. Benny walked in a few minutes later, nude, and they enjoyed making love.

THIRTY-THREE

FROM THE MIND OF ARASH KHAN, THE MAHAN TANTRIC:

After going through the purple portal, I find myself on the bridge of a huge spaceship. As I gaze around in awe, the other six goddesses of the Order of the Transcendent come through and join me on the bridge. "Where are we?" I ask.

A goddess to my left wearing all white, loose cotton clothing smiles at me. "This is your spaceship now, Lord Khan. You are the Mahan Tantric. Whatever you wish to name this spaceship, is yours and yours alone." Her white dreadlocks are so long that they almost reach down to her ankles.

"Well, I, ah," I sputter a bit, not knowing what to name a *spaceship*. "Maybe we'll call it just spaceship for now. I don't think there's a reason to name a spaceship; however, I might have a name for it sometime." I gaze around again in awe of the control crystals surrounding us and the glass that allows observance of the stars and planets around us. Turning back to face the six goddesses who are now my comrades, I say, "However, we will no longer be known as the Order of the Transcendent." I raise my hand above me, the white sleeve of my kurti loosens to reveal the kara on my right wrist. "We shall henceforth be known as the *Parliament of Power!*"

THIRTY-FOUR

Kelly and Benny left the dorms and went across campus toward the car park. "Which lot of the car park are we going to again?" Kelly asked.

"Lot seven," Benny answered. "That's what Jenny's note said."

"Jenny? Who's Jenny?" Kelly said.

Benny looked over at Kelly and smiled, holding her hand. "She's a friend of mine. She's very intelligent."

"Oh, yeah," Kelly continued, "I think I have some classes with her. Pleasant and nice young woman."

"Yeah, she is," Benny agreed.

From an entrance to one of the buildings, Mr. Malign saw Benny and Kelly walking hand in hand. As they got farther away from him, Mr. Malign started to follow them from a distance. The couple did not notice him behind them.

The couple arrived at the car park and Mr. Malign made sure he wasn't seen by the young woman and young man. "What's that stuff called again?" Kelly asked, indicating the purple and yellow liquid inside the syringe.

Benny shrugged. "It doesn't have a name. Just prepare to squirt your mind." He smiled and winked at her.

Kelly's pussy instantly got wet as he said this. "Uhhh, yeah," she moaned. "Put it in me. Feels so fucking amazing!" She moaned again, having a spontaneous full body orgasm.

Benny found a red convertible and sat Kelly down on the hood of the car. He sat next to her. She tilted her head back, closing her eyes as Benny plunged the needle into her vein. Only squirting half of the liquid into her arm, he pulled it out and squirted the remaining liquid into his mouth, drinking it down. Then he threw the syringe away, not needing it anymore.

Spirals began to appear under Benny and Kelly on the hood of the red convertible. They looked like cloth sacks that were eating them both up. When their heads sank lower than the hood of the car, they dissappeared thoroughly into the portals. Then the portals conjoined, coming together into one portal as Mr. Malign rushed toward it. He dove into the spinning spiral just before it closed, leaving the hood of the red convertible smooth and shining once again.

Benny and Kelly were spinning through black space together. White light gushed all around them. Their mouths moved but no sound escaped. Simultaneously, an incision appeared on the upper part of both of their craniums. It cut a circle around their scalps, sparks flew, and the skin began to peel back and expose their skulls. After which their scalps and top of their skulls blew away like hats, leaving their brains exposed. The white light still surrounded them, protecting them. Even though their brains were exposed, they stayed intact as they fell through the darkness and suddenly found themselves on the Rainbow of Reflection.

The Rainbow of Reflection was a glass walkway floating in space. Stars twinkled all around. Kelly and Benny stood next to each other on the circular part of the Rainbow of Reflection. Clouds were also floating through the Expanse. Benny walked over to where the glass walkway kept going and going into the distance. This road was hilly and stretched off into the distance farther than Benny could see. "Should we walk it?" Kelly asked, extending her hand to Benny.

Benny took Kelly's hand and they began to walk onto the Rainbow of Reflection. They were unsure of where it led or how far it went into the distance, but they had faith. As they trekked the Rainbow, it began to get gradually steeper. They both heard a sound they didn't recognize and stopped walking. Kelly and Benny were quiet as a creature emerged overtop of the hill in front of them. It looked like half of a person with just an upper body. It hovered with a spiral of Black Mist where its legs should have been. Its head was completely bandaged and the only facial feature that could be seen was bulging completely white eyes. It had a scrawny upper body and arms. The creature held a long slender knife in each hand.

"What the fuck is that?" Kelly asked, terrified.

"I dunno," Benny replied. "But at least there's only one of them."

Just as Benny said that, an army of the creatures poured up from behind the single one that was heading straight for Benny and Kelly. "Run!" Benny screamed.

The couple turned back and ran toward the platform they had arrived on. Before they knew it, Kelly and Benny were surrounded by the strange creatures. Benny and Kelly were overtaken by the creatures as they pounced on them both, dragging them down to the floor. Soon the couple were buried in the creatures. Benny's arm shot up through the bodies of the creatures as he and Kelly sank down and back through the Rainbow of Reflection.

THIRTY-FIVE

Rob, just as his blue Soulmind, stood on the Moon, looking down toward the Earth where Anna's yellow Soulmind had been pulled back through the atmosphere and into Vespyr's body. He watched as the spaceships of the Greys began to descend to the Earth since the seal had been broken and the Earth had ascended to the Fifth Dimension—the IM.

Turning back from the Earth, he looked at the Black Pyramid. Walking over to it, he slipped silently into it; finding himself in the inner chamber of the pyramid that was lit by four torches —one on each of the walls. Rob approached the sarcophagus slowly. He looked inside where the black sand was and crawled inside. As he laid down on his back, he felt a spiral of energy pulling his blue Soulmind down. He didn't resist. And as his blue Soulmind spun down, descending into the inner Earth, he instantly found himself standing on the platform of the Inner Earth surrounded by thousands and thousands of Grey aliens. Even existing purely in his blue Soulmind form, he was terrified of them, thinking they wished to exterminate his Soulmind completely. They did. And as they rushed toward him, bent on annihilating him—

Rob suddenly gasped, breathing in rich oxygen once again. He found himself at once in his physical body again. Paolo and Gabriella were standing over him with two ankhs touching his chest right above his heart. Rob looked down and his blue Soulmind energy was spiraling out of his heart space. "Holy shnikeys!" Rob exclaimed.

Gabriella and Paolo smiled down at Rob who was laying on the floor of their white temple space. They were both sitting in rock pose wearing all white and they both were wearing turbans as well. "Welcome back to the land of the living, our friend," Gabriella spoke.

"Whoa, I'm alive!" Robert exclaimed. "I was just surrounded by a bunch of Grey aliens that looked like they wanted to extinguish my very Soulmind."

Paolo spoke saying, "They did. Those Greys, or Zetas, are not to be trusted—never to be trusted!"

"I thought I was gonna die," Rob said. "Like go into space dust or something."

Gabriella laughed. "That's why we resurrected you, young man."

"I appreciate that," Rob replied.

"And I'll tell you what," Paolo continued, wafting his hand through the blue tendrils of Robert's Soulmind.

"Yeah?" Rob said.

"You can active anyone's Soulmind at Will," Gabriella explained. "Without having to make love to them. You can, that's okay also; but you have the ability now with the point of your finger or a snap of your fingers to instantly activate *anyone's* unactivated Soulmind. That power is now under your True Will."

"Whoa, that's radical," Rob replied.

Both Paolo and Gabriella laughed, raising their ankhs into the air.

NOVEMBER & DECEMBER

ONE

Mr. Malign was walking on clouds immersed in a sea of blue sky. Suddenly he was approached by Sebastian Archaic who was in the form of Michael Jackson. "How have you come to this place?" Sebastian asked.

"A portal," Mr. Malign answered.

"You were never meant to come here," Sebastian said sternly. "This is why you are now in the In-Between and not at Ground Zero Consciousness."

"What are you talking about?" Mr. Malign asked.

"I am Sebastian Archaic!" Sebastian announced.

"Really?" Mr. Malign said excited. "I've always wanted to meet you!"

"I am," Sebastian continued. "Why do you teach so much about Solstice Will I Am? That nigga channelled a lot of his poetry from my poetry." He waved his hand and the clouds and blue sky around them changed into a grassy hill at night. Looking up into the star-filled sky, he recited some of his poetry.

Sebastian grasped at the air and a tiny sun appeared between his fingers. He put it up to his lips and blew it up like a balloon then let it float away. As it floated up, the sun rose as it became day. He approached Mr. Malign and pinched the middle of his lips between his fingers. As he pulled his fingers away, he pulled a string of written words out of Mr. Malign's mouth. The written words were the same as the poetry he was reciting. Sebastian and Mr. Malign started to float up off of the ground and ascended into space. As they ascended, Sebastian continued reciting.

They both floated into space, surrounded by darkness and stars. They came to a stop a little above the glass walkway where Kelly and Benny had just been piled on by the strange creatures. Both Mr. Malign and Sebastian looked down as Benny and Kelly struggled underneath the creatures and were at once pulled back through to the Hollow Dimension—which was now the IM.

Mr. Malign looked at Sebastian quizzically. "Saul Williams wrote that poem that you just recited," he said.

"There are only two things you need to know, nigga," Sebastian continued, walking through space toward Mr. Malign. "One: I wrote that poem. And two: you don't belong here in MERARI." Sebastian flicked Mr. Malign's forehead with his finger. "Boop."

Mr. Malign's body crackled and sputtered like TV static then disappeared. Sebastian turned around on the black Expanse surrounded by stars and started to walk. "Where are my watermelons filled with fried chicken wings?" he said.

Mr. Malign woke up in his chair behind his desk in his classroom. He jumped up like he had just awoken from a dream. He looked around the room and it was empty. "Oh, man!" he exclaimed, breathing heavily and feeling his heart racing.

TWO

Benny screamed and his bed opened up like a gaping portal which shot blood out like a fountain. The geyser of blood made a stream that hit the ceiling and rained down into the room. Benny came shooting out of the stream and was spat to the floor. Vomiting onto the floor, he fell to his hands and knees and slid around in the slippery blood on the floor of his bedroom.

In Kelly's bedroom, her bed exploded in a shower of rose petals. The petals shot out like a fountain and hit the ceiling. Kelly came shooting out of the stream of rose petals and was spat to the floor. Rolling over, her eyes suddenly melted into giant tears and burst like giant dew drops. She was then covered by a rain of rose petals.

Benny was sleeping in his bed. The bedroom was back to normal. There was no sign that the blood had been there at all and Benny's chemistry set was intact on his little work station. Jason pounded on the door of Benny's bedroom, startling him awake. "Wake the fuck up, asshole!" Jason yelled. "Make me some food!"

Benny blinked and rolled over, rubbing the sleep out of his eyes.

"Make your own fucking food!" Benny yelled back.

"I can't, I'm too coked out," Jason replied. "Get yo ass out here, nigga!"

Benny pulled himself out of his bed and opened the bedroom door. He was confronted by Jason who was nude except for boxer shorts. "Are you coked out?" Benny asked.

"That's what I just said, innit?" Jason replied.

Benny walked past Jason toward the island in the kitchen. There was an open carton of easy mac on the counter. Its contents were strewn everywhere on the counter top. "What the fuck is that?" Benny asked, indicating the macaroni noodles on the counter.

"That's why I wanted you to make me food, Benny," Jason explained. "The mac attacked."

Benny shook his head and started to clean up the noodles. He scooped the noodles back into the cup. Then he noticed unsniffed lines of cocaine on the left side of the counter.

"You want a line?" Jason asked.

Benny shook his head. "Maybe later," he replied. Then he put water in the easy mac and placed it in the microwave.

"That Kelly is pretty sexy," Jason commented, sniffing and wiping his nose.

Benny looked at him for a long moment. "And?" he said.

"We could, ya know, like have a threesome—you, me, and Kelly," Jason said. "I would love to do that with you two."

The microwave timer dinged. Benny took the food out of the oven and shoved it in Jason's chest. "Here's your fucking food," he said. "You're welcome." Then he walked back into his room and slammed the door.

Jason scooped the mac into his mouth, and while he was chewing said, "All I wanted was my dick licked. It's not like I wanted the moon."

THREE

Benny stood in front of his Modern Poetry class with a new poem he had written in his hand. There were two words on the white board behind him: *poetry day*. After clearing his throat, he read and recited the following poem:

This is a rhyme about gettin paid, gettin paid
You are my muse, my spirit
And you've made me rich beyond reason
Because you've spit these colors into my eyes
Making my retinas shatter and my pupils dilate
In order to make a larger whole for your soul

Catch me if you can
But this ain't a race
And I'm not a rabbit
I remember when they used to call me 'turtle'
But now, I can stand up straight
Since the vertebrae be fused to the titanium of my soul
And I can drum out a bum bum bum
On the sticks, the clams, the snakes
That feather this expanse
Of unweathered talk
Of unspooned words
Of tortured wings
That will fall off once the sky becomes the color of wine
And I know, that you all know, that I know, that you know
That I am not you
But in that fact I am becoming everything
And that makes us the same
Part the ways
We are the parts
Of the world
And we are one
We are the sun

The fire
The living
And everything I have said here tonight
Will take flight into the darkest and most narrow
Tunnels that lead out of the spheres into another tunnel
And into you
My muse
My spirit
My guide
My myself
Because you are me
And I am you
And that is a picture of me
Even though it was developed as you
It bears my face

The constellationness of time conflagrations
Because the sky is aflame with air waves
That ripple with our voices
I still exist to grow roots in cosmopolitan gardens
To sprout no thought
Just phallic symbols
But I shall grab them
And jerk them till they spirt

Blood

Because I know they just exist here
To transform into vaginal imagery
My muse
My spirit
You've made me rich beyond reason

Because even though I can't have children
You aid me in giving birth
And for this I thank you

This shit ain't about gettin paid, gettin paid
And this shit
Does not
Rhyme

Thank you

Everyone in the class clapped and Benny went to sit back down at his desk in front of Kelly. Mr. Malign walked to the front of the class looking as if he was in deep thought. He pulled his head up and looked at Kelly. "Miss Moriarty," he said, "I know you have something for us."

"What? No, uh," she stuttered, "I think I'll pass."

"We all know you have a poem hidden in that brain of yours. Why not speak it," Mr. Malign replied. "Get your thin body up here, young lady."

Reluctantly, Kelly got up out of her chair. She didn't have a notebook or a piece of paper in hand. She recited from memory the following poem:

Clouds fly above the earth in a pattern of wind currents as the landscape underneath changes
From the Compass of a changing society that sees things differently and through their own personal haze
I don't crack
I blaze on through this world
Tearing the searing hearts of fire from this world of mystics
And finally see what is truly beyond the stars

I see what is truly beyond the authority
I see everything how it really is and what I must do
To bask in the glory of a completed and varnished frame of wood
The odor of fresh cedar
And the sound of crisp leaves
Is all I hear when the soft wind silently blows the grass through the
Golden winds of change
But I know that hibernation only lasts so long
And the sun comes out again after the long freeze
The warmth returns again to the bright landscape
And white wisps fly through the atmosphere in cyclic currents of
steadiness

What we must do is peel off our melting flesh and reveal the
scarred tissue
But not shun it
Model it
And caress it
Love it and cherish it
Laughter is only a cut to the ear, but scars can be beautiful if we are
not ashamed
Gash my heart and it will just uncover the fire therein
Eviscerate me and what will be left is intense light
Blazing through to the clouds above me rocketing toward the stars
In a spiral of longing
Our persistence may not carry us above the cosmos,
But we can and will set our sights toward the skies

The whole class burst into applause and Kelly awkwardly did a curtsy and scuttled back to her seat. At the end of class, as the students were packing up to go to their next class, Benny walked past Mr. Malign. He grabbed Benny's arm too tightly and said in a harsh whisper, "I know where your travels have taken you. I advise that you don't stick your nose in where it doesn't belong!"

Benny pulled his arm out of Mr. Malign's grip. "Don't touch me like that," Benny said sternly. "That hurt my arm. And I don't know what you're talking about!" He shook his head at Mr. Malign and quickly went to catch up with Kelly. When he got to her side, he said, "I didn't know you wrote poetry."

"Yeah, well, if you were ever actually interested in anything that I had to say maybe you'd know," Kelly said, frowning slightly at her lover.

"Oh, come on, Kelly," Benny responded, "you know I'm interested in you and what you're interested in."

Kelly shrugged. "The way I see it," she continued, "is that you're so absorbed with your own art and your own journey that I didn't feel like bothering to share my poetry with you."

"That's not fair, love," Benny said, trying to hold Kelly's hand. "I want to know everything about you. I love you."

"I don't feel like talking about this right now," Kelly said flatly.

"Okay," Benny said.

They stopped outside of Kelly's dorm room. She turned to her lover and said, "Do you even have time to pick up your camera anymore? Aren't we photographers?"

"Yeah," Benny said. "We're photographers, but we're all-around artists as well."

"What I'm saying here, Benny," Kelly continued with a sigh, "is that maybe you spend a little too much time looking through your own lens. Pick up another one and maybe you'll see something different." Then she leaned in and kissed Benny on the lips. After which she silently went back into her dorm room and closed the door.

FOUR

Benny was sitting at his desk with his chemistry setup pushed to one side. He was wearing full cross-dress. Hunched over a piece of paper, he was writing feverishly. The sketch he was drawing was a muffin. "That's it," he said, "the muffins hold the key to getting past those creatures of MERARI."

Benny jumped up from his chair and went to Kelly's dorm room. Once he was there, he knocked on the door. He was wearing a skirt, knee-high socks, and a tight shirt. Kelly's roommate, Marsha, opened the door. She looked at Benny as if he was out of his mind. "Is Kelly here?" he asked.

"Uh, yeah," Marsha said, "she's in her room."

Marsha let Benny into the dorm room and he knocked on the door of Kelly's bedroom. "Hey! Kelly! I know how to get past those creatures in Merari!"

Kelly opened the door slowly. "Shhh," she hushed him. "Keep your fucking voice down. People are going to think you're a nutcase." Then she looked down at what Benny was wearing. At the same time, they both realized they were wearing the same outfit. They didn't comment on this; Kelly just opened her door wider and let Benny into her room. Benny shut the door behind him.

"It's the muffins," he said.

"Muffins?" Kelly said.

"Yes! The muffins will allow us to get past those creatures," Benny explained.

"What are you saying?" Kelly asked.

"There is a recipe for magic muffins," he continued. "They give the eater new knowledge."

Kelly looked skeptical. Then her face lit up in recognition. "Oh, yeah! Alice said something about making me muffins. That can't just be a coincidence." She looked at Benny, smiled, and kissed him on the lips again.

"Good!" he said.

"She must have that recipe," Kelly continued.

"Can you get it?" Benny asked.

"I can try," Kelly returned.

"Let's do it!" Benny said, excited.

"Okay, go back to your room and wait for me," Kelly said, putting her hand on Benny's shoulder, then she smiled and squeezed his penis. "I'll get the recipe and come get you."

They kissed.

FIVE

Outside of Alice's dorm room, Kelly stood. She knocked on the door. Alice's roommate, who was also named Marsha, opened the door. "Uh-huh?" Marsha said.

"Is Alice here?" Kelly asked.

"No, not right now," Marsha answered. "Do you want me to tell her you came by?"

"It's cool," Kelly replied. "I just, uh, left one of my textbooks in her room. Can I grab it really fast?"

"Oh, yeah, that's okay," Marsha said, opening the door wider so Kelly could come in. Kelly went in quickly and into Alice's bedroom. Kelly closed the door behind her and frantically searched every drawer and shelf for the recipe. She even looked at loose papers in Alice's bookshelf. Moving her eyes all over, she scanned the room. Dropping to her knees, she felt around under the bed. There was a book there and she pulled it out. It was a hardcover book with photos of Britney Spears. Kelly shook her head in amusement. She opened the front cover of the book and the recipe, on a piece of looseleaf paper, fell out. After throwing the book on top of the bed, she darted out of the dorm room and back into the hallway.

Once she was outside of Benny's dorm room, Kelly scrawled out a note on a piece of paper. After which she slid the paper under the door. She knocked three times and then ran away down the hallway.

Inside Benny's dorm room, he was eating macaroni at the island and reading Saul Williams poetry. That was when he heard Kelly's knocks at the door. By the time he got up to open the door, Kelly was already around the corner of the hallway. As he closed the door, he noticed the note on the floor. The note read: *Benny—Meet me in the campus car park. Bring your camera. - Kelly*

Benny went to his room to get his camera. Pulling a box out from under his bed, his professional camera was inside. He pulled it out and hung it around his neck. Then he went to go meet Kelly in the car park.

Once he got there, it was dark and shadows danced on the cars from the glow casted from the lamps above the cars. Lights also flickered in the windows of the campus buildings. Mr. Malign lurked in the shadows watching the couple. Suddenly a bright flash illuminated Benny's still-feminine-looking form. Kelly had just taken a picture of him.

"No fair!" he said.

Kelly laughed. Then Benny began to chase her through the car park playfully. Benny also began to snap pictures of Kelly as she ran around laughing. After a while, they both got tired and stopped running. They were hunched over, panting, and caught their breath at the same time. Simultaneously they raised their cameras and took a picture of each other at the same time. They were counterparts, lovers. Then they both let their cameras fall back down to hanging around their necks. They both rubbed their eyes.

"Ready to make some muffins?" Benny asked Kelly.

She nodded.

When they arrived back at Benny's dorm room, the muffins were already baked and sitting on the island in the kitchen. Kelly and her lover glanced at each other and then they noticed that Jason's bedroom door was closed.

"Fucker baked my muffins," Benny said.

"At least it doesn't look like he ate any of them," Kelly said. They both walked over to look at the muffins, brushing shoulders. They both picked up a muffin at the same time. They smiled at each other and took a bite, enjoying the delicious sweetness of the muffins. As they ate, they sat down next to each other at the island. The muffins were so delicious that between the two of them, they ate all of them. Kelly burped loudly. Benny laughed and also burped.

"Are they speaking to us?" Kelly asked.

"I think they just did," Benny responded. They both laughed.

"They're telling us to be very quiet and absorb the Spiral-verse," Kelly continued.

Benny closed his eyes and crossed his legs up on the chair.

"They're not working," Kelly whined.

"Shhh," Benny hushed her. Then they sat in silence for a moment. After which Kelly leaned to one side and let loose a wet, juicy fart. Benny opened one eye and saw Kelly grinning at him. "That was beautiful and wonderful," he commented.

Kelly stared at Benny as she smiled. Stars appeared in her eyes as she was so taken by the love she felt for Benjamin Sanderson. His nostrils grew enormously large and then shrank back down to normal size. She grinned while watching this a couple times. "That's it!" she laughed.

"Hmm?" Benny asked.

"Your nose is the next portal," Kelly said decisively. She leaned forward and slid her fingers into his nostrils.

Benny chuckled. "I kinda like that," he said, sounding nasally. While his lover's fingers were still in his nose, he stared into Kelly Moriarty's eyes. Her eyes became circular analog wall clocks on which the second hand, minute hand, and hour hand spun backwards.

"The answers don't come from without, they come from within," they both said in unison.

After Kelly slid her fingers from Benny's nostrils, he opened his mouth wide, taking the hugest inhale he ever had taken in his life. The whole room collapsed inward and was sucked into his mouth. He sucked in the campus, the buildings, and the world. Only Kelly Moriarty and Benjamin Sanderson were standing in a space surrounded by white. As Kelly stretched her hand out toward Benny, both of their white Soulminds began to spiral from their hearts, braiding together and connecting them. "We know the secret through each other," they said in unison.

They suddenly heard a loud knocking, but they didn't turn their heads, they kept staring into each other's eyes as their white Soulminds surrounded them and connected them within the light.

They both heard Jason's voice saying, "Hey, fuckers! You better not be out there eating my marijuana muffins!"

Suddenly everything zipped back out of Benjamin's mouth and he and Kelly looked over to see Jason standing in front of his open bedroom door.

"I'm talking to you two lovers," Jason continued.

Benny and Kelly burst out laughing. They stood up off their chairs and hugged each other, still cackling with laughter. "You know that both of you are wearing the same clothes," Jason stated. He shrugged and Benjamin and Kelly began to kiss each other, sliding their tongues into each other's mouths. They caressed each other. Benny slid his hands over Kelly's breasts and Kelly caressed down Benny's body and massaged his penis.

Jason pulled out a bag of cocaine from his pocket and poured some out on the surface of the island. "You lovebirds want a line?" he asked.

Kelly turned and jumped up and down, her breasts bouncing. Jason handed her a small rolled up piece of paper. She leaned down over the white powder and sniffed it. "Benny, come hit this, asshole," Jason said.

"Stop calling me an asshole, rectal seepage," Benny said to Jason.

"I know, I was just joking around," Jason continued, smiling at his friend.

Kelly handed her lover the rolled up piece of paper and Benny sniffed a line of the white powder. After which they began to kiss passionately again. She pushed herself against her lover and she pulled him to the floor. Laughing hysterically, Kelly began to rub Benny's cock through his skirt. She got him erect and his penis popped out of his panties. His lover brought her mouth down to lick his penis. Jason began to stroke his own penis as he watched the two lovers making love.

Jason slowly walked over to Kelly and went down on his knees behind her. Her beautiful ass was up in the air as she continued to hold and lick Benny's penis in her mouth. Jason flipped her skirt up and pulled her panties down slowly. Jason began to slide two fingers into Kelly's wet cunt and she began to moan. She slid Benny's cock out of her mouth and said, "Mmm, yeah, I like that, that feels great."

Then Jason slid his fingers out and brought his face down to her vagina and started licking her, tasting her sweet juices on his tongue. After bringing his face back up, he rubbed the tip of his cock over the lips of her wet pussy and slid his cock inside of her. She started to slide her hand down Benny's cock as he closed his eyes and moaned loudly.

After pulling his cock out of Kelly's pussy, he rubbed the tip around her anus. "I don't really like it that way," she said. "You can put it in my vagina, but not that way. I just don't prefer that."

"Ahhh, come on," Jason said. "Let's just do anal a little bit."

"No!" Kelly said, looking down at her lover who had fallen asleep briefly. "You're not gonna stick that huge cock in my tiny asshole."

Both Kelly and Jason burst out laughing after she said that. As they laughed hysterically, they rolled around the floor together, brushing up against each other. Jason stood up and grabbed Kelly's wrist, pulling her to standing. Then he began to drag her to Benny's bedroom. She struggled against him, reaching down for Benjamin.

"What the fuck are you doing?" Kelly said. "Benny! Wake up, my love!" She turned back to Jason. "Let me the fuck go, Jason!"

As Jason dragged her into Benny's bedroom, Kelly continued to reach out for Benny, hoping he would wake up. Jason threw Kelly down onto Benny's bed face down. After getting on top of her, he put his dick between her ass cheeks. He thrusted in hard. Kelly screamed. "Ah, fuck," she moaned. Jason continued to thrust in and out of her tight hole.

"You like that? You like that big cock up your ass?" Jason said.

"Big mistake," Kelly said, reaching under Benjamin's bed. After pulling out the bowie knife that she knew was there, she swung it back over her shoulder, stabbing Jason in the chest. He fell off the bed and onto the floor, bowie knife sticking out of his chest. Blood gushed from the wound, and there was blood on his cock. Blood dripped between Kelly's thighs as she stood up.

"What the fuck! What the fuck! What the fuck!" Jason screamed as he felt the blade of the bowie knife pierced through his heart. Kelly leaned down and ripped the knife from Jason's chest. Jason yelled in pain as blood gushed and sprayed her face. She licked her lips. Then she jumped onto Jason, stabbing him over and over again in the face until it was mutilated and unrecognizable. She stood up over him, covered in blood, breathing heavily as she dropped the knife to the floor. Turning around slowly, she saw Benjamin standing there, staring with his mouth hanging open.

Benjamin looked down at Jason's mutilated body and then back up at his lover. Kelly walked over to her lover and held him tightly, sobbing into his chest. She convulsed, her body shaking violently as she wept. Benny held her tightly and kissed the top of her head. "Shh, I love you, sweetheart," Benny said.

Kelly looked up into her lover's face with tears in her eyes and smiled in spite of the pain she felt. "What are we gonna do with this?" she asked.

"We bury him, my love," Benny said.

"I'll get some garbage bags," Kelly said, disengaging from her lover's embrace and went into the kitchen to get some garbage bags.

She returned with two medium sized garbage bags. "We don't have any bigger bags?" Benny asked. Kelly shook her head. "That's okay," he continued. "Put one over his head and the other over his legs."

Kelly slid one bag over Jason's head and the other over his legs; leaving his midsection exposed. "It's not covering him all the way," Kelly said.

"No shit! Fuck it!" Benny said. "It's gonna have to be good for now. Help me pick him up."

"Help me pick him up," Kelly said.

Benjamin leaned down and attempted to help Kelly pick the body up; Benny by the legs and Kelly by the head. The first couple times they picked him up, he slipped out of the bags. After fumbling about, they finally got a grip on the body and carried him toward the door.

When they got to the door, Benny said, "Open the fucking door, Kelly!"

Kelly dropped Jason's head and opened the door. Blood seeped out of the bags and onto the floor. After picking the head up again, they guided the body into the hallway. They waddled like penguins down the hall toward the elevators. When they got to the elevators, Kelly dropped her side of the bags again and blood splattered on the floor and the walls. She pressed the down arrow on the elevator, smearing blood on the button.

"Let's take the stairs instead," Benny suggested.

Kelly shrugged and they walked over to the stairs and took Jason down that way instead. "Death is an interesting thing, isn't it," Kelly said as they walked down the stairs. "It's like the phallic," she continued. "The penis entering the vagina."

Benny shrugged as they went out the door which led to the car park on the RISD campus. "So what are we gonna do with this?" Benny asked as they walked through the car park, their breath blowing out in puffs of white air.

"Let's take him to the forest preserve over there," she indicated.

As they went toward the trees, Mr. Malign was watching them from around the corner of the dorm building. Once Kelly and Benny got into the shelter of the trees, they dropped Jason in the two garbage bags and caught their breath. Mr. Malign peeked at them from behind a tree.

"Oh, fuck," Kelly said.

"Hmm?"

"We don't have a shovel," Kelly continued. "How are we gonna bury him?"

Benny's white Soulmind began to spiral out of his heart and he put his hand inside and pulled out a silver spoon. "Would m'lady like a spoon?" he said.

Kelly stepped over to him and took the spoon from his hand. She looked at it and threw it at Benjamin's head; it bounced off and she smiled, the corner of his mouth twitching. "What the fuck am I gonna do with a spoon, Benny?" Kelly yelled at him.

"You could have just asked me for this shovel," he replied, leaning down to pick up the shovel that was next to him on the earth.

"Where did that come from?" Kelly asked.

"All things come from the Creator."

"When are you gonna sober up?" Kelly said, slapping Benny in the face. "We're alone! Gimme that!" She snatched the shovel from Benny and began to dig in the dirt. After a while of digging, she said, "I think that's deep enough, don't you?"

Benny shrugged and Kelly pulled Jason over to the hole in the dirt and let him fall inside. She looked down at herself. "So much blood," she said, shivering a little in the cold.

Benny approached Kelly and dipped his fingers in the blood that was on her face; then he opened her mouth and slid his fingers down her throat. She gagged. "Now do it to me," Benny said.

Kelly slid her blood-soaked fingers down Benny's throat, but he didn't gag. "Now what?" Kelly asked.

"Um... Words. Words," Benjamin said. "We are artists. And when we travel, it's a gift to every person in the world. This is for everyone who was ever called a faggot when they had the balls to be themselves! Now you."

"Uhh... This is for everyone who was told to shut the fuck up when they chose to speak instead of be silent!"

Benny said: "This is for everyone who was pushed back down after they chose to stand up!"

Kelly said: "This is for everyone with an opinion different than the majority!"

Benny said: "This is for every person who refused to conform or transform into the 'typical public school kid'!"

Kelly said: "This is for every child who was ever raped, but felt like it would be better to make light of it!"

Benny said: "This is for you! The ones who struggle! The ones who feel they have no voice! You do!"

"All you need to do is *speak with it!*" Kelly agreed.

As soon as Kelly uttered the last words of their poem, the hole where Jason laid still transformed into a spiraling and whirling vortex of purple energy. The wind whipped Benny's and Kelly's hair around their faces. "You ready?" Kelly asked.

Benjamin smiled and held Kelly's hand. "Yes, my love," he said. "Let's do it!"

After which they jumped into the spinning violet light. Mr. Malign ran out from behind the tree and jumped into the bright violet light after the two lovers.

The portal stayed open, shining its violet light into the night.

The Perfect Trinity

"The Perfect and the Perfect are one Perfect and not two;
nay, are none! Nothing is a secret key of this law."

\- Aleister Crowley, *The Book of the Law*

"When you arrive at Tar, you'll wear a golden crown
upon your head. And you'll possess the key
that opens all the labyrinths."

\- Alejandro Jodorowsky, *Fando y Lis*

SIX

I'm not sure what to make of my resurrection. Having the ability to activate anyone's Soulmind at Will without having to have sex with them is a strange new skill I've acquired. I don't know anyone else who has that ability as of yet.

After taking a flight back to Chicago, I went to Terry's house to find Mothman and Allister there as a happy couple. It's morning and I'm pouring myself a mug of green tea. I sigh from the exhaustion of all I've been through. Looking up, I see Mothman and Allister walking down the stairs together. "Morning," I say.

"Top O the morning," Allister says, smiling. She's wearing a long, silk robe that is red with silver dragons on it. Mothman is wearing a t-shirt and shorts. He yawns and wipes the sleep from his eyes.

"Robert!" Mothman says. "The fuck man. It's been too long since I've seen my bestie friend." He runs over and squeezes me in a big hug.

"You saw me yesterday when I got back," I wheeze, hugging my friend. Mothman lets me go from the hug after kissing me on the cheek; then he opens the refrigerator to look for something to eat.

Allister comes over and leans on the island across from me and stares into my eyes, smiling wide. "The Great Mother is here, Rob," she says.

I shake my head. "Who's that? The Great Mother. Do I know her?" I ask, not exactly sure who Allister is referring to.

Allister chuckles and I raise an eyebrow. Looking over my shoulder, I see Mothman getting some vegan sausages and roasted potatoes to heat up on the stove. After I turn back to Allister, she says, "I told the other students who have left our high school that she would be here," she continues. "That was my prophecy to them because their parents had been killed in that catastrophe. You know what I'm referring to."

I nod my head. "That was intense," I reply. "That Tock entity said some strange things to me before I destroyed him. You know I don't like hurting people, but I felt like I had no choice in that situation. The battle was raging, Maya was trying to kill Terry and destroy pretty much everything it seemed like. And Trick, Tock, and Tick—ah..." I hesitate. "They were just too evil to let live. You know what I mean."

Allister nods soberly. "Yes, Robert, I understand," she agrees. "However, like I was saying, the Great Mother—*is* Maya."

I gasp and Mothman stops cooking his food to turn and look at Allister. "What?" Mothman says. "You didn't tell me that! She's dangerous!"

My mouth hangs open. "You've never seen her," I continue. "How would you even know what she looks like? You only know of her from what me and Mothman have told you. We were the ones who had to deal with her."

Allister smiles again, looking between me and Mothman as we stare at her. "She has transformed into a higher being. She has a Soulmind now and is part of our Playground."

"What?" Mothman says. "How do you know that?"

"Sometimes I just know," Allister responds. "Terry and she made love and it activated her Soulmind, transforming her into a human."

"Whoa," I say, exchanging a glance with Mothman. "Terry is powerful."

"He is one of the most powerful beings I've ever met," Allister continues. "So Maya has been meditating in the forest preserve near the old high school. Some students still attend, but the ones who's parents were killed in the catastrophe became disillusioned by the monotony and began to live in the forest as a community. They were drawn to Maya, and they began to meditate collectively. Then she realized she could activate all of their Soulminds at Will. So she activated all of the young men's and young women's Soulminds at once, just the other day."

After taking a sip of my green tea I say, "Holy wow! I acquired that same ability through Paolo and Gabriella resurrecting me."

Mothman continues to stare at his lover, not sure what to make of what she is saying. The vegan sausages in the skillet begin to sizzle and he turns to push them around with a spoon so they will cook evenly. "If you can do that," Allister continues, "then you and her are the only ones with that skill currently."

"I wanted to see her again," I say, "but I figured she'd always want to be trying to destroy the Hollow Dimension. It's good to know that she doesn't want to anymore and that maybe her and I could be reunited. I do love her. Even when she was trying to create mayhem, I still loved her."

"I know, Rob," Allister says to me, looking deep into my eyes as I notice a spiral of blue light coming forth from my chest. "Do you want to go see her with me today?"

"Yes," I say without hesitation.

"I want to come with you both," Mothman says, chewing on a vegan sausage.

"Okay," Allister says. "We'll all three go see the new Maya and all the new members of our Playground."

When we arrive in the forest preserve where Maya is sitting meditating in front of a group of meditating young men and young women, I am shocked to see how much she has changed. She is wearing a black flowing dress and her green aura blazes all around her. Her aura is so huge that it stretches all the way into the treetops and encapsulates all of the meditating young Soulminds. Within Maya's green aura, all the colors of the other human's Soulminds dance as well. Allister and Mothman stand beside me.

There is a light dusting of snow on the ground. Allister had put on some warmer clothes, but wore her silk robe of red and silver dragons on it. She had put her hood up and now stands next to me with her arms out toward Maya.

Slowly Maya opens her eyes and looks up at us three. Her face lights up and she smiles when she sees me. "Rob, my love!" she exclaims with tears in her eyes. I can't help tearing up my-self. She jumps up and wraps me in a big hug. The new members of the Playground open their eyes and smile when they see us hugging. Maya kisses me on the lips and squeezes me again.

"Look at you, Maya," I say in awe. "You and your merry band of followers. You're different."

"Yes, I'm different, love," she says, "but these young Soul-minds are not my followers. We are all part of the Playground now. *No Bounce, No Play*; right, love?"

I laugh. "*No Bounce, No Play*."

Allister puts her hand on Maya's shoulder as me and her con-tinue to hold each other in an embrace. My blue Soulmind aura blazes around me. Maya's green Soulmind aura blazes around her. Mothman's orange Soulmind aura blazes around him. Allis-ter's green Soulmind aura blazes around her. All of our Soulmind energies begin to spiral out of our chests and braid together into a luminescent tapestry—Connected within the Light.

"You are no longer Maya," Allister says to my lover. "You are Gaia: the Great Mother!"

"Is the battle over?" I ask, turning to Allister.

She shakes her head. "No, this is just the beginning."

SEVEN

Mr. Malign was in space again. He was standing on a circular platform that was hovering. It was about ten feet in diameter. This platform was yellow with a red spiral on it. Suddenly Sebastian Archaic appeared in front of him. As he approached Mr. Malign, Solstice Will I Am appeared next to Sebastian wearing a sleeveless white shirt, tattered jeans, and a necklace shaped as the planet Saturn. Sebastian turned to face Solstice and said, "This poetry teacher wanted to see us again." Solstice Will I Am nodded to Sebastian and Sebastian Archaic approached Mr. Malign and said: "Cancel the apocalypse!"

Solstice and Sebastian stepped to the outside of the platform, still facing Mr. Malign. The outer ring began to slowly rotate counter-clockwise. The center where Mr. Malign was standing remained stationary. The outer ring began moving down, creating a cone shape. As the outer ring spiraled down, it created a slide. Mr. Malign, Solstice, and Sebastian all slid down the slide and back into Mr. Malign's poetry class. Sebastian Archaic put on a pair of spectacles and approached the white board. As Mr. Malign watched his white board, an image began to flicker and appear. The first image was of a crowd in front of a stage where a hiphoppa was performing. The crowd cheered, raising their hands into the air.

The second image that flickered on the white board was of a pastor preaching in a mega church. The crowd lifted their hands toward the heavens. Then the third image flickered on the white board; this was of a poet reciting his poetry. The crowd cheered and clapped and raised their hands to applaud the poet's beautiful writing. Then a fourth image flickered and appeared on the white board. Mr. Malign approached the white board to get a better view. The image was of a happy Buddha dancing with his hands in the air.

Suddenly Mr. Malign found himself in the back of a car. Sebastian Archaic was driving the car. Solstice Will I Am was in the passenger's seat. They drove through a forest of twisted trees. Hanging from the trees were countless round white fruit. They looked like giant teardrops. Both Solstice and Sebastian turned to look back at Mr. Malign and said in unison: "Each one teach one."

Suddenly there was a violent earthquake that began shaking the car. Sebastian punched the inside of the windshield and it began to spiderweb and then shattered. All three of them climbed out through the shattered windshield as the earthquake still raged around them. All three men stood watching as the car was taken by the earthquake. The trees around them were shaking violently. Mr. Malign was terrified as the ground continued to shake and all three of them struggled to keep their balance. Then instinctively, they all faced each other amidst the earthquake. They then high-fived in the air; and as their hands touched, their bodies dissipated instantly in a puff of Purple fog and Black Mist.

EIGHT

Benny and Kelly were on the Rainbow of Reflection again in the Dimension of MERARI. "Do you see any of those creatures?" Benny asked.

Kelly shook her head. "No, my love."

Benny's white Soulmind began to spiral out of his solar plexus and the white light of his aura illuminated around him—Kelly's aura and Soulmind were also blazing. The hilt of Benny's bowie knife popped out of his solar plexus and he grabbed it. Pulling it from his solar plexus chakra, it came out with a blade made of white light. He began to walk up the Rainbow of Reflection and Kelly followed close behind as a spiral of white light spiraled out of her solar plexus as well. The handle of a whip popped out of the spiral of white light at her third chakra. She pulled it out and the rest of the whip was made of her white Soulmind light.

Benny and Kelly held their Soulmind weapons as they heard a sound they didn't recognize. "What's that?" she asked.

Benny didn't say anything; he was on high alert as the strange creatures came rushing at the couple. Benny and Kelly ran forward through the crowd of creatures—her swinging her whip of light and Benny swinging his bowie knife of light.

The creatures were torn apart by their Soulmind weapons as they tried to make it through and not be overtaken by them. "Dear Goddess! Can you hear us now?" Benny said.

"Dear Goddess! Can you hear us now?" Kelly said.

Suddenly a giant burst of white light illuminated in front of the lovers, blowing the strange creatures off of the Rainbow of Reflection into space. The being that appeared before Kelly and Benny was Luce the Goddess of Light. Both Benny and Kelly dropped their Soulmind weapons and they disappeared into their auras. They bowed to Luce the Goddess of Light. Then a beam of white light spiraled from her heart and split into two, connecting her heart with both Benjamin's and Kelly's. All three smiled at each other in loving harmony. "Walk through me," the Goddess spoke.

Benjamin and Kelly leaned in to one another and kissed on the lips, then they walked through the Goddess and her bright white aura; continuing along the Rainbow of Reflection. Luce the Goddess of Light turned to watch Kelly and Benjamin as they approached the other end of the Rainbow of Reflection. The lovers, with the Goddess behind them, all looked up and saw a tower of stone at the far end of the Rainbow of Reflection. After Kelly Moriarty and Benjamin Sanderson approached this tower, they noticed a strange indentation on the front of the stone. This indentation was in the shape of a circle with three triangles pointing up around the top edge, and four triangles pointing down around the bottom edge of the circle. There were also two arrows; one pointing off of each side, east and west.

Both the young man and young woman touched the indentation in the stone together. After they thoroughly studied the indentation in the stone, a purple spiral of light appeared below them. This light shone up around them. After they both portaled through this violet light, they found themselves standing in a forest of twisted trees. They stepped forward out of the portal onto the ground amidst the trees. Benny and Kelly held hands as they walked forward. Suddenly Sebastian Archaic appeared before them.

Sebastian smiled as he approached the lovers. "My name is Sebastian Archaic," he said. The three of them approached each other smiling. When they came together, they joined hands and recited in unison:

We are the Forevers of this land
But what if there comes a time when I have nothing left to give you
Will you come and claim my heart
My scepter
However, I now know that I am part of this world
There is a war, a silly war of clashing egos
But there are the important battles that are necessary to fight
And so I gladly take up my sword to cut the established to ribbons

We are the meeting of Spirit

By what means do we arrive at this meeting place
Shall it be by train
By bus
By car
By bike
By portal
Or shall it be by our own feet quietly pattering the road
Leading to the gates
Or by our words
Our voices uttering the songs of our lives
To become kin to whomever else is listening
To whomever has eyes to hear it
And ears to see it

After they recited this poem in unison, the landscape changed into a barren desert. Sebastian, Kelly, and Benny were standing there as they looked around. The sky was gray at first and then a bright shining star appeared in the center of the sky. The star descended toward the desert sand in between the three companions. The star transformed into a nude young woman. "Darren is helping all three of you lovers," the young woman said.

Sebastian exchanged a glance at his two companions. "Who's Darren?" Sebastian asked.

"He loves you three here now, and all humans—ones with Soulminds and ones who *will* have Soulminds," the young woman continued. "Actually, *all* humans have Soulminds. The Creator is in all of his creations. And as humans, we are meant to continue creativity as an extension of being creators ourselves. The refusal to be creative is self-will and counter to our true nature as human Soulminds."

"Every man and every woman is a Star," they all said in unison.

After they spoke this together. A beam of purple light shot up around all four of them and stretched high into the heavens. Then all four of them together began to ascend toward the sky. As they moved up through the purple light, Sebastian said, "You all have much more to accomplish. Even as you travel through this world and beyond. Through every Dimension—all humans are Pan-Dimensional beings."

Benjamin looked at Kelly and said, "You are my Sun."

"And you are my Moon," Kelly returned with a smile.

"You are my angel, my GoddessGod," Benjamin continued.

"As you are my GodGoddess," Kelly said.

"Together we are an angel of the ShadowLight," they said in unison.

Suddenly Benny's clothes transformed into a brilliant, flowing white dress. Kelly's clothes transformed into a brilliant white pants-suit. The lovers spiraled through the purple light and a portal opened up on the floor of Benny's bedroom at RISD. They walked out of the violet light hand in hand. Both Benjamin

Sanderson and Kelly Moriarty were still wearing their white clothes—both androgynous.

They kissed and Benny looked down and noticed blood making her white pants red between her legs. Silently Kelly began to pull her pants down and kicked them across the floor. Then she took her shirt off slowly and stood before Benjamin. He marveled at her beauty—she was radiant, shining. Then he pulled his dress over his head and placed it on the floor with Kelly's white clothes as well. They embraced and began kissing. They slid their tongues into each other's mouths as they guided each other over to the bed. Kelly laid down on her back as Benjamin put his face between her legs. He tasted her—licking between her pussy lips. He found her clitoris with the tip of his tongue and flicked it. Kelly moaned with pleasure and ecstasy.

Benjamin then laid down onto his back as Kelly mounted him. She got on top and guided his cock into her vagina. She moaned more as she slid down onto his cock. The red juice slid down his shaft in a pleasurable way. They both moaned in ecstatic ecstasy. "I want you to orgasm with me," Kelly said.

Benjamin nodded his head as his mouth hung open; he breathed slowly and deeply as they made love. "Cum with me," Kelly Moriarty said. She could feel the orgasm building in her vagina and clitoris. They both moaned in unison and orgasmed with the most intense white light that shot forth from their Soulminds. This white light of their Soulminds braided together and shot out the tops of their heads—their crown chakras—and a pink lotus bloomed above them in the room. As this giant pink lotus bloomed above them, also a pink lotus bloomed above Kelly's head and Benny's head.

"We are together," they both said in unison, "aligned with the Divine. Our Soulminds divine when we pantomime the dance of time."

They continued to make love as their white Soulminds enveloped them, pulling them off of the bed. They floated in the air, still making love. The room around them disappeared in a wash of purple light and suddenly they were hovering above a beautiful plateau. Their bodies were connected in a v-shape. The pink lotuses were still on top of their crown chakras and the other giant pink lotus floated above them in its beauty.

Suddenly a young woman appeared walking toward them across the plateau. Both Kelly and Benny looked to see who it was approaching them. They instantly recognized her as Jenny—the young woman who was one of their classmates. "Both of you come find me," Jenny said.

After Jenny said this, both Kelly and Benjamin were consumed in the consummation of their Soulminds.

NINE

Kelly and Benny woke up in their bed at the same time. They were still nude and looked into each other's eyes. They smiled at each other and kissed on the lips. "Do you want to go see Jenny?" Kelly asked.

"Yes," Benny responded. "Let's take a quick shower together, throw on some clothes, and we'll go to her dorm room."

Benny and Kelly sat at the kitchen table in Jenny's dorm room. They had been having a fun conversation and laughing together as friends do. "I'm glad you lovebirds came to see me," Jenny said. "I love talking with you two. Mr. Malign gave me this. I'm not sure where he got it from, but it is for both of you." She pulled an object out of the pocket in her hoodie and placed it on the table between the three of them.

Kelly and Benny stared at the object. It matched exactly the indentation on the stone pillar that was in the middle of the Rainbow of Reflection. "He had this?" Kelly said.

Jenny shrugged. "He told me he had it in his desk in his modern poetry classroom. He also told me that he had given up trying to get to MERARI. And that this is now for you. Together."

"What will happen?" Benjamin asked.

Kelly Moriarty and Jenny shrugged. "I am waiting for the climactic moment when the Purple Fog meets the Black Mist," they said in unison.

Benny nodded his head. They all stood up from the table and Kelly slid the object—the key thing—into the pocket of the hoodie she was wearing. "There is somewhere where you two should go together," Jenny continued. "There is a train I know of that goes there." She then leaned in toward the two lovers. She kissed Kelly on the lips and then she kissed Benny on the lips. "We are all immortal, Pan-Dimensional beings with Soulminds," she said. "Our energy lives on for eternity. It never dissolves. Hold on to this and your energetic Love. Never let that Love die. This is the secret of Forever."

All three of them leaned in and kissed each other at the same time.

TEN

In the morning, the Chai Shop opened up and Eden went in to get a tea. There was a pleasant young woman working there. "The hours on your door are different than when you actually opened up this morning," Eden commented to the woman.

"Yes, I'm going to be updating that soon," the young woman said. "The couple who used to own this Chai Shop actually went into space with some androgynous person named Caspian."

"Huh?" Eden said. "They went into *space*?"

"Yes," the young woman continued. "Caspian has his own spaceship. The couple who owned this place became hisher lovers. So they became his companions and wanted to visit some other planets."

"That's possible?" Eden asked.

The young woman nodded and handed Eden, or Mystery, a chai tea. Mystery took it graciously and sipped the delicious liquid. "Do you like to read?" the young woman asked.

Mystery nodded as she sipped the sweet tea. The young woman smiled and indicated their library of books. "Thanks," Eden replied and went into the room full of books. She was instantly drawn to one particular bookshelf. Her eyes scanned over the shelves as her pink and red Soulmind began to spiral out of her heart center. The energy wafted, braided, and undulated as it brought her up to two books that were side by side on the self. One of the books was small with a dark blue cover; its title read: *Initiation Human and Solar*. The book next to it had a light blue cover and its title read: *At the Sign of the Square and Compasses*.

ELEVEN

Kelly and Benny sat on the train. Everything around them was glowing as if in a dream, surreal. They sat and looked out the window at the landscape flowing by. Hearing the soft laughter of children, Kelly Moriarty and Benjamin Sanderson turned to look. Three young girls rushed up to the couple, offering chocolates for sale. They eagerly held the box out to them. Kelly dug around in her pocket. As she was doing so, she noticed over the young girls' shoulders their mothers sitting in the seats across the aisle.

The floor under the mothers began to crack and withered arms began to come up underneath them as if they were trying to free themselves from under the train car. Kelly presented a dollar to the young girls and received a chocolate bar in exchange. The young girls giggled and scurried off toward the next train car. Kelly stood from her seat to follow them. She took Benny's hand and led him along with her.

After the couple crossed into the other train car, they saw tables in between the seats—like booths at a restaurant. However, the seats were filled with young girls and boys playing chess. The chess boards transformed into the backs of turtles. These turtles had only one eye and they all turned their heads to look at Benny and Kelly. "Do you feel dizzy?" Kelly asked.

Benny turned to her and nodded. They pressed their foreheads together and closed their eyes. They still held hands; and when they opened their eyes, they saw a nude girl walking toward them dragging a giant wooden cross. At the end of the aisle was a small mound of dirt. The girl suddenly turned around and began dragging the cross toward this mound of dirt. As Kelly and Benny watched, holding hands, the girl picked up the giant cross and placed it in the mound of dirt. Semen began to gush out of the top of the cross, soaking the three of them.

The young girl turned back to Benny and Kelly, raising her hands up toward them. A silver cup—The Grail—appeared in her hands. The Grail was empty, but soon filled with the white, milky semen. Before Kelly and Benny took The Grail from the young girl's hands, they looked out of the window of the train car. They saw the sky suddenly become dark and lightning rippled over and across it. Then they saw a great battle raging—a great war—World War Three—the war on Consciousness.

Brutal violence rippled through the fields; people being pumped full of bullets; people being gutted with knives. Kelly and Benny saw people dying of starvation; trying to eat leather for nutrition. Flies swarmed over the bodies of the dead. Then storms tore through the landscape; storms of hail, fire, and ice.

Benny and Kelly looked at each other in terror. As they shivered, they embraced each other. Everything around them dissolved and they were back in their seat in the other train car. They held each other and sobbed; the chocolate bar between them on the seat. They kissed passionately as the tears streamed down their faces. They both reached down at the same time and touched the chocolate bar. Together, they held it up and unwrapped it. Snapping off a piece of the chocolate, Benjamin held it out to Kelly and she took a bite. Kelly took the other piece and placed it lovingly in Benjamin's mouth. As they chewed the chocolate, they kissed again, sliding their tongues into each other's mouths; tasting the sweet and bitter of the dark chocolate. It was lovely.

They laughed and held hands together. "This is strange," Kelly said.

"Strange?" Benny asked.

"I really love you," she said.

"I love you," he returned. "Oh, this is where Jenny mentioned for us to go," Benjamin continued as the train came to a stop. The two lovers left the train together, still holding hands. Once they were off of the train, it disappeared behind them. In front of them was a grassy hill. The clouds above Kelly and Benny parted and a beam of sunshine illuminated down toward the grassy hill. The lovers looked at each other, smiling widely. Hand in hand they danced and frolicked up to the top of the grassy hill.

As they were bathed in the white light, their white Soulminds began to emanate and spiral from their heart chakras; their white auras illuminated around them as they danced together on the grass, under the warmth of the sun.

They held both of their hands—right in left, and left in right. And as they spun, a portal of purple light appeared in between them; opening a portal below them. Jessica Thorn came up through the portal in between them, smiling as her purple Soulmind spiraled from her chest and illuminated a huge violet aura around her. Her purple Soulmind and aura then encapsulated the three of them, combining her violet Soulmind with their white Soulminds. The white light combined with Jessica's Soulmind; and she felt her and Terry also Connected within the Light. Now all three of them—Jessica, Kelly, and Benny—were all three Connected within the Light.

Jessica opened up her hands, palms up, and a green seed appeared in the center of both palms. Kelly and Benny opened their mouths at the same time. Jessica then placed one seed on Benny's tongue, and one seed on Kelly's tongue. Benny and Kelly closed their mouths tightly and swallowed the seeds.

"I have come to tell you that you are the catalyst," Jessica said. "You will and have made it possible for the war to begin and end. Without you it would be impossible to start the revolution of the mind. You see, what is required is not yet in the IM—the Hollow Dimension—you will release this Purple Fog and Black Mist."

"Is this good?" Benny and Kelly said in unison.

"I have seen it," Jessica continued. "We four—Terry, I, and you lovers—we are all lovers now. And you have and will make it possible for the Spirit to reign once more."

"Is this an army?" Kelly asked.

Jessica nodded. "Terry and I—we call it the Playground. We are All part of the Playground. Remember this—*No Bounce, No Play!*"

"*No Bounce, No Play!*" Kelly and Benny said simultaneously.

"This is far from over," Jessica continued. "You are destined to cross paths with Terry Broswald in the future. You both are poets—beautiful poets. So, continue to recite your poetry to the stars, to the sun, to the moon, and to All!"

Suddenly Jessica blasted a pillar of purple and white Soul-mind light around all three of them. They ascended through the pillar portal. Kelly and Benny flew out of the pillar portal and into the forest preserve that was near RISD. The two lovers stood there staring at each other. Then they smiled as Terry appeared behind Kelly, and Jessica appeared behind Benny. Kelly turned to look at Terry; Benny turned to look at Jessica. All four of them kissed on the lips at the same time. Then Terry touched Kelly's third eye as Jessica touched Benny's third eye. Both Benny and Kelly saw the same vision instantaneously: a violent storm at sea; millions of people floated in the water and were thrown by the waves; Chicago was burning and being destroyed; a giant battle field with wounded men littering it; from the West came the Black Mist; from the East came the Purple Fog.

When Benny and Kelly opened their eyes again, Terry and Jessica were gone. The two lovers embraced and kissed. They held hands as they walked back toward the campus at RISD. "I thought you almost left me there for a moment," Benny said.

Kelly laughed and smiled. "I'd never leave you, love," she said. "You can be a silly young man sometimes." She poked his nose playfully.

"Thank you," Benjamin replied.

"Is there another portal we must go through?" Kelly asked.

"We are Pan-Dimensional beings with Soulminds," Benjamin replied. "We are the portal. We are the World—or all worlds, all Dimensions."

Kelly's white Soulmind began to spiral out of her heart chakra. Benny's Soulmind weapon, the bowie knife, popped out of her Soulmind and she grasped the handle. She swung it forward and sliced Benny right below his ribs. Then she took the Soulmind weapon and made a cut below her own ribs. White Soulmind light shot out from both of them, spiraling around the two lovers. The white light encapsulated both of them and they exploded into a shower of star light.

Instantly they found themselves on the circular platform of the Rainbow of Reflection. "You still have that object, right?" Benny asked Kelly. "That key thing."

Kelly nodded and pulled the stone key out of the pocket of her hoodie and handed it to Benny. As they walked toward the stone pillar in the middle of the Rainbow of Reflection, those strange creatures began to pour over the top of the first hill toward them both. When the creatures saw the stone key, they became frightened and began leaping off of the glass walkway on either side. "Look! They're scared of the key!" Kelly said.

Benjamin Sanderson and Kelly Moriarty walked fearlessly through the throng of creatures as they kept leaping off into space. "This is the moment," Kelly continued as they approached the stone pillar that towered high above them.

"This is not the Climactic Moment yet," Benjamin said. "This will make it possible for The Climactic Moment to happen." He held the stone key out toward Kelly and she touched the other side of it as they both placed it into the indentation in the stone. It stayed in place as they backed away from the stone pillar. They kissed and then held hands as they watched the tower/

pillar begin to shake. As it started to move upwards, Black Mist began to pour out of one side, and Purple Fog began to pour out of the other side.

From the space that had opened up as the pillar ascended, came flooding white light. Hand in hand, Kelly and Benny walked into it.

Instantly Kelly found herself plummeting down out of the sky and through the clouds. She was high above a mountain range that had small grassy valleys between them. Her arms and legs flailed out in all directions. Suddenly she smacked the ground ridiculously hard. She had landed in one of the grassy valleys between the mountains. As she began to push herself up, a hand was extended out to her. Looking up to see who it was, she recognized Sebastian Archaic.

"You have wings," Sebastian said.

The moment he said that, giant white wings expanded from behind his back and from behind Kelly's back. They stretched out and out East and West. Then Kelly's wings transformed into purple butterfly wings. Sebastian's wings also transformed into purple butterfly wings.

"We've always had them," Kelly and Sebastian said in unison.

Benny opened his eyes and he was in a small living room. The room was dim and he was sitting on a couch. The floor and the couch were covered with skeletons. Benny looked up at the window. Bright violet light streamed in through the curtains. A severed hand appeared and pulled the curtains aside, letting more of the light into the room. His white Soulmind began to spiral from his chest as a spiral of purple energy started to open below him. The purple energy went up and through his white aura and the light from the window went through him as well.

Benny fell into the palms of a thousand young people—all members of the Playground. They gently guided him to the ground as he looked up into the night sky. A bright moon shone overhead. All of the young Soulminds surrounded him and held him within their Love. As the young Soulminds of the Playground gazed up into the sky, stars appeared; they pulsed as if they were breathing.

The Moon then was crescented on both sides while its center remained unseen. Benjamin faintly heard his mother calling his name. The members of the Playground parted the way and Benjamin walked forward toward his mother's voice. She then appeared to him under the soft glow of the Moon. The Playground watched as they came together. They at once kissed and then began to recite together:

Our Father
Hallowed be thy name
Thy Kingdom cum
My Will be done
On Earth as it is heaven

All the young Soulminds of the Playground began to chant along with them:

Give us this day our daily bread
And forgive us our trespasses
As we Forgive those who trespass against us
And lead us not into Temptation
Deliver us from Evil
For ours is the Kingdom
The Power
The Glory

Forever and Forever
All
The Perfect and the Perfect are one Perfect
And not Two
Nay are None
God and I are One

Benjamin and his mother embraced. As they embraced, her form changed and Benjamin found himself embracing Kelly. She had giant purple butterfly wings stretching out from her shoulder blades. He also had giant purple butterfly wings stretching out from his shoulder blades.

The Moon above them suddenly changed to the Sun and the young Soulminds of the Playground were surrounding them on all sides in a ring. All the colors of their Soulminds collectively—even Benny's and Kelly's—became a beautiful tapestry of light.

"Cut open the sky and finally let me become One with Everything," Benjamin said.

"Please let me love you with a knife," Kelly said.

"For today and always I am the Dead King of caked-on makeup," Benjamin Sanderson continued. "I hide from the formations of dogma on the earth we have cracked for one Sanctis Symphony. And the dead sing praises to the ones who sent them to the grave. Deprivation results in Enlightenment of All the Senses."

Then Kelly said: "Why is everything so difficult when the nail is driven through the spine?"

Then immediately they took flight into the air, flapping their purple butterfly wings. They danced in the air, flying and smiling, laughing and kissing each other. "Look," Kelly said, pointing down toward the valley below. Benjamin looked down to see that the group of young Soulminds who were members of the

Playground were shifting and flickering. In their place appeared a group of tall aliens with gray juicy skin. Their black liquidy eyes were staring up at the two lovers as they flew and danced in the air between the earth and the sun. They were all holding harpoon guns.

When the Greys let the harpoons fly, they impaled Benjamin and Kelly. Blood gushed from their wounds as they looked at each other. Their wings still flapped and they held each other's hands as they flew slowly back down to the grass below them. Once they were back on the ground, their toes felt the soft grass. They were both still impaled by the harpoons. However, their love for each other never ceased.

"Every man and every woman is a star," Kelly said.

"Every woman and every man is a star," Benny said.

"I Love you, Benjamin," she said.

"I Love you, Kelly," he said.

Benny pulled the harpoons from Kelly's body and she pulled the ones from his. As she laid there bleeding on the ground, a spiral of white Soulmind light spiraled from his heart. Their shared Soulmind weapon popped out of the light and he grasped the handle of the bowie knife. He pulled it out and the light blade shimmered as a puddle of blood expanded around Kelly. A puddle of blood expanded below Benjamin's feet as he bled. He kneeled down on top of his lover and plunged the Soulmind blade into her solar plexus, then he cut down, making a gash.

Kelly screamed as white Soulmind light illuminated from the gash. Benjamin handed the Soulmind weapon to his lover and she stabbed him in the solar plexus chakra. He screamed as she cut a gash downward. White Soulmind light gushed forth. Kelly then stood up and embraced her lover as purple butterflies began to flutter all around them. As they embraced, they recited in unison:

If there is ever a time you can't find me
Don't worry
I'm doing aright
I may have crawled into a cave somewhere
Or a house
Counting my chakras
Countless of them
Mumbling something about Muffins
Wondering how many Dimensions I can explore in a lifetime

See, we found our reason to live again
Our children
And they have me giving birth
To Moons I never knew I had
We know we can see the future
We've decided to grow our hair
We will see this Terry
In the Sanctuary of All Possible Worlds
As well as all individual Dimensions
We are All Pan-Dimensional beings
All with Soulminds

See he
Led me
To her
Jessica Thorn
HeShe is our shining Star
That dances in the heavens
And will never go out
Because all men and women
All Soulminds

Are Immortal

At the beginning of Time is the Logos
And the Logos is the Word
And the Word is the Logos
We recite poetry
Recite and it shall be Created
The Nilotic took his own rib and created us
Then we took our own ribs
To create each other
Now our one rib less
Leaves us shape-less
Mind-less
Sex-less

We are All Connected within the Light

Kelly and Benjamin fell into the grass, kissing. As they laid in the pool of their own blood, they stared into each other's eyes with the most intense Love—Unconditional Love. They continued reciting:

Now one plus one equals zero
Our bond is shattered but unbroken
We consummated our Love
And now we commence
Toward the cosmos with every being we've ever known
And every being we will know

Grass and flowers began to grow up and consume their bodies as they continued reciting their poem.

This is our child
Our legacy
Now one plus one equals infinity
I know the maths sound strange
We seem to find ourselves aligning with divinity
We don't struggle
We accept
I, I, and we are the holy trinity
And we androgynously are living proof
That there is Truth in immortality
We live as gods, regardless
For whatever our task will be
We shall carry the cross
And crucify ourselves
It will make them have more faith in us
We will hang from that cross
They will all pierce our sides with spears
We will bleed the cosmos out of chaos

The flowers and grass pulled Benny and Kelly down into the earth. Their bodies were ringed with vines and flowers. They kissed again and looked into each other's eyes and felt as if they were dancing among the stars.

Our bodies could die on those crosses
Bury us in a tomb
We will rise on the 7th hour
And speak in the 7th octave
We go toe-to-toe with Eternity
Until we are the saviors of the young Soulminds

Maybe not the saviors, but something

Nothing
We are definitely made for something
We cannot die
Some may question the Love we have for each other
And All
And the Love between Terry and Jessica
It only makes us question them:

How have you saved the children

Then Benny and Kelly were pulled into the earth. Just before they were consumed, a portal of purple light shot up from below them, saving their lives. It was the combination of Soul-mind energies between Terry Broswald and Jessica Thorn. Kelly Moriarty and Benjamin Sanderson were then taken by orgasmic ecstasy.

TWELVE

The couple that Jessica had been staying with had dropped her off at the base of Mount Shasta. She stood in the grass, silently calling Terry toward her. Suddenly the giant spaceship Tenchi appeared over her head. She looked up and shielded her eyes from the bright lights underneath it. A blue beam of light descended from the bottom of the spaceship. On this beam of light, Terry and Vespyr rode down to meet Jessica Thorn on the grass at the base of Mount Shasta.

Jessica was so overcome with joy to see Terry that she burst into tears, hugging him and kissing him all over his face. "My love!" she exclaimed. They both had tears in their eyes. Vespyr stood, a giant alien princess of Tar next to them. She was smiling as well, tears gathering at the corners of her eyes.

"Who is this?" Jessica asked, gazing up at the giant woman with long beautiful red hair.

"This is Vespyr," Terry said, smiling. "Our new lover!"

Vespyr bent down and kissed Jessica on the lips. Jessica was startled at first but then relaxed, enjoying the kiss of the Taran princess. Terry enjoyed watching them kiss.

"Just one more thing," he said, raising his hand into the air. Terry's white and purple Soulmind began to braid out of his heart. Jessica's purple and white Soulmind began to braid out of her heart. And Vespyr's green Soulmind began to braid out of her heart. All three braided together and they felt orgasmic bliss.

At the Chai Shop, Eden, or Mystery, was flipping through the book *At the Sign of the Square and Compasses*. Suddenly a black circle opened up beneath her—it was Terry using the Matter-Relocation pod to bring her to him. Eden cried out as the black tentacles encapsulated her, crushing her bones into a puff of Black Mist. The book with the blue cover fell to the floor of the library of the Chai Shop.

In another puff of Black Mist, Eden appeared next to Vespyr, Terry, and Jessica. "Holy shit!" Eden exclaimed, catching her breath. She looked around at her lovers. They all now stood at the base of Mount Shasta with the great spaceship Tenchi floating above them all.

The Black Mist was approaching them from the West; the Purple Fog was approaching them from the East. Vespyr stood in front of Terry with her great green aura surrounding her. Jessica stood behind him to his left with her purple and white aura blazing. Eden stood behind him to his right with her red and pink aura blazing.

"Do you know that there may or may not be any ultimate truth?" Vespyr asked.

Terry nodded.

"Are you aware of your own True Will—your Love?" Vespyr said.

He nodded.

"Do you Dare to continue this adventure—this cosmic romance—beyond the stars and even beyond the Beyond?" Vespyr said.

Terry nodded again.

"Do you meditate and know that all humans and all beings—all entities everywhere—have Soulminds?"

He nodded and a spiral of white and purple light began to spiral from his chest. The hilt of his machete popped out of his heart space. After pulling it out, he stabbed the blade of light down into Vespyr's green spiral coming out of her heart. He cut down all the way to her sacral chakra. Bright rays of darkness mixed with green Soulmind light and the pin-pricks of stars shone from the gash. It split open, revealing the darkness and the light.

Right before the Purple Fog met the Black Mist, Terry crawled inside of Vespyr—pulling himself in and through.

"Now ye shall know that the chosen priest & apostle of infinite space is the prince-priest the Beast; and in his woman called the Scarlet Woman is all power given. They shall gather my children into their fold: they shall bring the glory of the stars into the hearts of men."

- Aleister Crowley, *The Book of the Law*

[If any of you *ever* try to make a religion out of *stuff* and *thangs*, I will be heated at you.]

Avtar Simrit is a modern mystic and an artist. His writings and art are inspired by mystical inquiry as well as all inner and outer journeys. Avtar's main artistic mediums are the written word, Hip Hop music, and video. To check out his music and other work, visit the author's website: www.mc-pan.com.